For Lara

SATURDAY

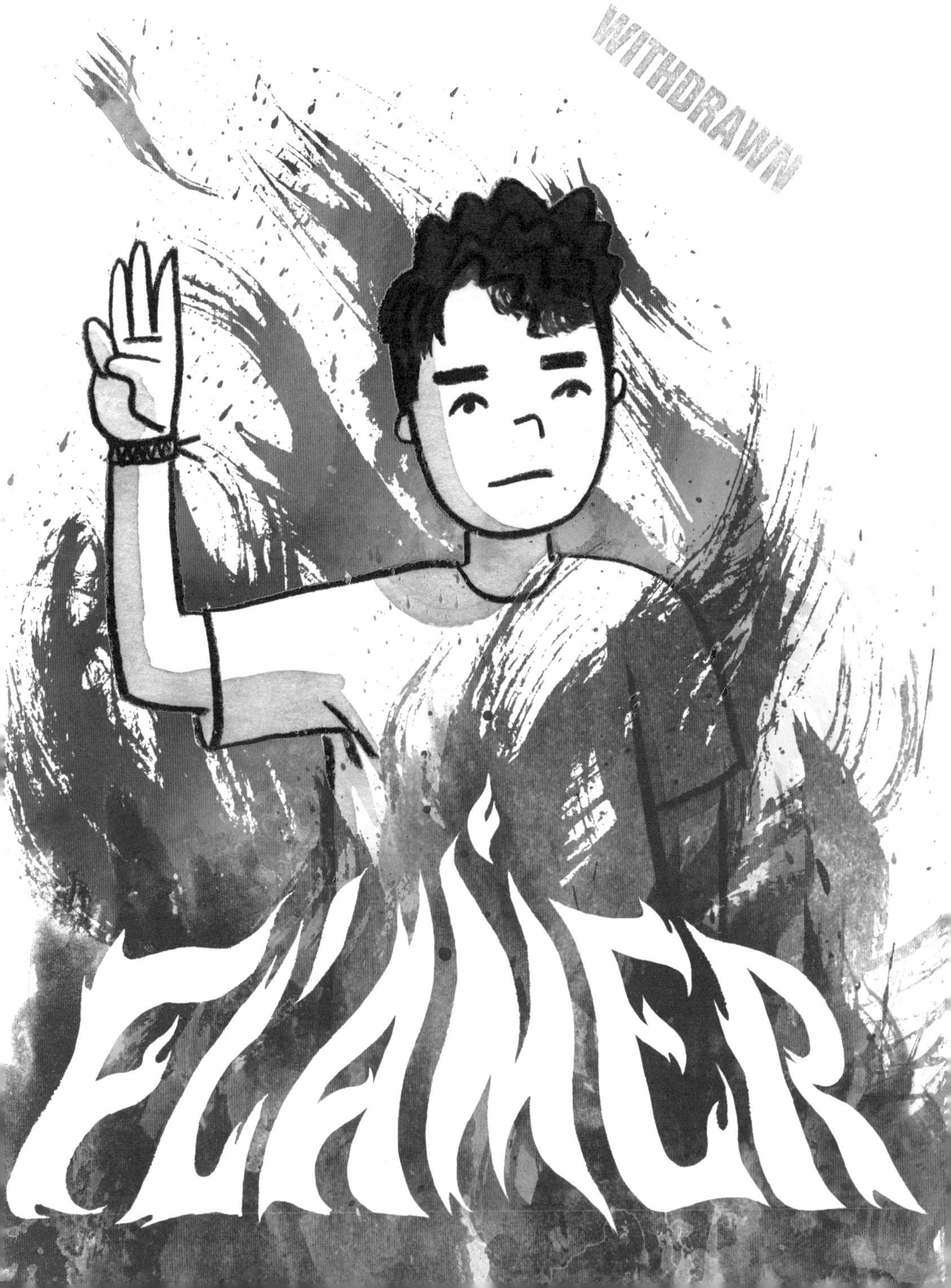
FLAMER

Henry Holt and Company, *Publishers since 1866*
Henry Holt® is a registered trademark of Macmillan Publishing Group, LLC
120 Broadway, New York, NY 10271 • fiercereads.com

Library of Congress Cataloging-in-Publication Data is available.

Our books may be purchased in bulk for promotional, educational, or business use. Please
contact your local bookseller or the Macmillan Corporate and Premium Sales Department at
(800) 221-7945 ext. 5442 or by email at MacmillanSpecialMarkets@macmillan.com.

First edition, 2020 / Designed by Mallory Grigg and Colleen AF Venable
This book was made with black colored pencil and ink washes on bristol paper.
Printed in China by 1010 Printing International Limited, North Point, Hong Kong

ISBN 978-1-62779-641-5 (hardcover)
10 9 8 7 6 5 4 3 2 1

ISBN 978-1-250-75614-5 (paperback)
10 9 8 7 6 5 4 3 2 1

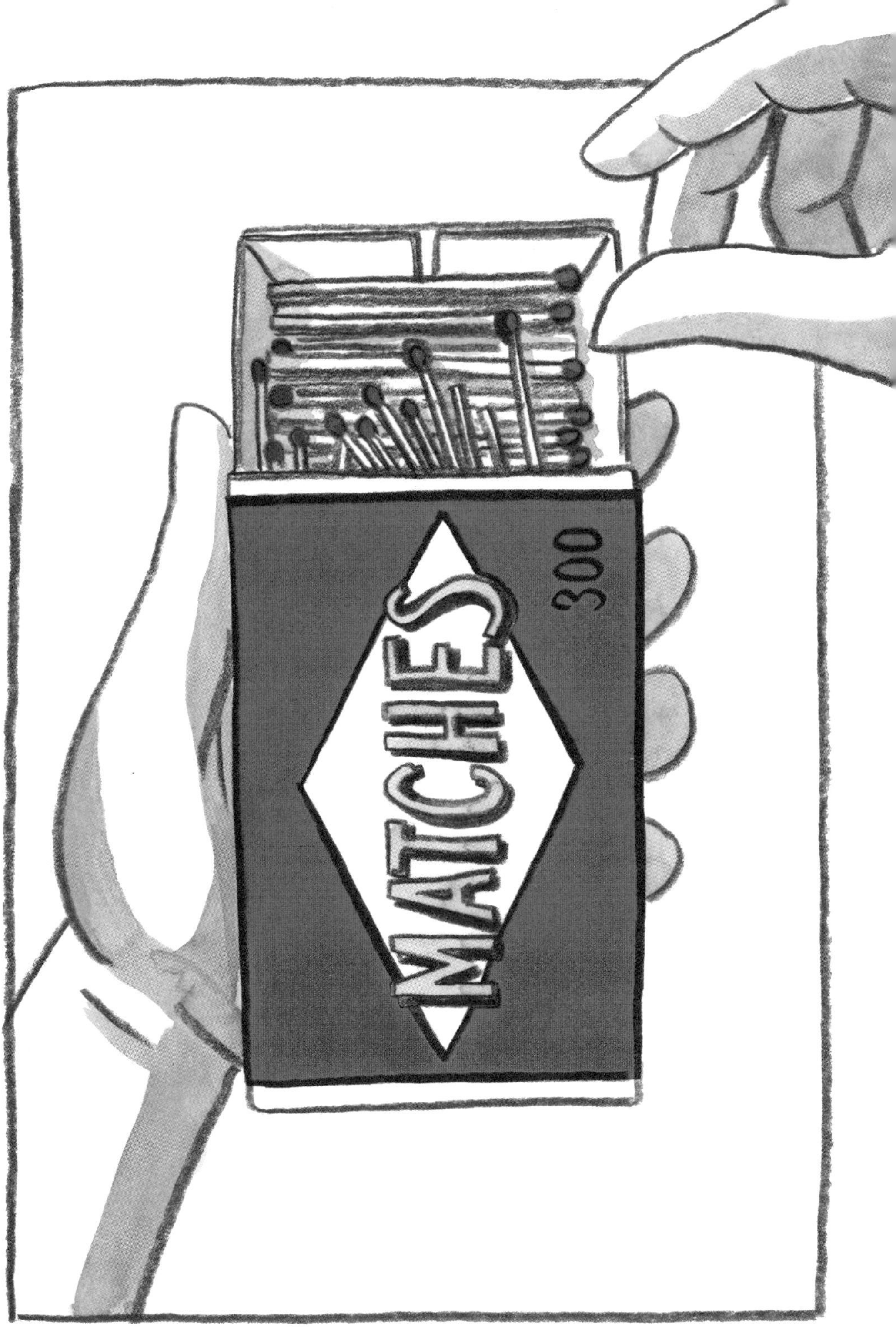
MATCHES
300

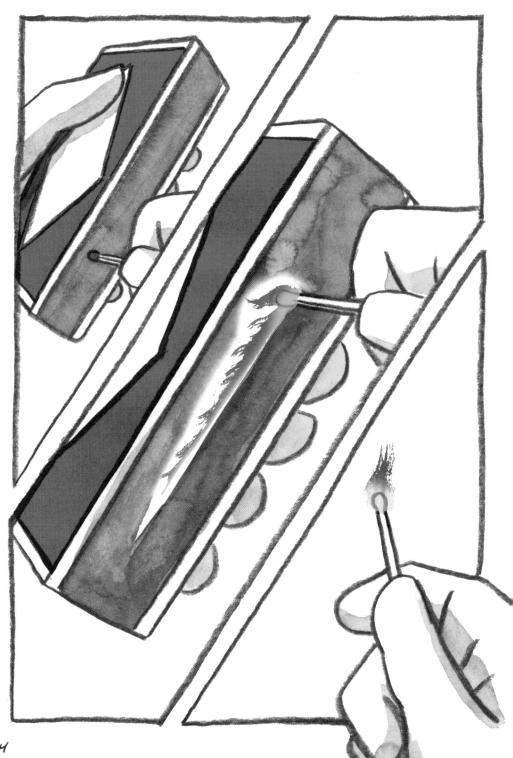

4

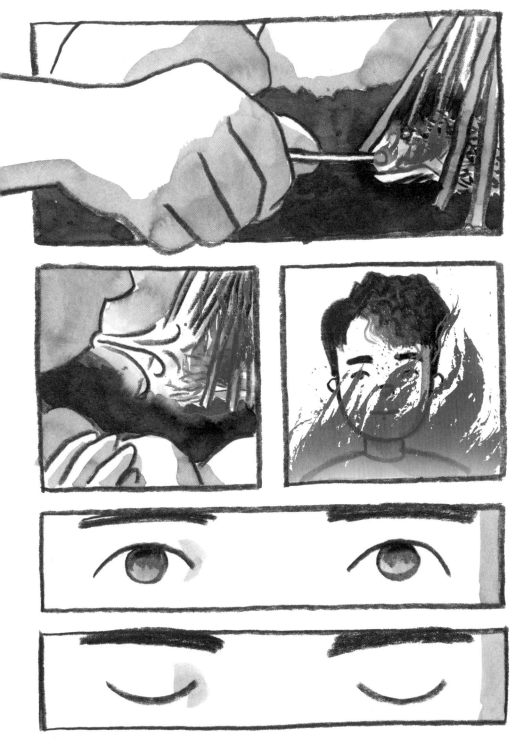

5

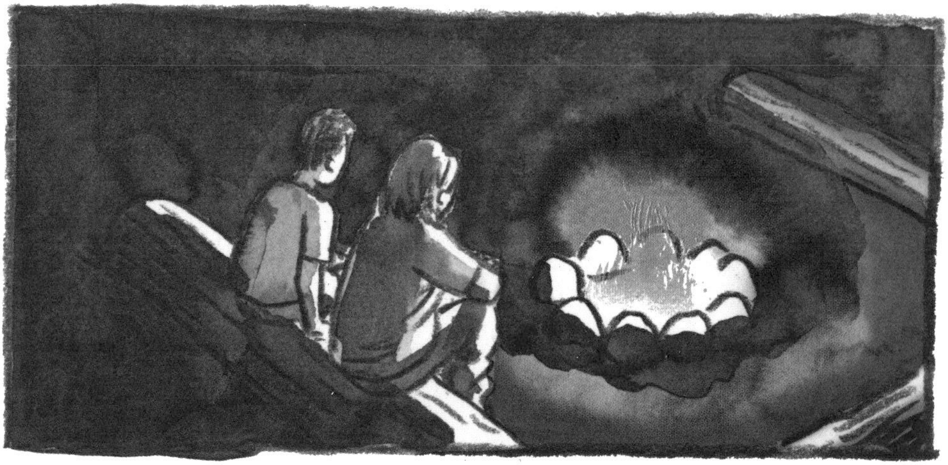

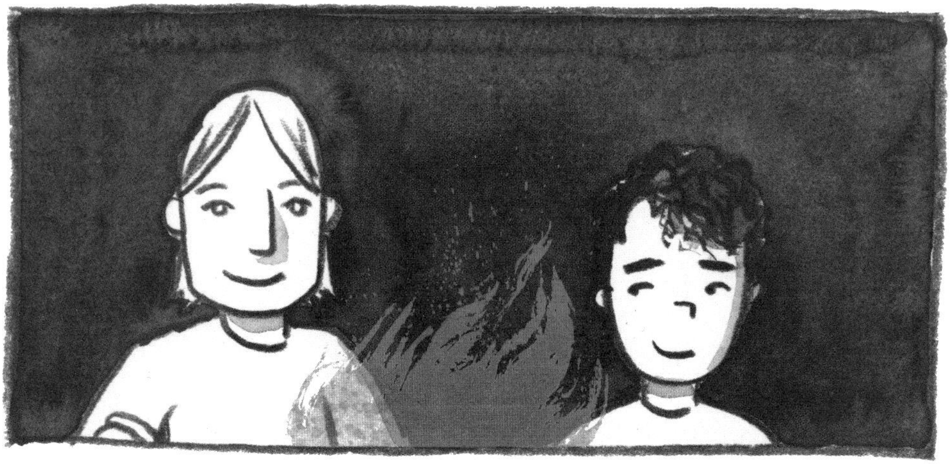

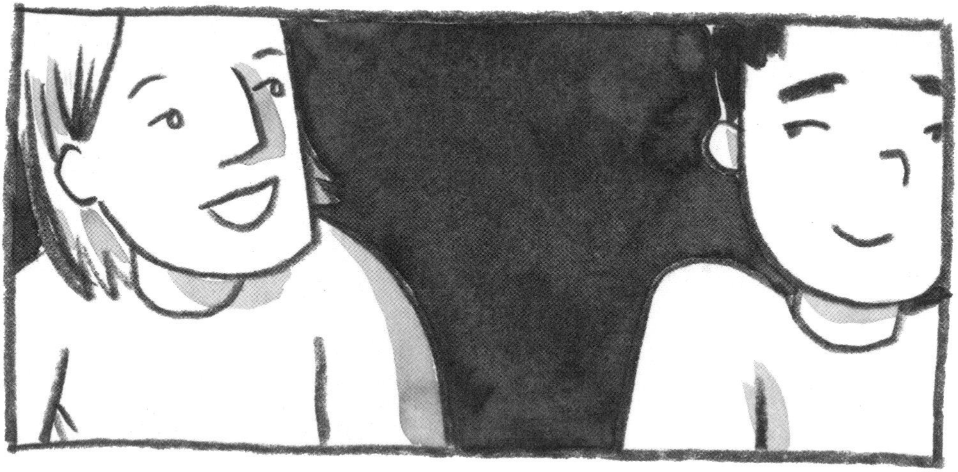

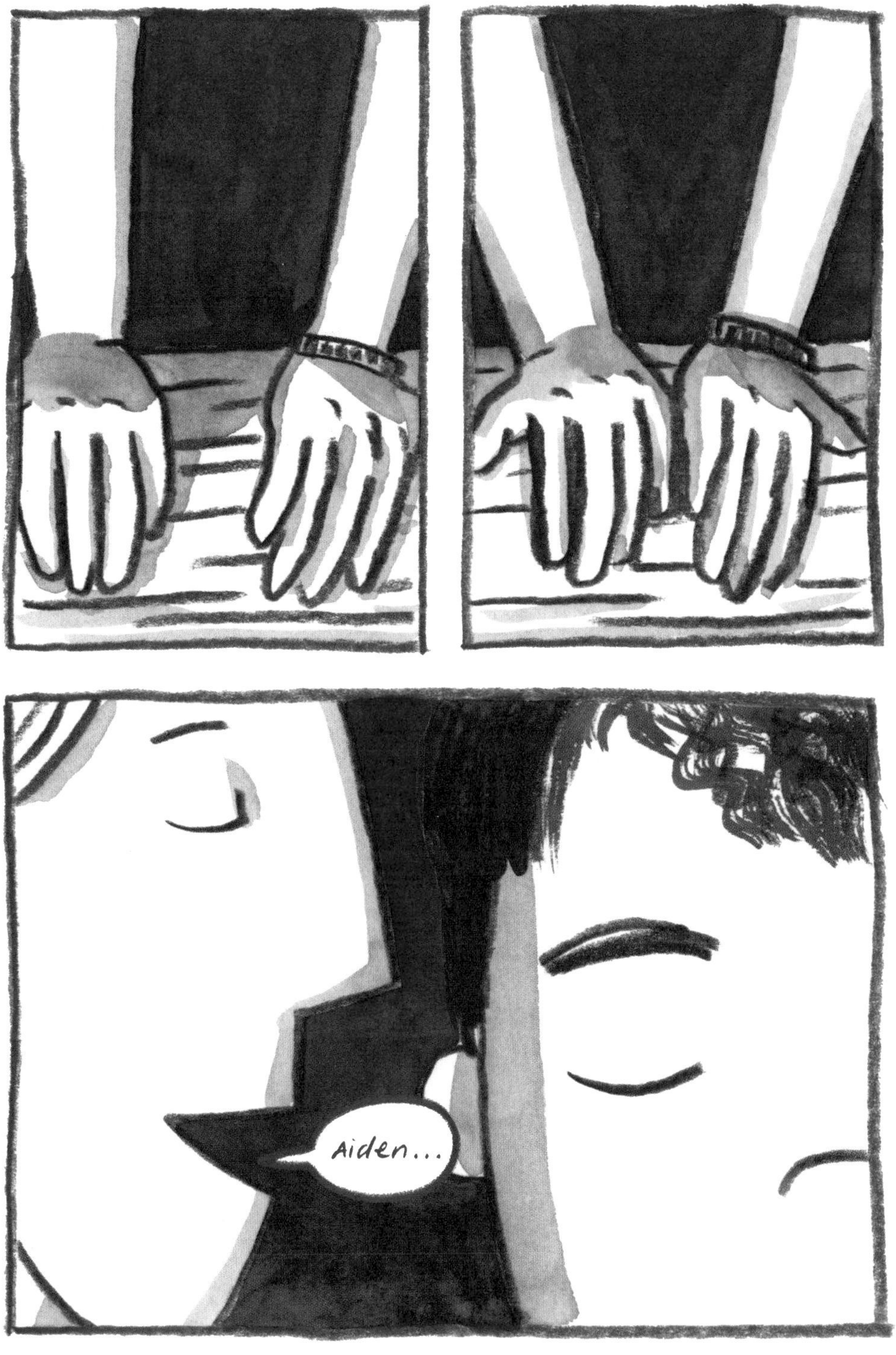
Aiden...

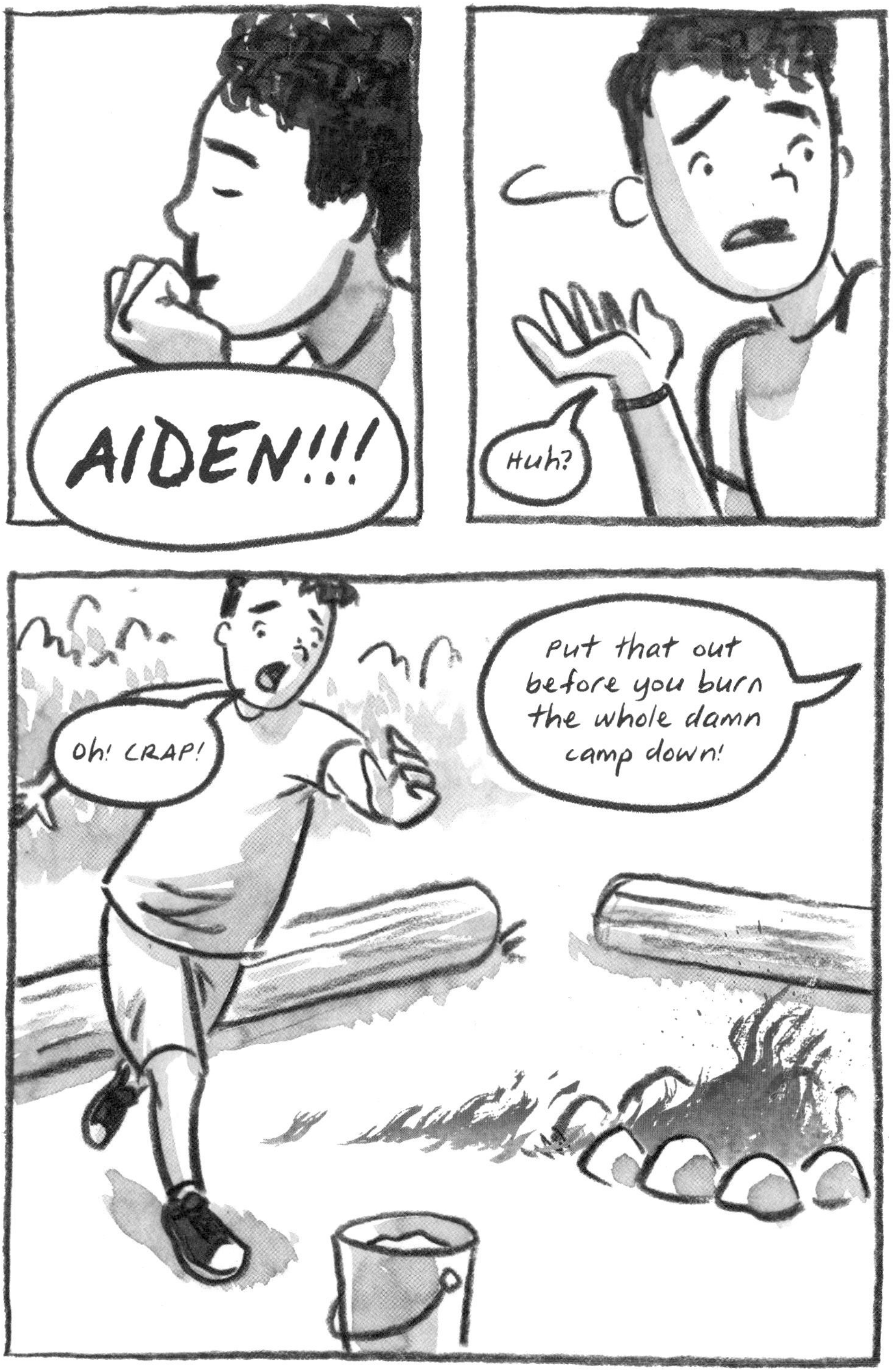
AIDEN!!!
Huh?
Oh! CRAP!
Put that out before you burn the whole damn camp down!

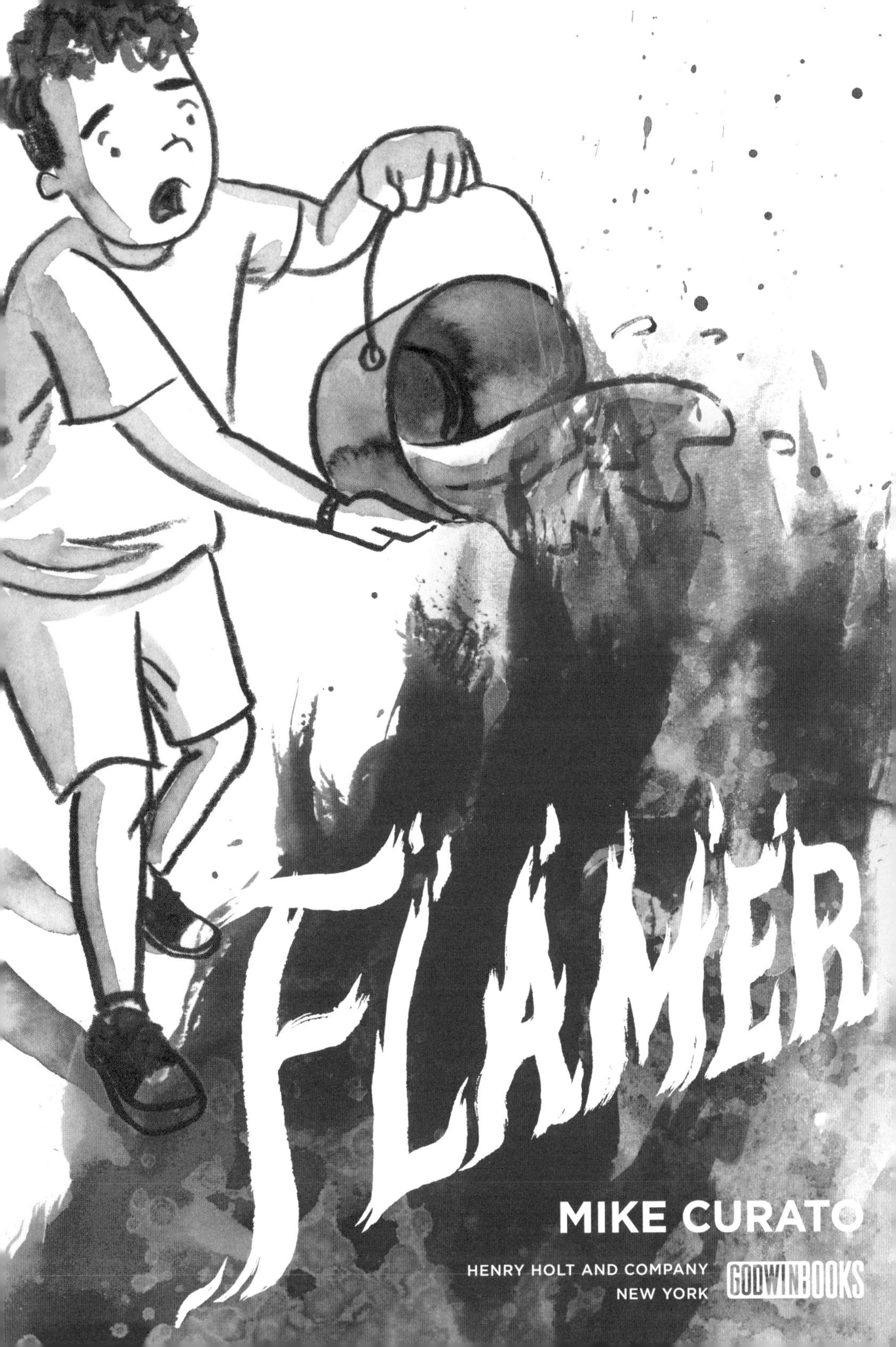

FLAMER

MIKE CURATO

HENRY HOLT AND COMPANY
NEW YORK
GODWIN BOOKS

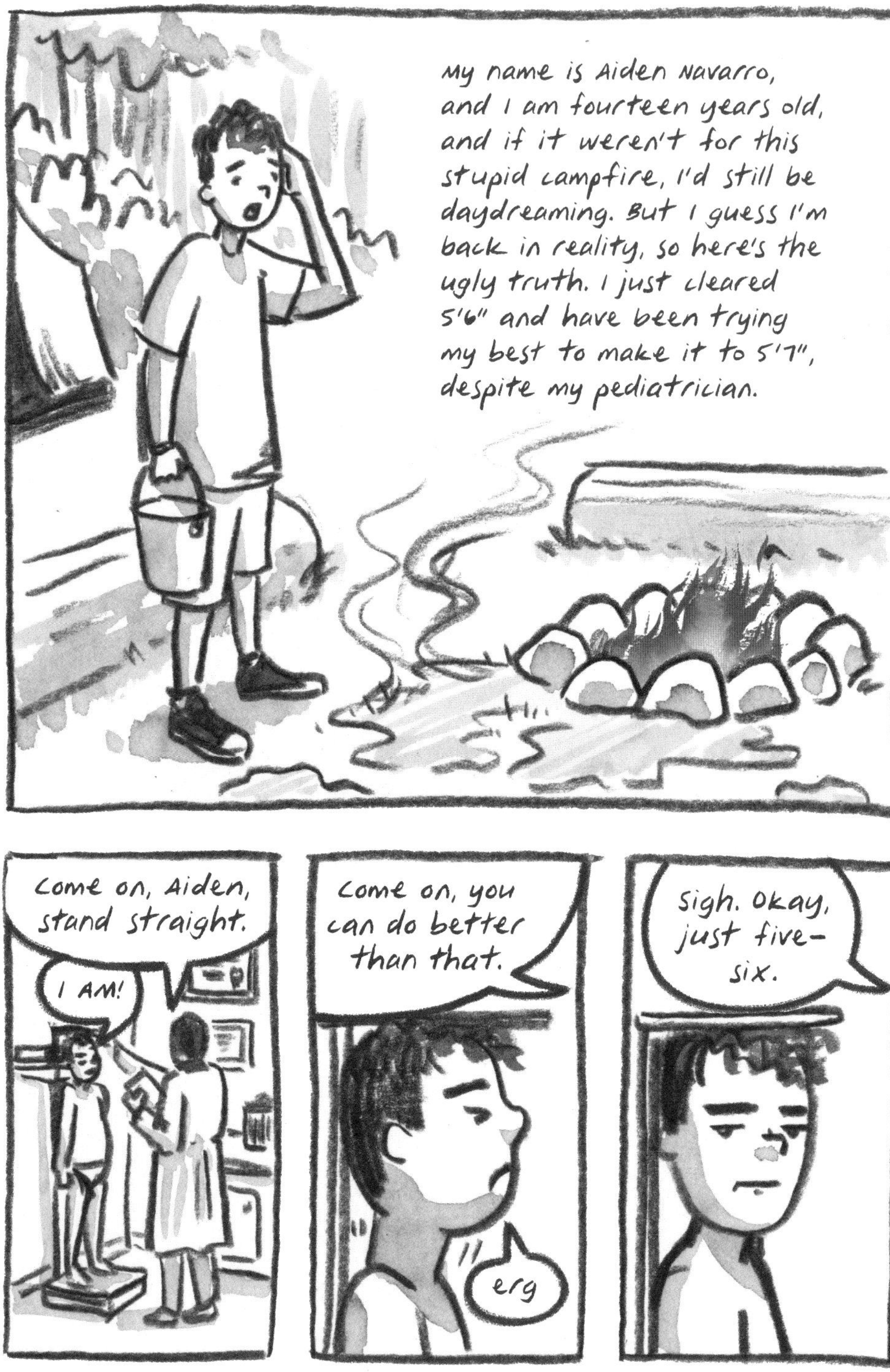
My name is Aiden Navarro, and I am fourteen years old, and if it weren't for this stupid campfire, I'd still be daydreaming. But I guess I'm back in reality, so here's the ugly truth. I just cleared 5'6" and have been trying my best to make it to 5'7", despite my pediatrician.
Come on, Aiden, stand straight.
I AM!
Come on, you can do better than that.
erg
Sigh. Okay, just five-six.

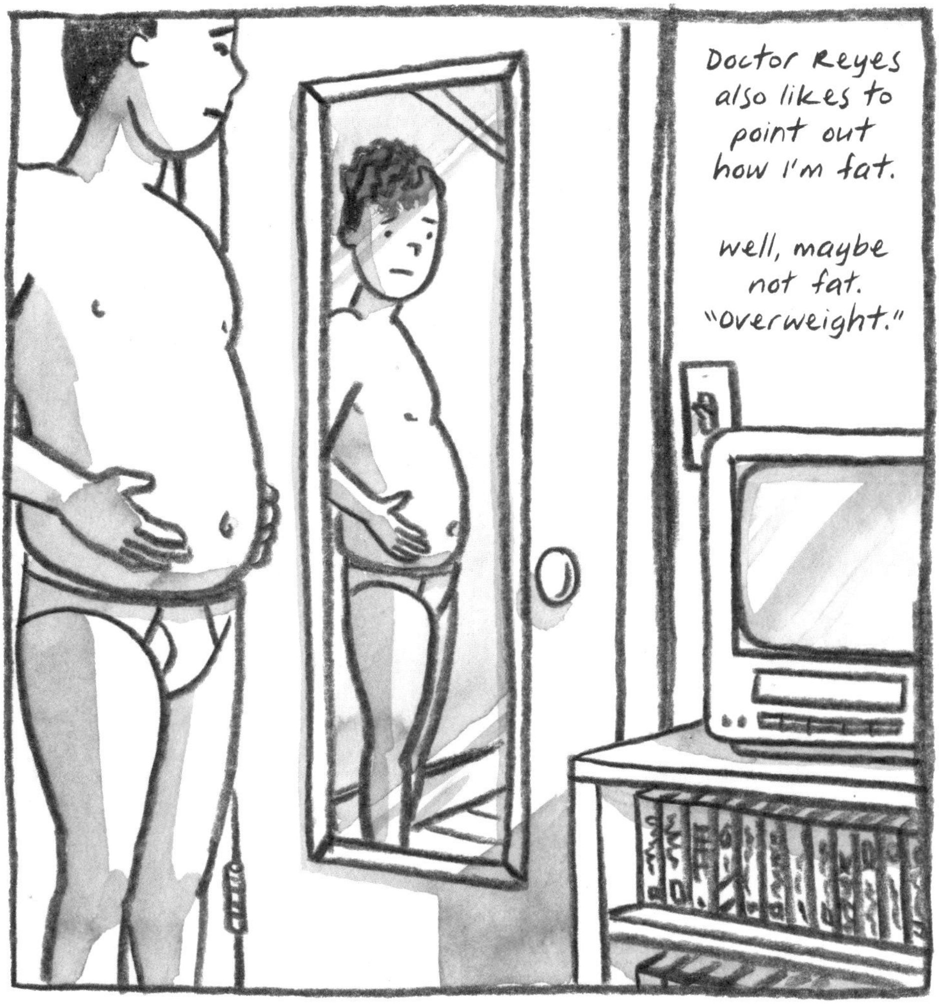
Doctor Reyes also likes to point out how I'm fat.
well, maybe not fat. "overweight."

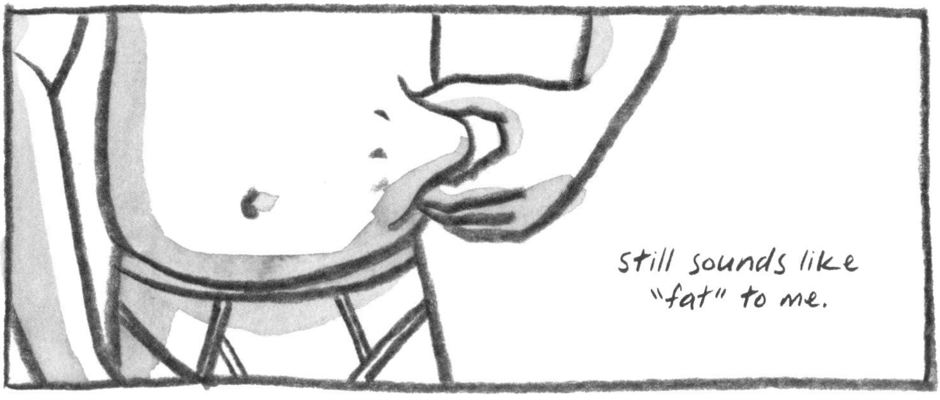
still sounds like "fat" to me.

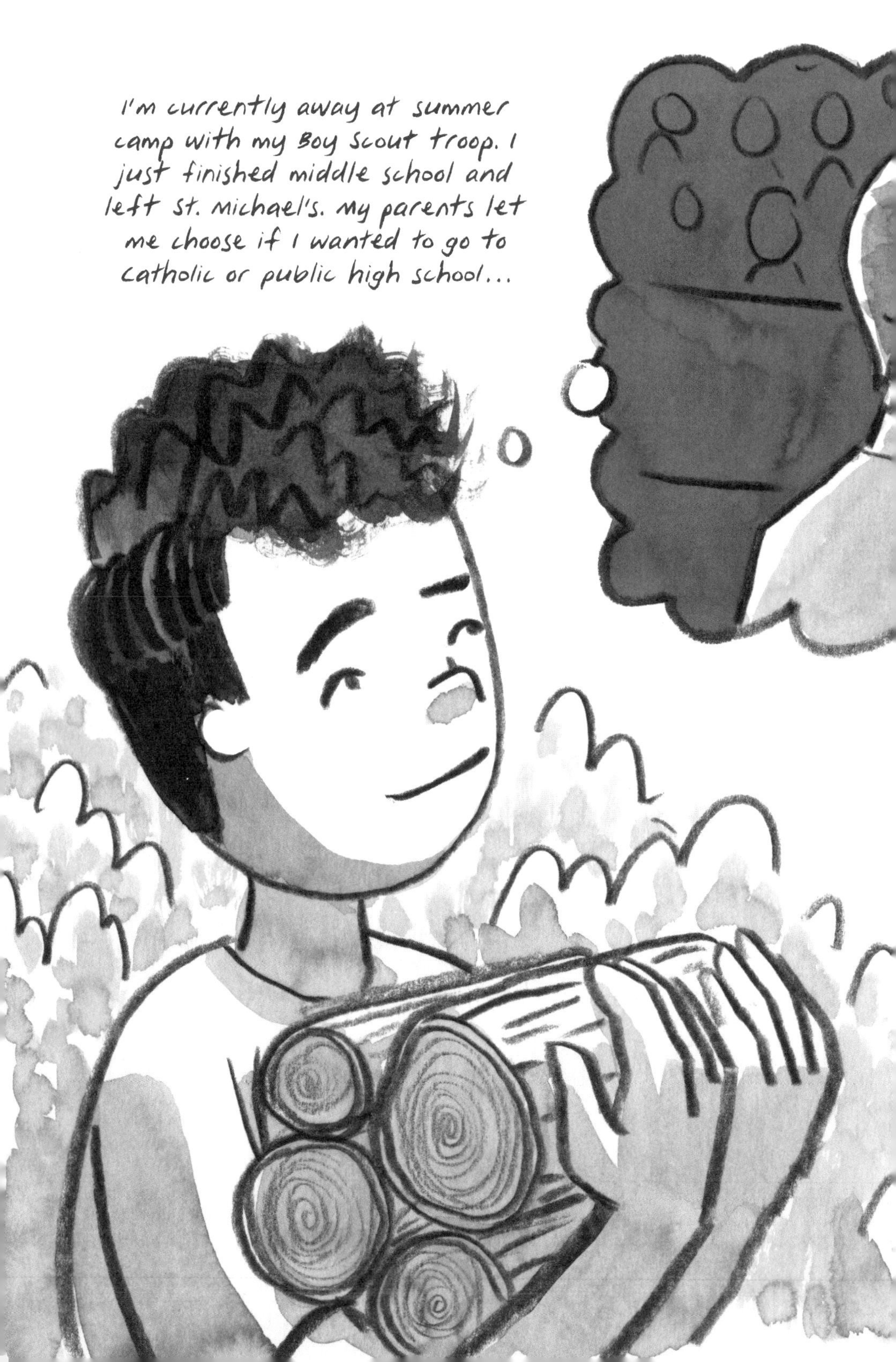
I'm currently away at summer camp with my Boy Scout troop. I just finished middle school and left St. Michael's. My parents let me choose if I wanted to go to Catholic or public high school...

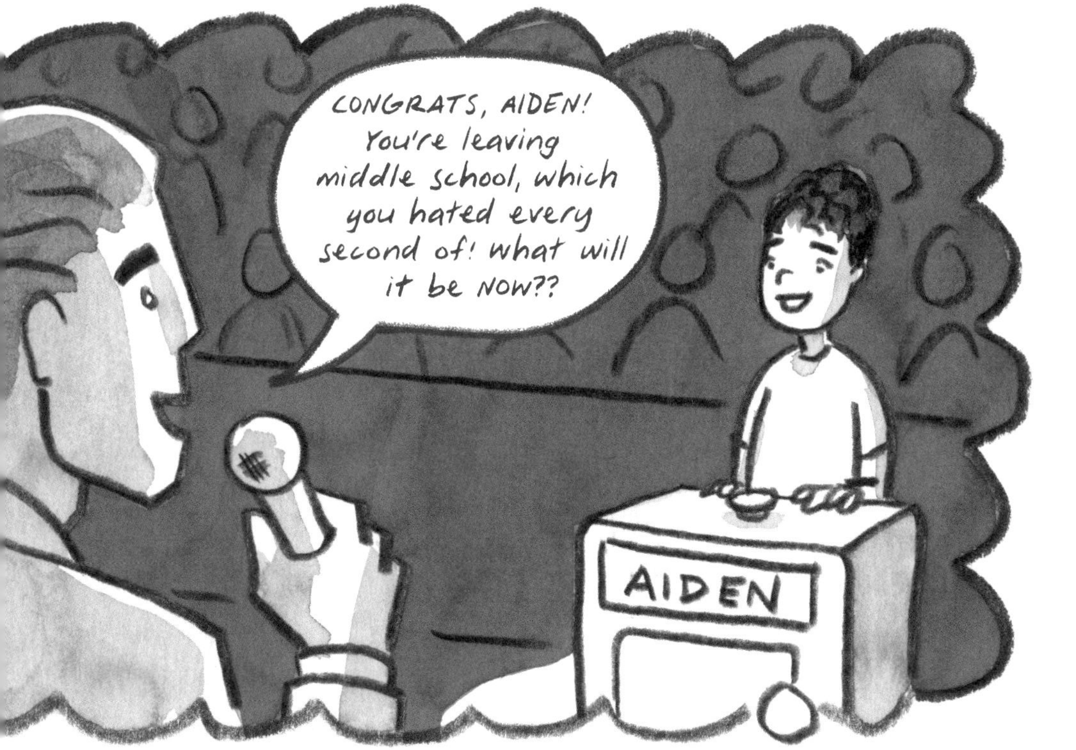
CONGRATS, AIDEN! You're leaving middle school, which you hated every second of! what will it be NOW??
AIDEN

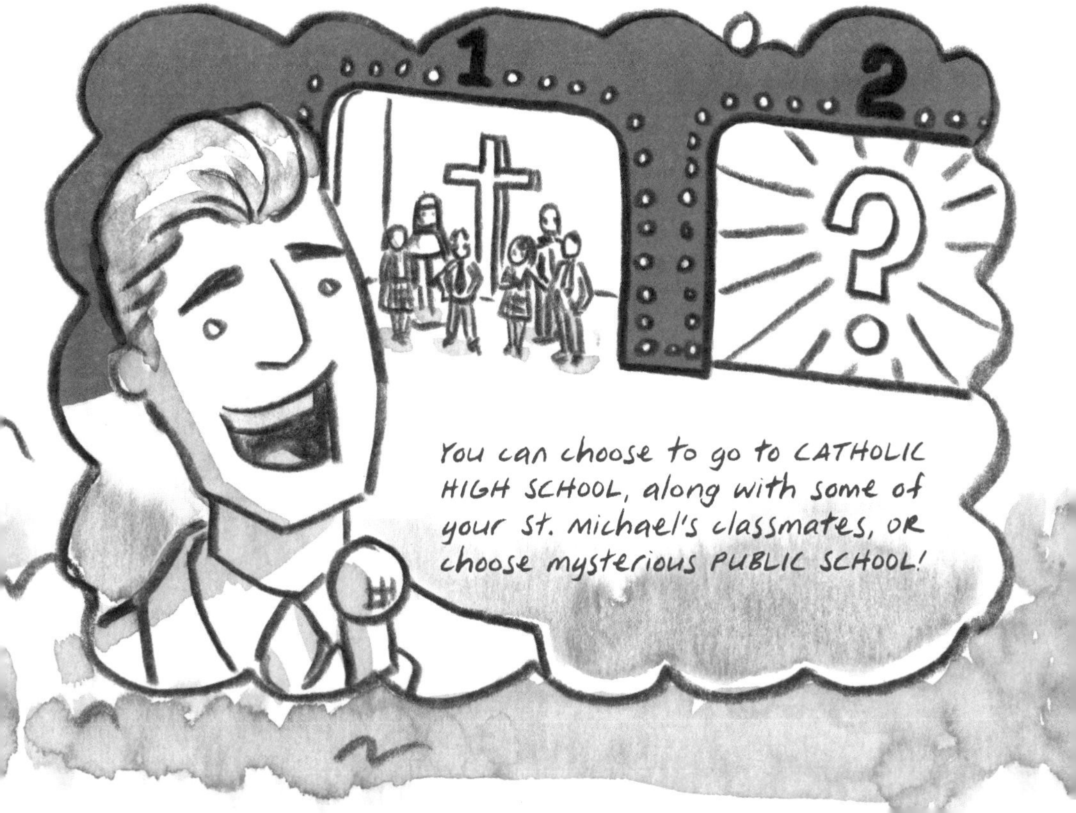
1
2
You can choose to go to CATHOLIC HIGH SCHOOL, along with some of your St. Michael's classmates, OR choose mysterious PUBLIC SCHOOL!

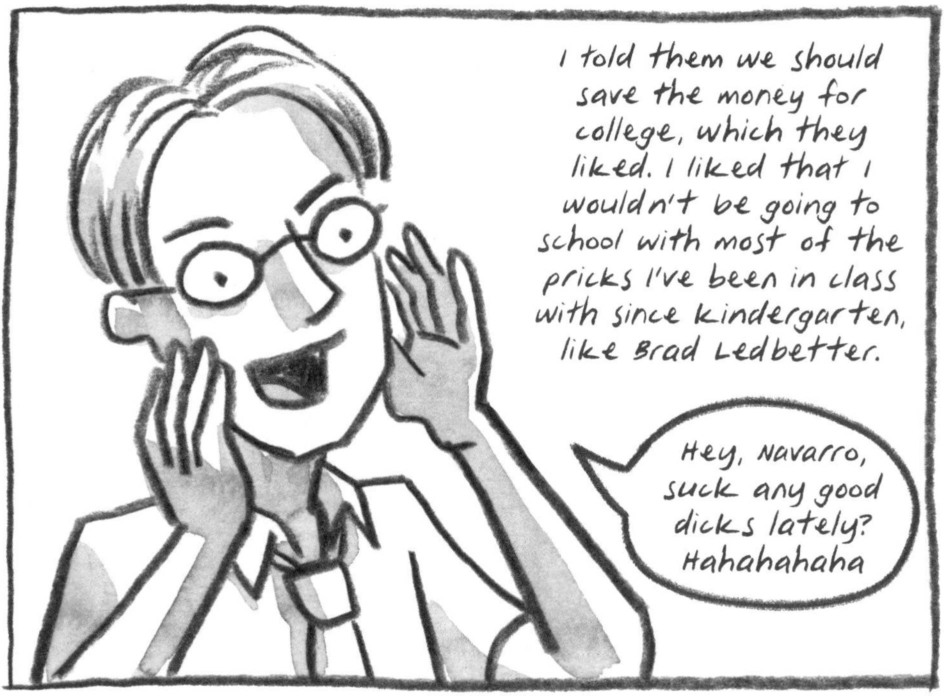
I told them we should save the money for college, which they liked. I liked that I wouldn't be going to school with most of the pricks I've been in class with since kindergarten, like Brad Ledbetter.
Hey, Navarro, suck any good dicks lately? Hahahahaha

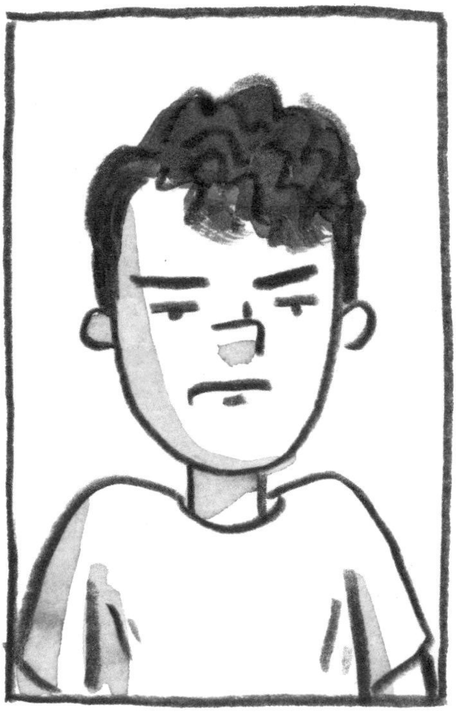

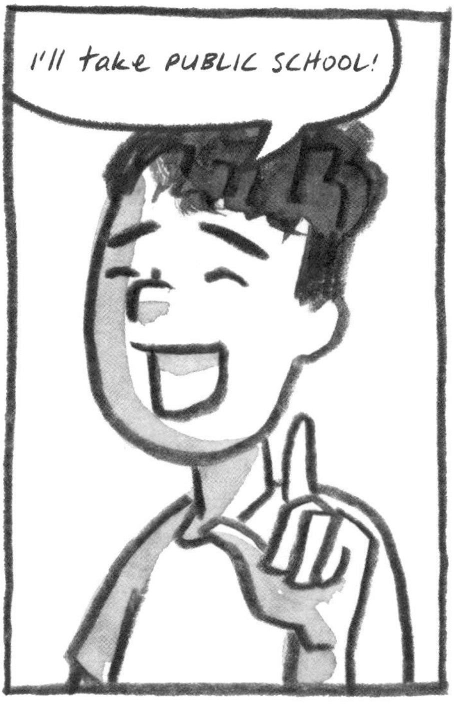
I'll take PUBLIC SCHOOL!

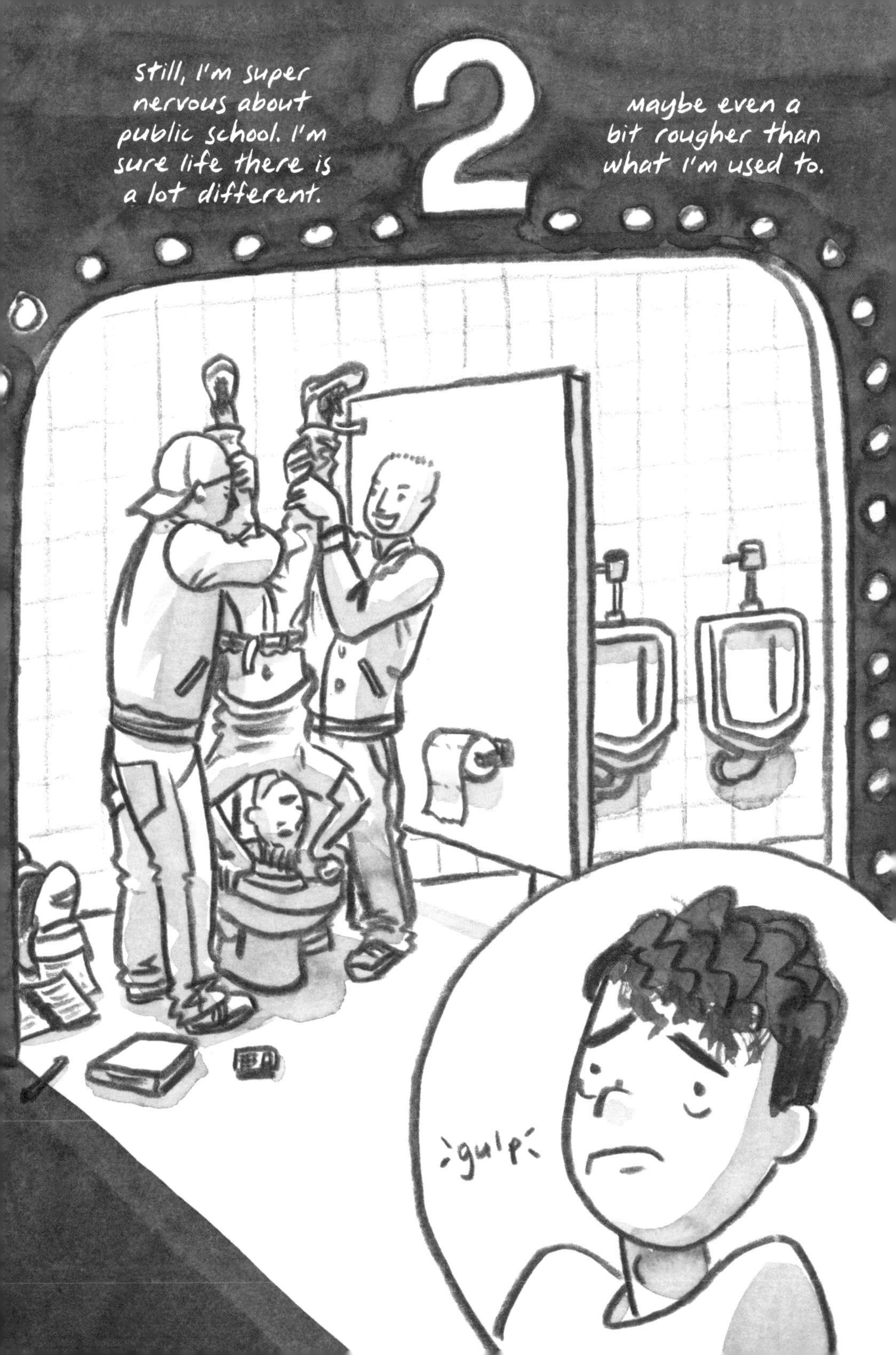
Still, I'm super nervous about public school. I'm sure life there is a lot different.
2
Maybe even a bit rougher than what I'm used to.
gulp

Also, I've been wearing the same uniform every day for almost a decade. I've recently been informed that I don't know how to dress myself, but I think it's all a matter of opinion.

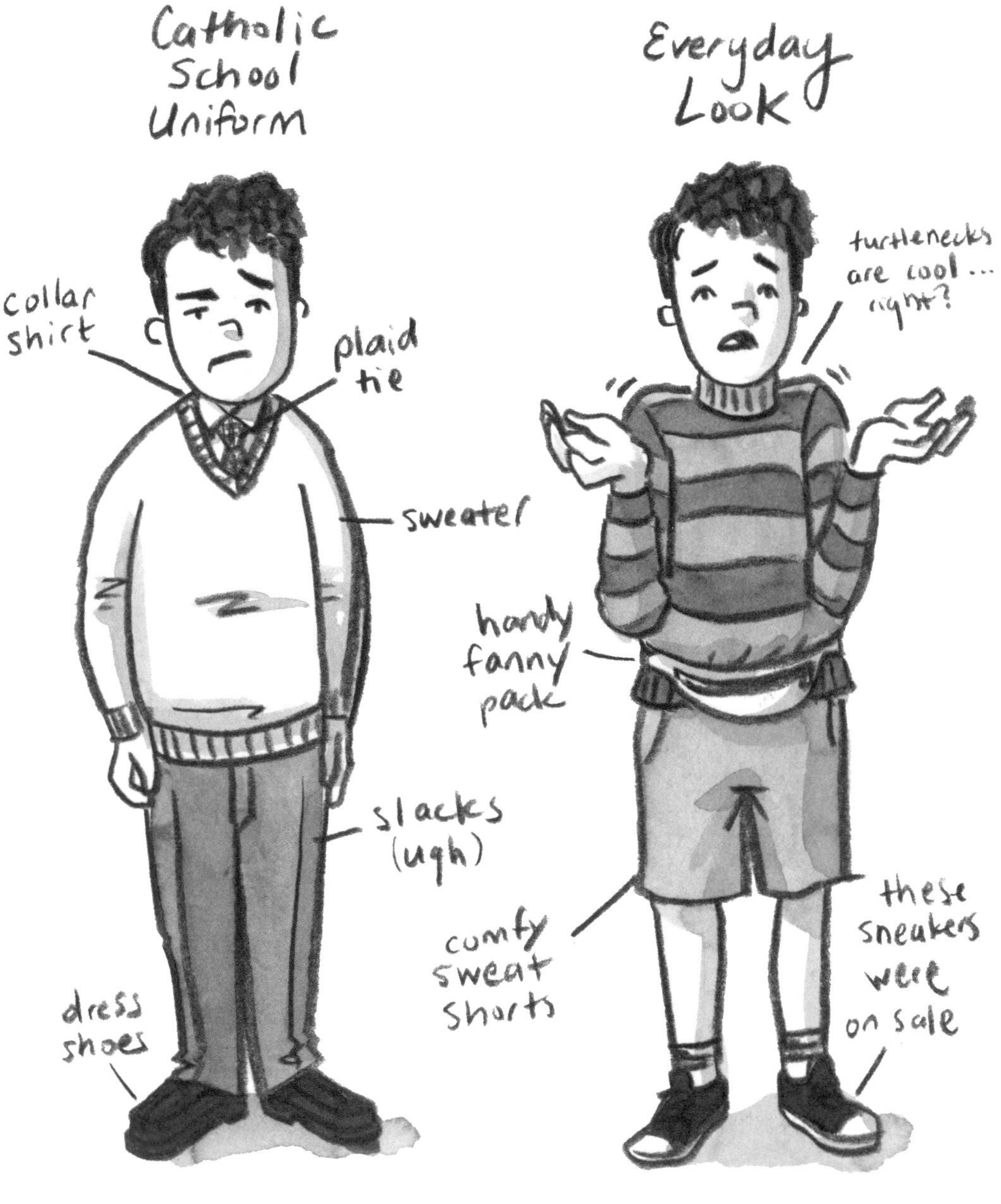
Catholic School Uniform
collar shirt
plaid tie
sweater
slacks (ugh)
dress shoes
Everyday Look
turtlenecks are cool... right?
handy fanny pack
comfy sweat shorts
these sneakers were on sale

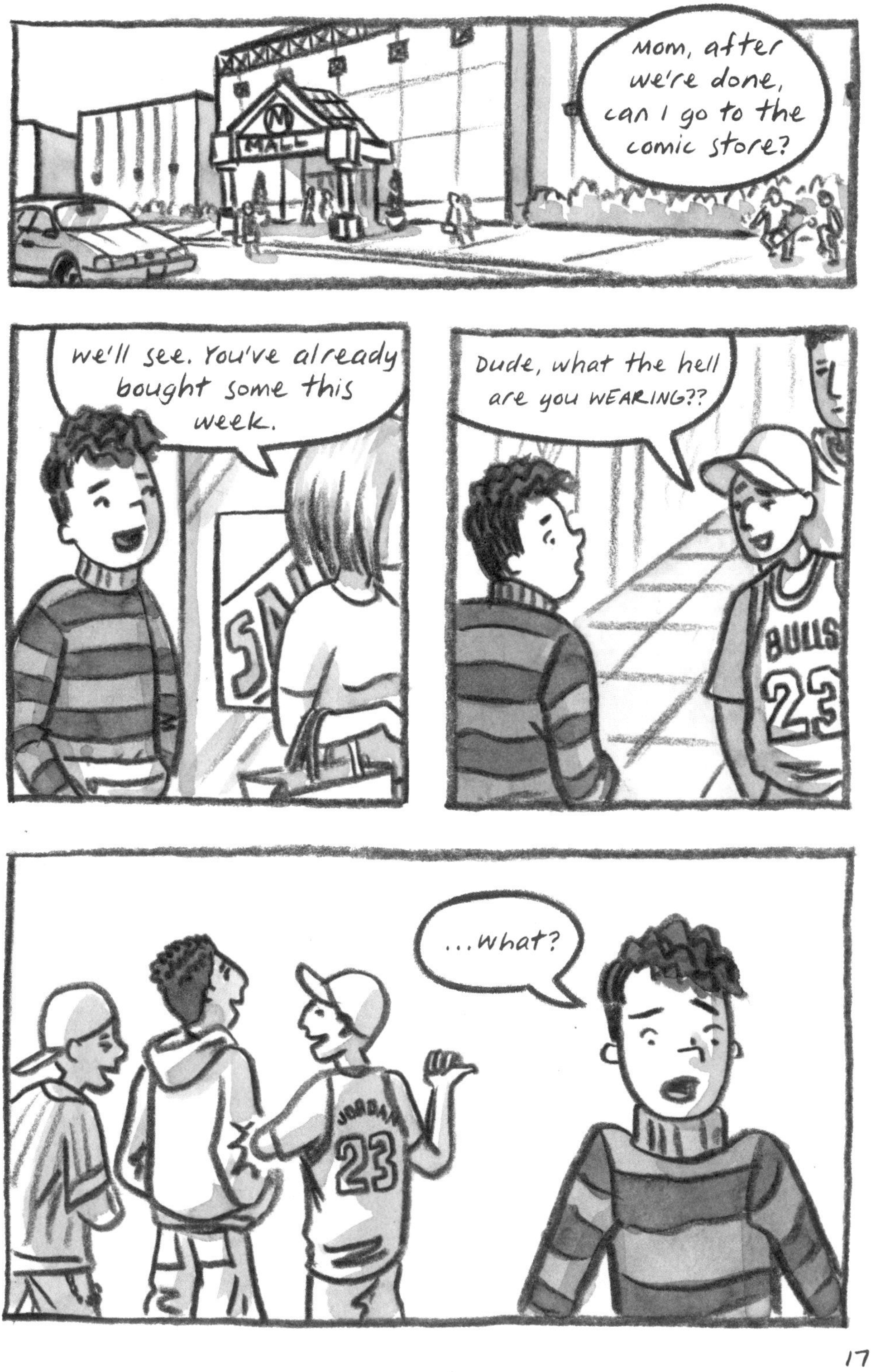
MALL
Mom, after we're done, can I go to the comic store?
We'll see. You've already bought some this week.
Dude, what the hell are you WEARING??
BULLS
23
JORDAN
23
...what?

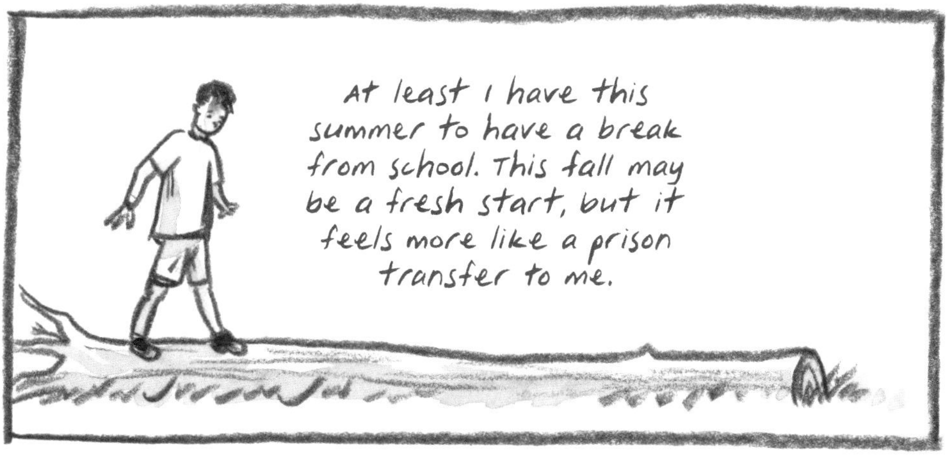
At least I have this summer to have a break from school. This fall may be a fresh start, but it feels more like a prison transfer to me.

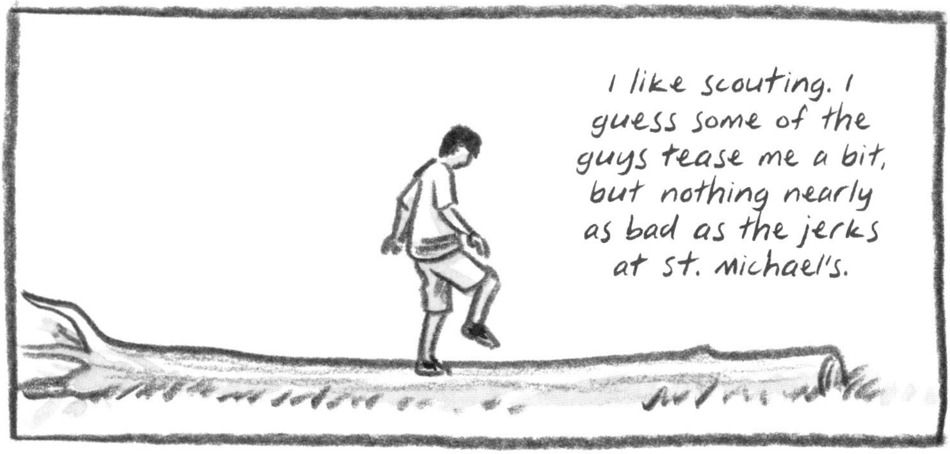
I like scouting. I guess some of the guys tease me a bit, but nothing nearly as bad as the jerks at St. Michael's.

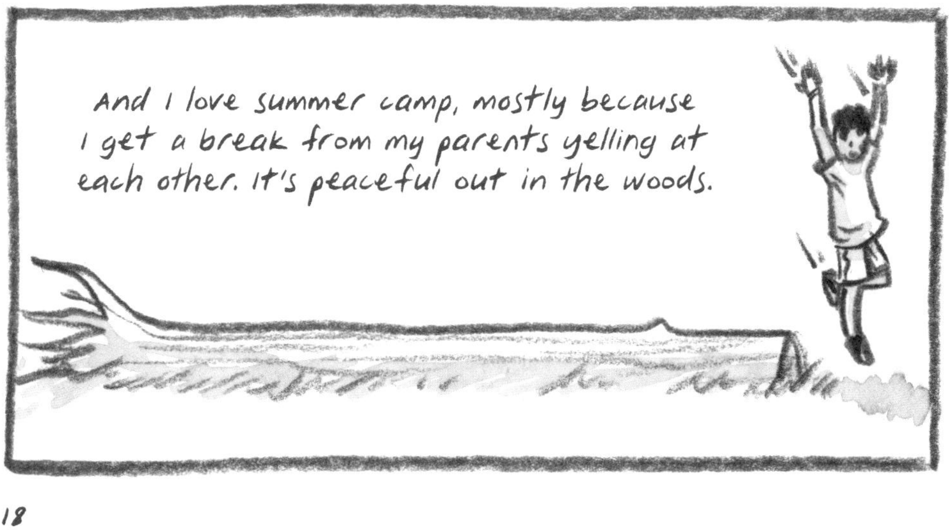
And I love summer camp, mostly because I get a break from my parents yelling at each other. It's peaceful out in the woods.

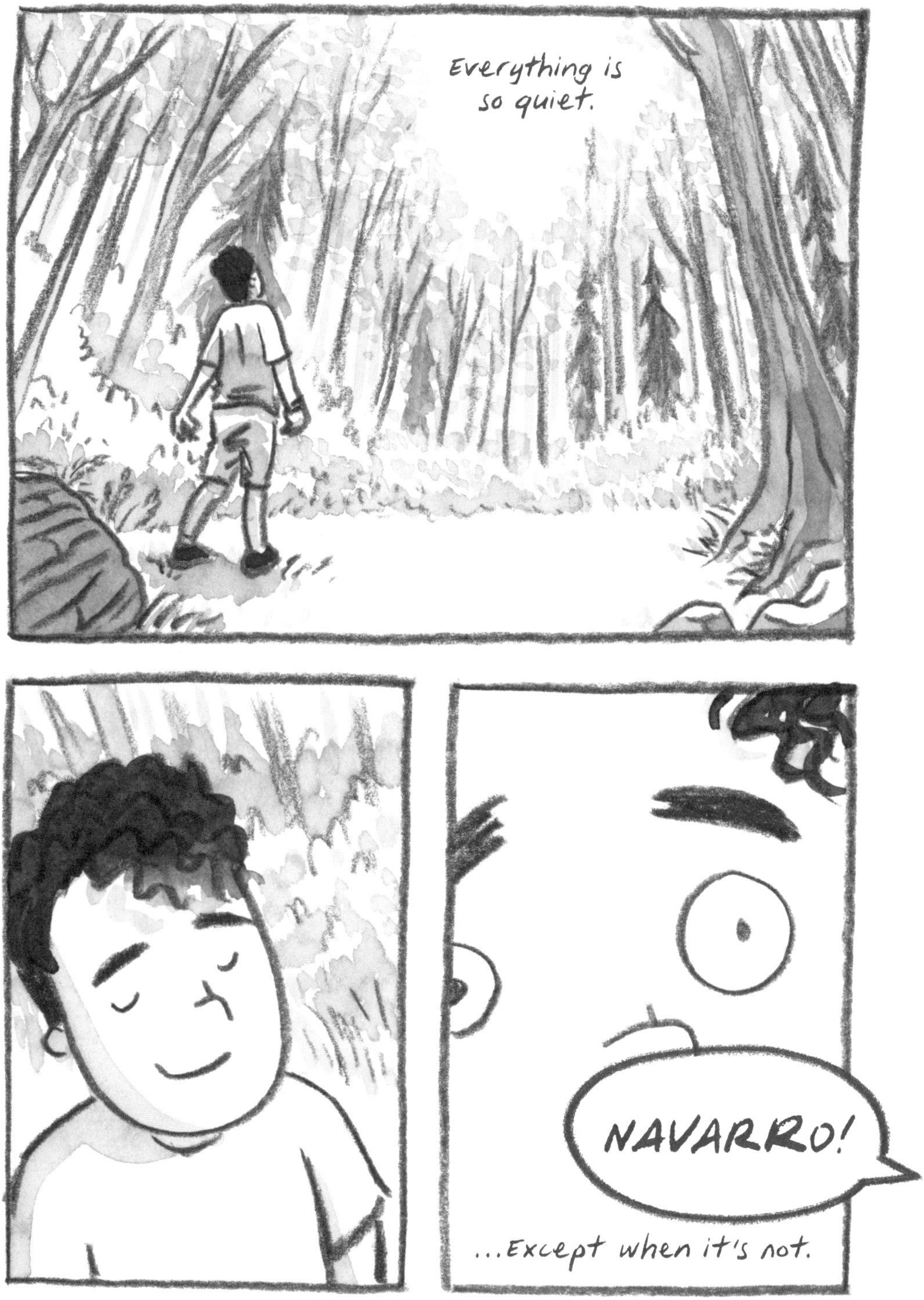
Everything is so quiet.
NAVARRO!
...Except when it's not.

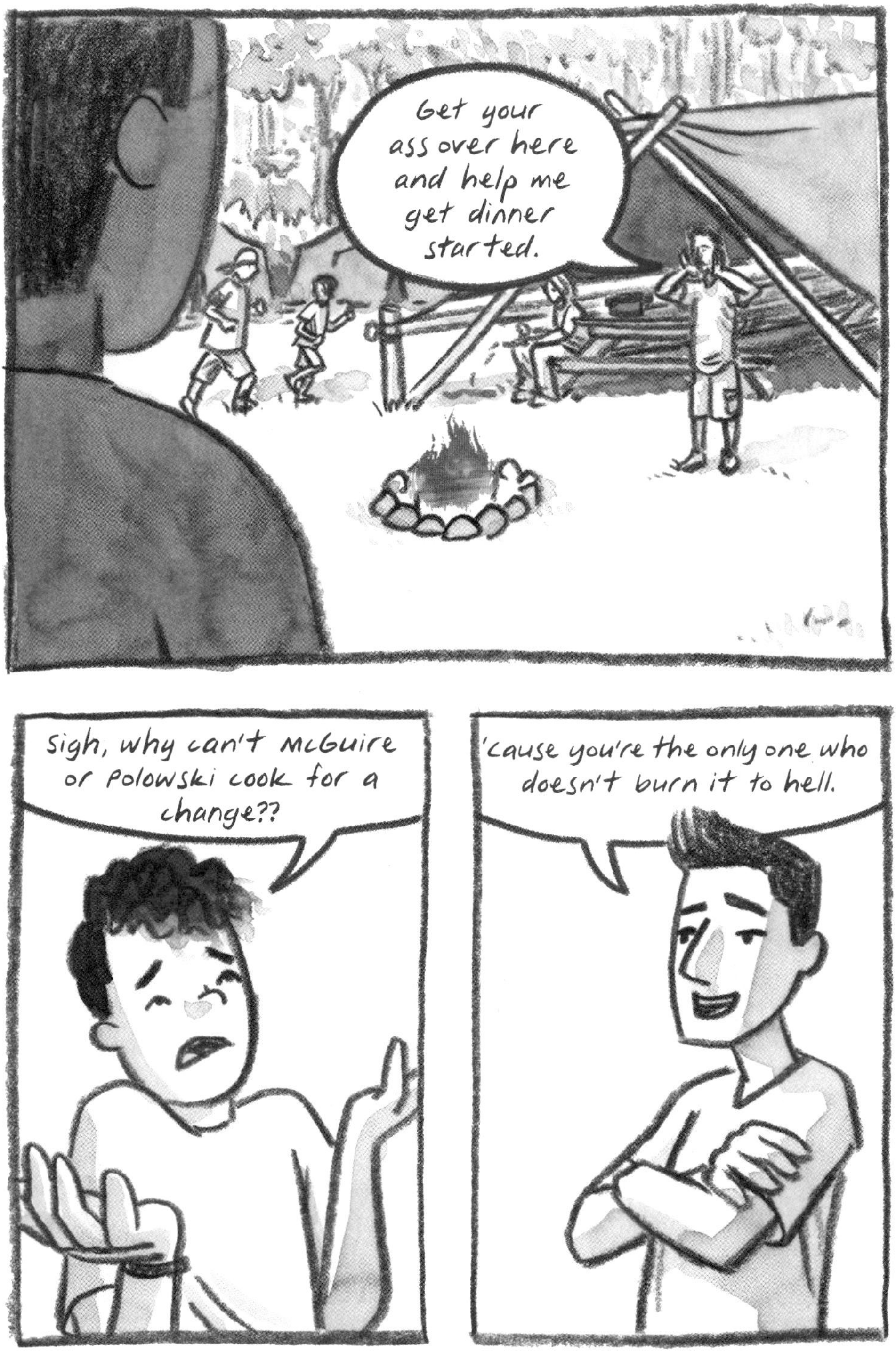
Get your ass over here and help me get dinner started.
Sigh, why can't McGuire or Polowski cook for a change??
'Cause you're the only one who doesn't burn it to hell.

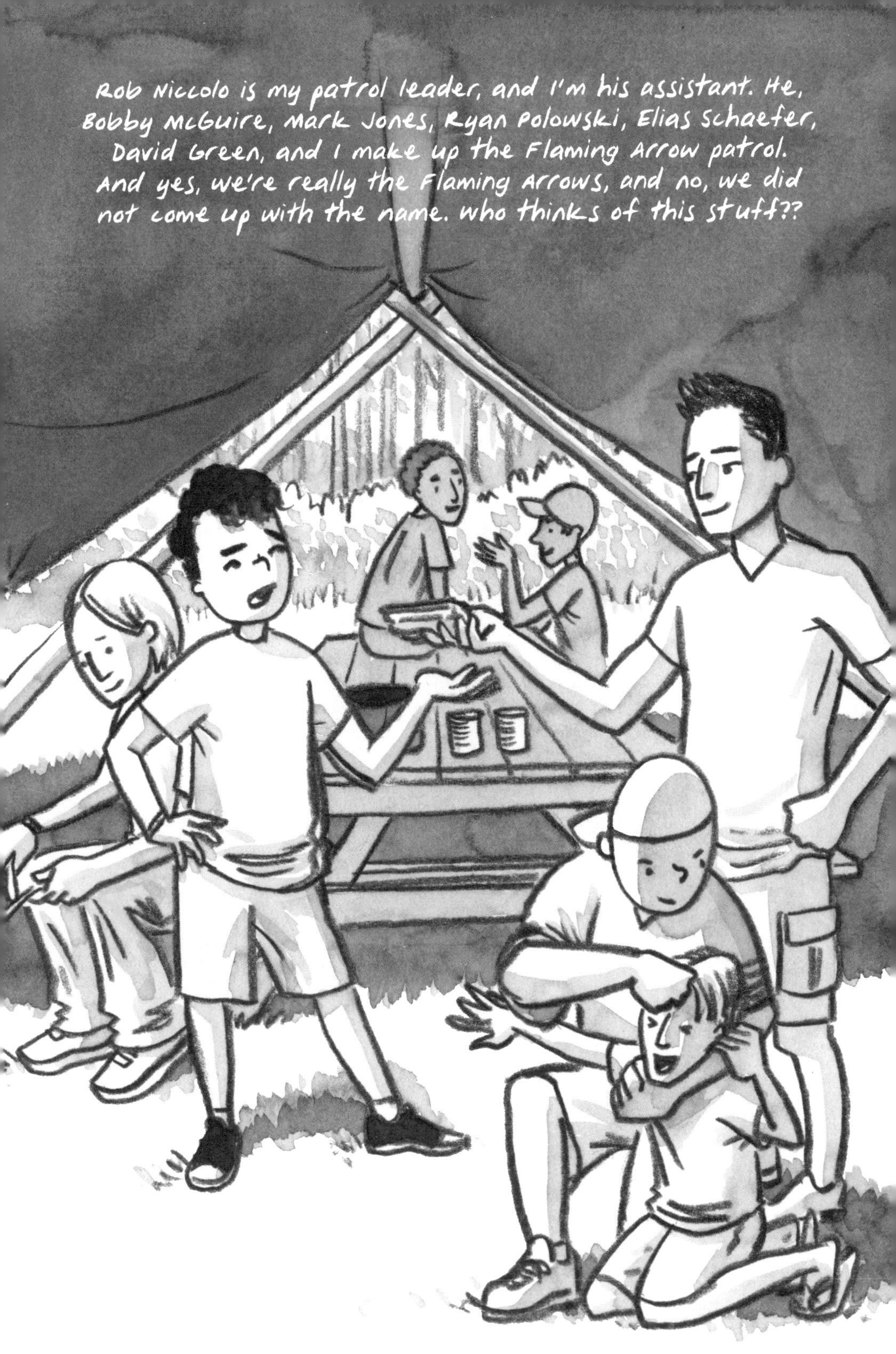
Rob Niccolo is my patrol leader, and I'm his assistant. He, Bobby McGuire, Mark Jones, Ryan Polowski, Elias Schaefer, David Green, and I make up the Flaming Arrow patrol. And yes, we're really the Flaming Arrows, and no, we did not come up with the name. Who thinks of this stuff??

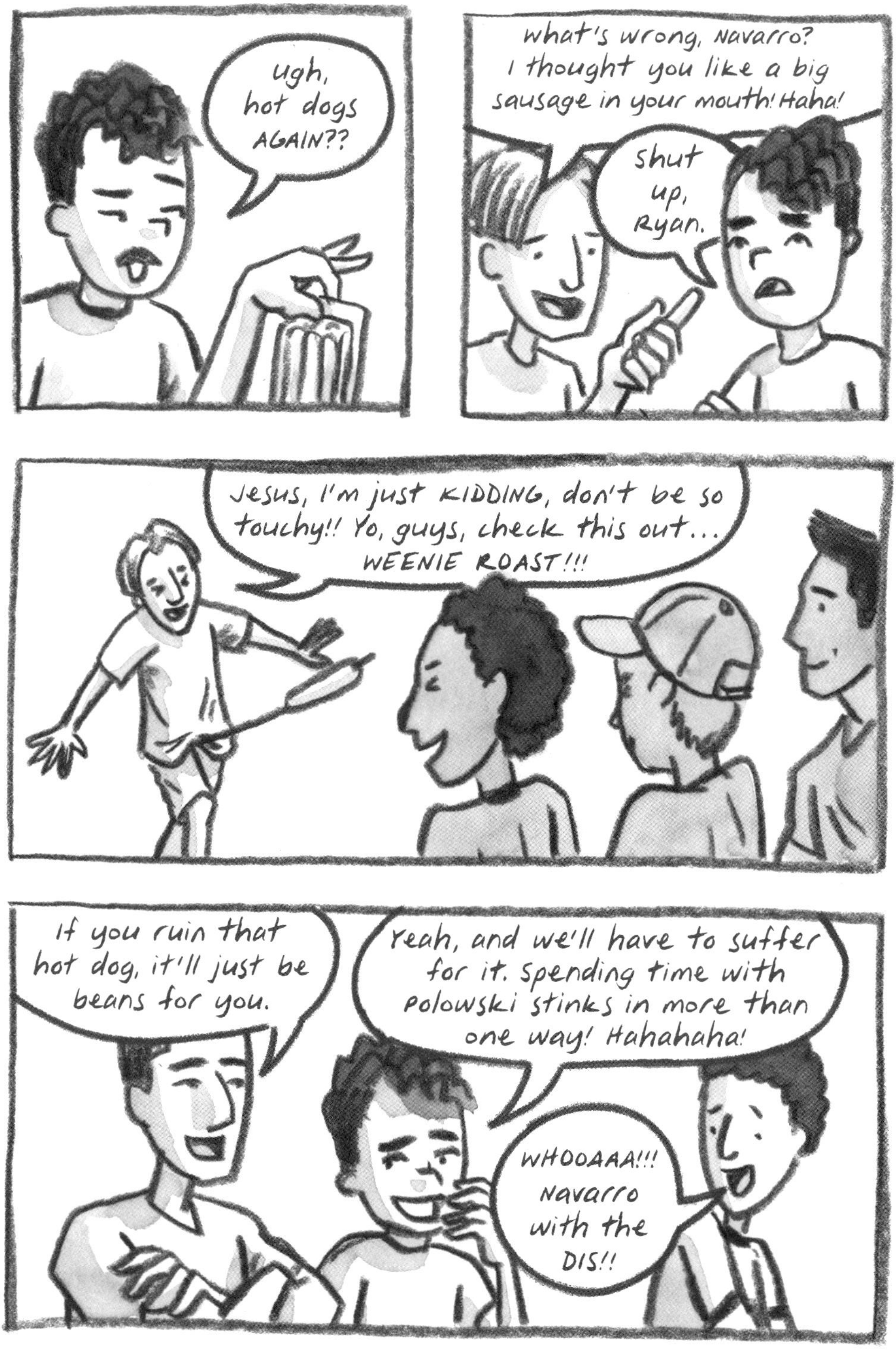
ugh, hot dogs AGAIN??
what's wrong, Navarro? I thought you like a big sausage in your mouth! Haha!
Shut up, Ryan.
Jesus, I'm just KIDDING, don't be so touchy!! Yo, guys, check this out... WEENIE ROAST!!!
If you ruin that hot dog, it'll just be beans for you.
Yeah, and we'll have to suffer for it. Spending time with Polowski stinks in more than one way! Hahahaha!
WHOOAAA!!! Navarro with the DIS!!

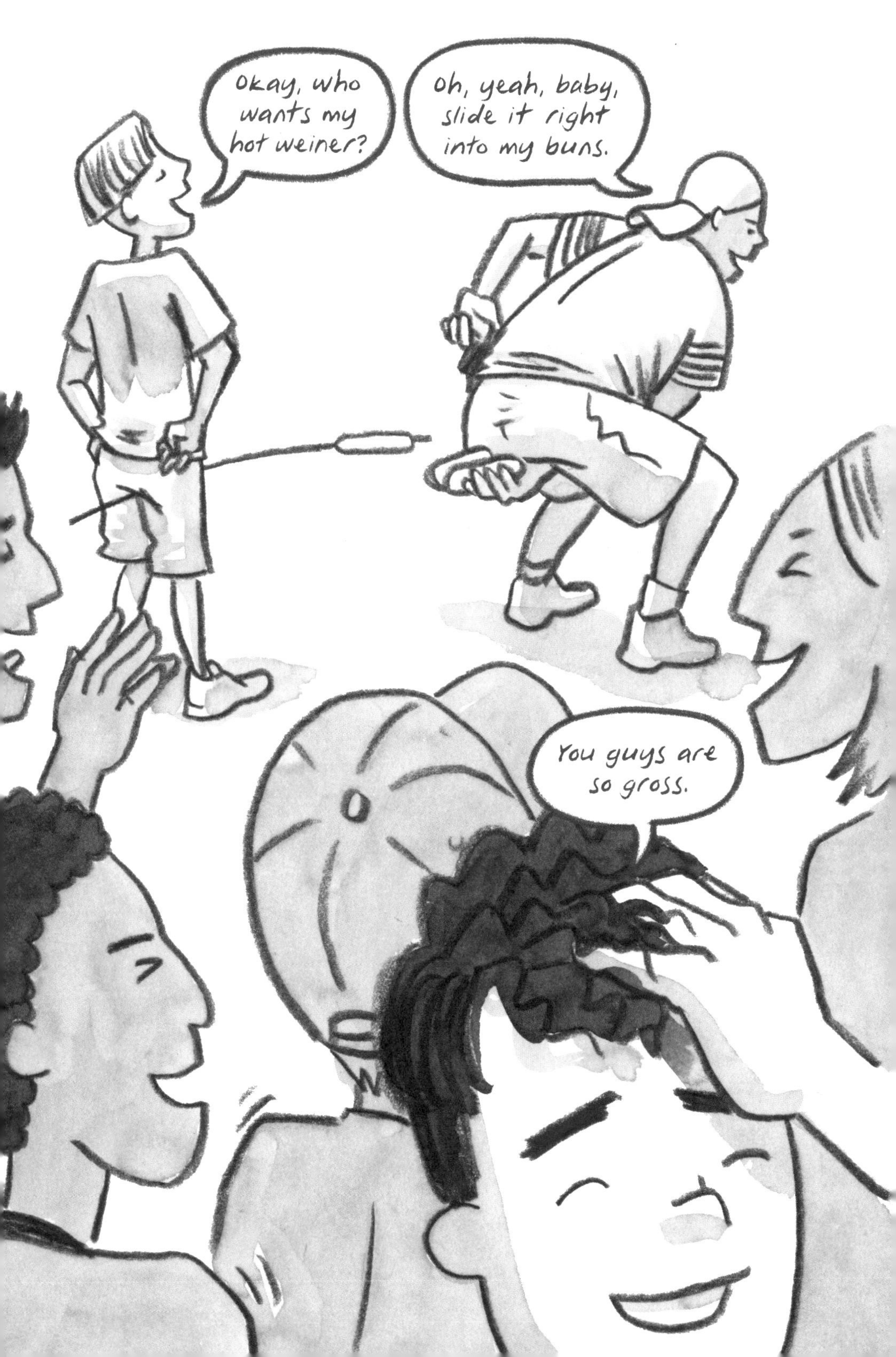
Okay, who wants my hot weiner?
Oh, yeah, baby, slide it right into my buns.
You guys are so gross.

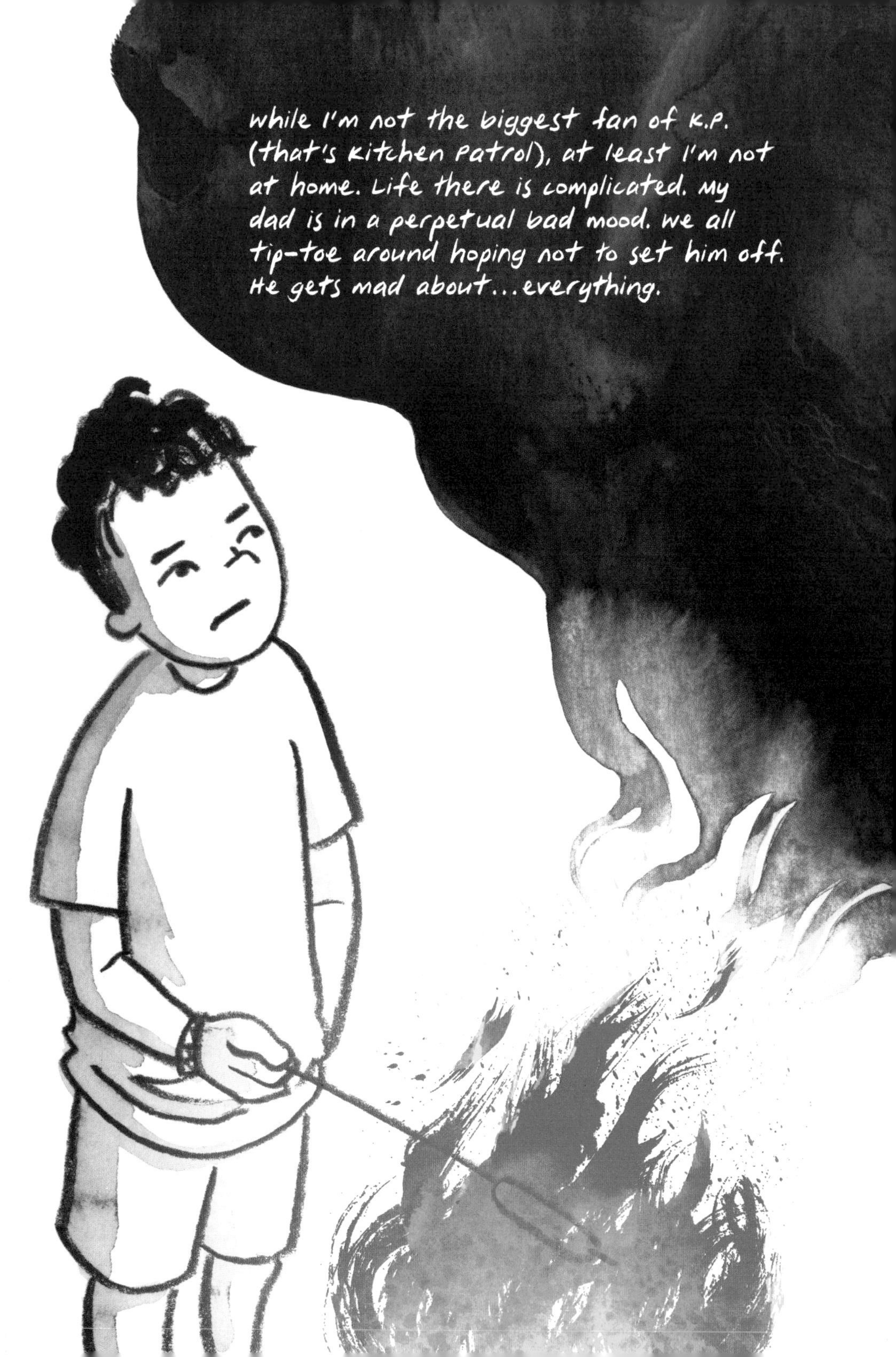
while I'm not the biggest fan of K.P. (that's kitchen patrol), at least I'm not at home. Life there is complicated. My dad is in a perpetual bad mood. we all tip-toe around hoping not to set him off. He gets mad about...everything.

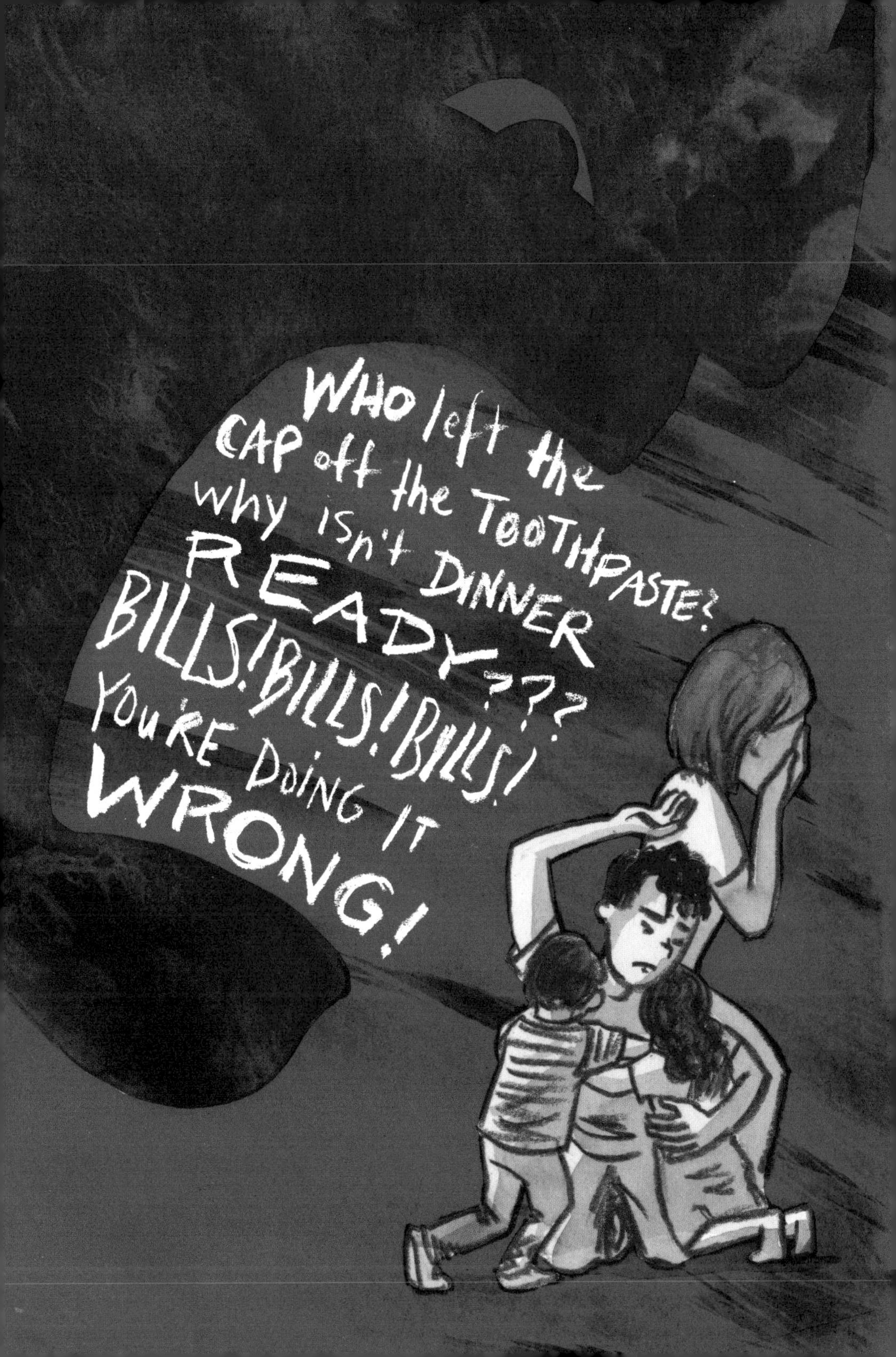
WHO left the
CAP off the TOOTHPASTE?
why isn't DINNER
READY???
BILLS! BILLS! BILLS!
YOU'RE DOING IT
WRONG!

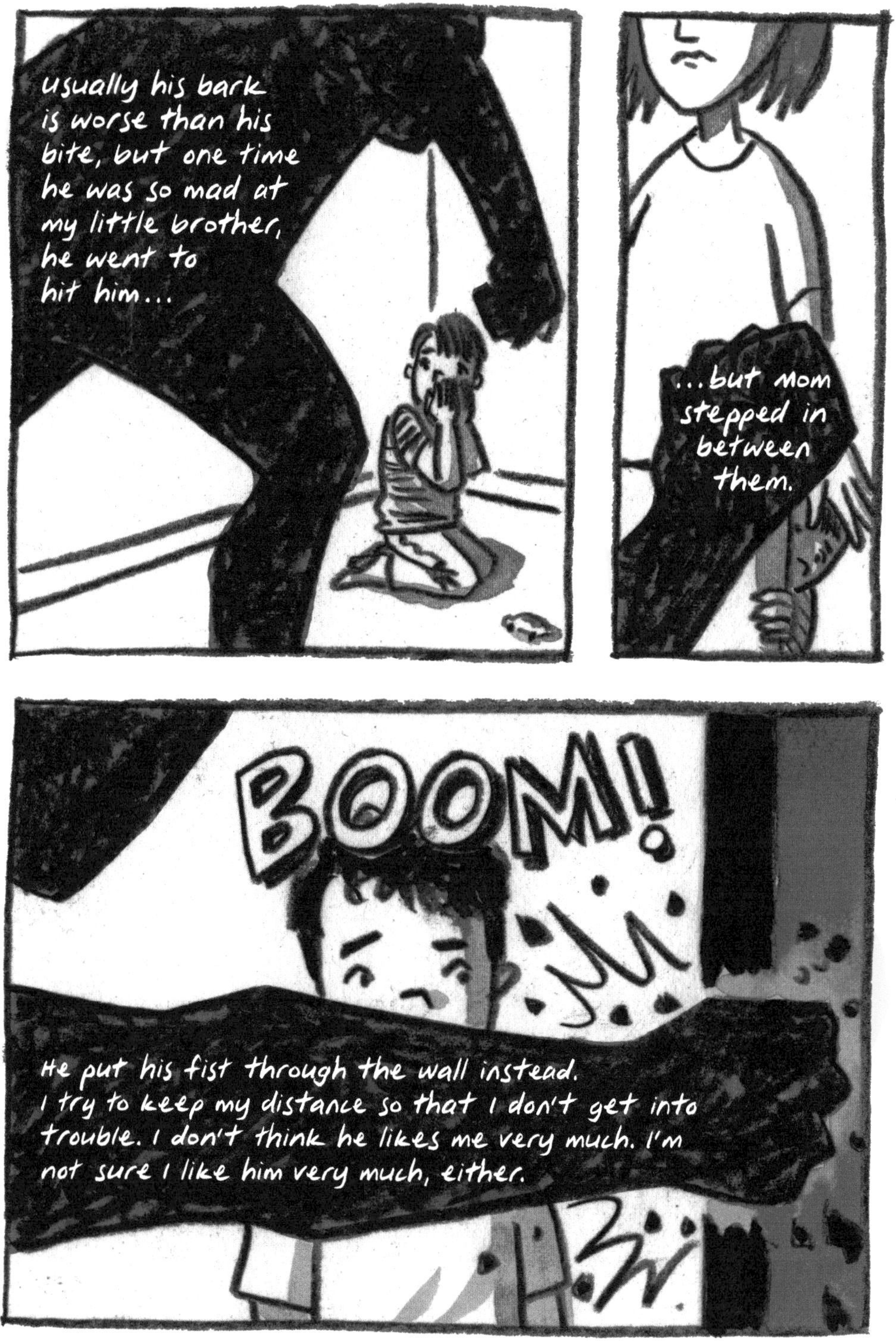
usually his bark is worse than his bite, but one time he was so mad at my little brother, he went to hit him...
...but mom stepped in between them.
BOOM!
He put his fist through the wall instead. I try to keep my distance so that I don't get into trouble. I don't think he likes me very much. I'm not sure I like him very much, either.

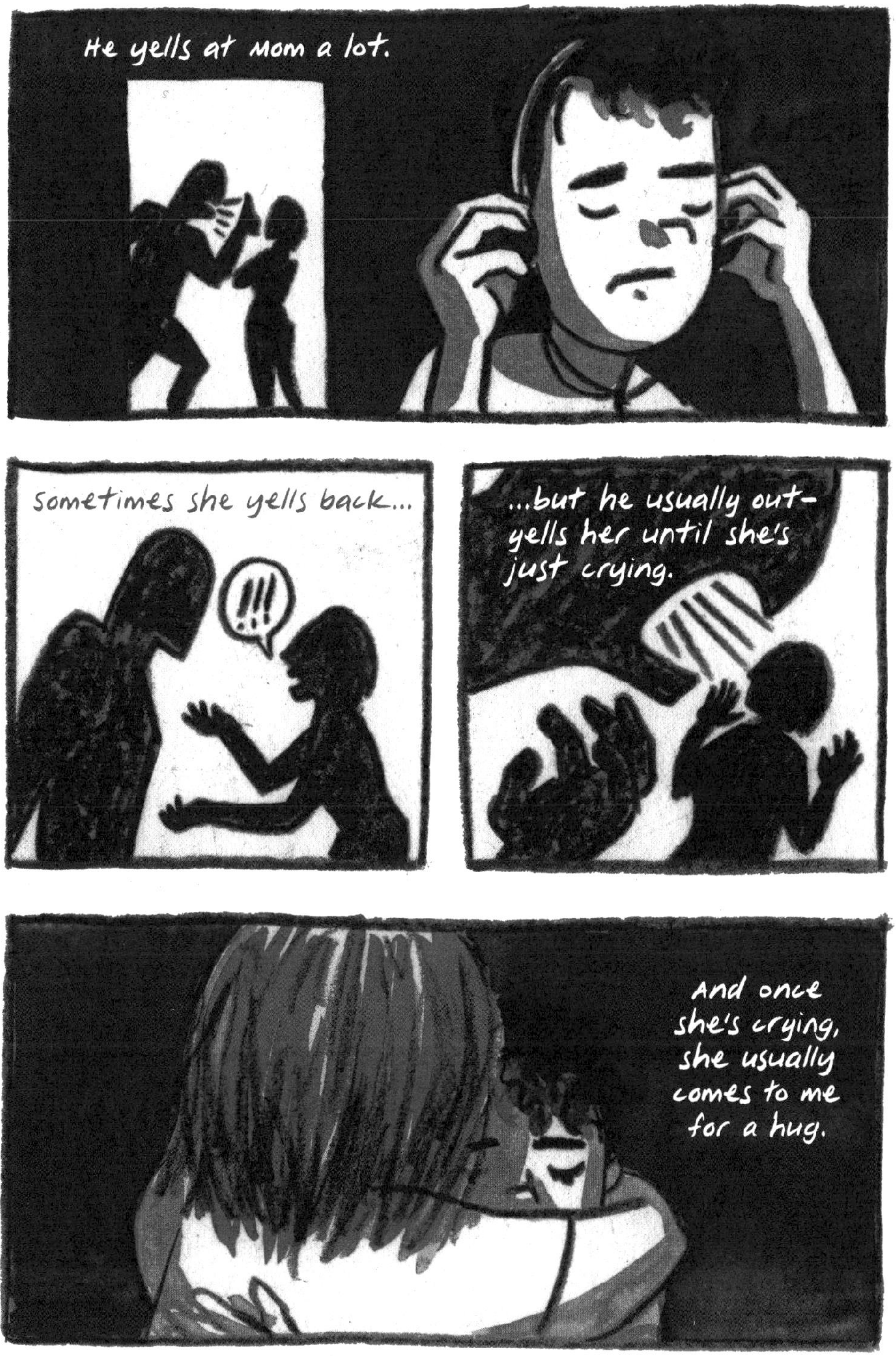
He yells at Mom a lot.
Sometimes she yells back...
!!!
...but he usually out-yells her until she's just crying.
And once she's crying, she usually comes to me for a hug.

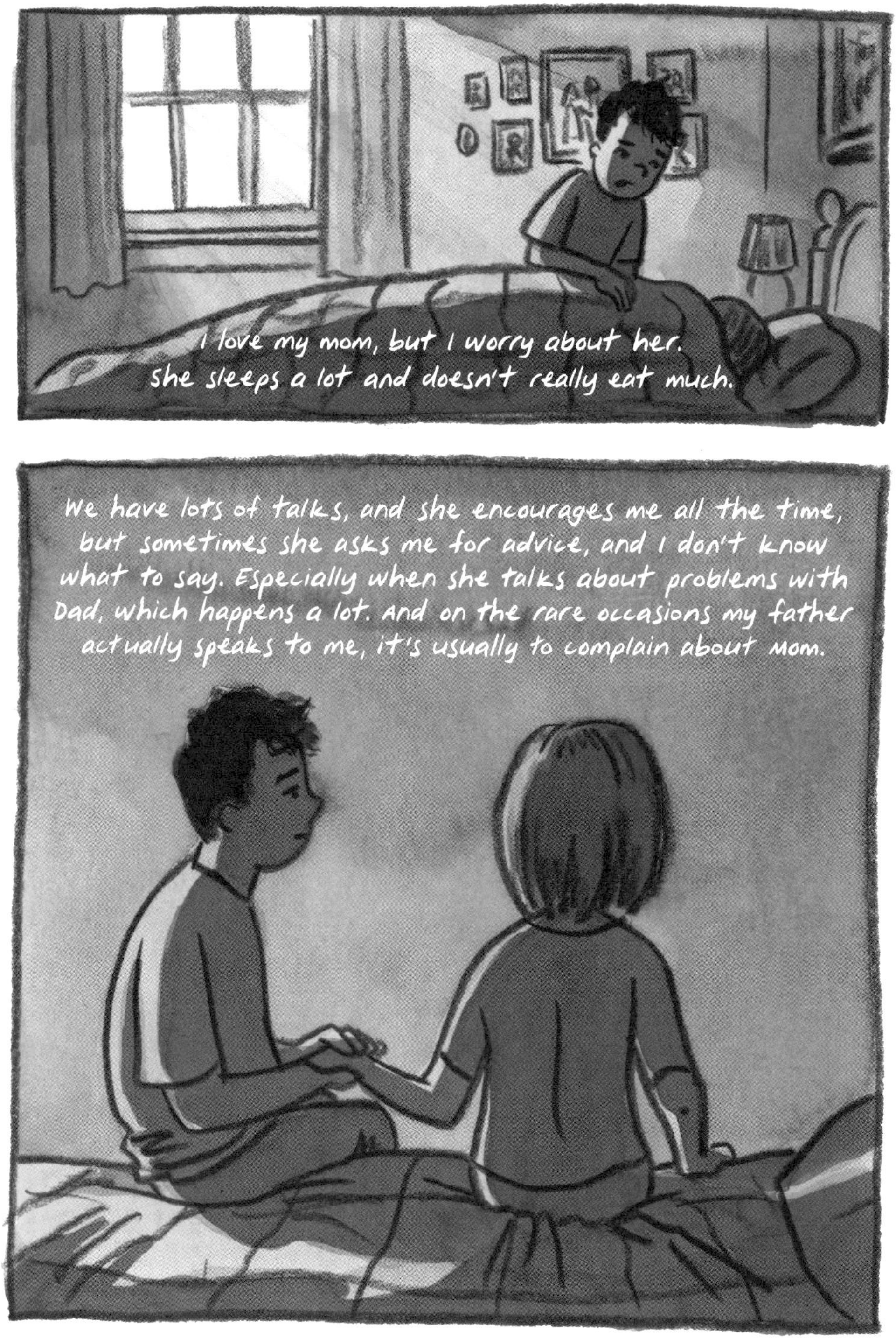
I love my mom, but I worry about her. She sleeps a lot and doesn't really eat much.
We have lots of talks, and she encourages me all the time, but sometimes she asks me for advice, and I don't know what to say. Especially when she talks about problems with Dad, which happens a lot. And on the rare occasions my father actually speaks to me, it's usually to complain about Mom.

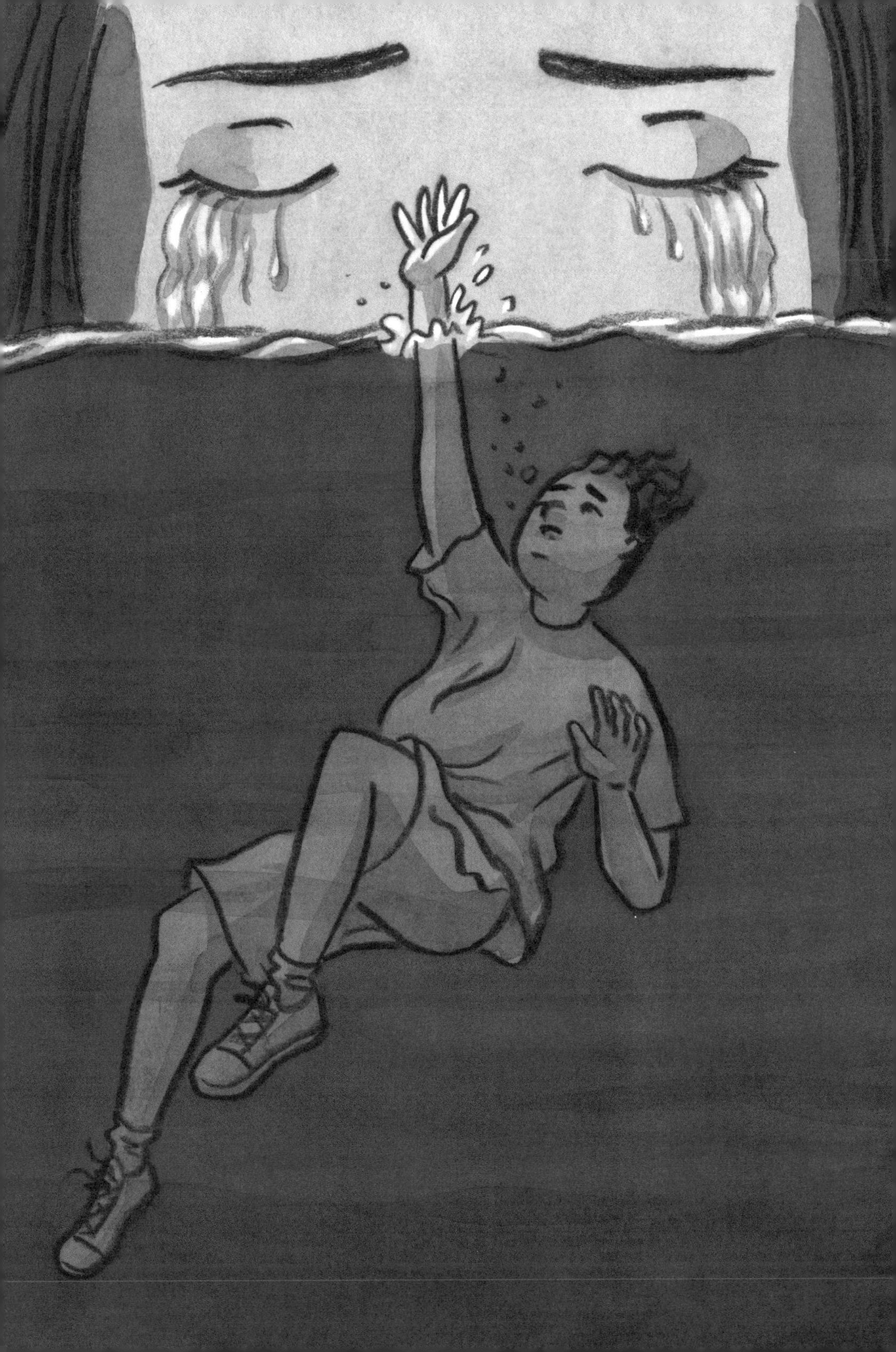

I don't know what it is about me that makes people want to share everything with me. Even here at camp, though I'm not the tallest, or strongest, or coolest, for some reason everyone comes to me with their problems...

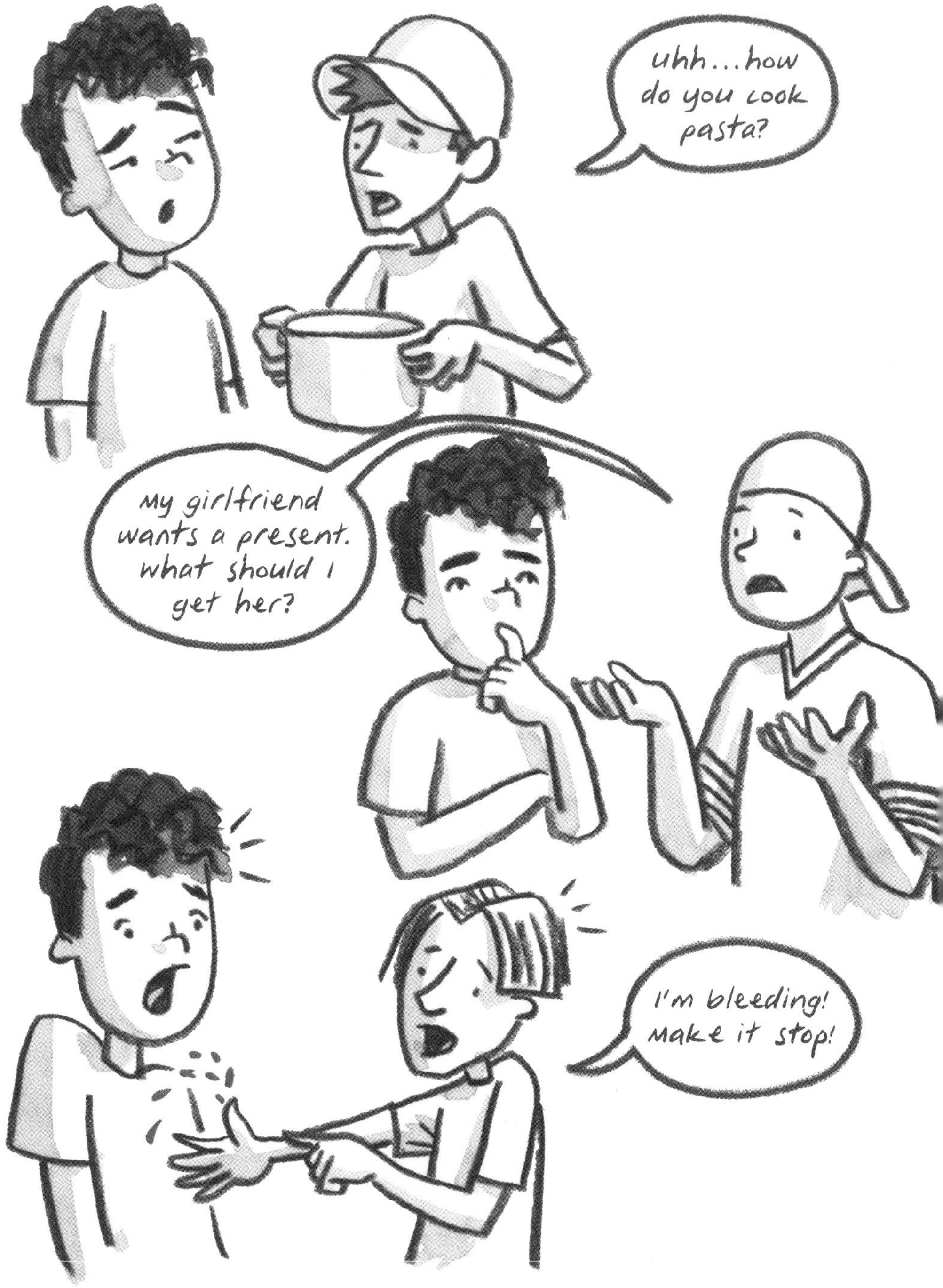
uhh...how do you cook pasta?
My girlfriend wants a present. What should I get her?
I'm bleeding! Make it stop!

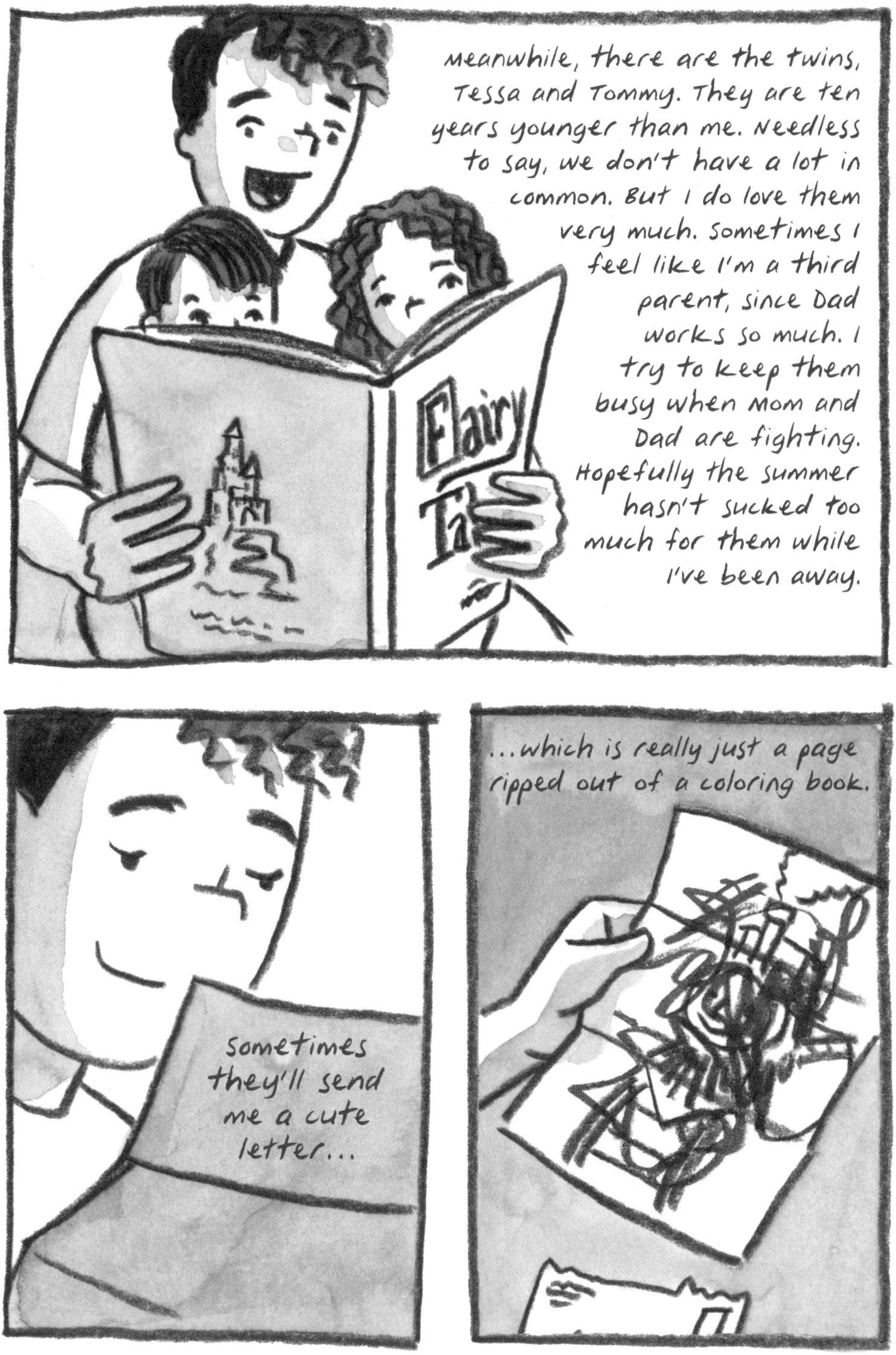
Meanwhile, there are the twins, Tessa and Tommy. They are ten years younger than me. Needless to say, we don't have a lot in common. But I do love them very much. Sometimes I feel like I'm a third parent, since Dad works so much. I try to keep them busy when Mom and Dad are fighting. Hopefully the summer hasn't sucked too much for them while I've been away.
Fairy
Sometimes they'll send me a cute letter...
...which is really just a page ripped out of a coloring book.

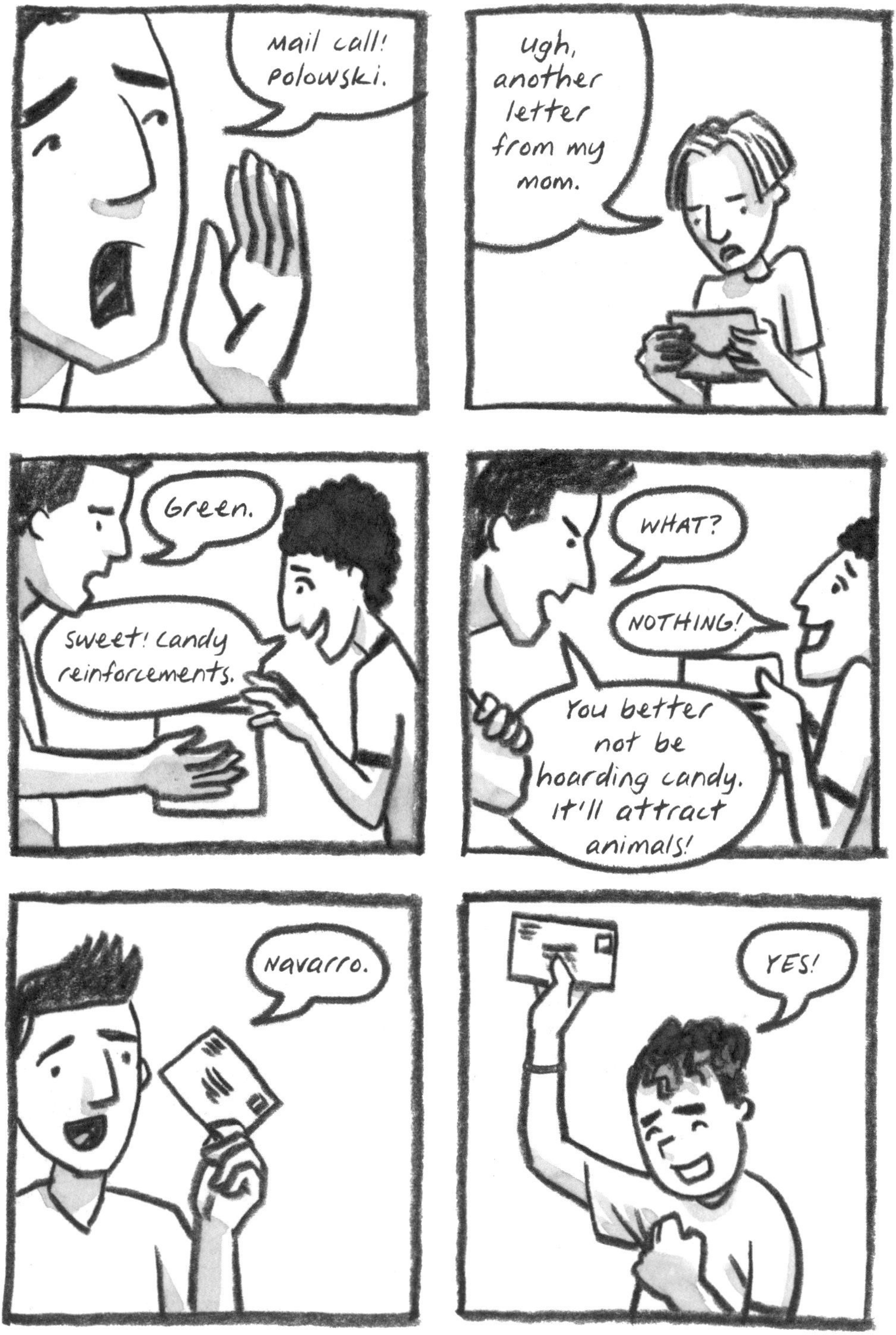
Mail call! Polowski.
Ugh, another letter from my mom.
Green.
Sweet! Candy reinforcements.
WHAT?
NOTHING!
You better not be hoarding candy. It'll attract animals!
Navarro.
YES!

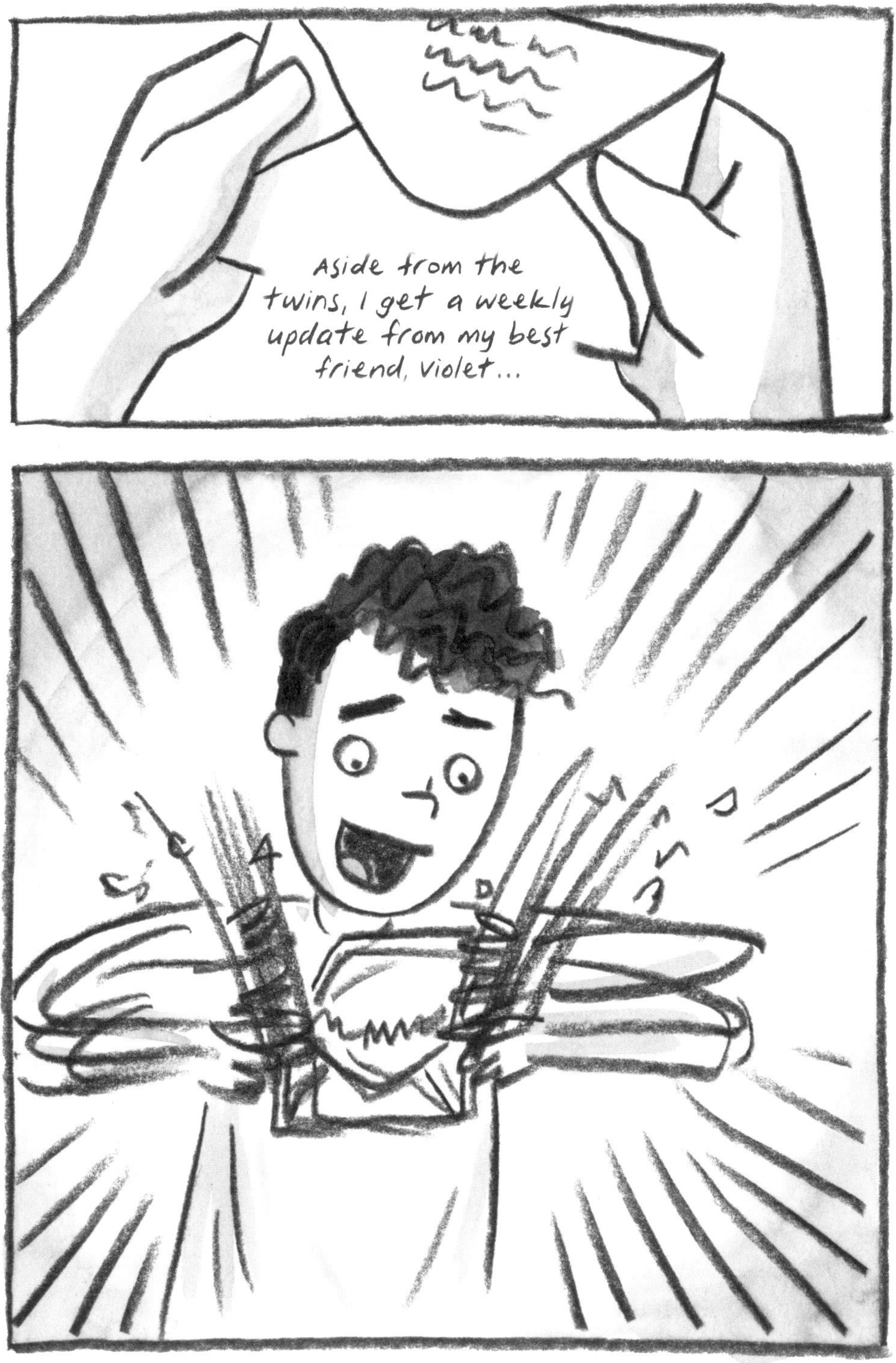
Aside from the twins, I get a weekly update from my best friend, Violet...

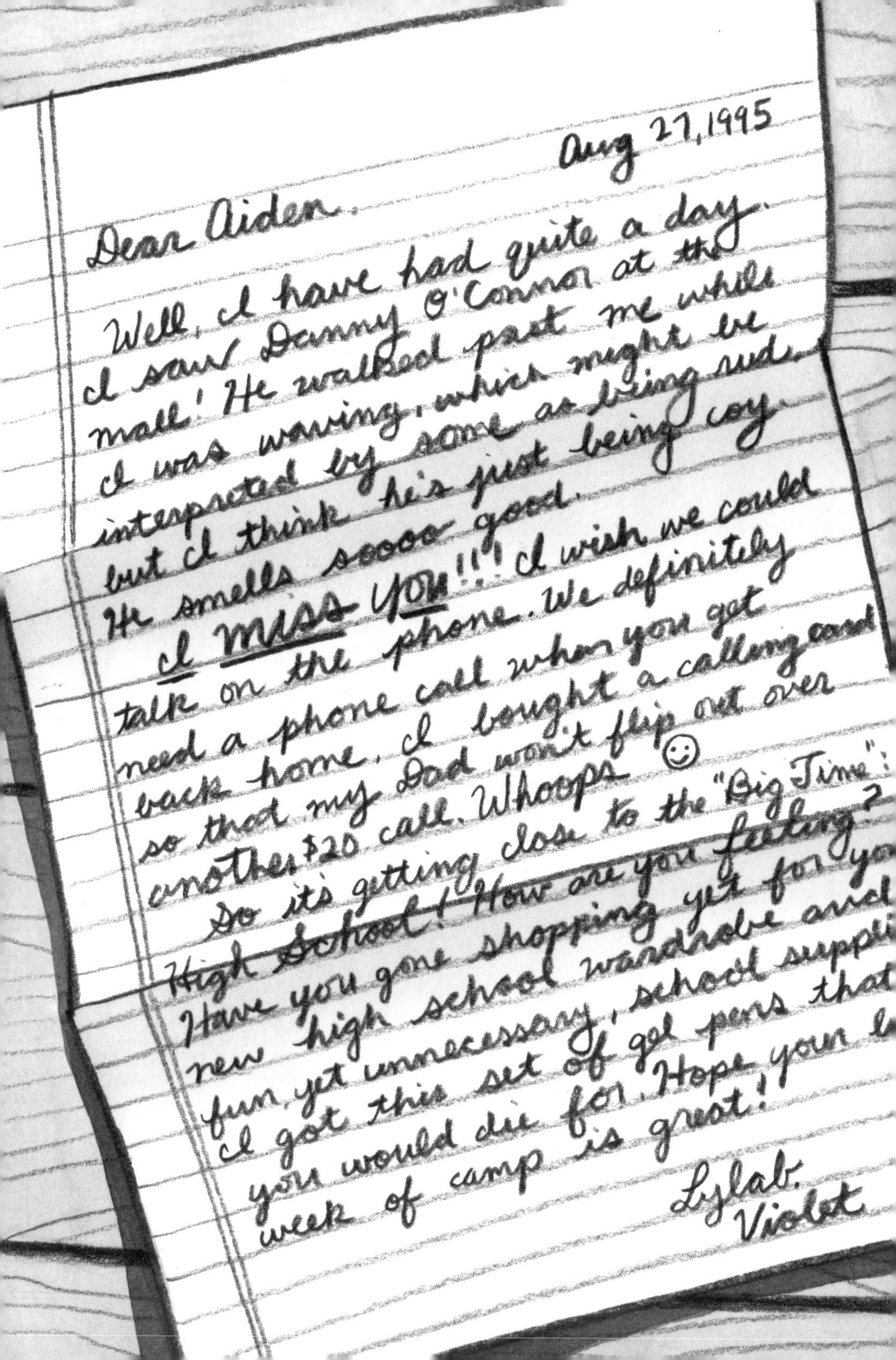

Aug 27, 1995

Dear Aiden,

Well, I have had quite a day. I saw Danny O'Connor at the mall! He walked past me while I was waving, which might be interpreted by some as being rude, but I think he's just being coy. He smells soooo good.

I MISS YOU!!! I wish we could talk on the phone. We definitely need a phone call when you get back home. I bought a calling card so that my Dad won't flip out over another $20 call. Whoops ☺

So it's getting close to the "Big Time": High School! How are you feeling? Have you gone shopping yet for yo new high school wardrobe and fun, yet unnecessary, school suppli I got this set of gel pens tha you would die for. Hope your l week of camp is great!

Lylab.
Violet

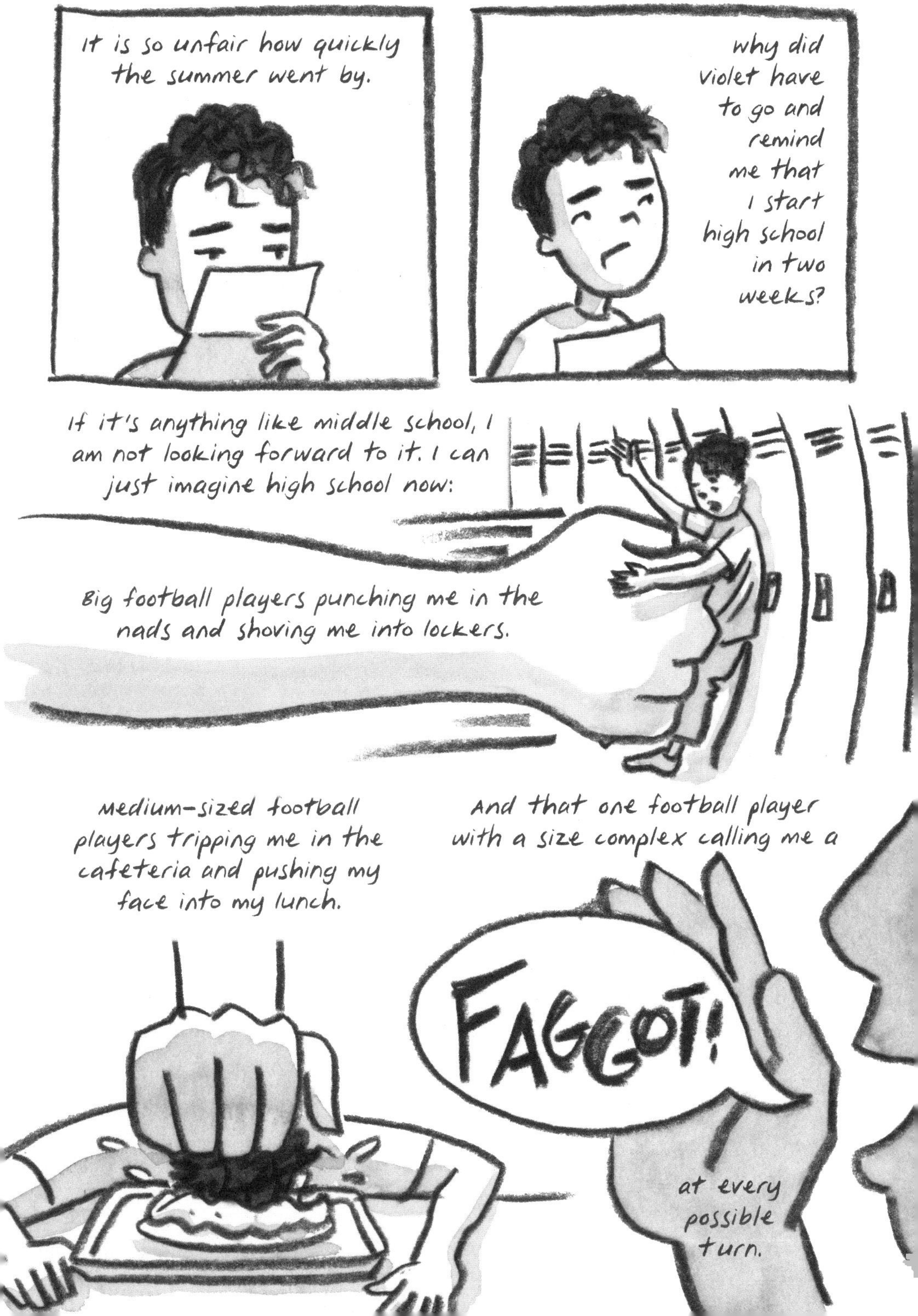
It is so unfair how quickly the summer went by.
why did violet have to go and remind me that I start high school in two weeks?
If it's anything like middle school, I am not looking forward to it. I can just imagine high school now:
Big football players punching me in the nads and shoving me into lockers.
Medium-sized football players tripping me in the cafeteria and pushing my face into my lunch.
And that one football player with a size complex calling me a
FAGGOT!
at every possible turn.

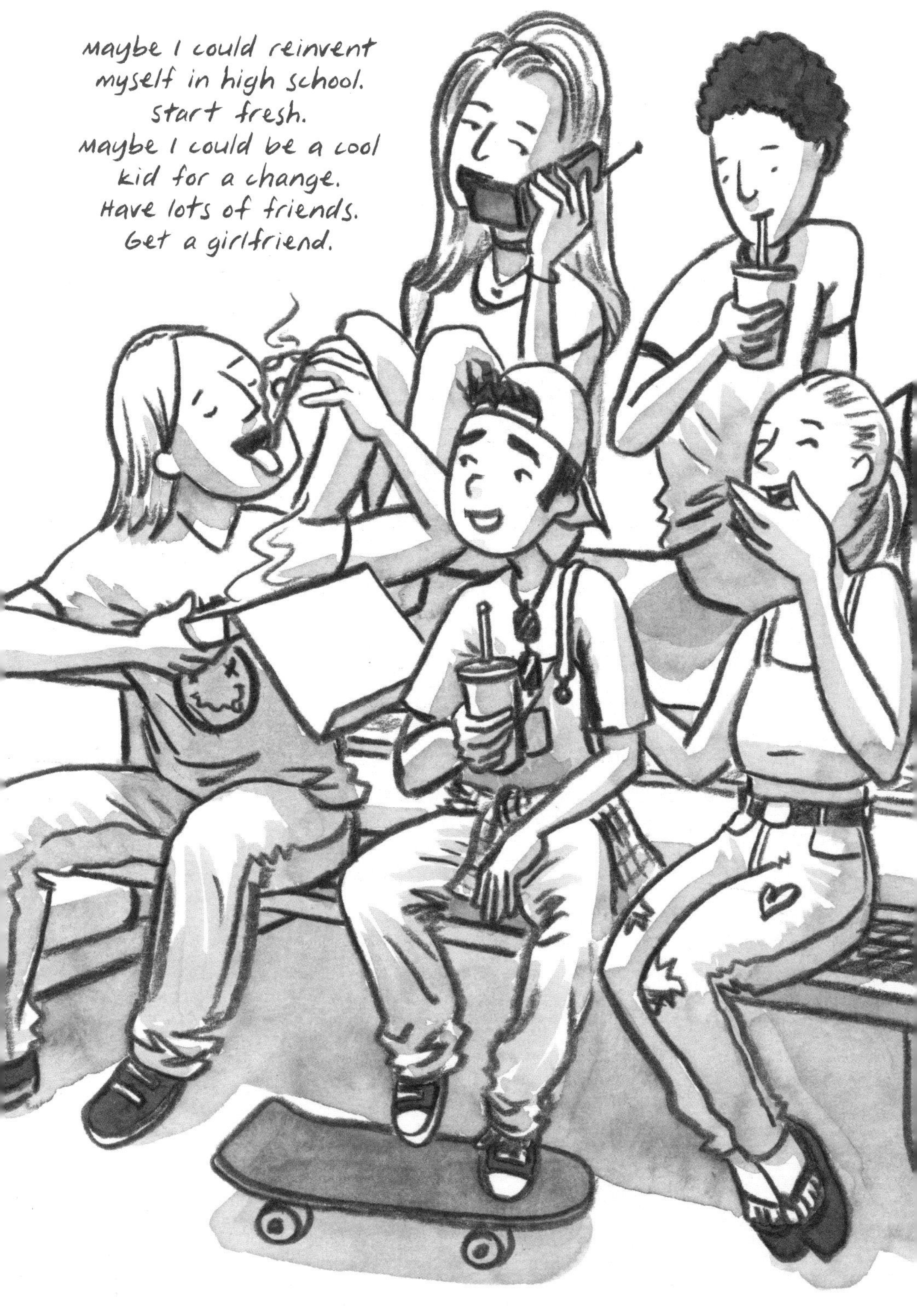
Maybe I could reinvent
myself in high school.
Start fresh.
Maybe I could be a cool
kid for a change.
Have lots of friends.
Get a girlfriend.

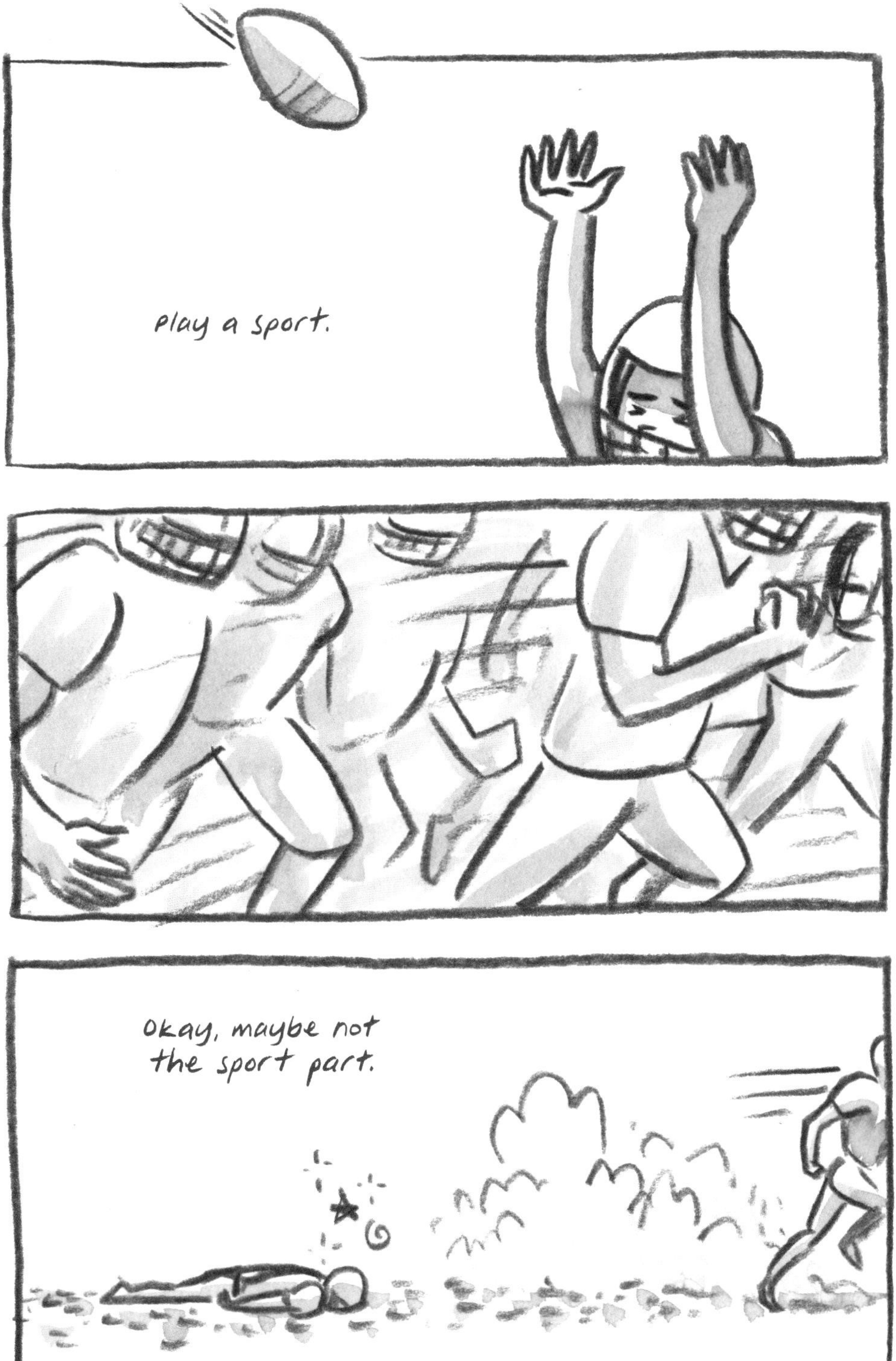
Play a sport.
Okay, maybe not
the sport part.

I'd rather just stay here at camp.
I understand how it works, unlike high school.

PATROL

TROOP

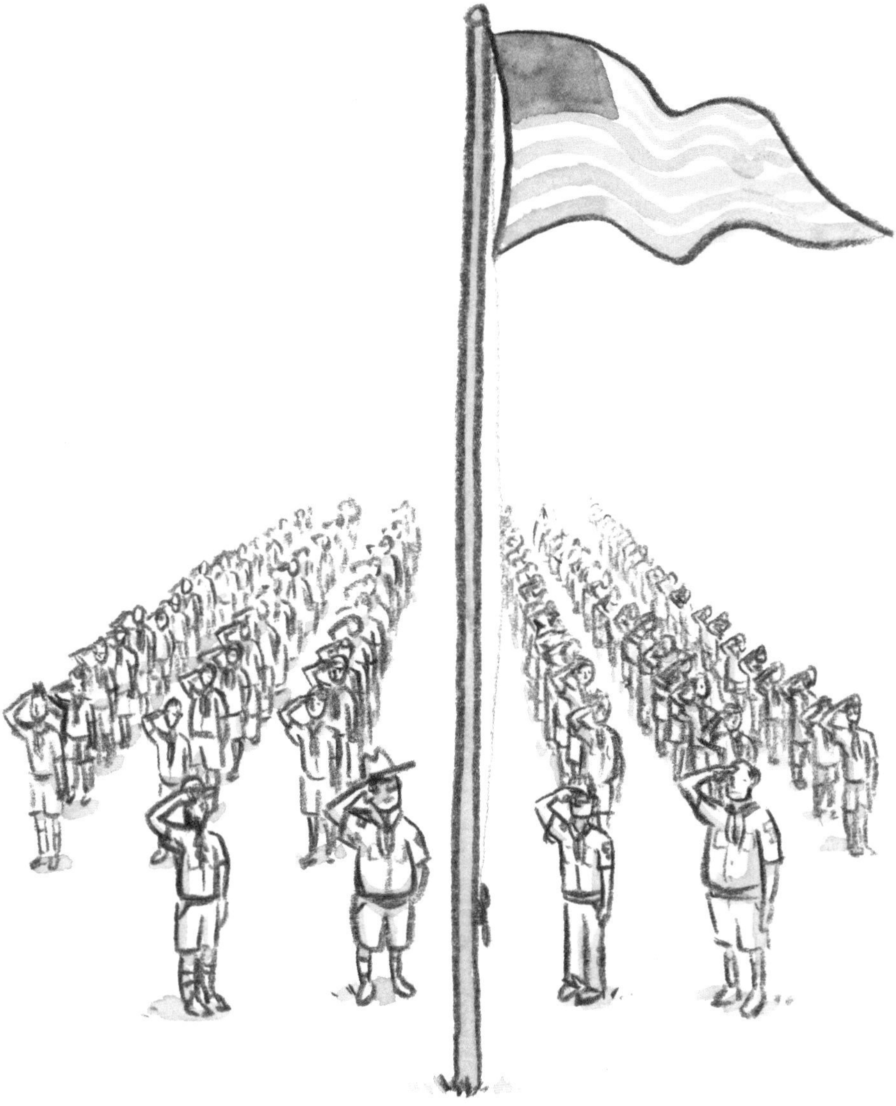

CAMP

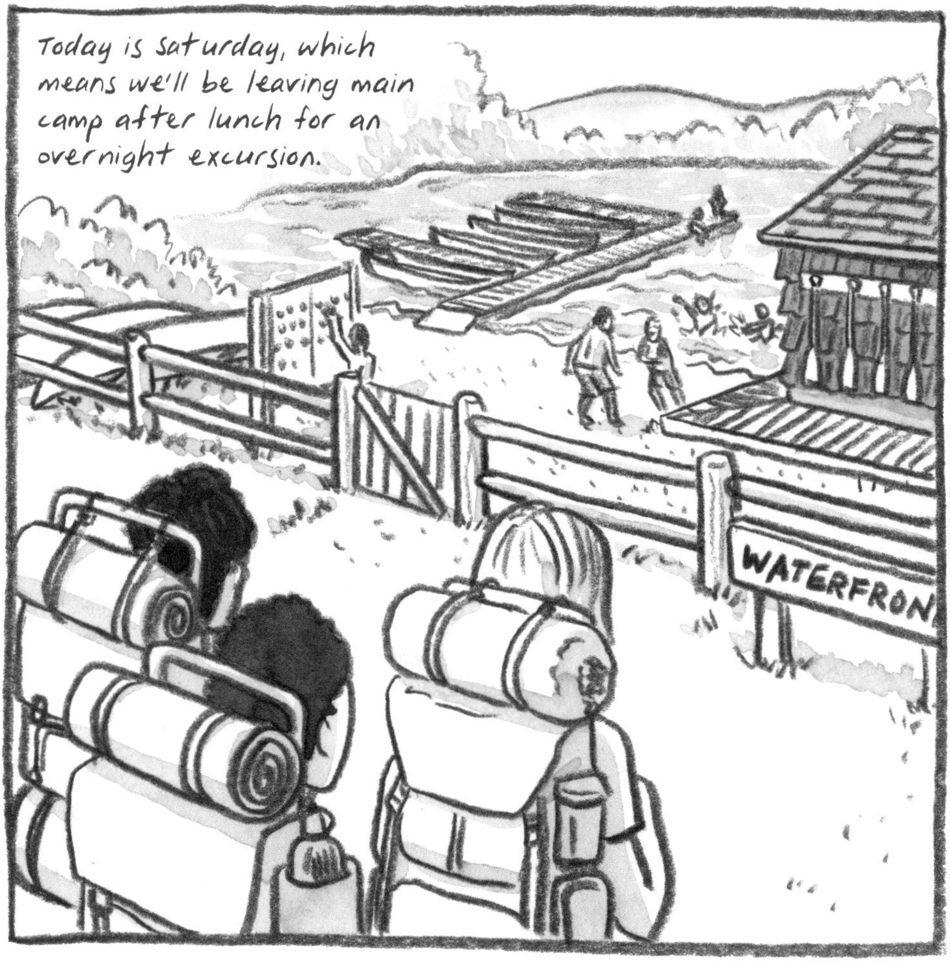
Today is saturday, which means we'll be leaving main camp after lunch for an overnight excursion.
WATERFRON

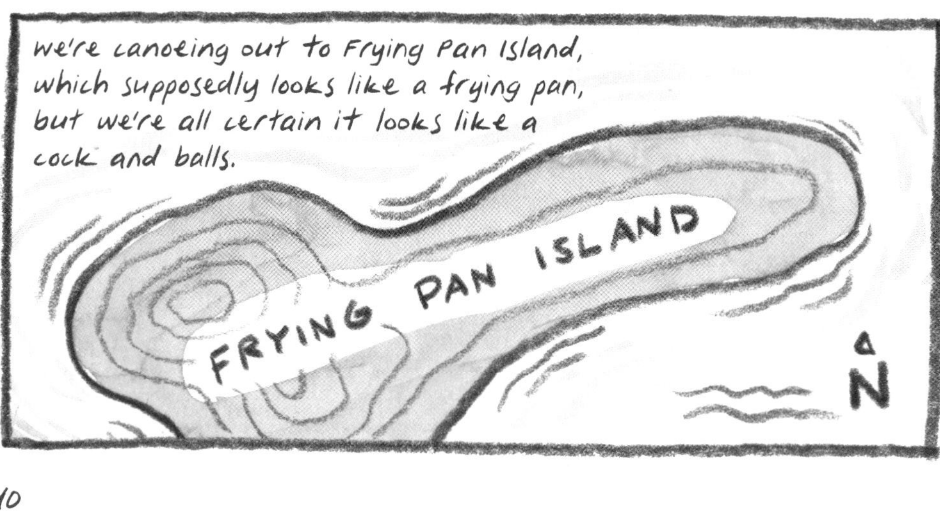
we're canoeing out to Frying Pan Island, which supposedly looks like a frying pan, but we're all certain it looks like a cock and balls.
FRYING PAN ISLAND
N

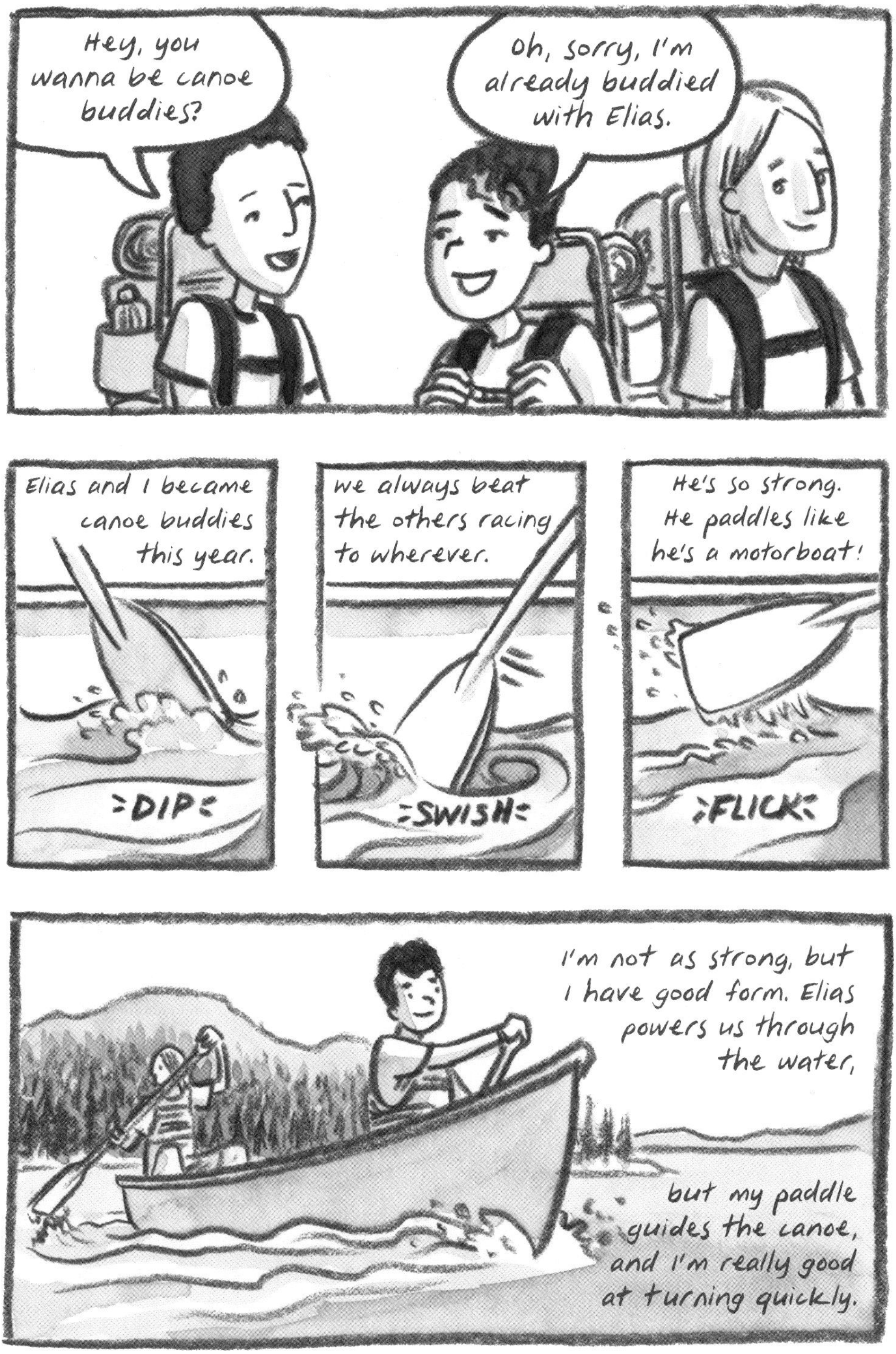
Hey, you wanna be canoe buddies?
Oh, sorry, I'm already buddied with Elias.
Elias and I became canoe buddies this year.
DIP
We always beat the others racing to wherever.
SWISH
He's so strong. He paddles like he's a motorboat!
FLICK
I'm not as strong, but I have good form. Elias powers us through the water,
but my paddle guides the canoe, and I'm really good at turning quickly.

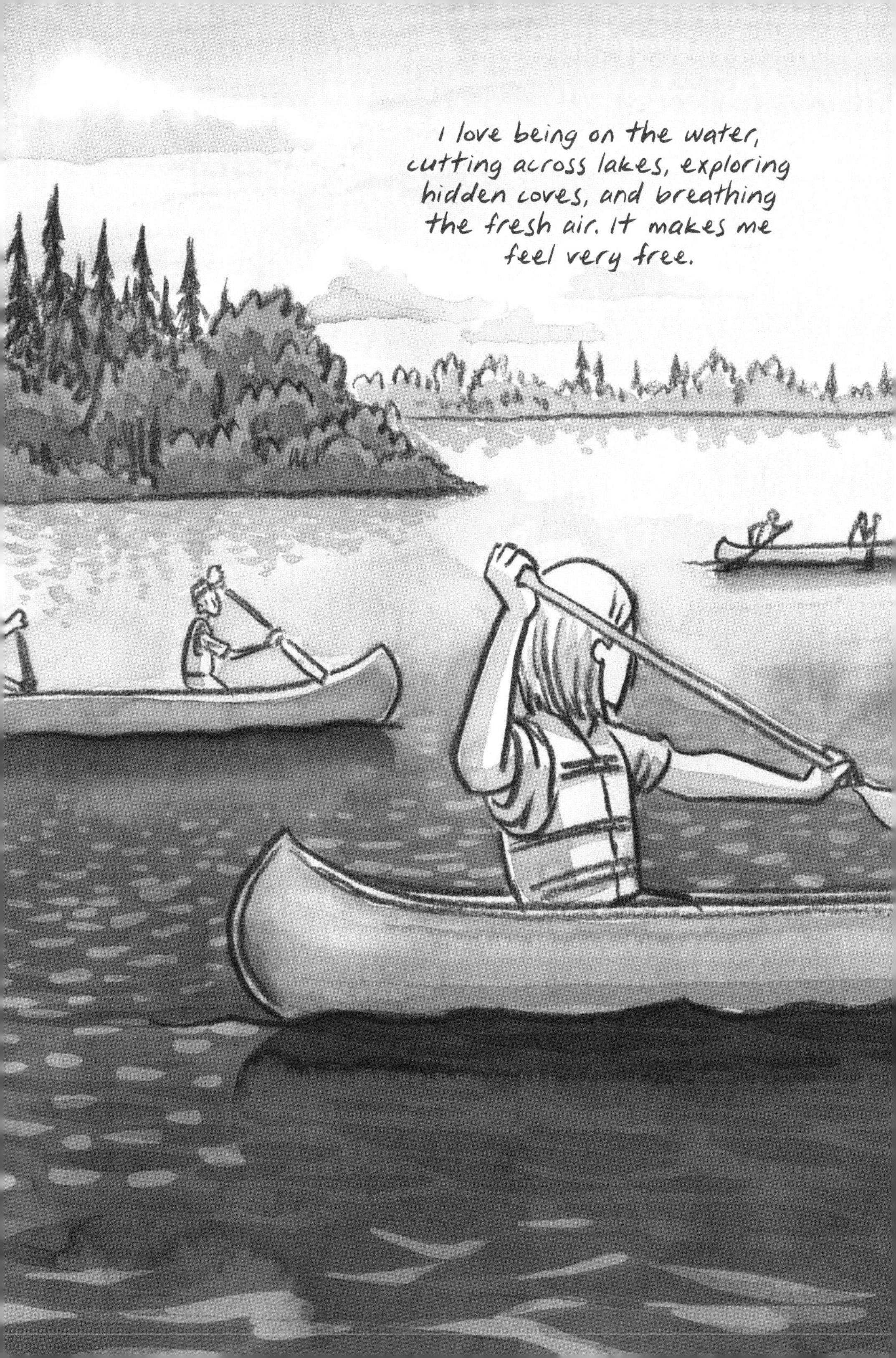
I love being on the water, cutting across lakes, exploring hidden coves, and breathing the fresh air. It makes me feel very free.

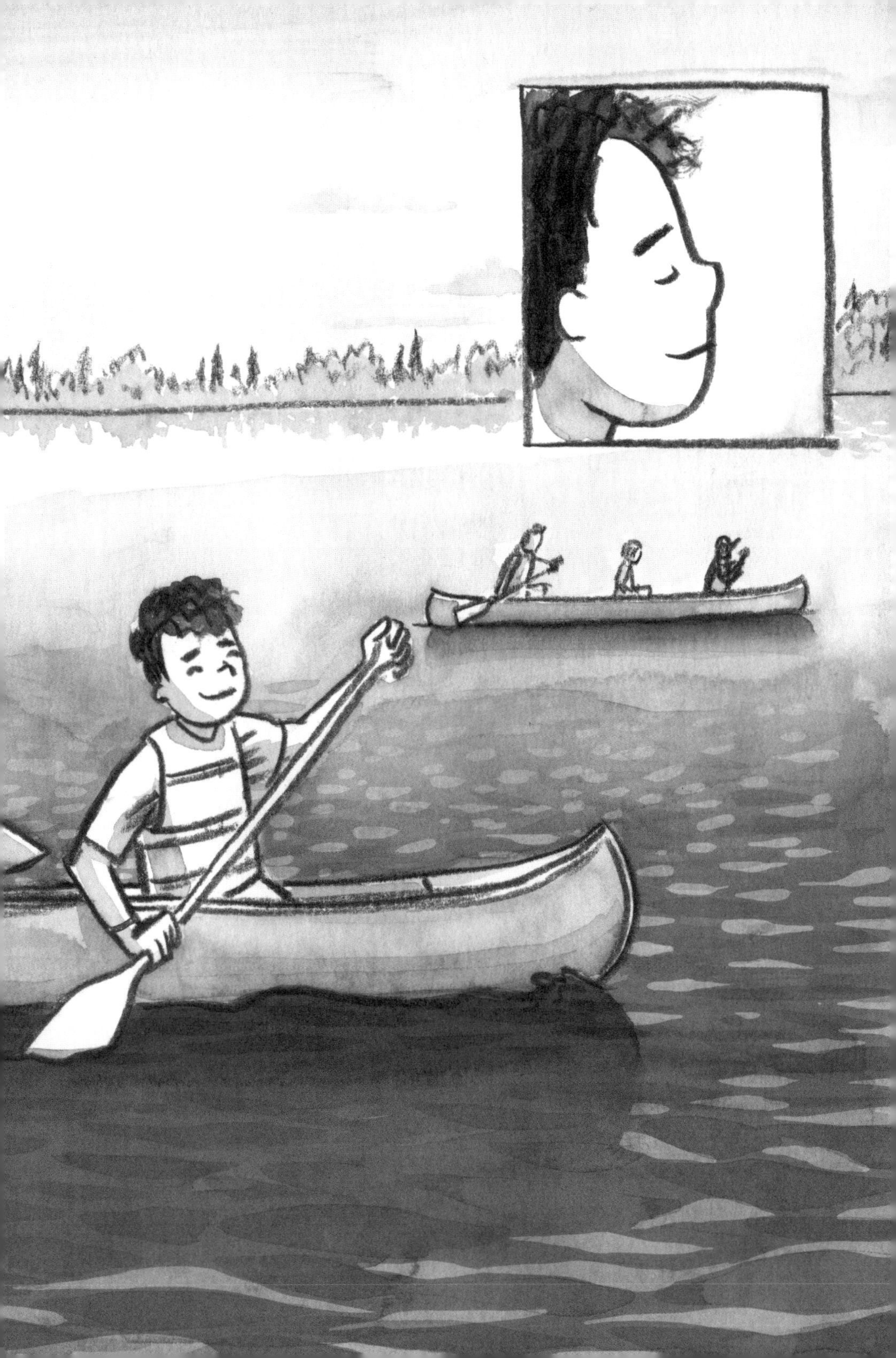

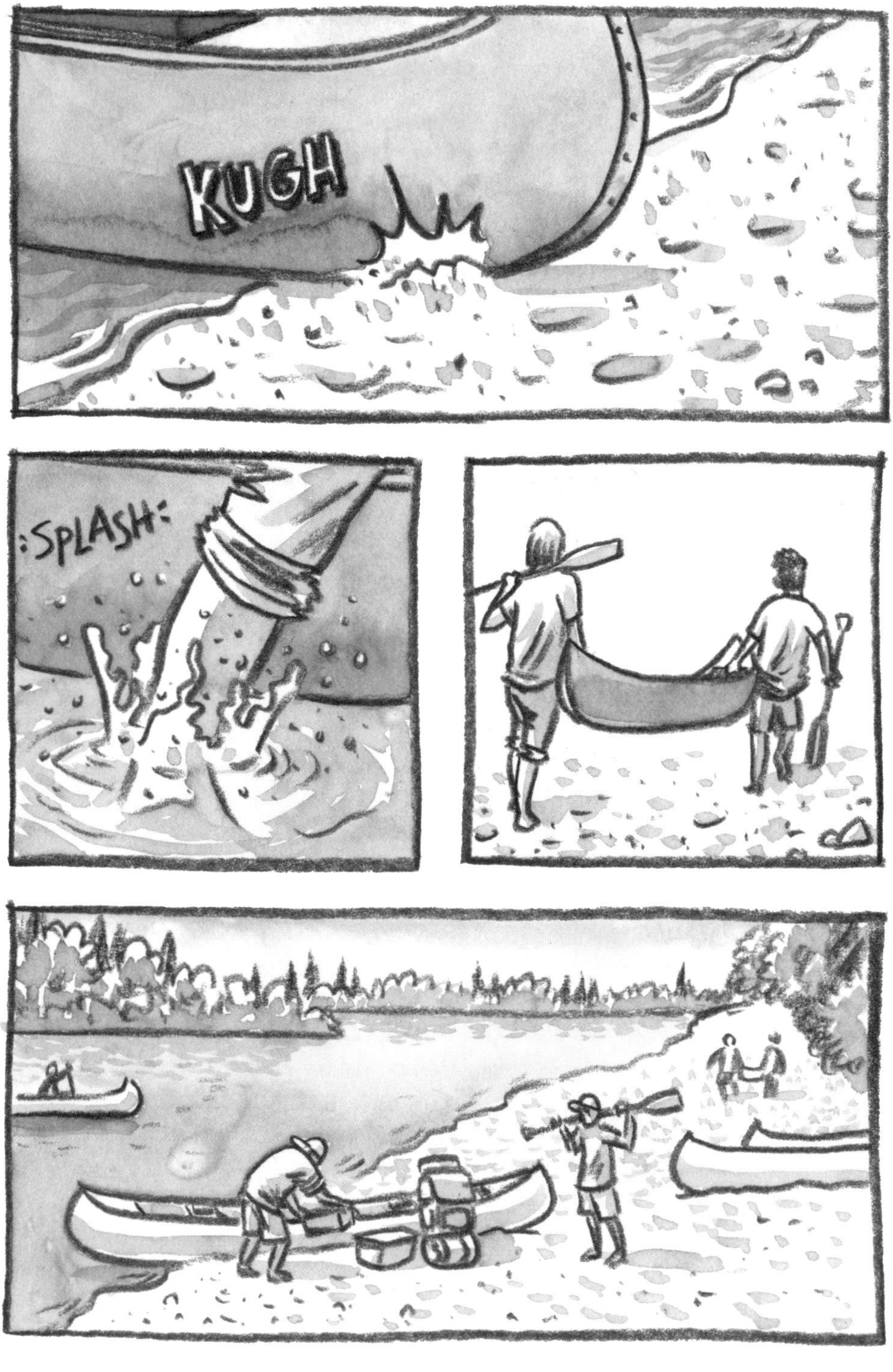
KUGH
SPLASH

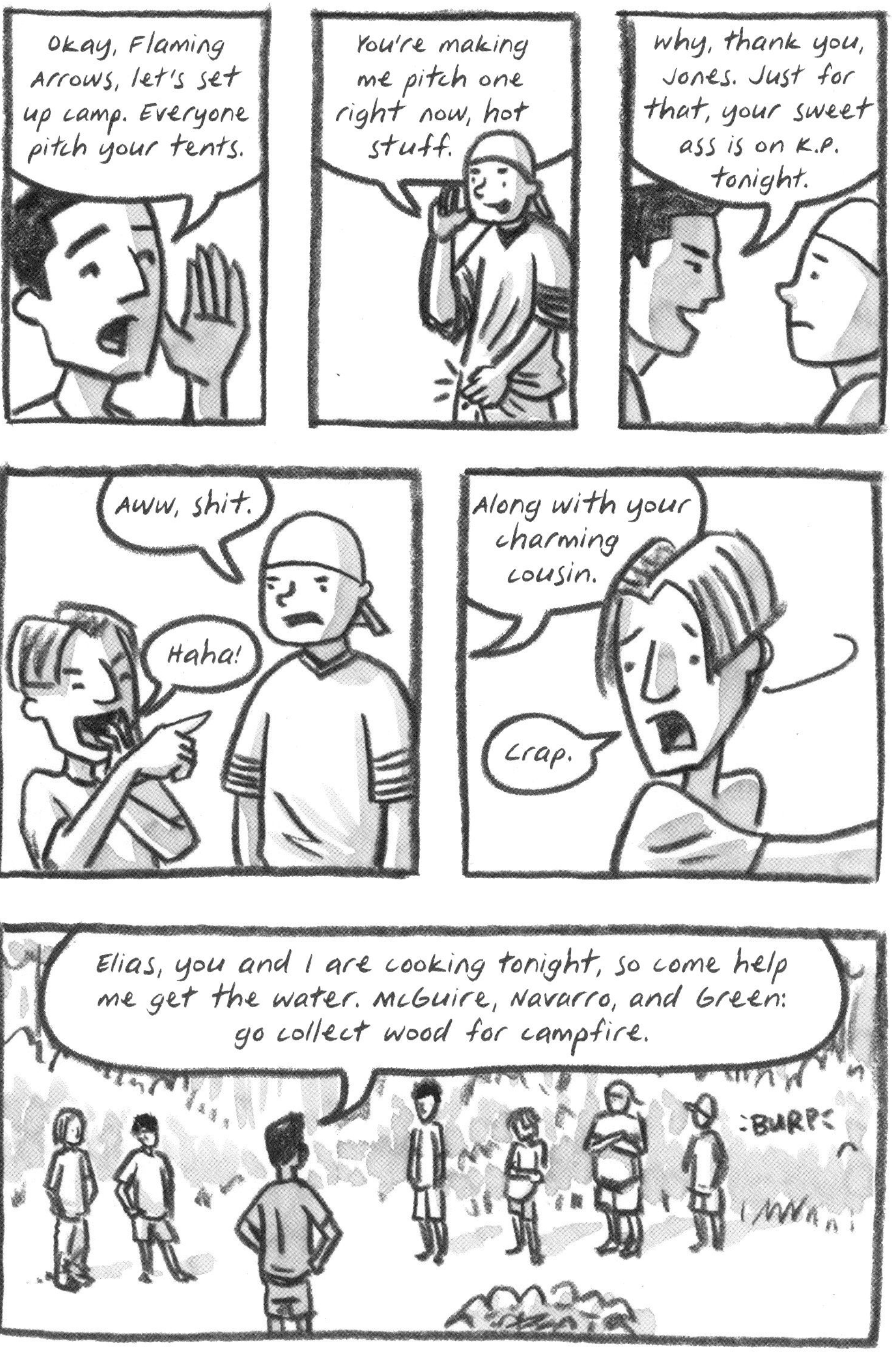
Okay, Flaming Arrows, let's set up camp. Everyone pitch your tents.
You're making me pitch one right now, hot stuff.
Why, thank you, Jones. Just for that, your sweet ass is on K.P. tonight.
Aww, shit.
Haha!
Along with your charming cousin.
Crap.
Elias, you and I are cooking tonight, so come help me get the water. McGuire, Navarro, and Green: go collect wood for campfire.
BURP

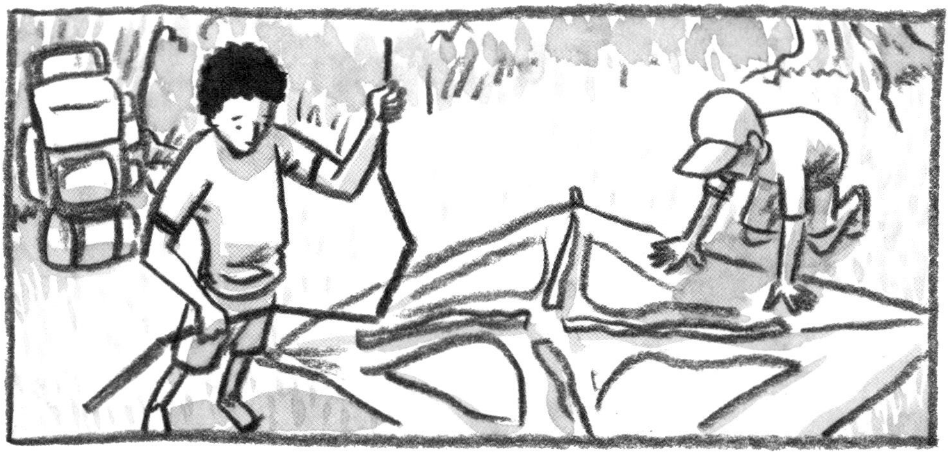

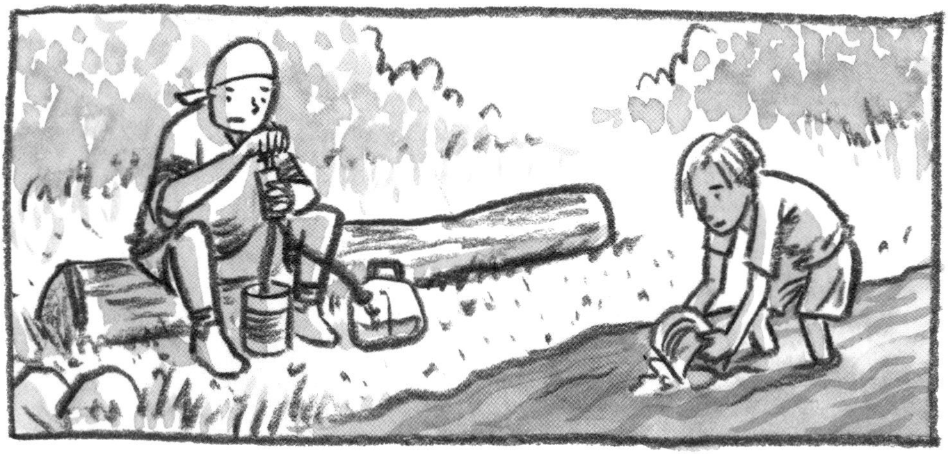

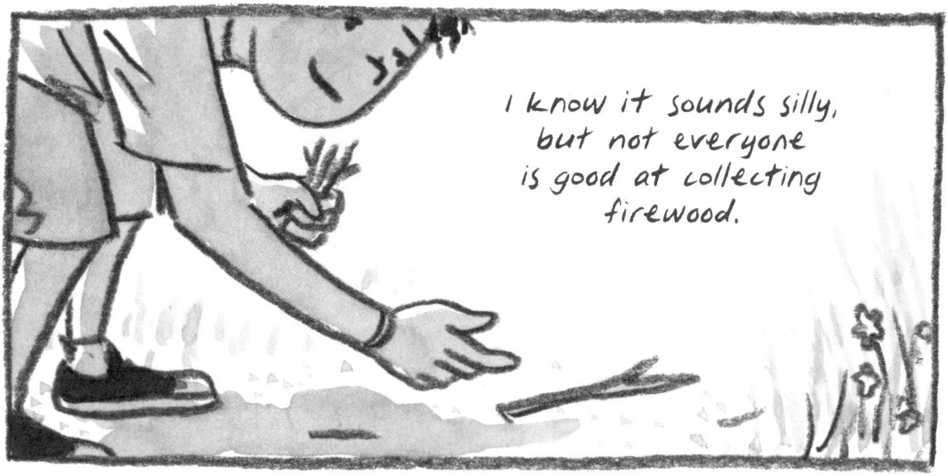
I know it sounds silly, but not everyone is good at collecting firewood.

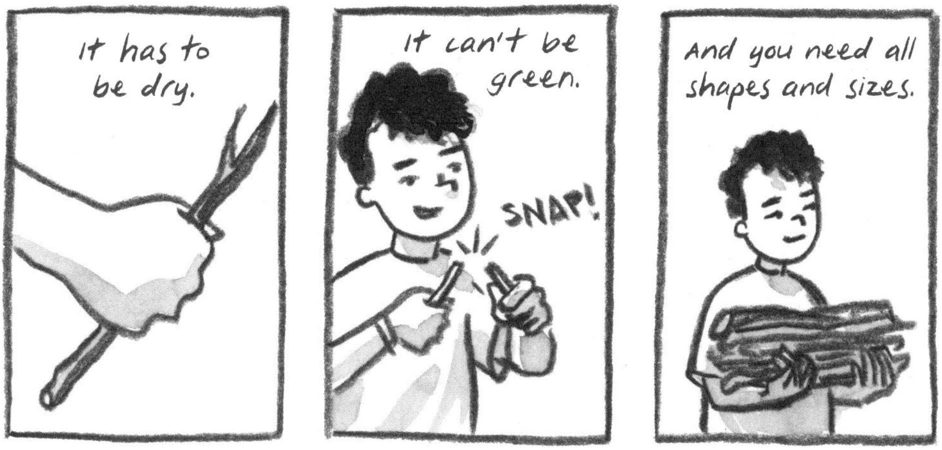
It has to be dry.
It can't be green.
SNAP!
And you need all shapes and sizes.

There's kindling—the tiny stuff. You can't just light a match and set a log ablaze. You've got to start small.

Then there's a range of medium-sized sticks.

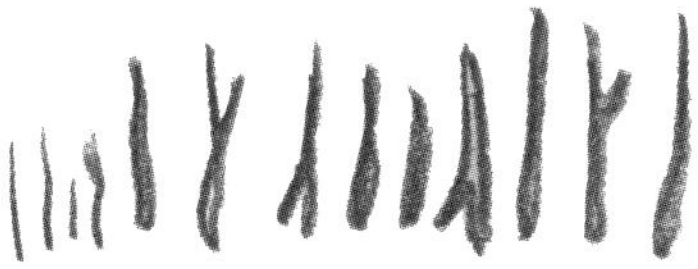

kindling

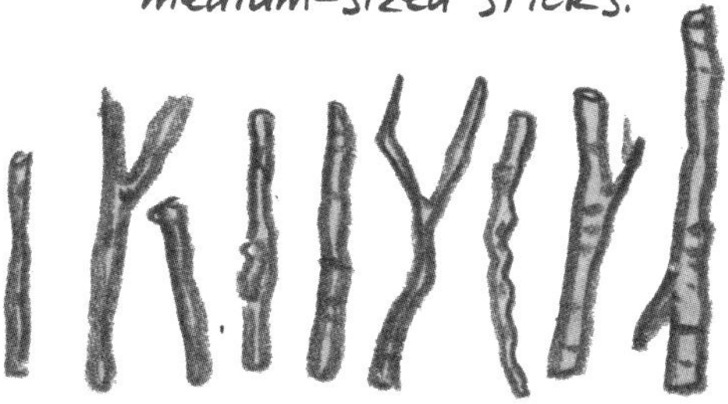

medium

Then you've got logs. Of course, split wood always burns faster.

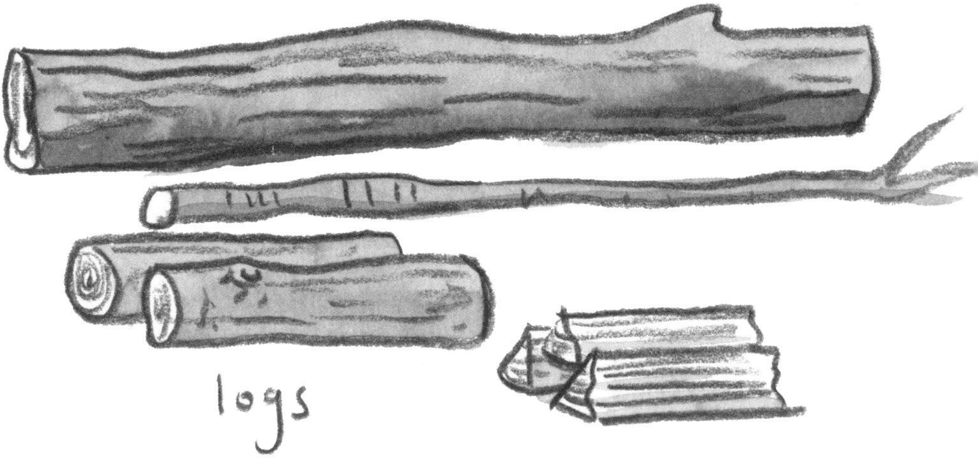

logs

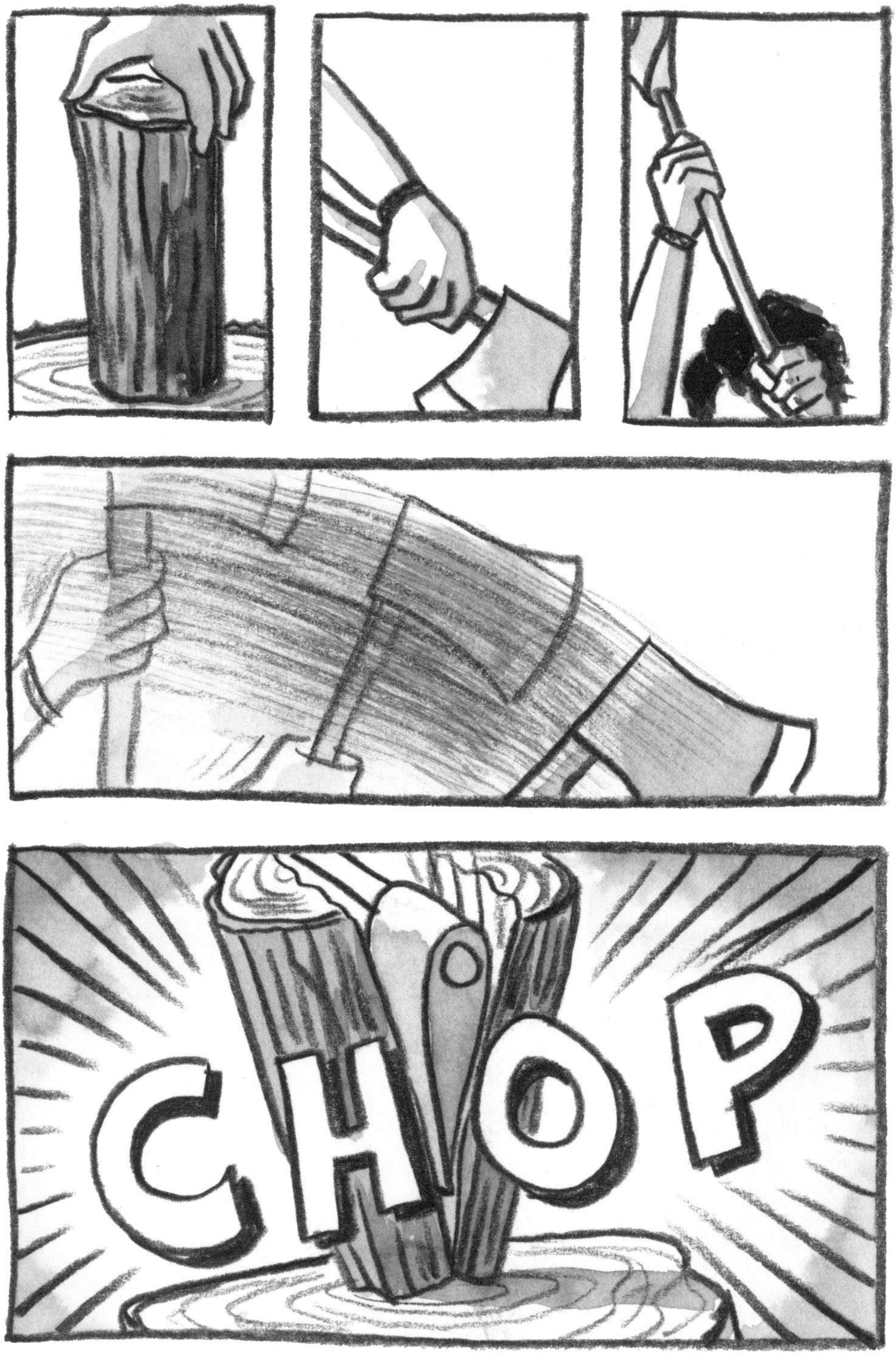
CHOP

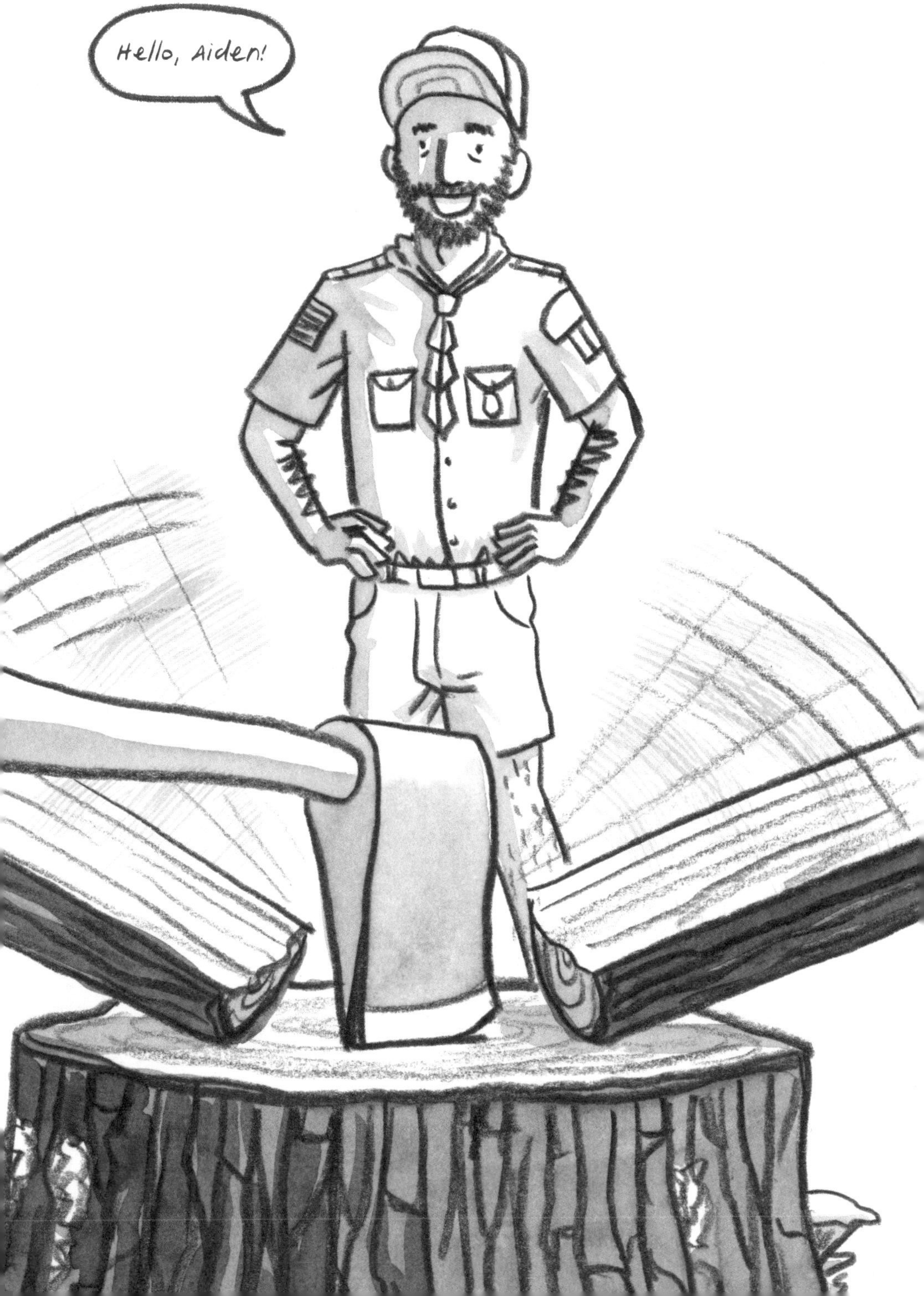
Hello, Aiden!

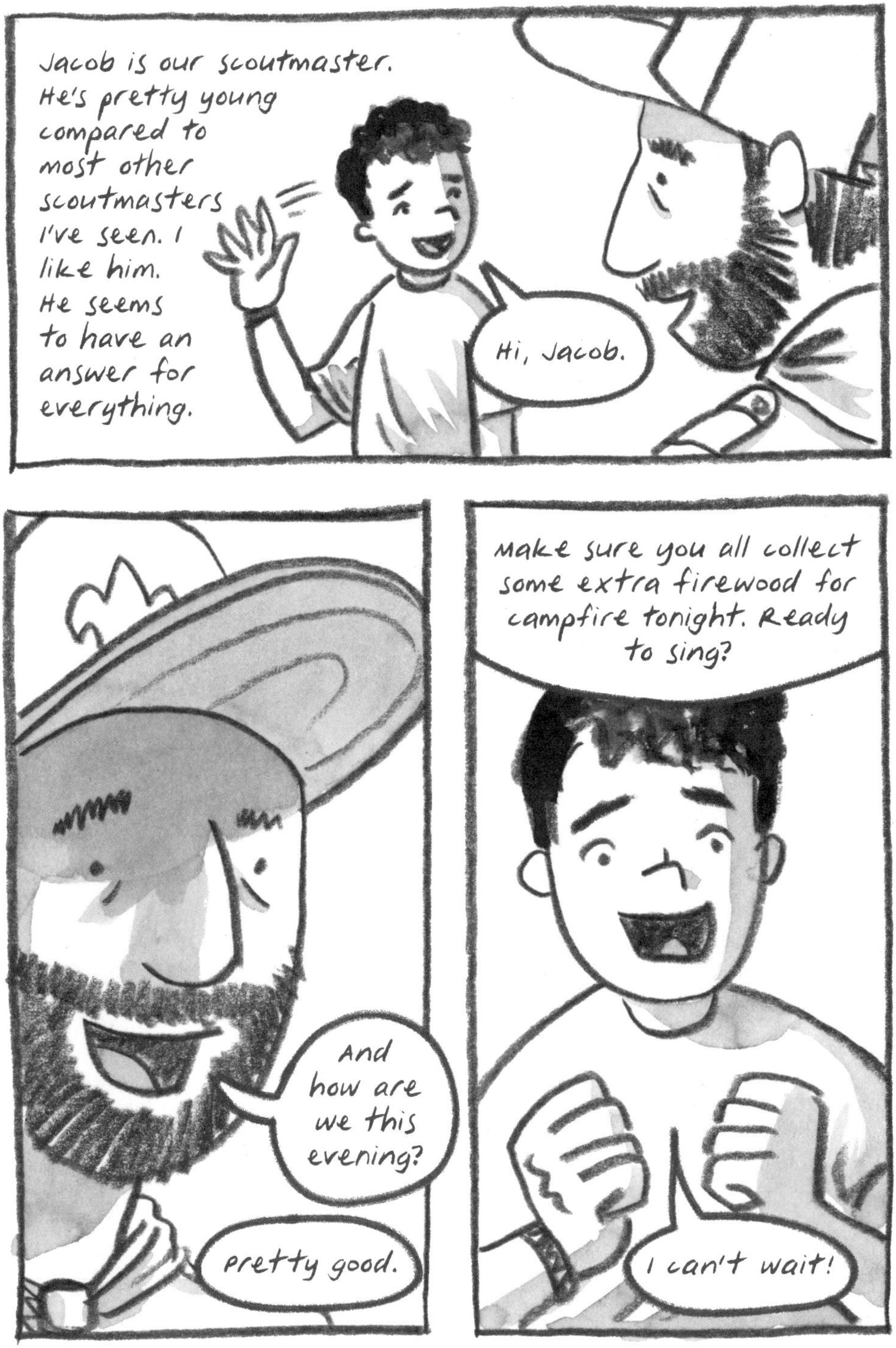
Jacob is our scoutmaster. He's pretty young compared to most other scoutmasters I've seen. I like him. He seems to have an answer for everything.
Hi, Jacob.
And how are we this evening?
Pretty good.
Make sure you all collect some extra firewood for campfire tonight. Ready to sing?
I can't wait!

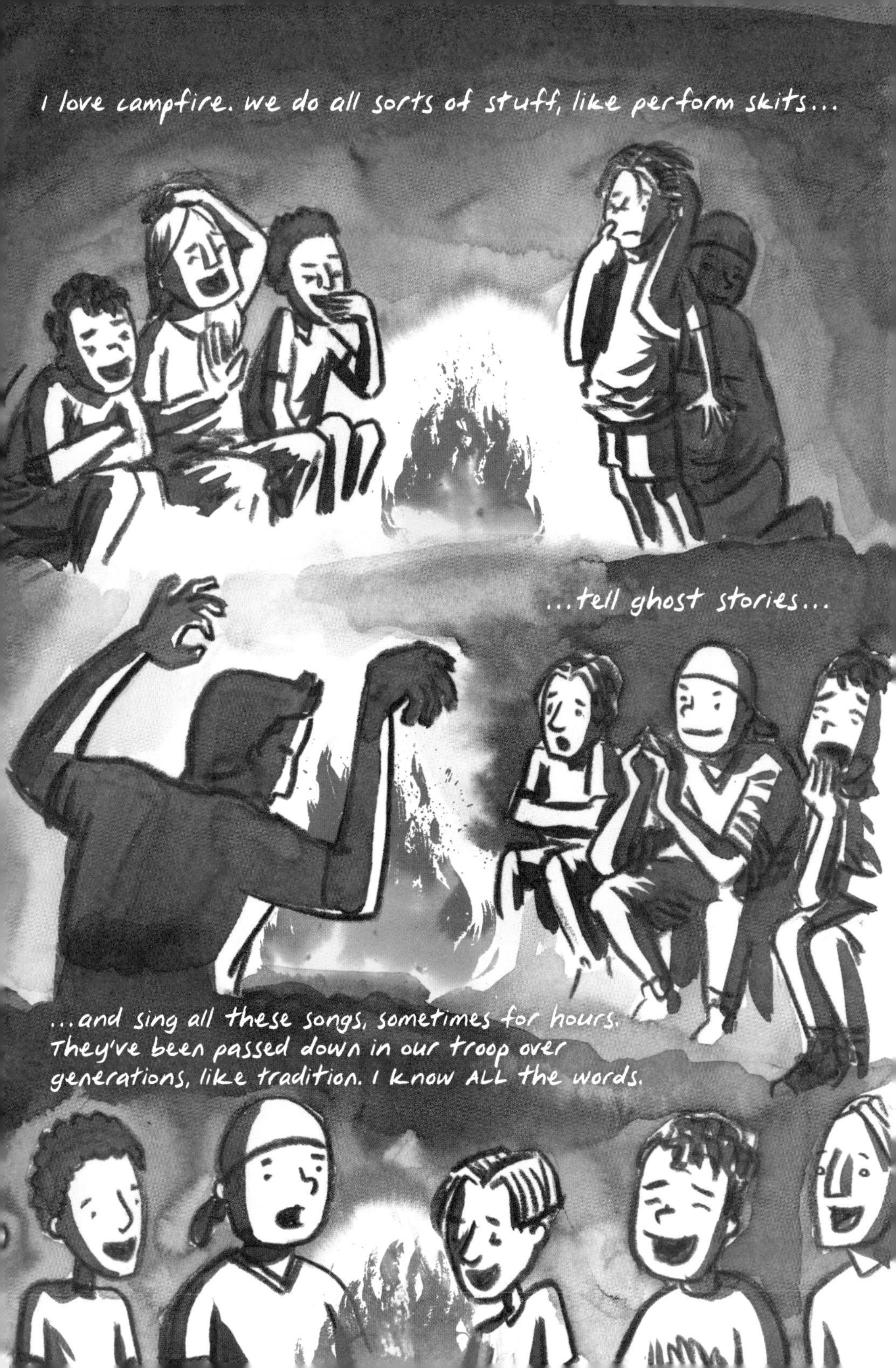
I love campfire. We do all sorts of stuff, like perform skits...
...tell ghost stories...
...and sing all these songs, sometimes for hours. They've been passed down in our troop over generations, like tradition. I know ALL the words.

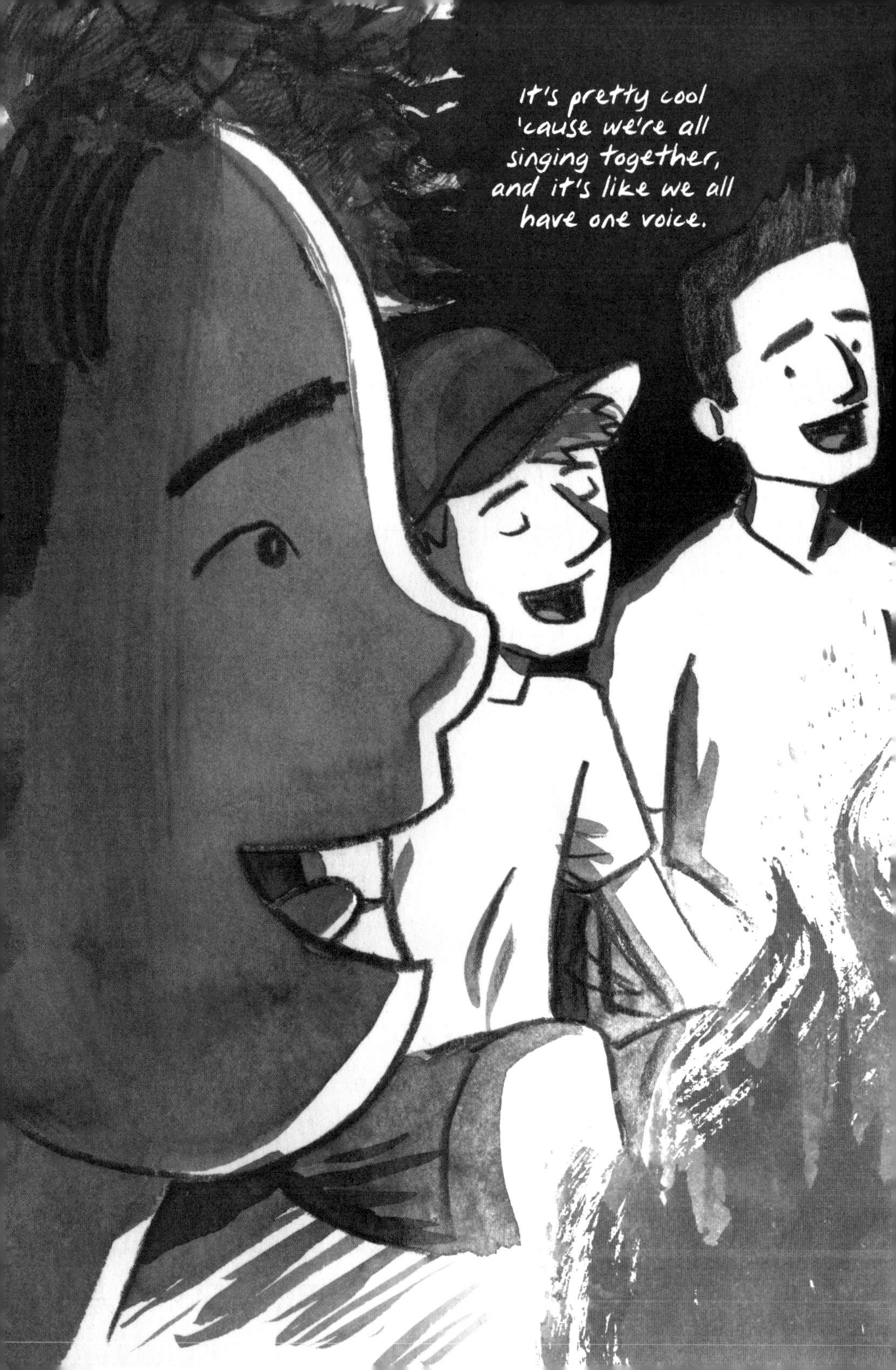
It's pretty cool 'cause we're all singing together, and it's like we all have one voice.

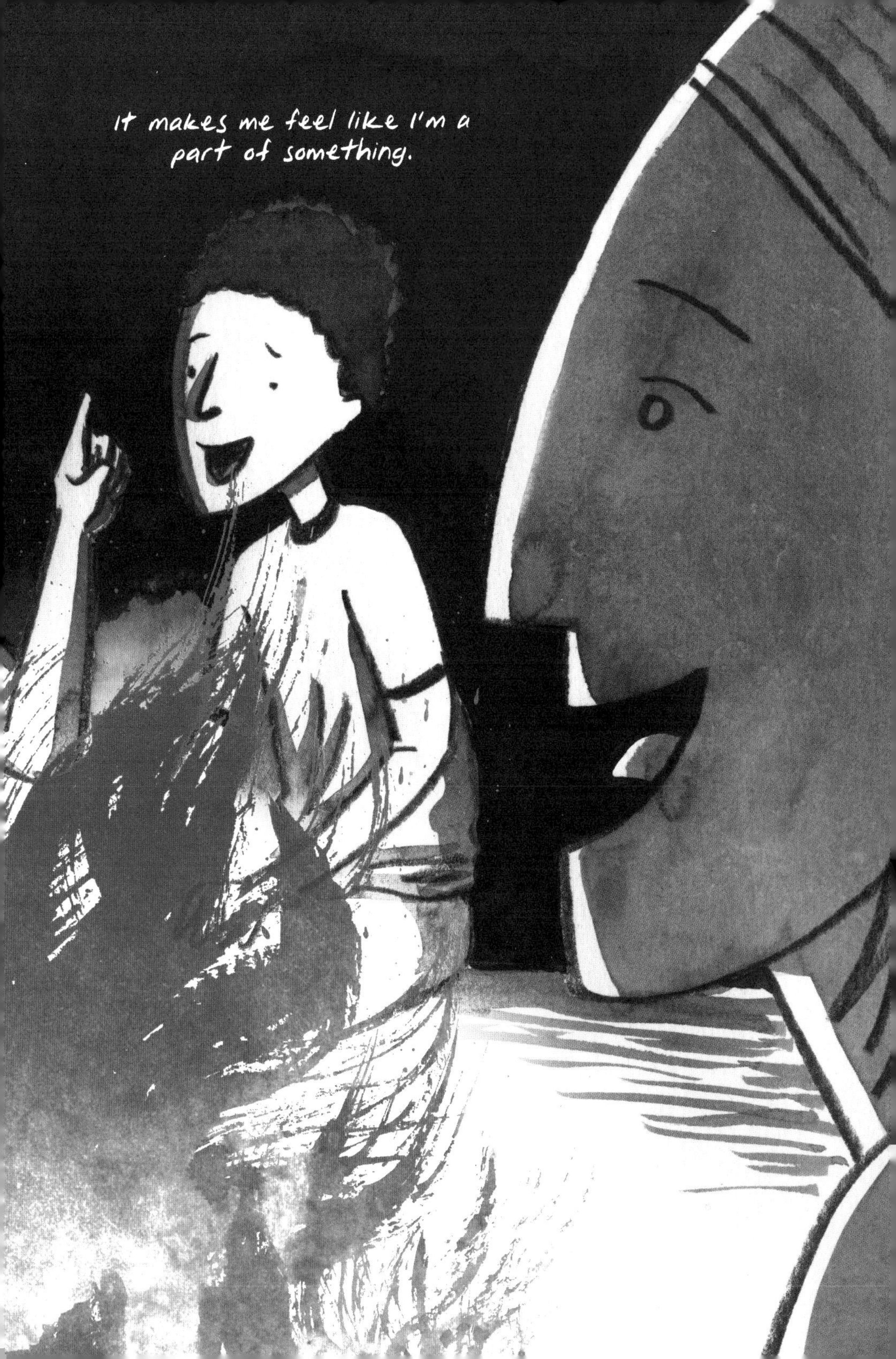
It makes me feel like I'm a part of something.

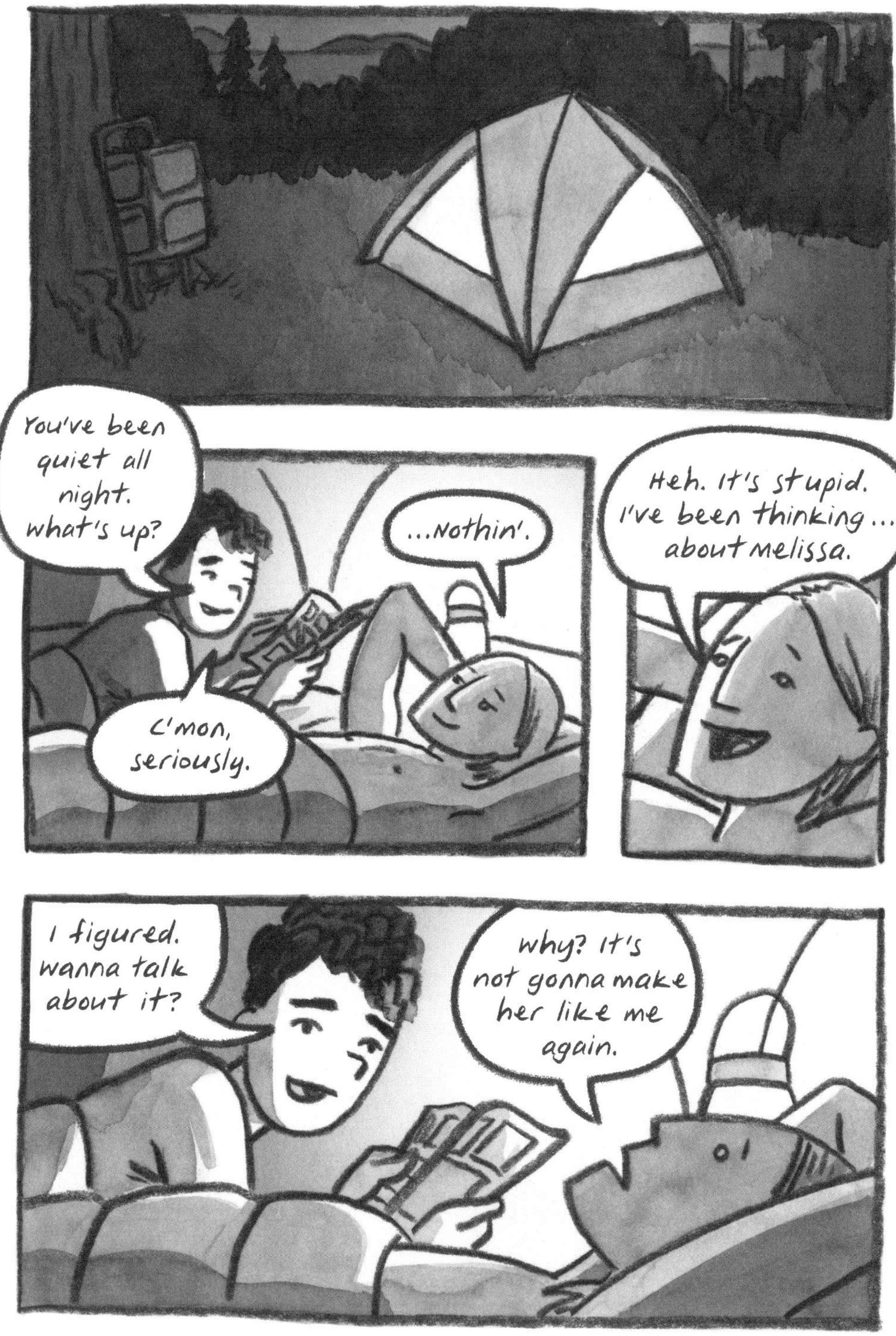
You've been quiet all night. what's up?
...Nothin'.
C'mon, seriously.
Heh. It's stupid. I've been thinking... about Melissa.
I figured. wanna talk about it?
why? It's not gonna make her like me again.

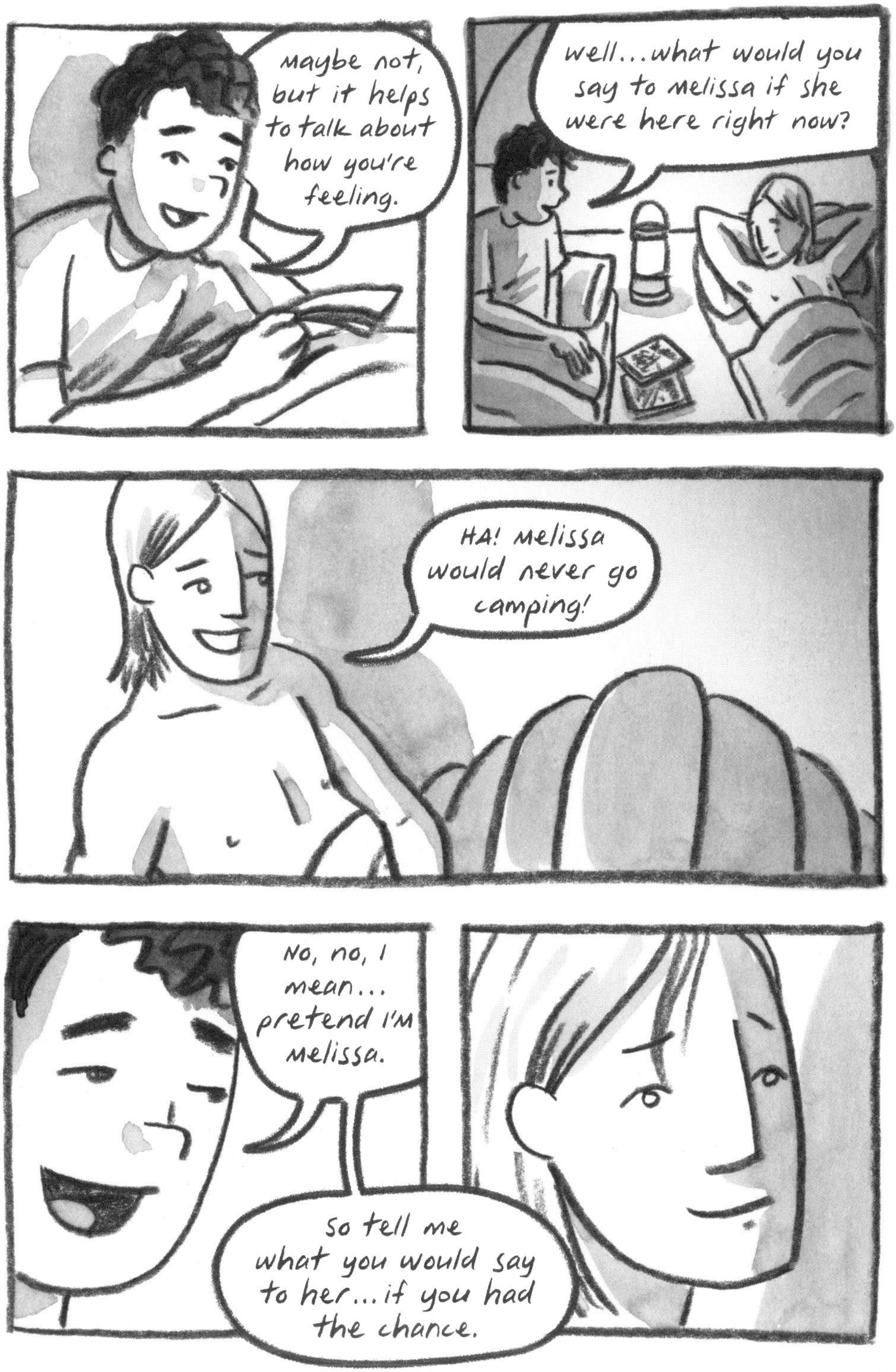
maybe not, but it helps to talk about how you're feeling.
well...what would you say to melissa if she were here right now?
HA! Melissa would never go camping!
No, no, I mean... pretend I'm Melissa.
So tell me what you would say to her...if you had the chance.

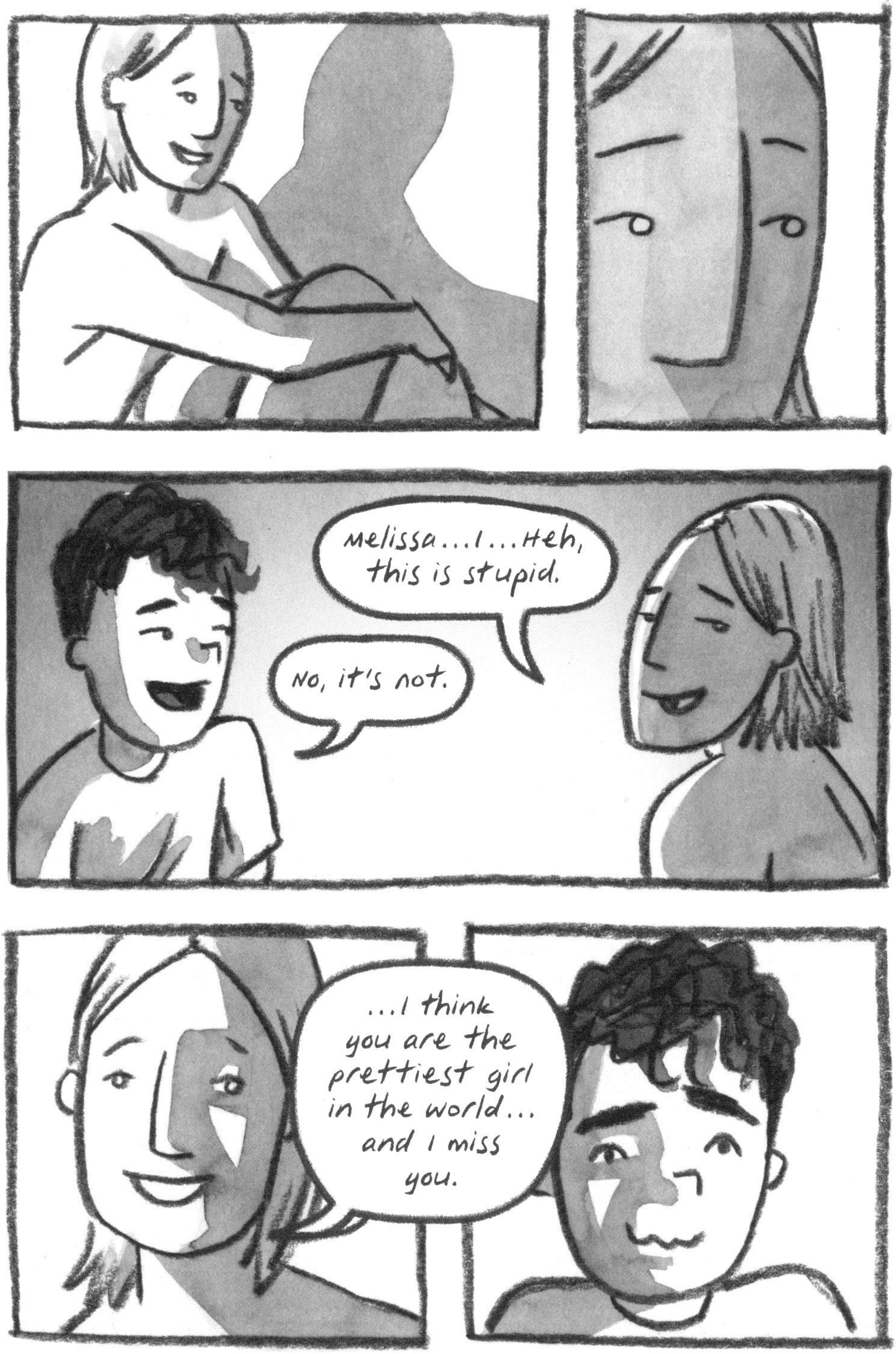
Melissa...I...Heh, this is stupid.
No, it's not.
...I think you are the prettiest girl in the world... and I miss you.

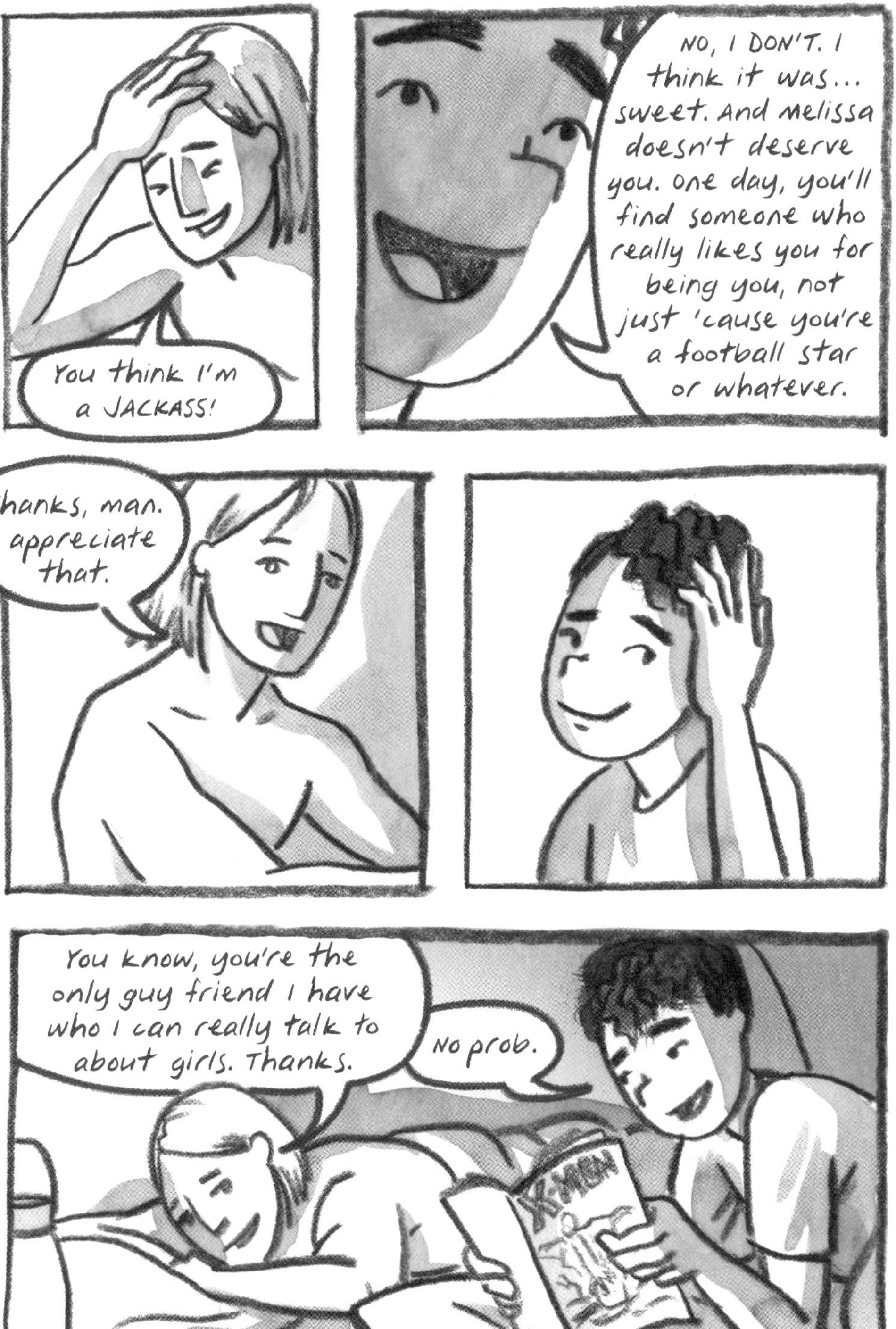
You think I'm a JACKASS!
NO, I DON'T. I think it was... sweet. And Melissa doesn't deserve you. One day, you'll find someone who really likes you for being you, not just 'cause you're a football star or whatever.
Thanks, man. I appreciate that.
You know, you're the only guy friend I have who I can really talk to about girls. Thanks.
No prob.
X-MEN

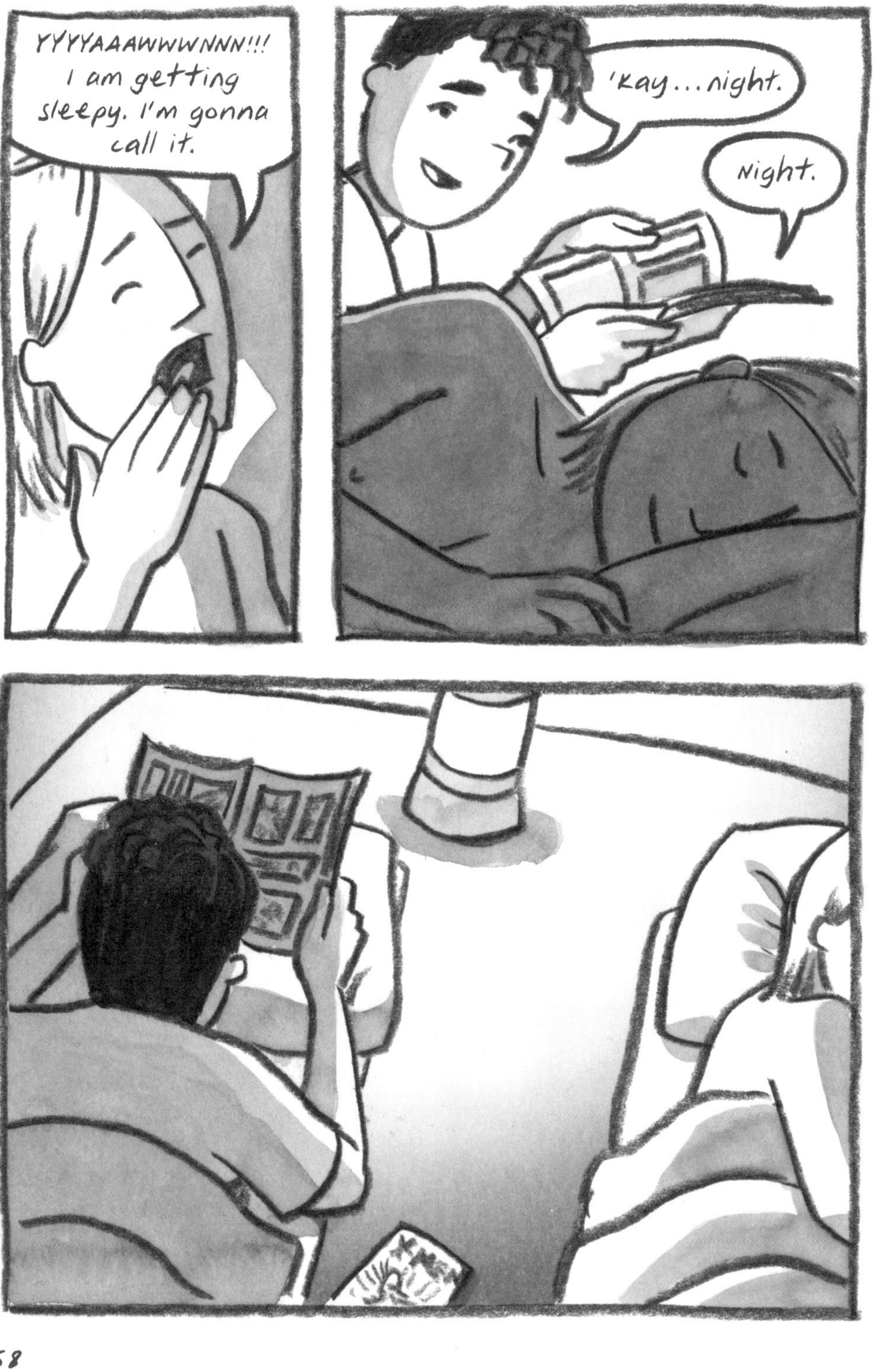
YYYYAAAWWWNNN!!! I am getting sleepy. I'm gonna call it.
'Kay... night.
Night.

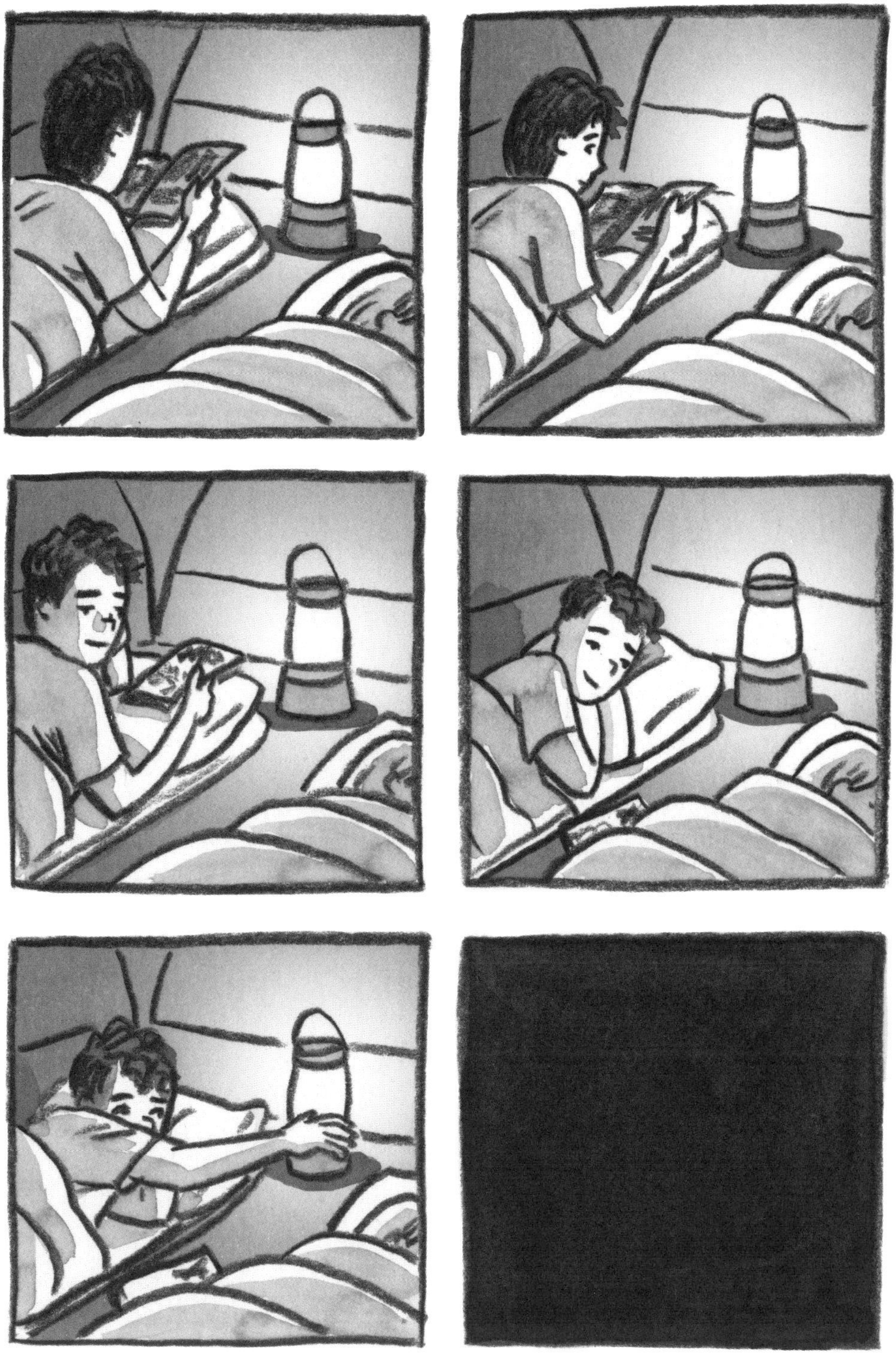

SUNDAY

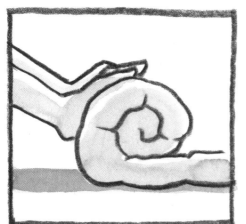

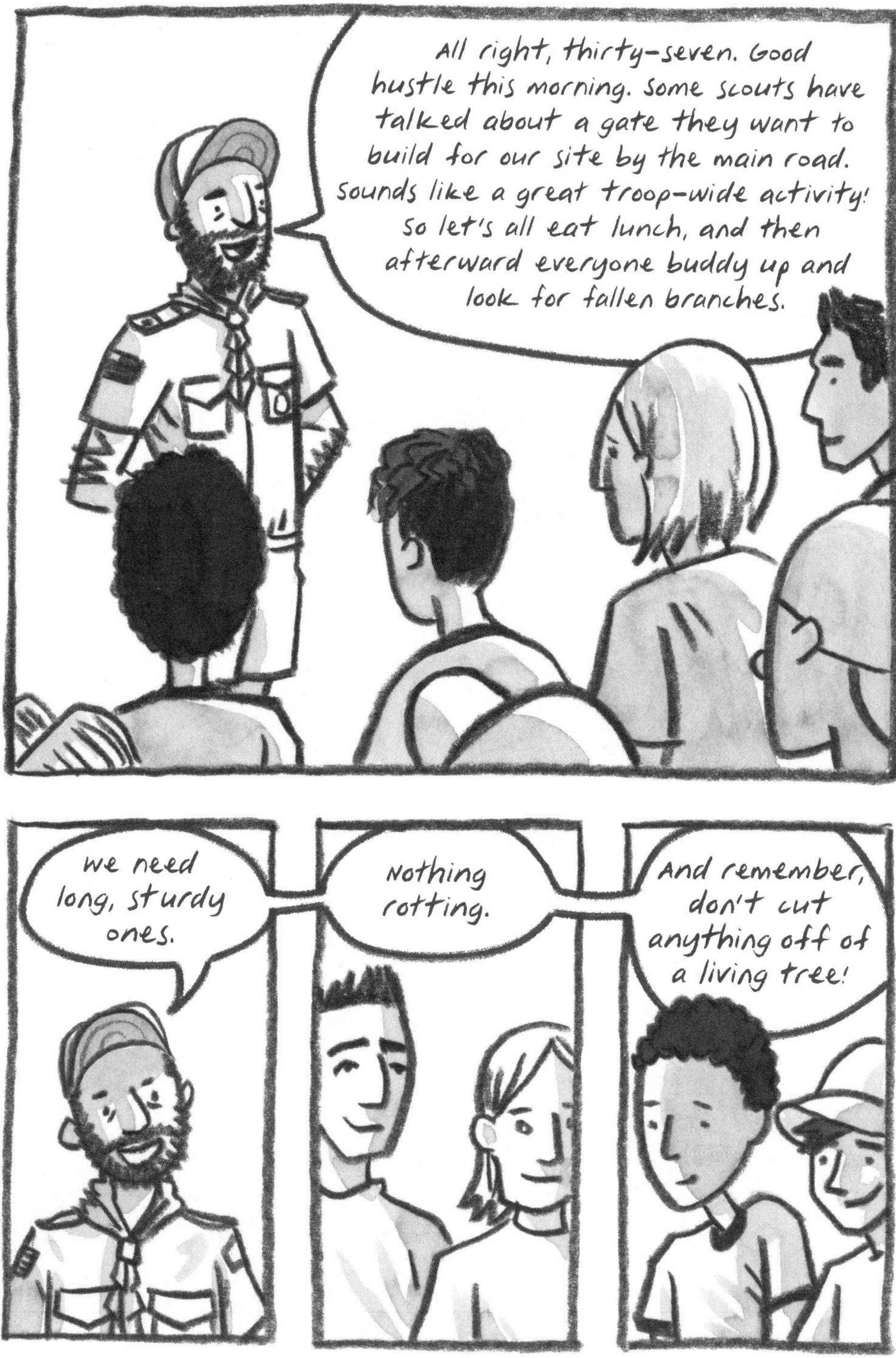
All right, thirty-seven. Good hustle this morning. Some scouts have talked about a gate they want to build for our site by the main road. Sounds like a great troop-wide activity! So let's all eat lunch, and then afterward everyone buddy up and look for fallen branches.
We need long, sturdy ones.
Nothing rotting.
And remember, don't cut anything off of a living tree!

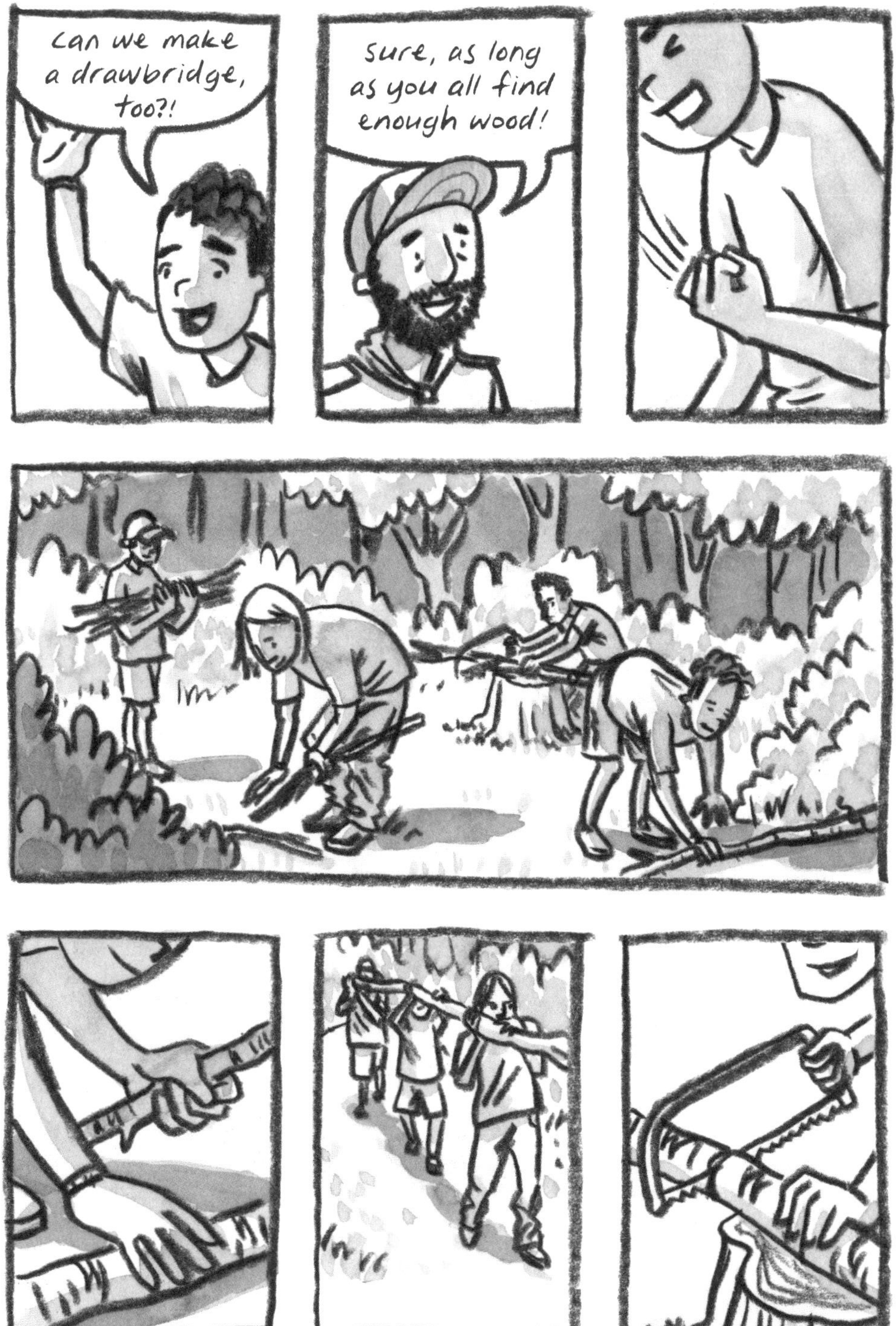
can we make a drawbridge, too?!
sure, as long as you all find enough wood!

square knot

clove hitch

timber hitch

round lashing

shear lashing

square lashing

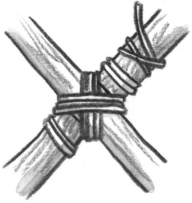

diagonal lashing

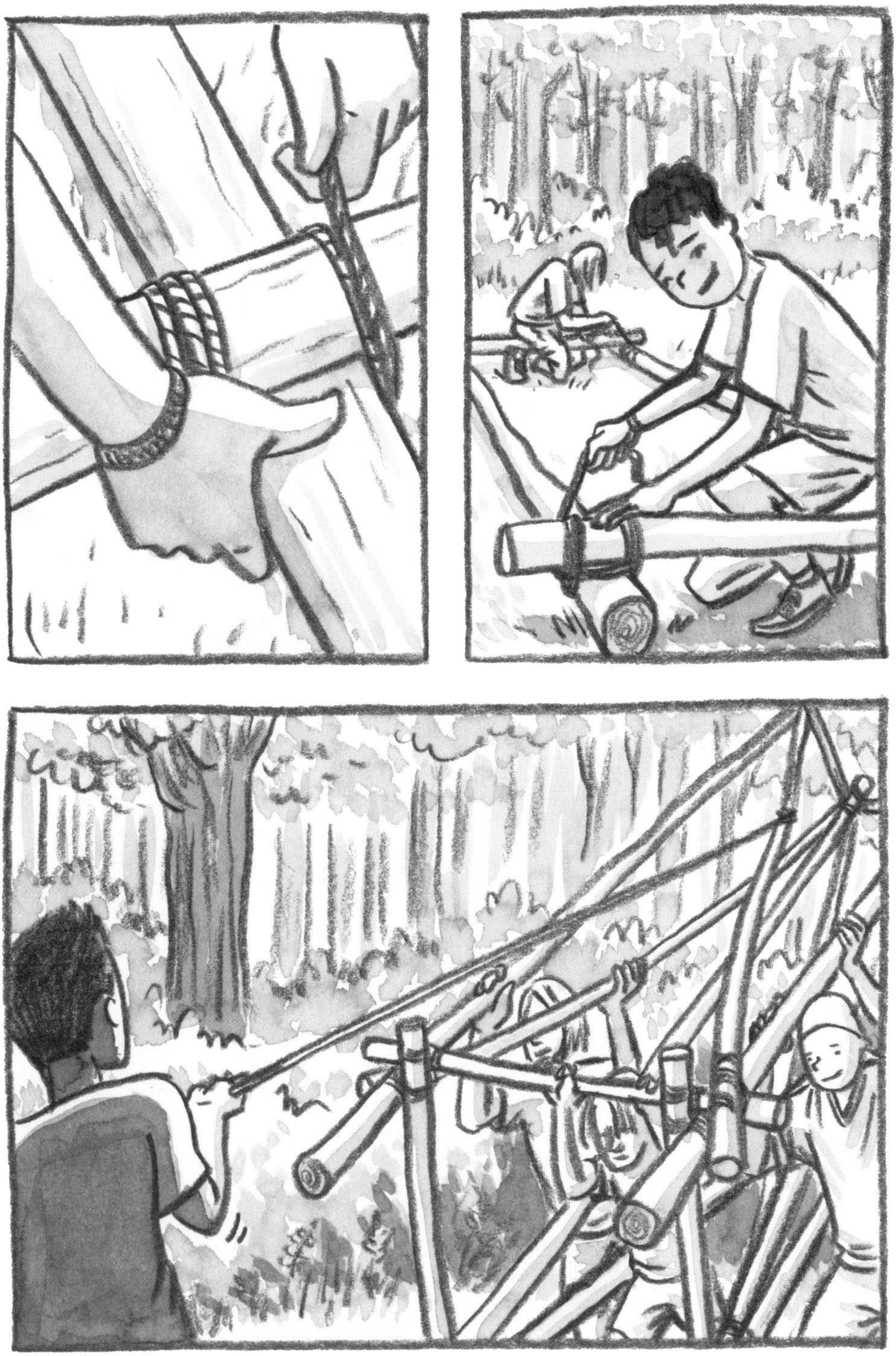

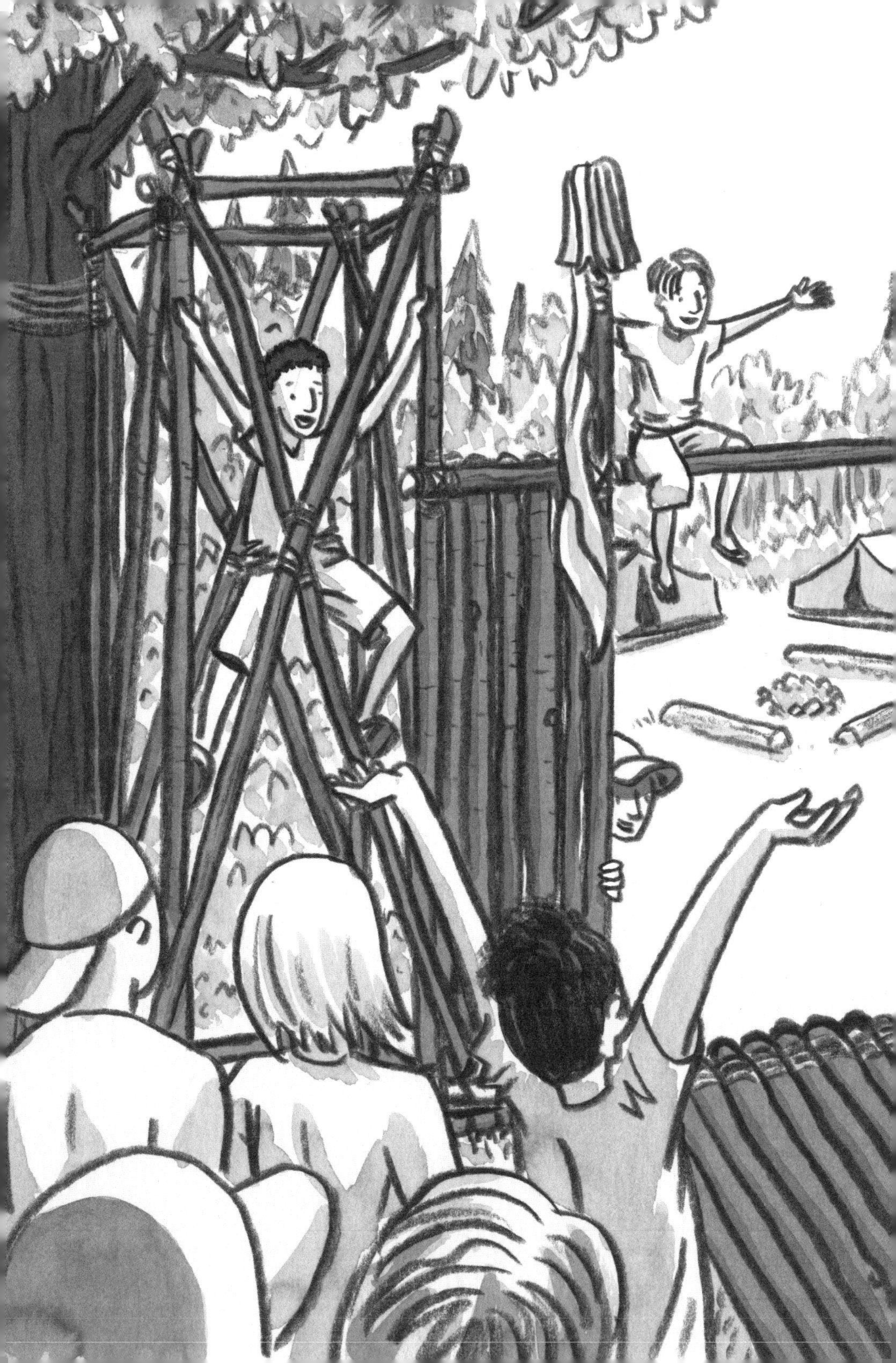

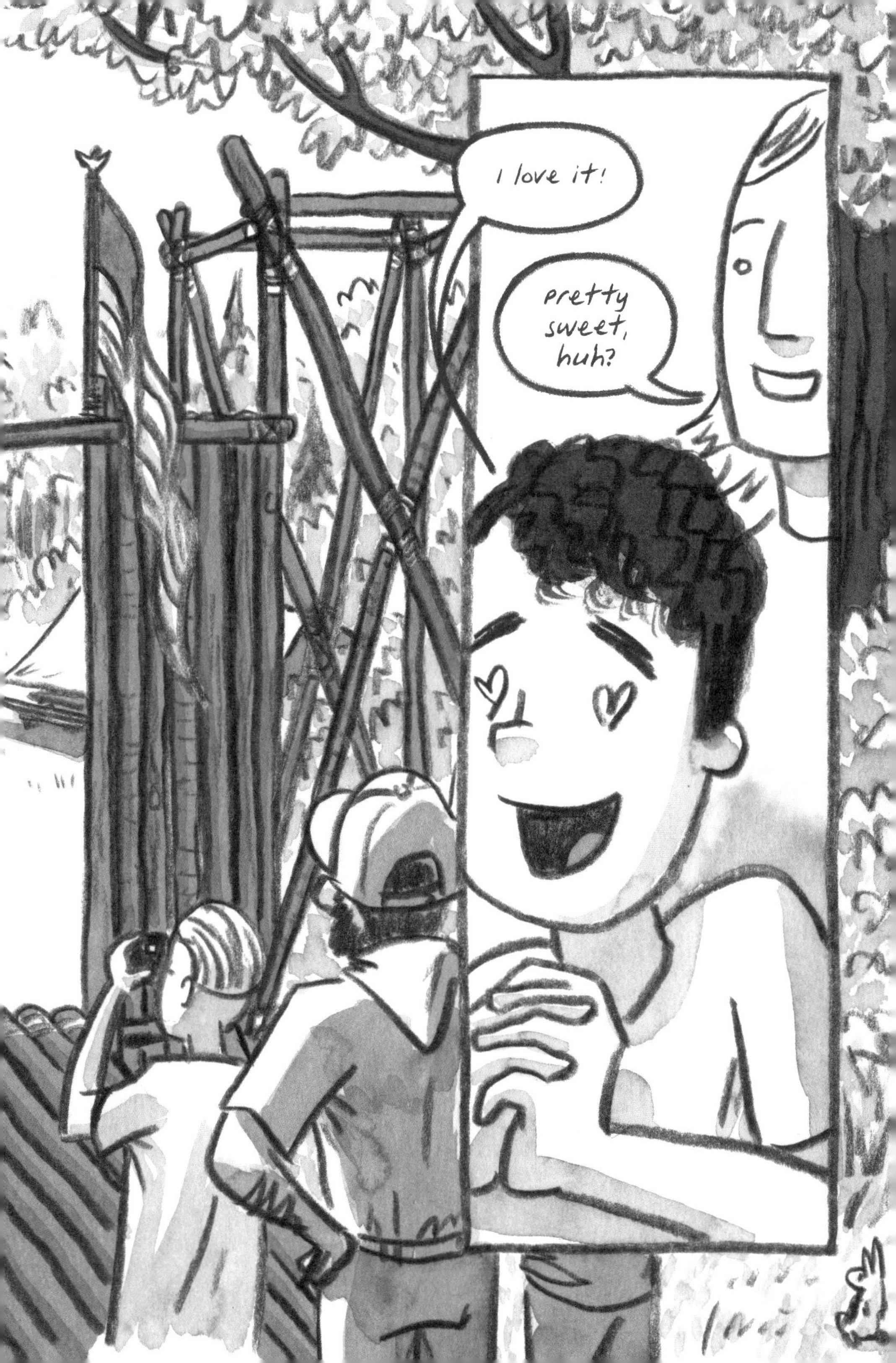
I love it!
pretty sweet, huh?

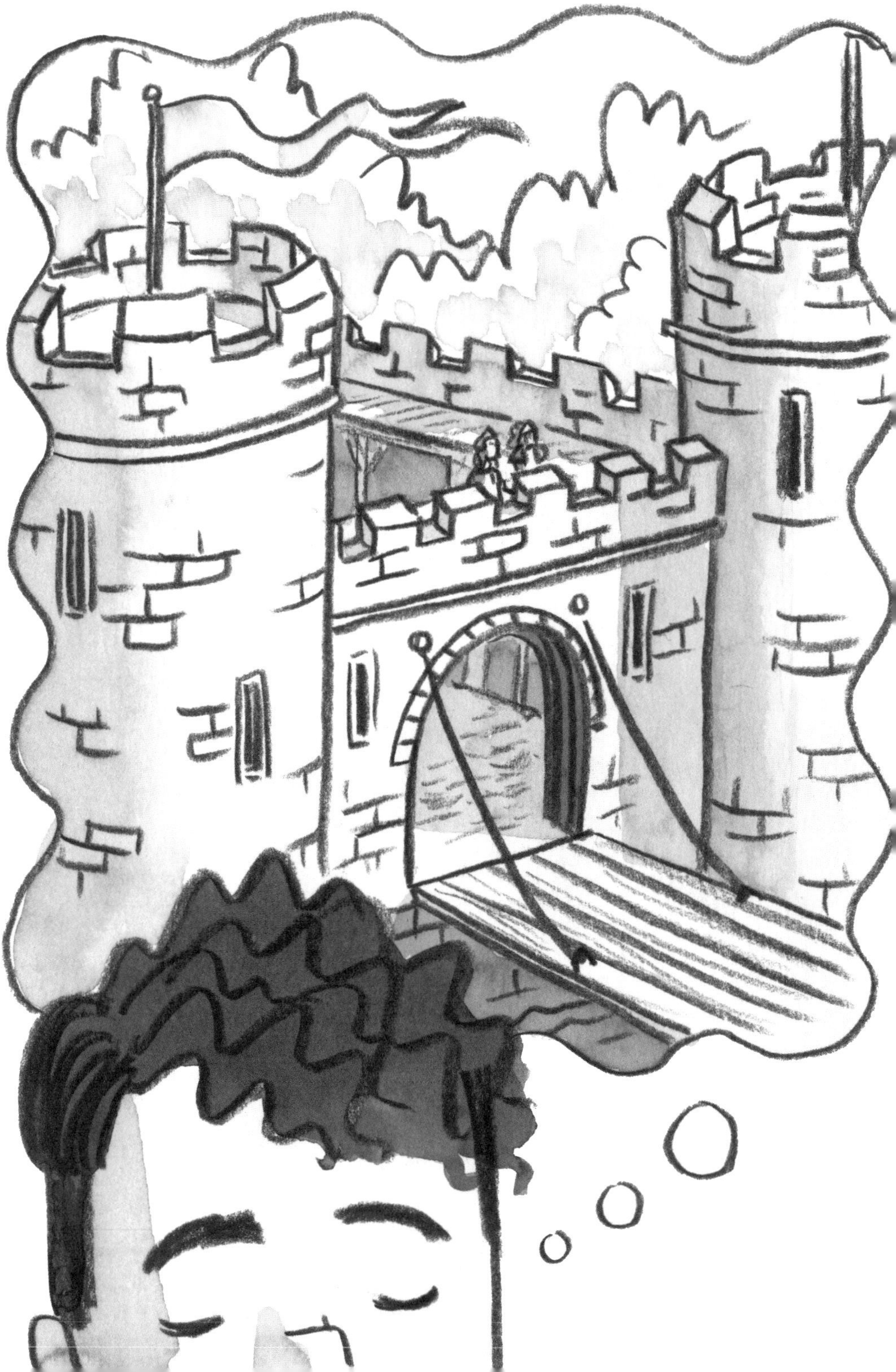

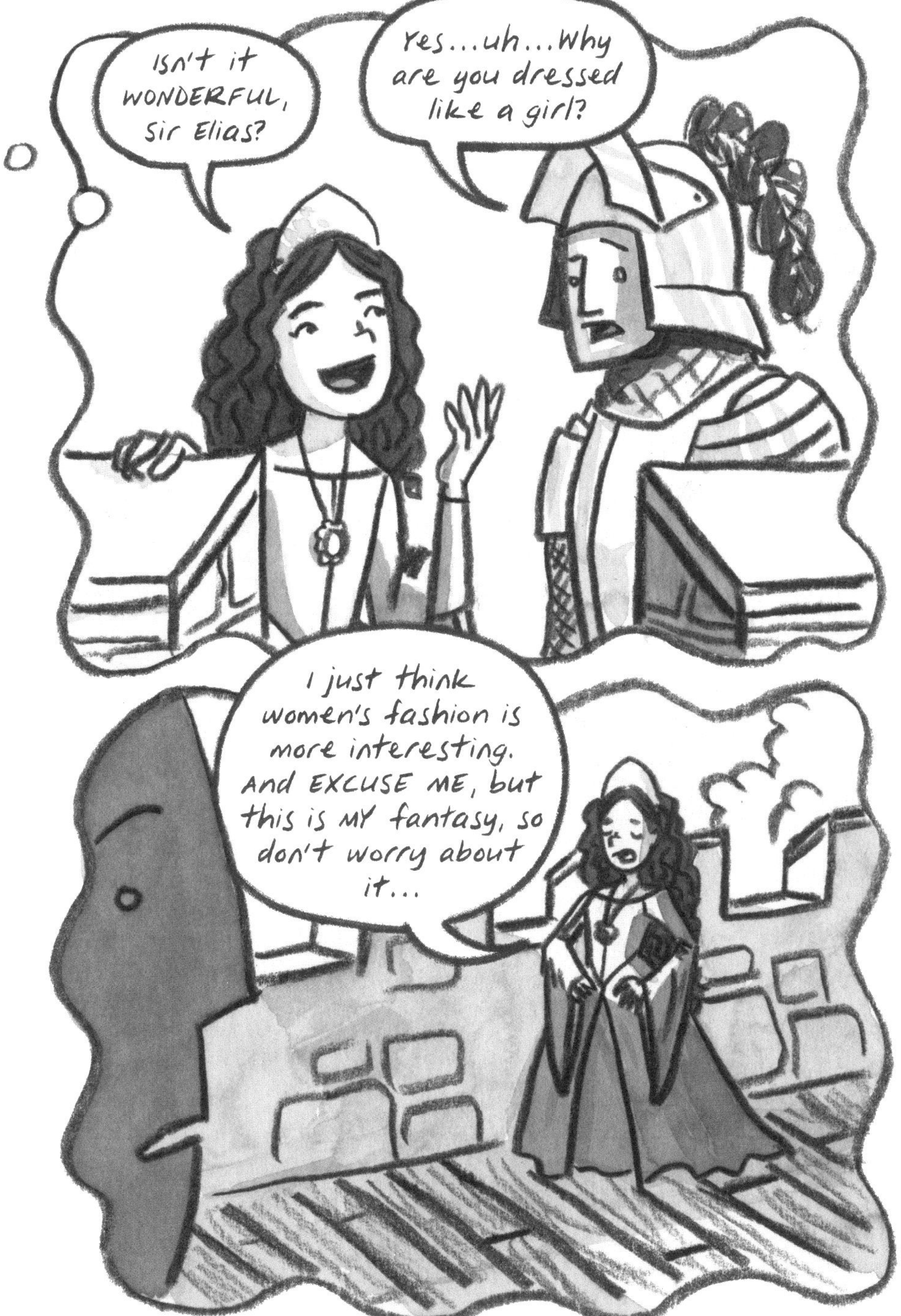
Isn't it WONDERFUL, Sir Elias?
Yes...uh...Why are you dressed like a girl?
I just think women's fashion is more interesting. And EXCUSE ME, but this is MY fantasy, so don't worry about it...

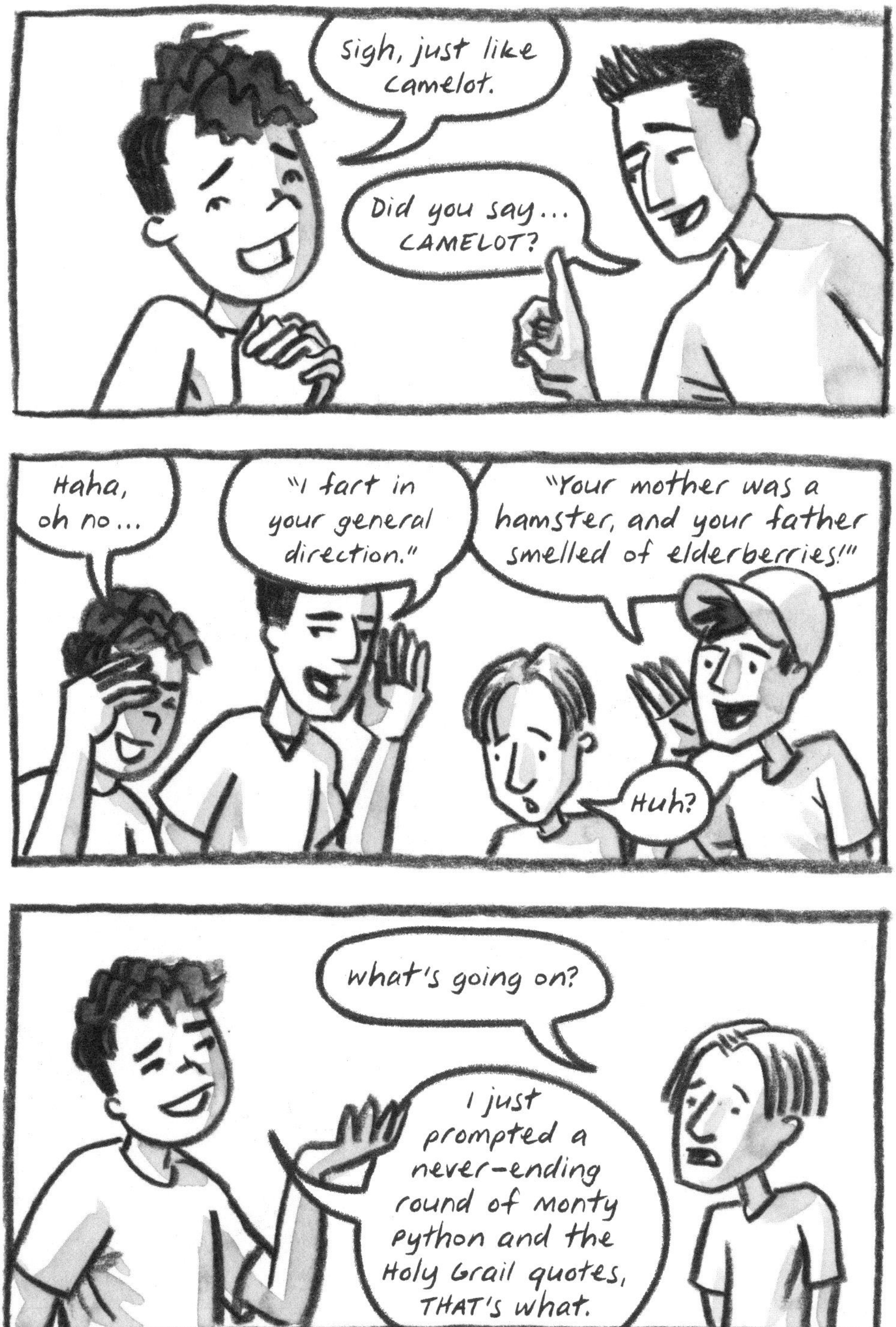
Sigh, just like Camelot.
Did you say... CAMELOT?
Haha, oh no...
"I fart in your general direction."
"Your mother was a hamster, and your father smelled of elderberries!"
Huh?
What's going on?
I just prompted a never-ending round of Monty Python and the Holy Grail quotes, THAT'S what.

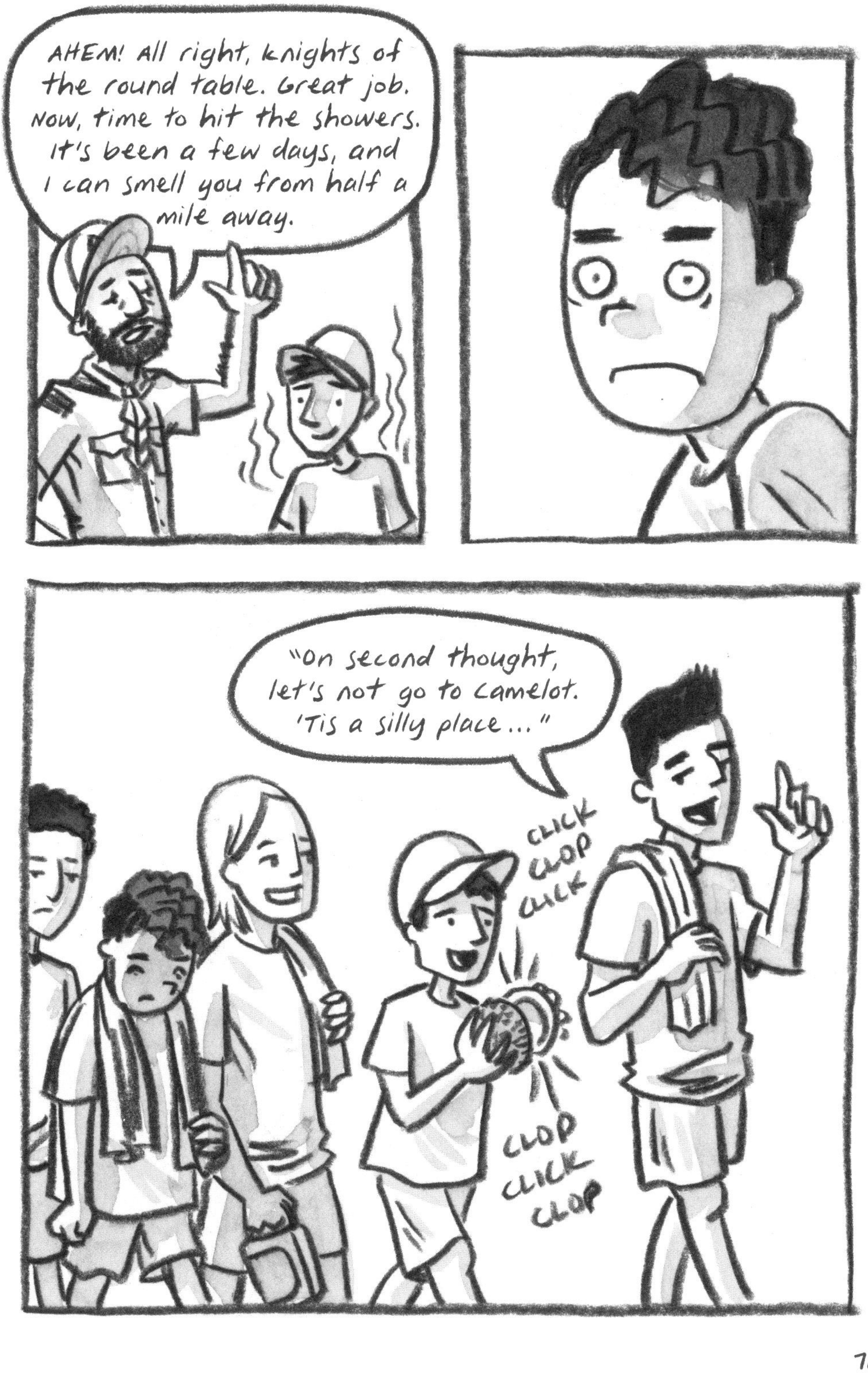
AHEM! All right, knights of the round table. Great job. Now, time to hit the showers. It's been a few days, and I can smell you from half a mile away.
"On second thought, let's not go to Camelot. 'Tis a silly place..."
CLICK CLOP CLICK
CLOP CLICK CLOP

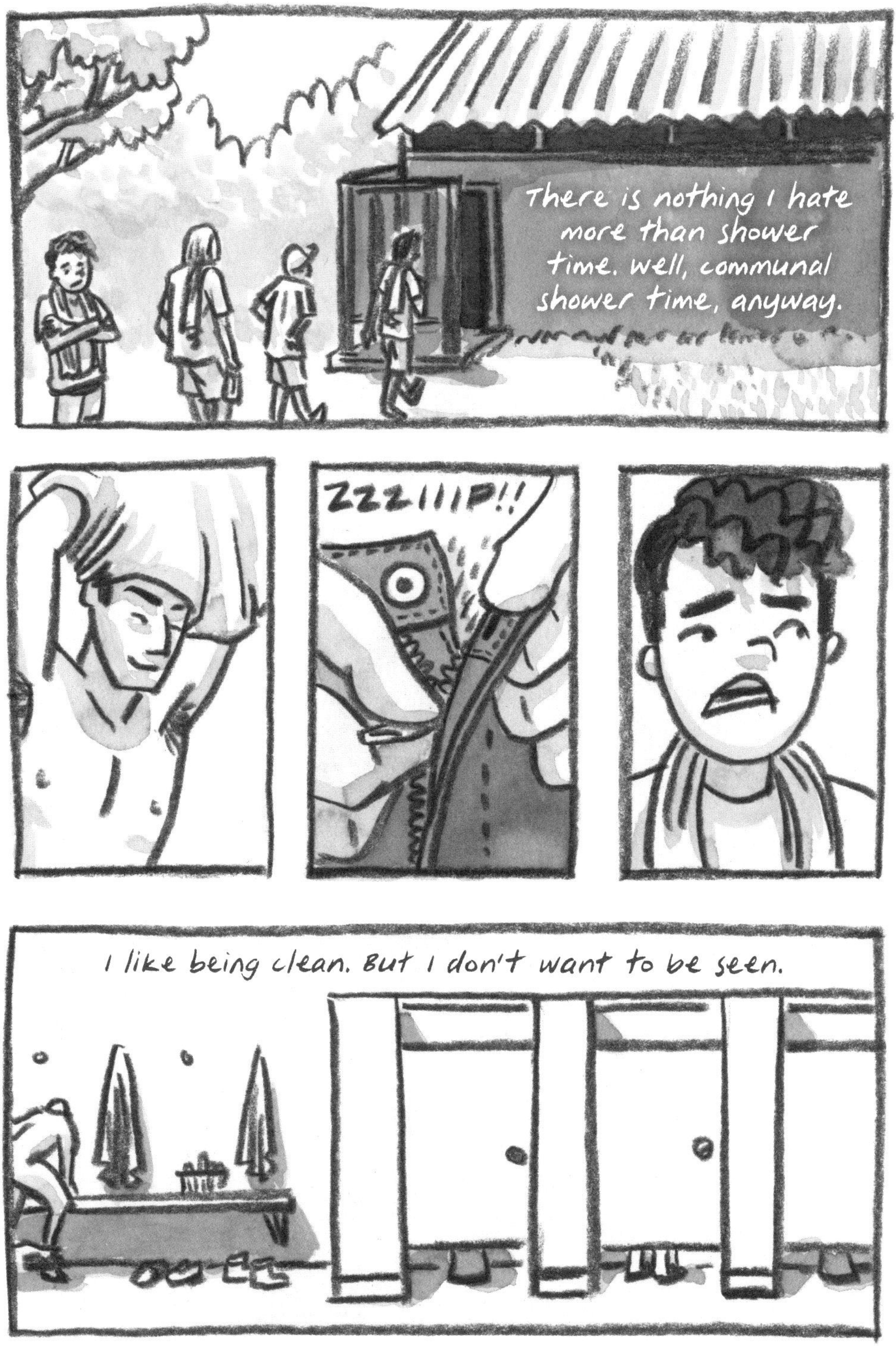
There is nothing I hate more than shower time. Well, communal shower time, anyway.
ZZZIIIP!!
I like being clean. But I don't want to be seen.

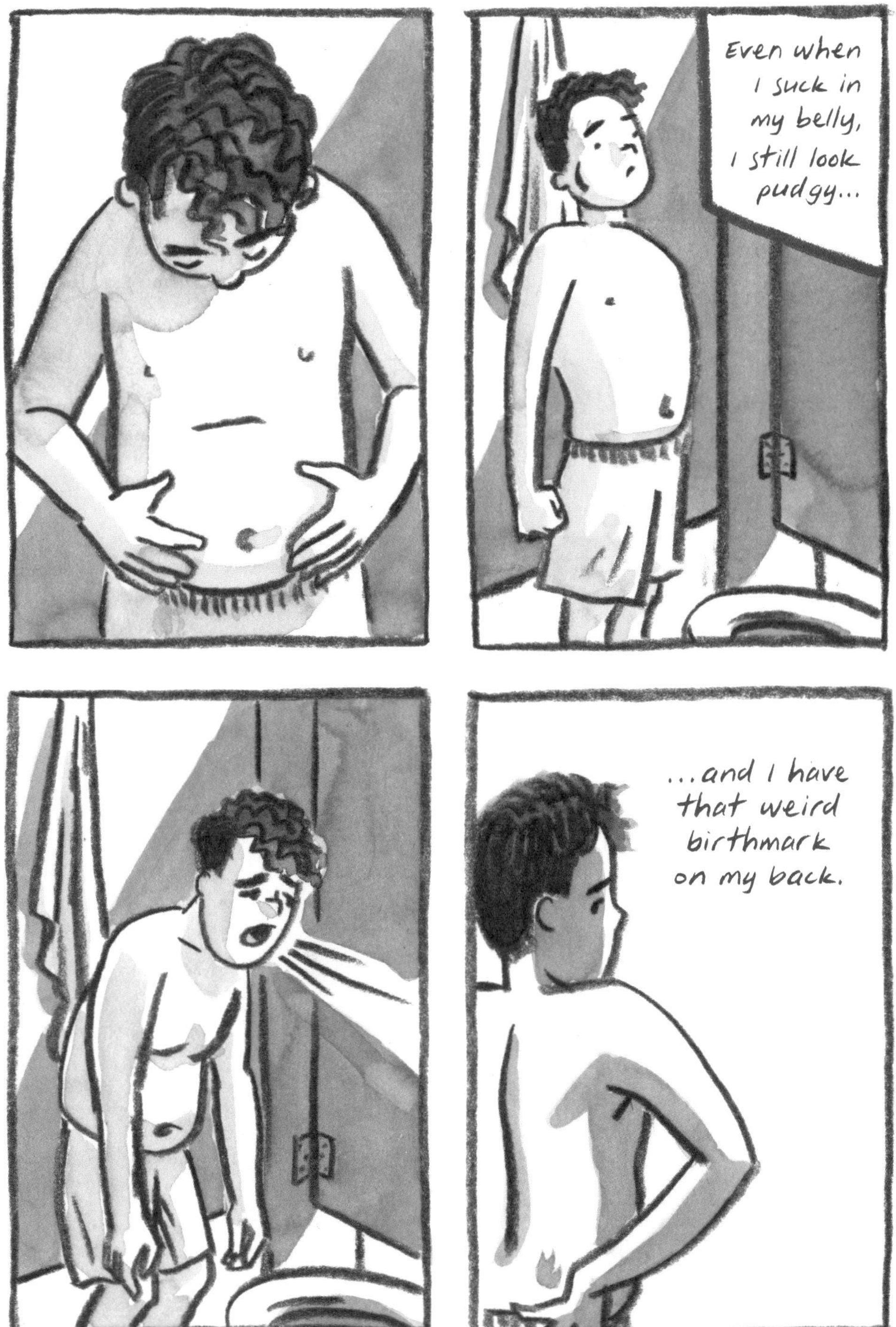
Even when
I suck in
my belly,
I still look
pudgy...
...and I have
that weird
birthmark
on my back.

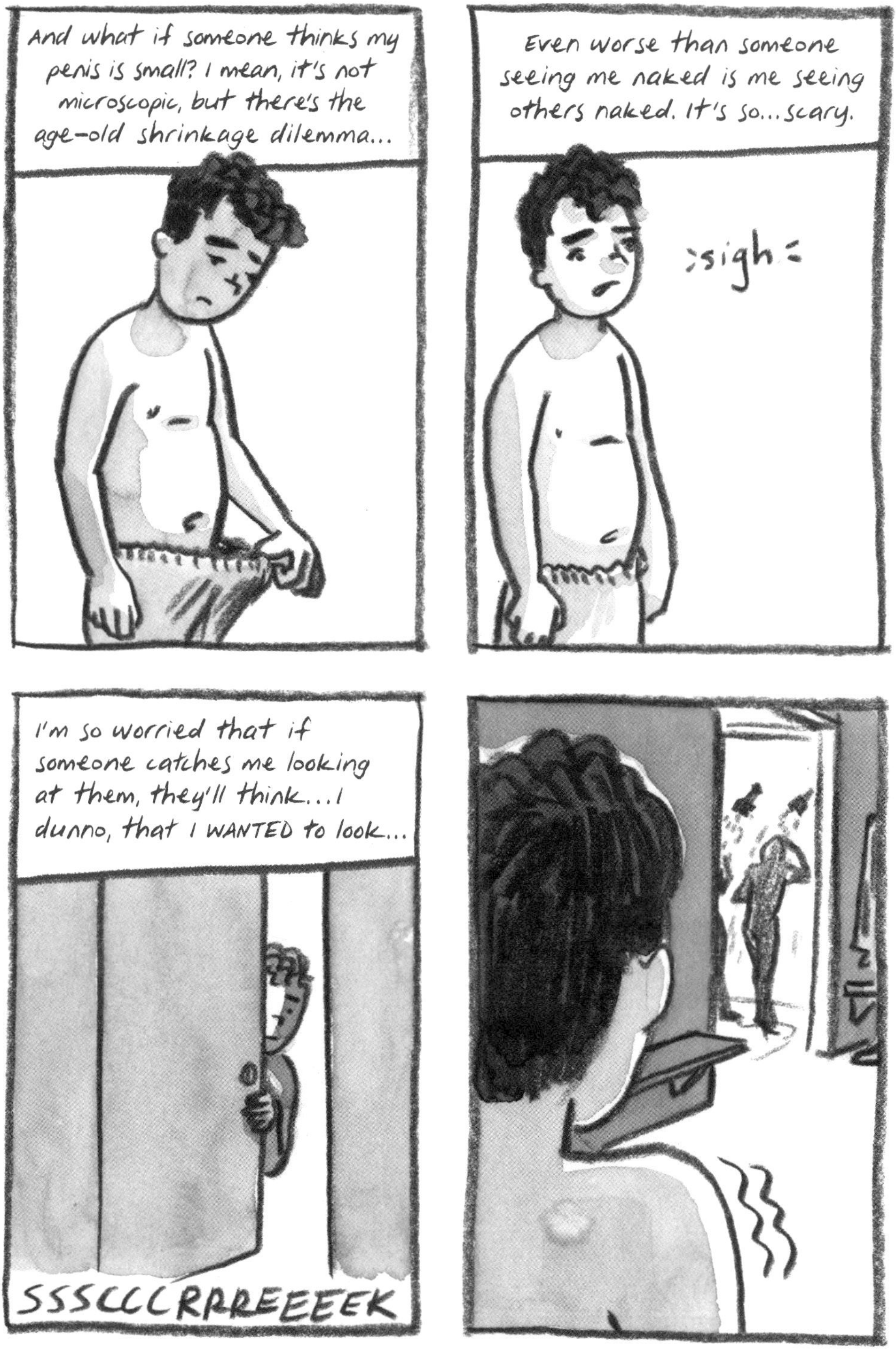
And what if someone thinks my penis is small? I mean, it's not microscopic, but there's the age-old shrinkage dilemma...
Even worse than someone seeing me naked is me seeing others naked. It's so... scary.
:sigh:
I'm so worried that if someone catches me looking at them, they'll think... I dunno, that I WANTED to look...
SSSCCCRRREEEEK

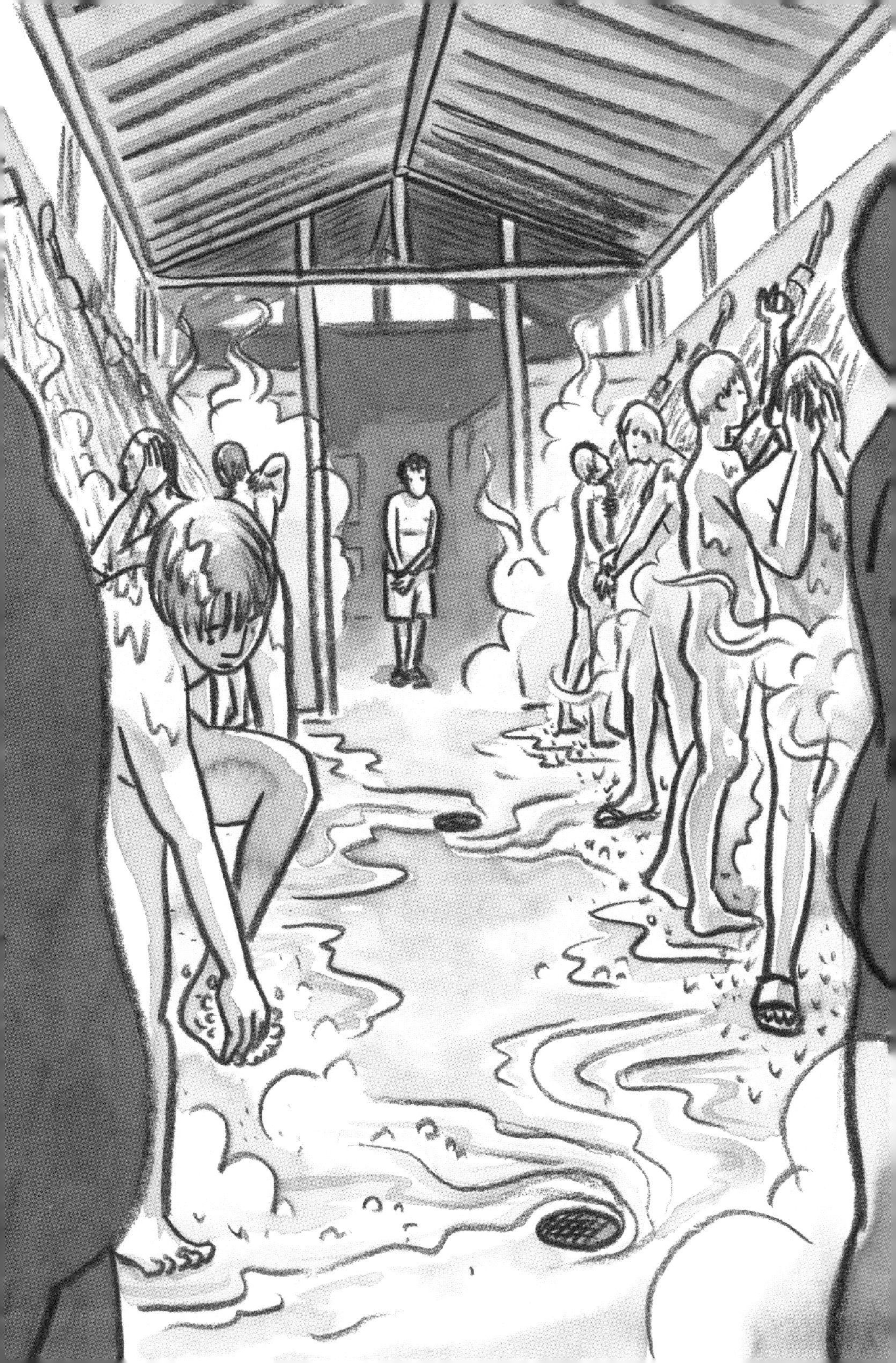

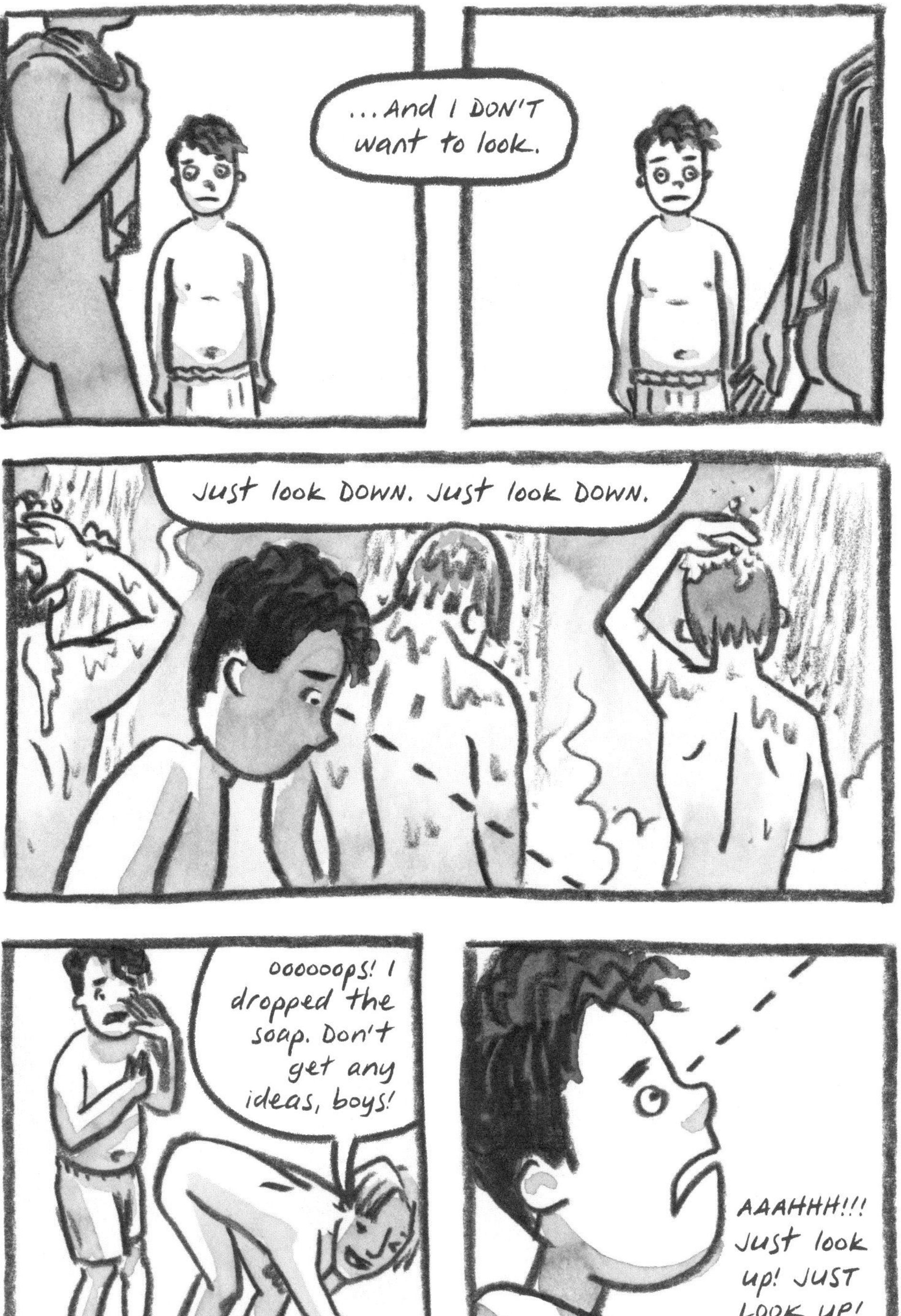
...And I DON'T want to look.
JUST look DOWN. JUST look DOWN.
ooooooops! I dropped the soap. Don't get any ideas, boys!
AAAHHH!!! Just look up! JUST LOOK UP!

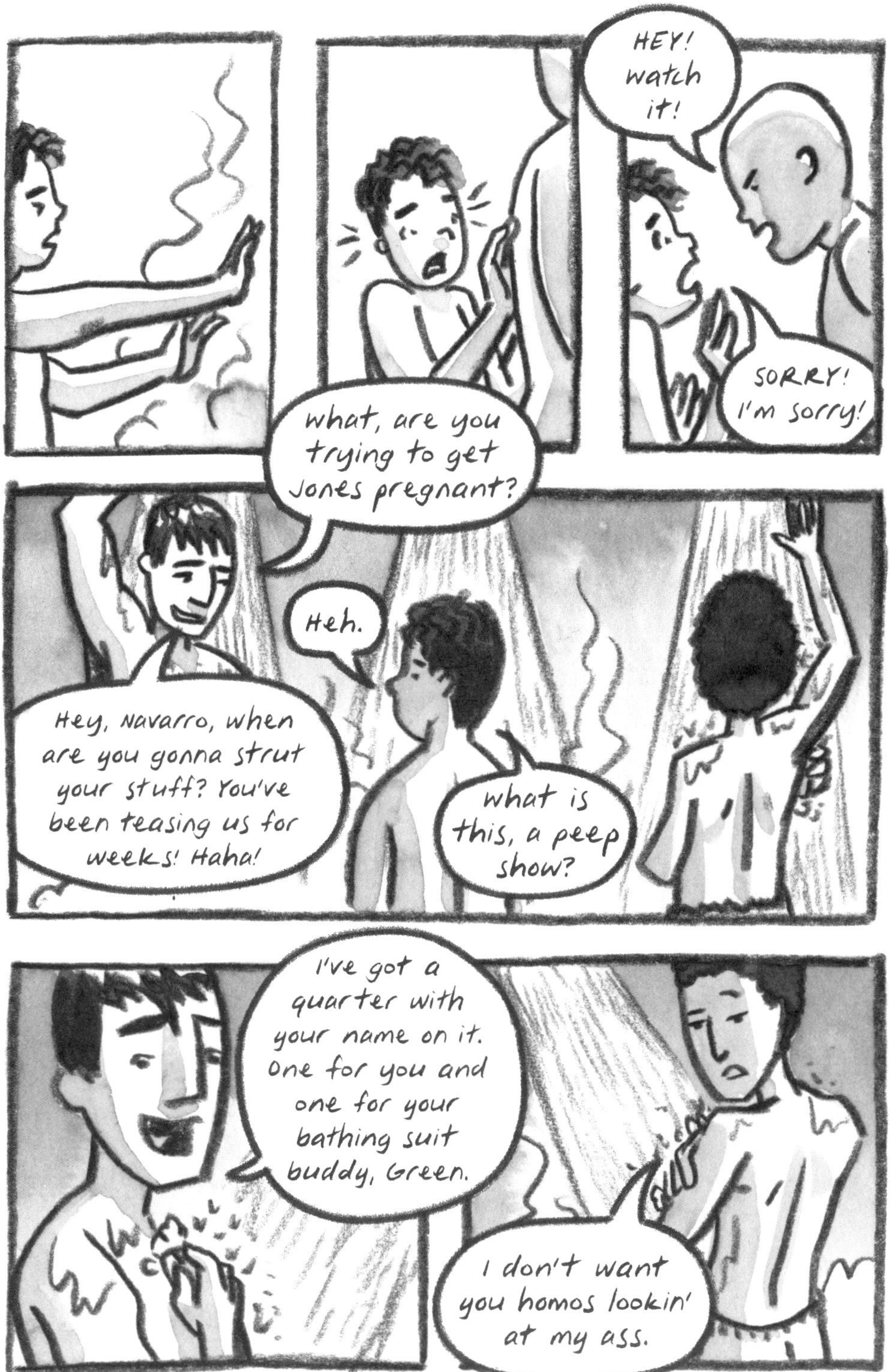
HEY! watch it!
SORRY! I'm sorry!
what, are you trying to get Jones pregnant?
Heh.
Hey, Navarro, when are you gonna strut your stuff? You've been teasing us for weeks! Haha!
what is this, a peep show?
I've got a quarter with your name on it. One for you and one for your bathing suit buddy, Green.
I don't want you homos lookin' at my ass.

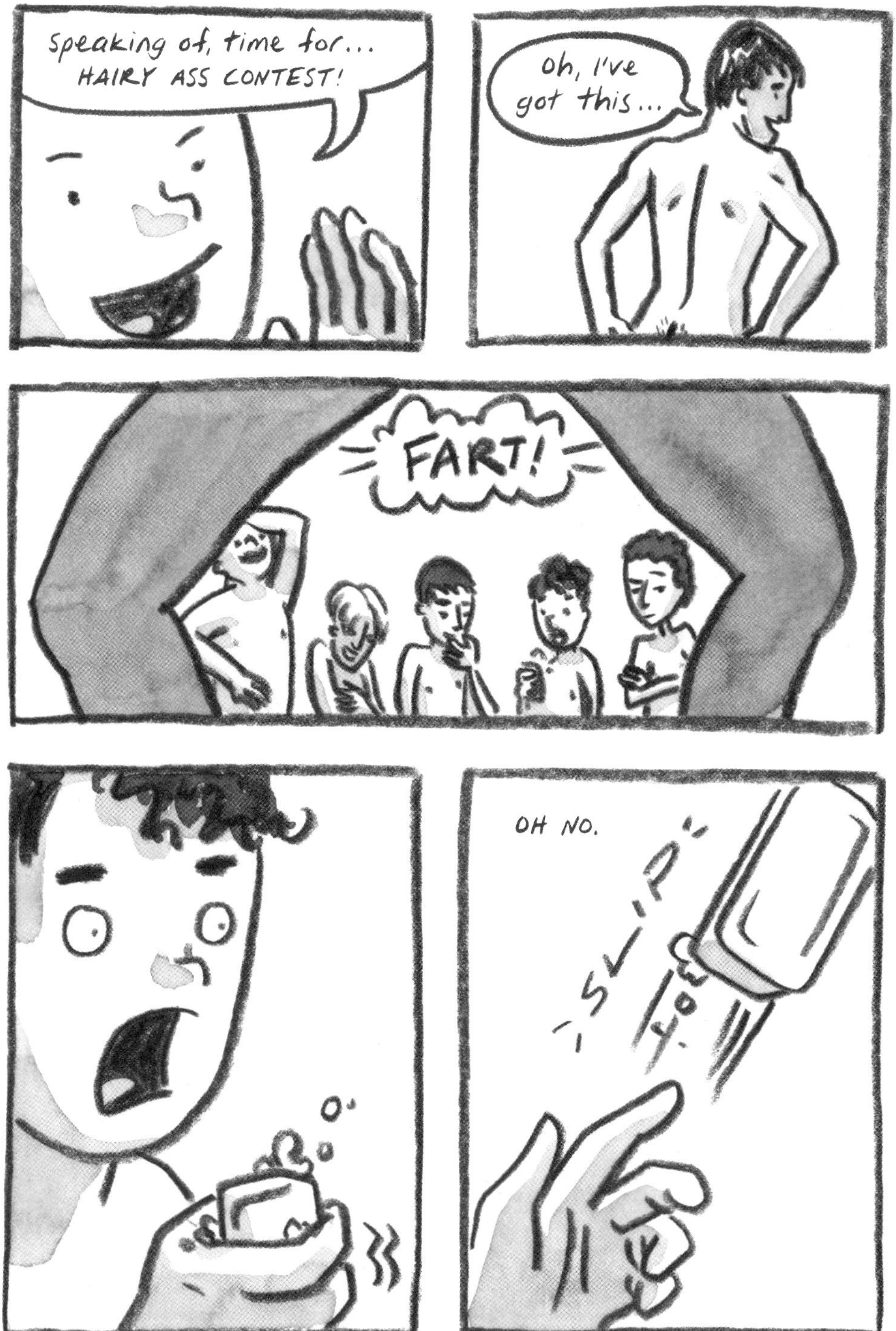

speaking of, time for...
HAIRY ASS CONTEST!
Oh, I've got this...
FART!
OH NO.
SLIP

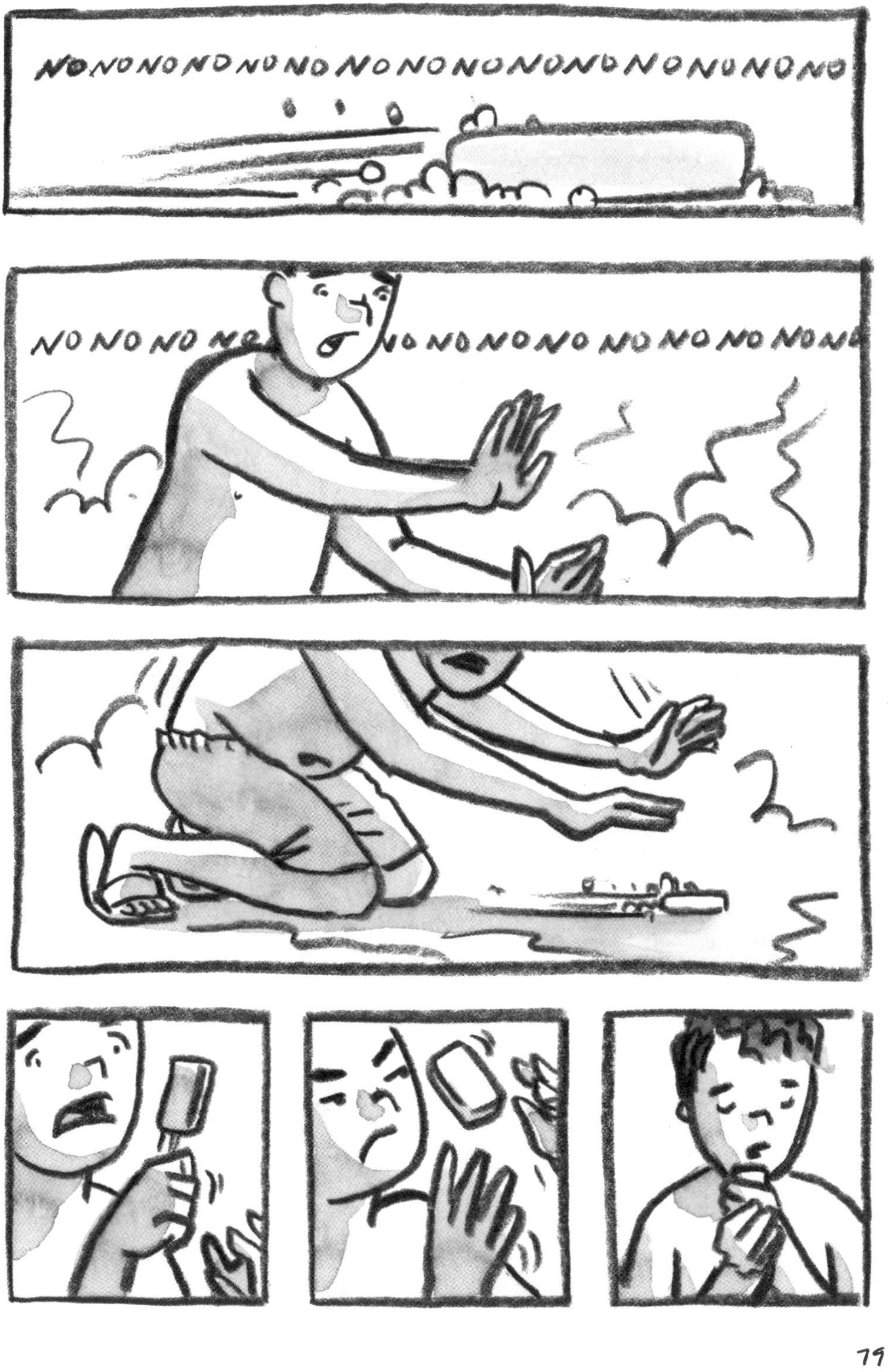
NONONONONONONONONONONONONONONONONO
NONONONO
NONONONONONONONONO

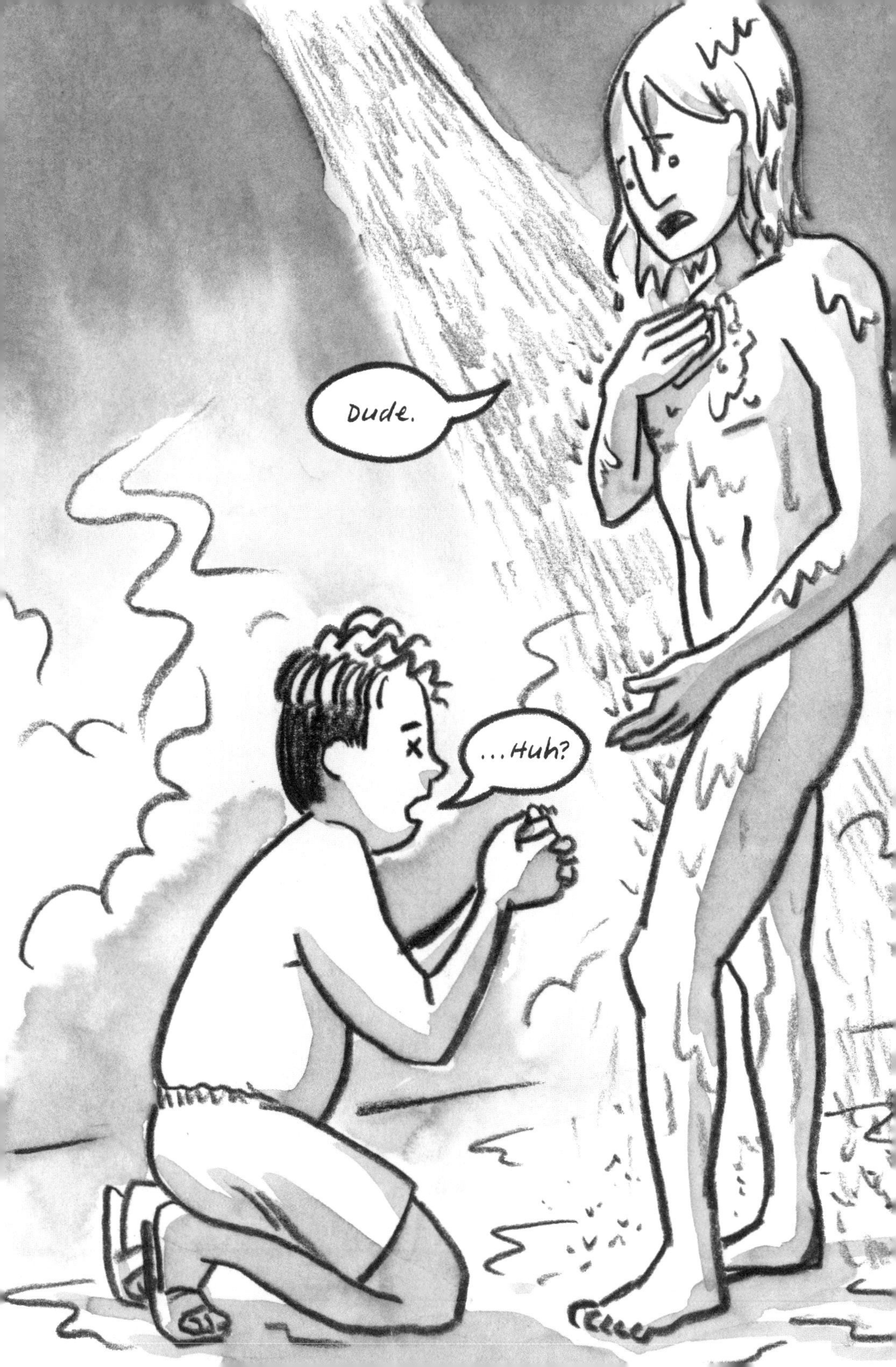
Dude.
...Huh?

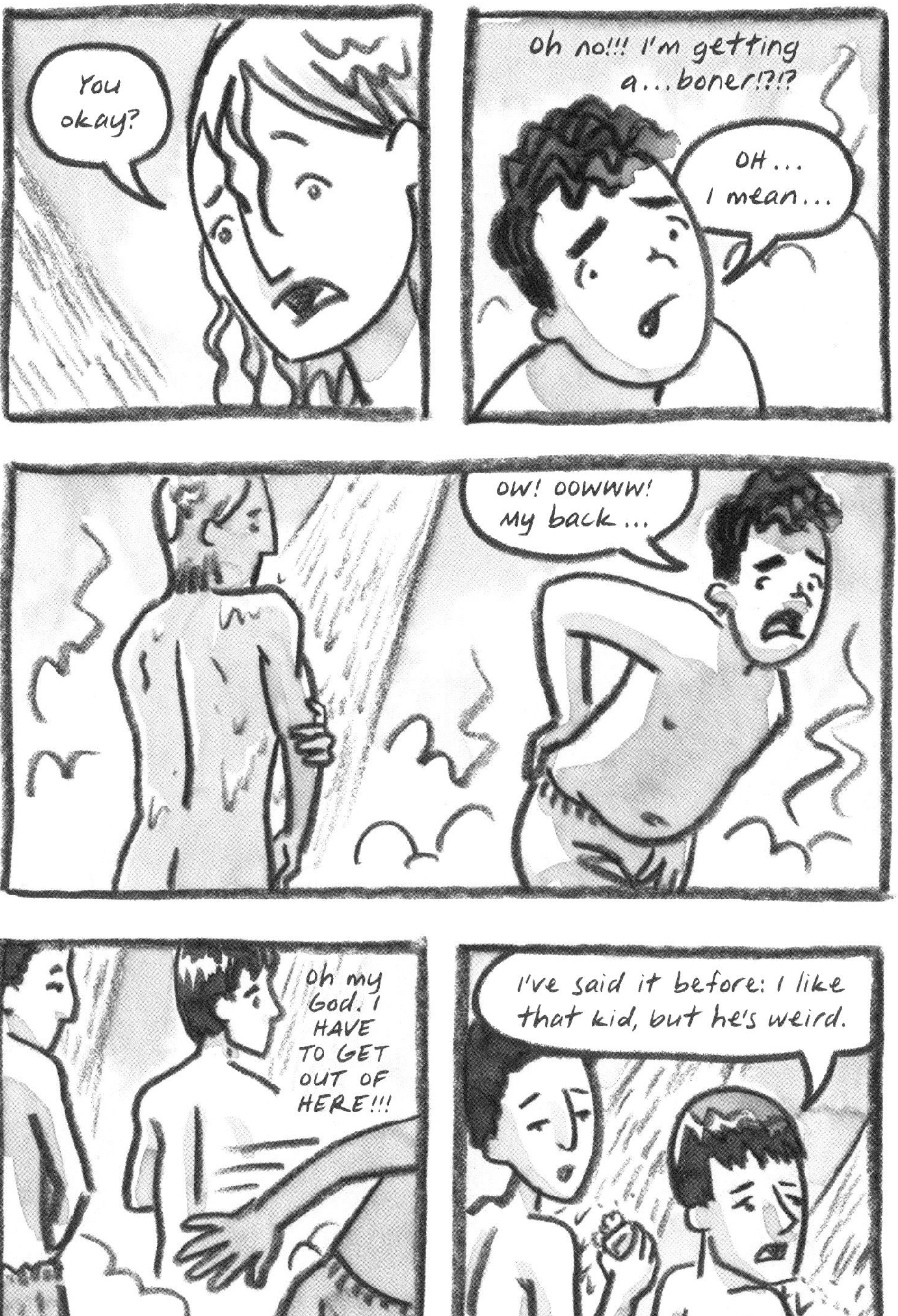
You okay?
Oh no!!! I'm getting a...boner!?!?
OH... I mean...
OW! OOWWW! My back...
Oh my God. I HAVE TO GET OUT OF HERE!!!
I've said it before: I like that kid, but he's weird.

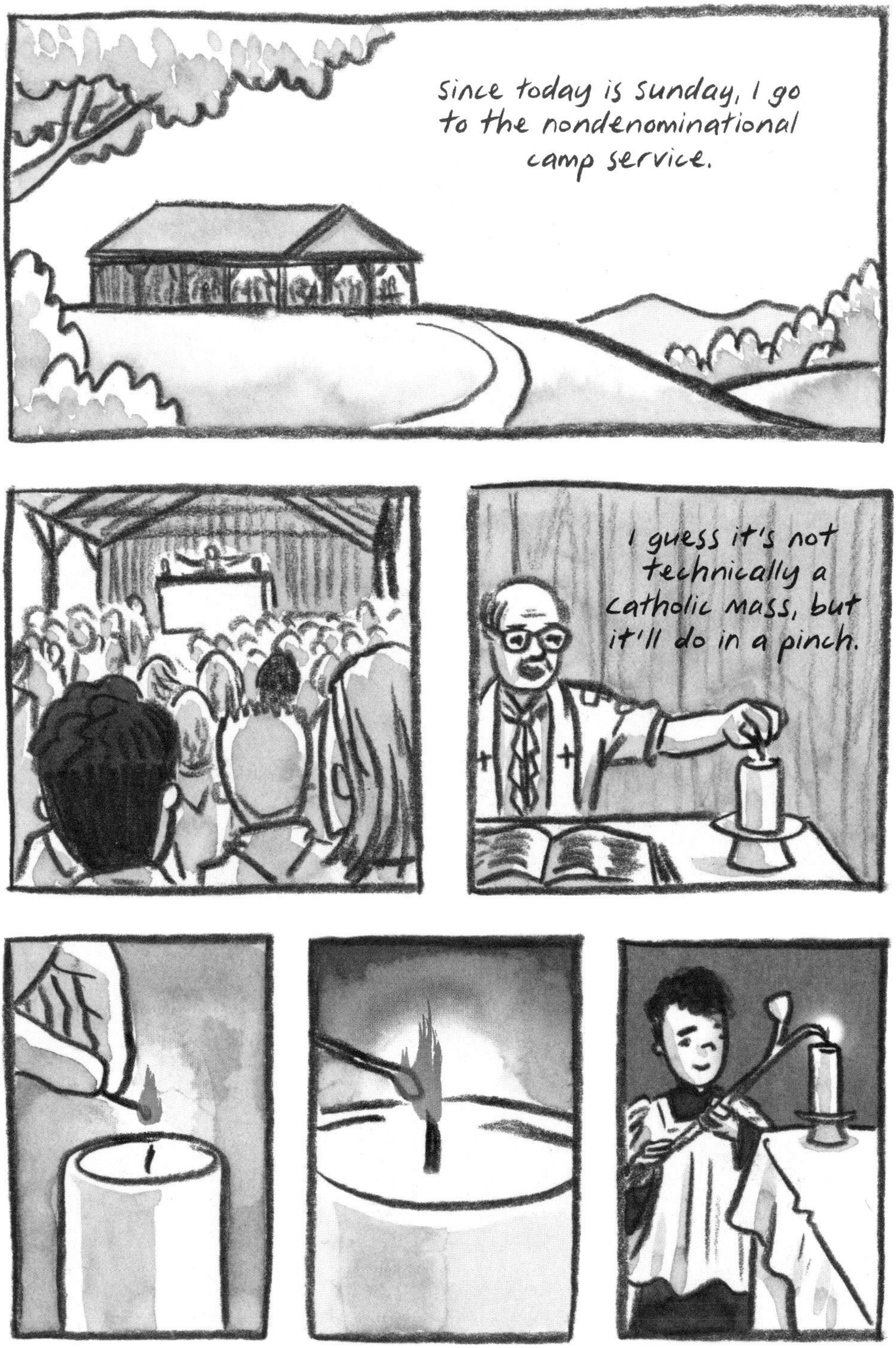
Since today is Sunday, I go to the nondenominational camp service.
I guess it's not technically a Catholic mass, but it'll do in a pinch.

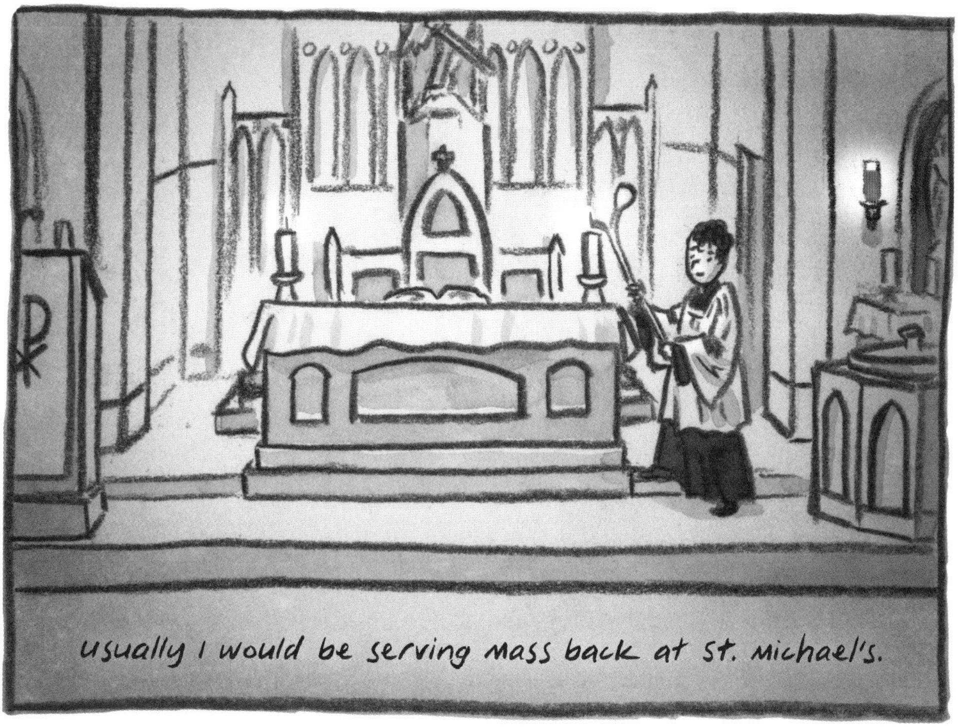
usually I would be serving mass back at St. Michael's.

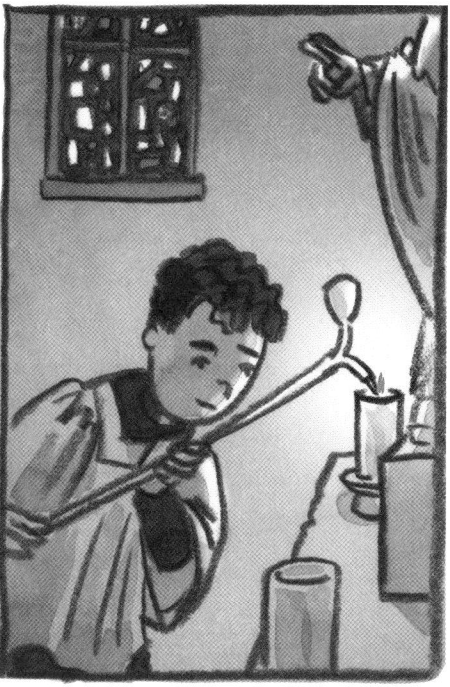

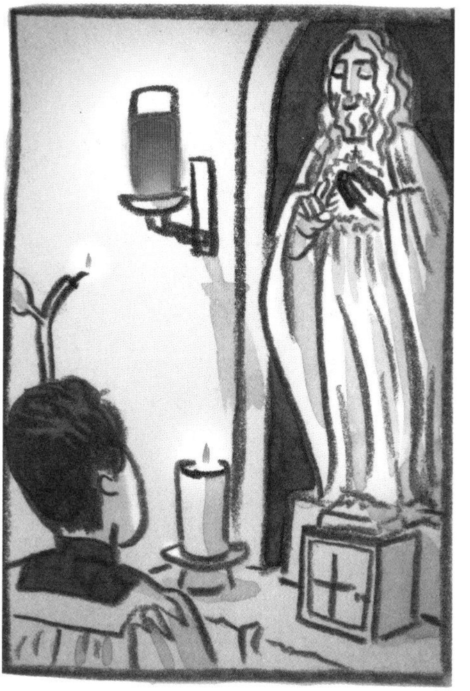

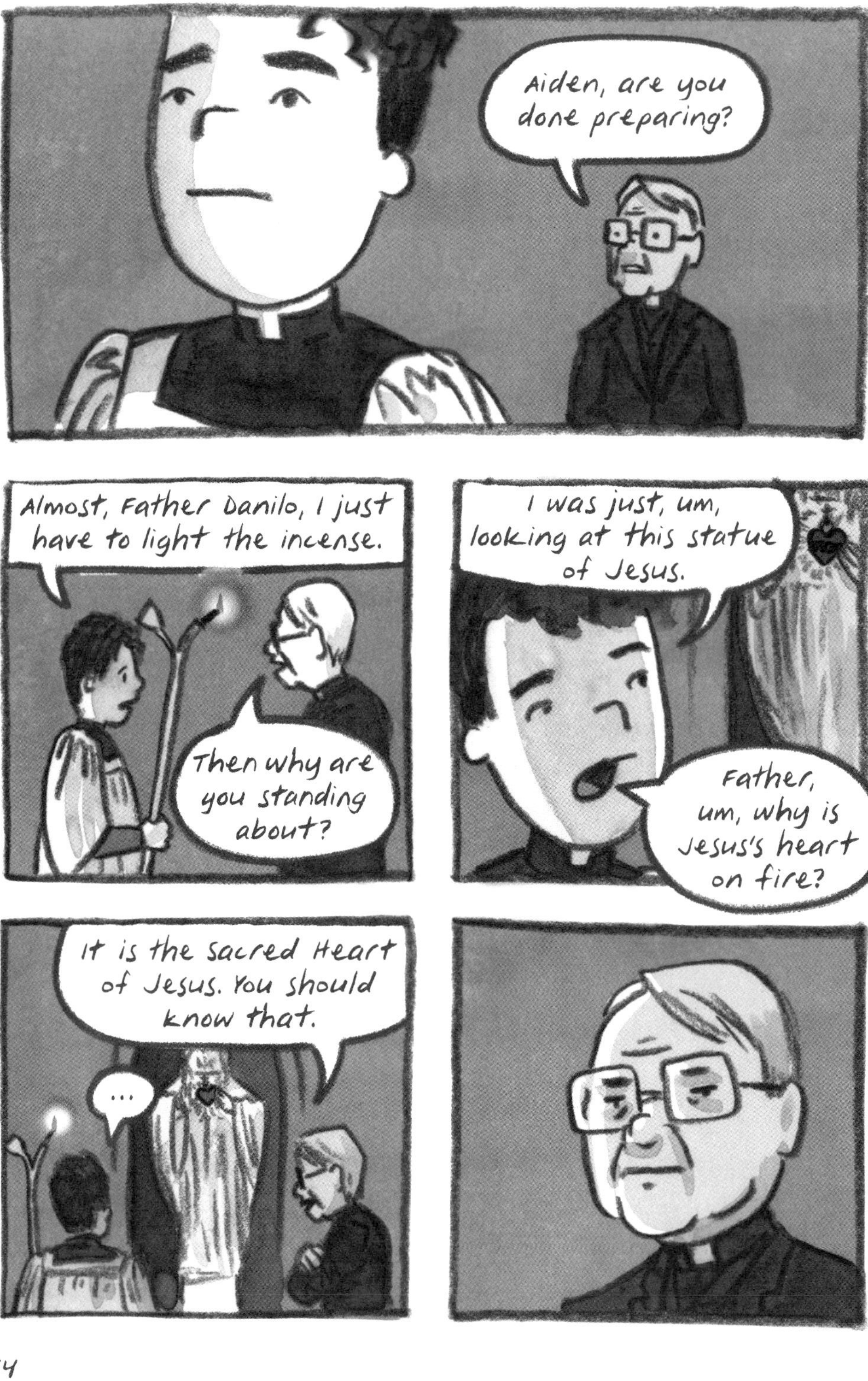
Aiden, are you done preparing?
Almost, Father Danilo, I just have to light the incense.
Then why are you standing about?
I was just, um, looking at this statue of Jesus.
Father, um, why is Jesus's heart on fire?
It is the Sacred Heart of Jesus. You should know that.
...

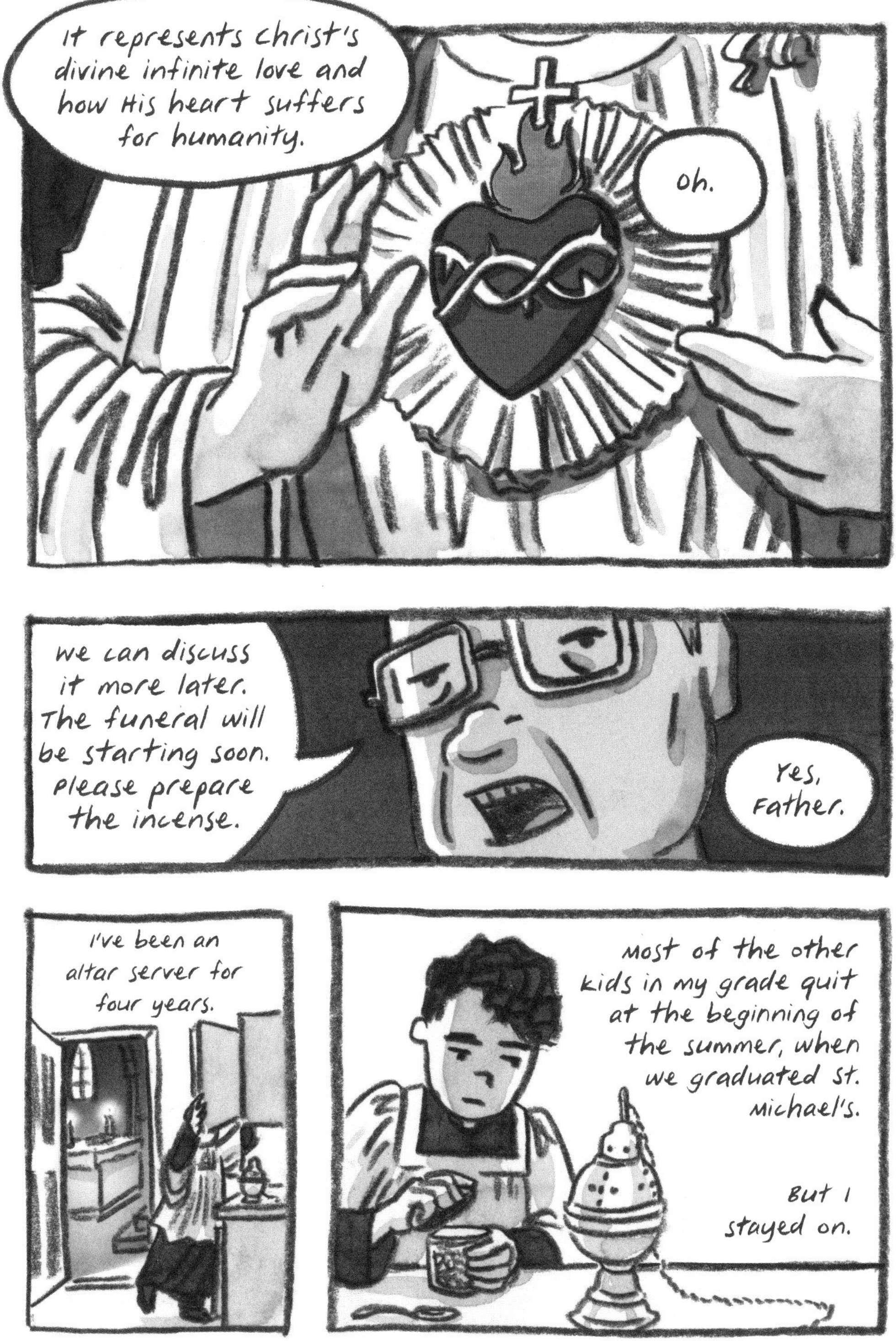
It represents Christ's divine infinite love and how His heart suffers for humanity.
Oh.
We can discuss it more later. The funeral will be starting soon. Please prepare the incense.
Yes, Father.
I've been an altar server for four years.
Most of the other kids in my grade quit at the beginning of the summer, when we graduated St. Michael's.
But I stayed on.

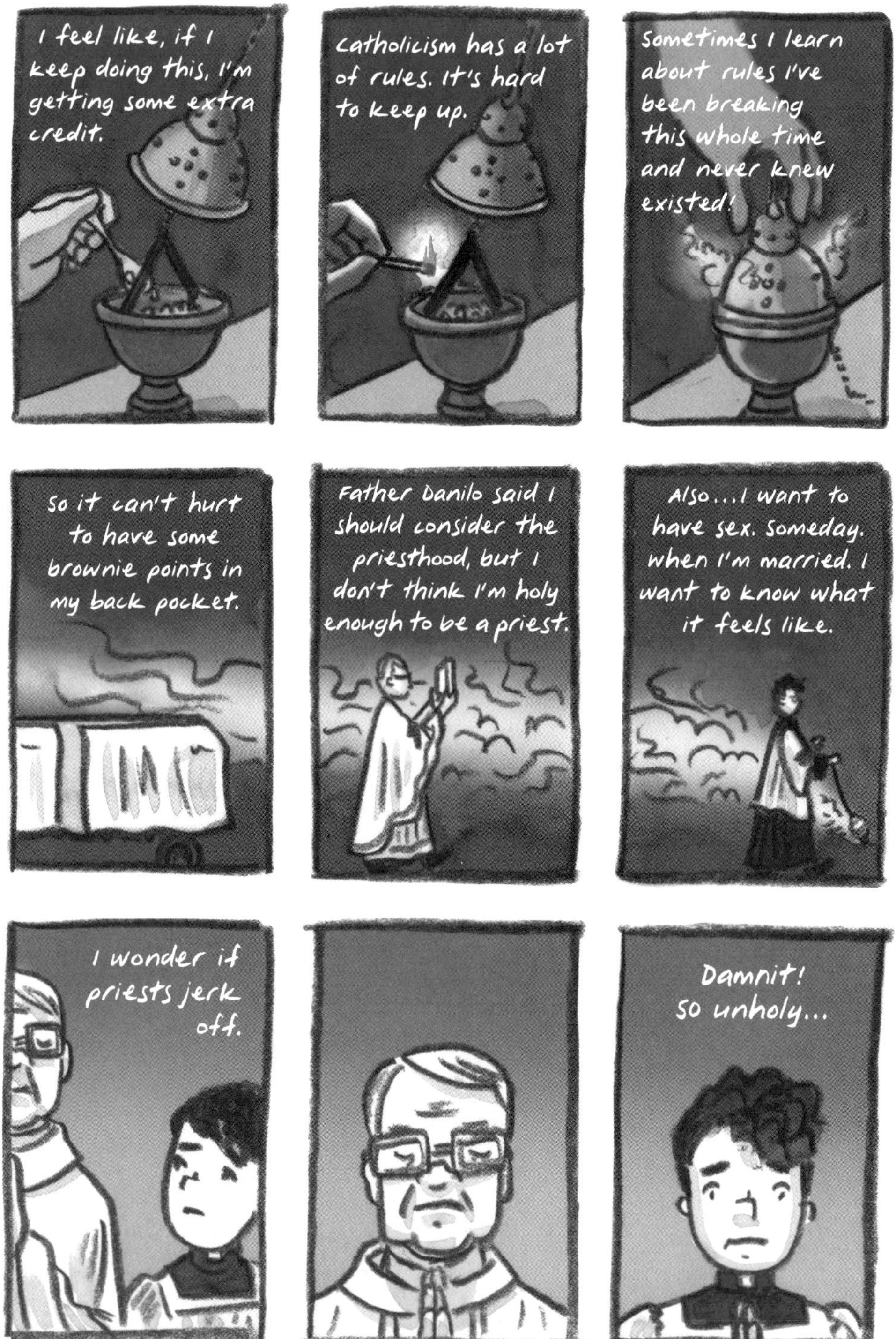
I feel like, if I keep doing this, I'm getting some extra credit.
Catholicism has a lot of rules. It's hard to keep up.
Sometimes I learn about rules I've been breaking this whole time and never knew existed!
So it can't hurt to have some brownie points in my back pocket.
Father Danilo said I should consider the priesthood, but I don't think I'm holy enough to be a priest.
Also...I want to have sex. Someday. When I'm married. I want to know what it feels like.
I wonder if priests jerk off.
Damnit! So unholy...

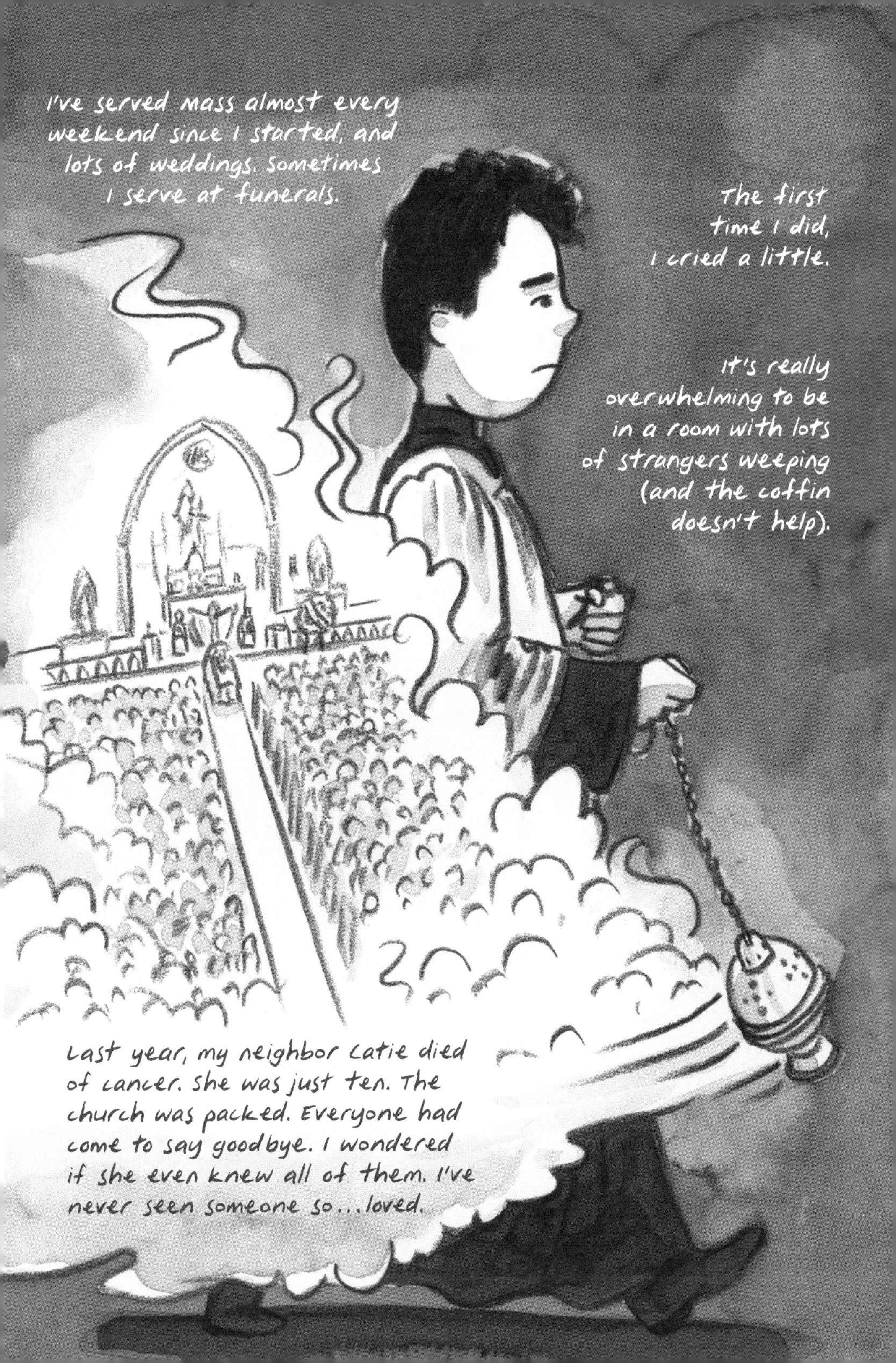
I've served mass almost every weekend since I started, and lots of weddings. Sometimes I serve at funerals.
The first time I did, I cried a little.
It's really overwhelming to be in a room with lots of strangers weeping (and the coffin doesn't help).
Last year, my neighbor Catie died of cancer. She was just ten. The church was packed. Everyone had come to say goodbye. I wondered if she even knew all of them. I've never seen someone so...loved.

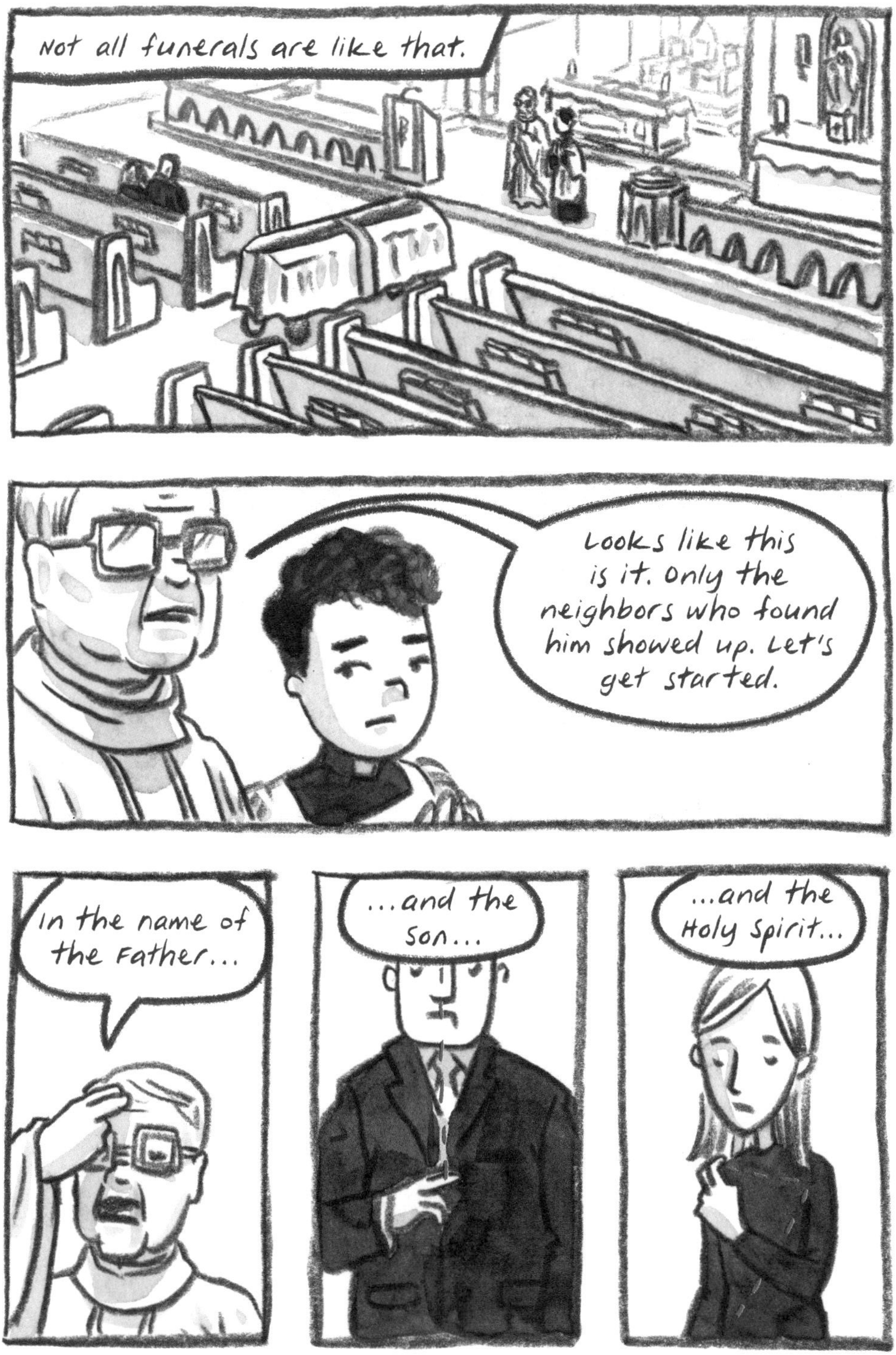
Not all funerals are like that.
Looks like this is it. Only the neighbors who found him showed up. Let's get started.
In the name of the Father...
...and the Son...
...and the Holy Spirit...

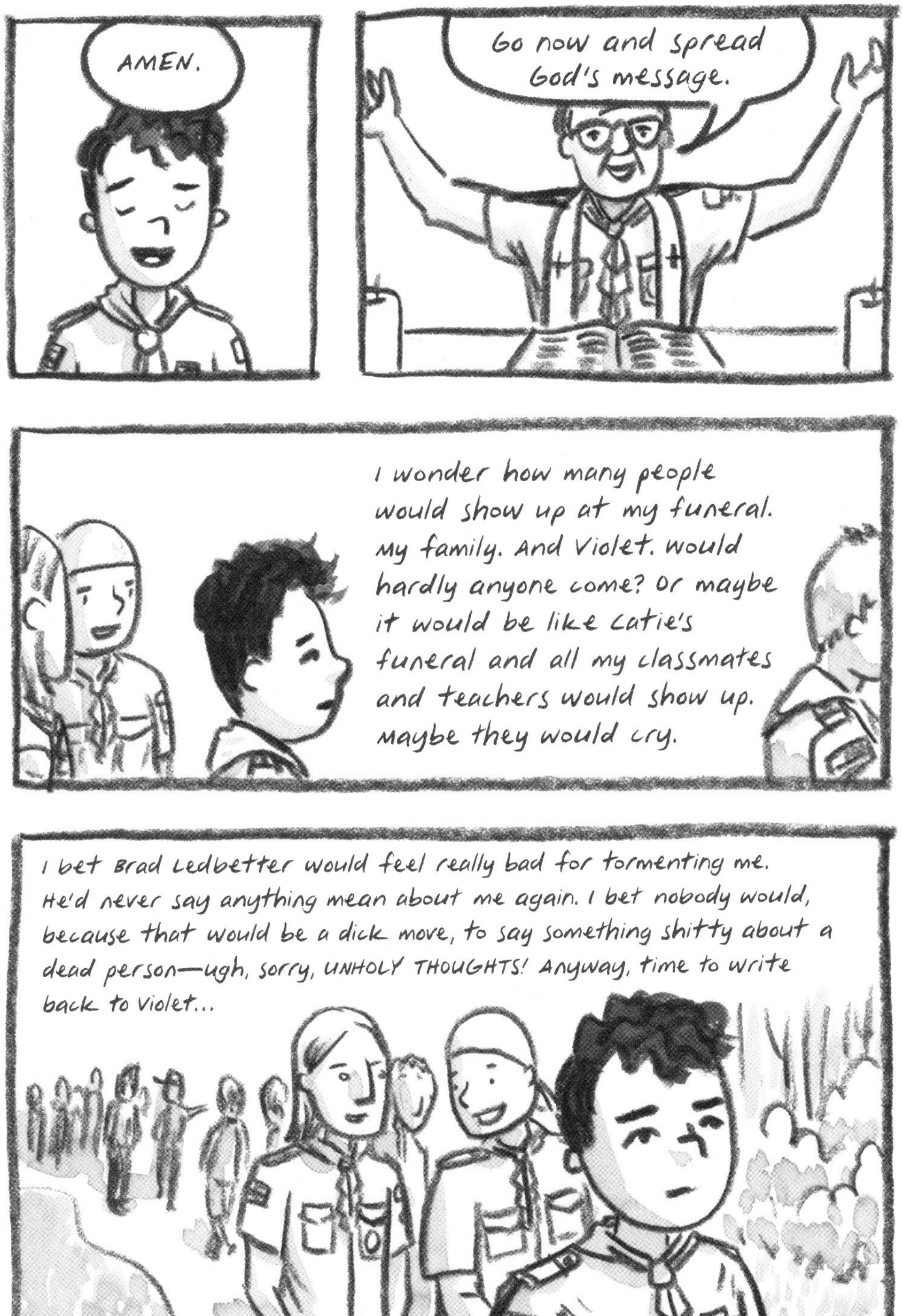
AMEN.
Go now and spread God's message.
I wonder how many people would show up at my funeral. My family. And Violet. Would hardly anyone come? Or maybe it would be like Catie's funeral and all my classmates and teachers would show up. Maybe they would cry.
I bet Brad Ledbetter would feel really bad for tormenting me. He'd never say anything mean about me again. I bet nobody would, because that would be a dick move, to say something shitty about a dead person—ugh, sorry, UNHOLY THOUGHTS! Anyway, time to write back to Violet...

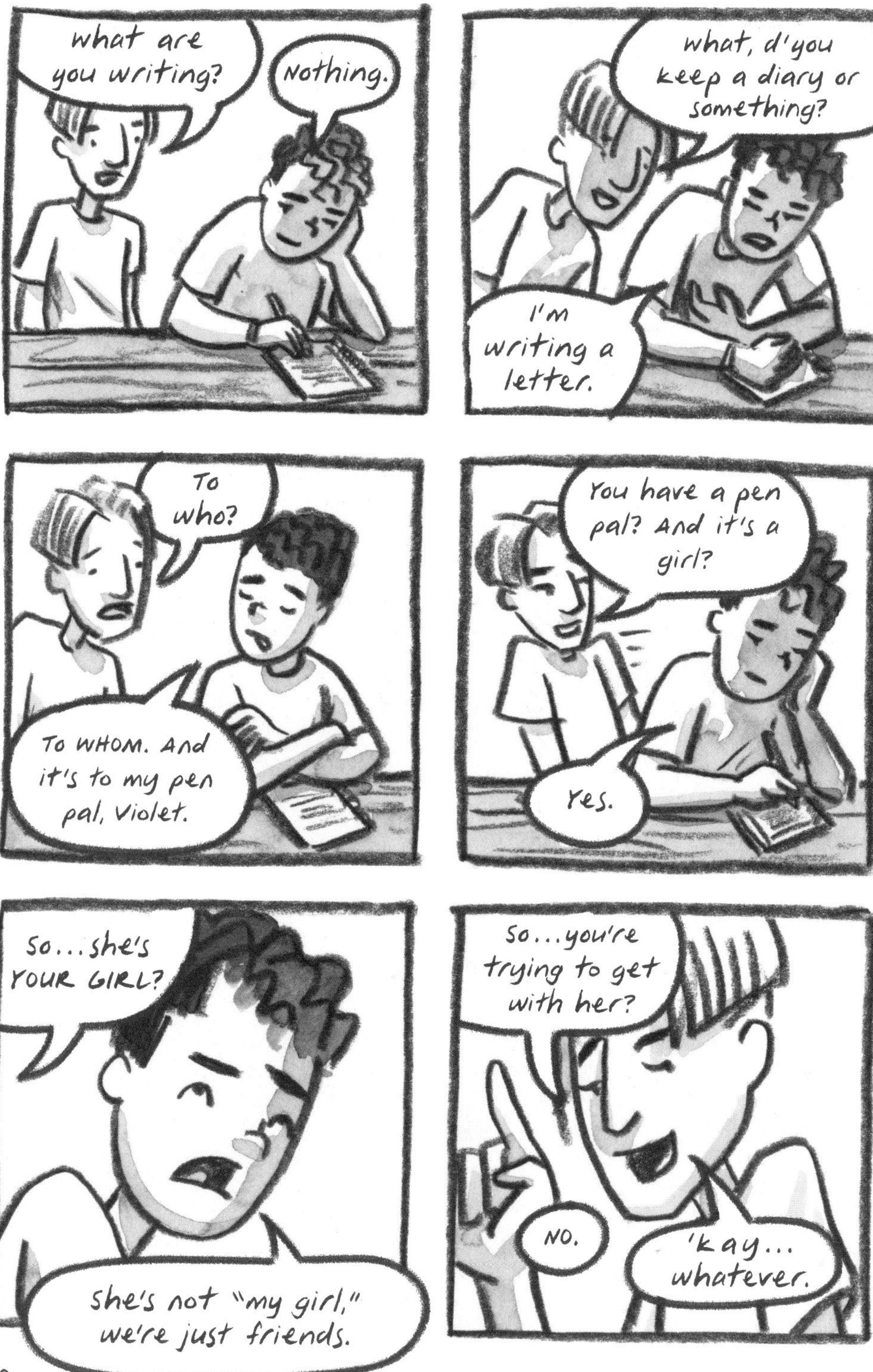
what are you writing?
Nothing.
what, d'you keep a diary or something?
I'm writing a letter.
To who?
TO WHOM. And it's to my pen pal, Violet.
You have a pen pal? And it's a girl?
Yes.
So...she's YOUR GIRL?
she's not "my girl," we're just friends.
So...you're trying to get with her?
NO.
'kay... whatever.

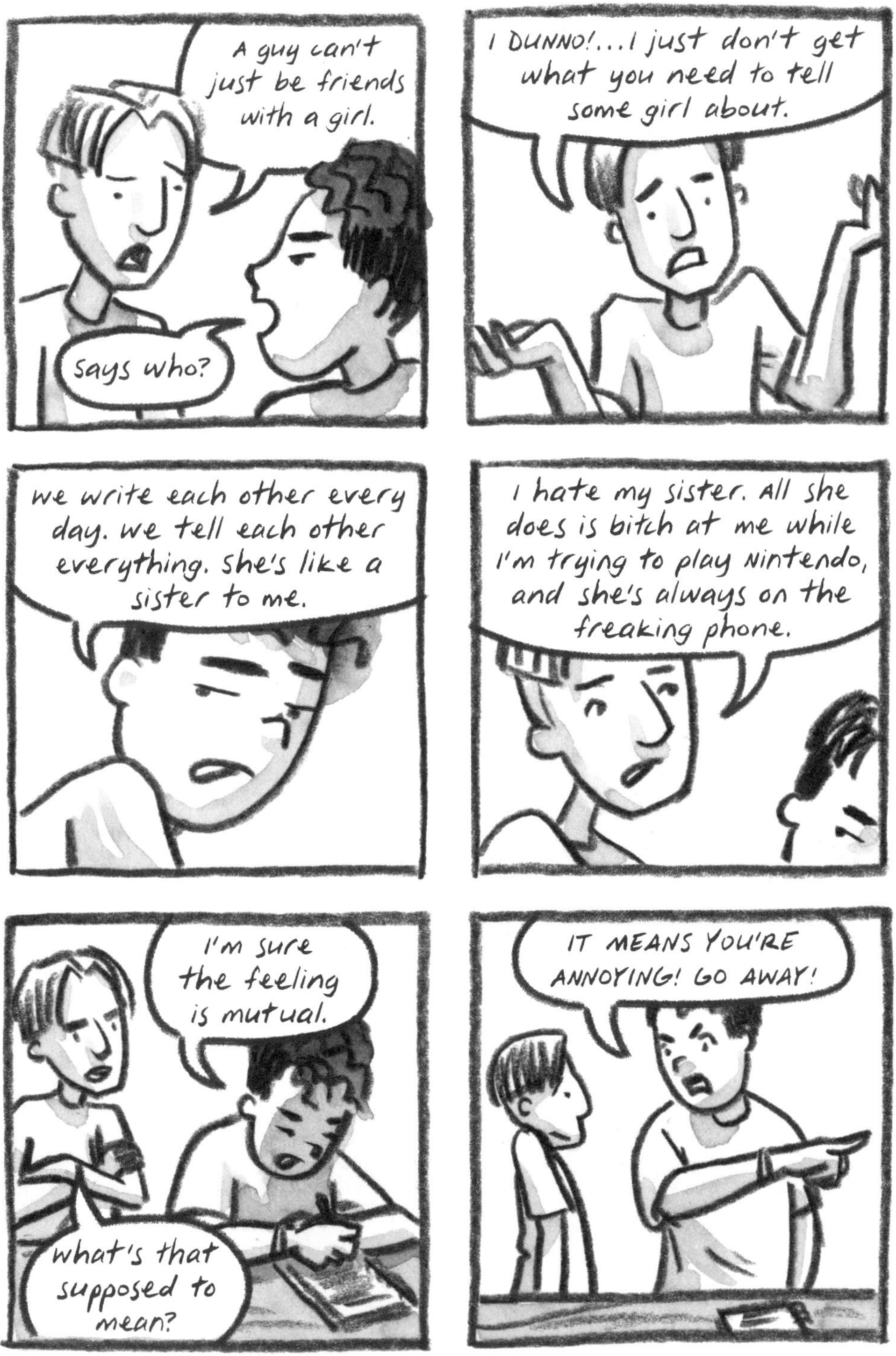
A guy can't just be friends with a girl.
Says who?
I DUNNO!...I just don't get what you need to tell some girl about.
We write each other every day. We tell each other everything. She's like a sister to me.
I hate my sister. All she does is bitch at me while I'm trying to play Nintendo, and she's always on the freaking phone.
I'm sure the feeling is mutual.
What's that supposed to mean?
IT MEANS YOU'RE ANNOYING! GO AWAY!

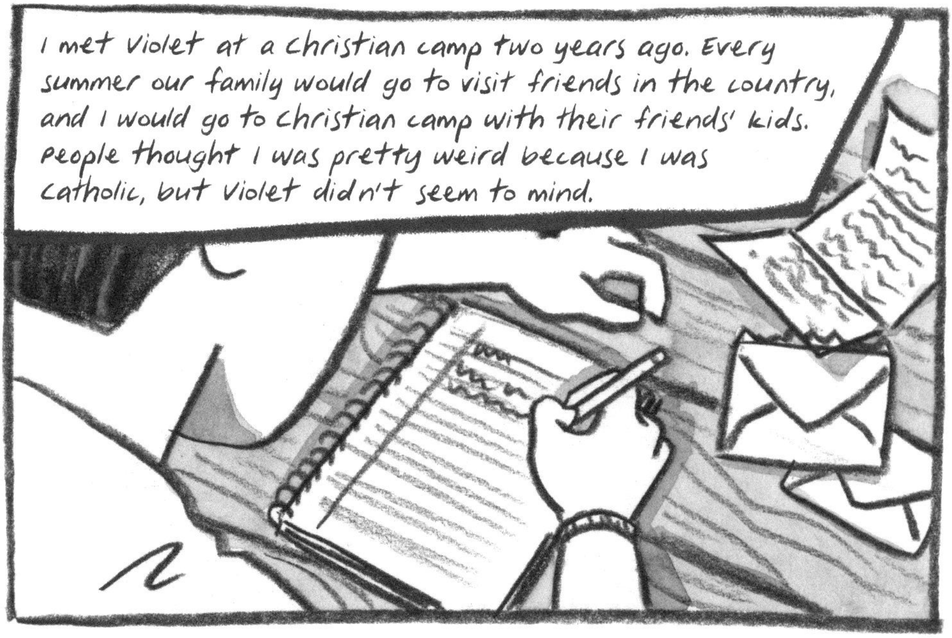
I met Violet at a Christian camp two years ago. Every summer our family would go to visit friends in the country, and I would go to Christian camp with their friends' kids. People thought I was pretty weird because I was Catholic, but Violet didn't seem to mind.

She was the first person I met who had the same zany sense of humor as me. We would busy ourselves singing spoof songs and consuming huge amounts of candy and soda at the trading post. One time Violet double-dog dared me to sniff some pepper. We were curious if it made you sneeze a lot like in cartoons. Apparently, the cartoons were accurate.

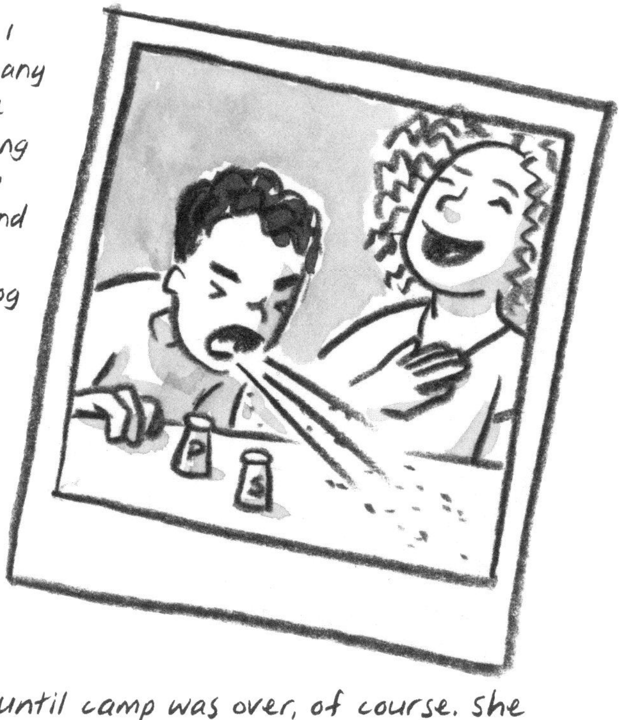
P
S

We were inseparable. Until camp was over, of course. She lives really far away, but we became pen pals instantly.

RIIIP!
Aug 25, 1945
Dear Violet,
What's up? I can't wait
your next letter! Camp is
ok. There's been a lot
I wish we could talk. Ugh.
Ryan is being a total loser.
He's asking me how I'm
friends with a girl (eyeroll!)
He thinks I'M the weirdo.
Anyway, we just went on an
overnight trip to Frying Pan
Elias and I are going
She's the only person I tell all my secrets to. We joke about how one of us could totally blackmail the other... except neither of us has any money.
Plus, we both know just as many secrets about the other!
Her letters mean the world to me. They are always the highlight of my week. I absolutely live for mail call.

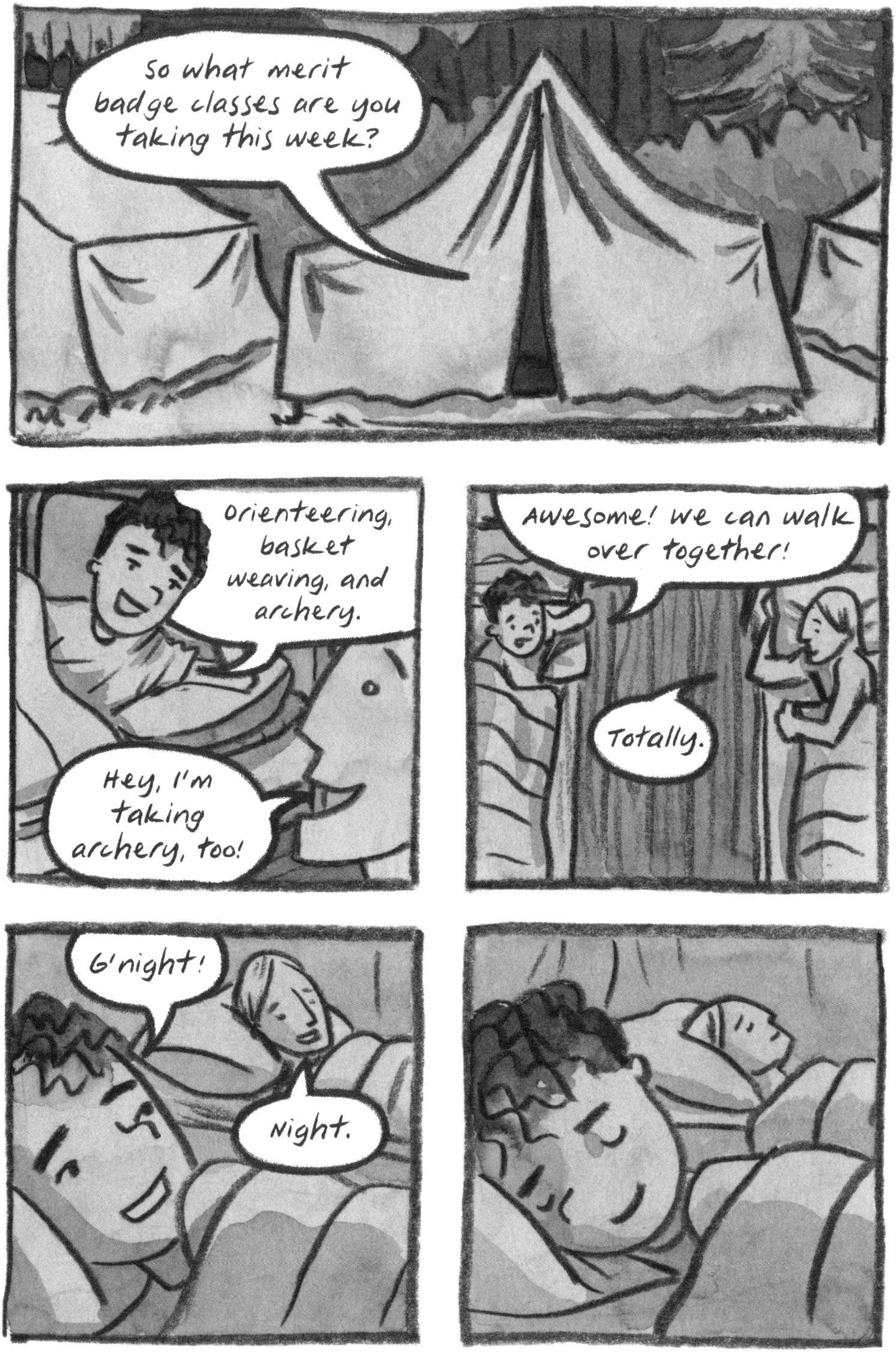
So what merit badge classes are you taking this week?
Orienteering, basket weaving, and archery.
Hey, I'm taking archery, too!
Awesome! We can walk over together!
Totally.
G'night!
Night.

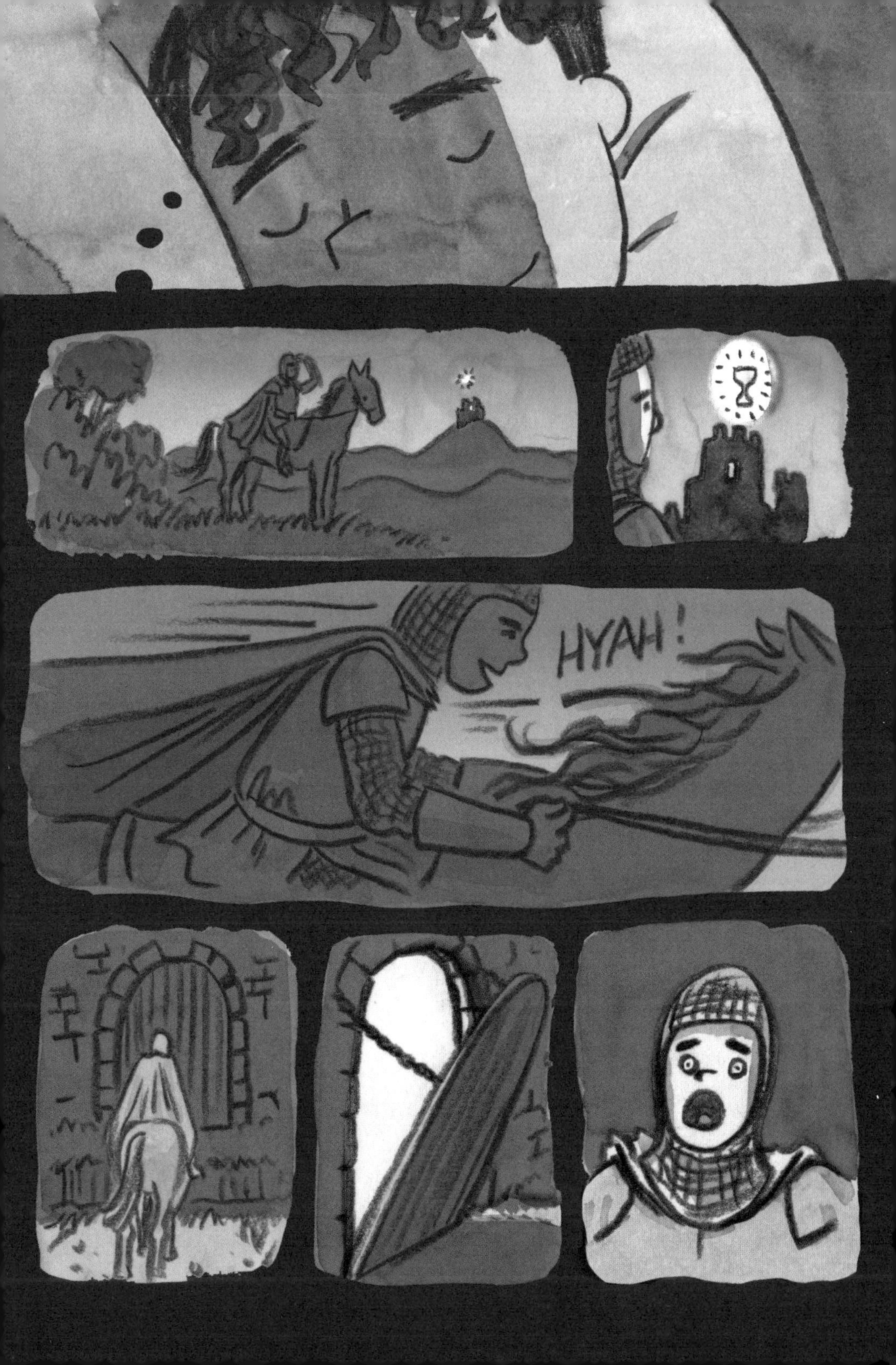
HYAH!

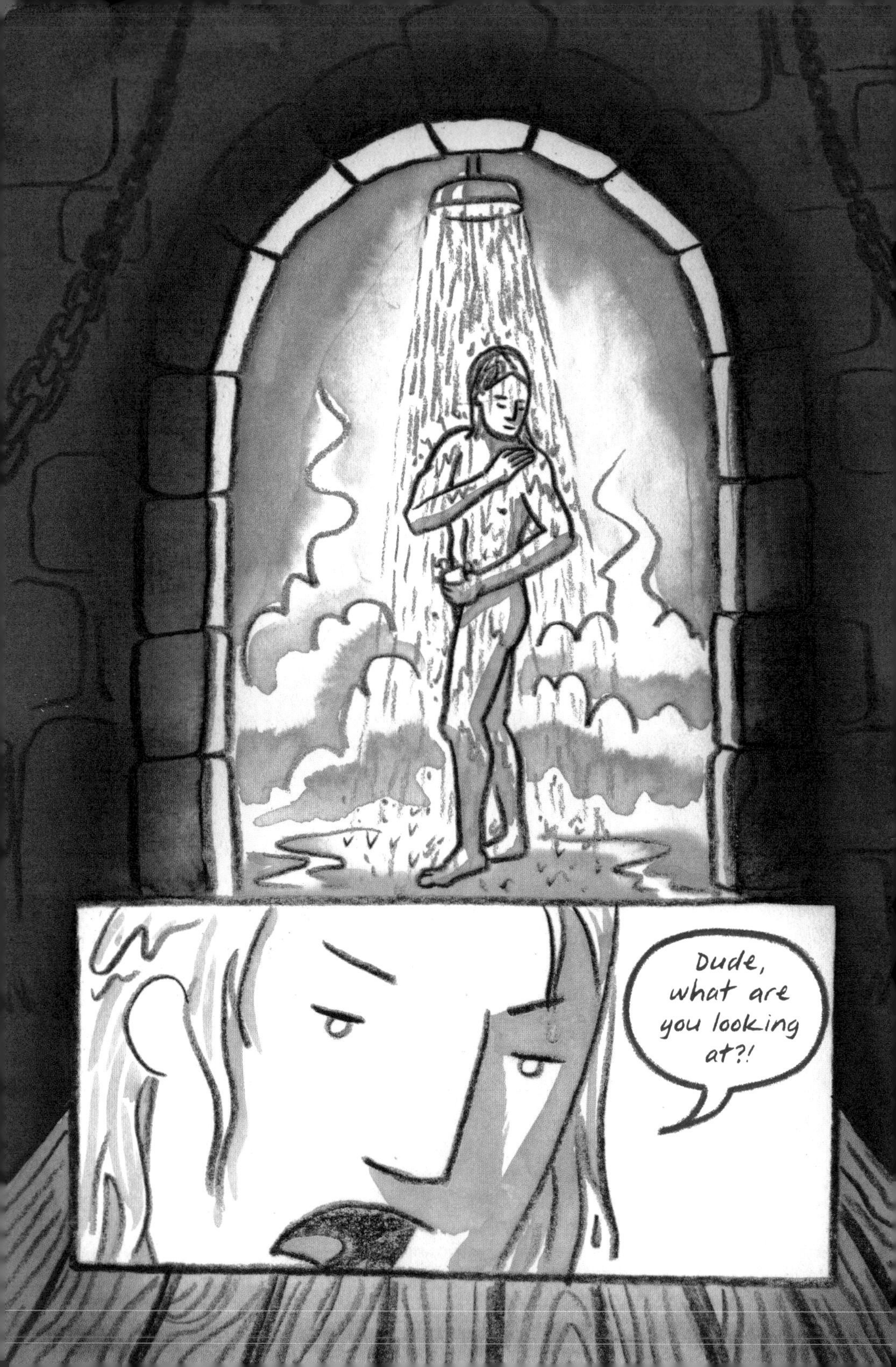
Dude, what are you looking at?!

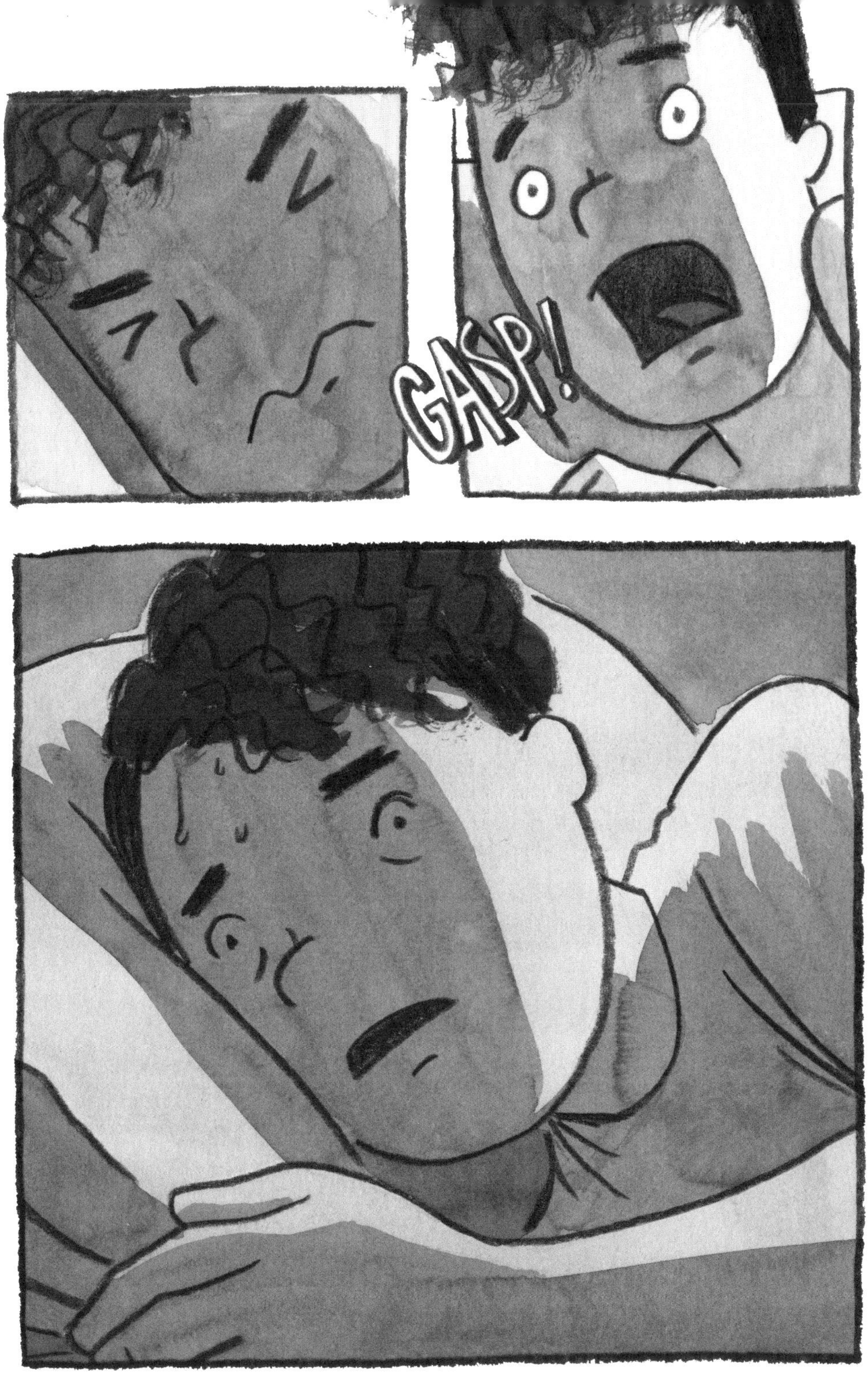
GASP!

MONDAY

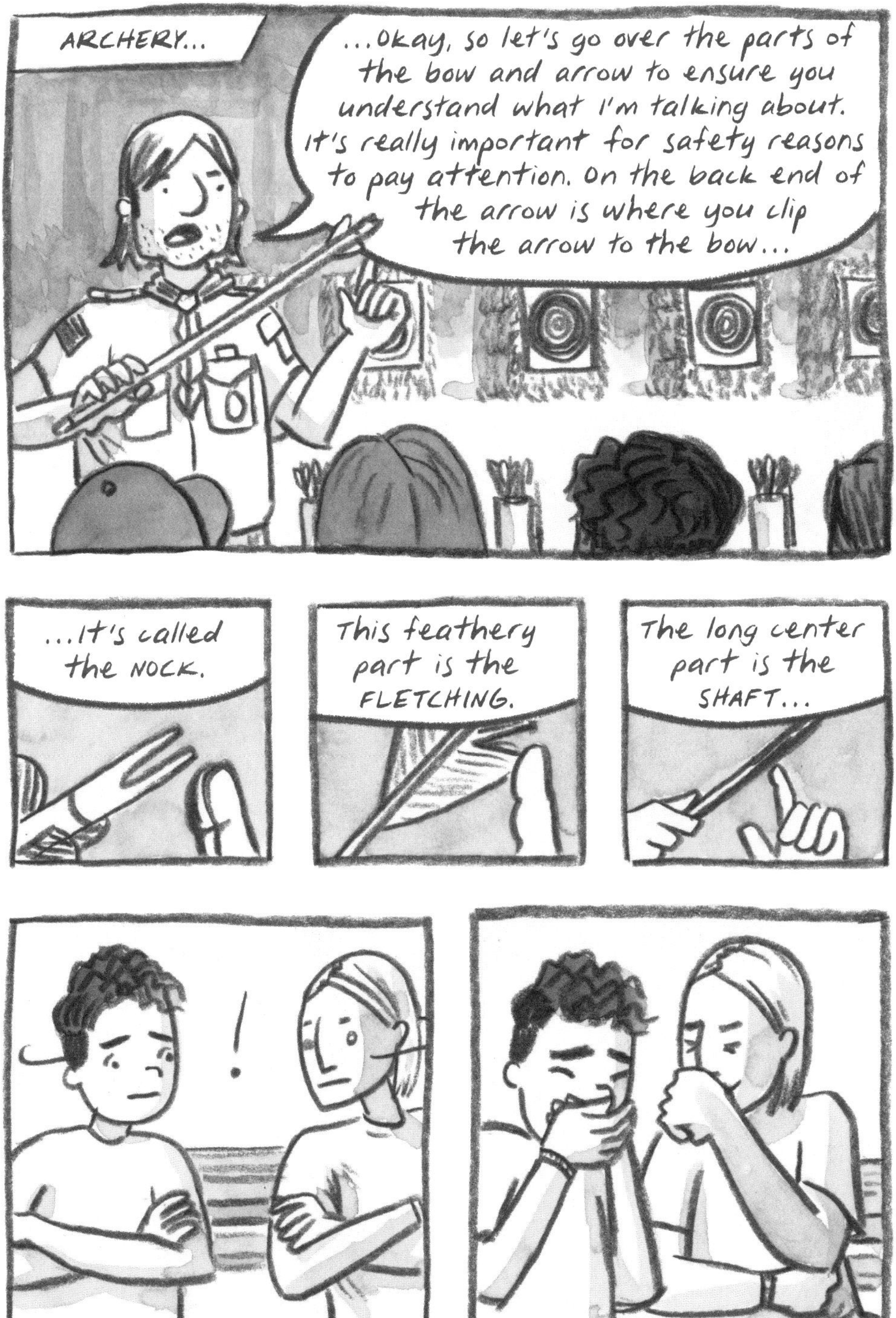
ARCHERY...
...Okay, so let's go over the parts of the bow and arrow to ensure you understand what I'm talking about. It's really important for safety reasons to pay attention. On the back end of the arrow is where you clip the arrow to the bow...
...It's called the NOCK.
This feathery part is the FLETCHING.
The long center part is the SHAFT...
!

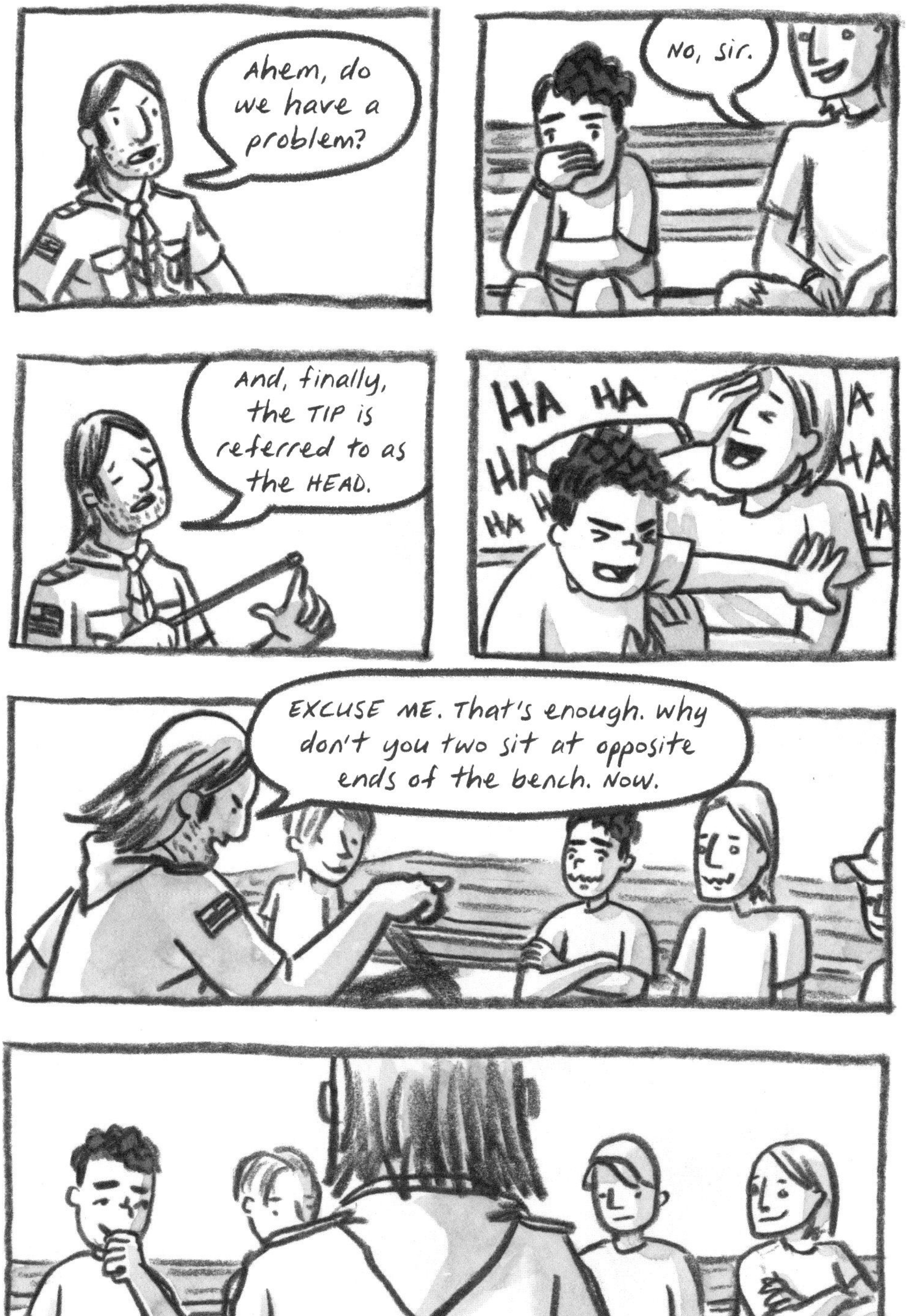
Ahem, do we have a problem?
No, sir.
And, finally, the TIP is referred to as the HEAD.
HA HA
HA
HA H
A
HA
HA
EXCUSE ME. That's enough. Why don't you two sit at opposite ends of the bench. Now.

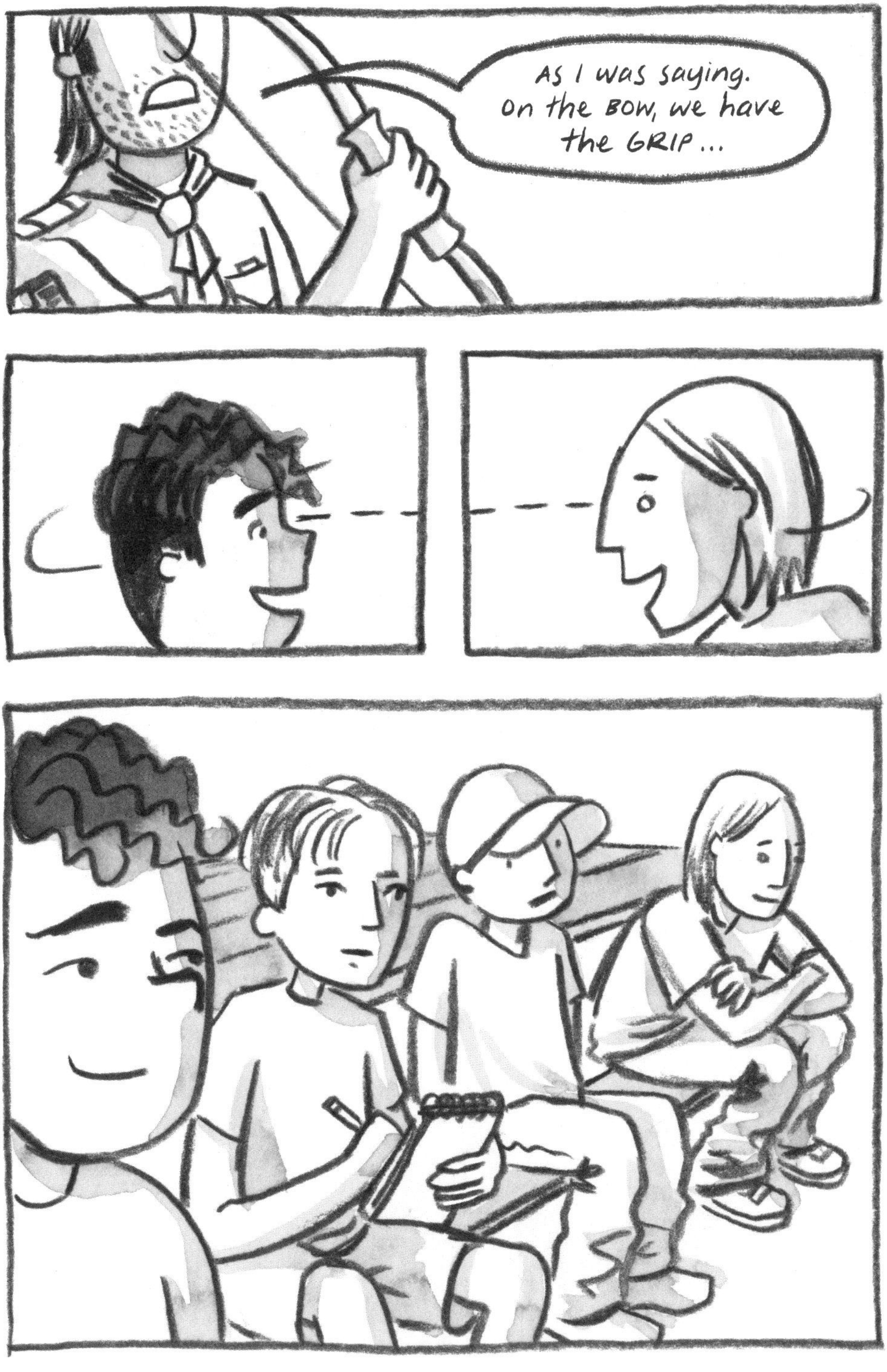
As I was saying. On the BOW, we have the GRIP...

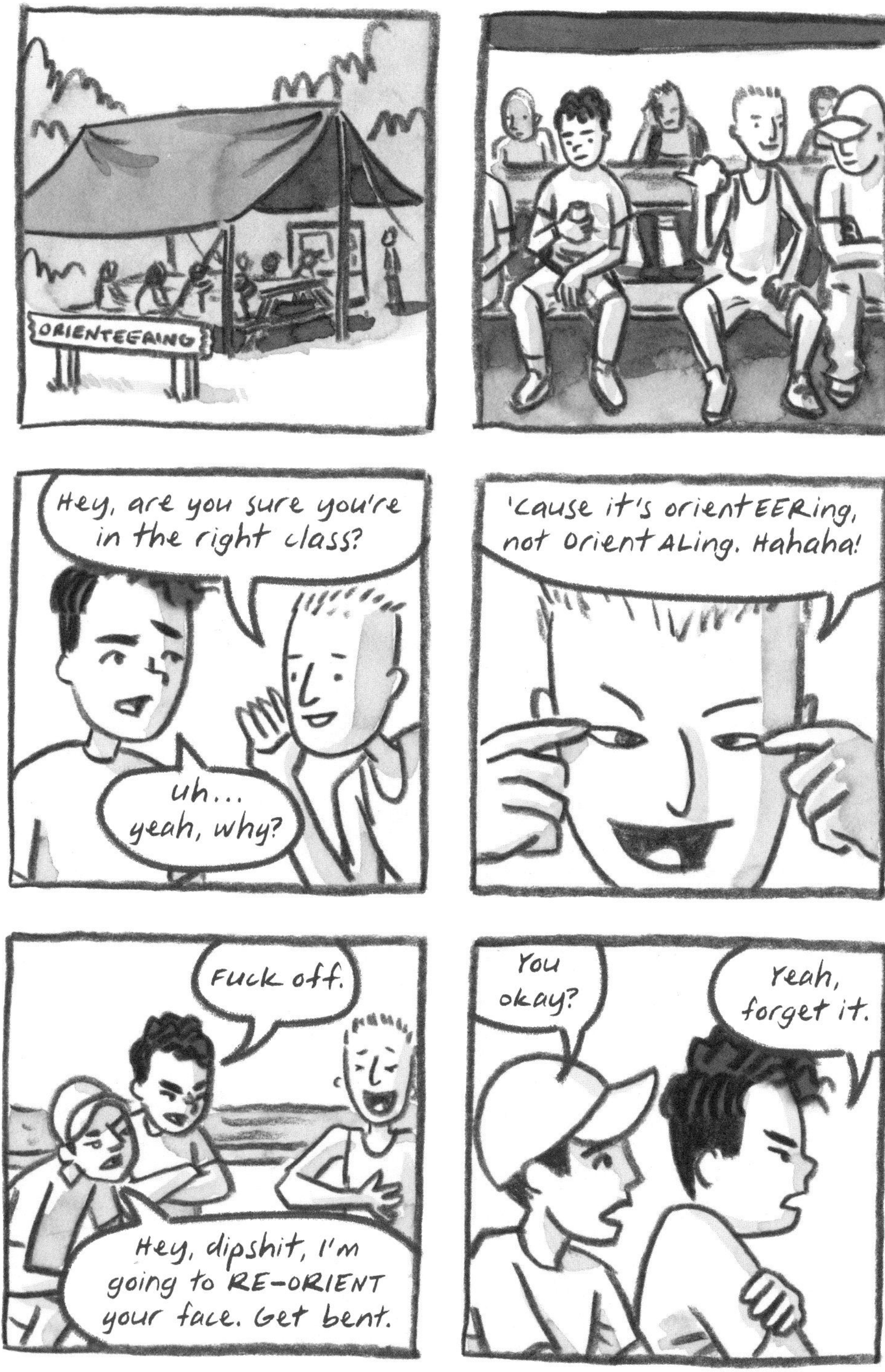
ORIENTEERING
Hey, are you sure you're in the right class?
uh... yeah, why?
'Cause it's orientEERing, not orientALing. Hahaha!
Fuck off.
Hey, dipshit, I'm going to RE-ORIENT your face. Get bent.
You okay?
Yeah, forget it.

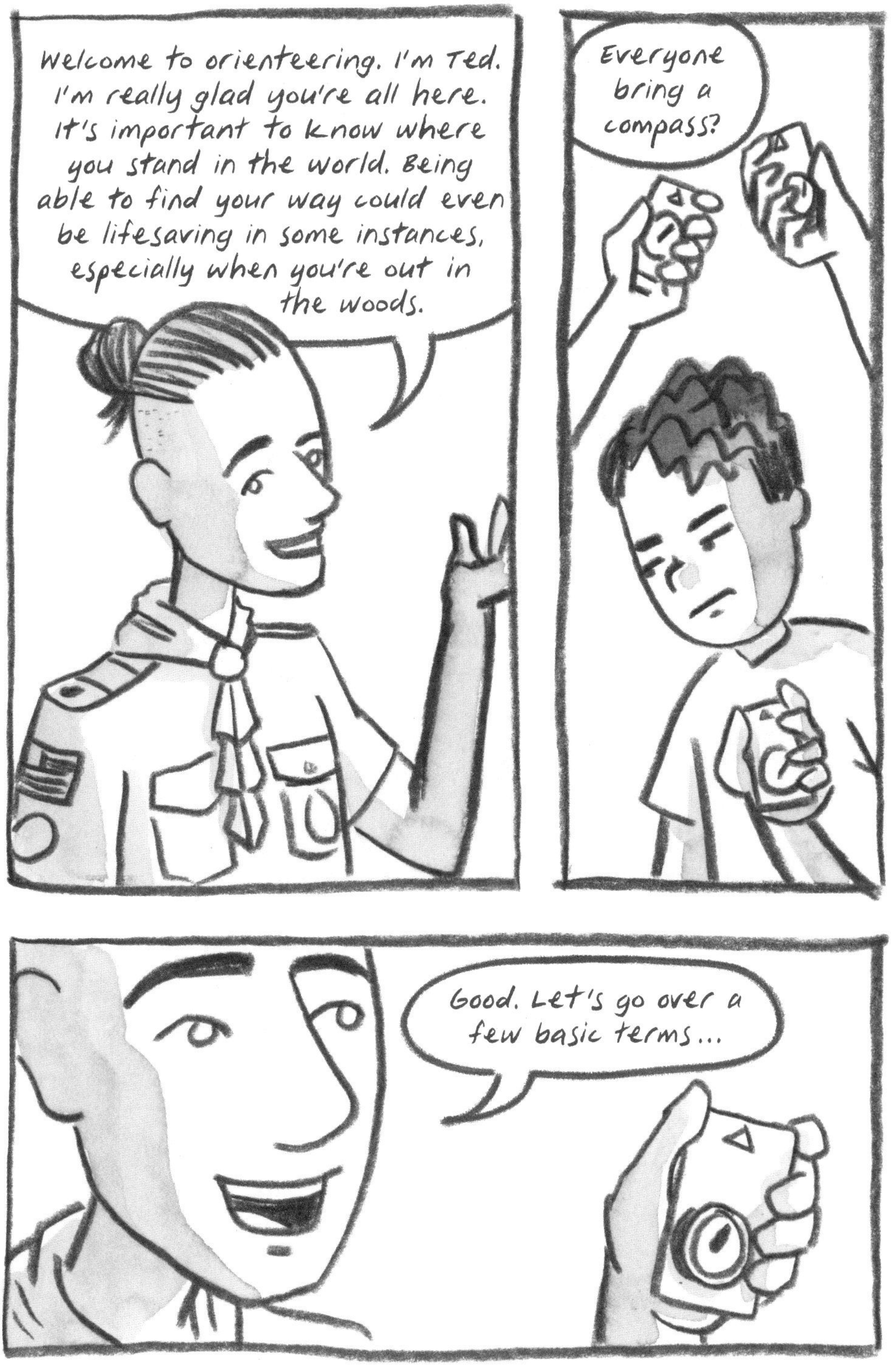
Welcome to orienteering. I'm Ted. I'm really glad you're all here. It's important to know where you stand in the world. Being able to find your way could even be lifesaving in some instances, especially when you're out in the woods.
Everyone bring a compass?
Good. Let's go over a few basic terms...

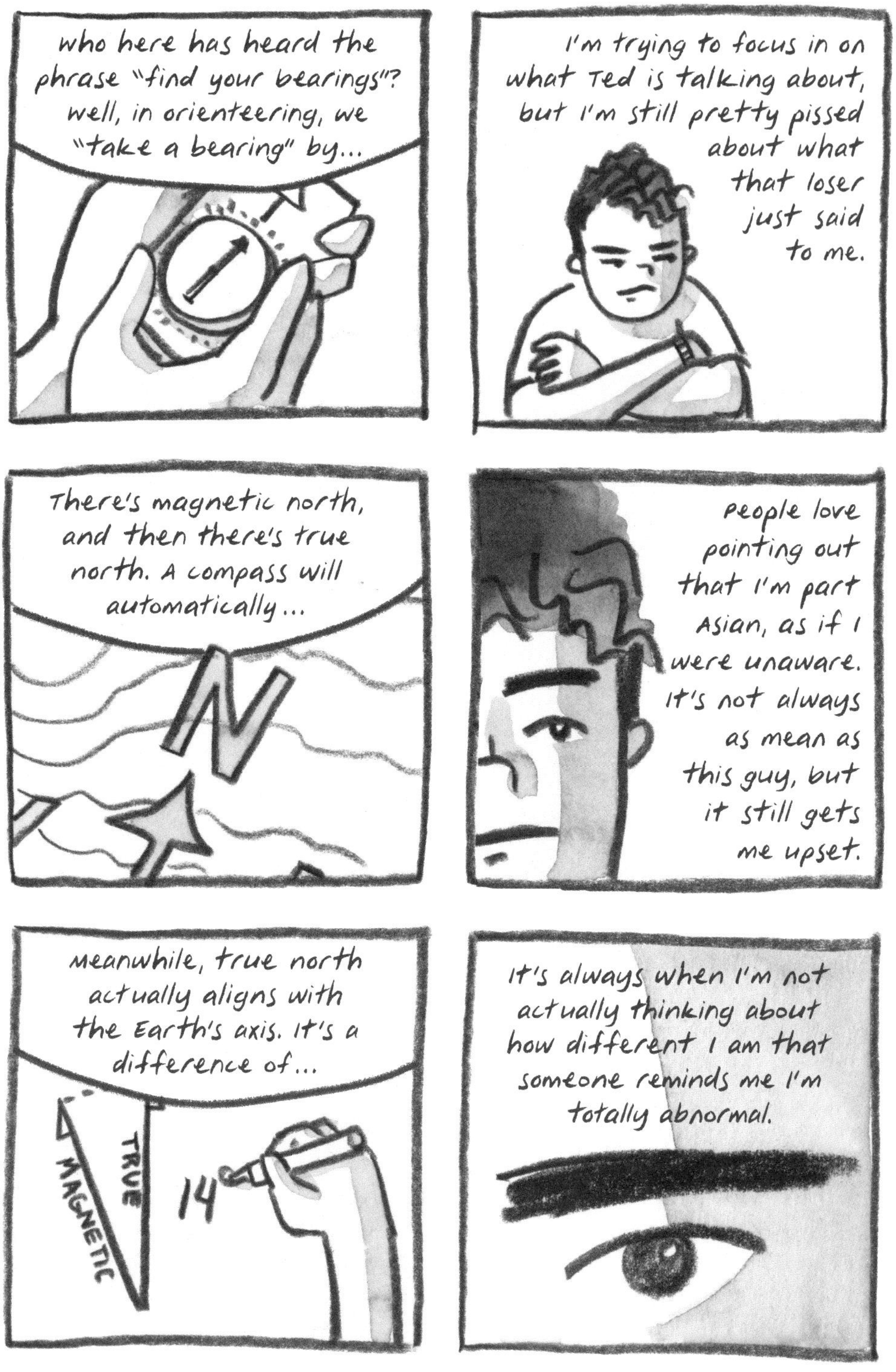
who here has heard the phrase "find your bearings"? well, in orienteering, we "take a bearing" by...
I'm trying to focus in on what Ted is talking about, but I'm still pretty pissed about what that loser just said to me.
There's magnetic north, and then there's true north. A compass will automatically...
N
People love pointing out that I'm part Asian, as if I were unaware. It's not always as mean as this guy, but it still gets me upset.
Meanwhile, true north actually aligns with the Earth's axis. It's a difference of...
TRUE
MAGNETIC
14°
It's always when I'm not actually thinking about how different I am that someone reminds me I'm totally abnormal.

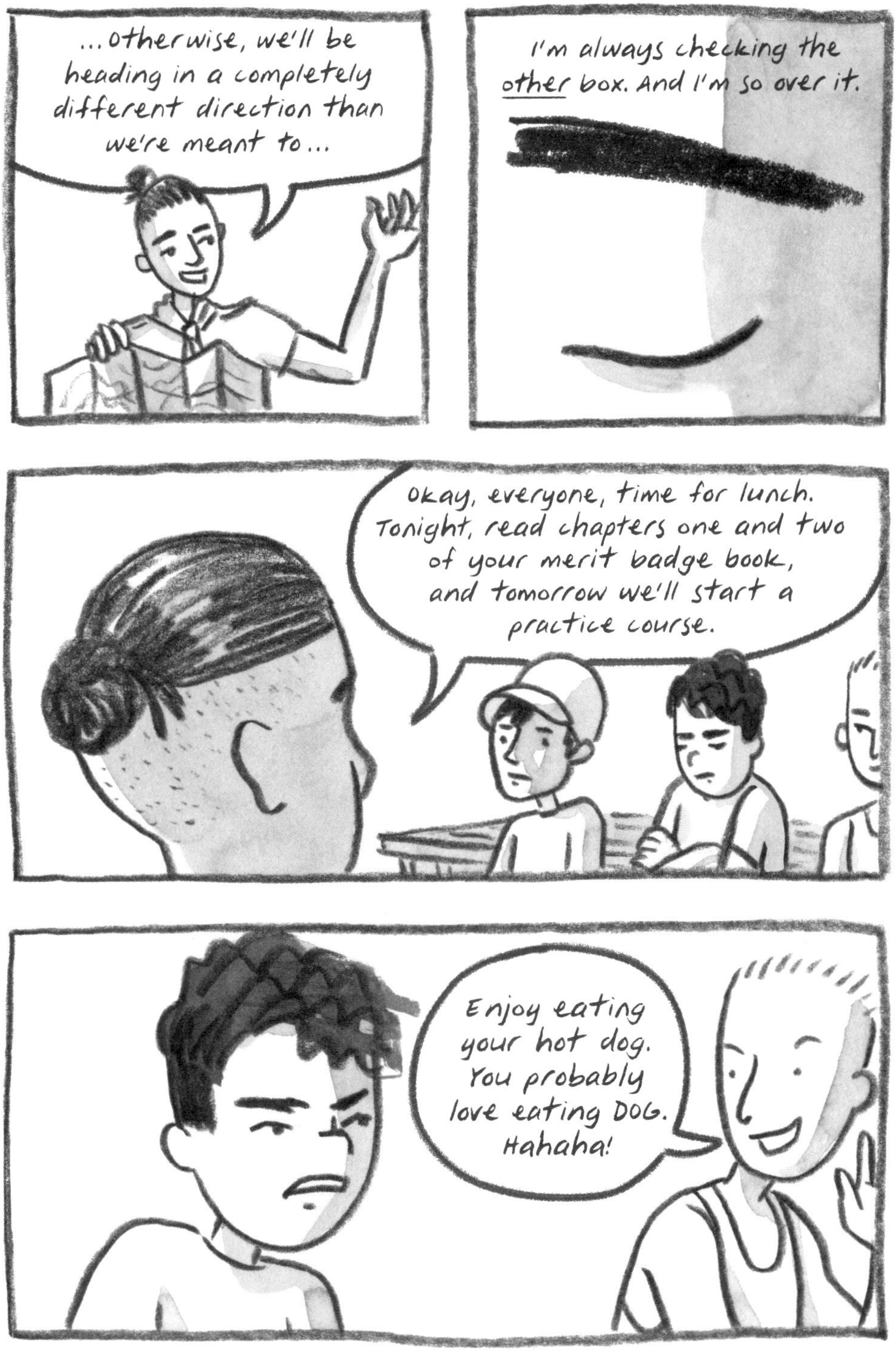
...otherwise, we'll be heading in a completely different direction than we're meant to...
I'm always checking the other box. And I'm so over it.
Okay, everyone, time for lunch. Tonight, read chapters one and two of your merit badge book, and tomorrow we'll start a practice course.
Enjoy eating your hot dog. You probably love eating DOG. Hahaha!

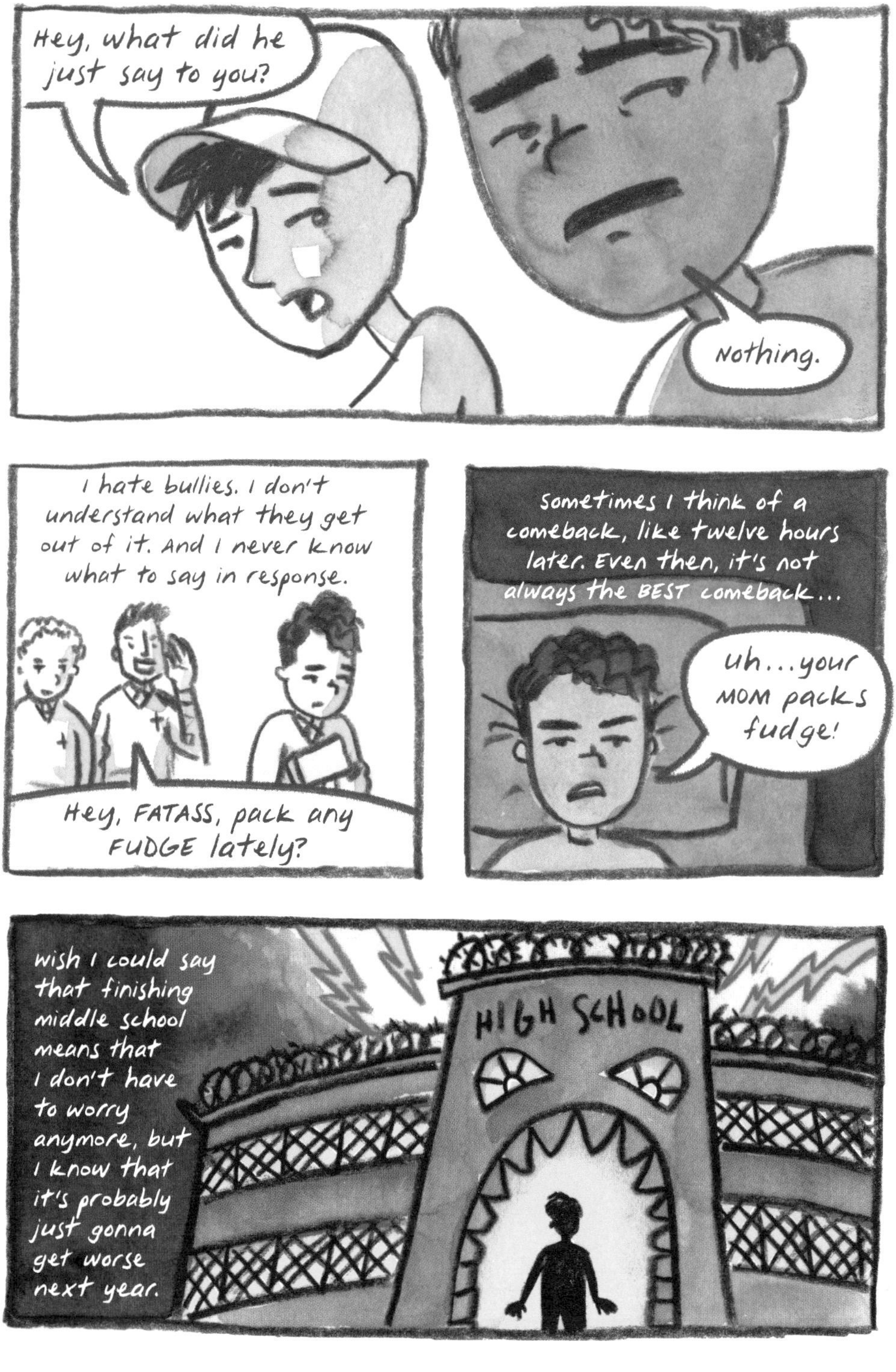
Hey, what did he just say to you?
Nothing.
I hate bullies. I don't understand what they get out of it. And I never know what to say in response.
Hey, FATASS, pack any FUDGE lately?
Sometimes I think of a comeback, like twelve hours later. Even then, it's not always the BEST comeback...
uh...your MOM packs fudge!
wish I could say that finishing middle school means that I don't have to worry anymore, but I know that it's probably just gonna get worse next year.
HIGH SCHOOL

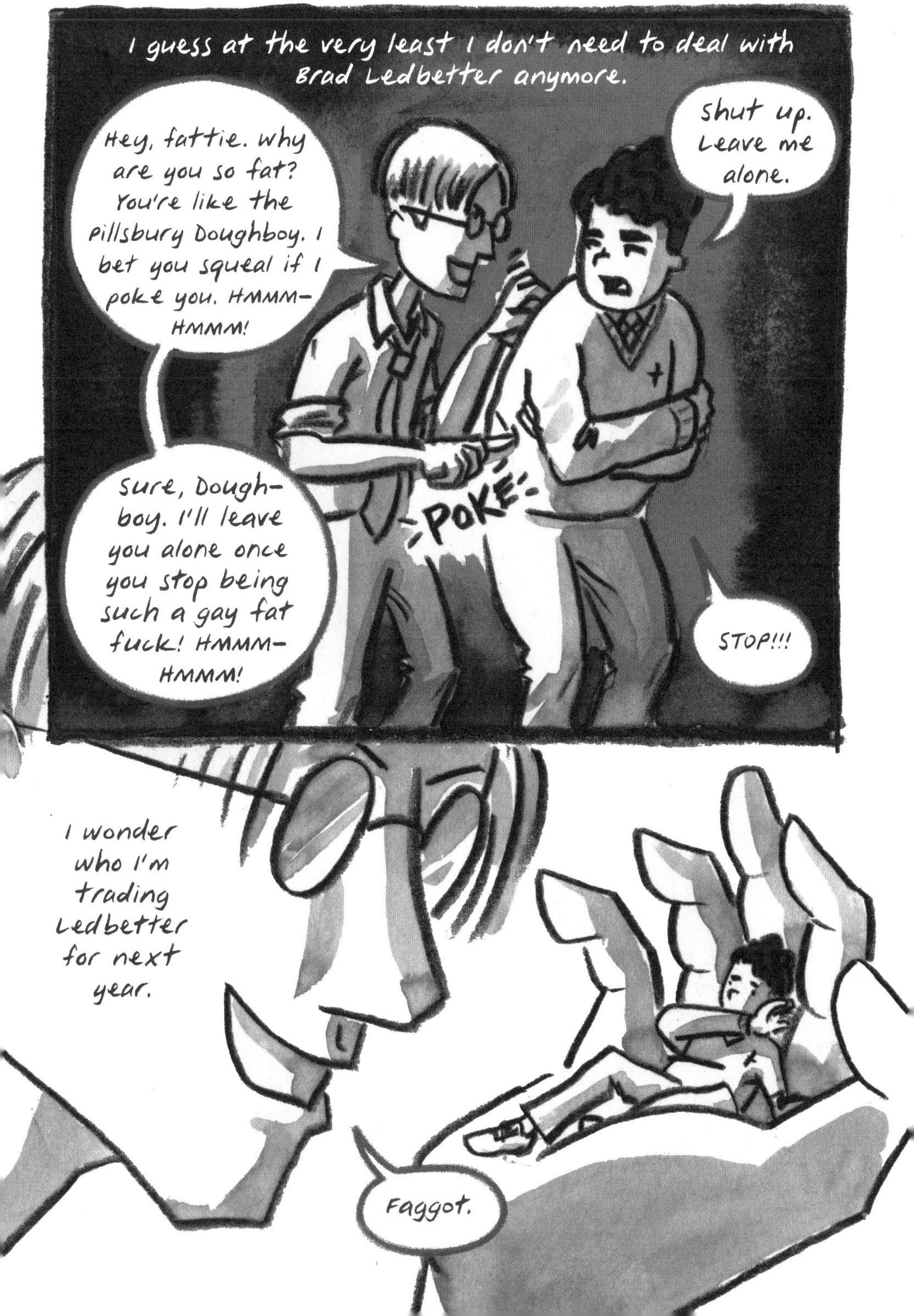
I guess at the very least I don't need to deal with Brad Ledbetter anymore.
Hey, fattie. Why are you so fat? You're like the Pillsbury Doughboy. I bet you squeal if I poke you. HMMM-HMMM!
Shut up. Leave me alone.
Sure, Doughboy. I'll leave you alone once you stop being such a gay fat fuck! HMMM-HMMM!
POKE
STOP!!!
I wonder who I'm trading Ledbetter for next year.
Faggot.

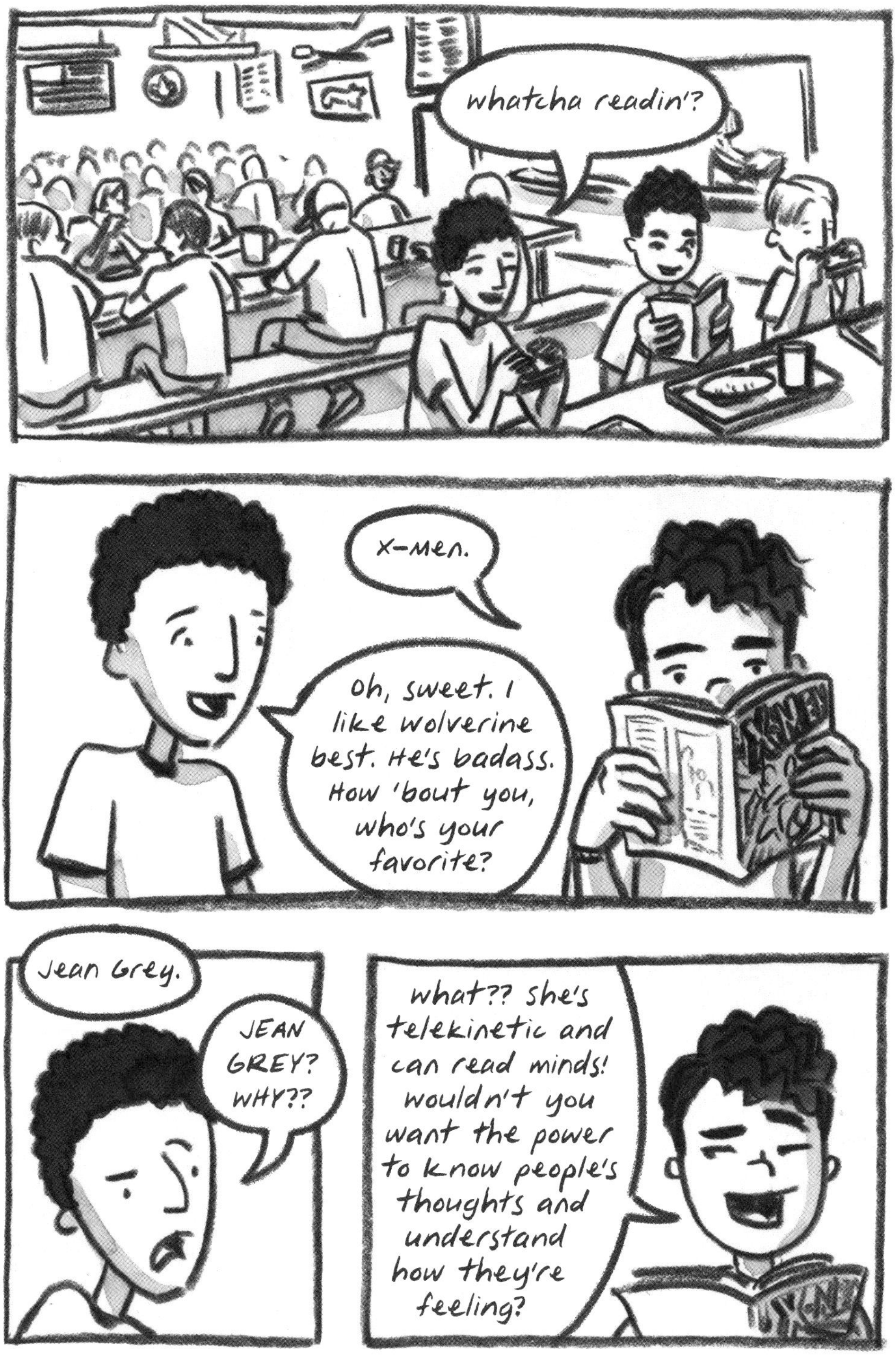
whatcha readin'?
X-Men.
Oh, sweet. I like wolverine best. He's badass. How 'bout you, who's your favorite?
Jean Grey.
JEAN GREY? WHY??
what?? she's telekinetic and can read minds! wouldn't you want the power to know people's thoughts and understand how they're feeling?

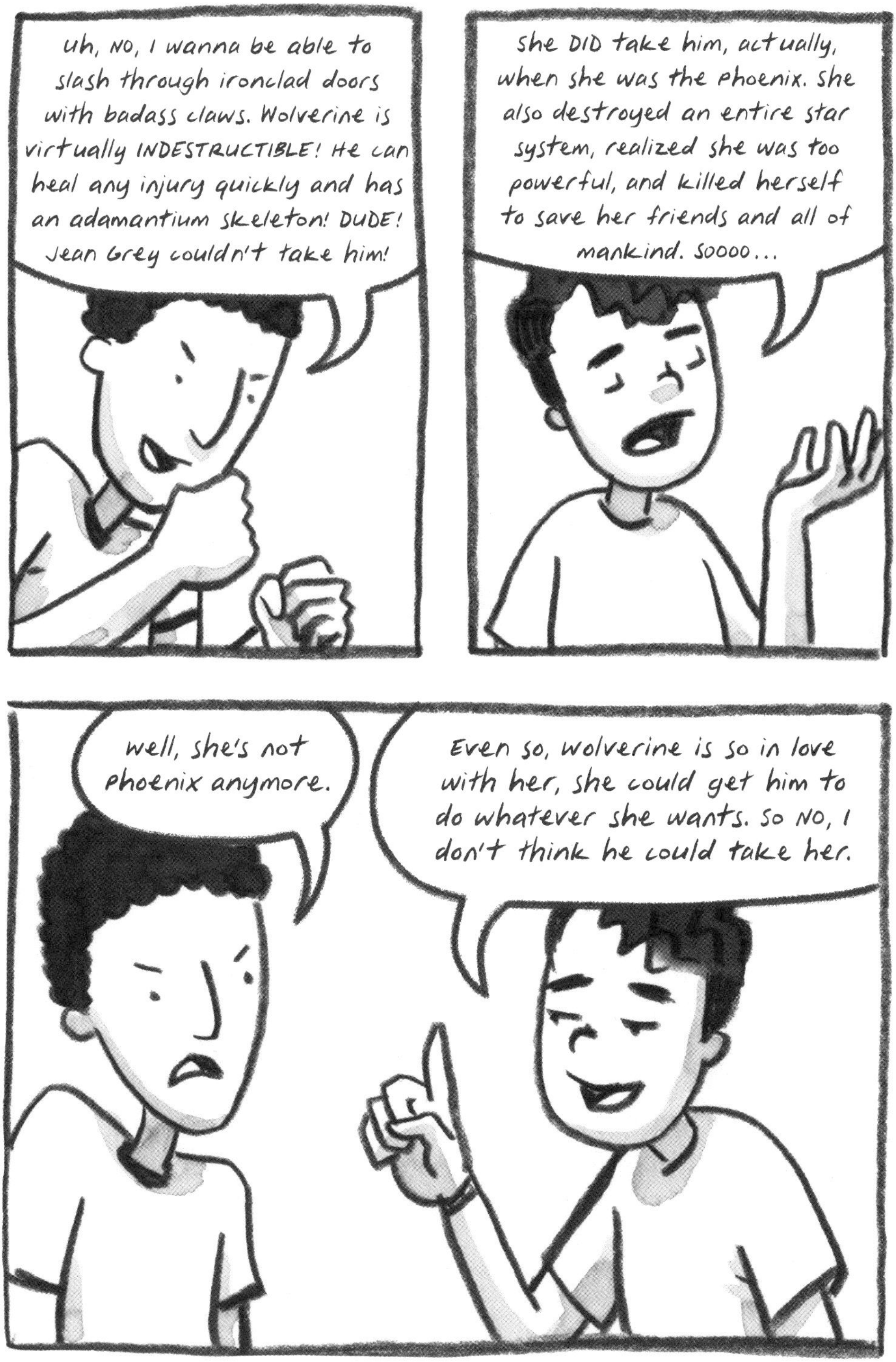
Uh, NO, I wanna be able to slash through ironclad doors with badass claws. Wolverine is virtually INDESTRUCTIBLE! He can heal any injury quickly and has an adamantium skeleton! DUDE! Jean Grey couldn't take him!
She DID take him, actually, when she was the Phoenix. She also destroyed an entire star system, realized she was too powerful, and killed herself to save her friends and all of mankind. Soooo...
Well, she's not Phoenix anymore.
Even so, Wolverine is so in love with her, she could get him to do whatever she wants. So NO, I don't think he could take her.

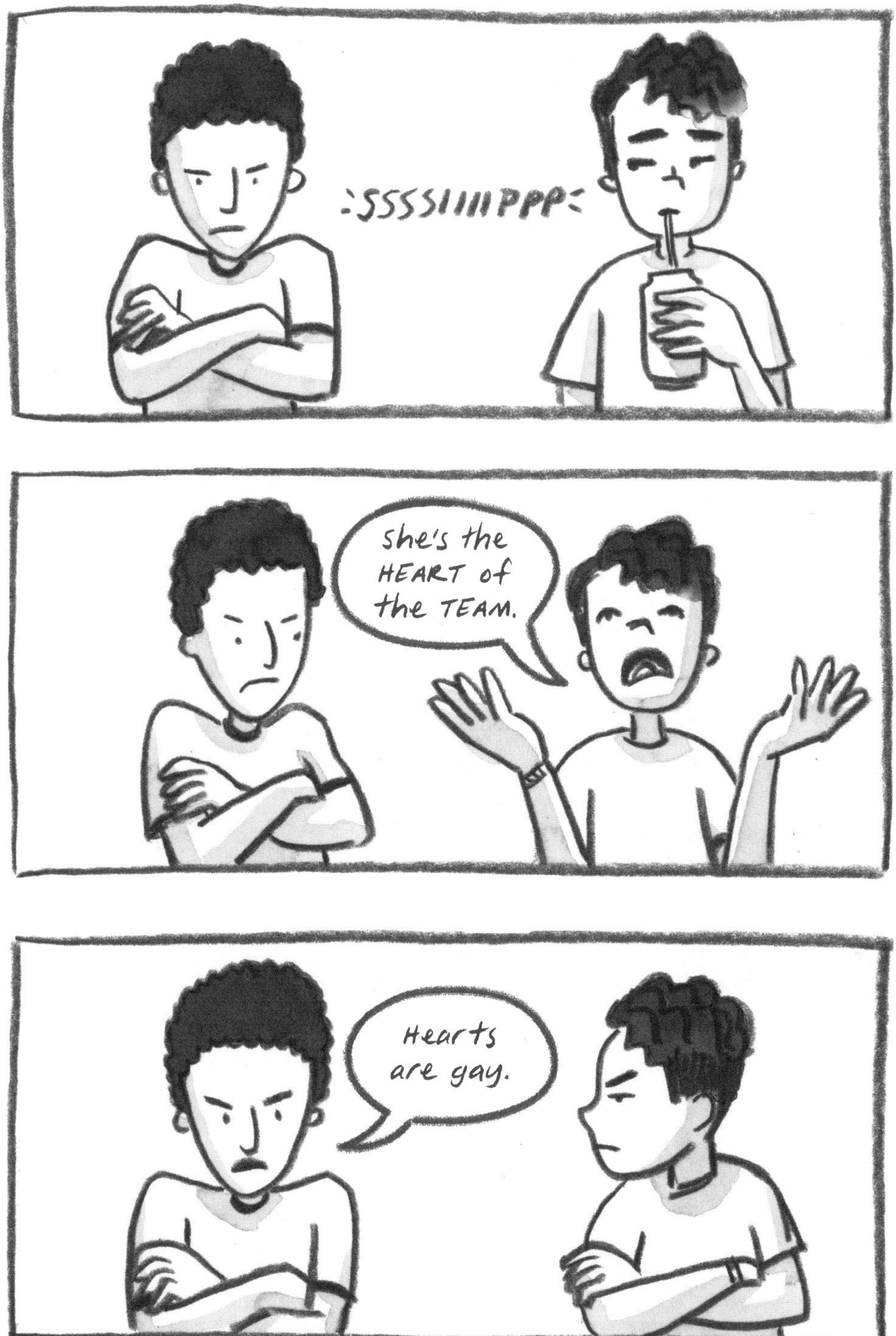
:SSSSIIIIPPP:
she's the HEART of the TEAM.
Hearts are gay.

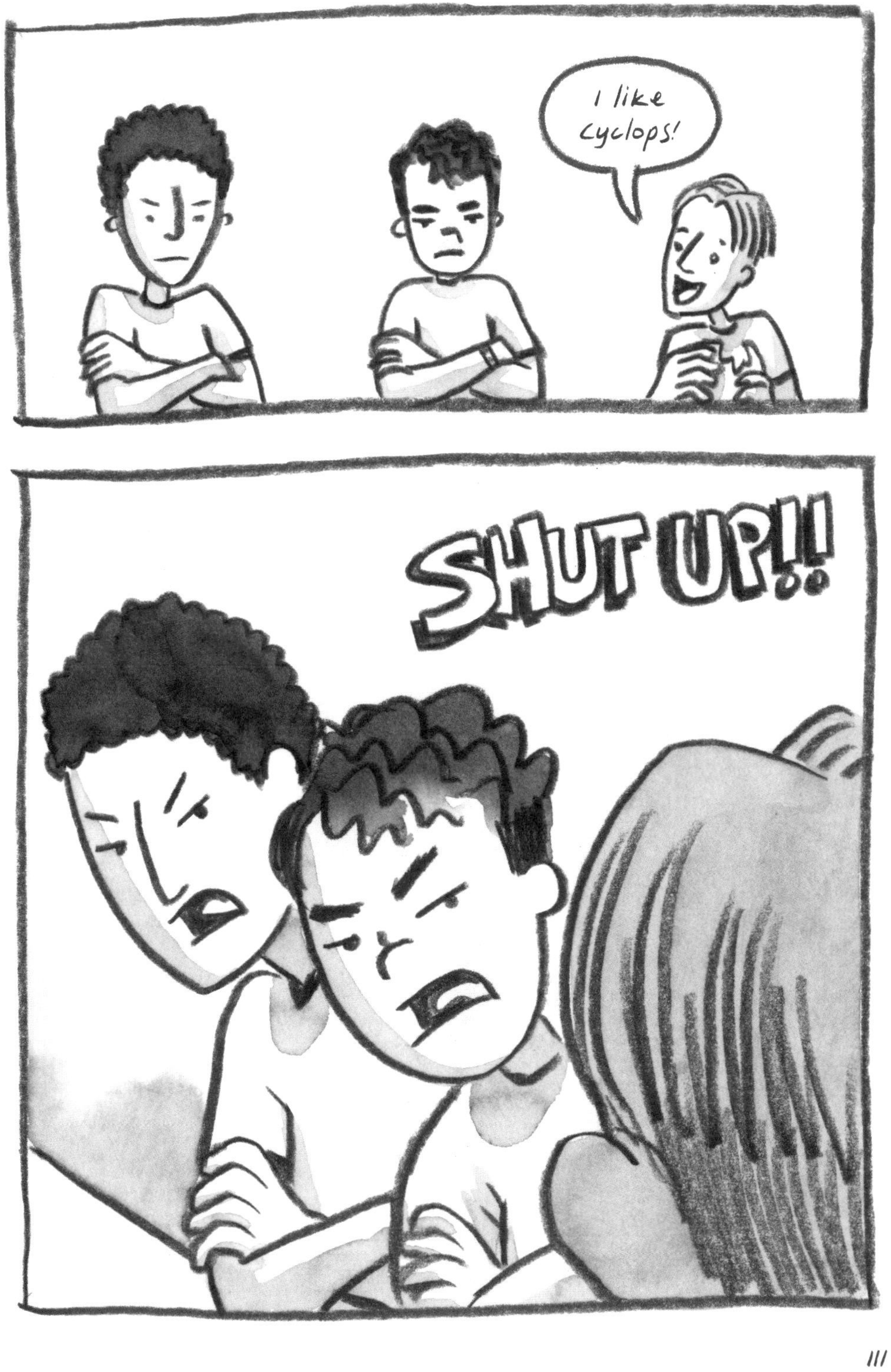
I like cyclops!
SHUT UP!!

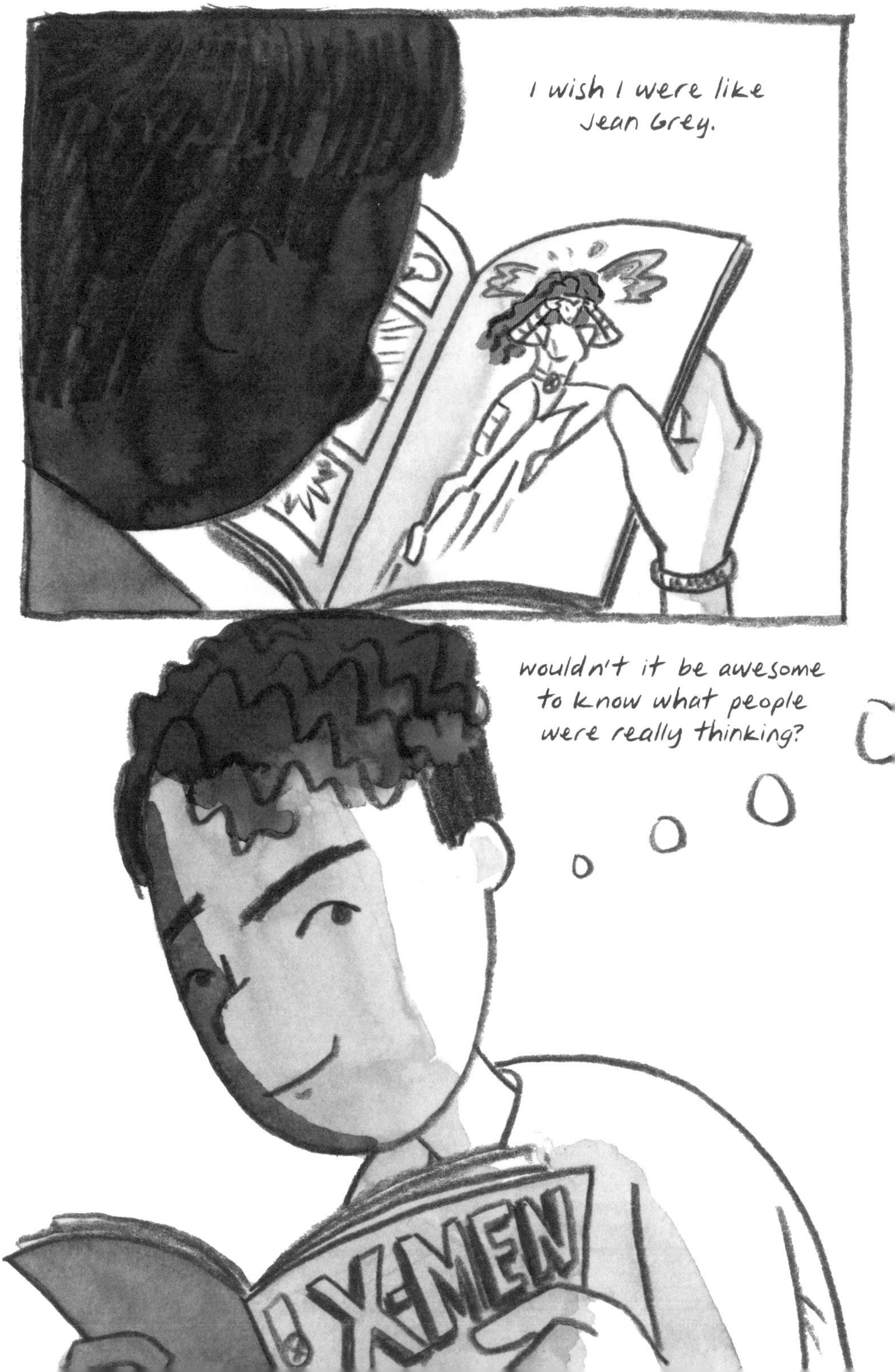
I wish I were like Jean Grey.
wouldn't it be awesome to know what people were really thinking?
X-MEN

And if they were thinking something bad about me...

I could make them pay.

They would be scared of me!

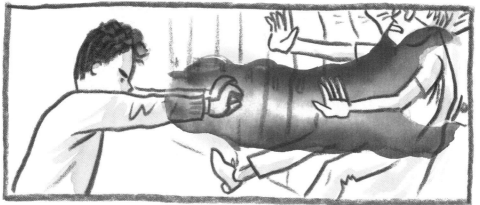

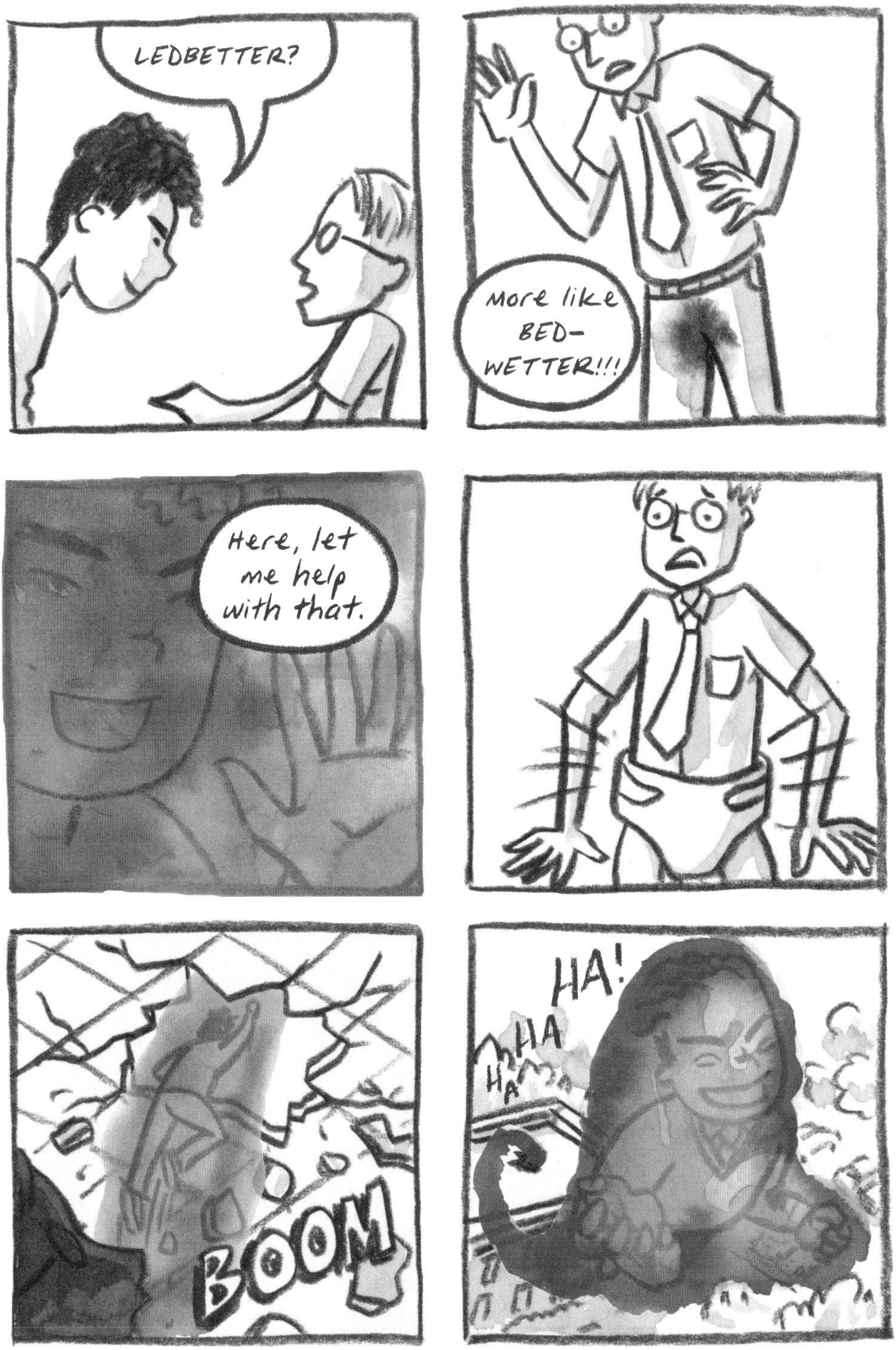
LEDBETTER?
More like BED-WETTER!!!
Here, let me help with that.
BOOM
HA!
HA
HA
HA

Although, if I were wolverine,

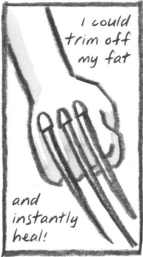

I could trim off my fat

and instantly heal!

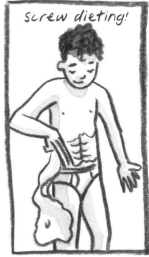

screw dieting!

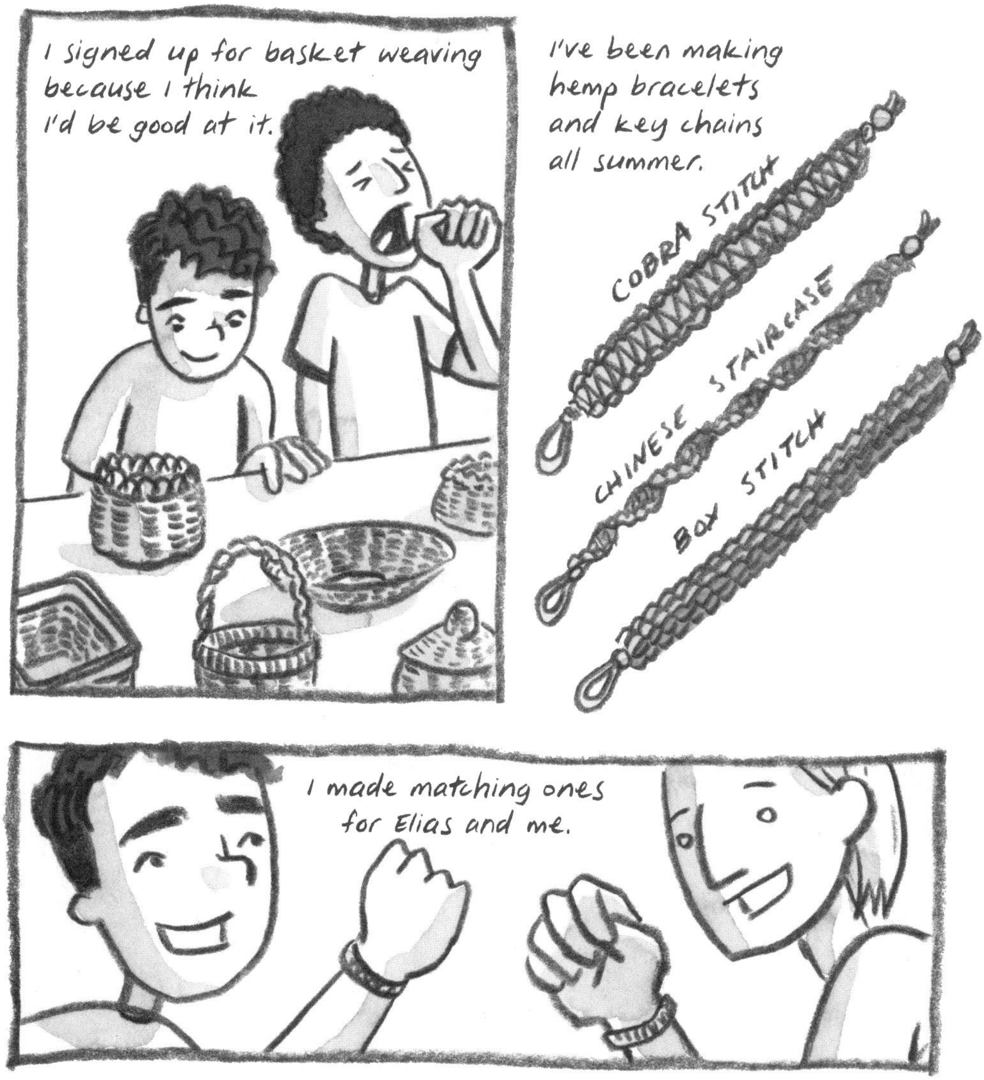
I signed up for basket weaving because I think I'd be good at it.
I've been making hemp bracelets and key chains all summer.
COBRA STITCH
CHINESE STAIRCASE
BOX STITCH
I made matching ones for Elias and me.

It's nice to know that all I have to do is learn one or two types of knots, then repeat that over and over, and in the end you get something really cool. I also already had to learn lots of knots for scouts. I like making them. It's really calming. I figured basket weaving would be the same sort of thing, but with reeds.

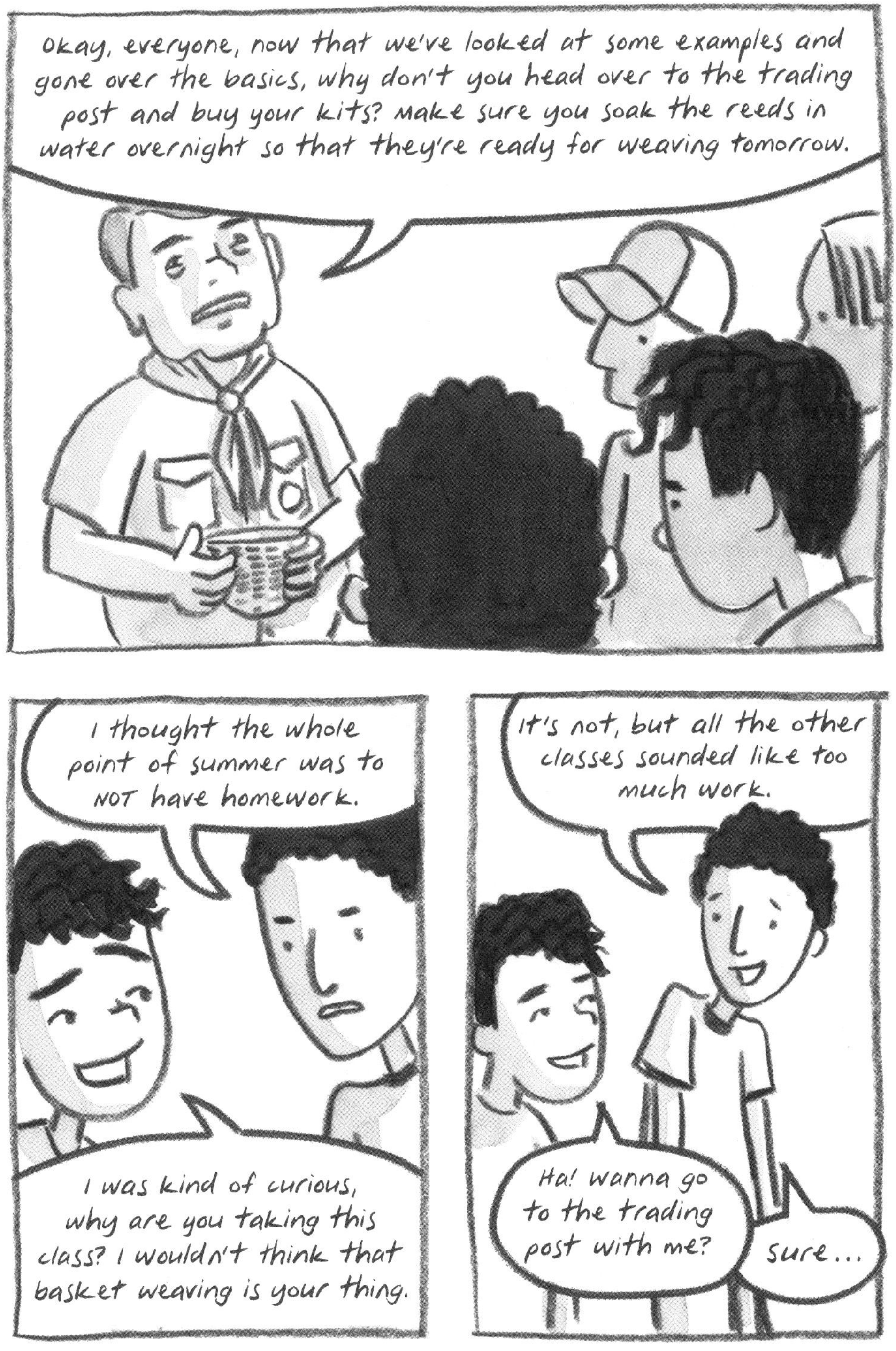
Okay, everyone, now that we've looked at some examples and gone over the basics, why don't you head over to the trading post and buy your kits? Make sure you soak the reeds in water overnight so that they're ready for weaving tomorrow.
I thought the whole point of summer was to NOT have homework.
I was kind of curious, why are you taking this class? I wouldn't think that basket weaving is your thing.
It's not, but all the other classes sounded like too much work.
Ha! Wanna go to the trading post with me?
Sure...

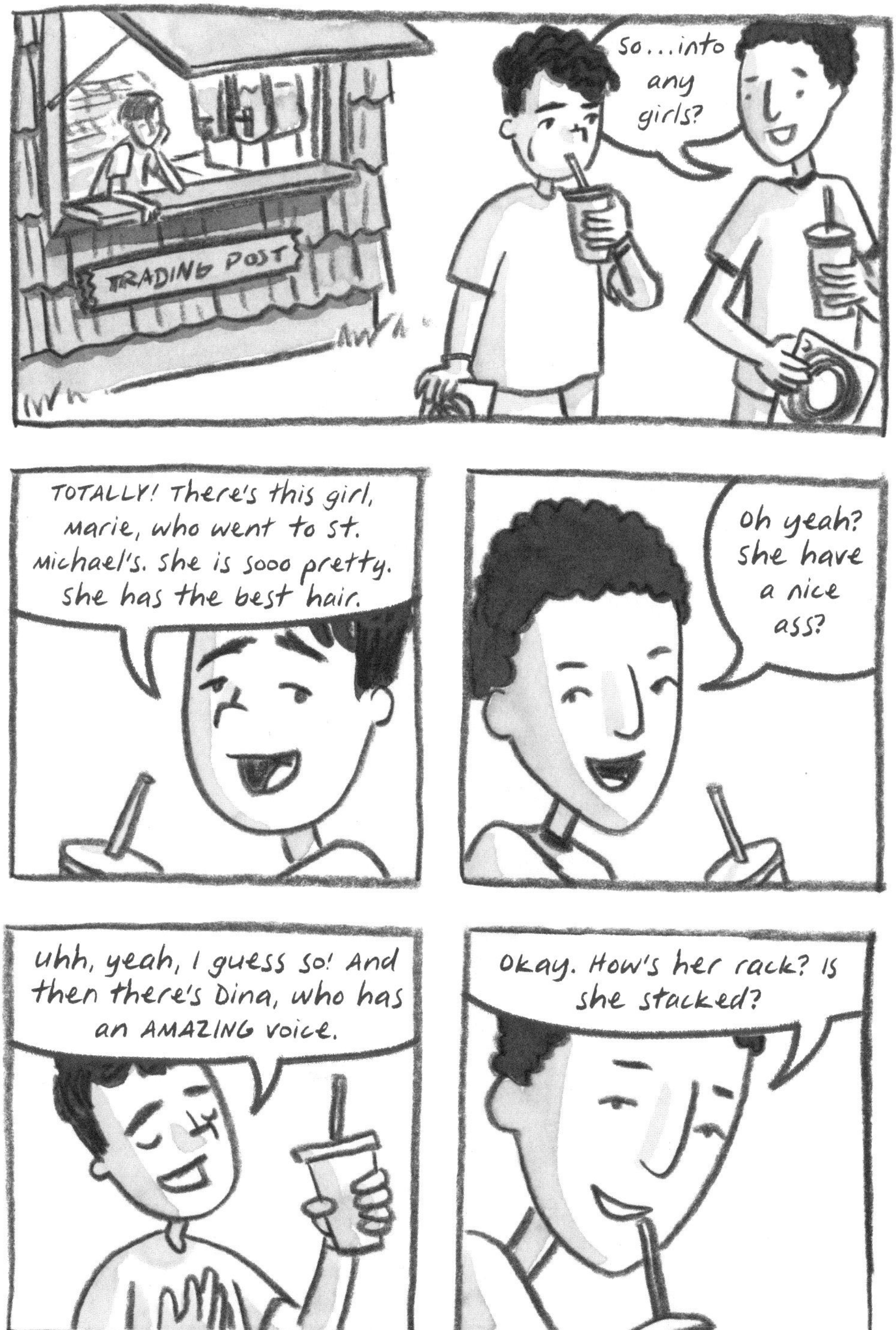

TRADING POST
So...into any girls?
TOTALLY! There's this girl, Marie, who went to St. Michael's. She is sooo pretty. She has the best hair.
Oh yeah? She have a nice ass?
Uhh, yeah, I guess so! And then there's Dina, who has an AMAZING voice.
Okay. How's her rack? Is she stacked?

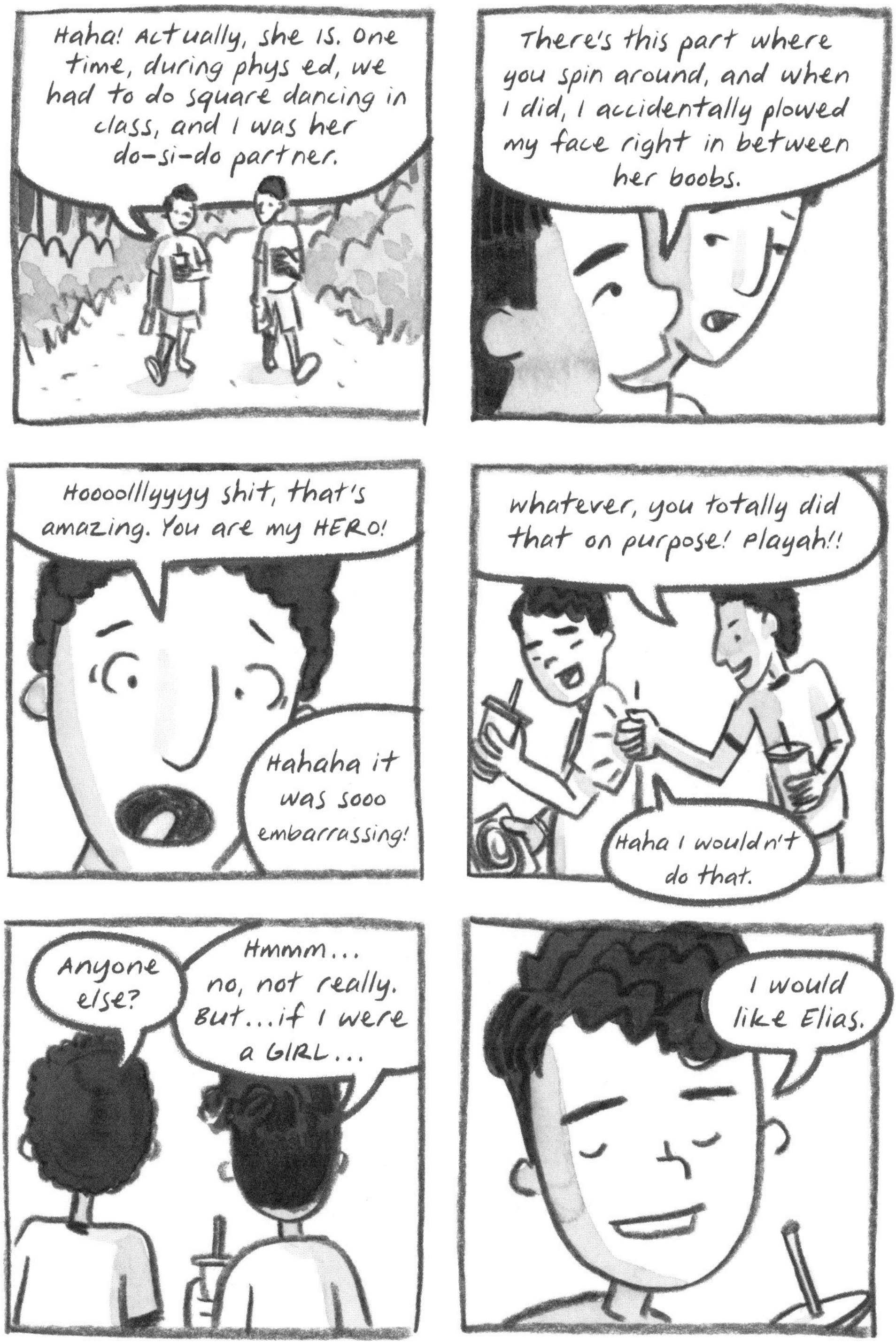
Haha! Actually, she IS. One time, during phys ed, we had to do square dancing in class, and I was her do-si-do partner.
There's this part where you spin around, and when I did, I accidentally plowed my face right in between her boobs.
Hoooolllyyyy shit, that's amazing. You are my HERO!
Hahaha it was sooo embarrassing!
Whatever, you totally did that on purpose! Playah!!
Haha I wouldn't do that.
Anyone else?
Hmmm... no, not really. But...if I were a GIRL...
I would like Elias.

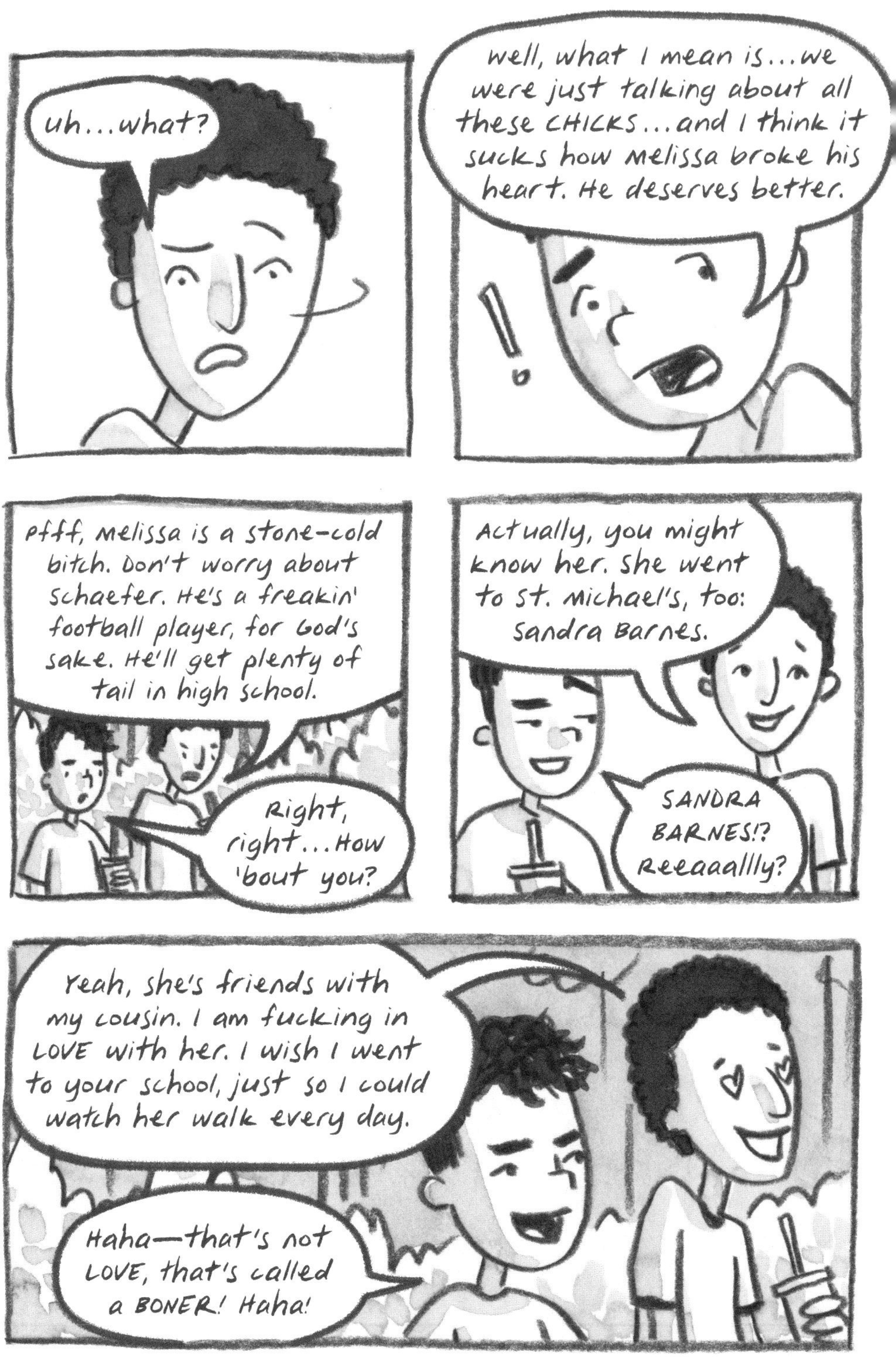
uh...what?
well, what I mean is...we were just talking about all these CHICKS...and I think it sucks how Melissa broke his heart. He deserves better.
Pfff, Melissa is a stone-cold bitch. Don't worry about Schaefer. He's a freakin' football player, for God's sake. He'll get plenty of tail in high school.
Right, right...How 'bout you?
Actually, you might know her. She went to St. Michael's, too: Sandra Barnes.
SANDRA BARNES!? Reeaaallly?
Yeah, she's friends with my cousin. I am fucking in LOVE with her. I wish I went to your school, just so I could watch her walk every day.
Haha—that's not LOVE, that's called a BONER! Haha!

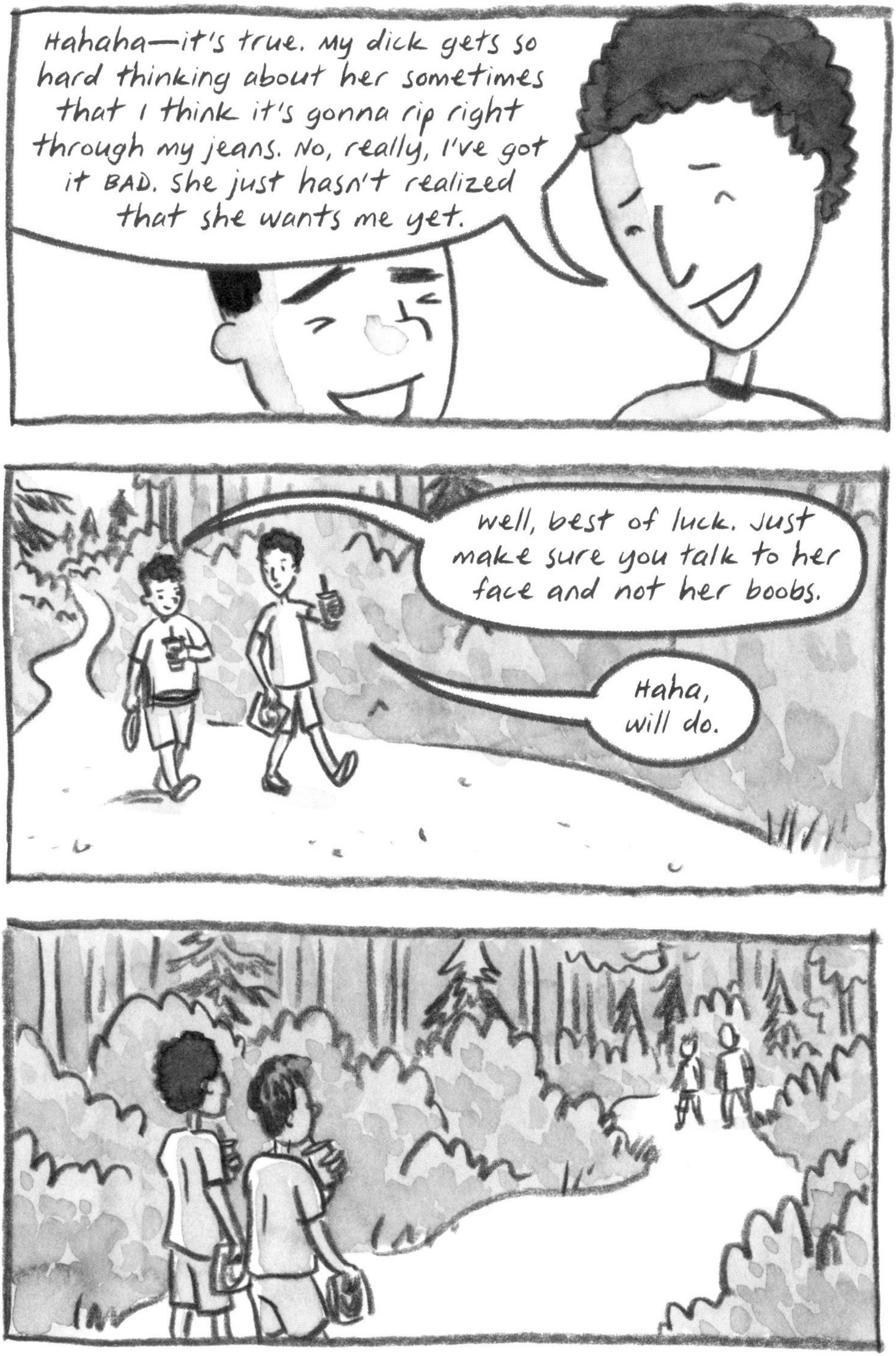
Hahaha—it's true. My dick gets so hard thinking about her sometimes that I think it's gonna rip right through my jeans. No, really, I've got it BAD. She just hasn't realized that she wants me yet.
Well, best of luck. Just make sure you talk to her face and not her boobs.
Haha, will do.

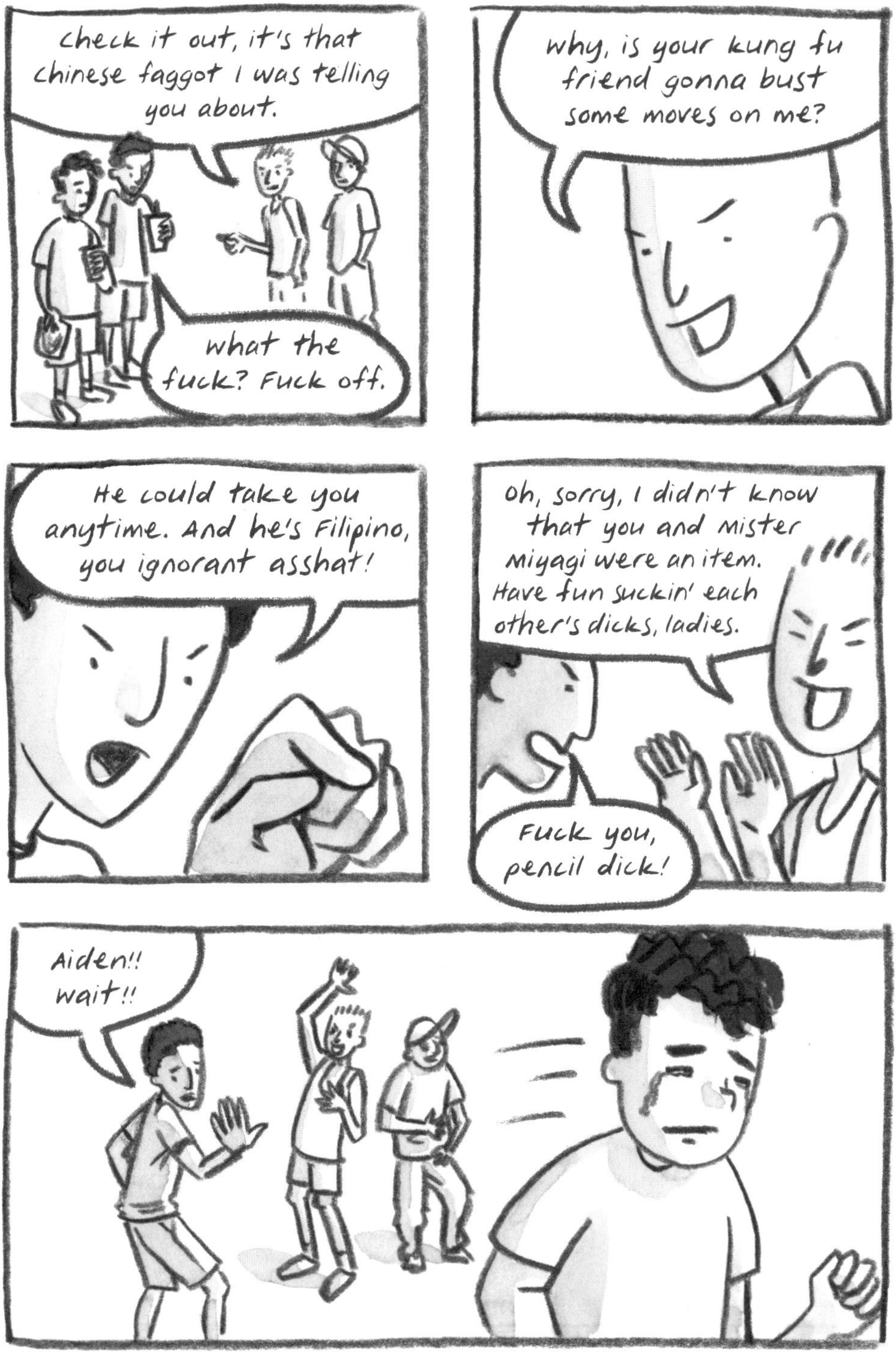
check it out, it's that chinese faggot I was telling you about.
what the fuck? Fuck off.
why, is your kung fu friend gonna bust some moves on me?
He could take you anytime. And he's Filipino, you ignorant asshat!
Oh, sorry, I didn't know that you and Mister Miyagi were an item. Have fun suckin' each other's dicks, ladies.
Fuck you, pencil dick!
Aiden!! wait!!

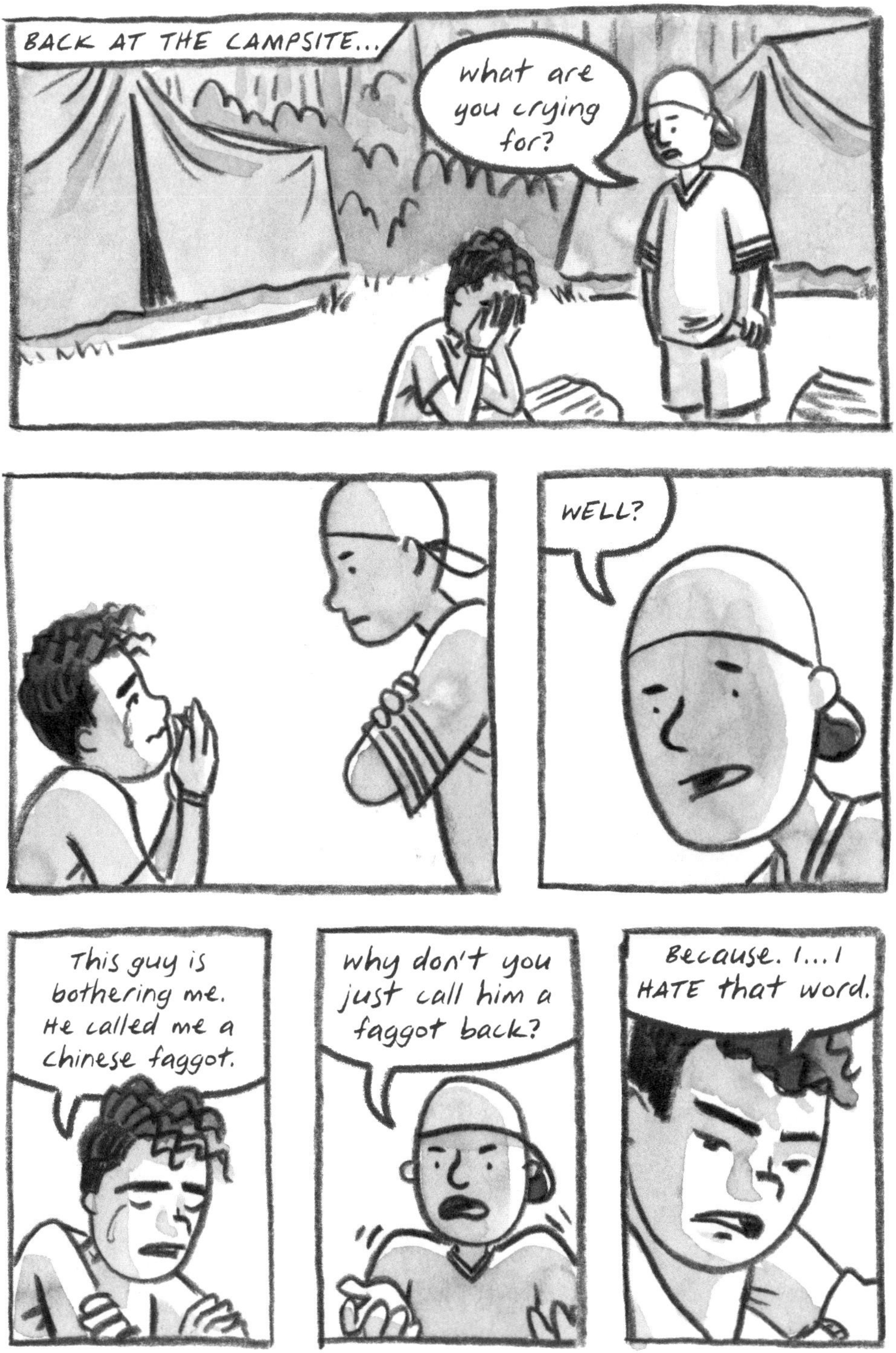
BACK AT THE CAMPSITE...
what are you crying for?
WELL?
This guy is bothering me. He called me a chinese faggot.
why don't you just call him a faggot back?
Because. I...I HATE that word.

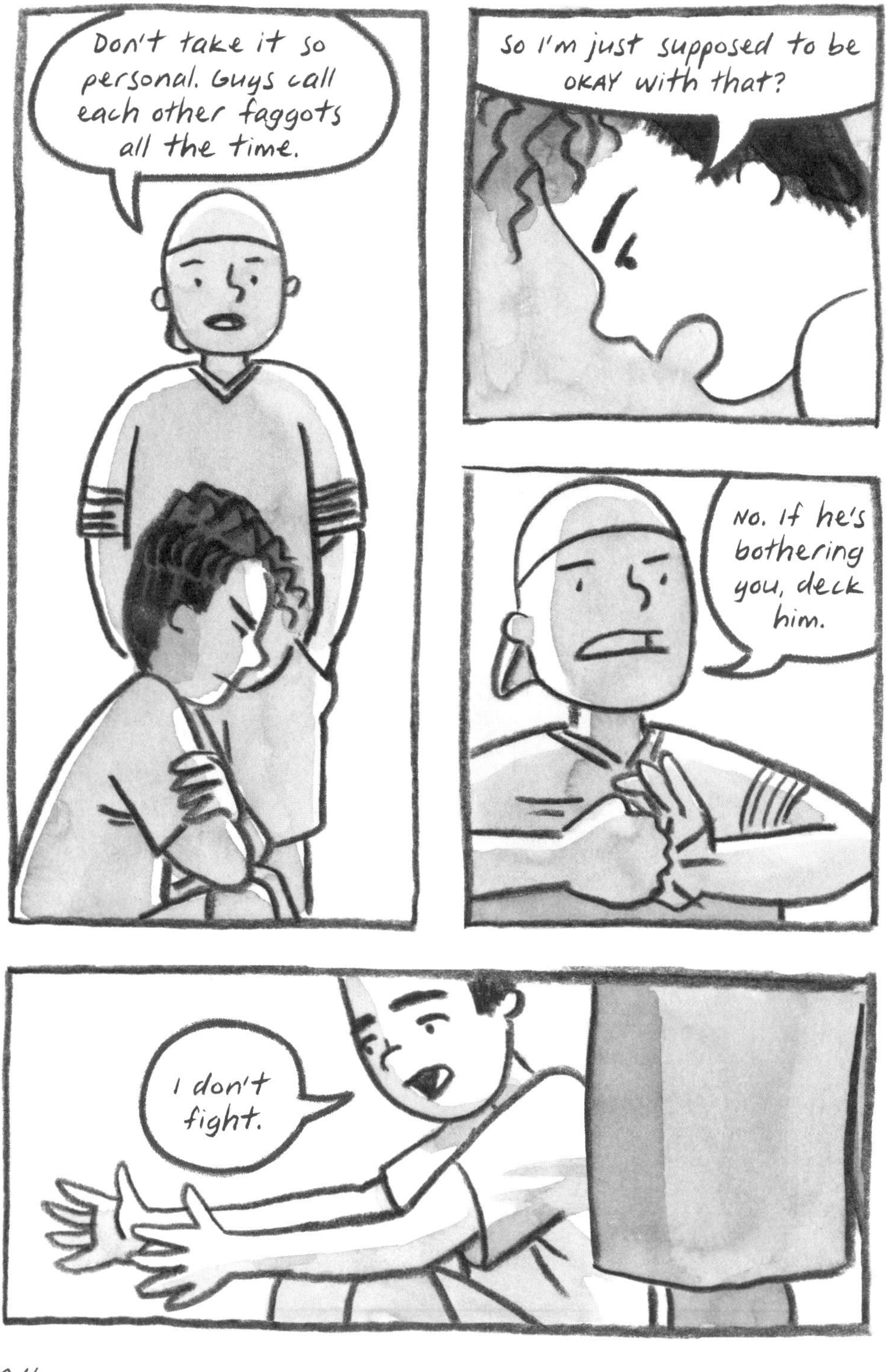

Don't take it so personal. Guys call each other faggots all the time.
So I'm just supposed to be OKAY with that?
No. If he's bothering you, deck him.
I don't fight.

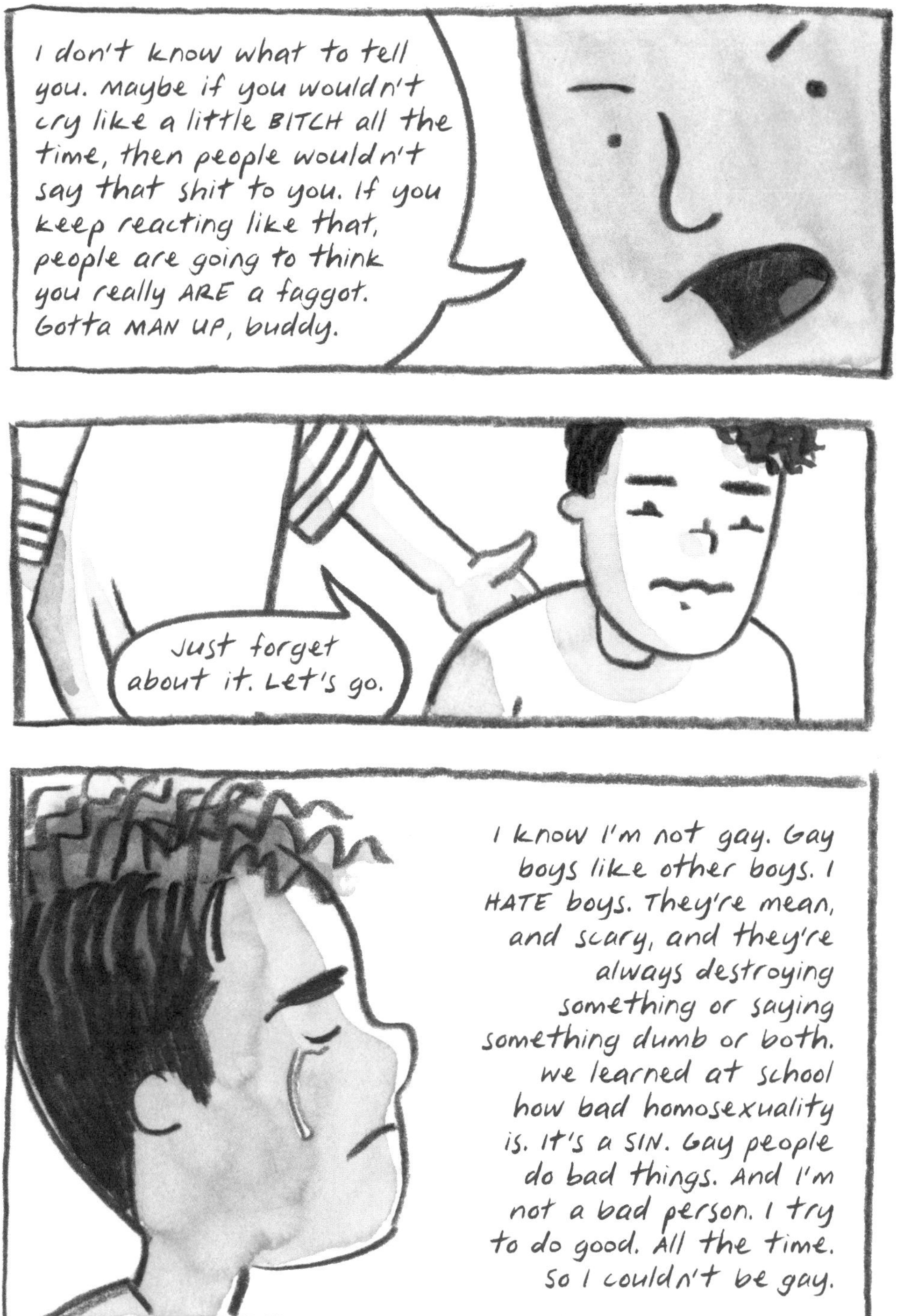
I don't know what to tell you. Maybe if you wouldn't cry like a little BITCH all the time, then people wouldn't say that shit to you. If you keep reacting like that, people are going to think you really ARE a faggot. Gotta MAN UP, buddy.
Just forget about it. Let's go.
I know I'm not gay. Gay boys like other boys. I HATE boys. They're mean, and scary, and they're always destroying something or saying something dumb or both. We learned at school how bad homosexuality is. It's a SIN. Gay people do bad things. And I'm not a bad person. I try to do good. All the time. So I couldn't be gay.

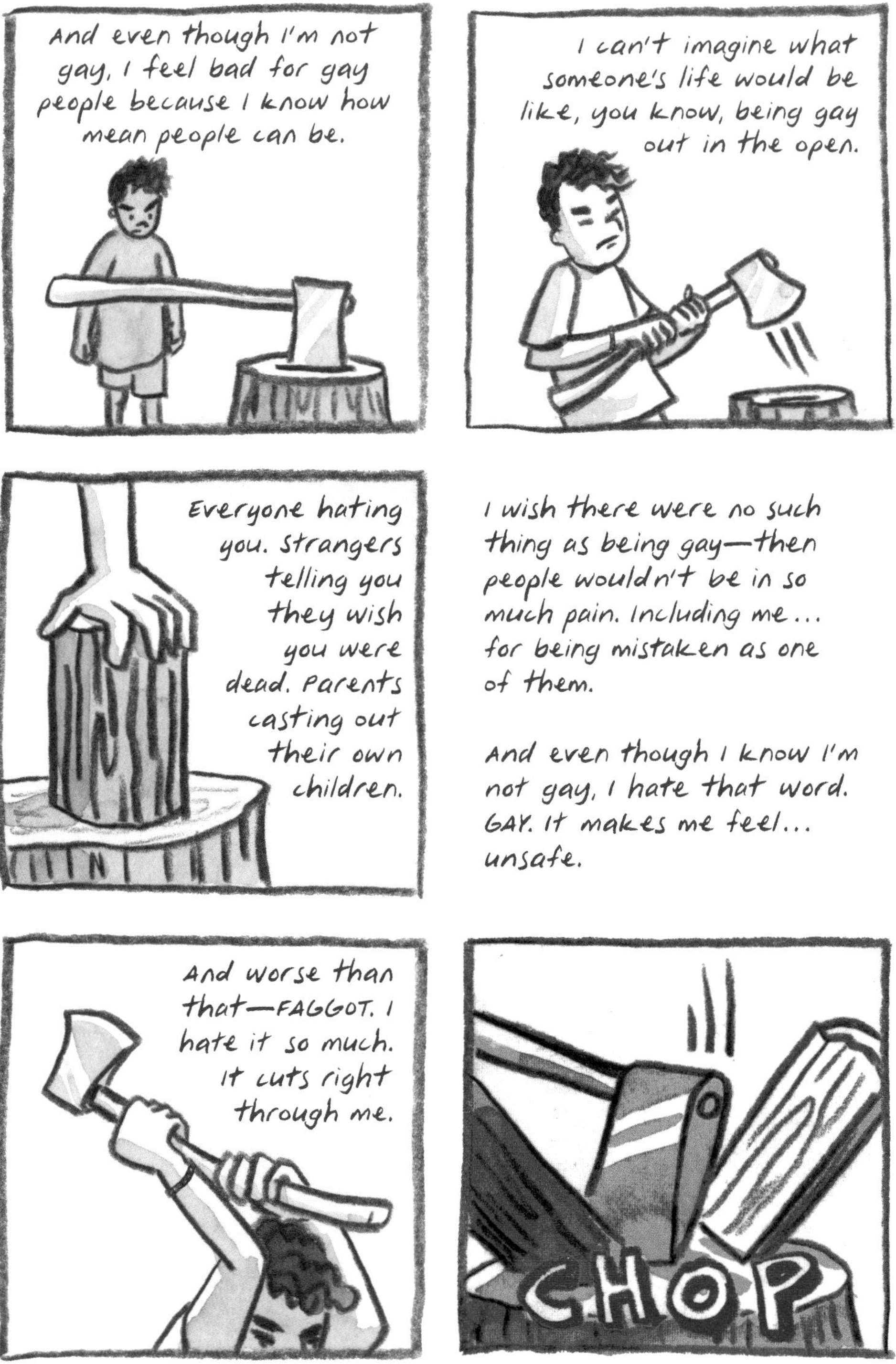
And even though I'm not gay, I feel bad for gay people because I know how mean people can be.
I can't imagine what someone's life would be like, you know, being gay out in the open.
Everyone hating you. Strangers telling you they wish you were dead. Parents casting out their own children.
I wish there were no such thing as being gay—then people wouldn't be in so much pain. Including me... for being mistaken as one of them.
And even though I know I'm not gay, I hate that word. GAY. It makes me feel... unsafe.
And worse than that—FAGGOT. I hate it so much. It cuts right through me.
CHOP

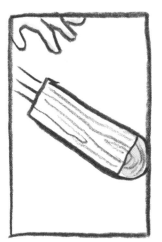

:CLUNK!:-

I read in a book once that "faggot" actually refers to a bundle of sticks.

In medieval times, homosexuals were burned alive at the stake. As if they were human firewood. I can't imagine dying like that.

But then, I can't imagine how much hotter the flames of hell would be.

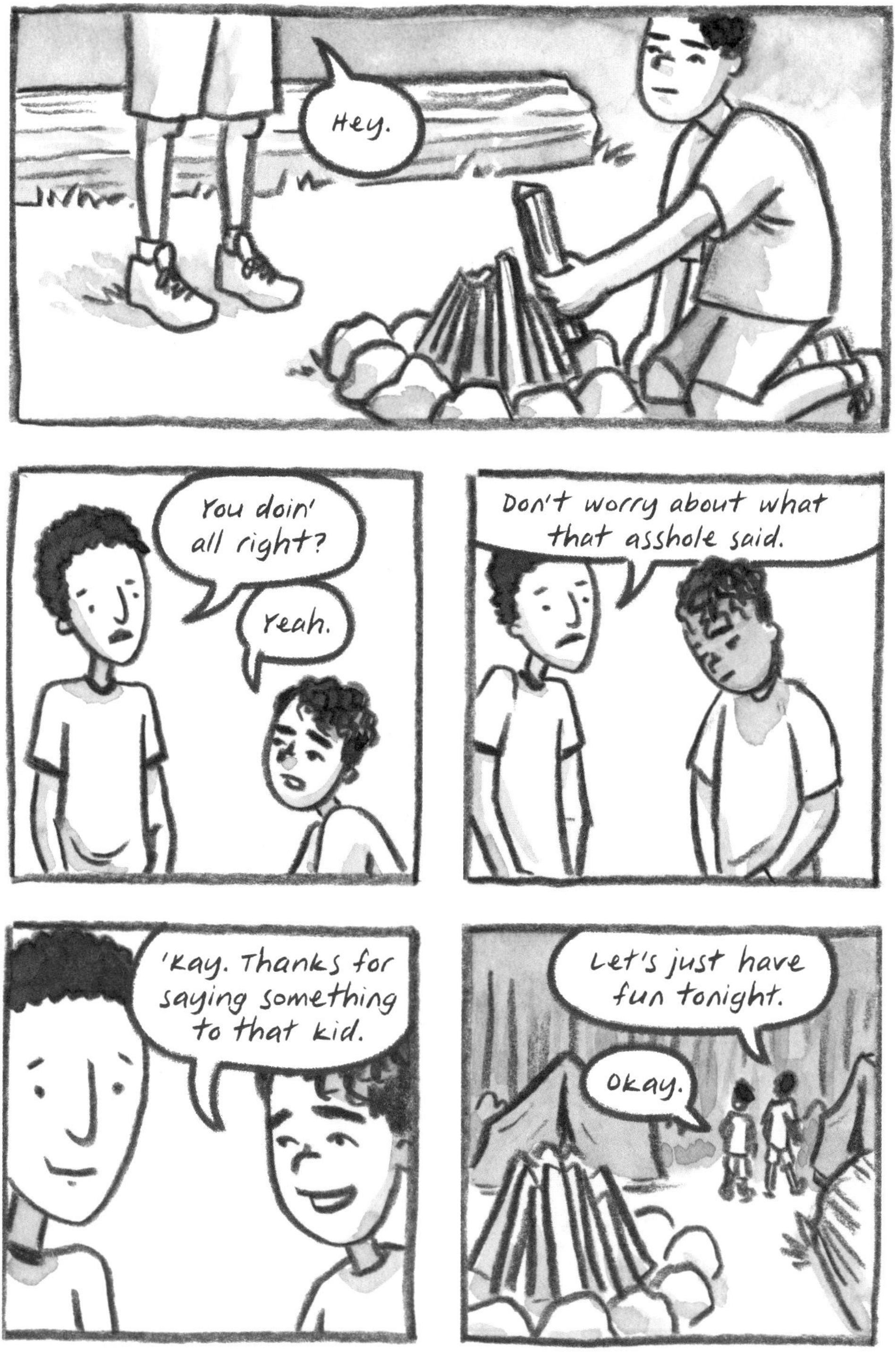
Hey.
You doin' all right?
Yeah.
Don't worry about what that asshole said.
'Kay. Thanks for saying something to that kid.
Let's just have fun tonight.
Okay.

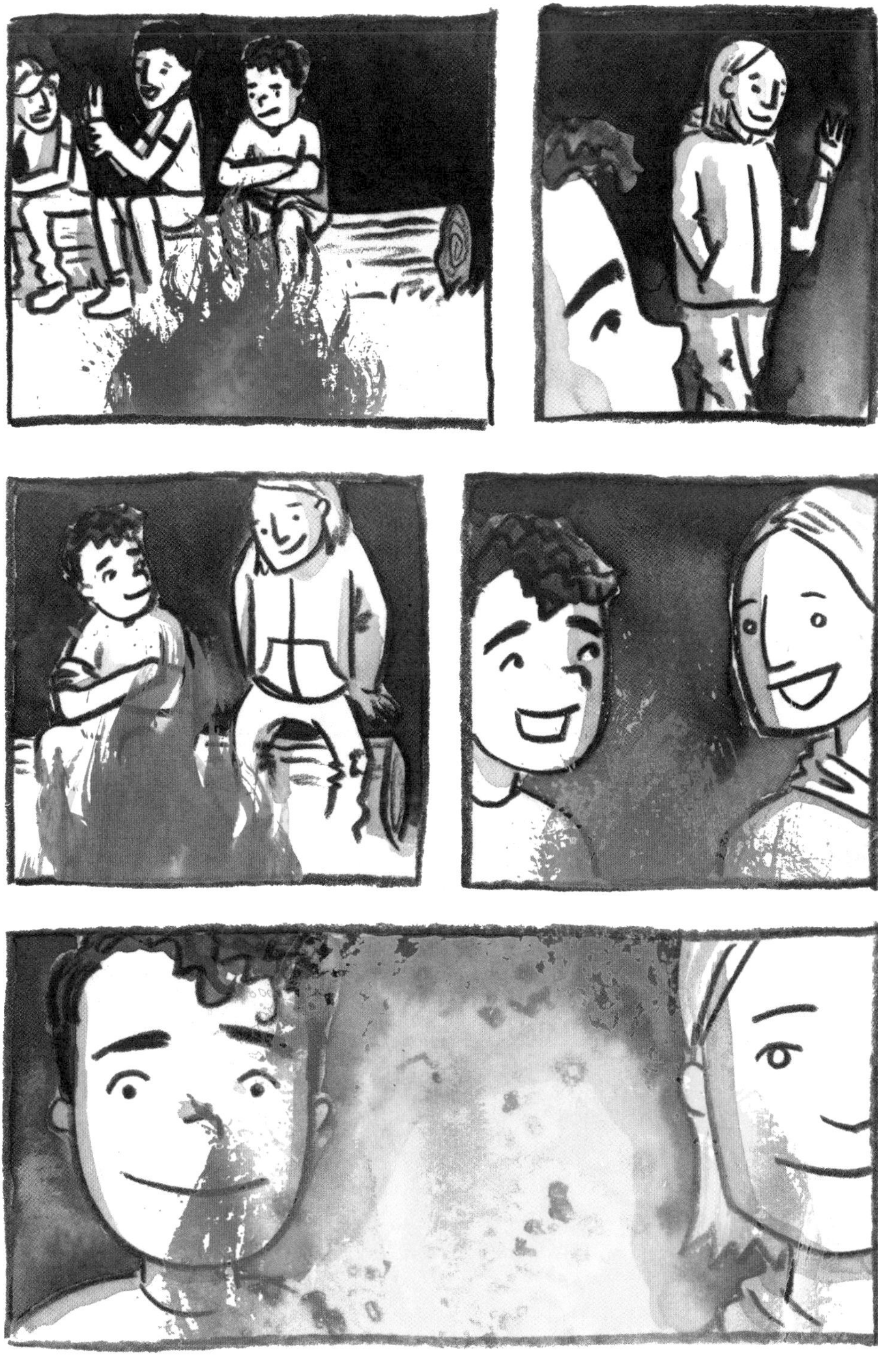

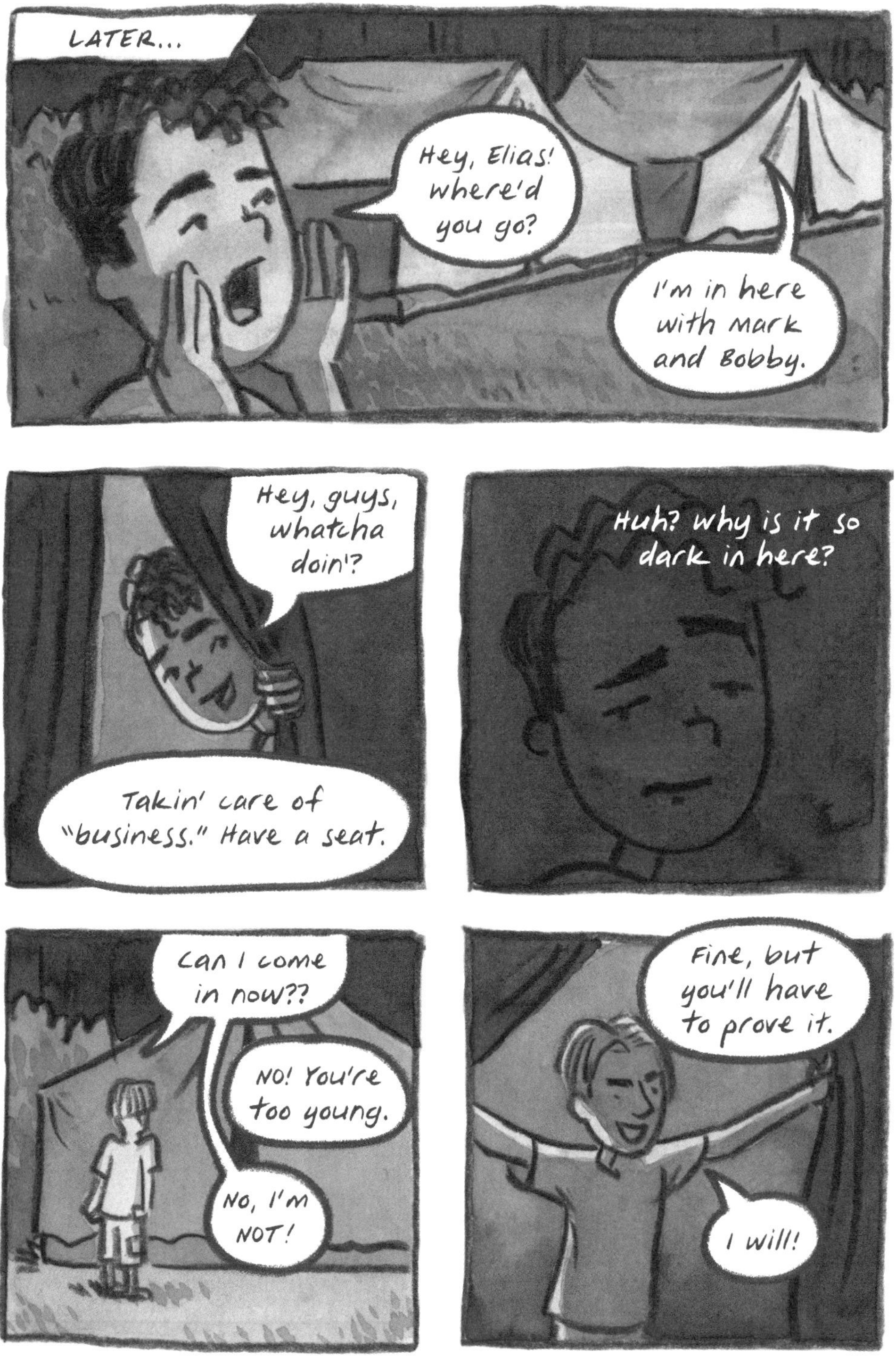
LATER...
Hey, Elias! where'd you go?
I'm in here with mark and Bobby.
Hey, guys, whatcha doin'?
Takin' care of "business." Have a seat.
Huh? why is it so dark in here?
can I come in now??
NO! You're too young.
No, I'm NOT!
Fine, but you'll have to prove it.
I will!

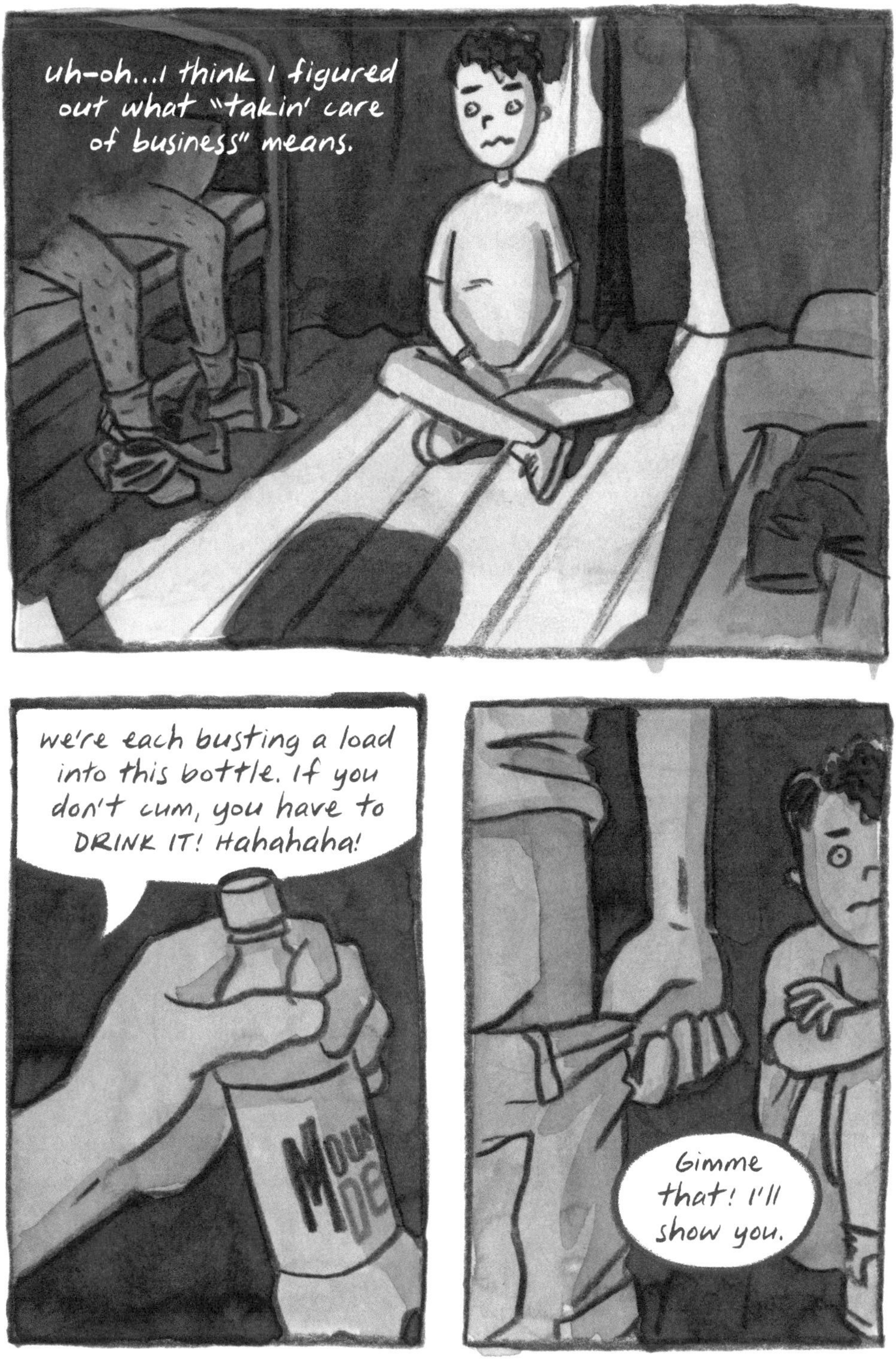
uh-oh...I think I figured out what "takin' care of business" means.
we're each busting a load into this bottle. If you don't cum, you have to DRINK IT! Hahahaha!
Gimme that! I'll show you.

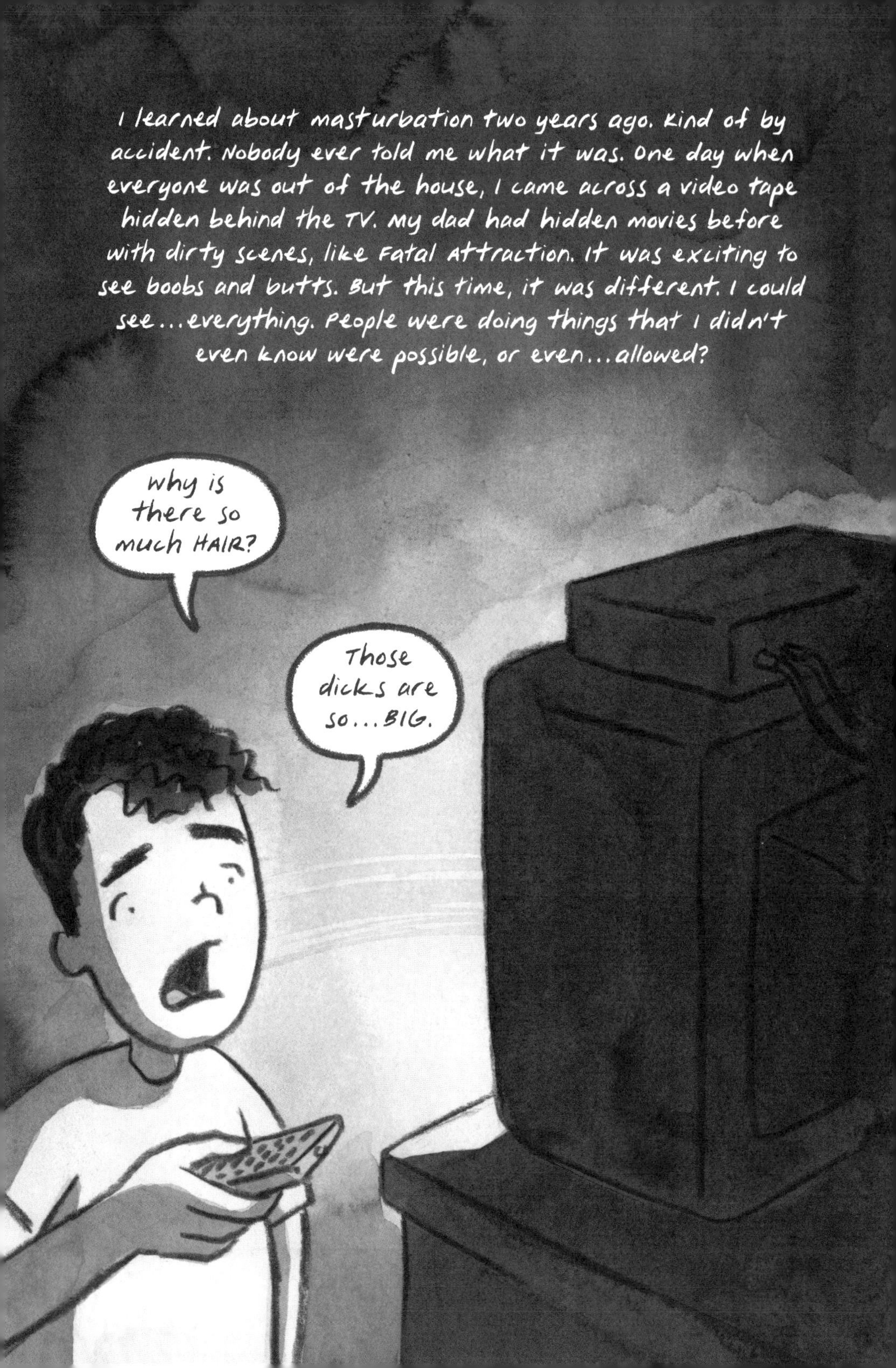
I learned about masturbation two years ago. Kind of by accident. Nobody ever told me what it was. One day when everyone was out of the house, I came across a video tape hidden behind the TV. My dad had hidden movies before with dirty scenes, like Fatal Attraction. It was exciting to see boobs and butts. But this time, it was different. I could see...everything. People were doing things that I didn't even know were possible, or even...allowed?
Why is there so much HAIR?
Those dicks are so...BIG.

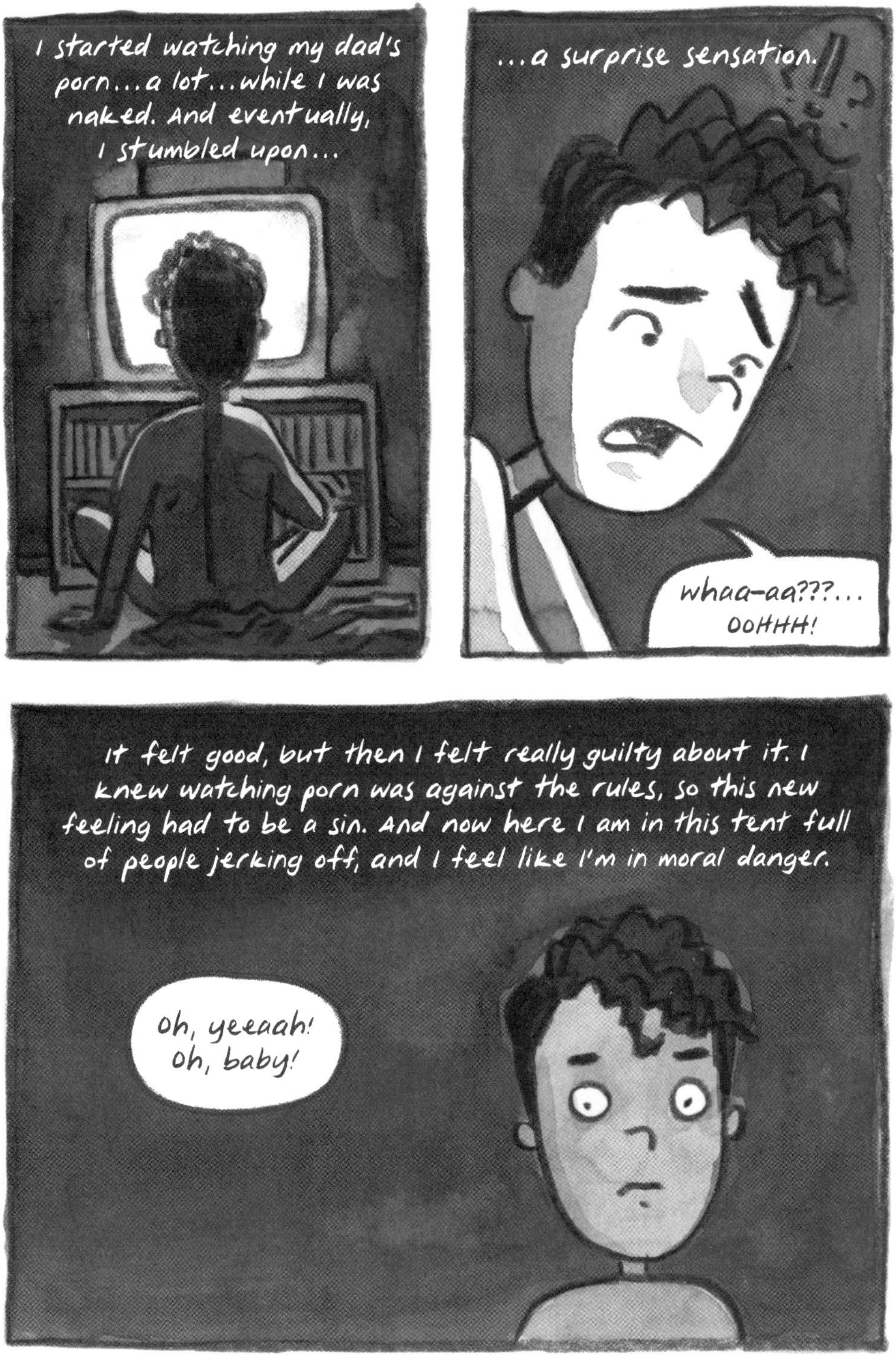
I started watching my dad's porn...a lot...while I was naked. And eventually, I stumbled upon...
...a surprise sensation.
?!?
Whaa-aa???... OOHHH!
It felt good, but then I felt really guilty about it. I knew watching porn was against the rules, so this new feeling had to be a sin. And now here I am in this tent full of people jerking off, and I feel like I'm in moral danger.
Oh, yeeaah! Oh, baby!

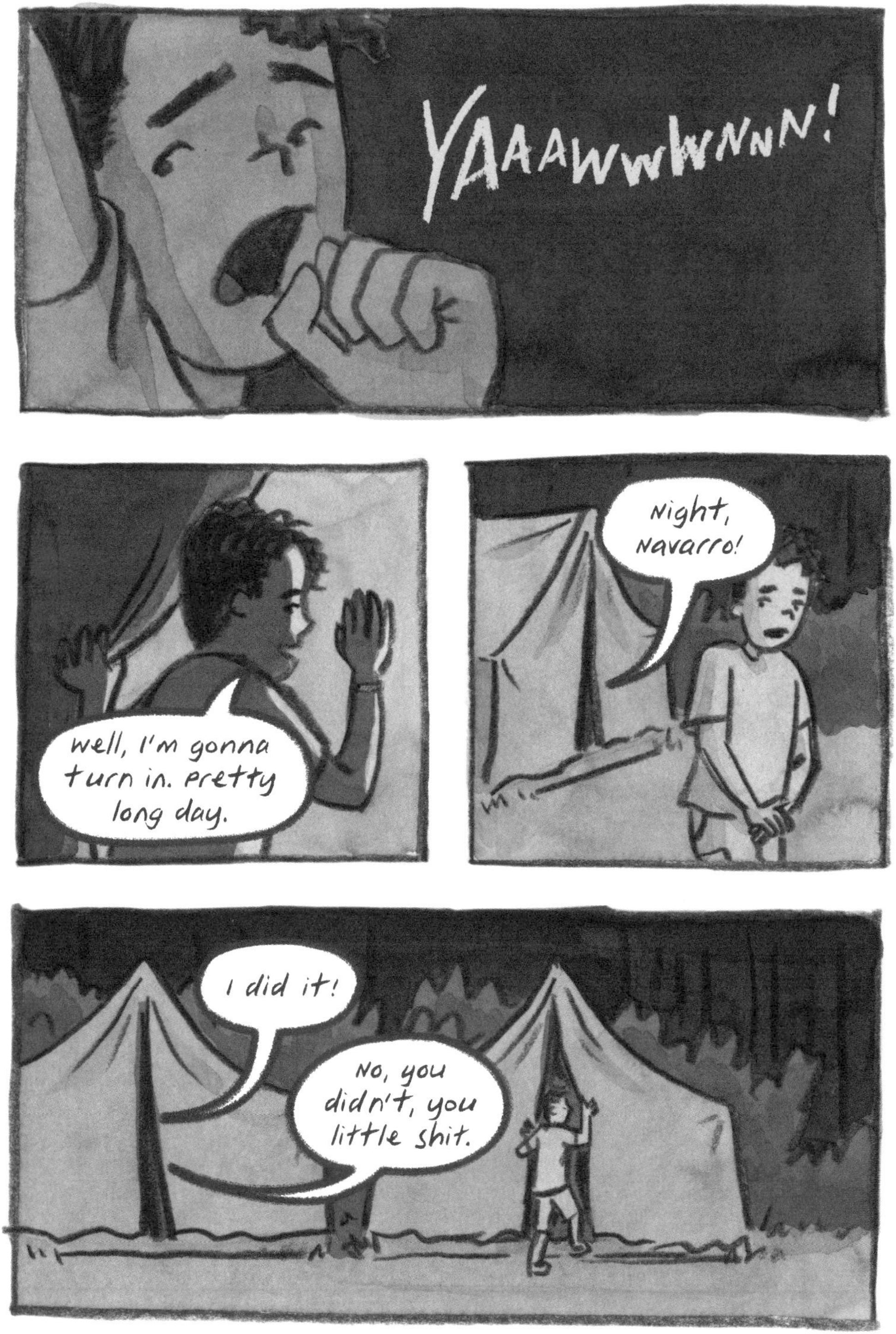
YAAAWWWNNN!
Well, I'm gonna turn in. Pretty long day.
Night, Navarro!
I did it!
No, you didn't, you little shit.

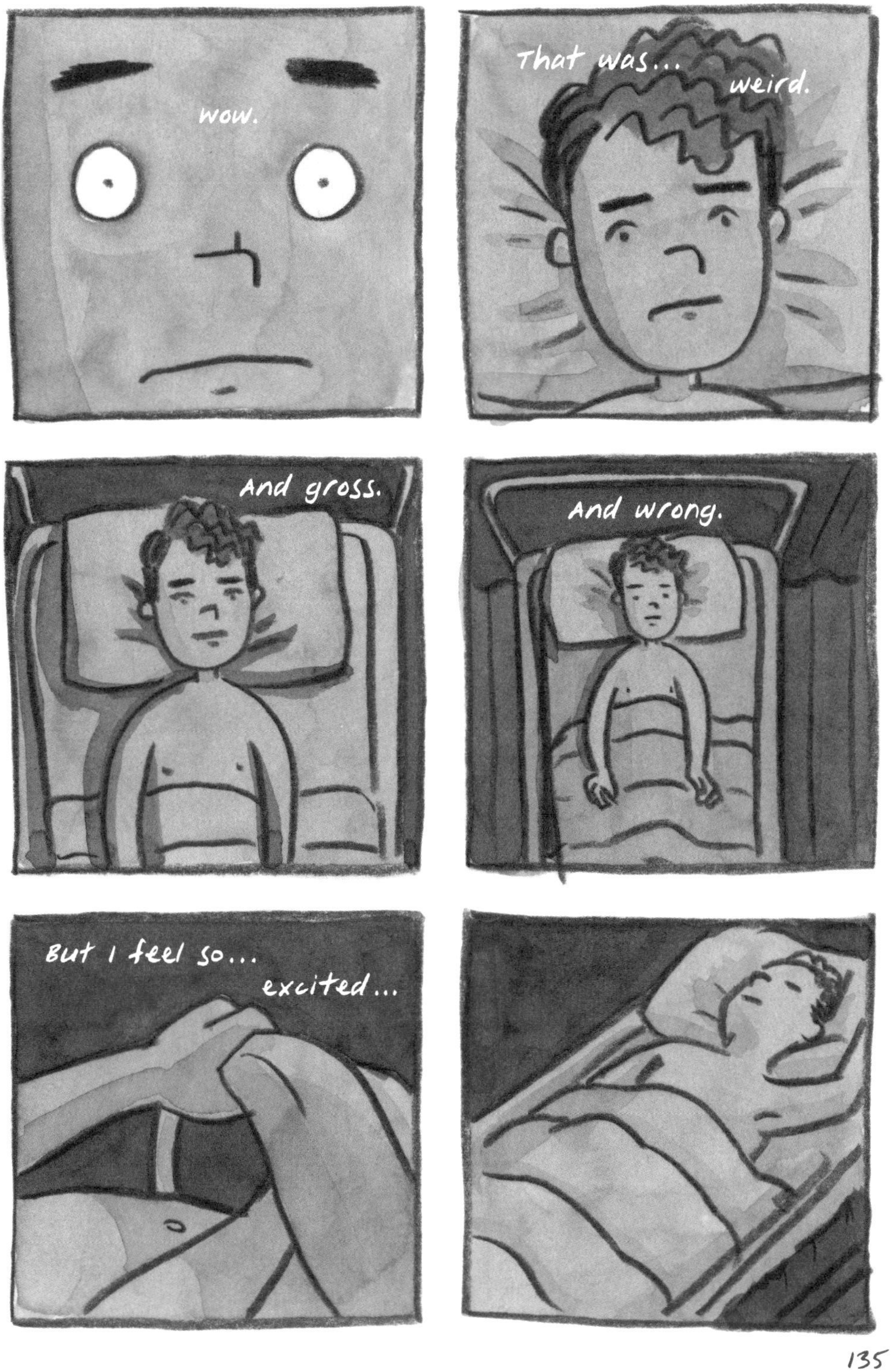
wow.
That was... weird.
And gross.
And wrong.
But I feel so... excited...

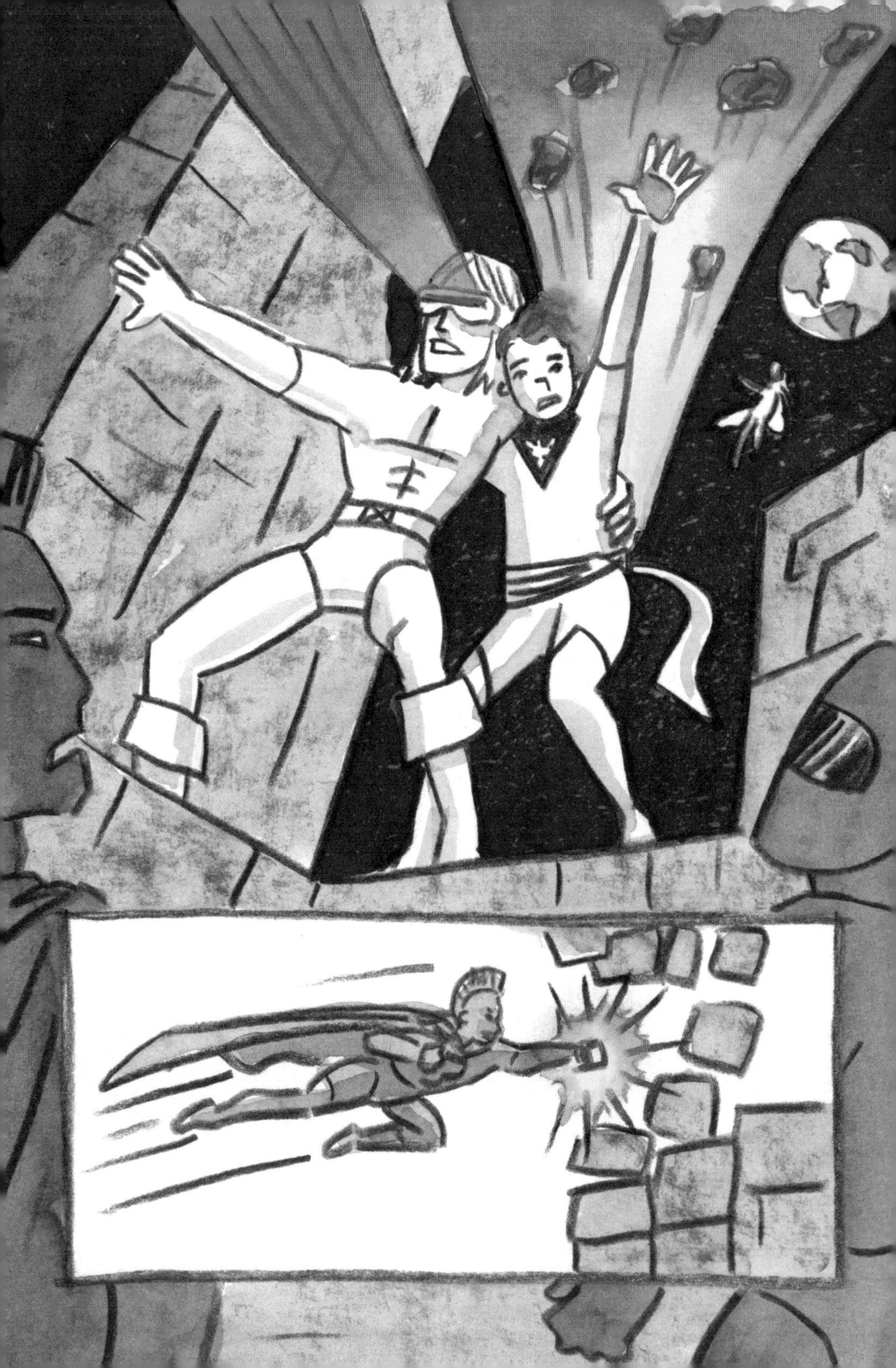

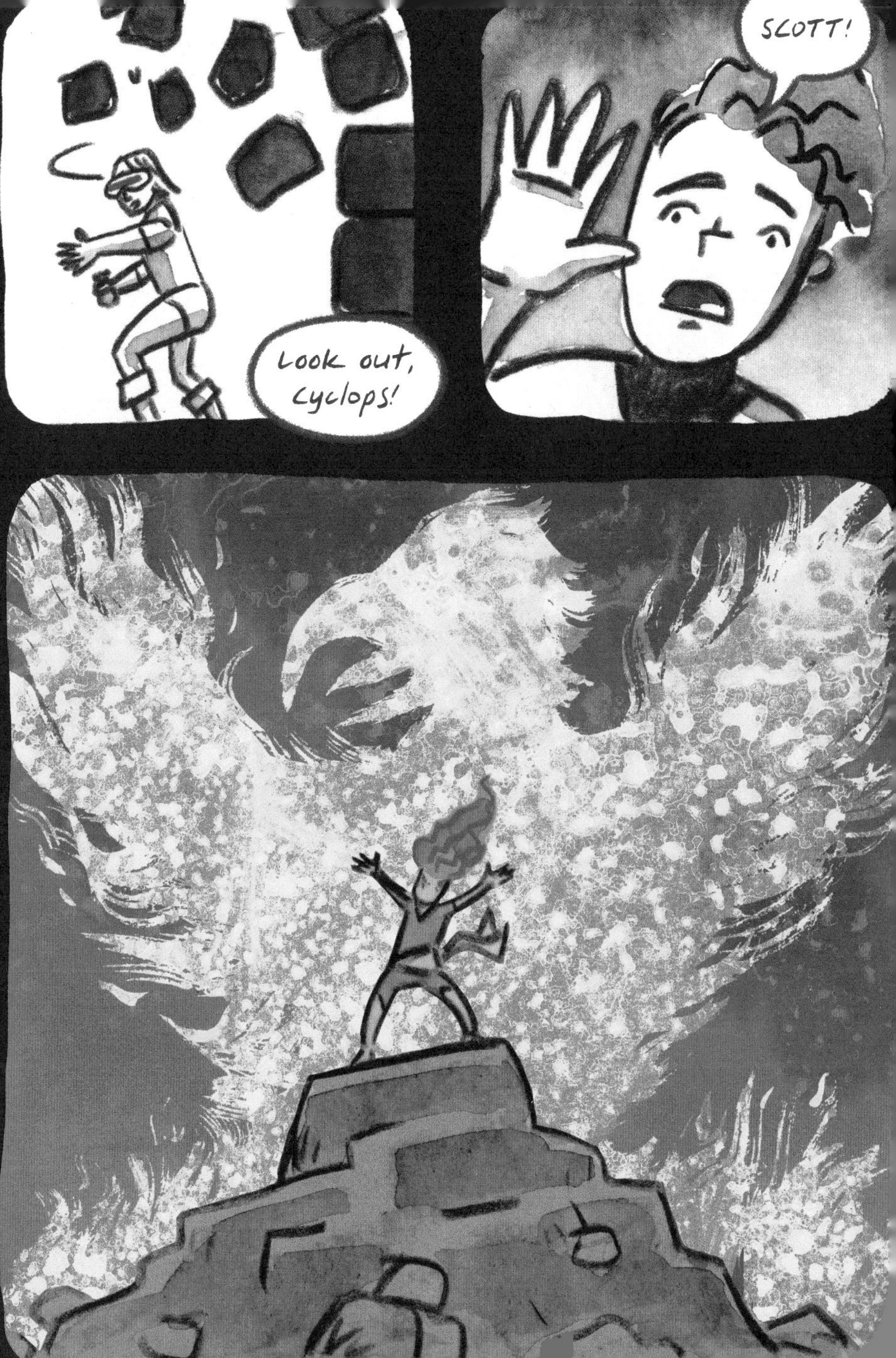
Look out, Cyclops!
SCOTT!

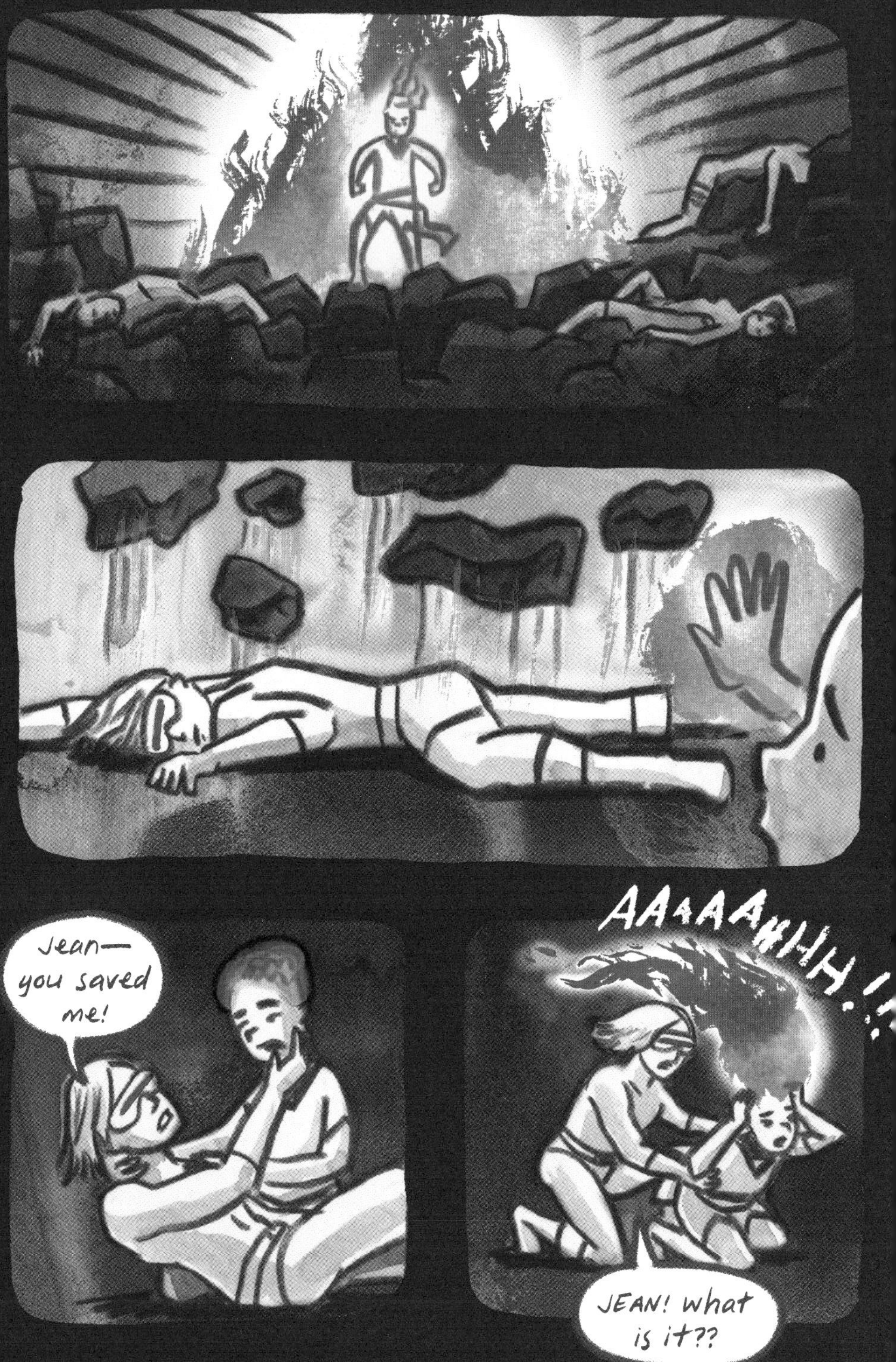
Jean—
you saved
me!
AAAAAAHHH!!!
JEAN! what
is it??

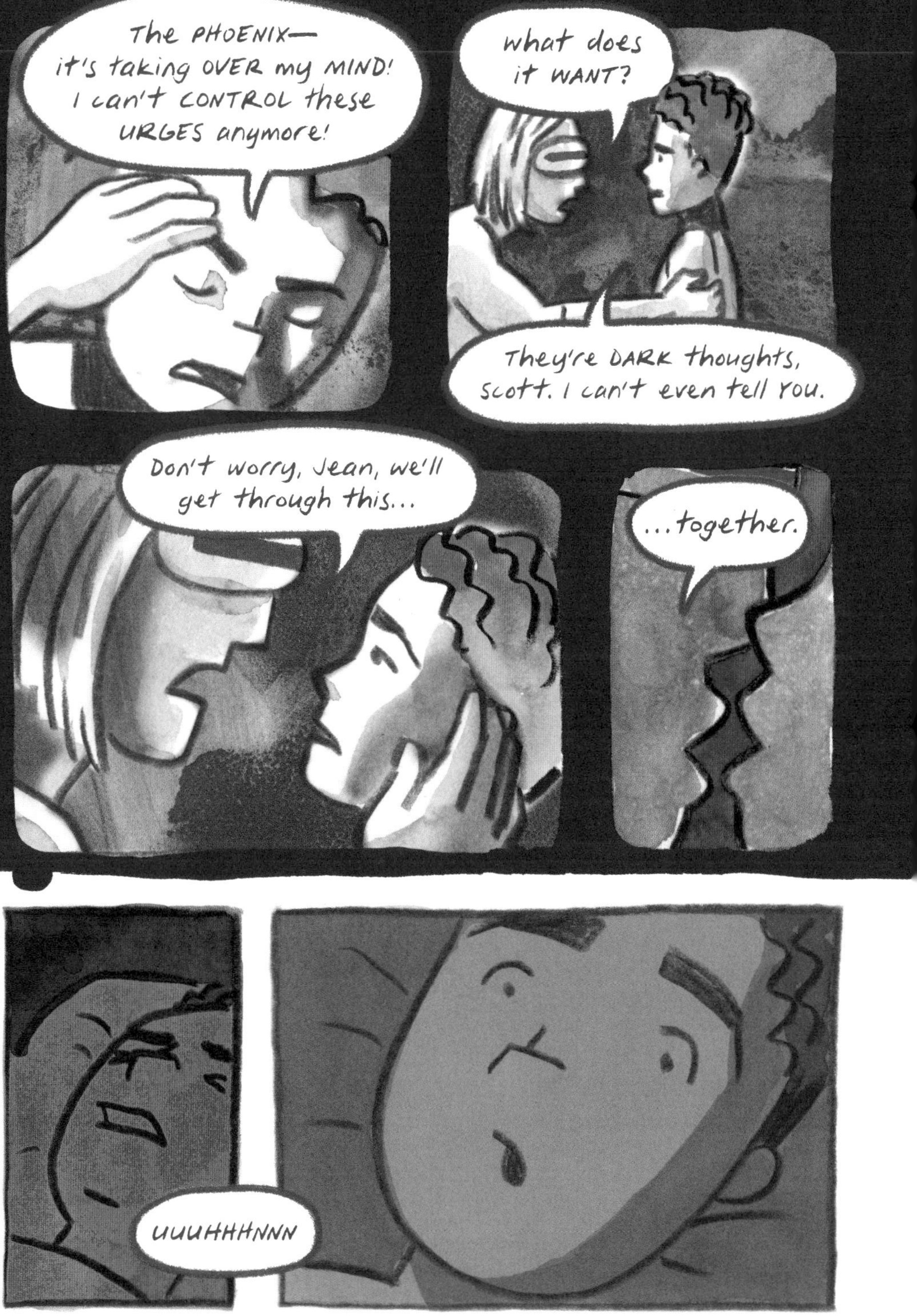
The PHOENIX—
it's taking OVER my MIND!
I can't CONTROL these
URGES anymore!
what does
it WANT?
They're DARK thoughts,
scott. I can't even tell you.
Don't worry, Jean, we'll
get through this...
...together.
UUUHHHNNN

TUESDAY

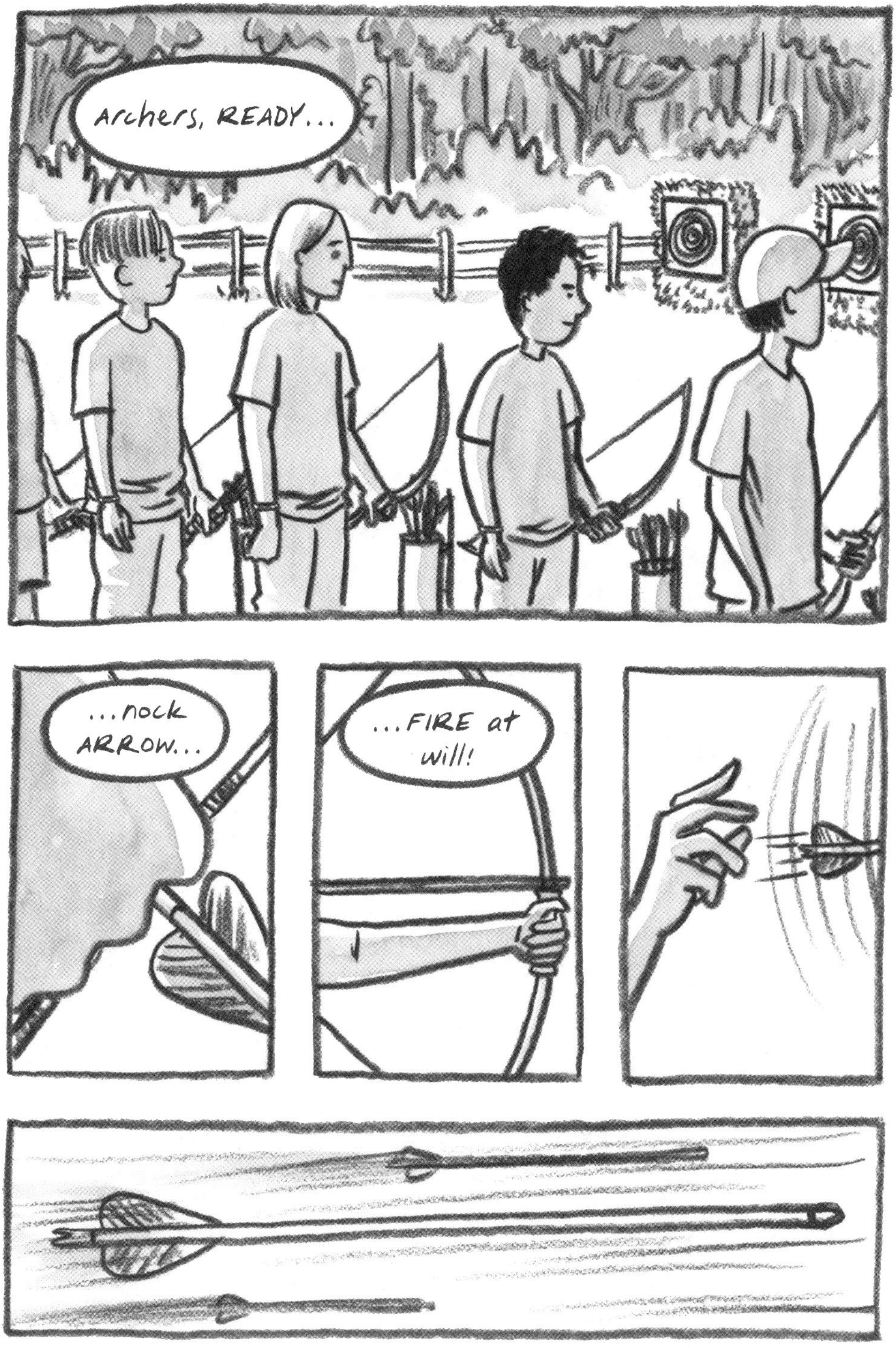
Archers, READY...
...nock ARROW...
...FIRE at will!

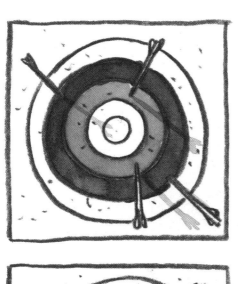

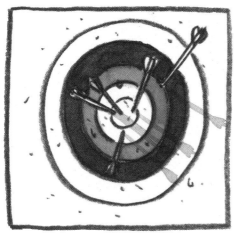

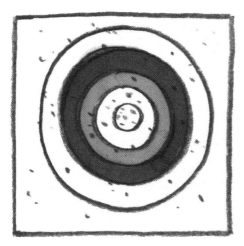

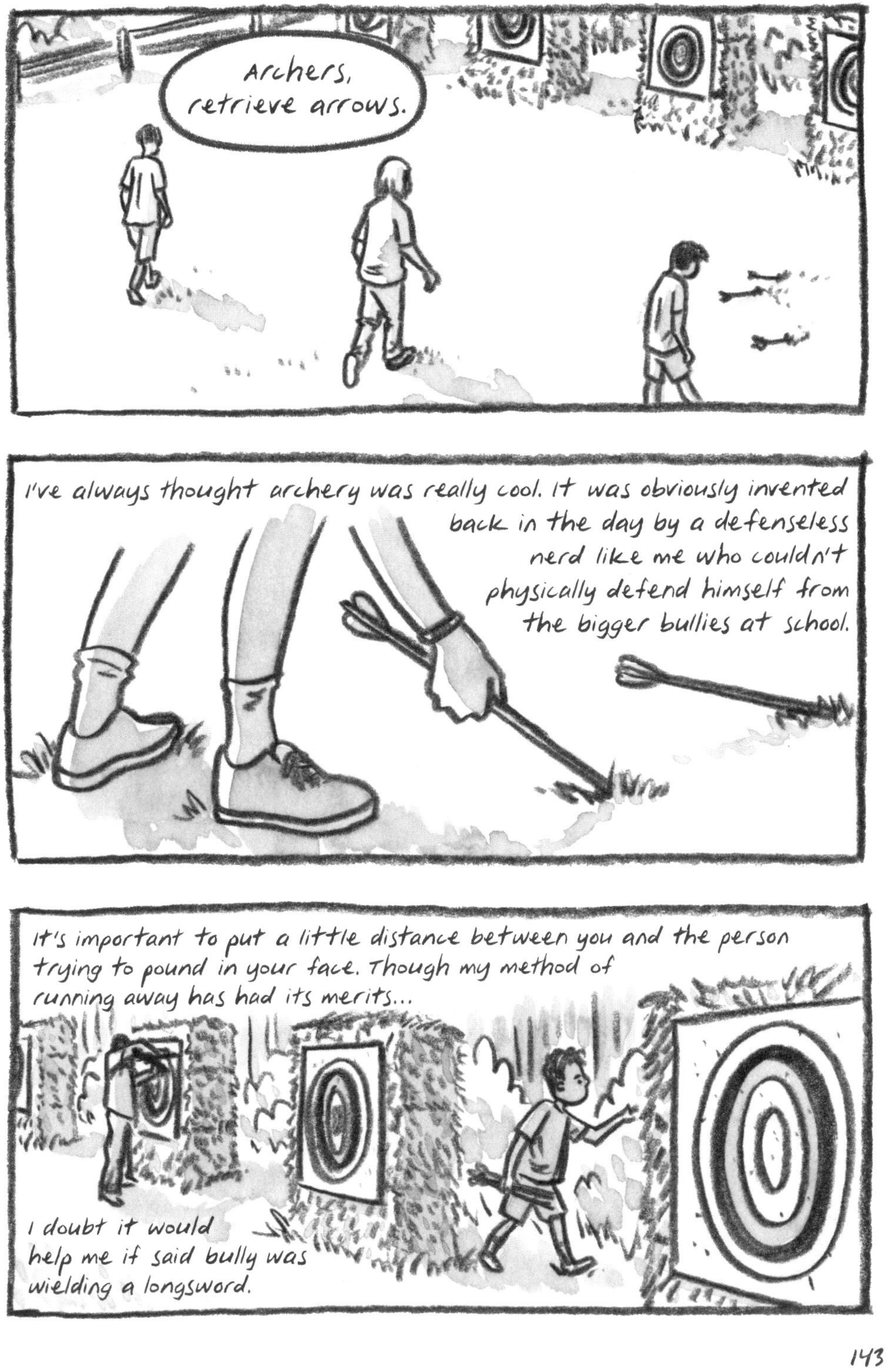
Archers, retrieve arrows.
I've always thought archery was really cool. It was obviously invented back in the day by a defenseless nerd like me who couldn't physically defend himself from the bigger bullies at school.
It's important to put a little distance between you and the person trying to pound in your face. Though my method of running away has had its merits...
I doubt it would help me if said bully was wielding a longsword.

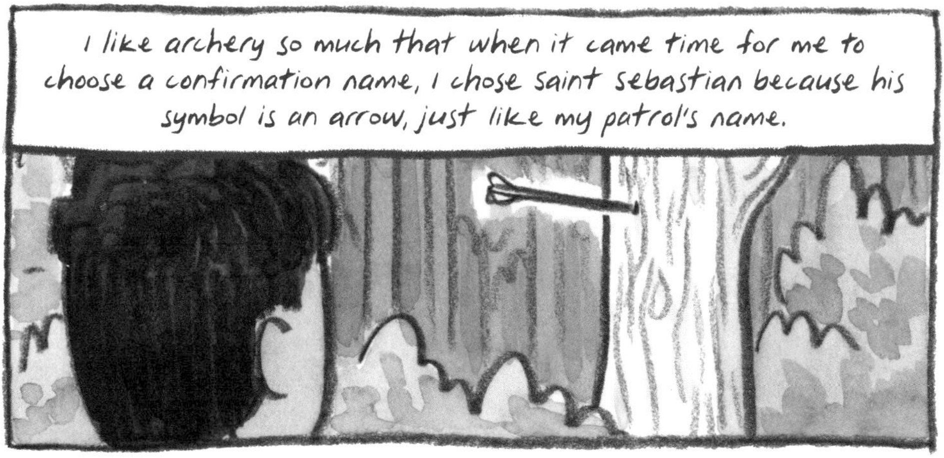
I like archery so much that when it came time for me to choose a confirmation name, I chose Saint Sebastian because his symbol is an arrow, just like my patrol's name.

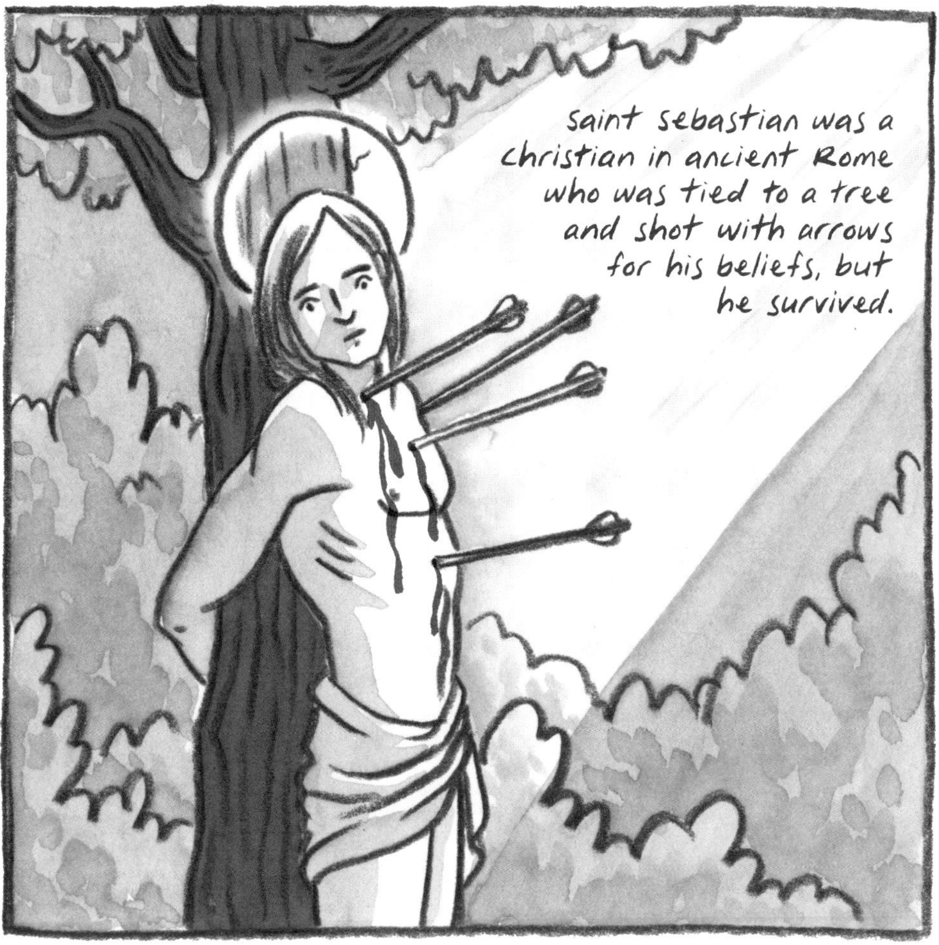
Saint Sebastian was a Christian in ancient Rome who was tied to a tree and shot with arrows for his beliefs, but he survived.

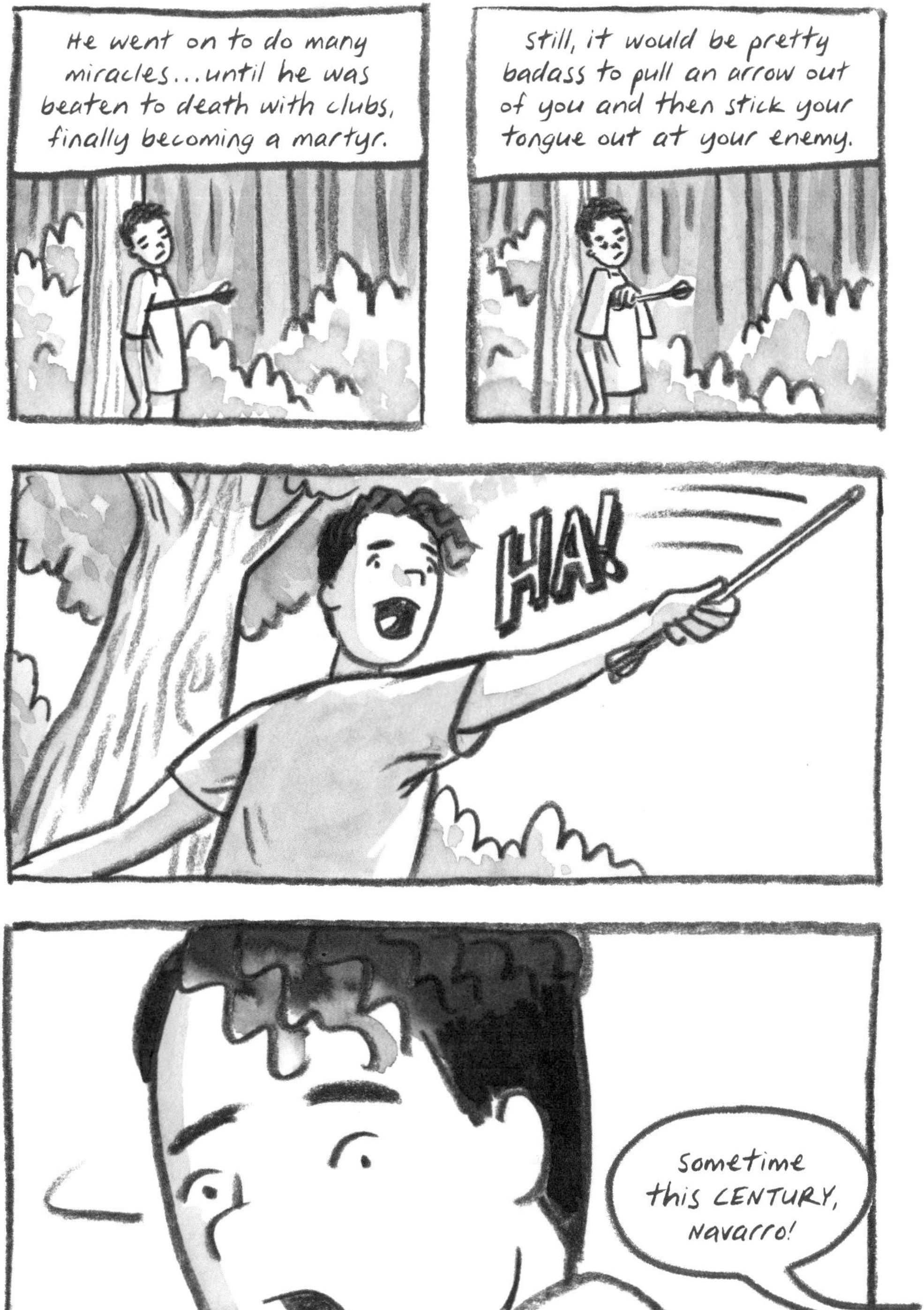
He went on to do many miracles...until he was beaten to death with clubs, finally becoming a martyr.
Still, it would be pretty badass to pull an arrow out of you and then stick your tongue out at your enemy.
HA!
Sometime this CENTURY, Navarro!

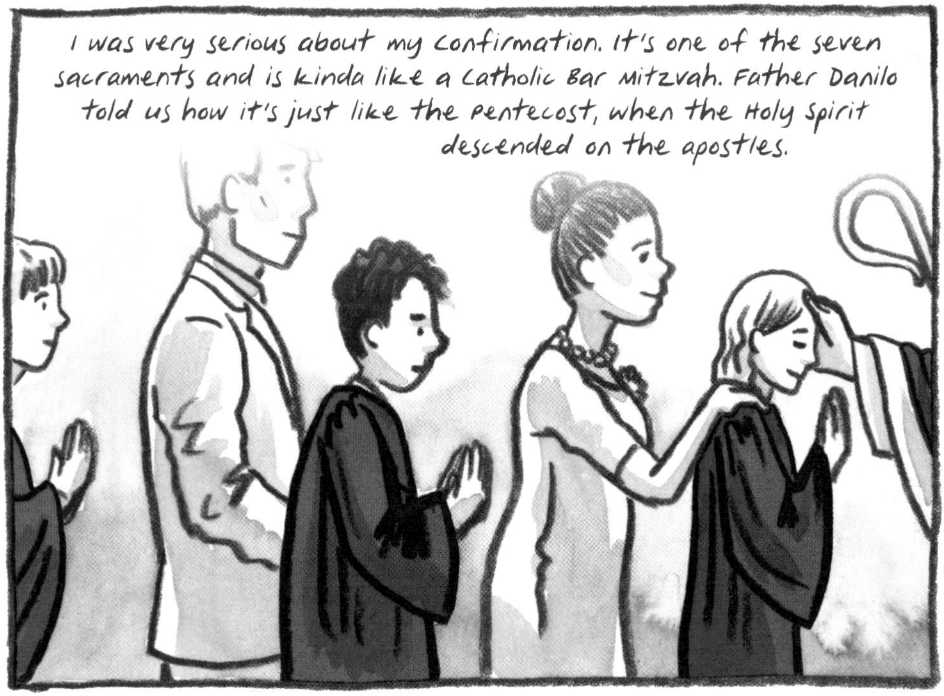
I was very serious about my confirmation. It's one of the seven sacraments and is kinda like a Catholic Bar Mitzvah. Father Danilo told us how it's just like the Pentecost, when the Holy Spirit descended on the apostles.

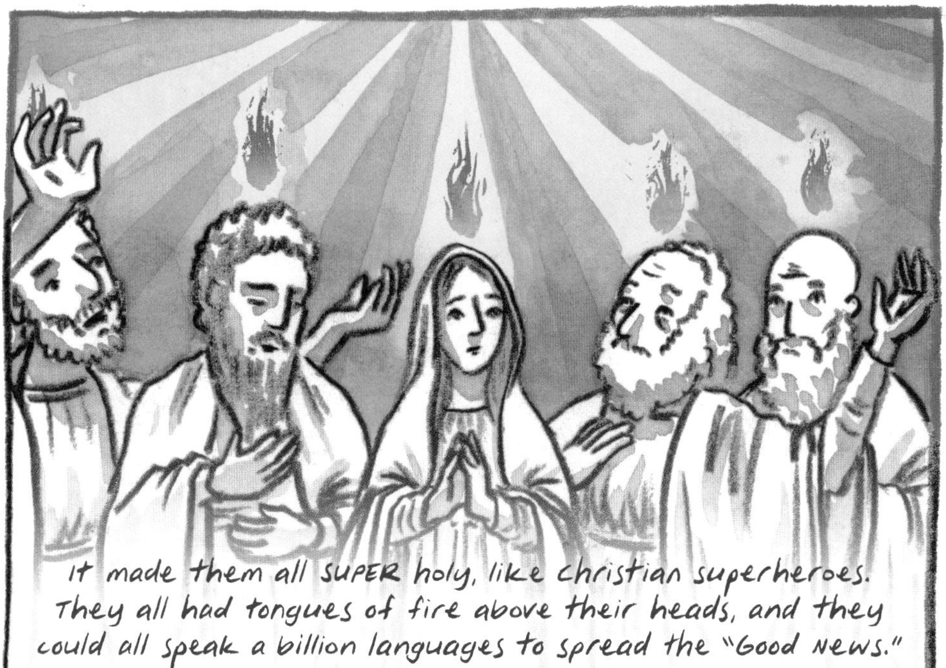
It made them all SUPER holy, like Christian superheroes. They all had tongues of fire above their heads, and they could all speak a billion languages to spread the "Good News."

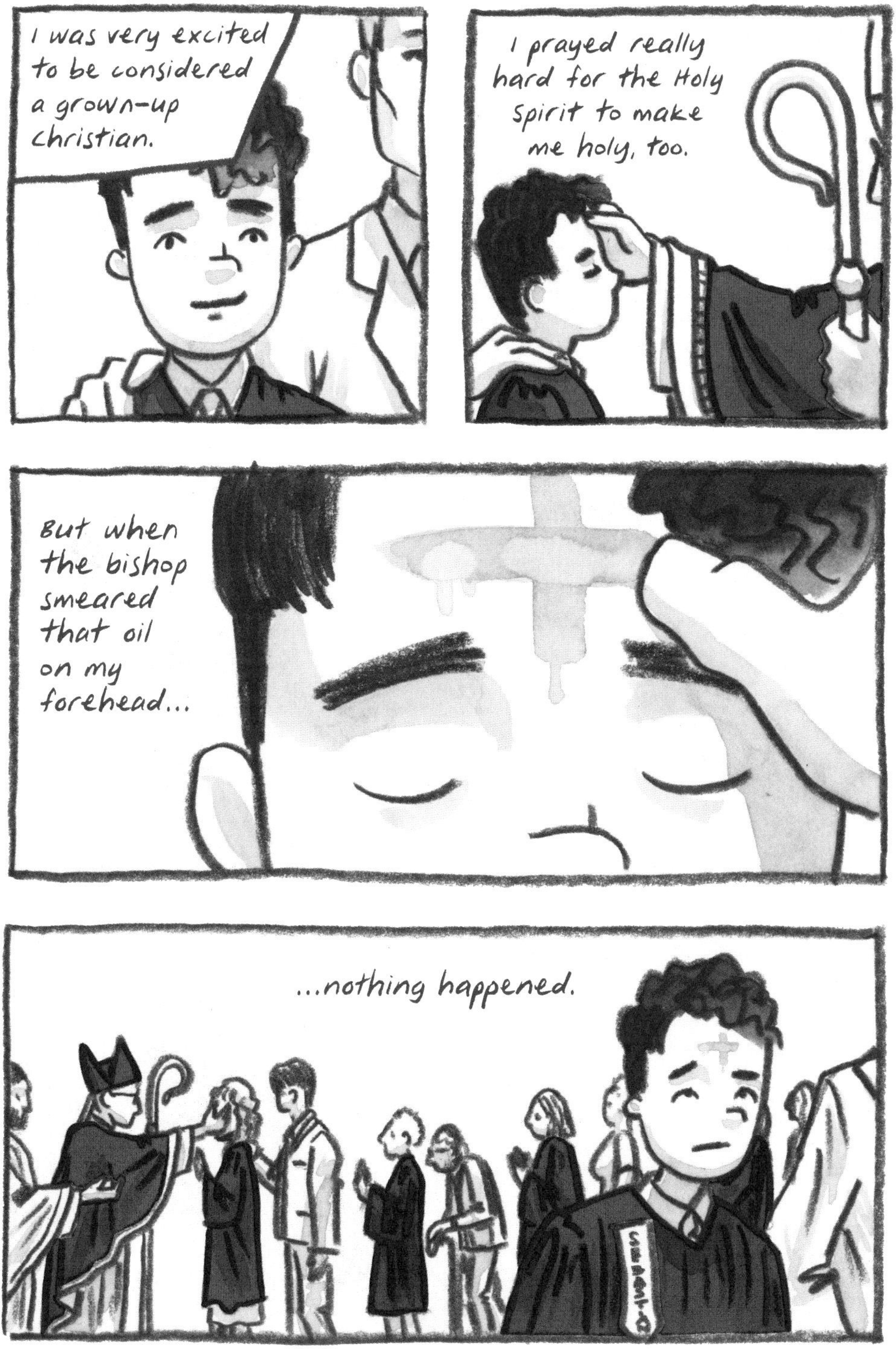
I was very excited to be considered a grown-up Christian.
I prayed really hard for the Holy Spirit to make me holy, too.
But when the bishop smeared that oil on my forehead...
...nothing happened.

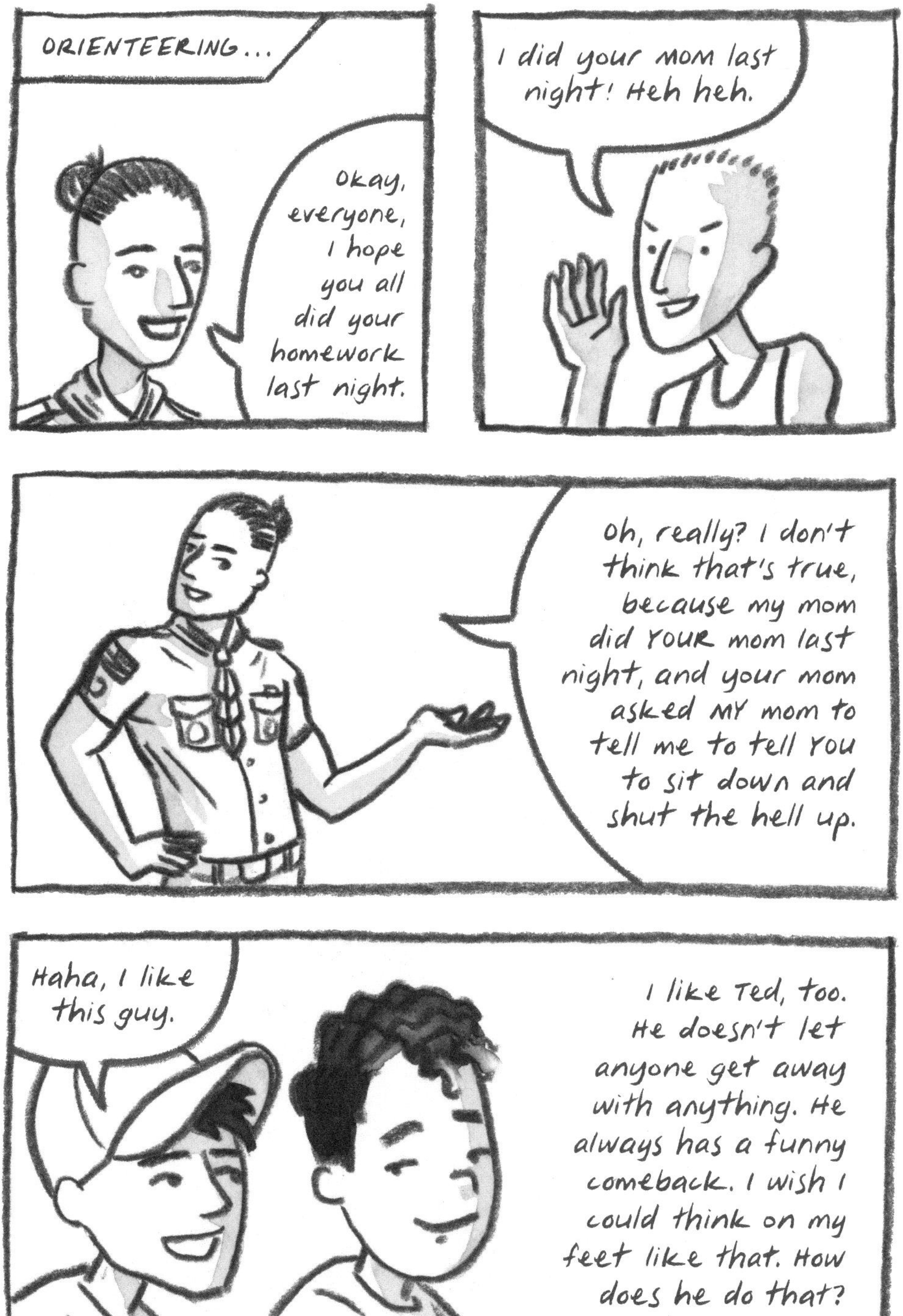
ORIENTEERING...
Okay, everyone, I hope you all did your homework last night.
I did your mom last night! Heh heh.
Oh, really? I don't think that's true, because my mom did YOUR mom last night, and your mom asked MY mom to tell me to tell YOU to sit down and shut the hell up.
Haha, I like this guy.
I like Ted, too. He doesn't let anyone get away with anything. He always has a funny comeback. I wish I could think on my feet like that. How does he do that?

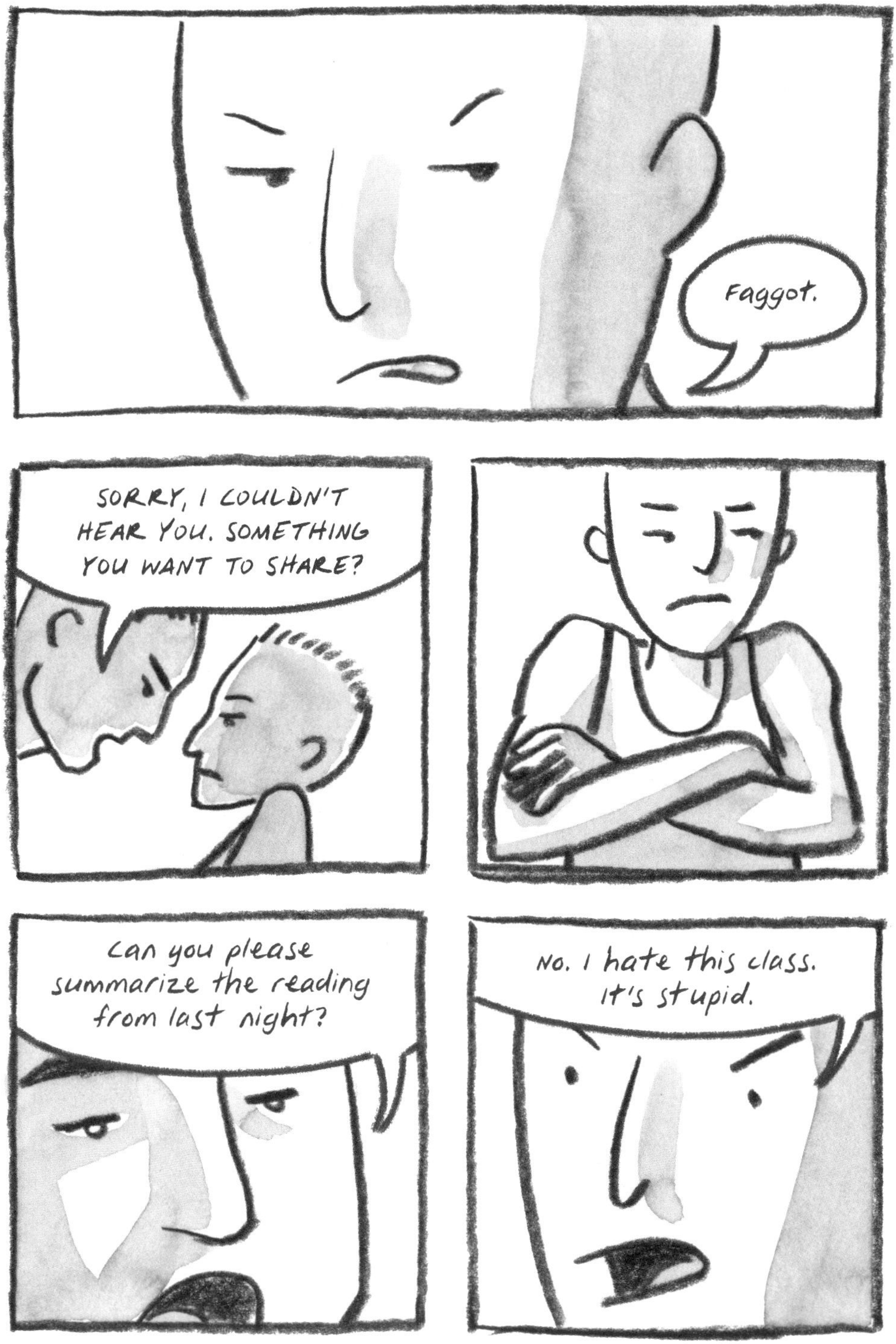
Faggot.
SORRY, I COULDN'T HEAR YOU. SOMETHING YOU WANT TO SHARE?
Can you please summarize the reading from last night?
No. I hate this class. It's stupid.

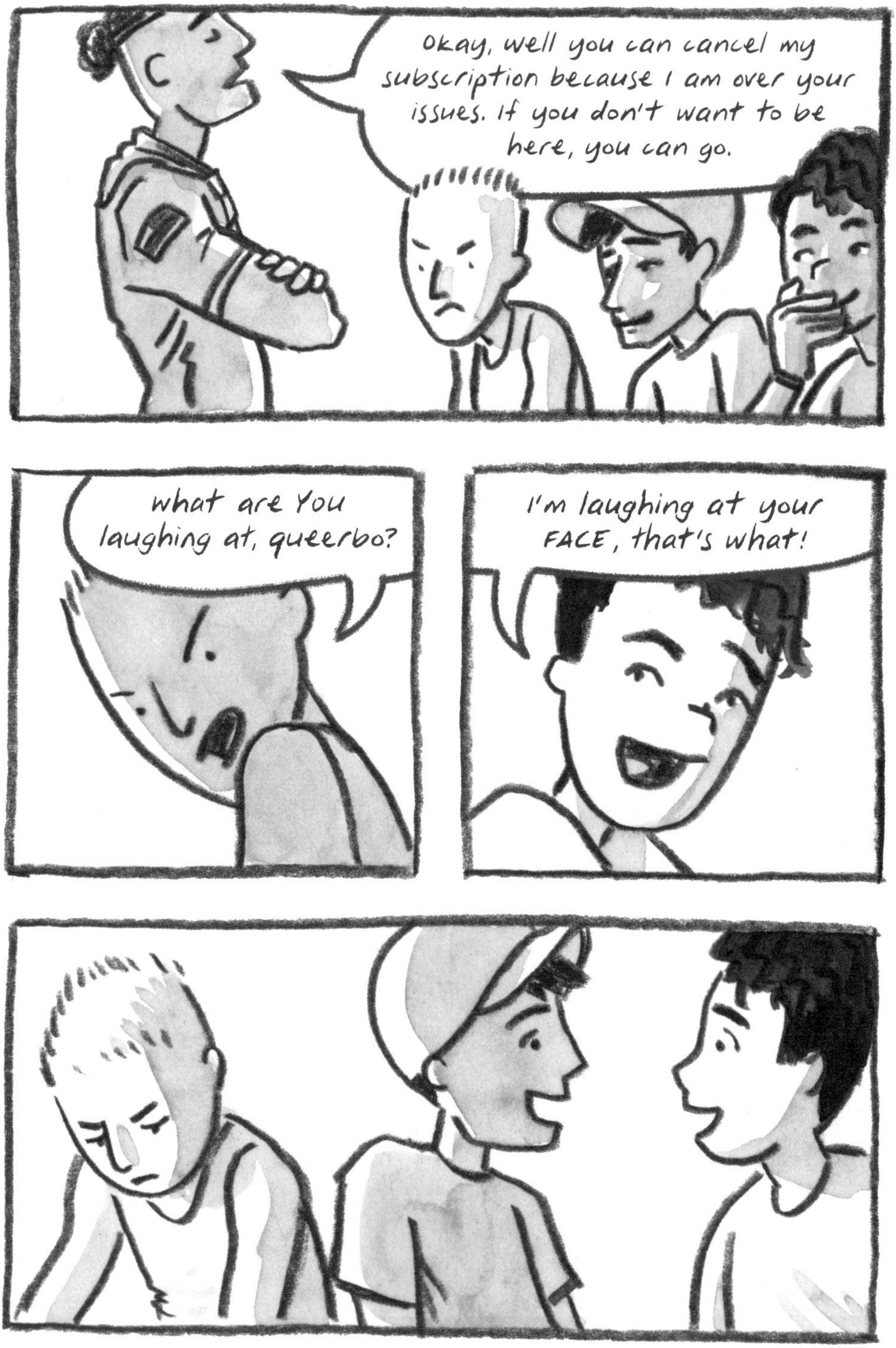
Okay, well you can cancel my subscription because I am over your issues. If you don't want to be here, you can go.
what are You laughing at, queerbo?
I'm laughing at your FACE, that's what!

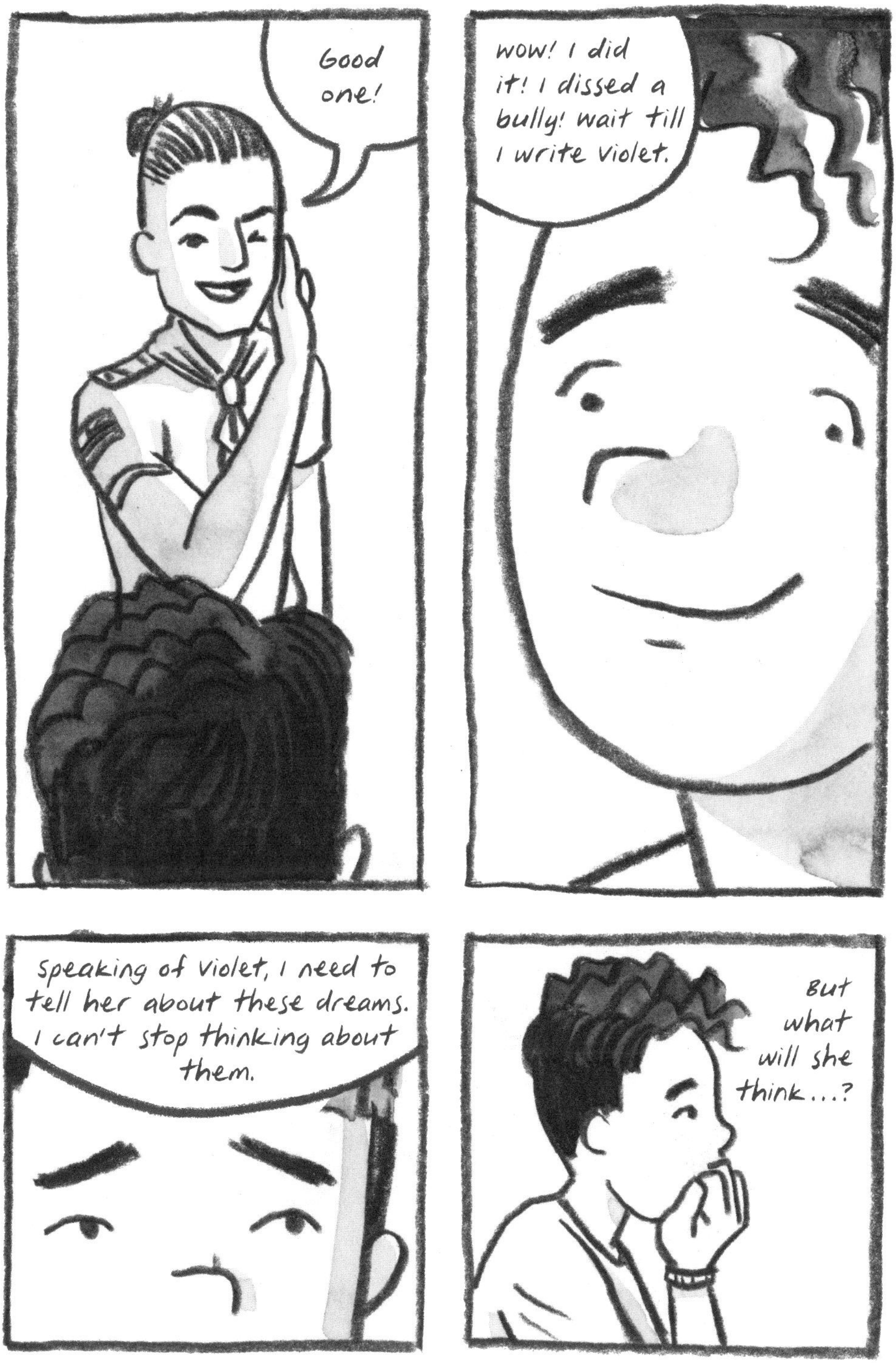
Good one!
WOW! I did it! I dissed a bully! Wait till I write Violet.
Speaking of Violet, I need to tell her about these dreams. I can't stop thinking about them.
But what will she think...?

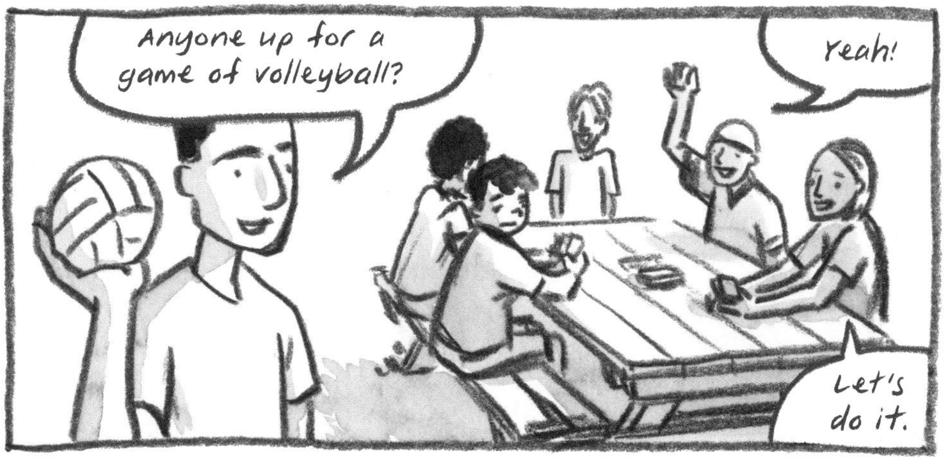
Anyone up for a game of volleyball?
Yeah!
Let's do it.

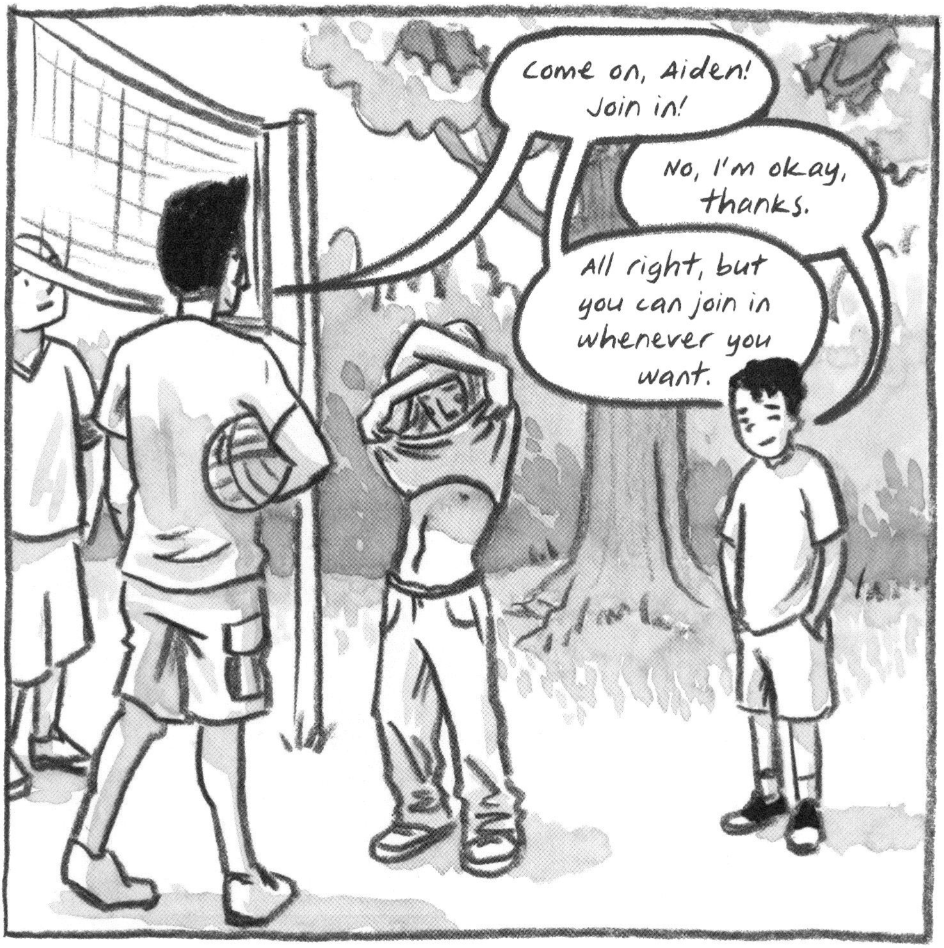
Come on, Aiden! Join in!
No, I'm okay, thanks.
All right, but you can join in whenever you want.

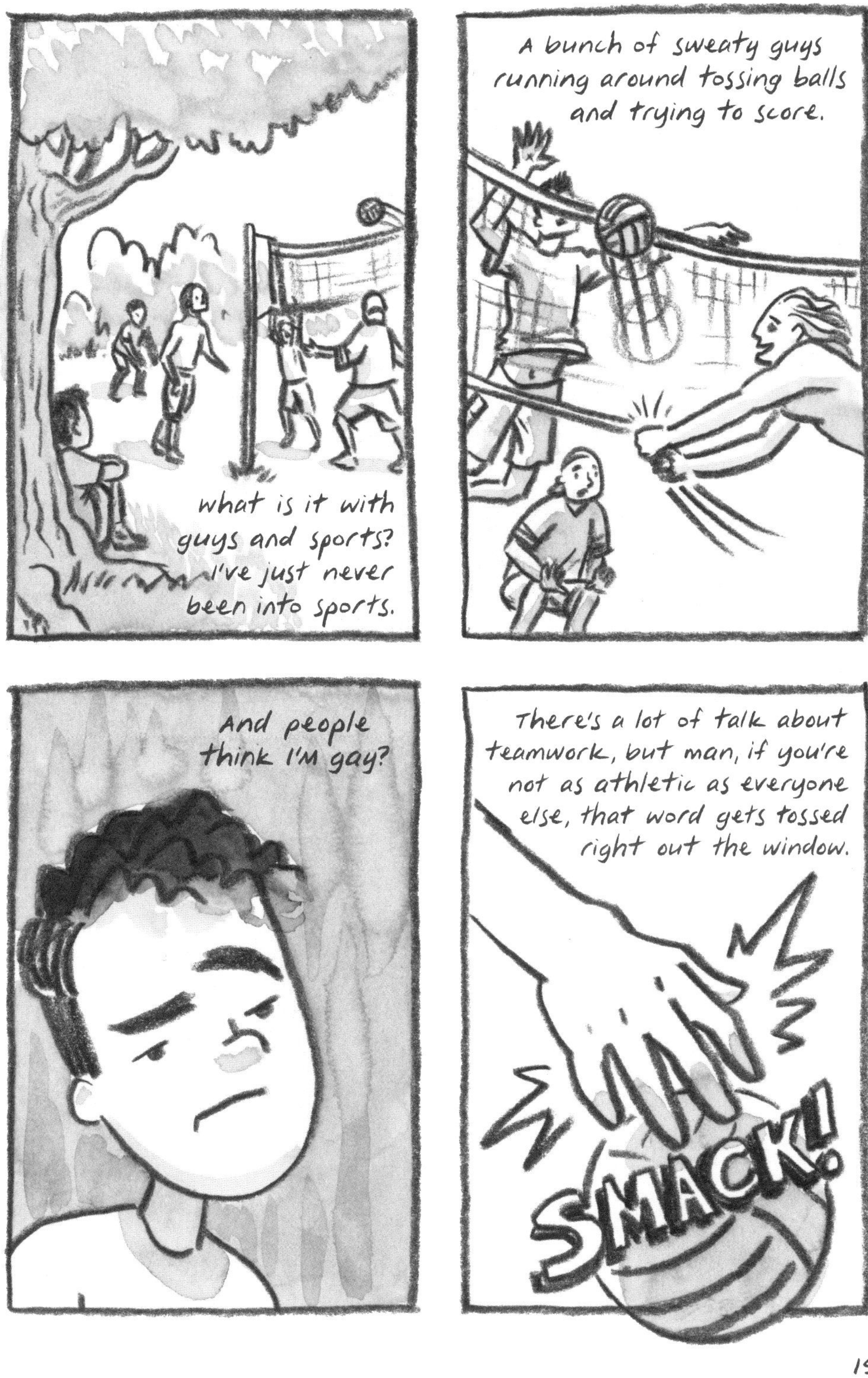
what is it with guys and sports? I've just never been into sports.
A bunch of sweaty guys running around tossing balls and trying to score.
And people think I'm gay?
There's a lot of talk about teamwork, but man, if you're not as athletic as everyone else, that word gets tossed right out the window.
SMACK!

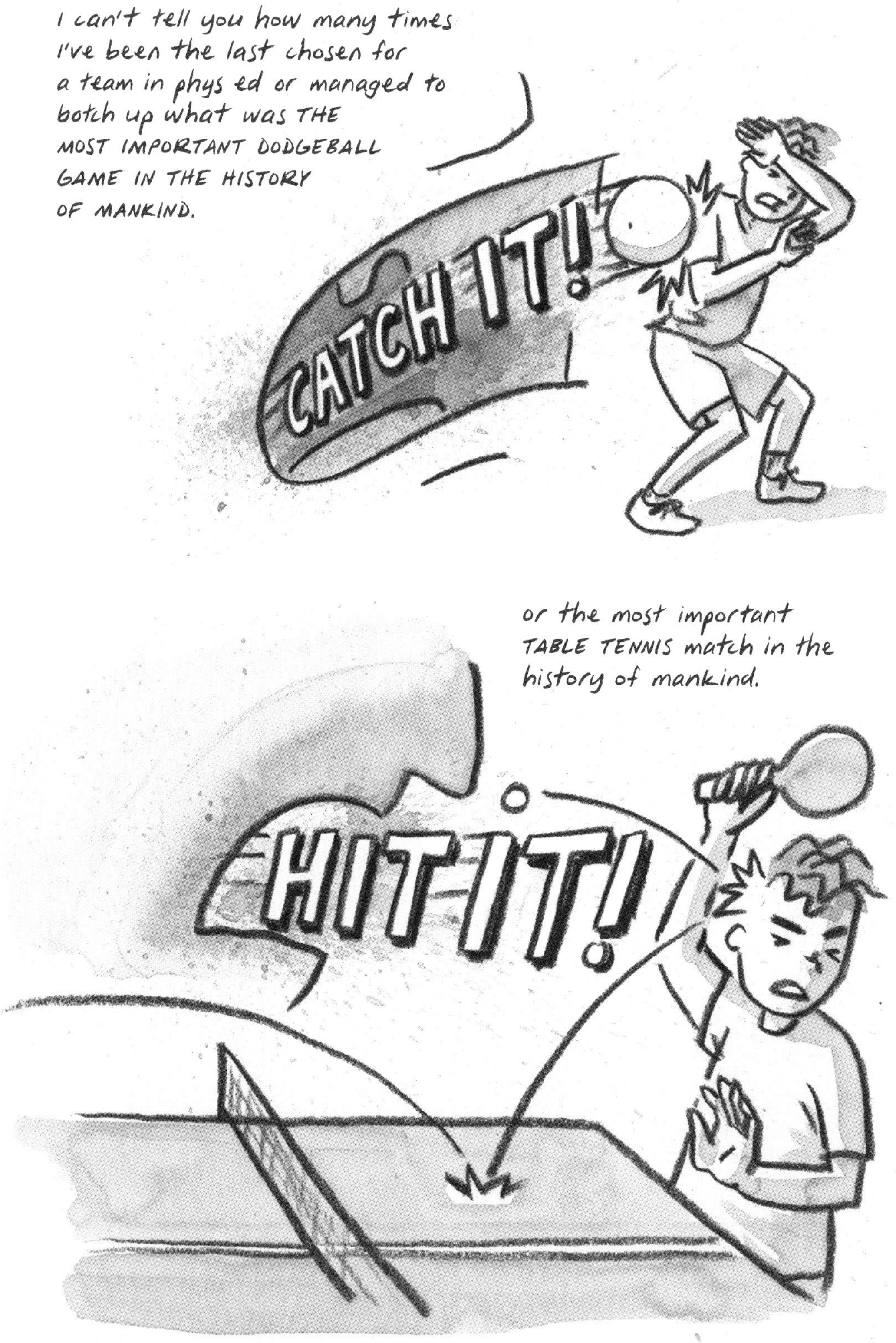
I can't tell you how many times I've been the last chosen for a team in phys ed or managed to botch up what was THE MOST IMPORTANT DODGEBALL GAME IN THE HISTORY OF MANKIND.
CATCH IT!
or the most important TABLE TENNIS match in the history of mankind.
HIT IT!

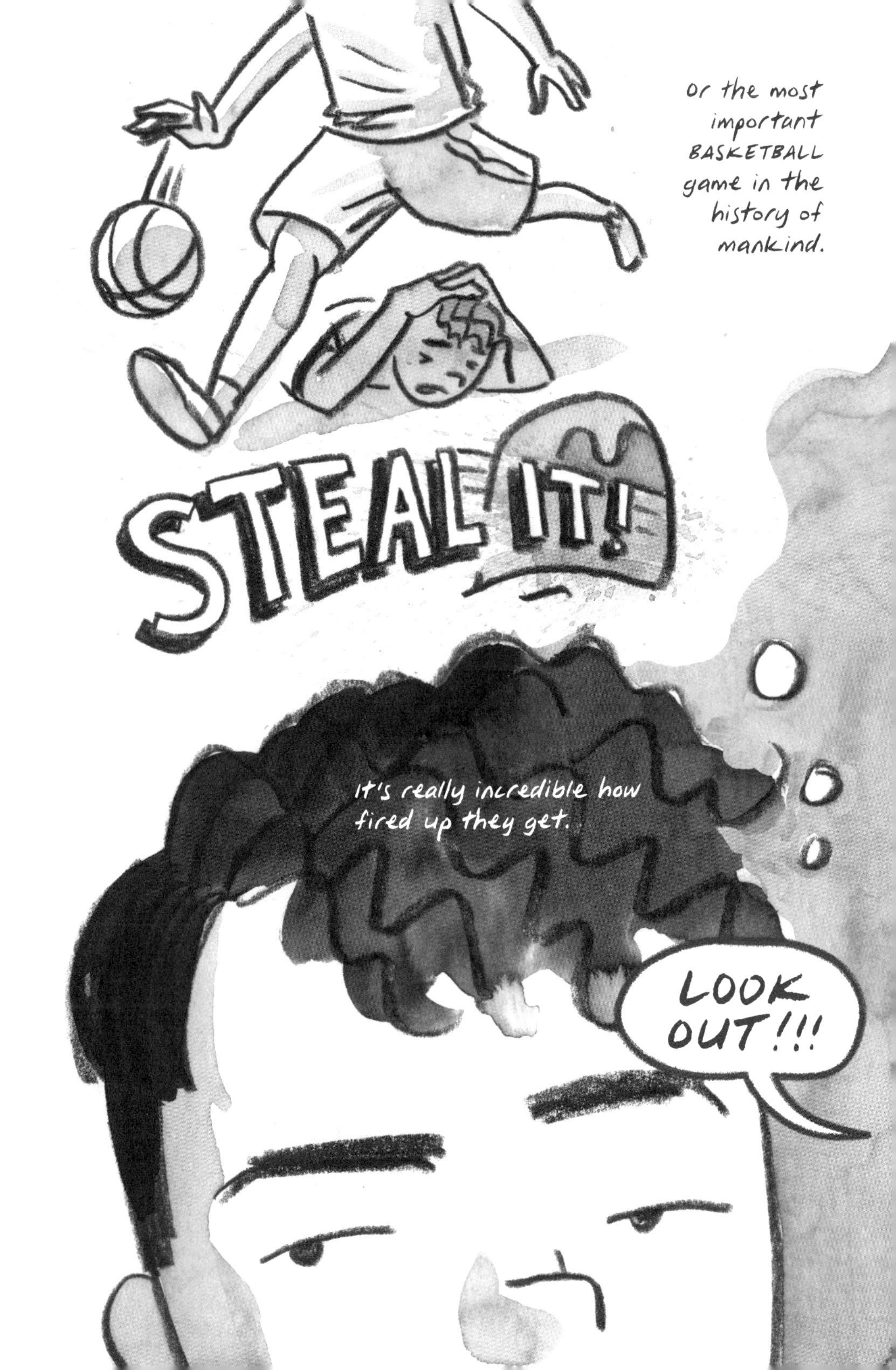
or the most important BASKETBALL game in the history of mankind.
STEAL IT!
It's really incredible how fired up they get.
LOOK OUT!!!

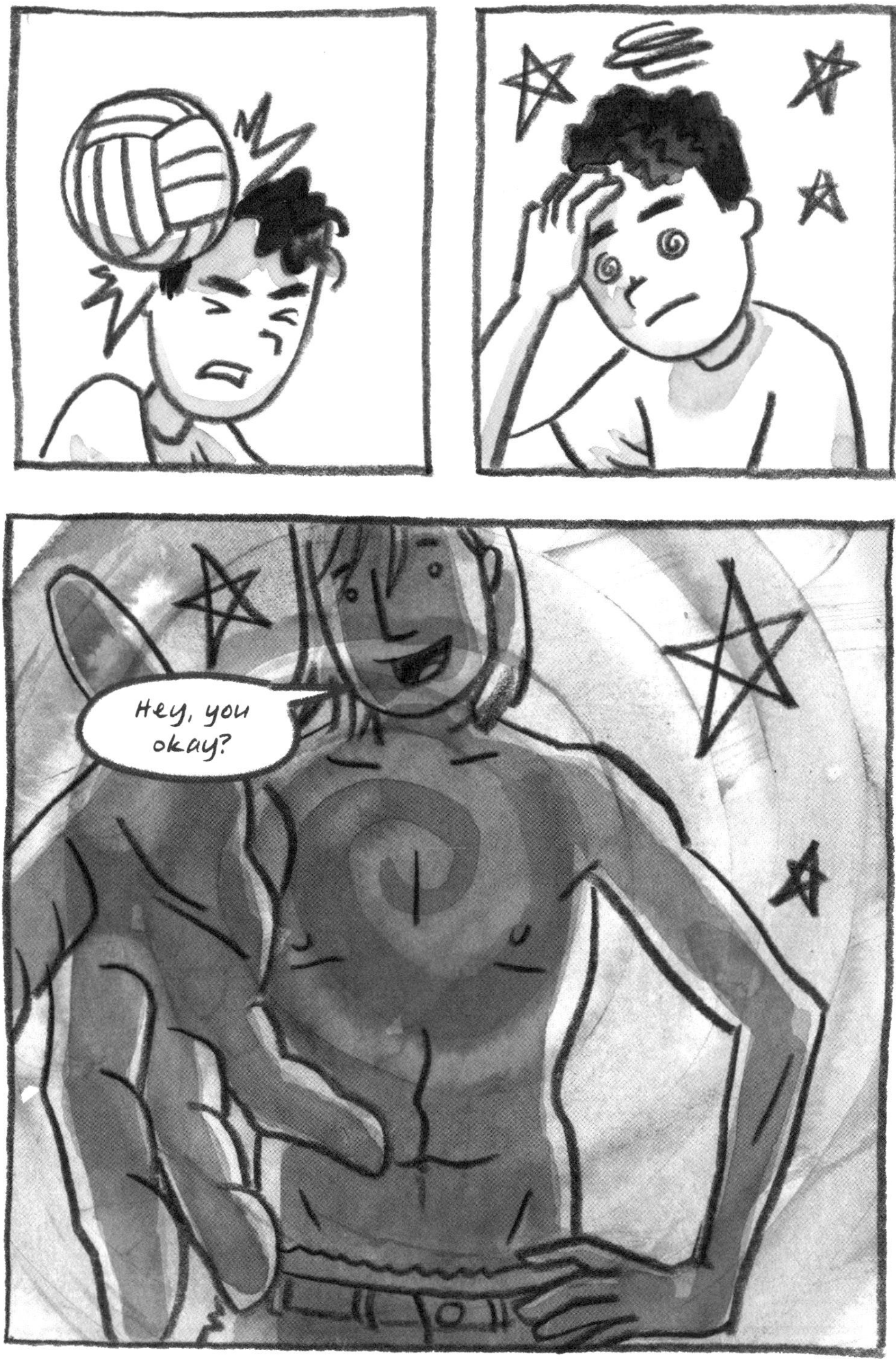
Hey, you okay?

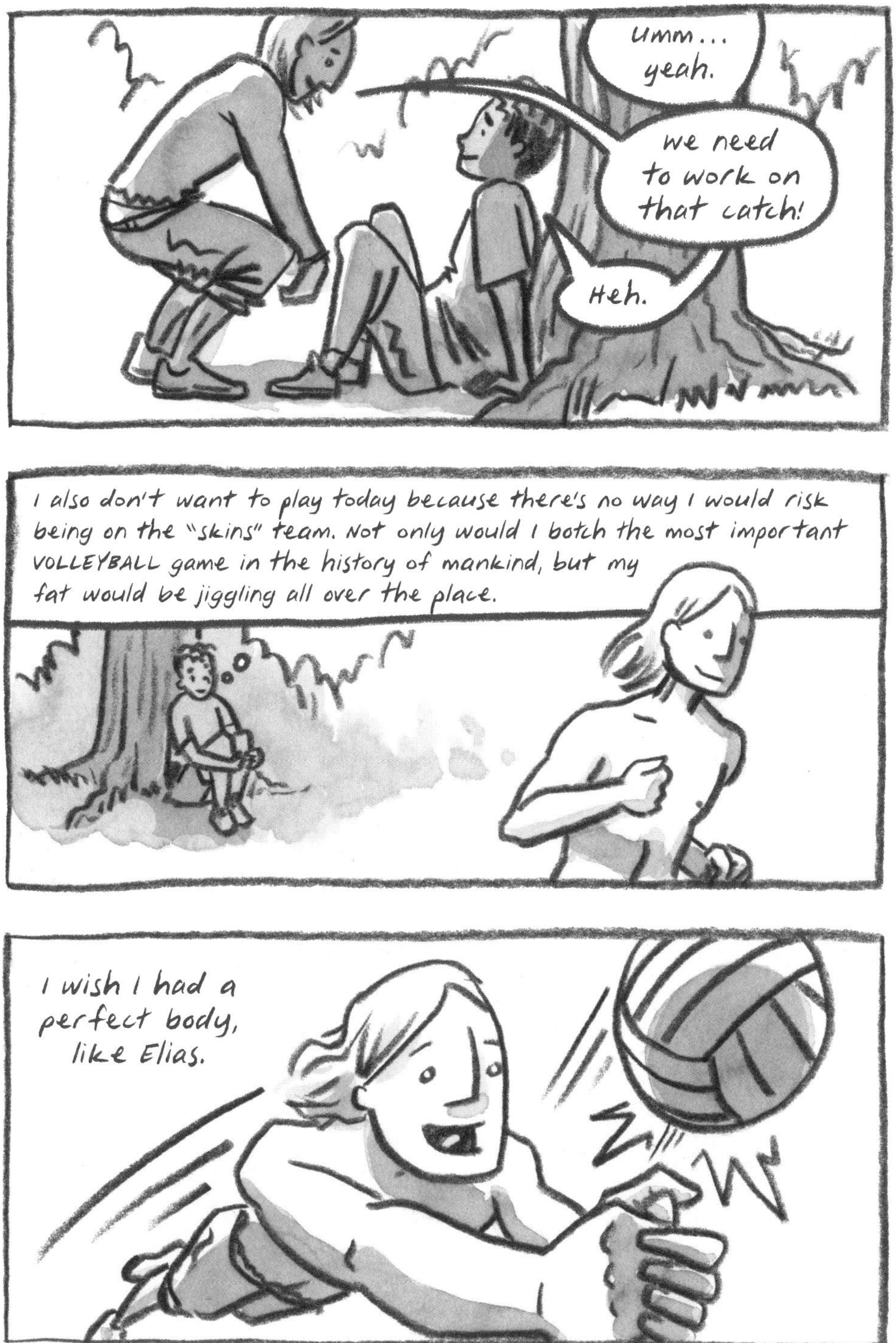
umm... yeah.
we need to work on that catch!
Heh.
I also don't want to play today because there's no way I would risk being on the "skins" team. Not only would I botch the most important VOLLEYBALL game in the history of mankind, but my fat would be jiggling all over the place.
I wish I had a perfect body, like Elias.

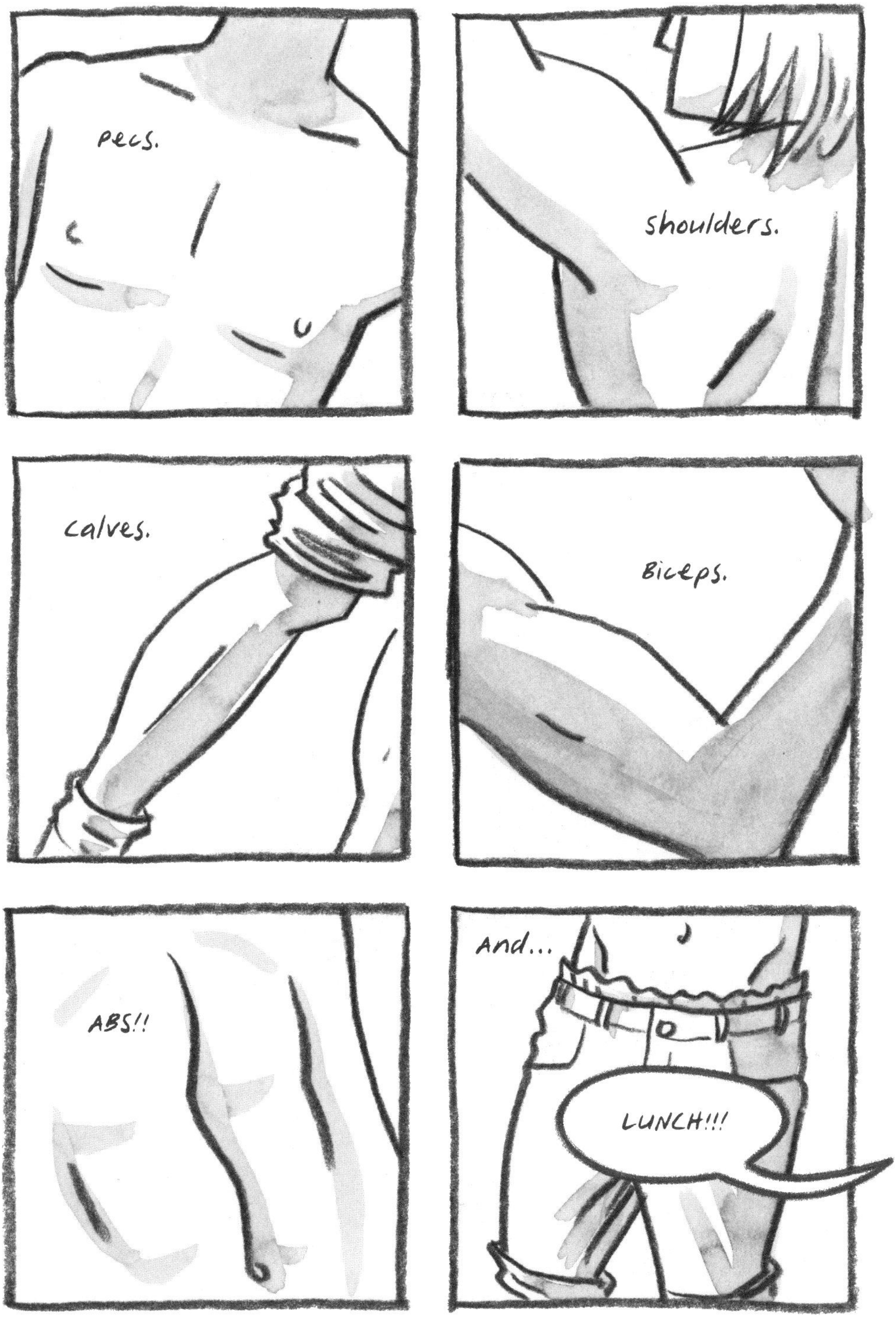
pecs.
shoulders.
calves.
Biceps.
ABS!!
And...
LUNCH!!!

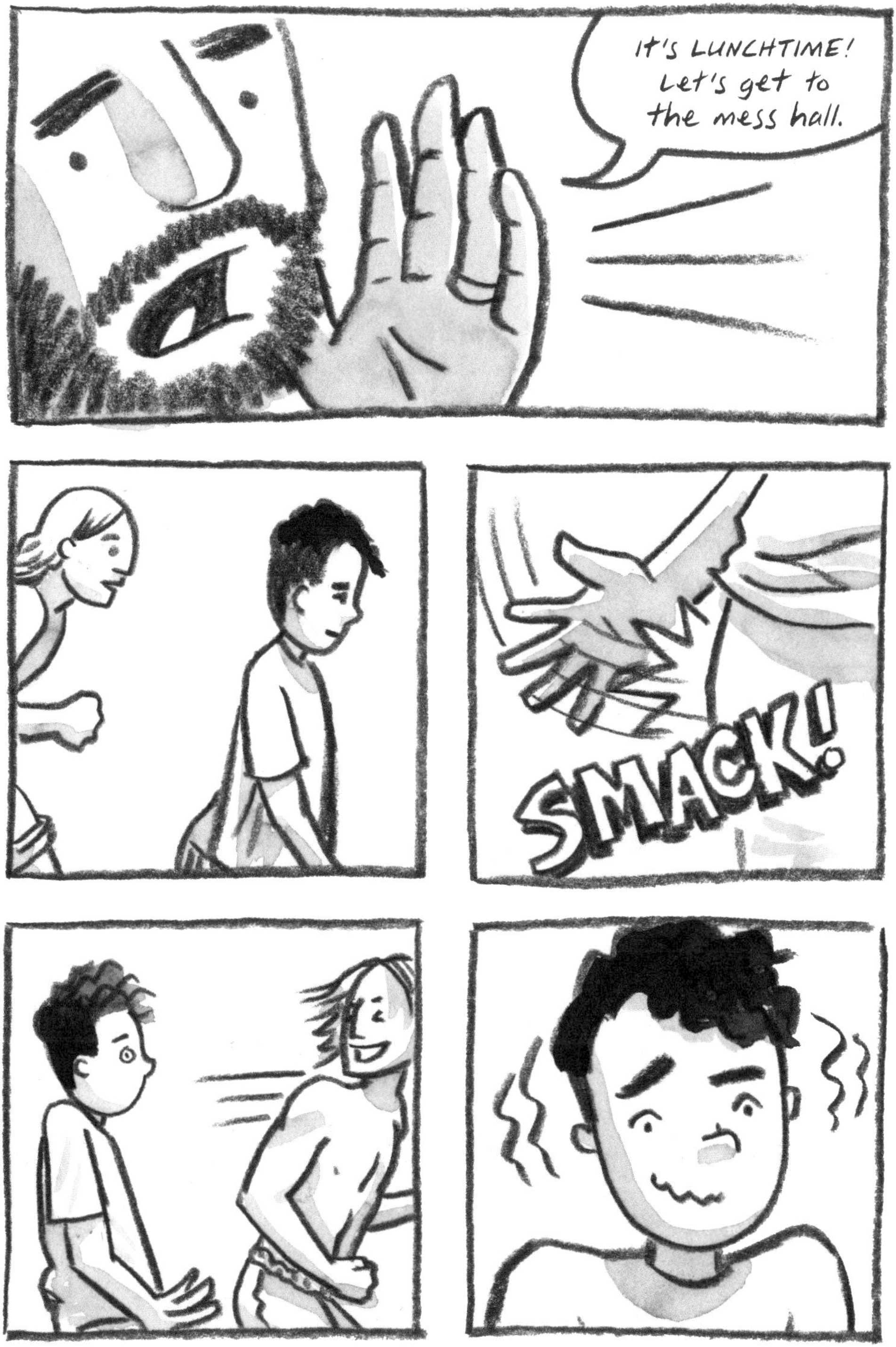
It's LUNCHTIME! Let's get to the mess hall.
SMACK!

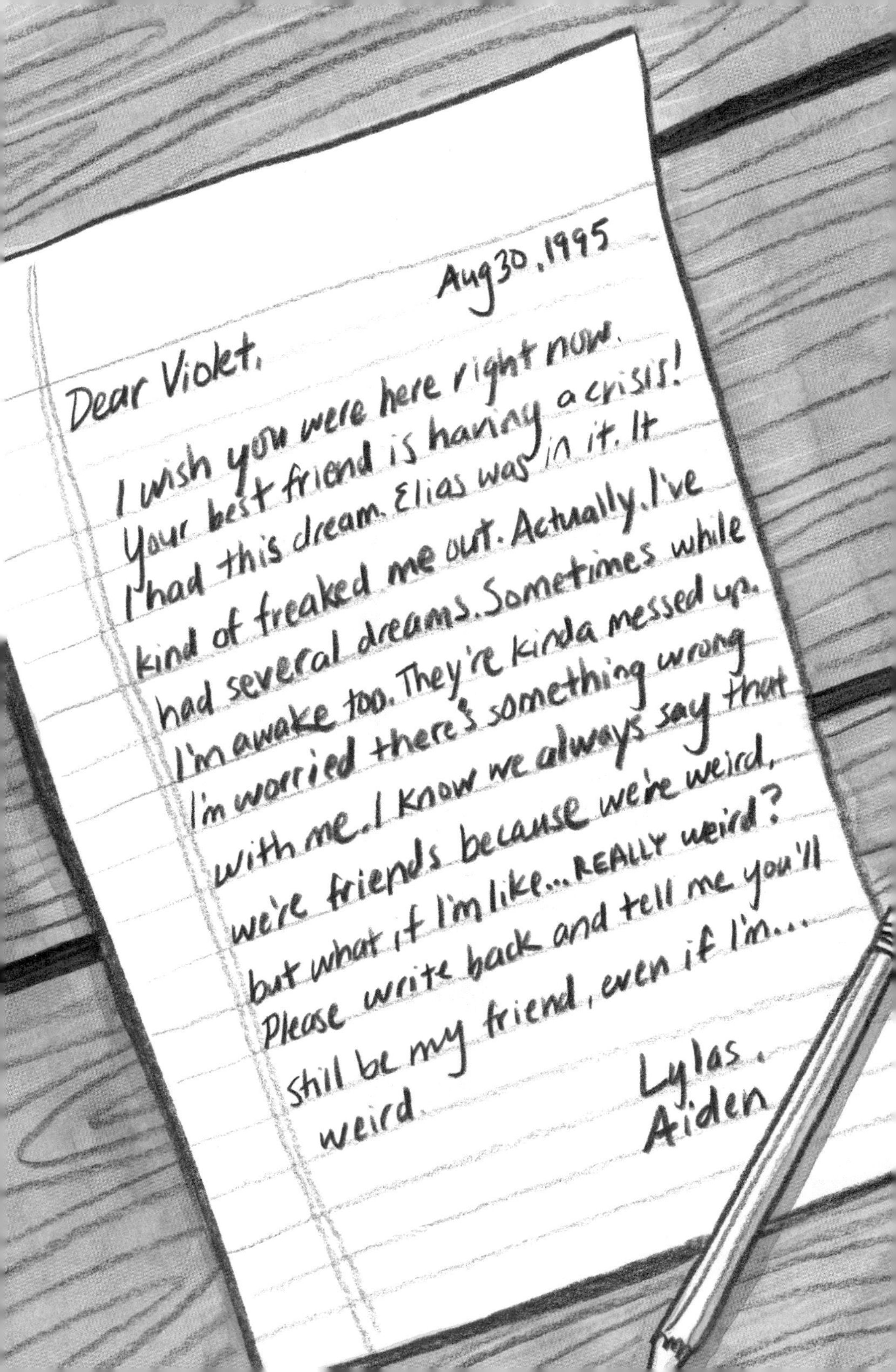

Aug 30, 1995

Dear Violet,

I wish you were here right now.
Your best friend is having a crisis!
I had this dream. Elias was in it. It
kind of freaked me out. Actually, I've
had several dreams. Sometimes while
I'm awake too. They're kinda messed up.
I'm worried there's something wrong
with me. I know we always say that
we're friends because we're weird,
but what if I'm like... REALLY weird?
Please write back and tell me you'll
still be my friend, even if I'm...
weird.

Lylas.
Aiden

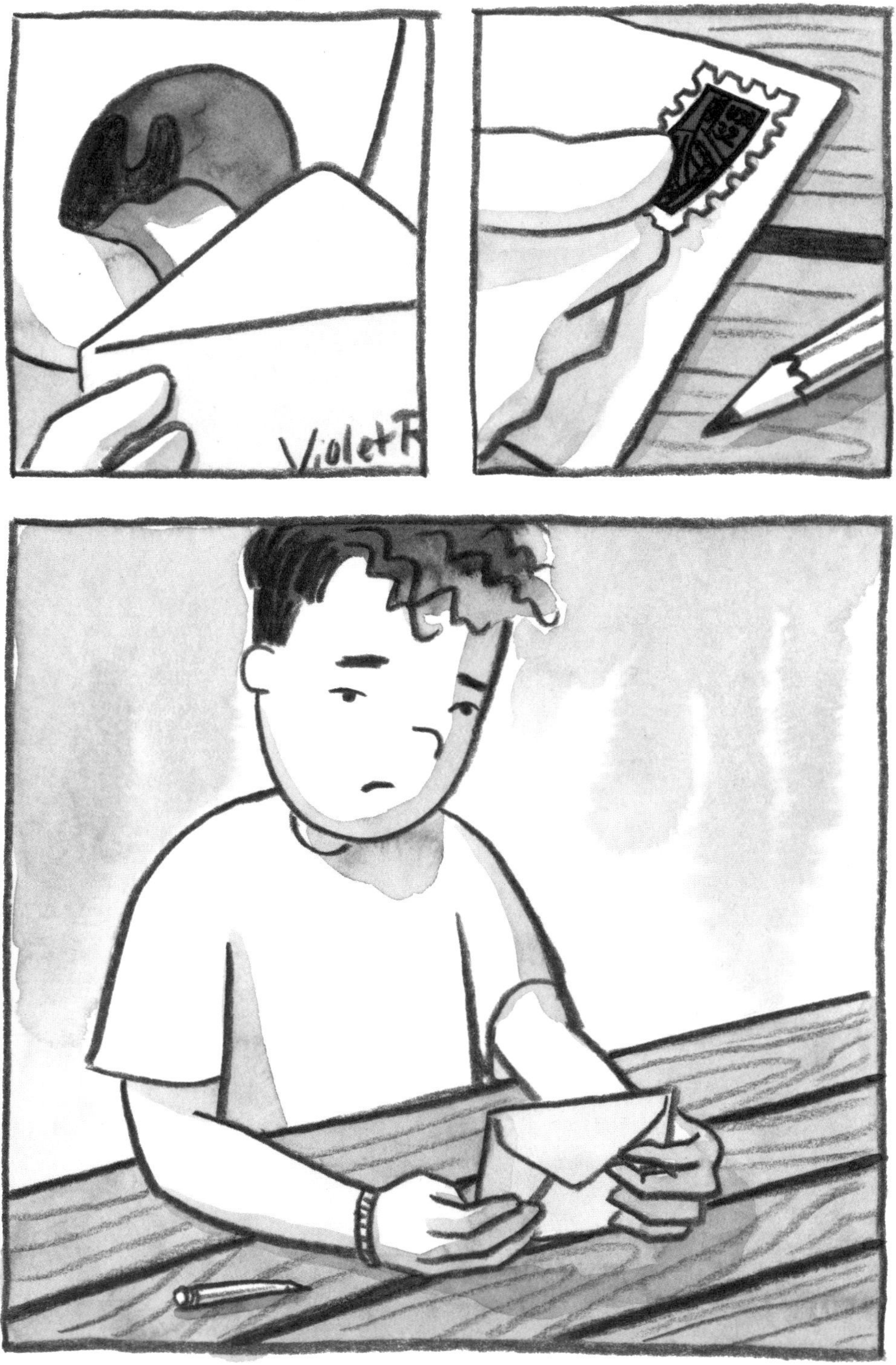
Violet R

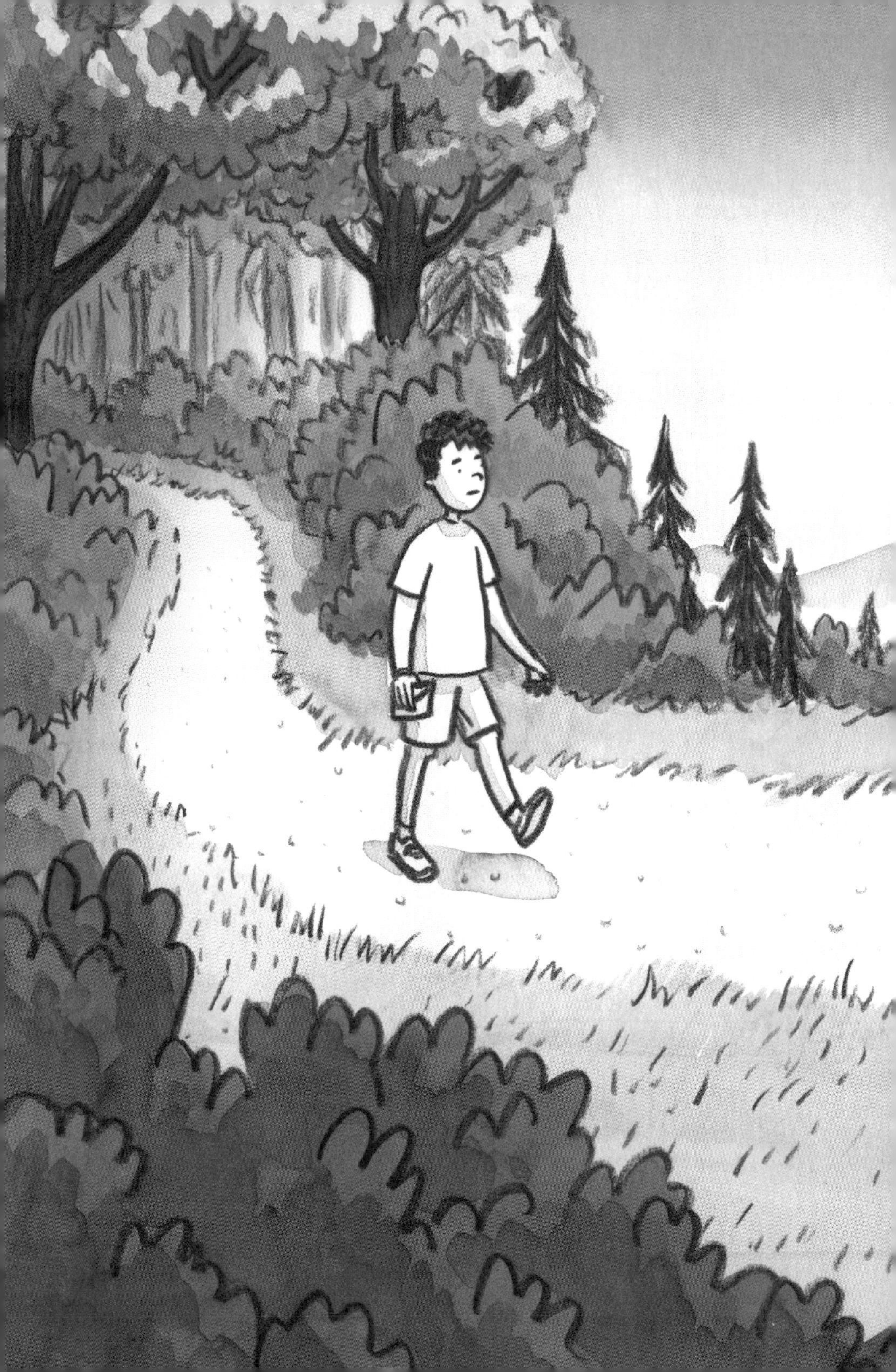

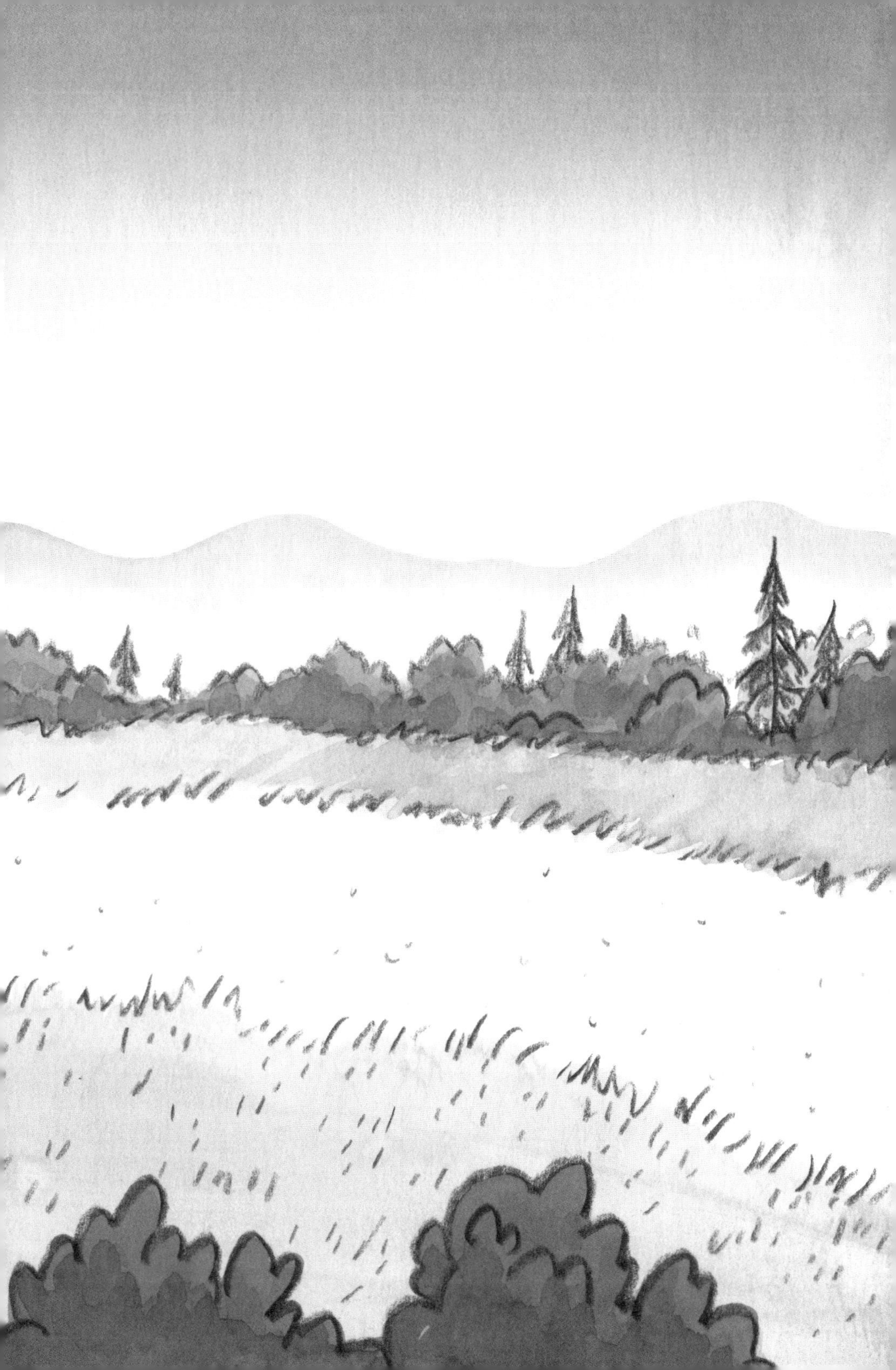

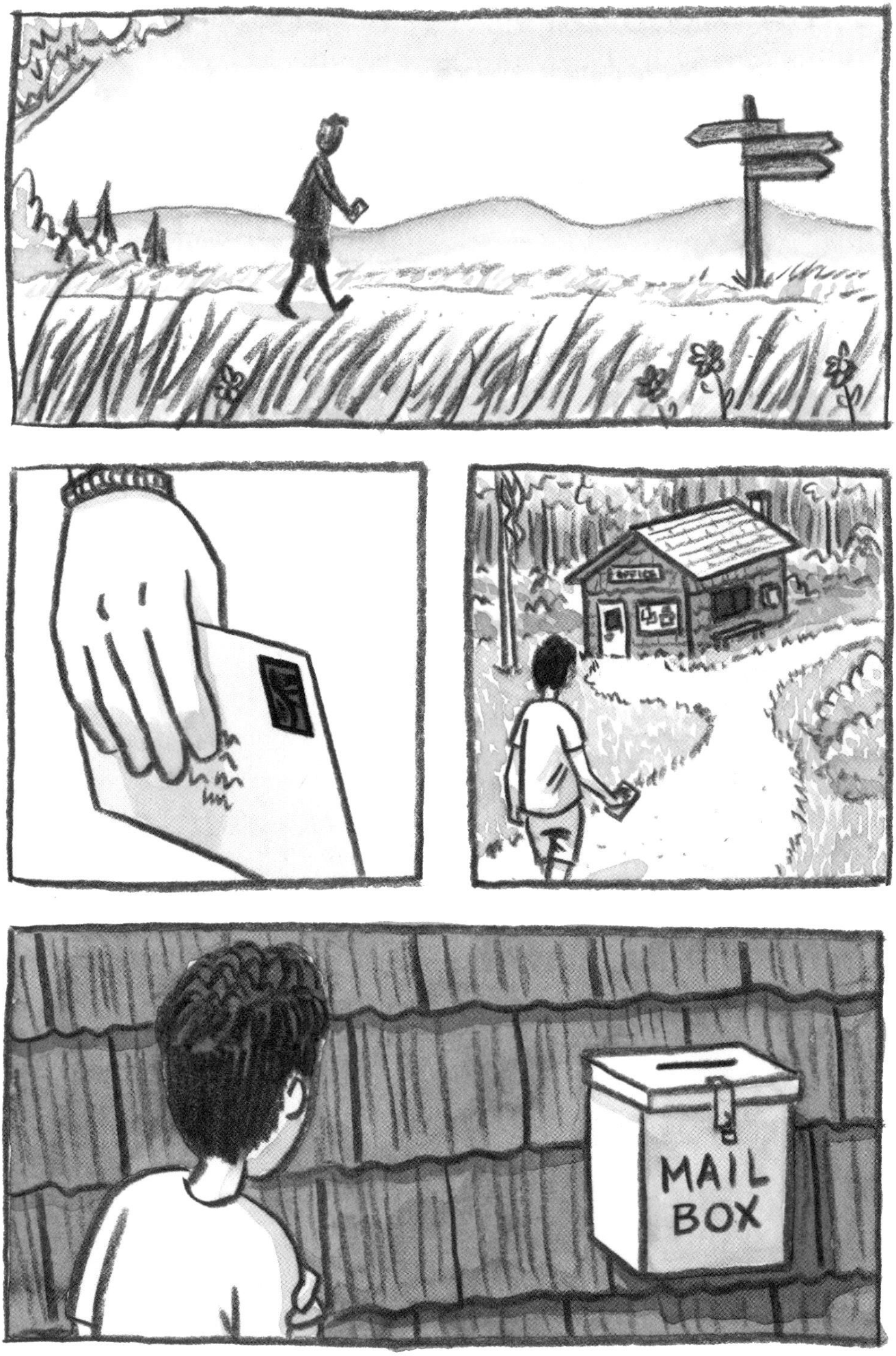
MAIL
BOX

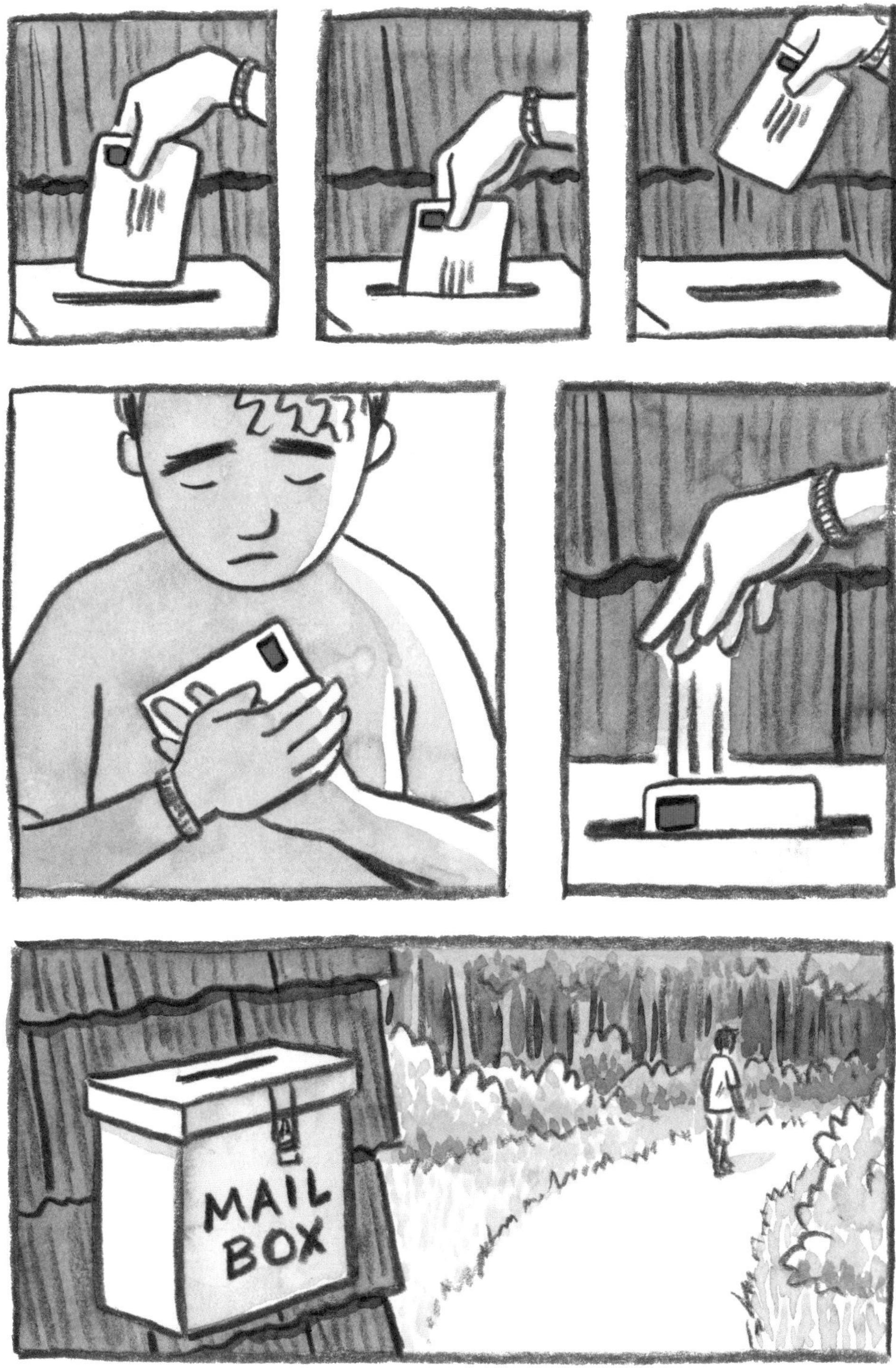
MAIL
BOX

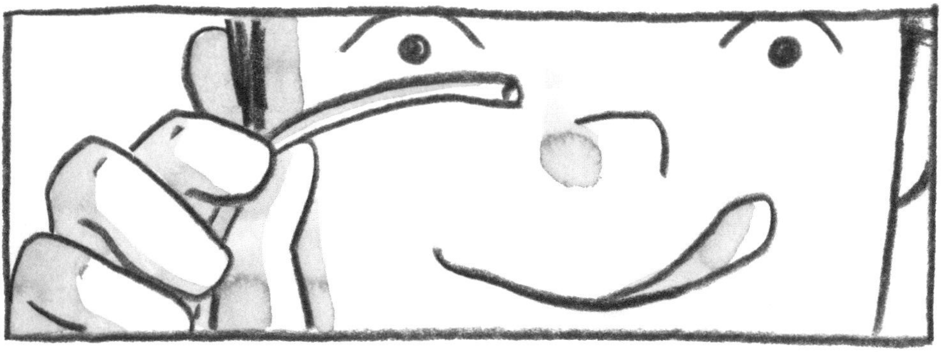

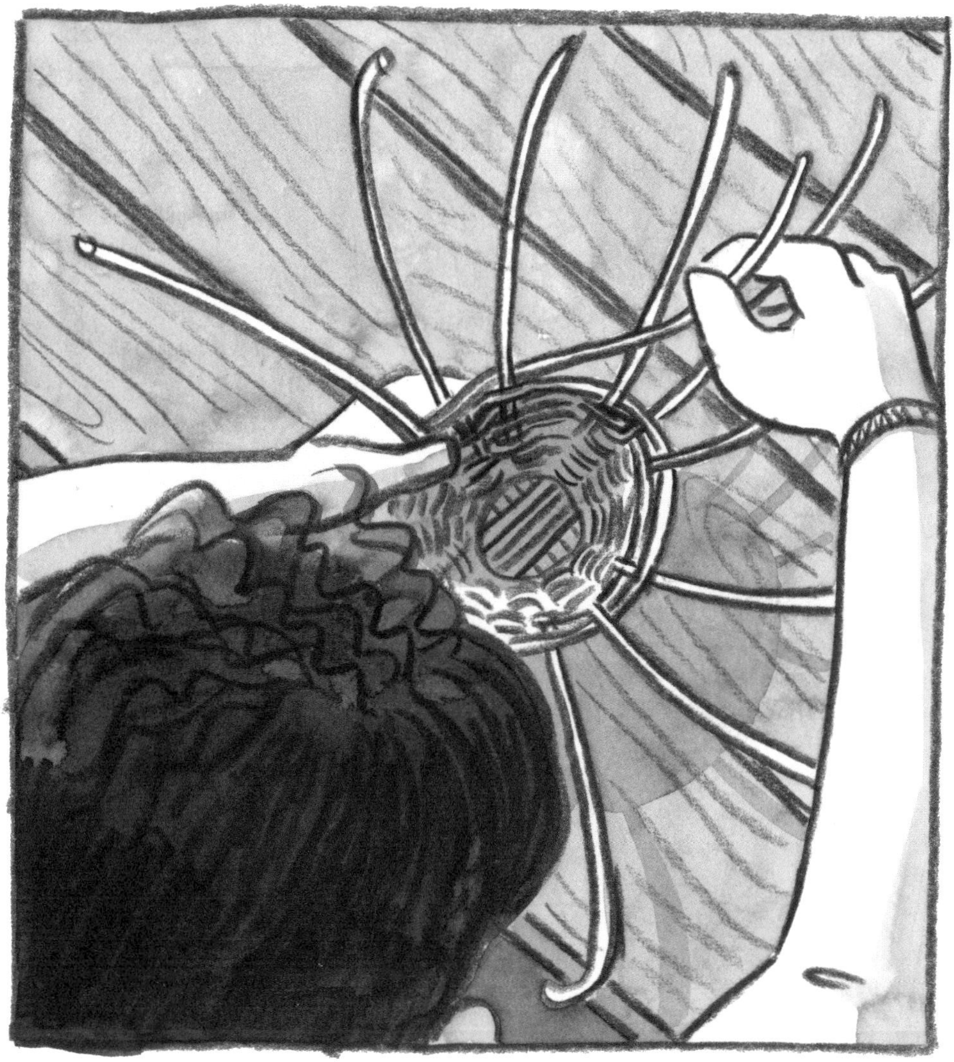

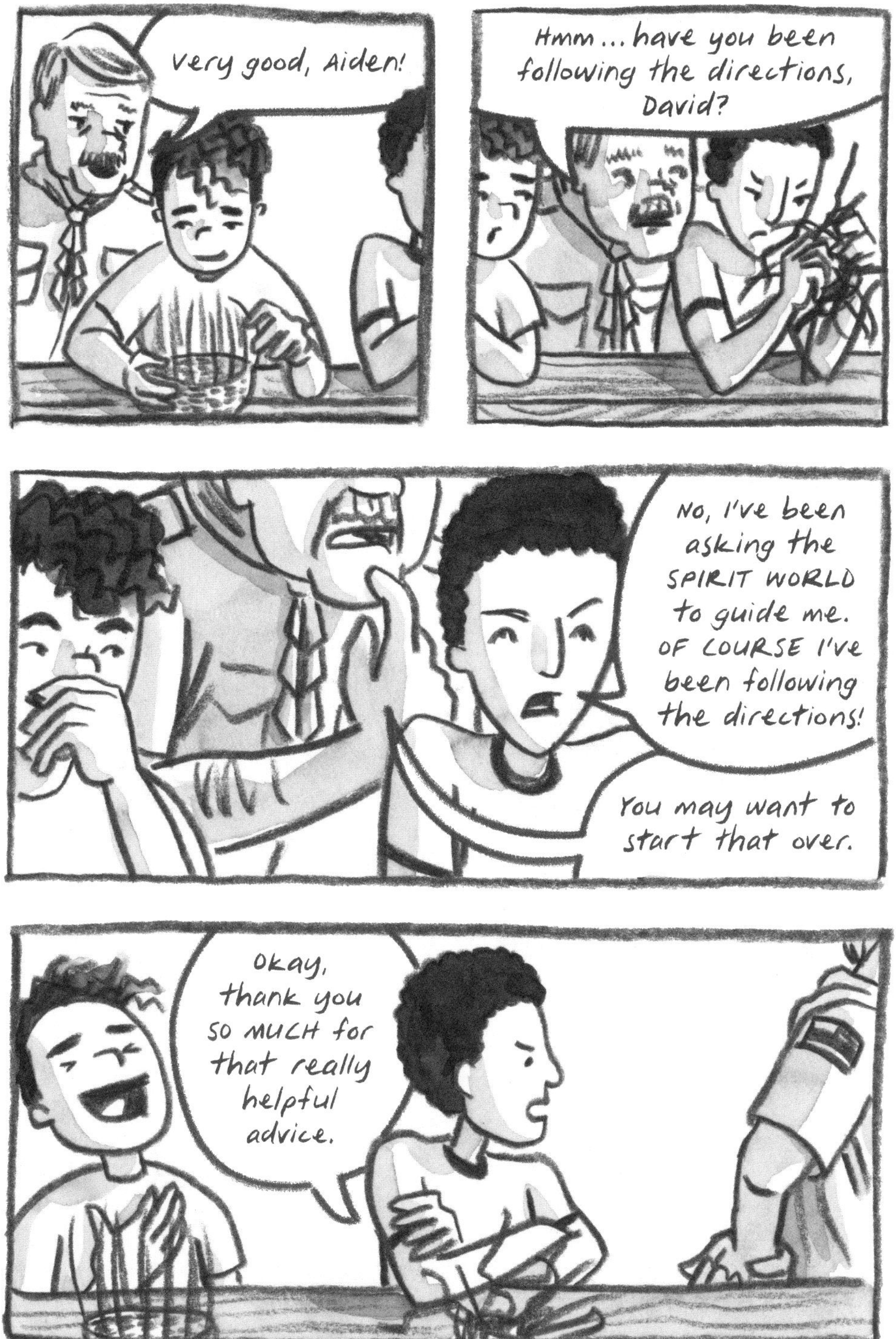
Very good, Aiden!
Hmm... have you been following the directions, David?
No, I've been asking the SPIRIT WORLD to guide me. OF COURSE I've been following the directions!
You may want to start that over.
Okay, thank you so MUCH for that really helpful advice.

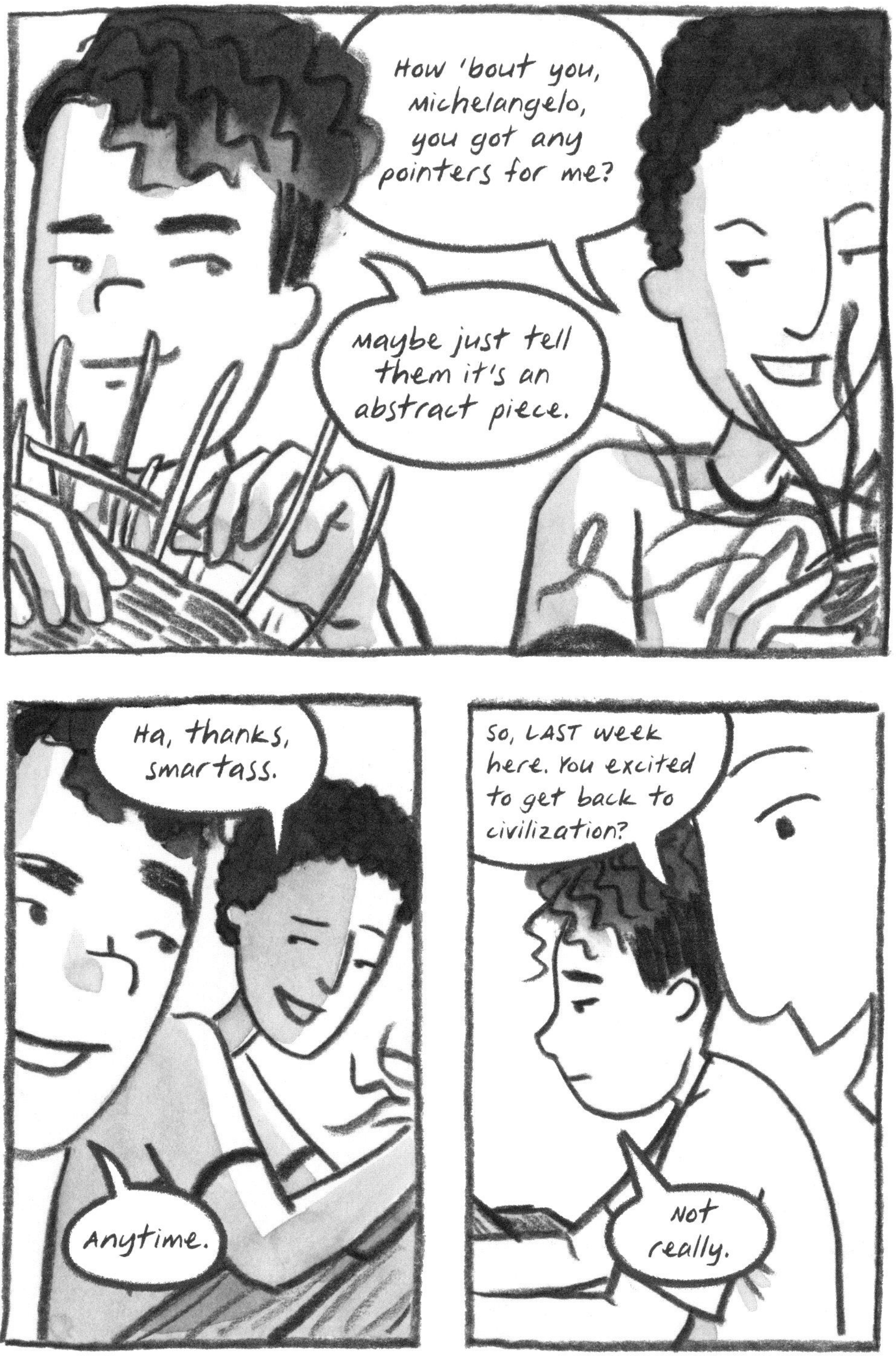
How 'bout you, Michelangelo, you got any pointers for me?
Maybe just tell them it's an abstract piece.
Ha, thanks, smartass.
Anytime.
So, LAST week here. You excited to get back to civilization?
Not really.

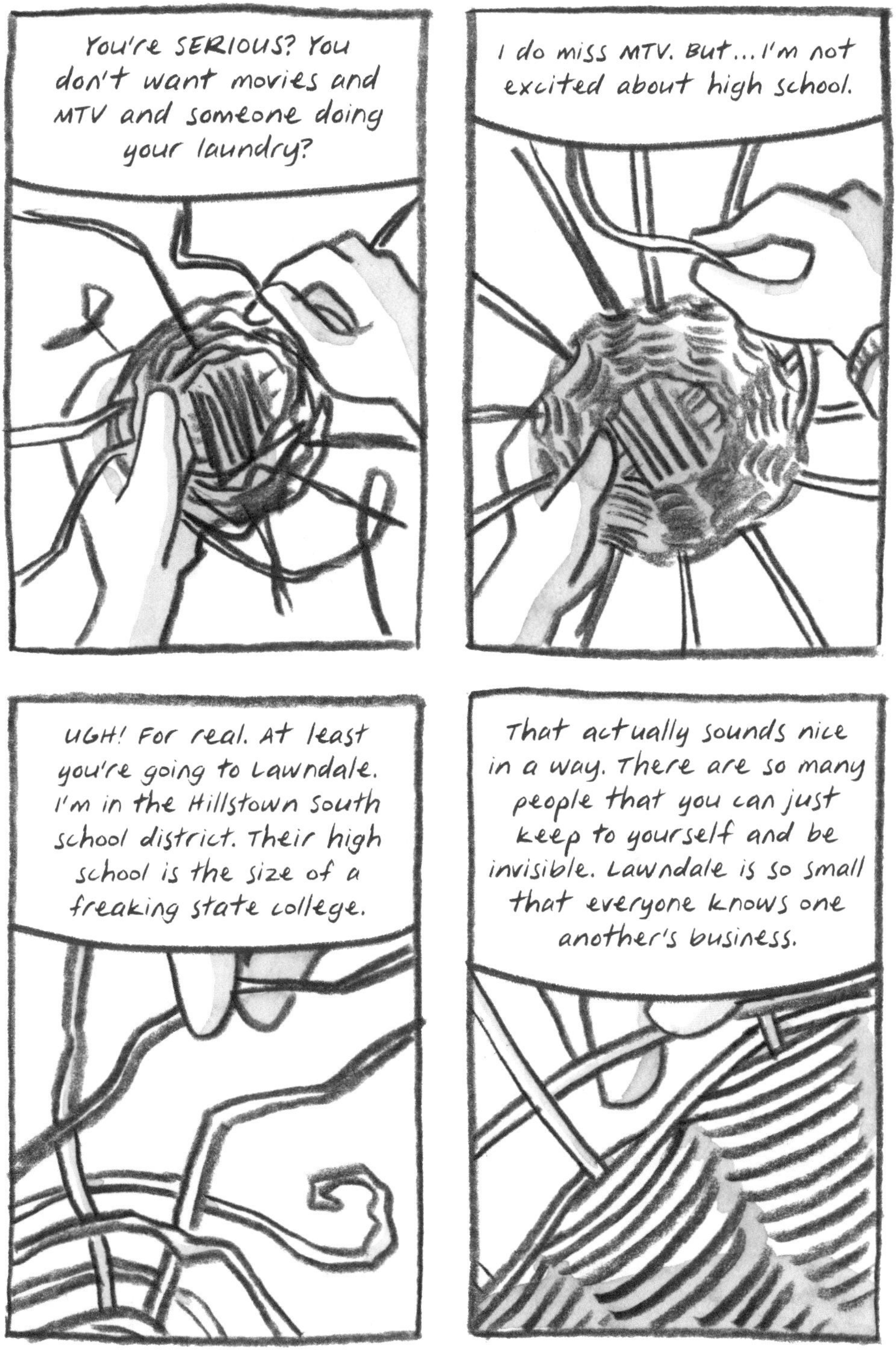
You're SERIOUS? You don't want movies and MTV and someone doing your laundry?
I do miss MTV. But... I'm not excited about high school.
UGH! For real. At least you're going to Lawndale. I'm in the Hillstown South school district. Their high school is the size of a freaking state college.
That actually sounds nice in a way. There are so many people that you can just keep to yourself and be invisible. Lawndale is so small that everyone knows one another's business.

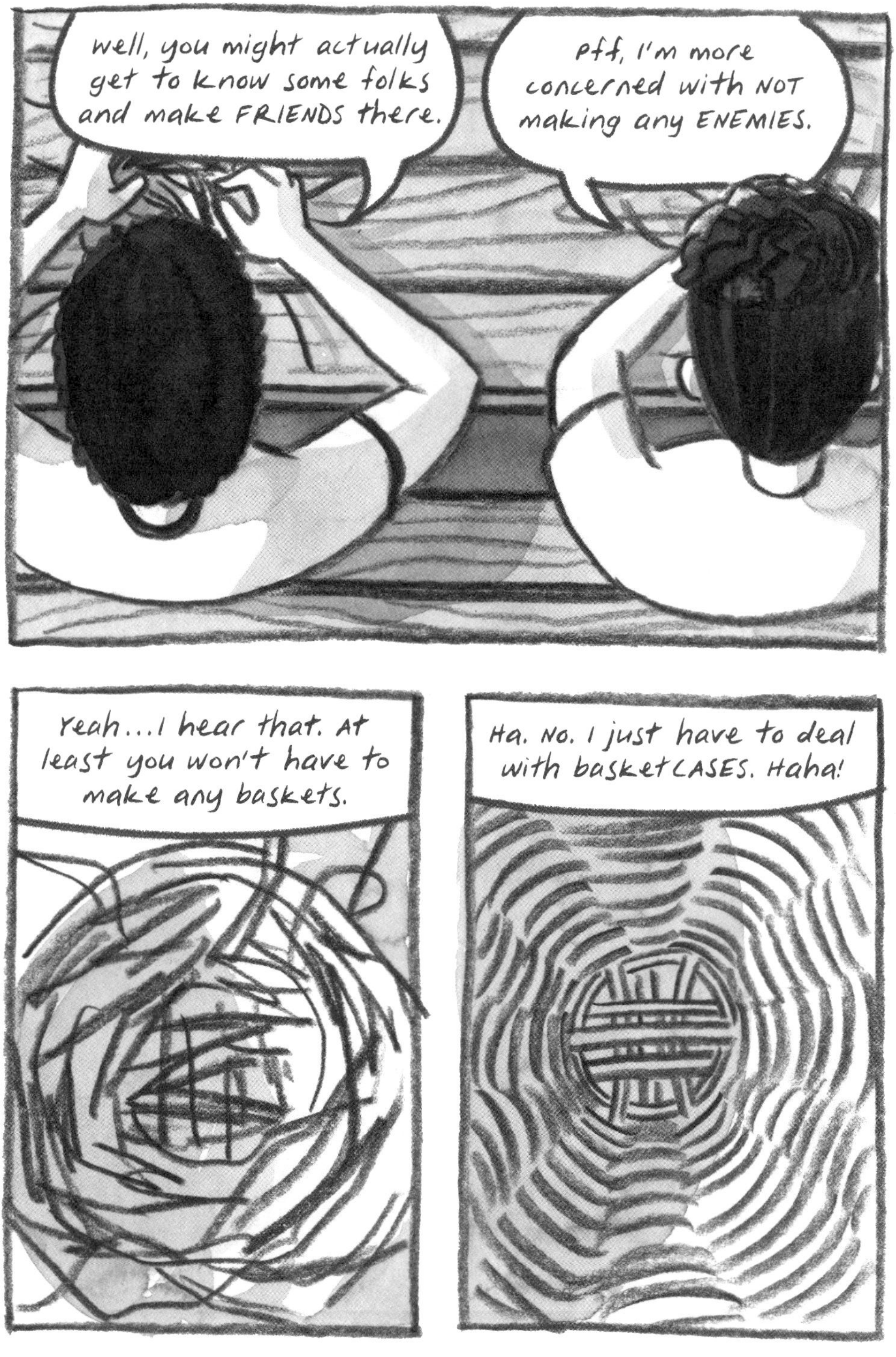
well, you might actually get to know some folks and make FRIENDS there.
pff, I'm more concerned with NOT making any ENEMIES.
Yeah...I hear that. At least you won't have to make any baskets.
Ha. No. I just have to deal with basketCASES. Haha!

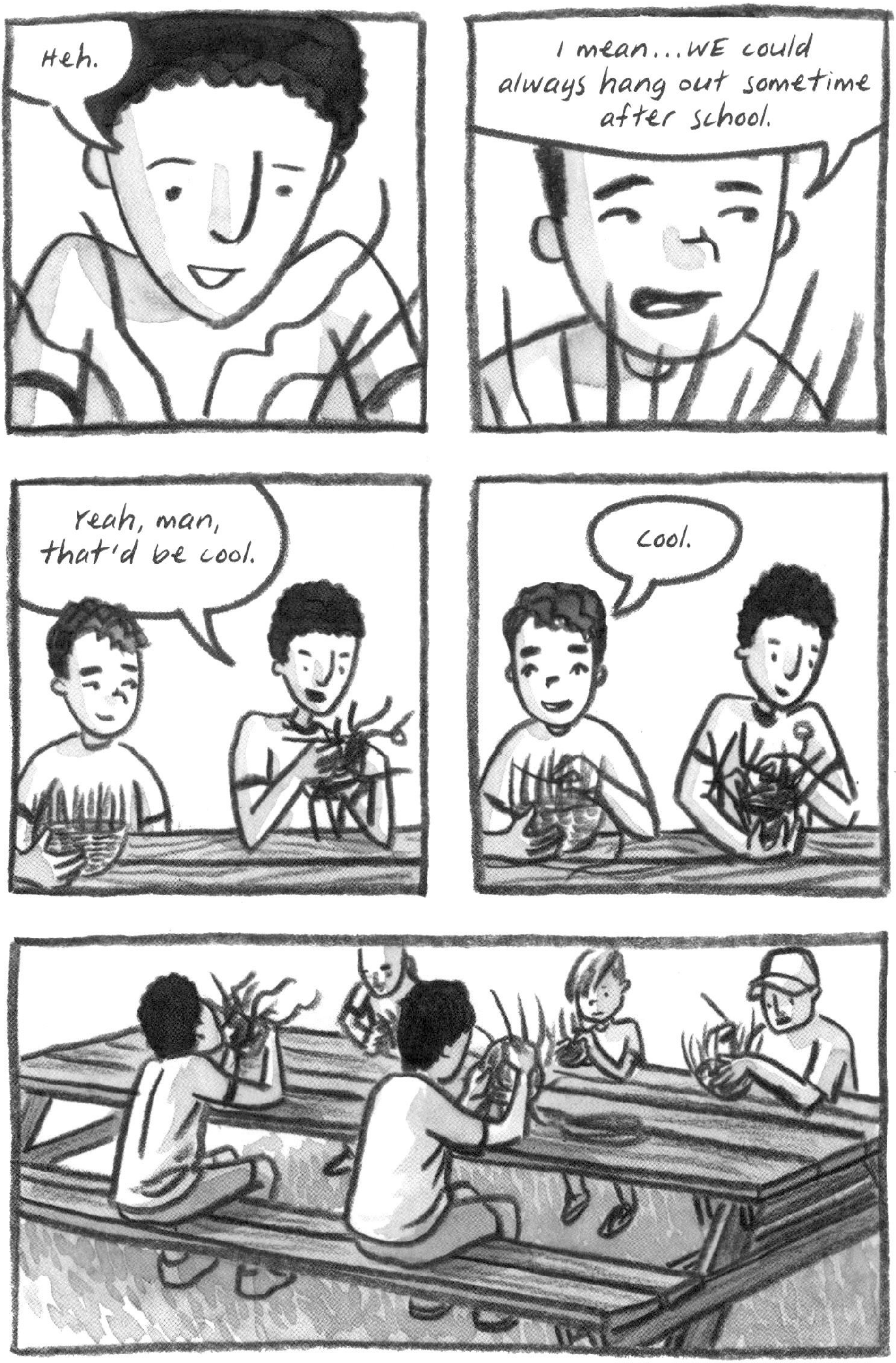
Heh.
I mean...WE could always hang out sometime after school.
Yeah, man, that'd be cool.
Cool.

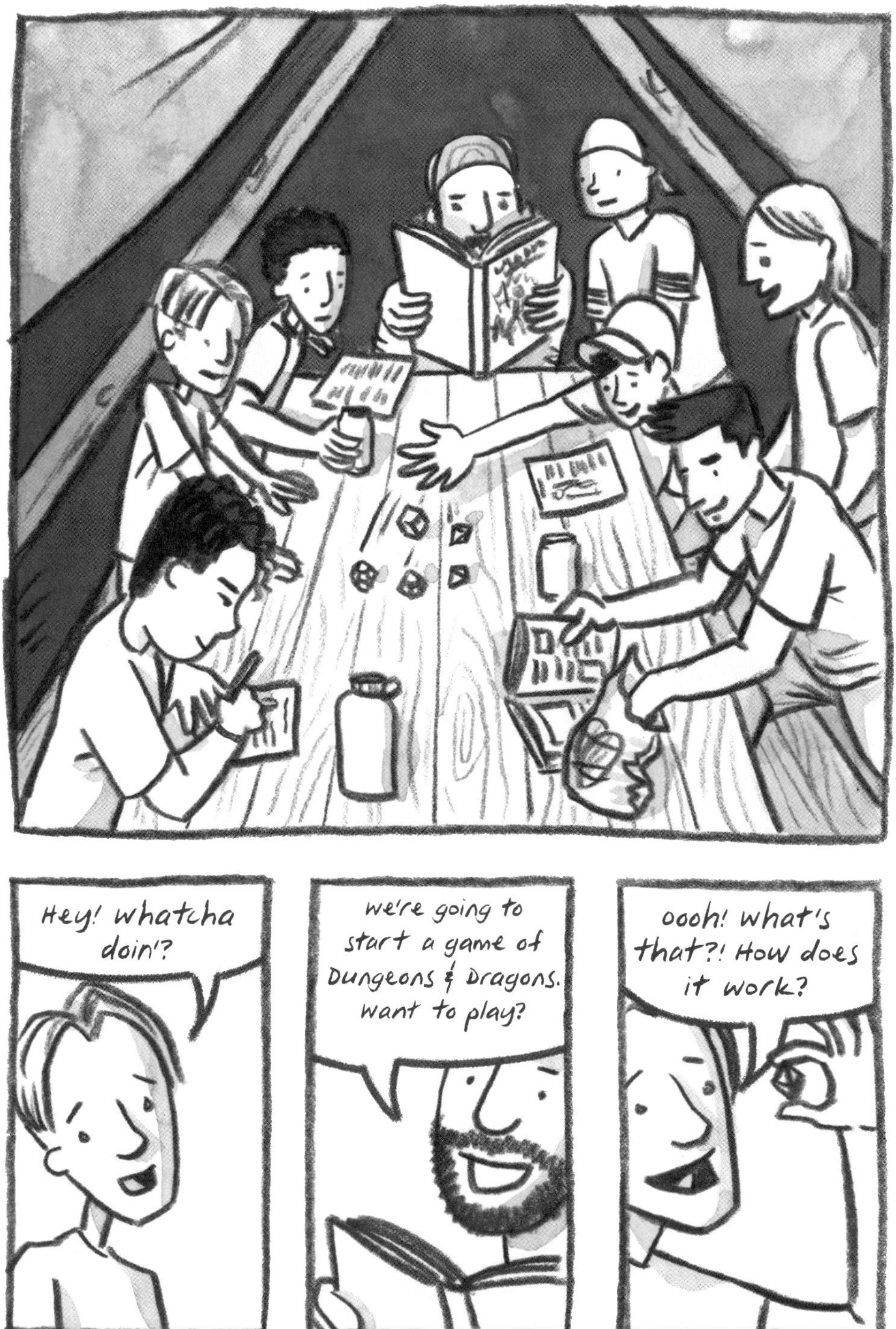
Hey! whatcha doin'?
we're going to start a game of Dungeons & Dragons. want to play?
oooh! what's that?! How does it work?

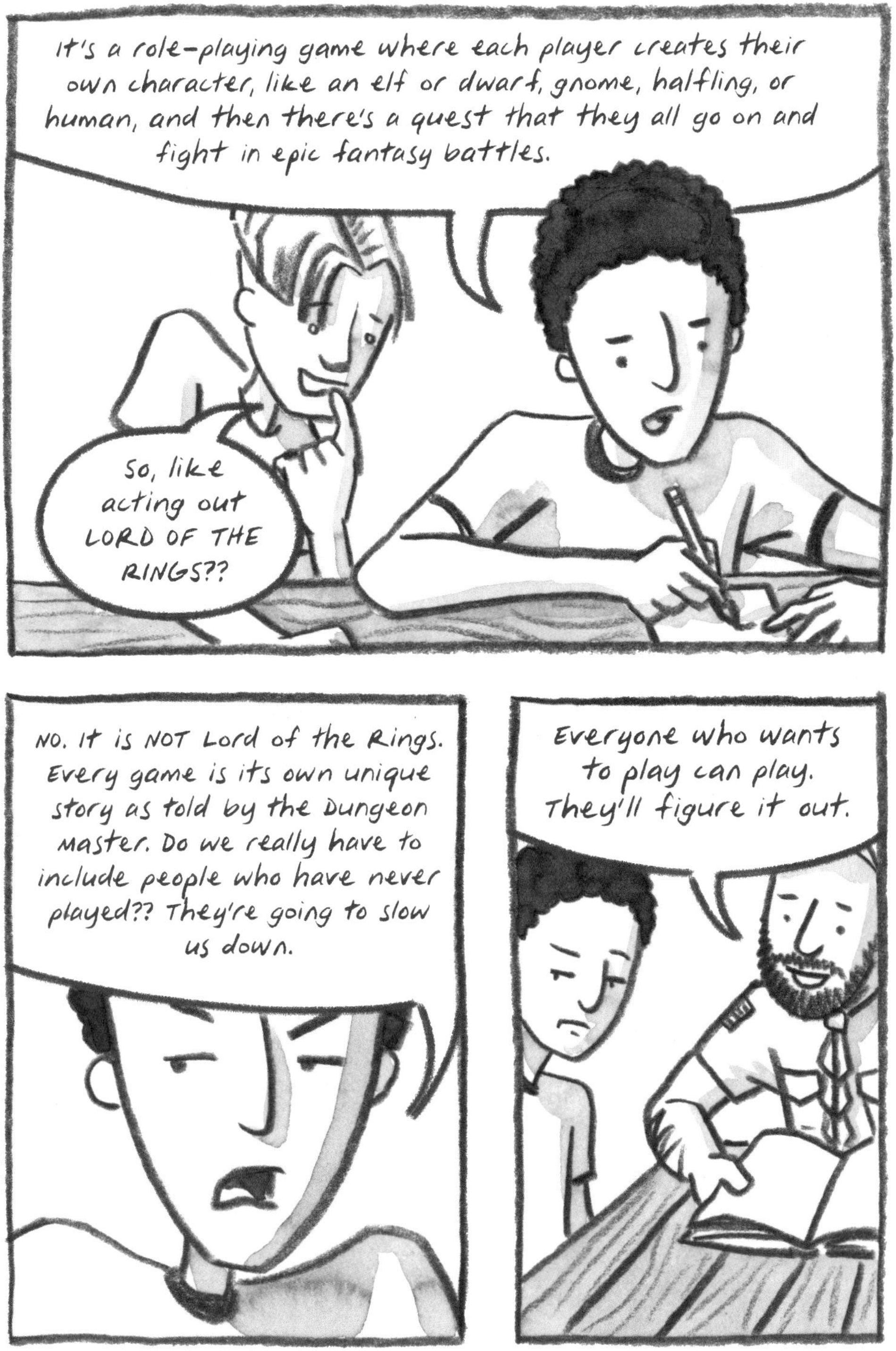
It's a role-playing game where each player creates their own character, like an elf or dwarf, gnome, halfling, or human, and then there's a quest that they all go on and fight in epic fantasy battles.
So, like acting out LORD OF THE RINGS??
No. It is NOT Lord of the Rings. Every game is its own unique story as told by the Dungeon Master. Do we really have to include people who have never played?? They're going to slow us down.
Everyone who wants to play can play. They'll figure it out.

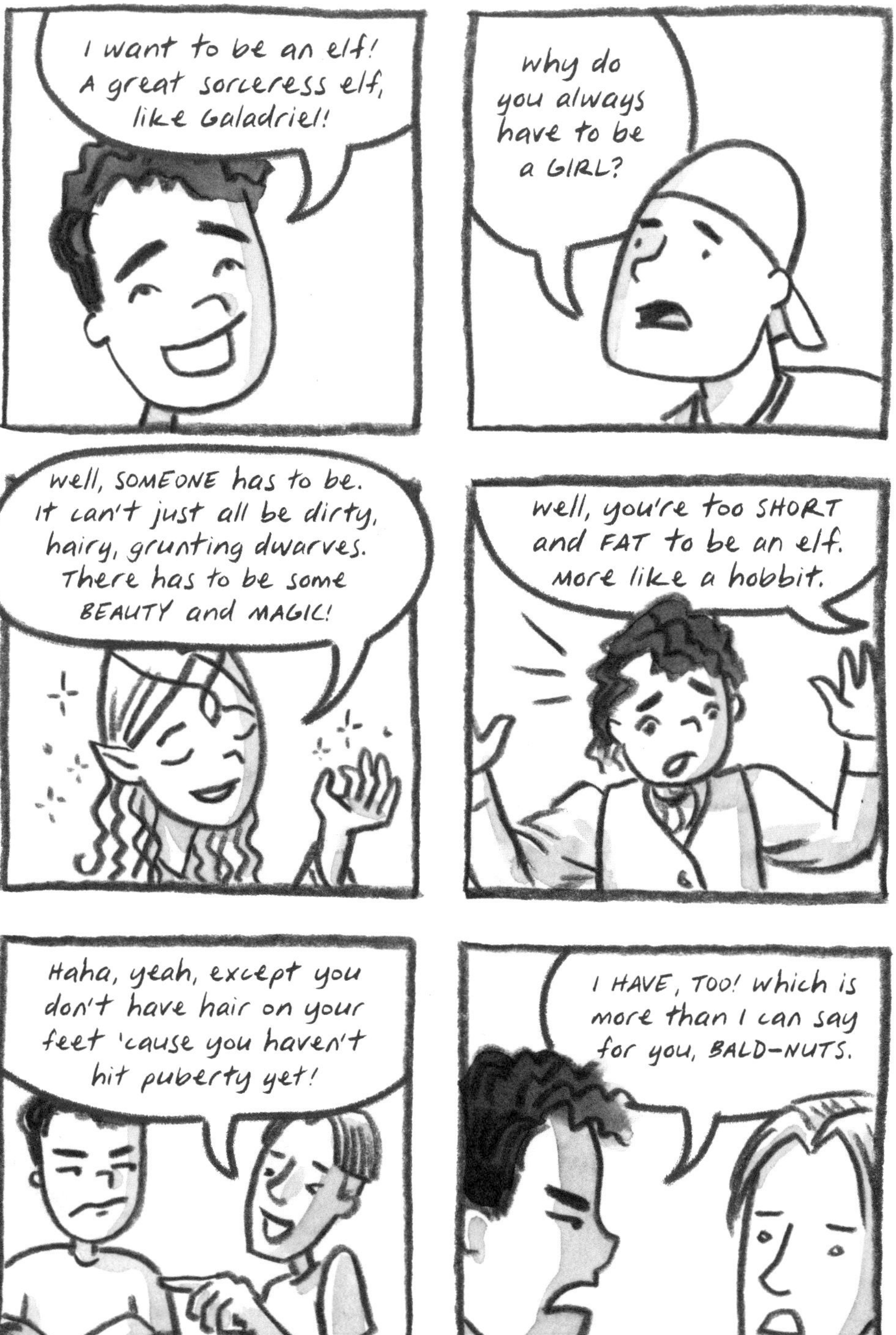
I want to be an elf! A great sorceress elf, like Galadriel!
why do you always have to be a GIRL?
well, SOMEONE has to be. It can't just all be dirty, hairy, grunting dwarves. There has to be some BEAUTY and MAGIC!
well, you're too SHORT and FAT to be an elf. More like a hobbit.
Haha, yeah, except you don't have hair on your feet 'cause you haven't hit puberty yet!
I HAVE, TOO! which is more than I can say for you, BALD-NUTS.

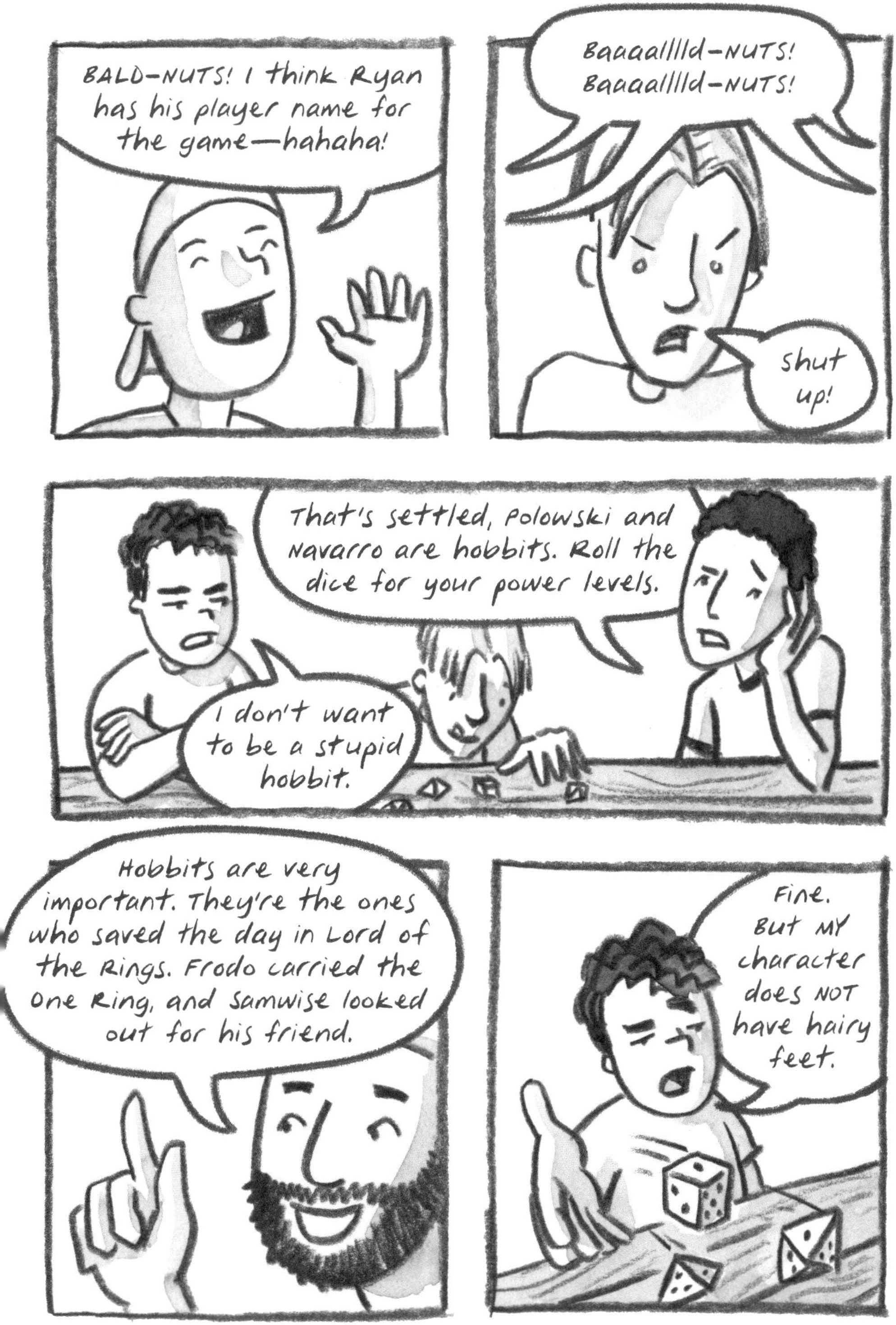
BALD-NUTS! I think Ryan has his player name for the game—hahaha!
Baaaallllld-NUTS! Baaaallllld-NUTS!
Shut up!
That's settled, Polowski and Navarro are hobbits. Roll the dice for your power levels.
I don't want to be a stupid hobbit.
Hobbits are very important. They're the ones who saved the day in Lord of the Rings. Frodo carried the One Ring, and Samwise looked out for his friend.
Fine. But MY character does NOT have hairy feet.

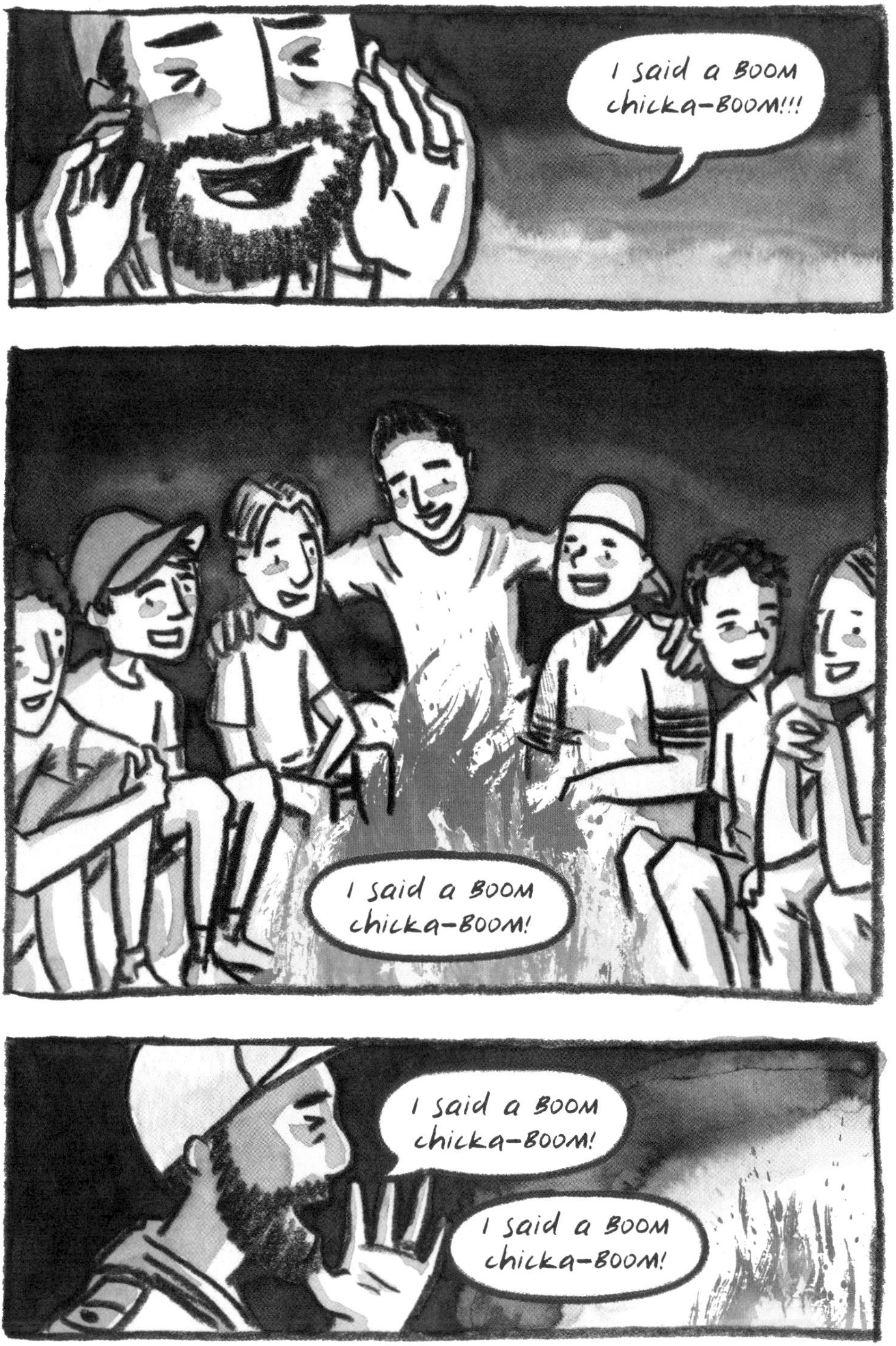
I said a BOOM chicka-BOOM!!!
I said a BOOM chicka-BOOM!
I said a BOOM chicka-BOOM!
I said a BOOM chicka-BOOM!

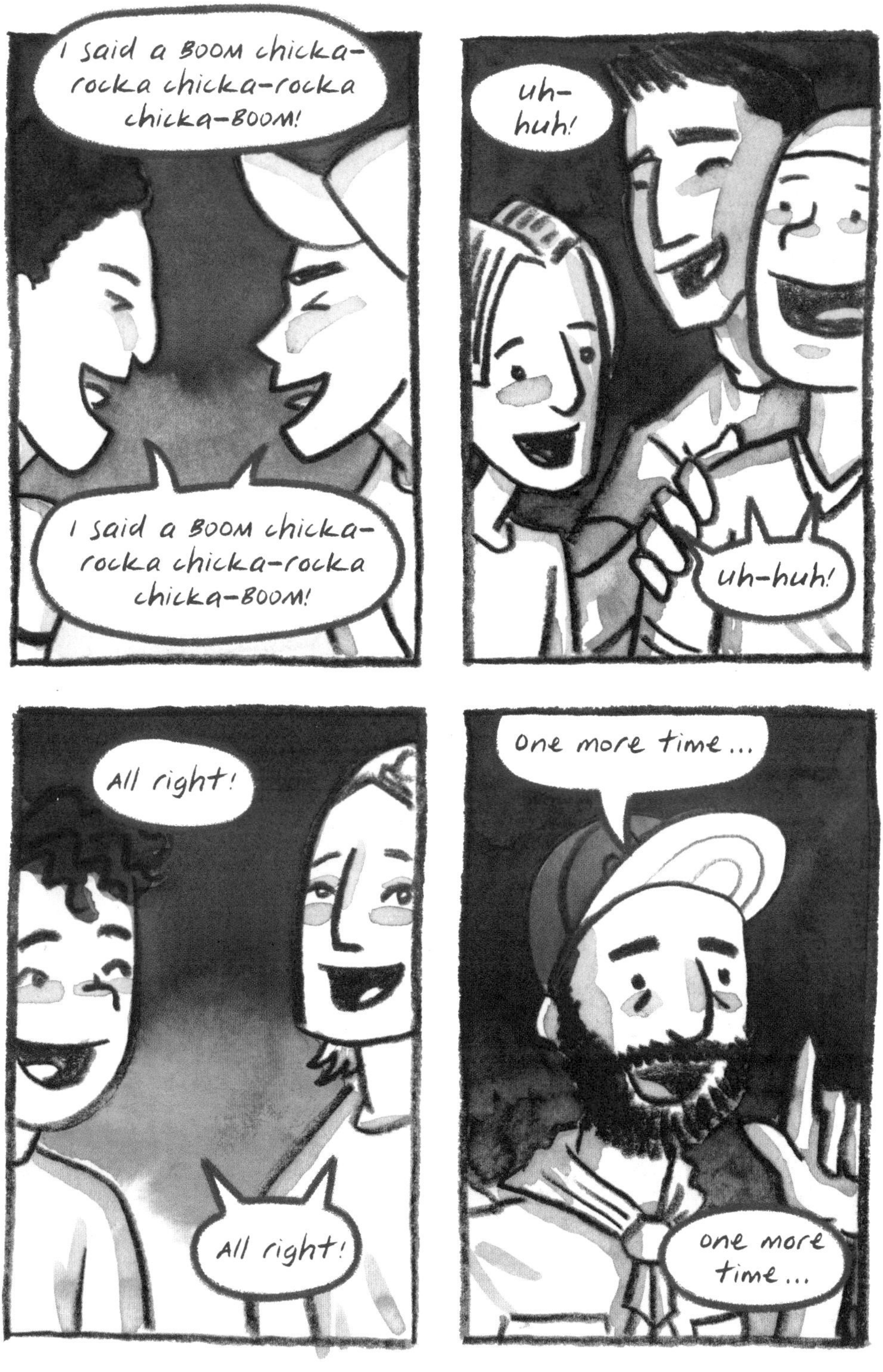
I said a BOOM chicka-rocka chicka-rocka chicka-BOOM!
I said a BOOM chicka-rocka chicka-rocka chicka-BOOM!
uh-huh!
uh-huh!
All right!
All right!
One more time...
one more time...

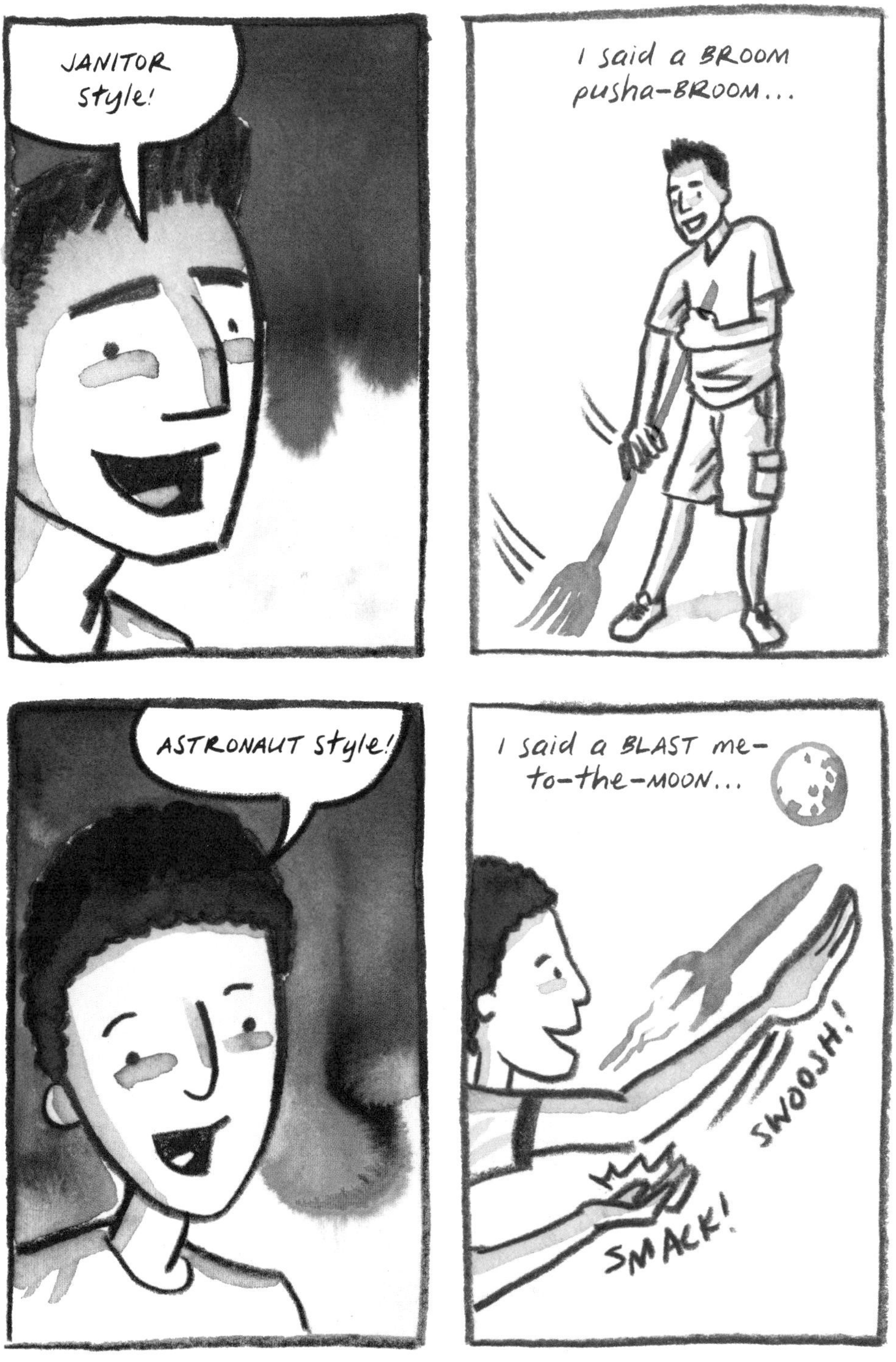
JANITOR style!
I said a BROOM pusha-BROOM...
ASTRONAUT style!
I said a BLAST me-to-the-MOON...
SWOOSH!
SMACK!

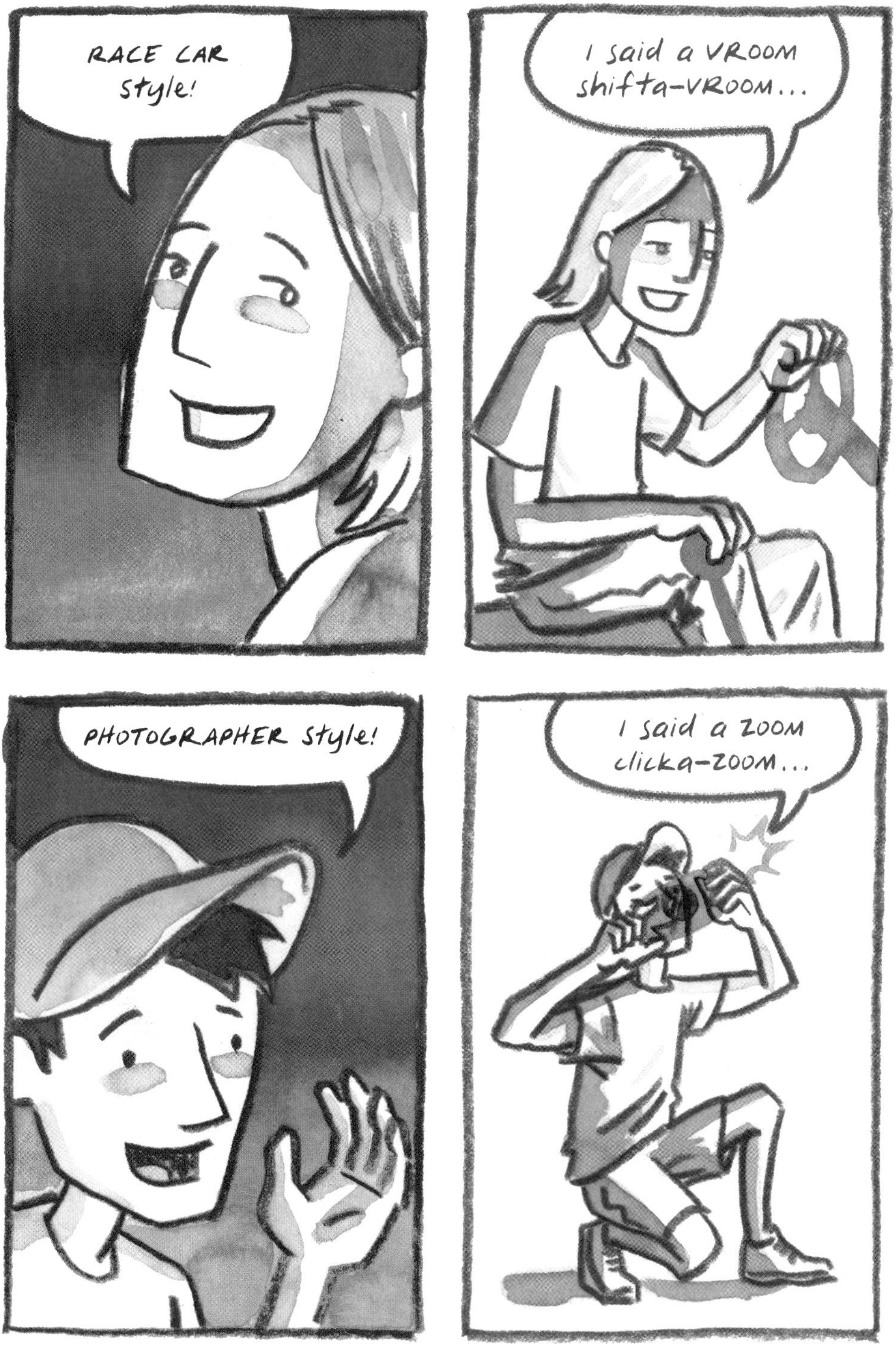
RACE CAR style!
I said a VROOM shifta-VROOM...
PHOTOGRAPHER style!
I said a ZOOM clicka-ZOOM...

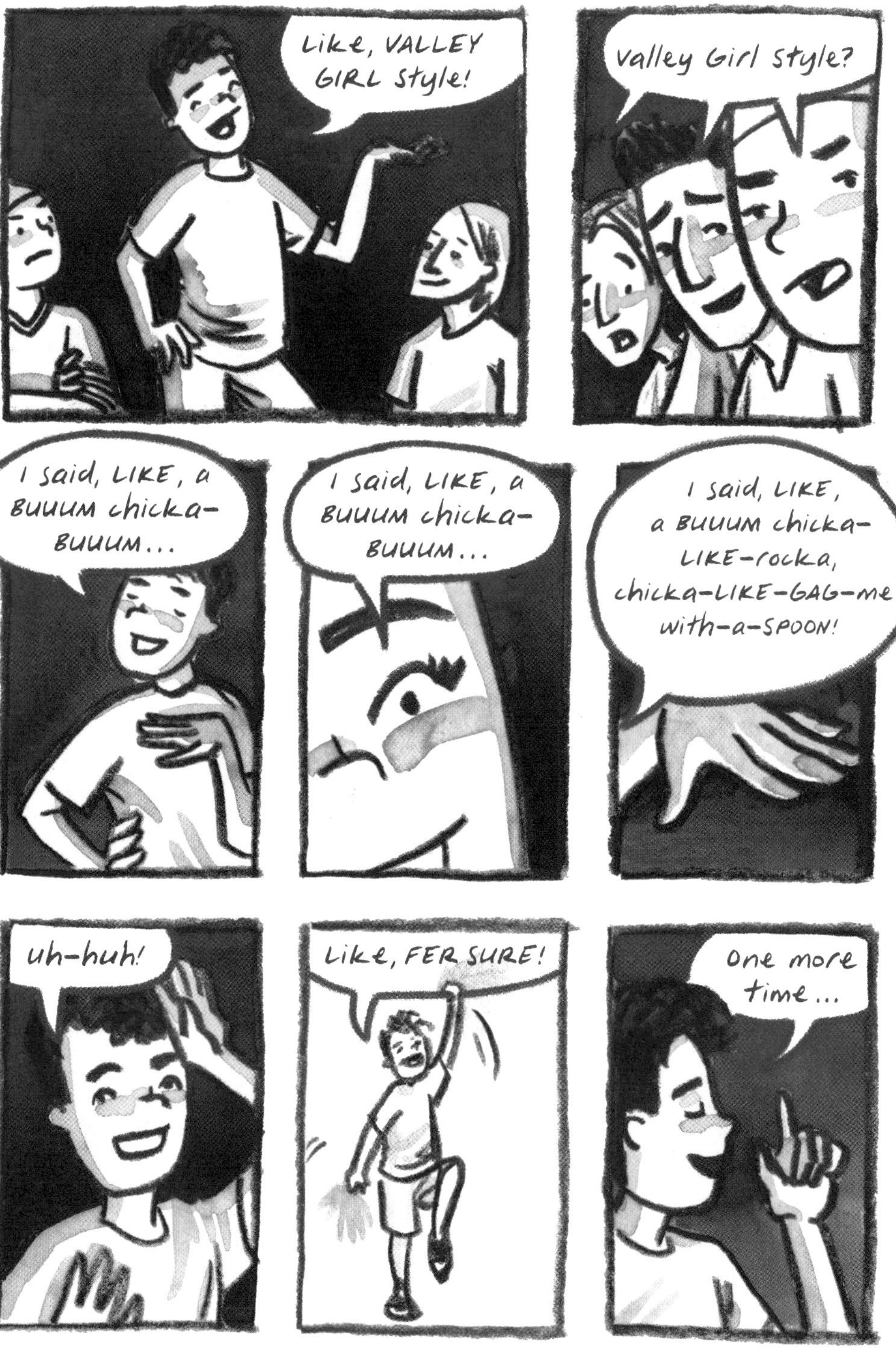
Like, VALLEY GIRL style!
Valley Girl style?
I said, LIKE, a BUUUM chicka-BUUUM...
I said, LIKE, a BUUUM chicka-BUUUM...
I said, LIKE, a BUUUM chicka-LIKE-rocka, chicka-LIKE-GAG-me with-a-SPOON!
uh-huh!
Like, FER SURE!
One more time...

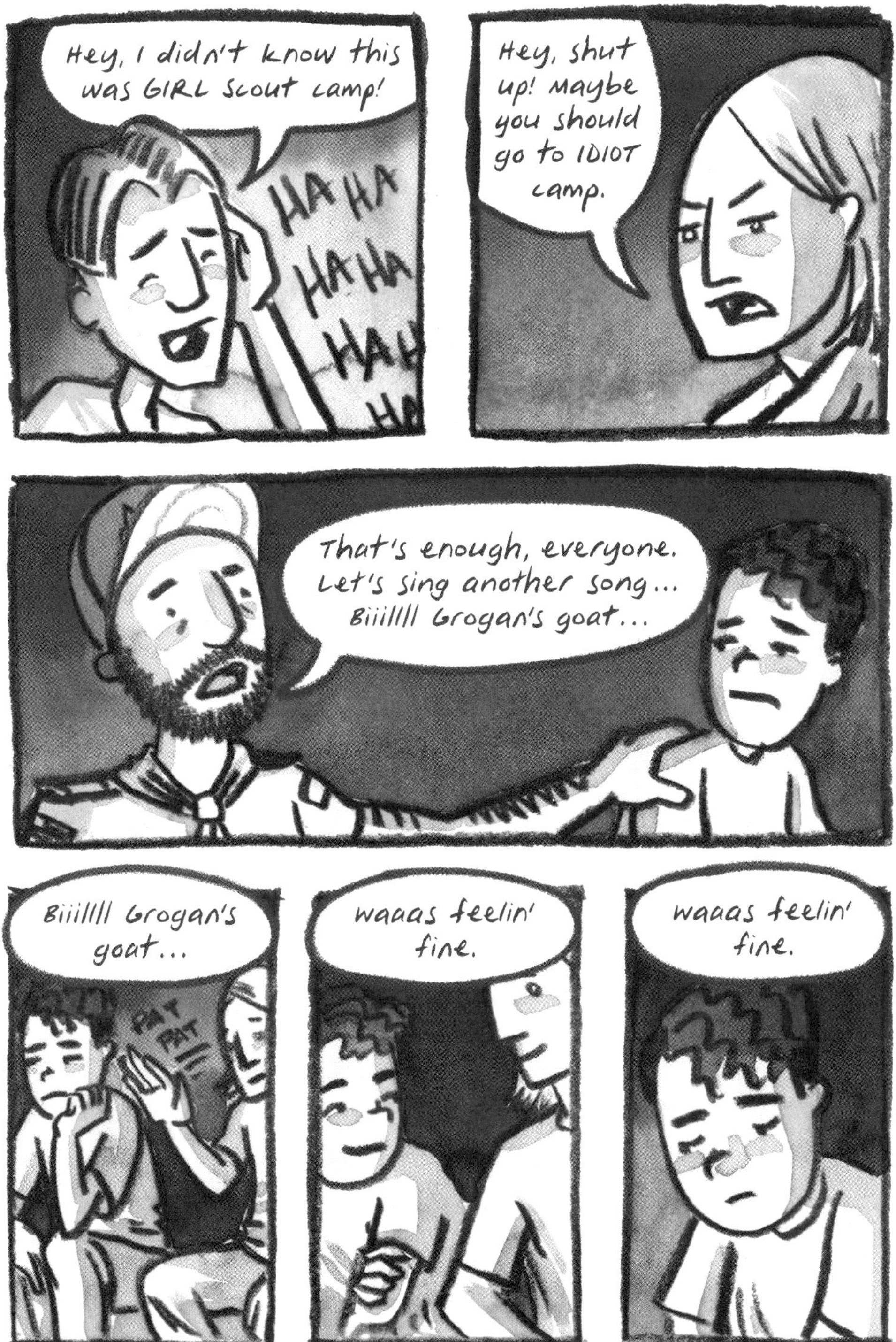
Hey, I didn't know this was GIRL Scout camp!
HA HA HA HA HA
Hey, shut up! Maybe you should go to IDIOT camp.
That's enough, everyone. Let's sing another song... Biiillll Grogan's goat...
Biiillll Grogan's goat...
PAT PAT
waaas feelin' fine.
waaas feelin' fine.

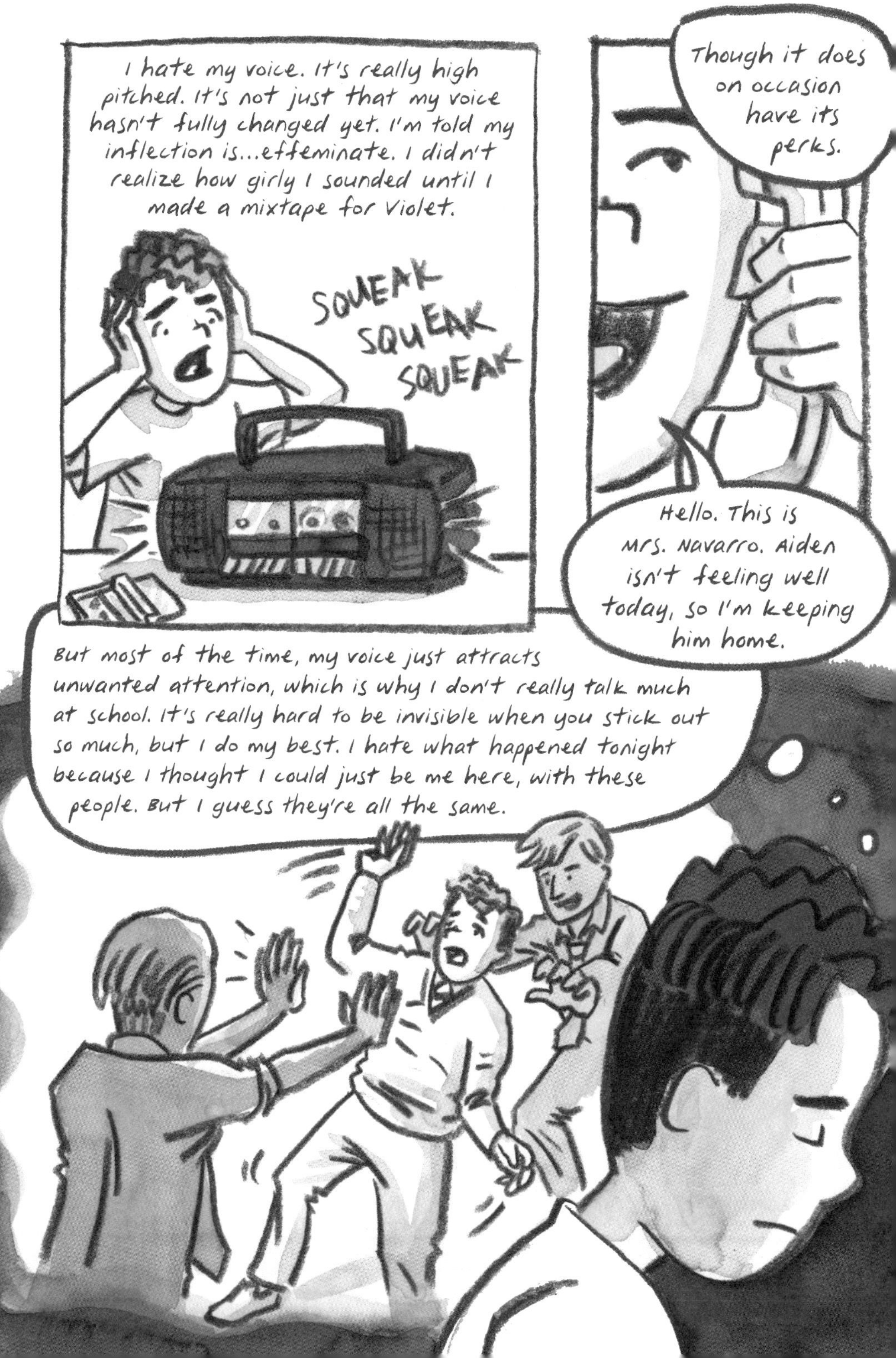
I hate my voice. It's really high pitched. It's not just that my voice hasn't fully changed yet. I'm told my inflection is...effeminate. I didn't realize how girly I sounded until I made a mixtape for Violet.
SQUEAK SQUEAK SQUEAK
Though it does on occasion have its perks.
Hello. This is Mrs. Navarro. Aiden isn't feeling well today, so I'm keeping him home.
But most of the time, my voice just attracts unwanted attention, which is why I don't really talk much at school. It's really hard to be invisible when you stick out so much, but I do my best. I hate what happened tonight because I thought I could just be me here, with these people. But I guess they're all the same.

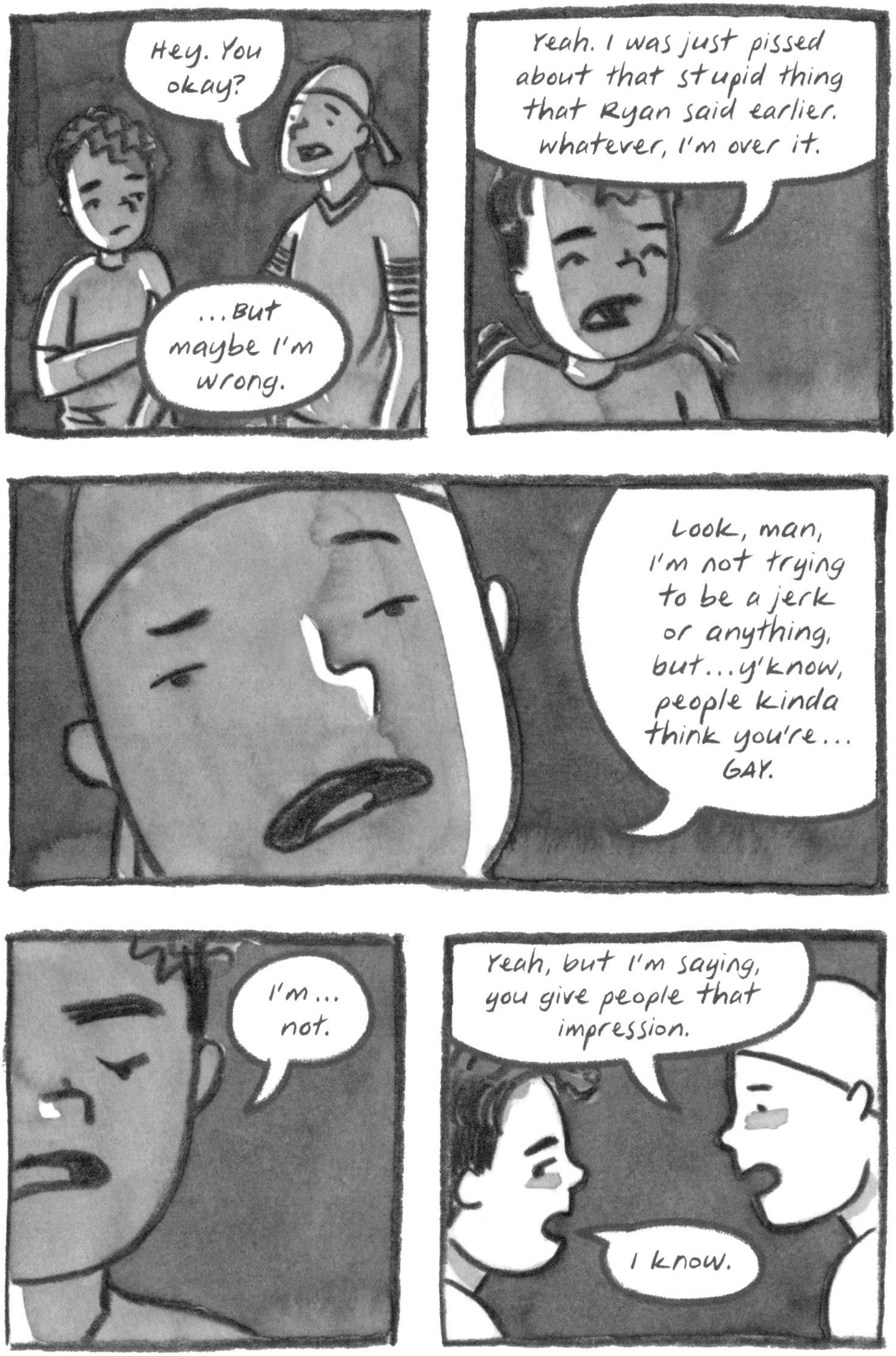
Hey. You okay?
...But maybe I'm wrong.
Yeah. I was just pissed about that stupid thing that Ryan said earlier. whatever, I'm over it.
Look, man, I'm not trying to be a jerk or anything, but...y'know, people kinda think you're... GAY.
I'm... not.
Yeah, but I'm saying, you give people that impression.
I know.

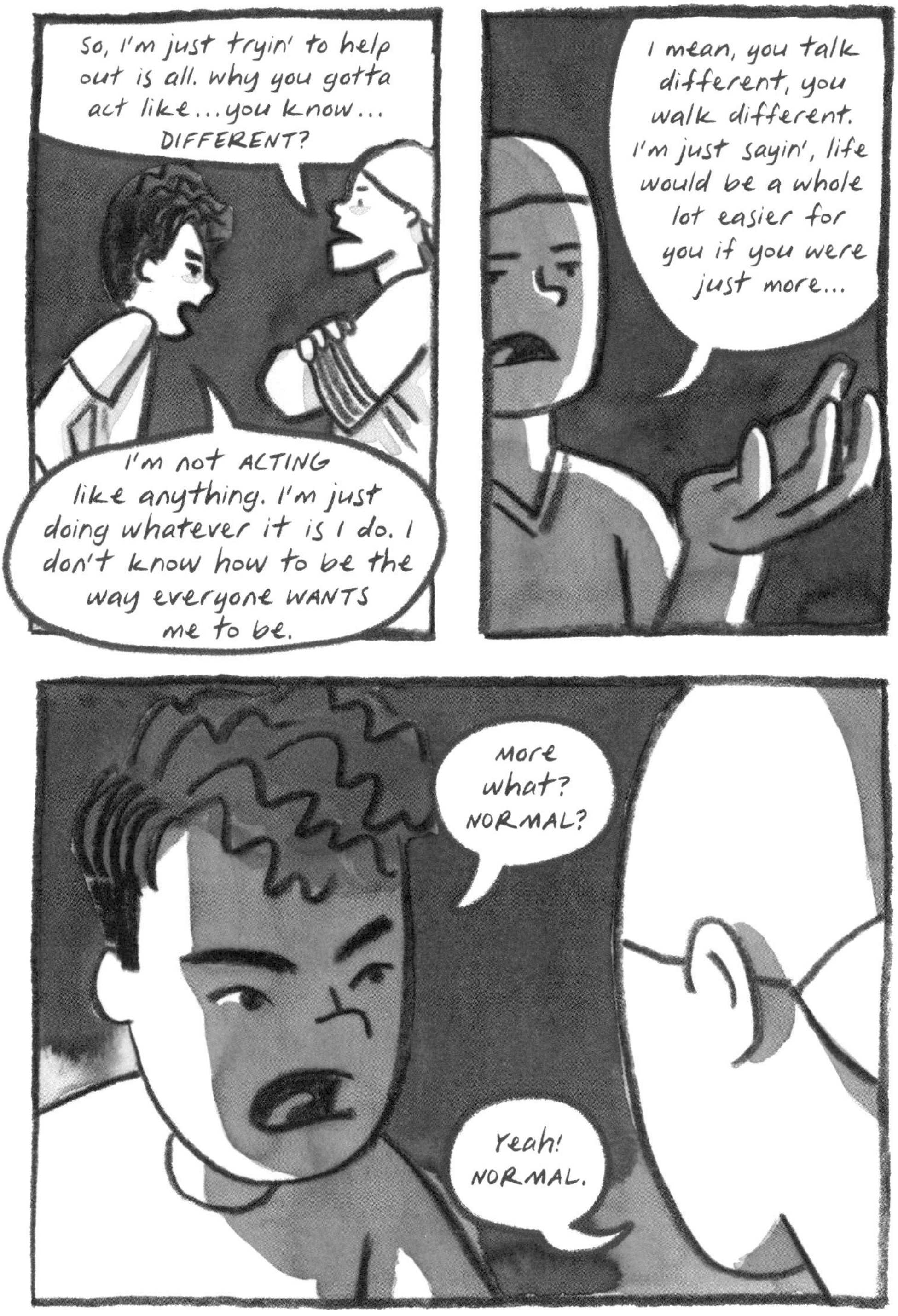
So, I'm just tryin' to help out is all. why you gotta act like... you know... DIFFERENT?
I'm not ACTING like anything. I'm just doing whatever it is I do. I don't know how to be the way everyone WANTS me to be.
I mean, you talk different, you walk different. I'm just sayin', life would be a whole lot easier for you if you were just more...
More what? NORMAL?
Yeah! NORMAL.

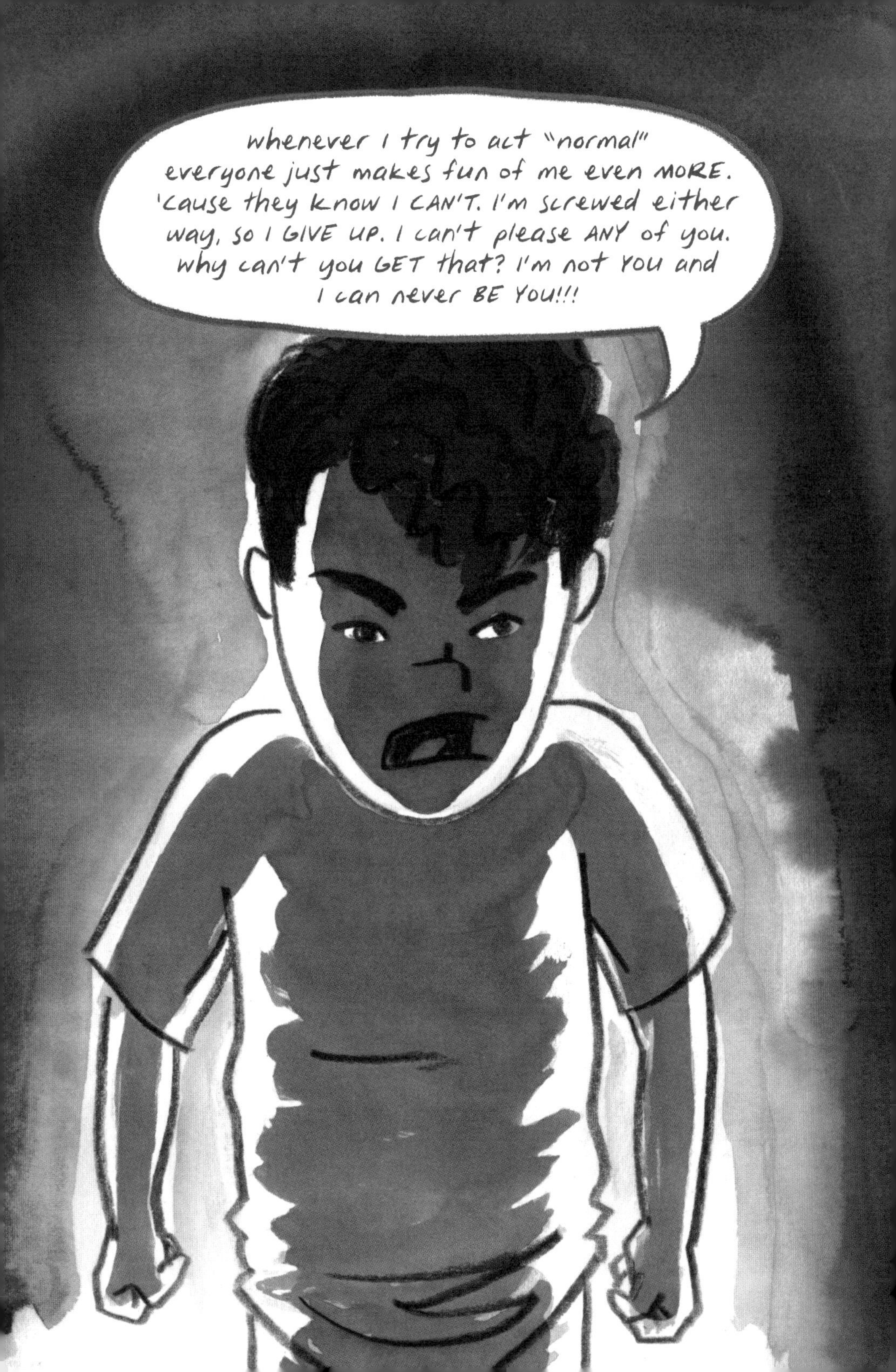
whenever I try to act "normal" everyone just makes fun of me even MORE. 'cause they know I CAN'T. I'm screwed either way, so I GIVE UP. I can't please ANY of you. why can't you GET that? I'm not YOU and I can never BE YOU!!!

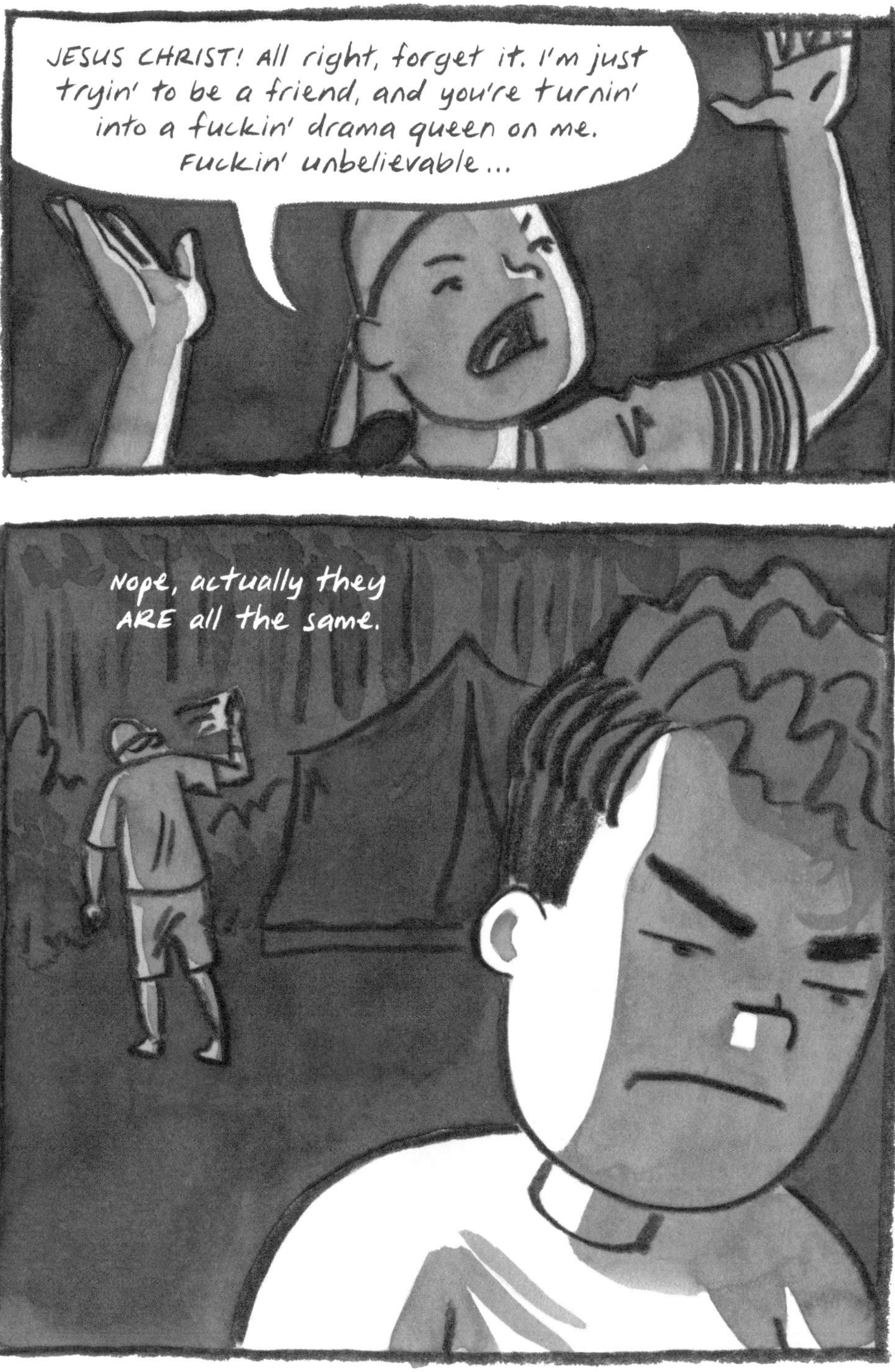
JESUS CHRIST! All right, forget it. I'm just tryin' to be a friend, and you're turnin' into a fuckin' drama queen on me. Fuckin' unbelievable...
Nope, actually they ARE all the same.

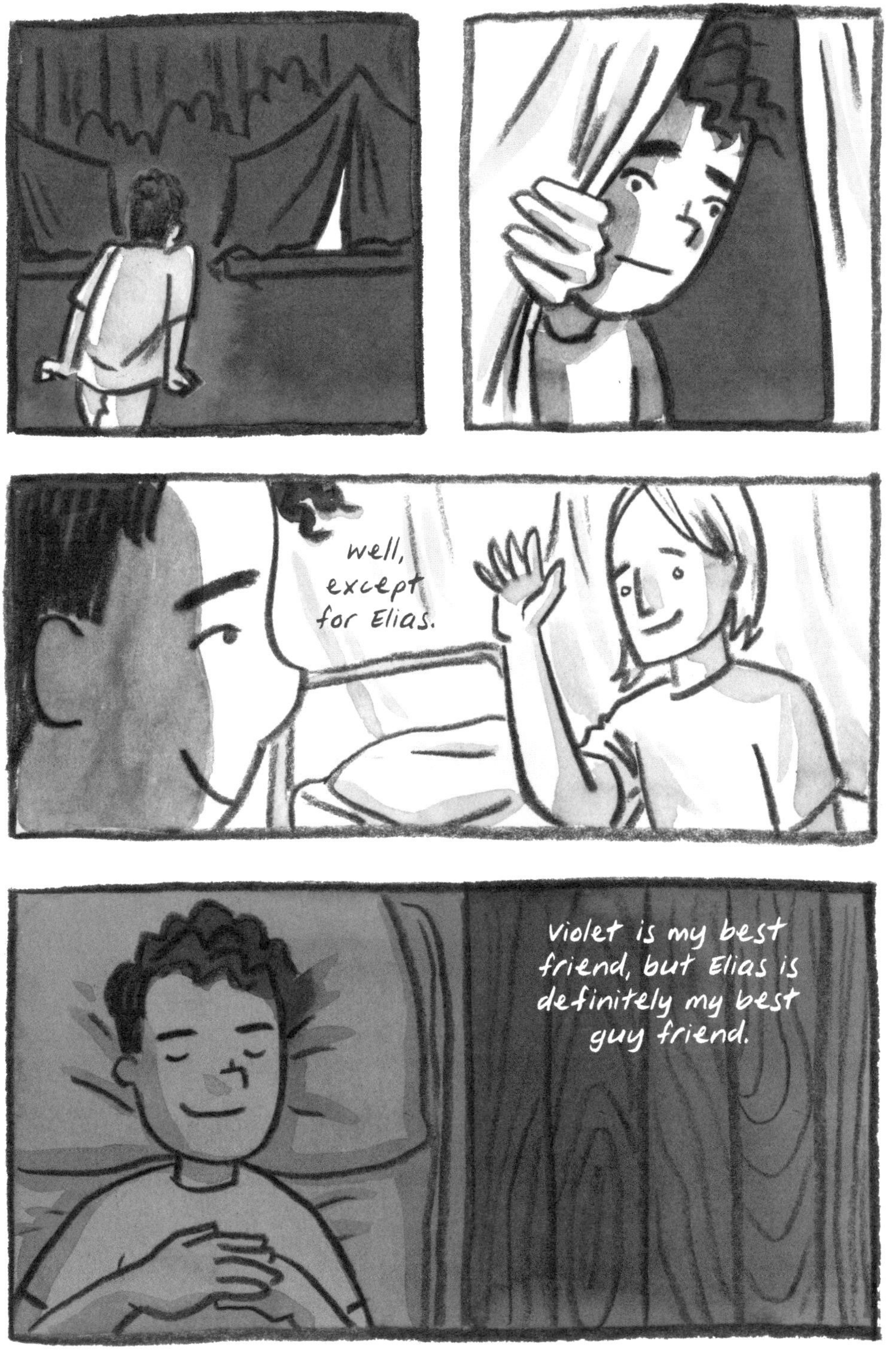

well, except for Elias.
Violet is my best friend, but Elias is definitely my best guy friend.

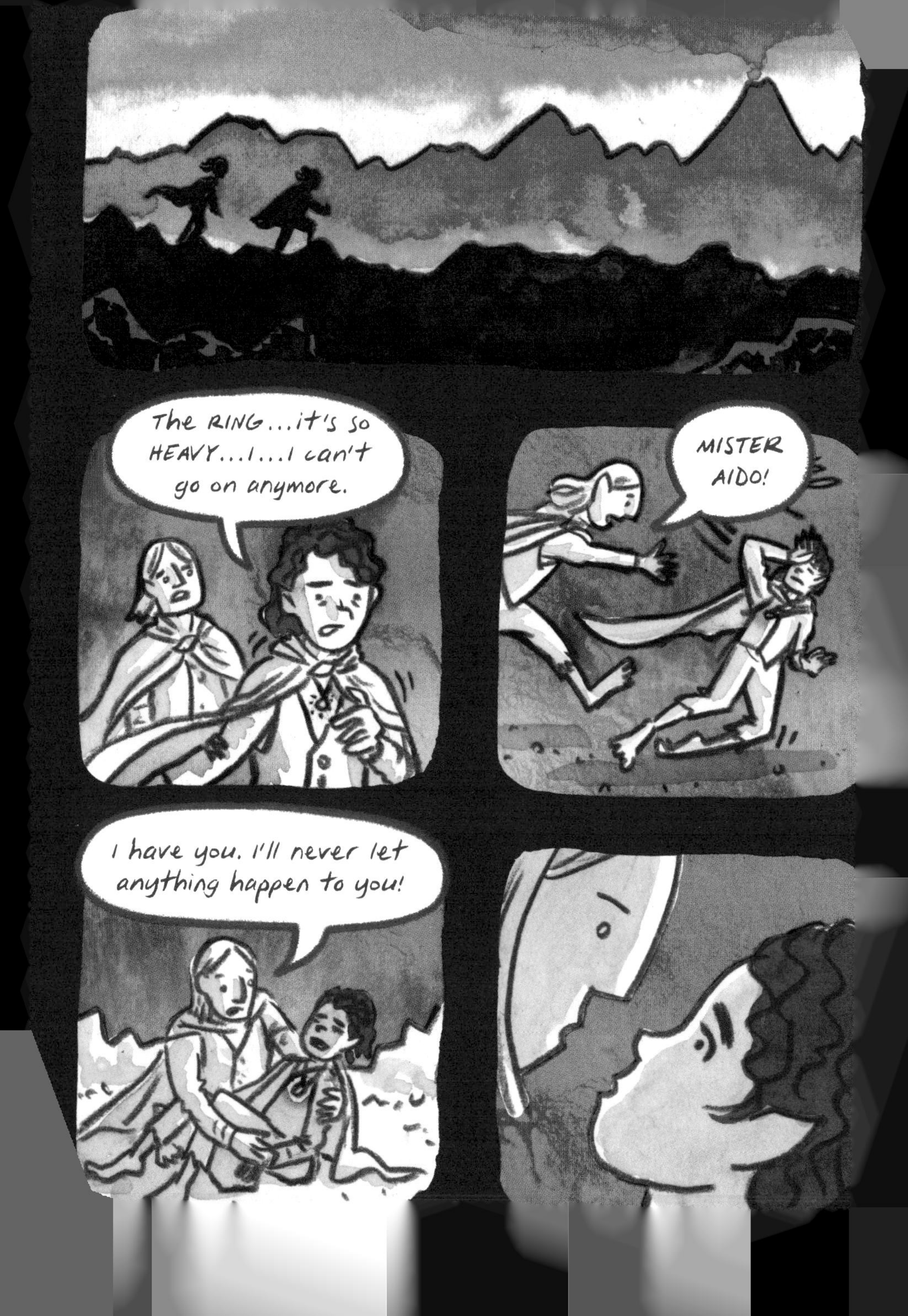
The RING...it's so HEAVY...I...I can't go on anymore.
MISTER AIDO!
I have you. I'll never let anything happen to you!

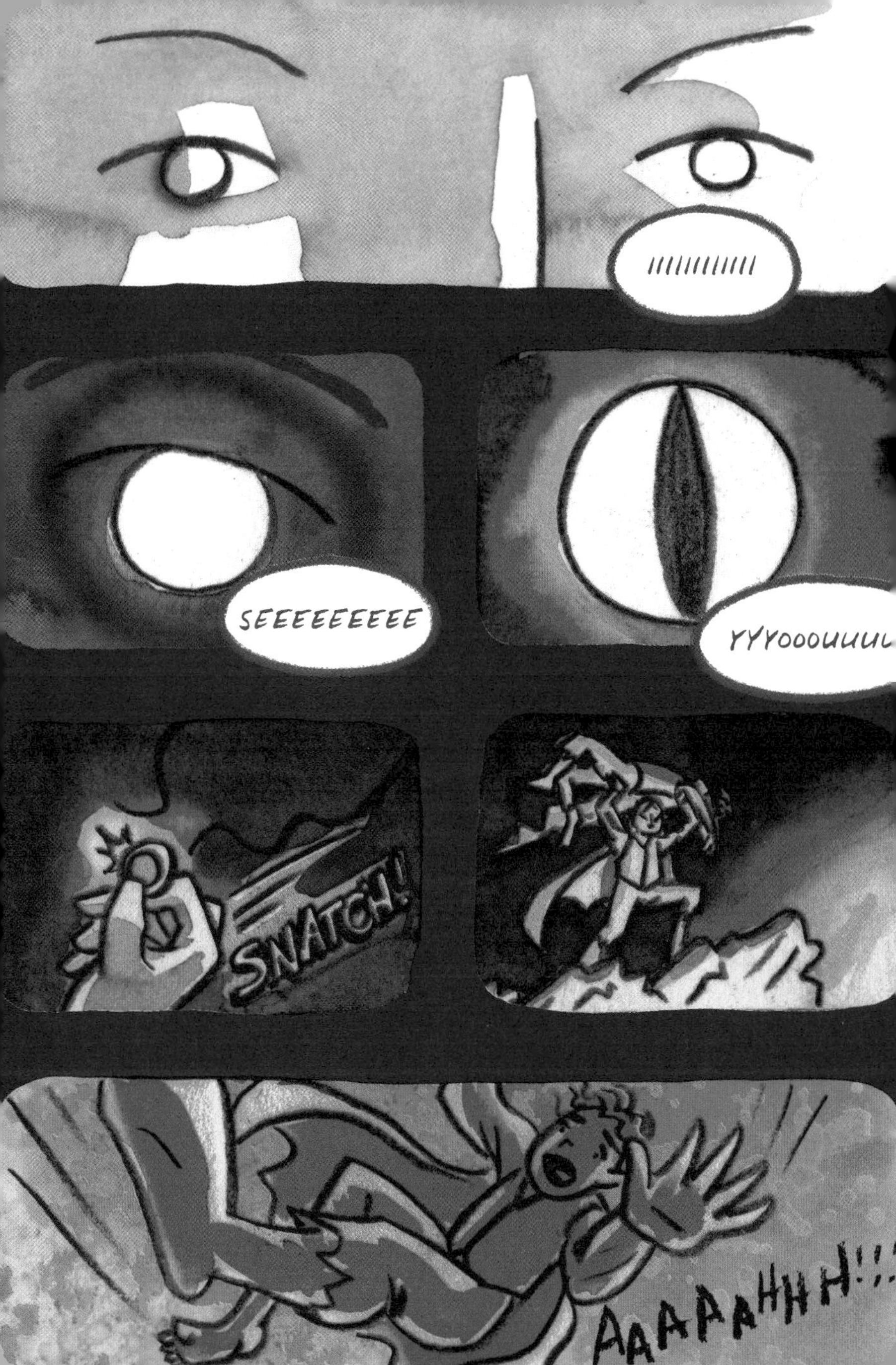

!!!!!!!!!!!!
SEEEEEEEEE
YYYOOOUUUU
SNATCH!
AAAAHHH!!!

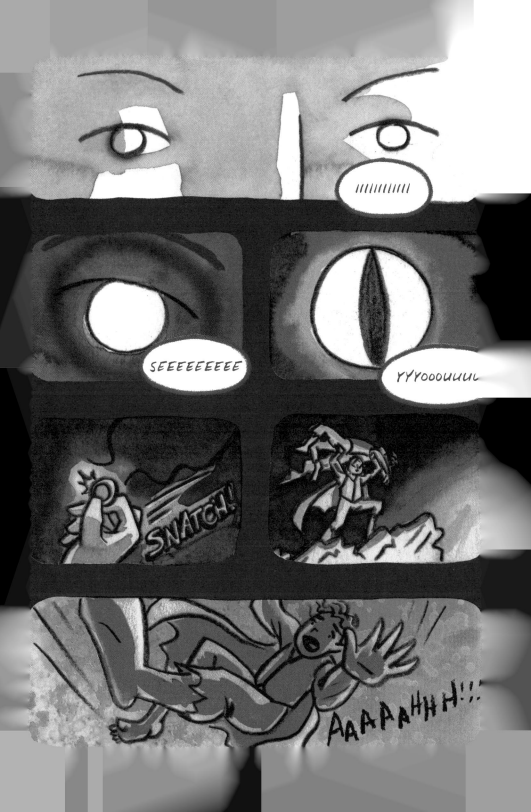

WEDNESDAY

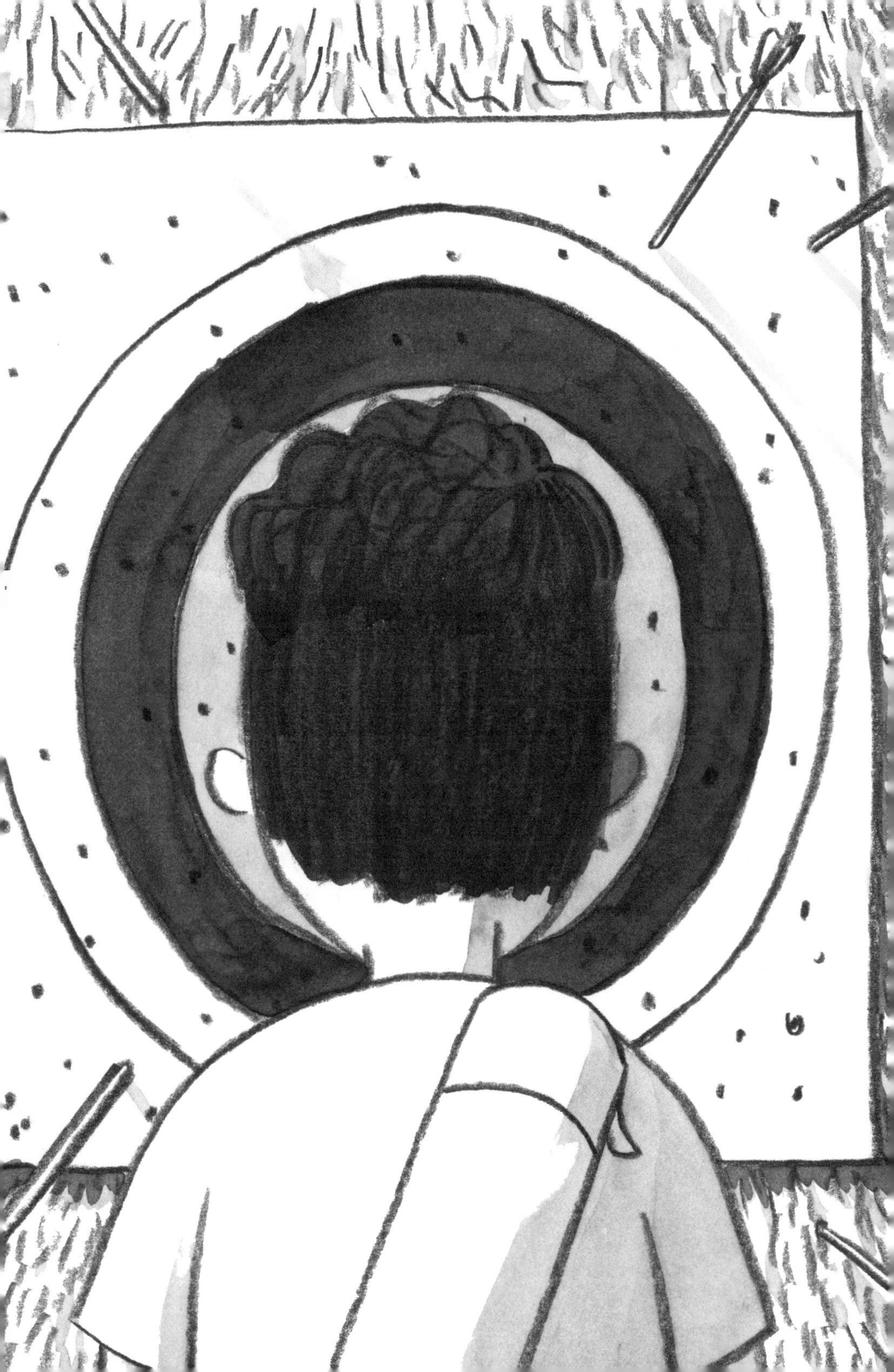

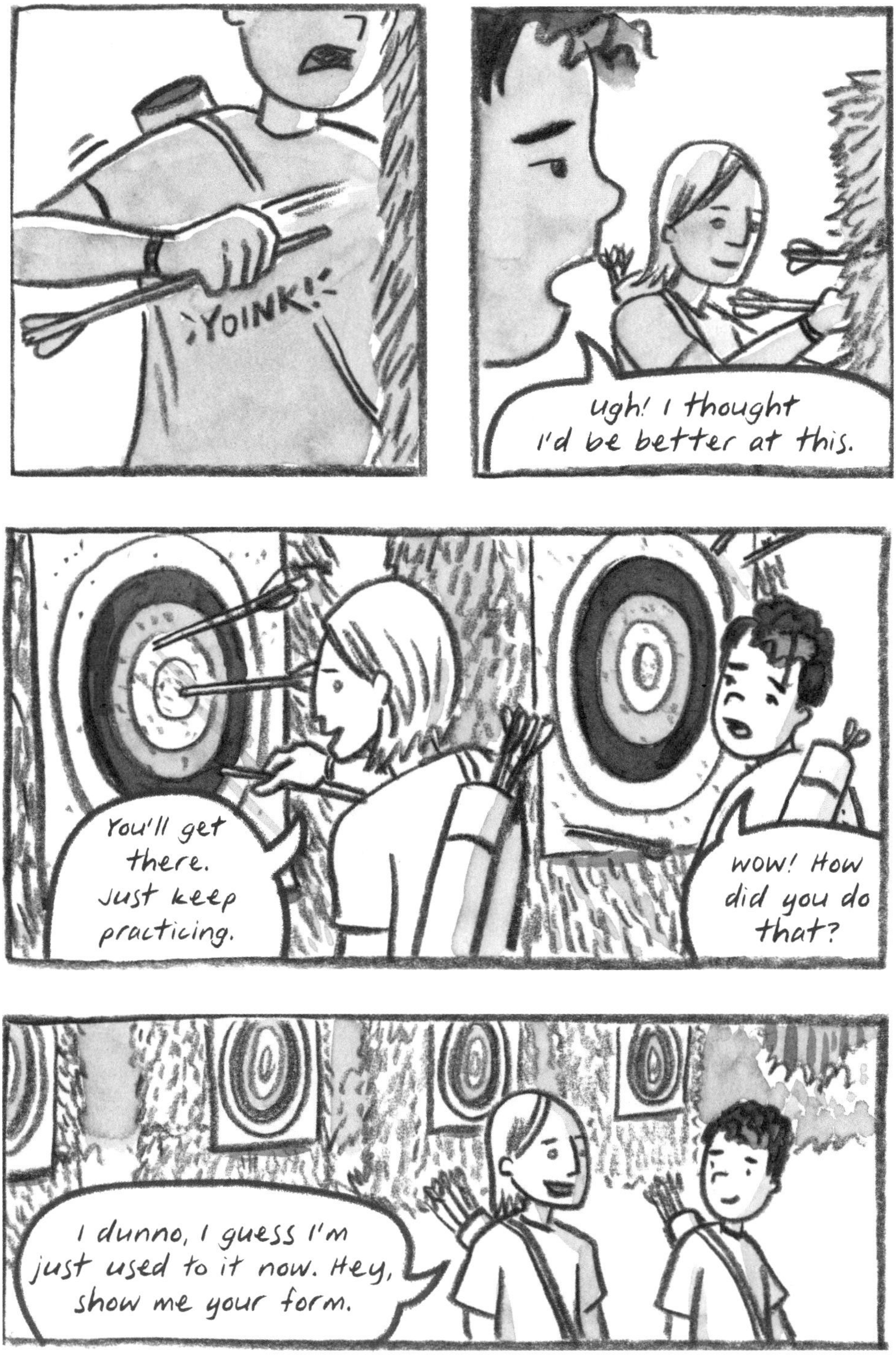
YOINK!
ugh! I thought I'd be better at this.
You'll get there. Just keep practicing.
wow! How did you do that?
I dunno, I guess I'm just used to it now. Hey, show me your form.

I don't think you're aiming high enough.

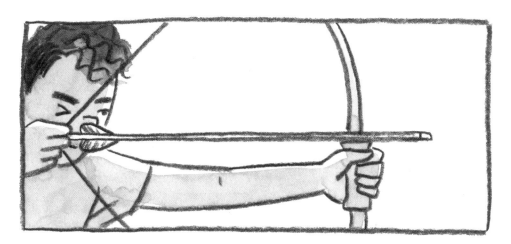

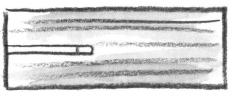

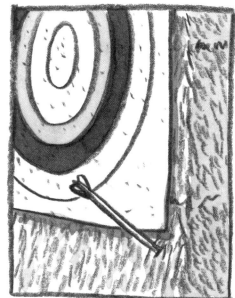

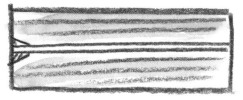

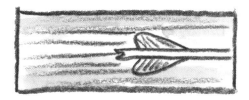

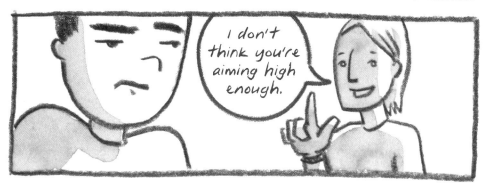

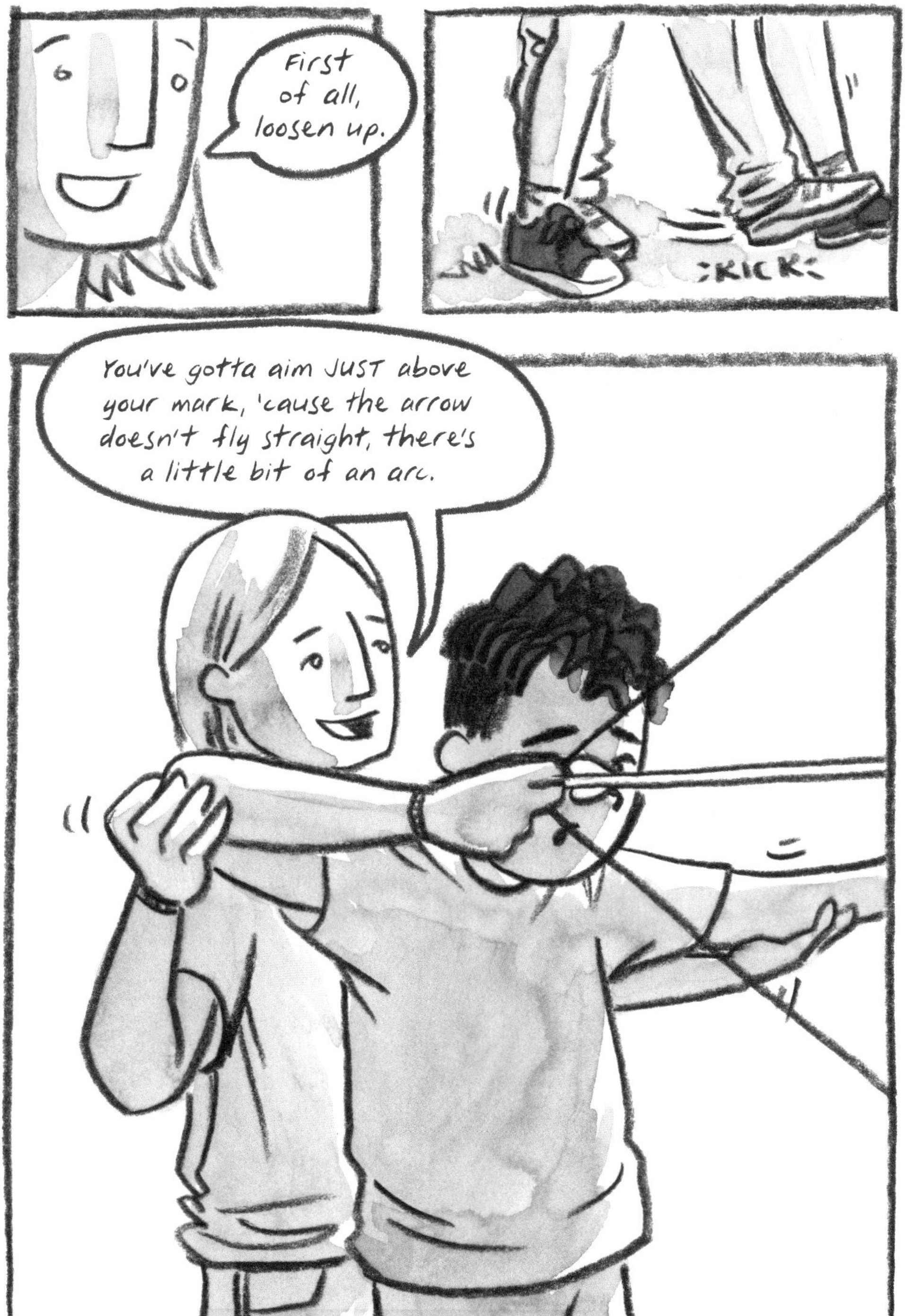
First of all, loosen up.
:KICK:
You've gotta aim JUST above your mark, 'cause the arrow doesn't fly straight, there's a little bit of an arc.

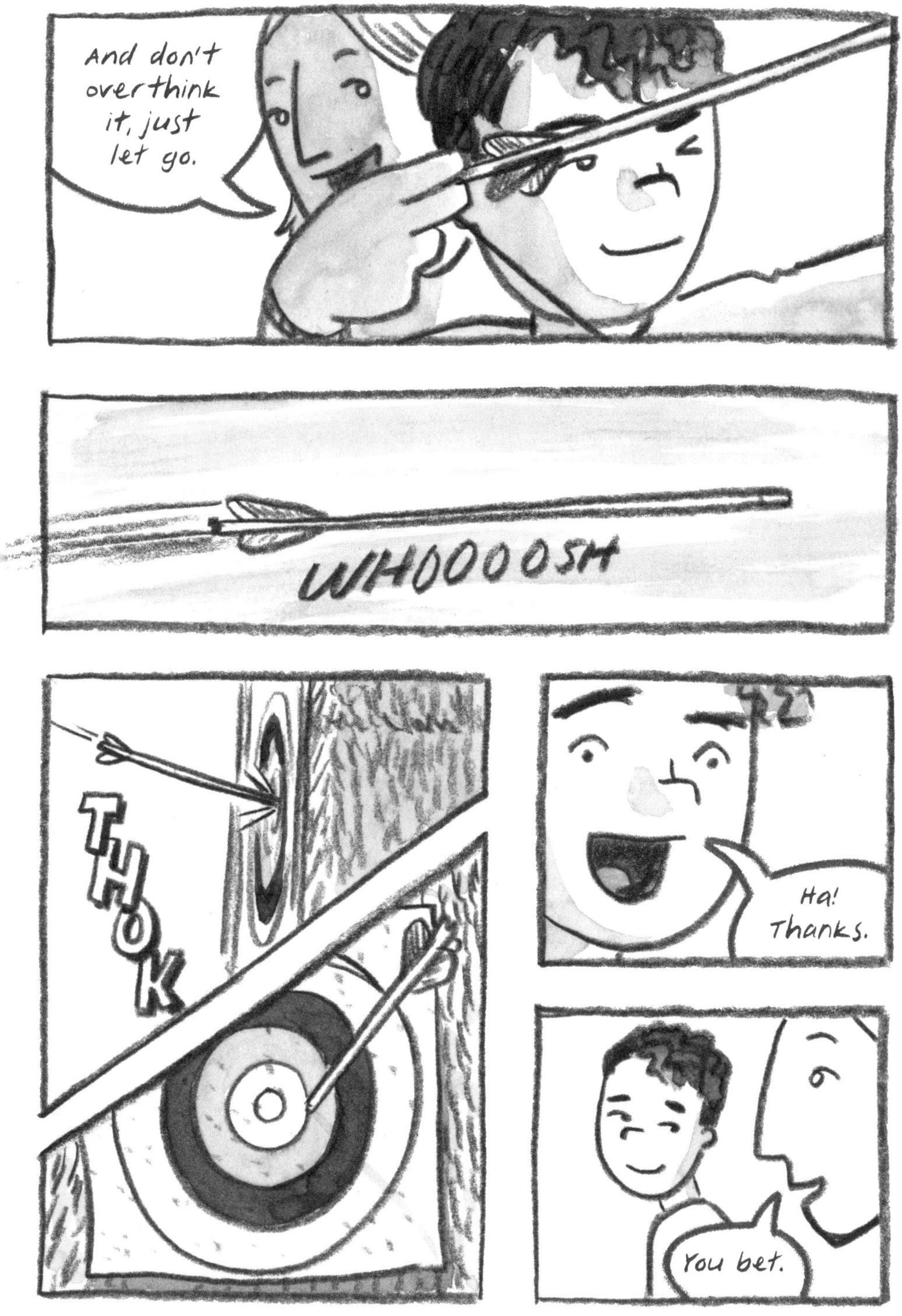
And don't overthink it, just let go.
WHOOOOSH
THOK
Ha! Thanks.
You bet.

Good mooooooorning, miss maaaary.

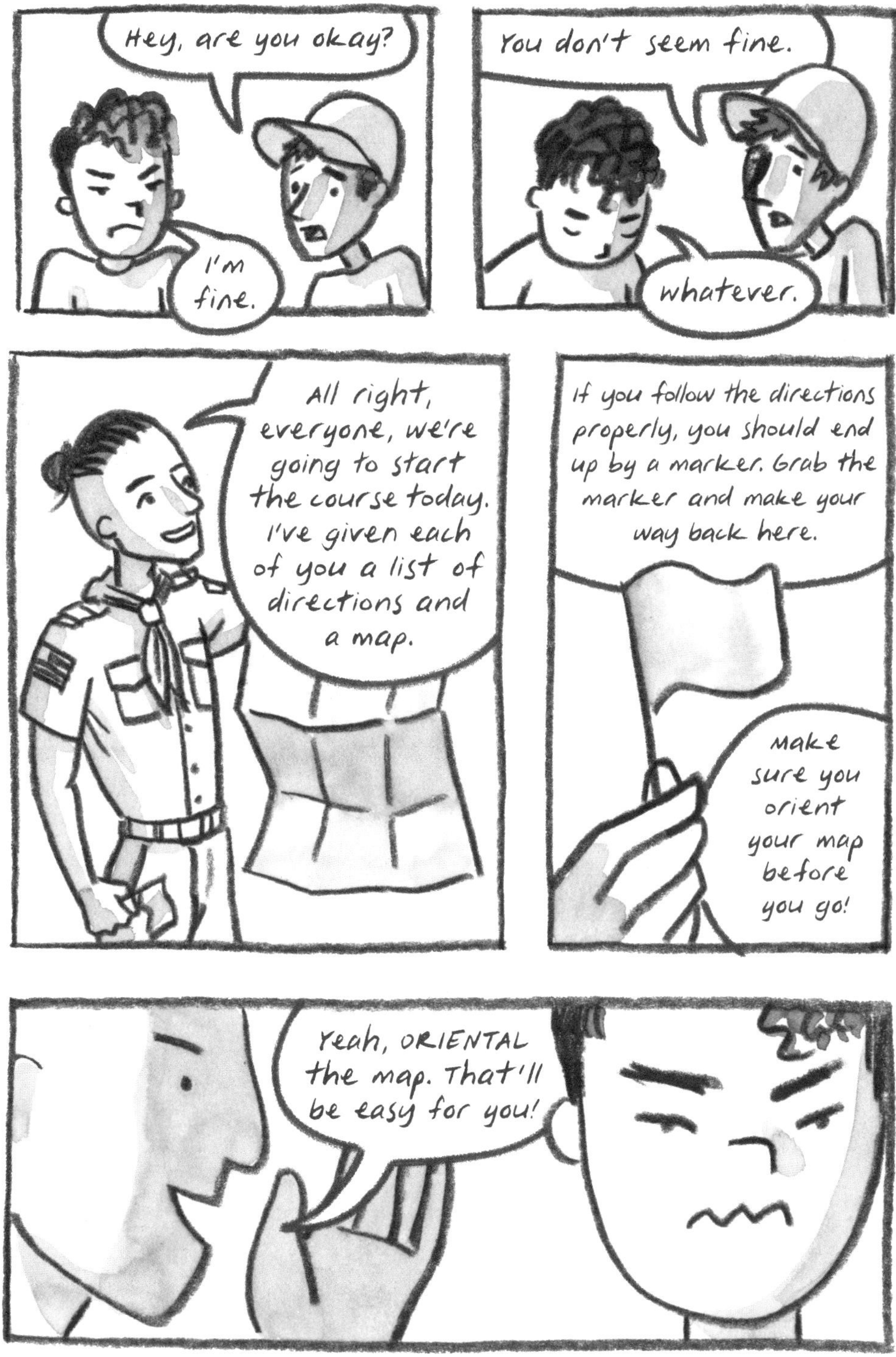
Hey, are you okay?
I'm fine.
You don't seem fine.
whatever.
All right, everyone, we're going to start the course today. I've given each of you a list of directions and a map.
If you follow the directions properly, you should end up by a marker. Grab the marker and make your way back here.
Make sure you orient your map before you go!
Yeah, ORIENTAL the map. That'll be easy for you!

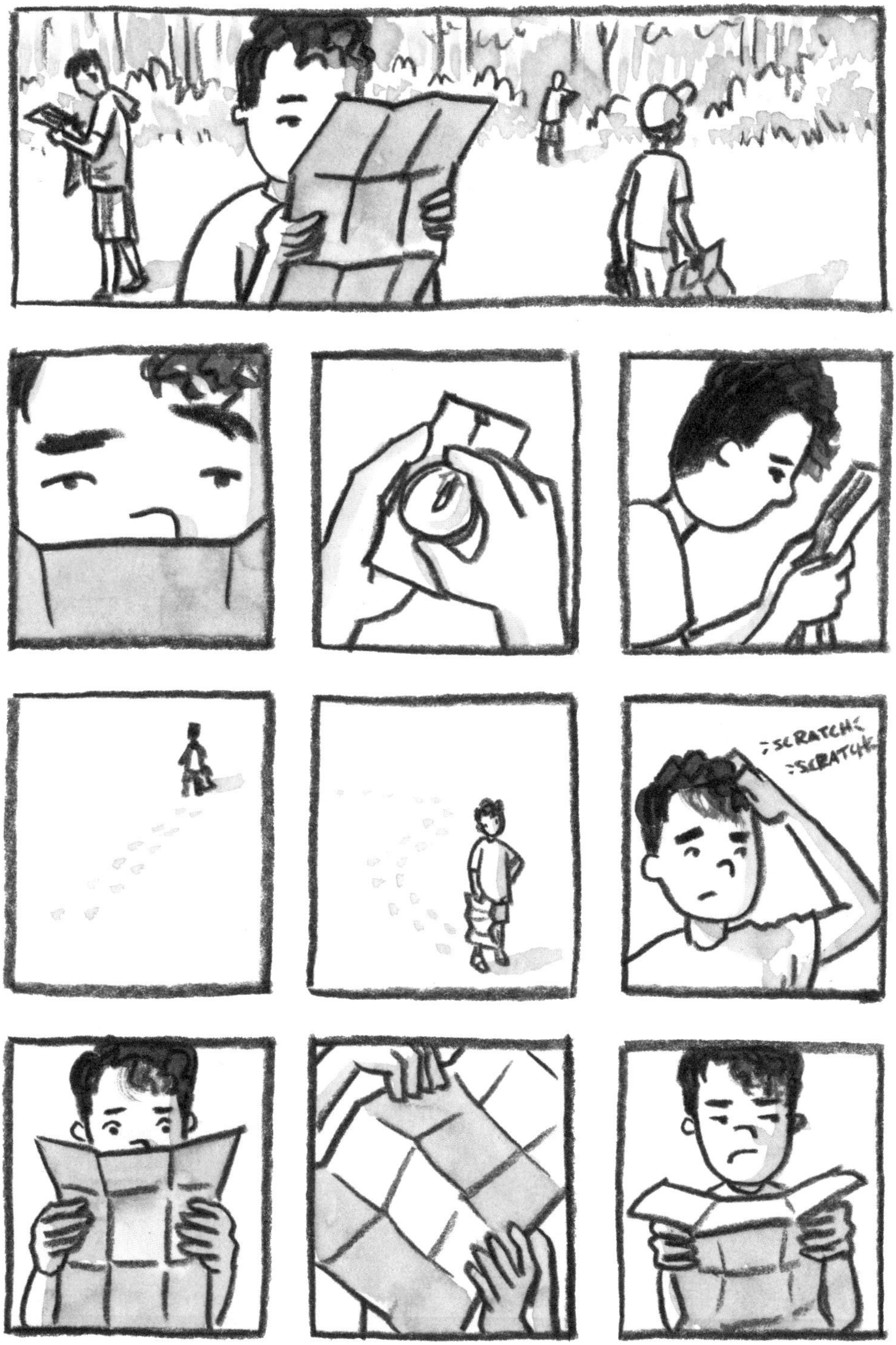
SCRATCH
SCRATCH

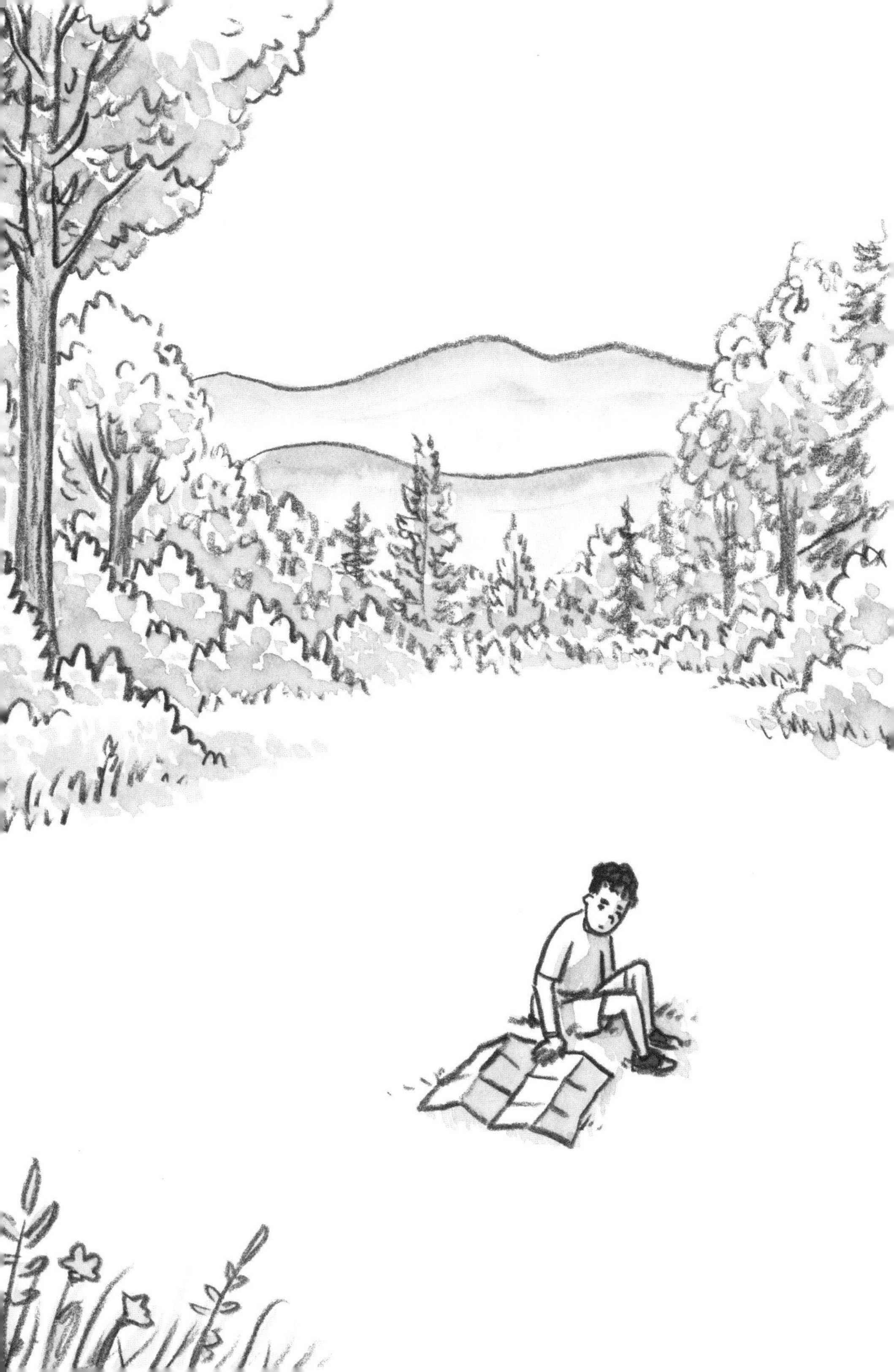

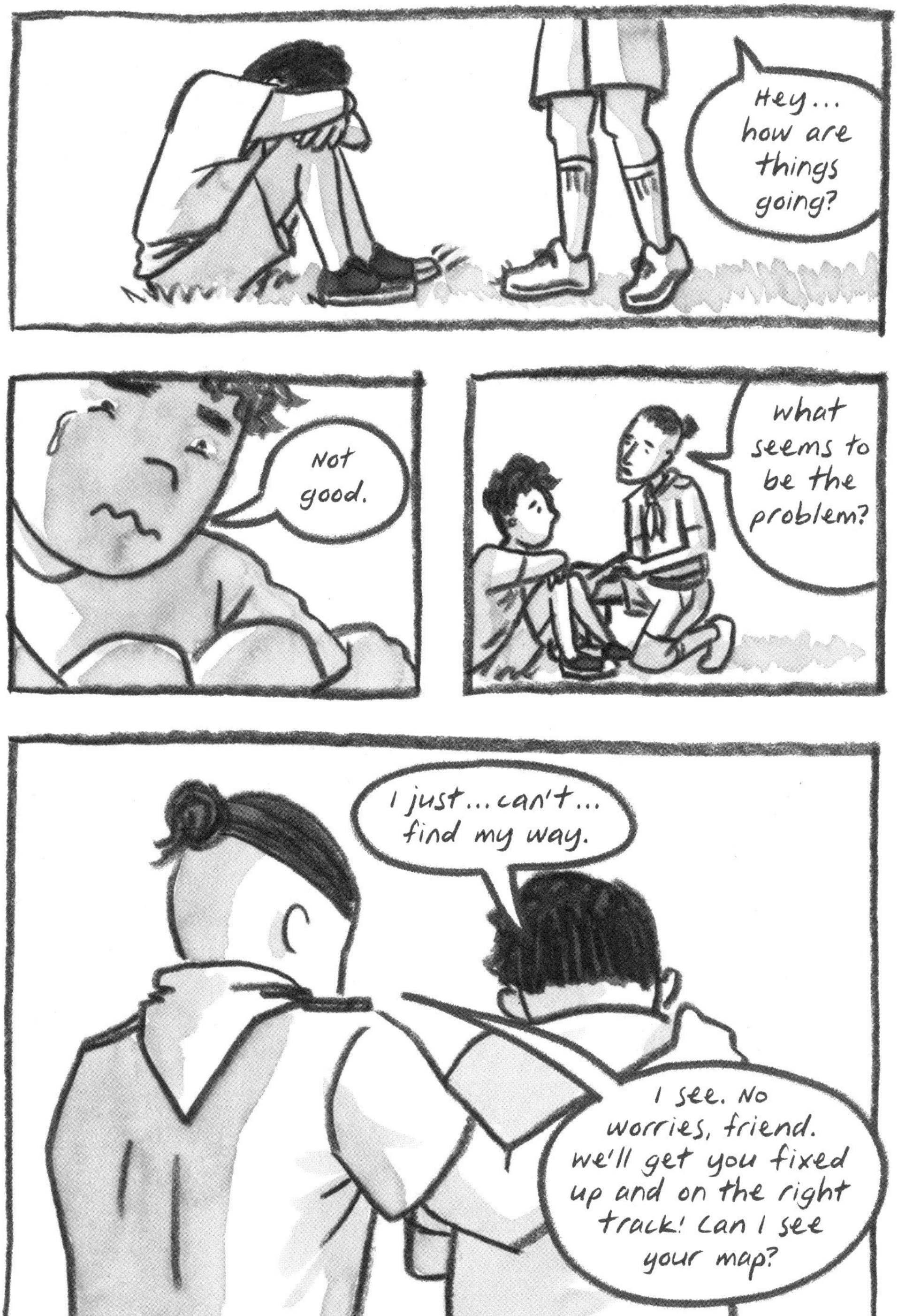
Hey... how are things going?
Not good.
What seems to be the problem?
I just... can't... find my way.
I see. No worries, friend. We'll get you fixed up and on the right track! Can I see your map?

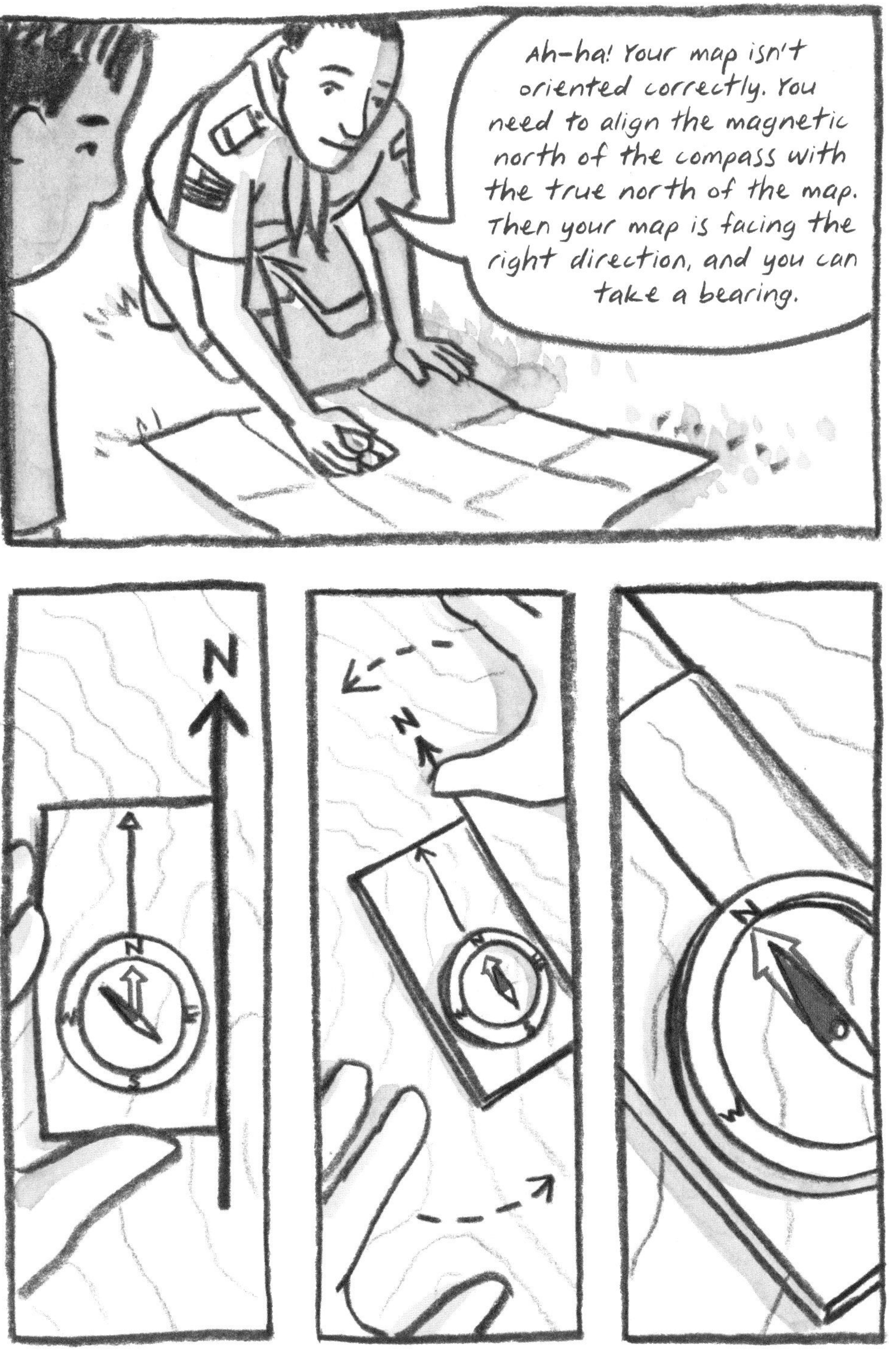
Ah-ha! Your map isn't oriented correctly. You need to align the magnetic north of the compass with the true north of the map. Then your map is facing the right direction, and you can take a bearing.
N
N
N
S
N

Now that the map is oriented properly, we can take a bearing between two points.
B
A
Align the edge of the compass to connect your points, with the directional arrow of the compass pointing to the destination.
A
Now turn the dial till "N" lines up with the red end of the needle.
Now you walk in the direction of your compass arrow and make sure the red end of the needle is always pointing to "N," your true north.

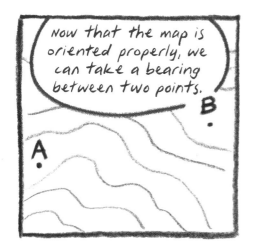

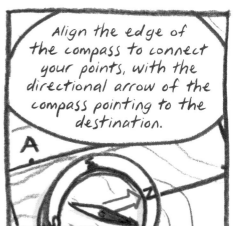

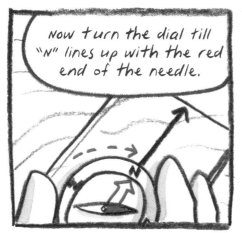

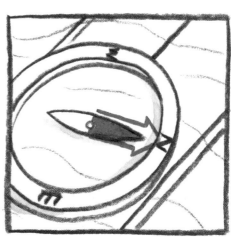

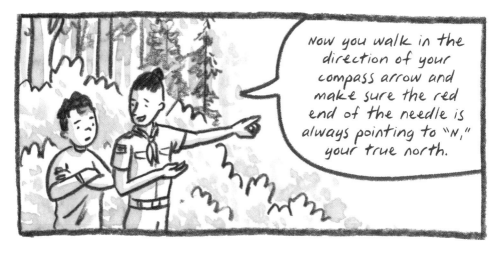

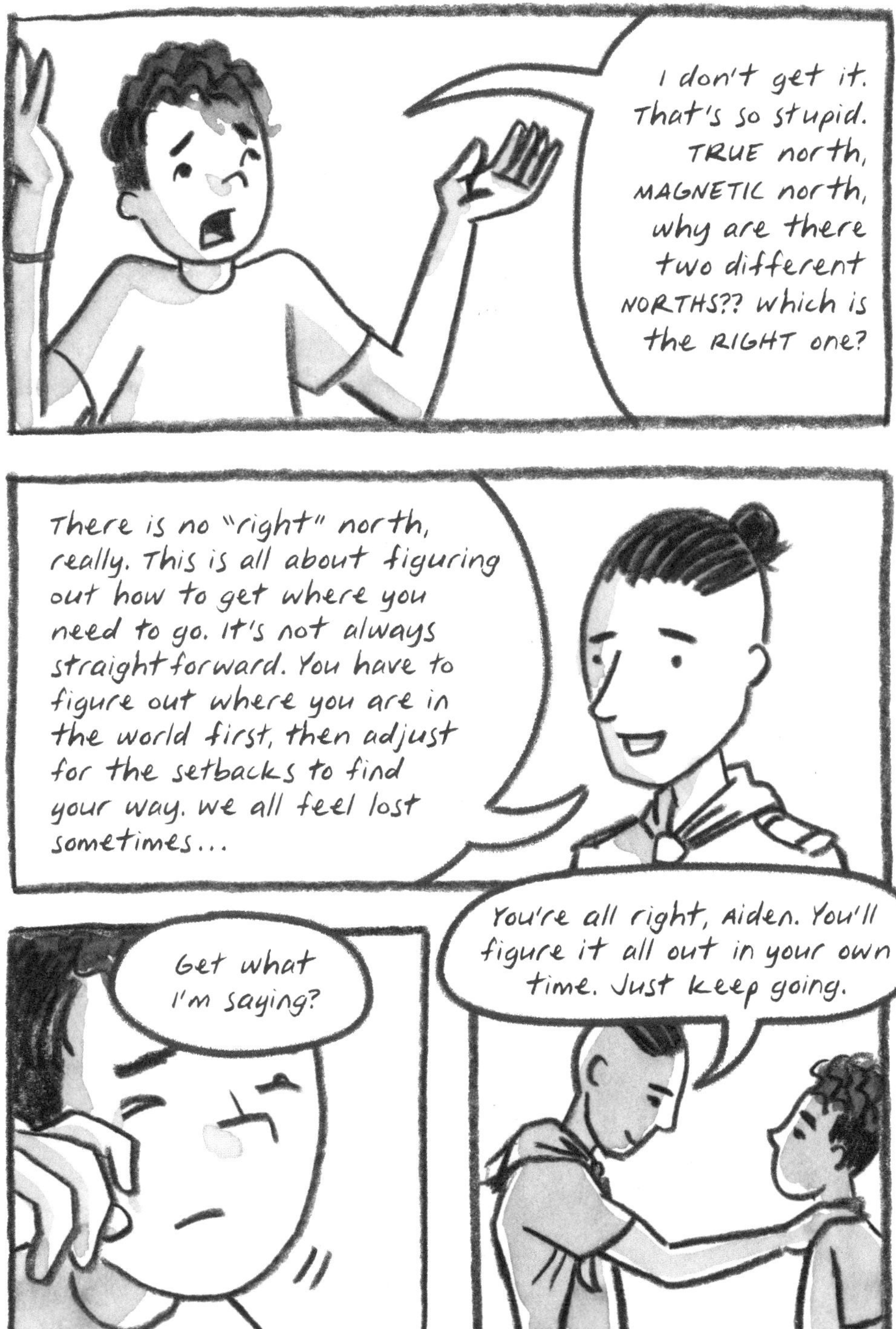
I don't get it. That's so stupid. TRUE north, MAGNETIC north, why are there two different NORTHS?? which is the RIGHT one?
There is no "right" north, really. This is all about figuring out how to get where you need to go. It's not always straightforward. You have to figure out where you are in the world first, then adjust for the setbacks to find your way. we all feel lost sometimes...
Get what I'm saying?
You're all right, Aiden. You'll figure it all out in your own time. Just keep going.

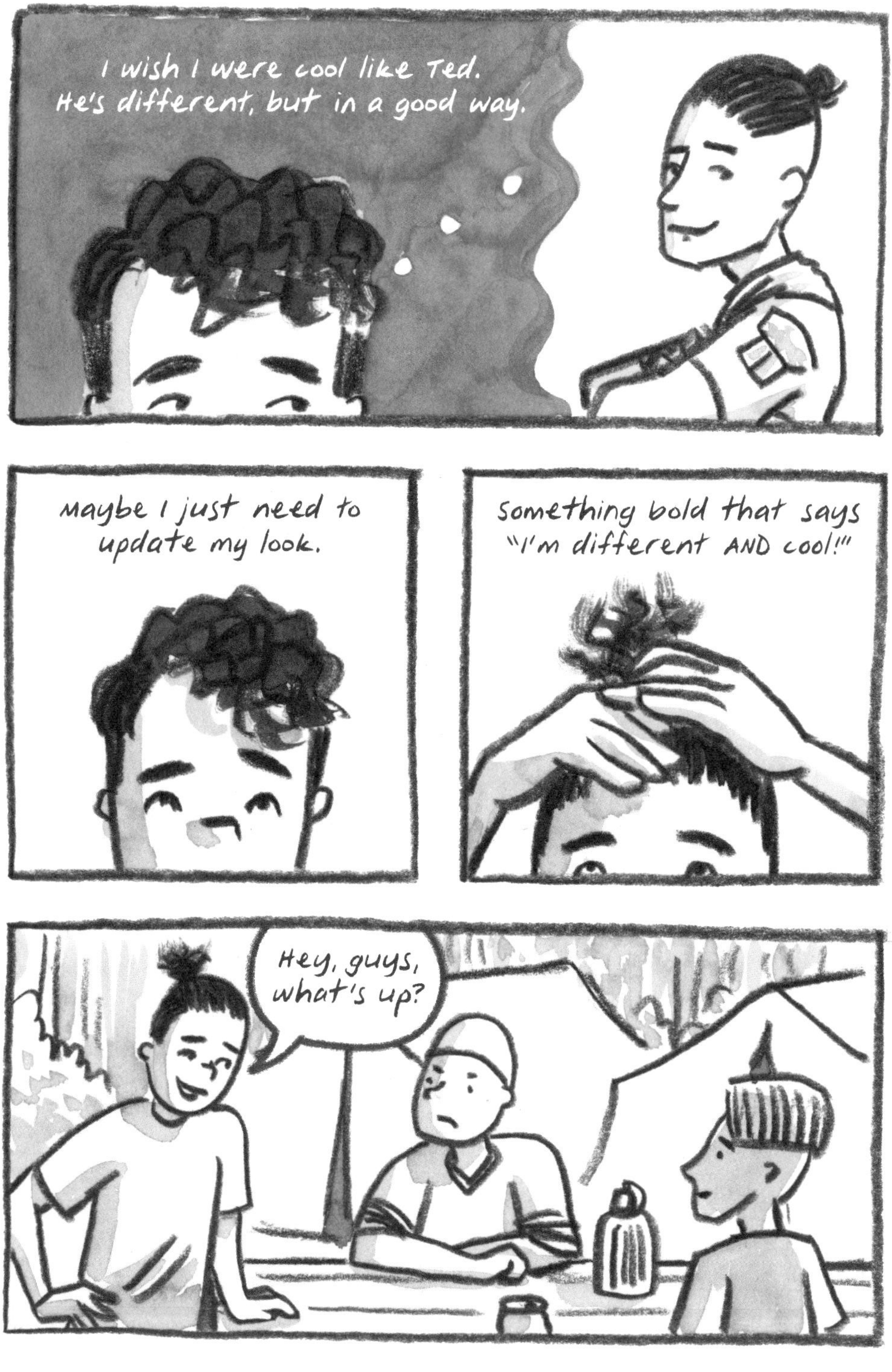
I wish I were cool like Ted. He's different, but in a good way.
Maybe I just need to update my look.
Something bold that says "I'm different AND cool!"
Hey, guys, what's up?

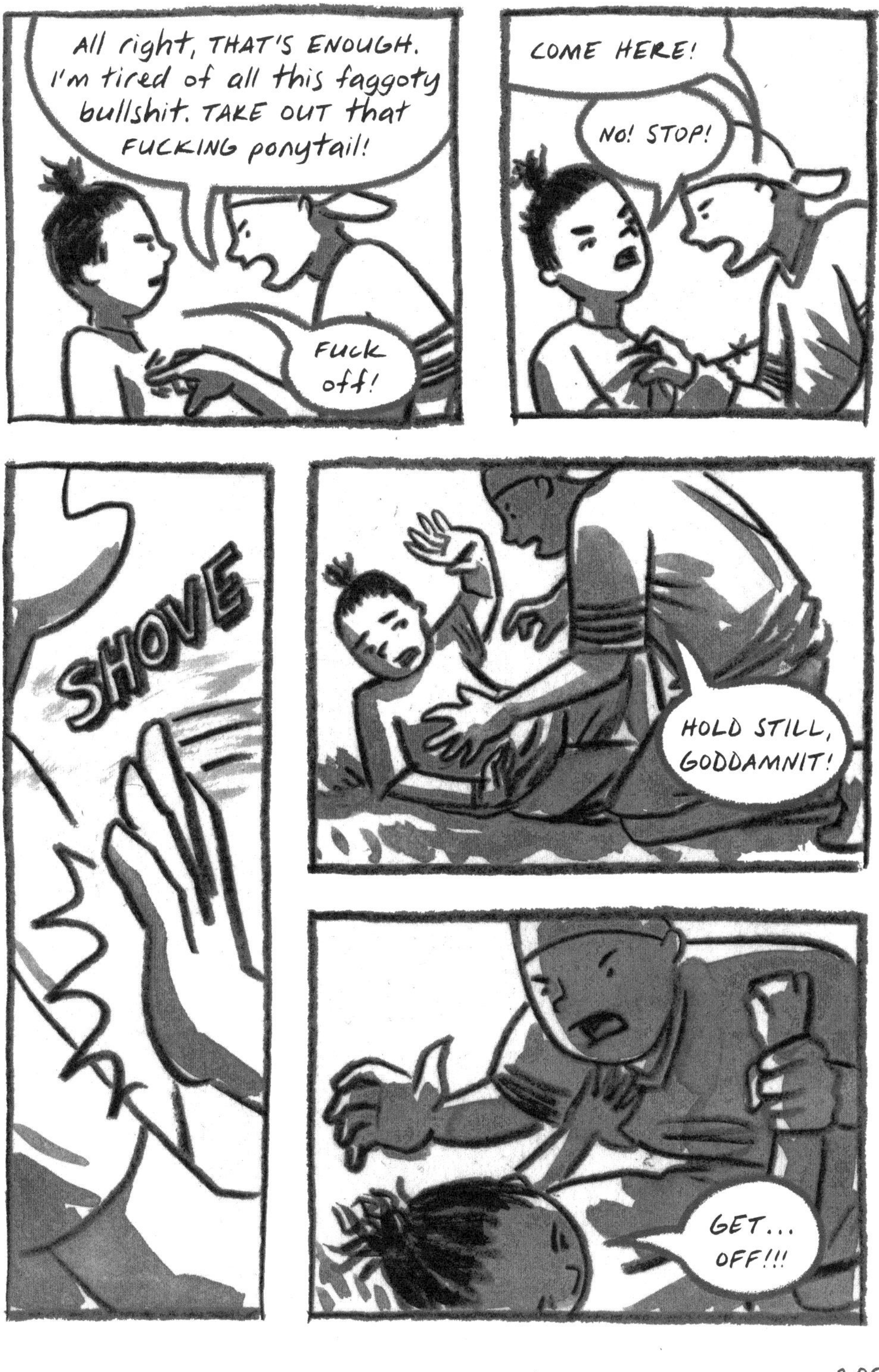
All right, THAT'S ENOUGH. I'm tired of all this faggoty bullshit. TAKE OUT that FUCKING ponytail!
Fuck off!
COME HERE!
NO! STOP!
SHOVE
HOLD STILL, GODDAMNIT!
GET... OFF!!!

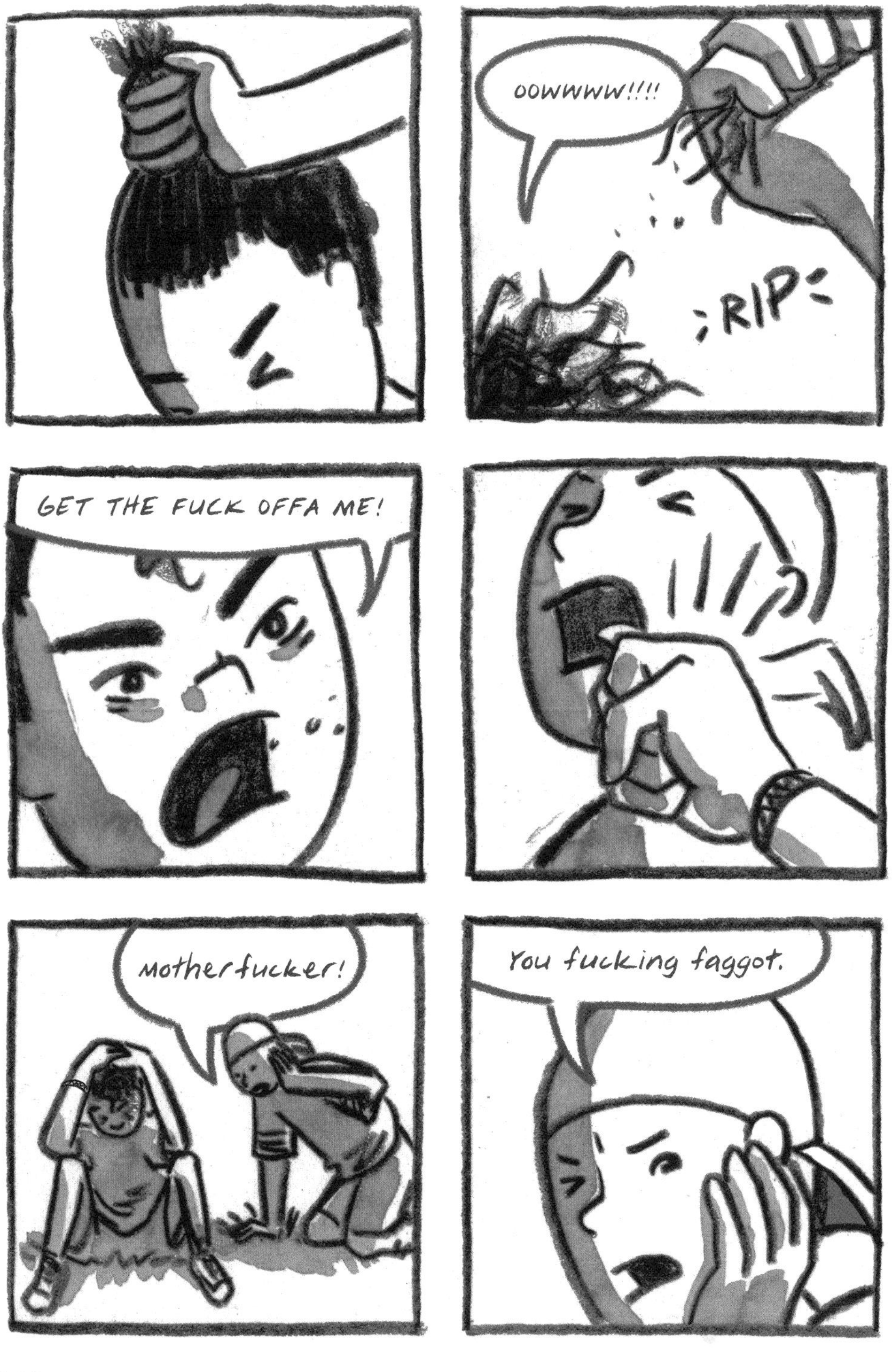
OOWWWW!!!!
RIP
GET THE FUCK OFFA ME!
Motherfucker!
You fucking faggot.

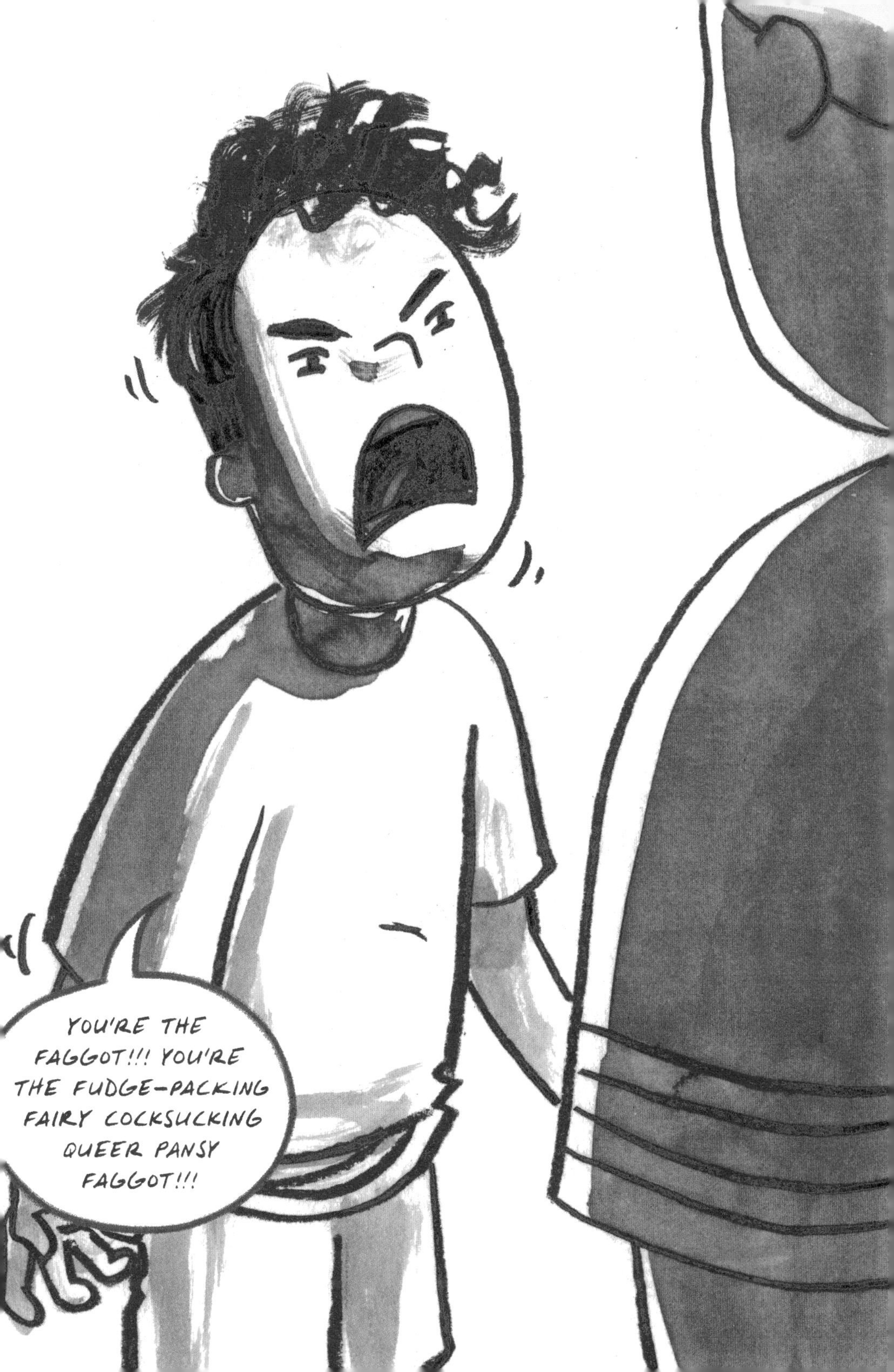
YOU'RE THE FAGGOT!!! YOU'RE THE FUDGE-PACKING FAIRY COCKSUCKING QUEER PANSY FAGGOT!!!

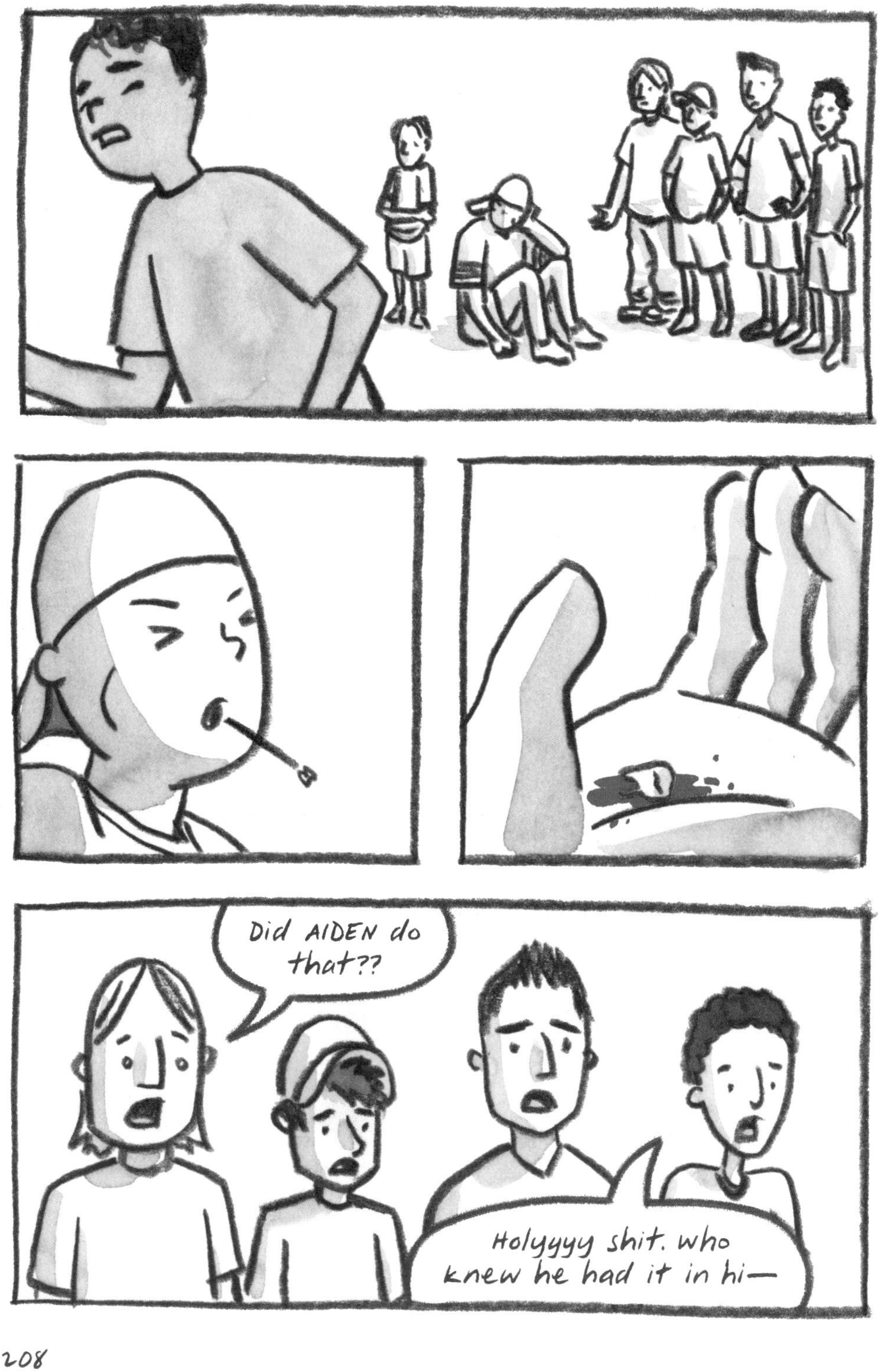
Did AIDEN do that??
Holyyyy shit. who knew he had it in hi—

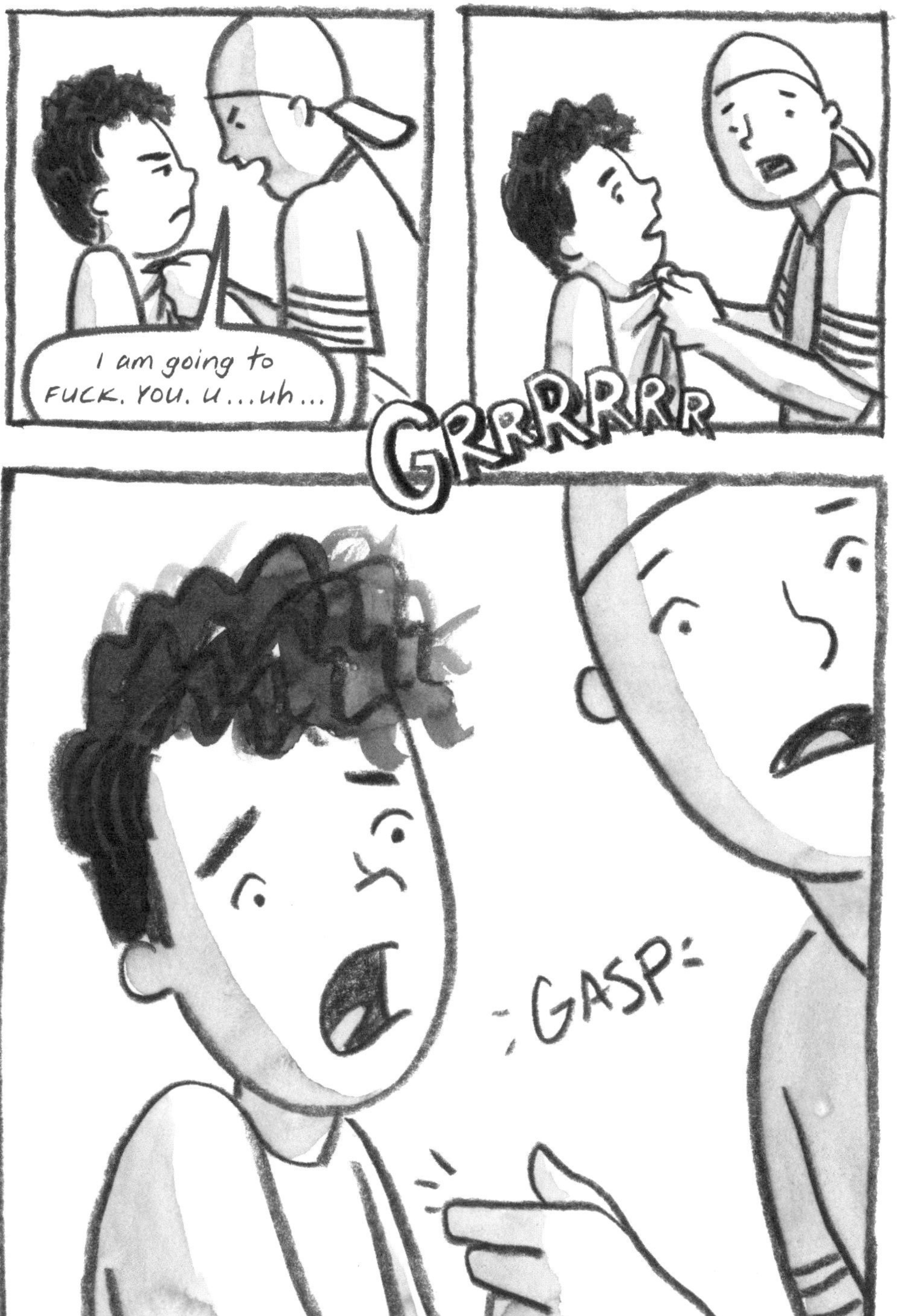
I am going to FUCK. YOU. U...uh...
GRRRRRR
GASP

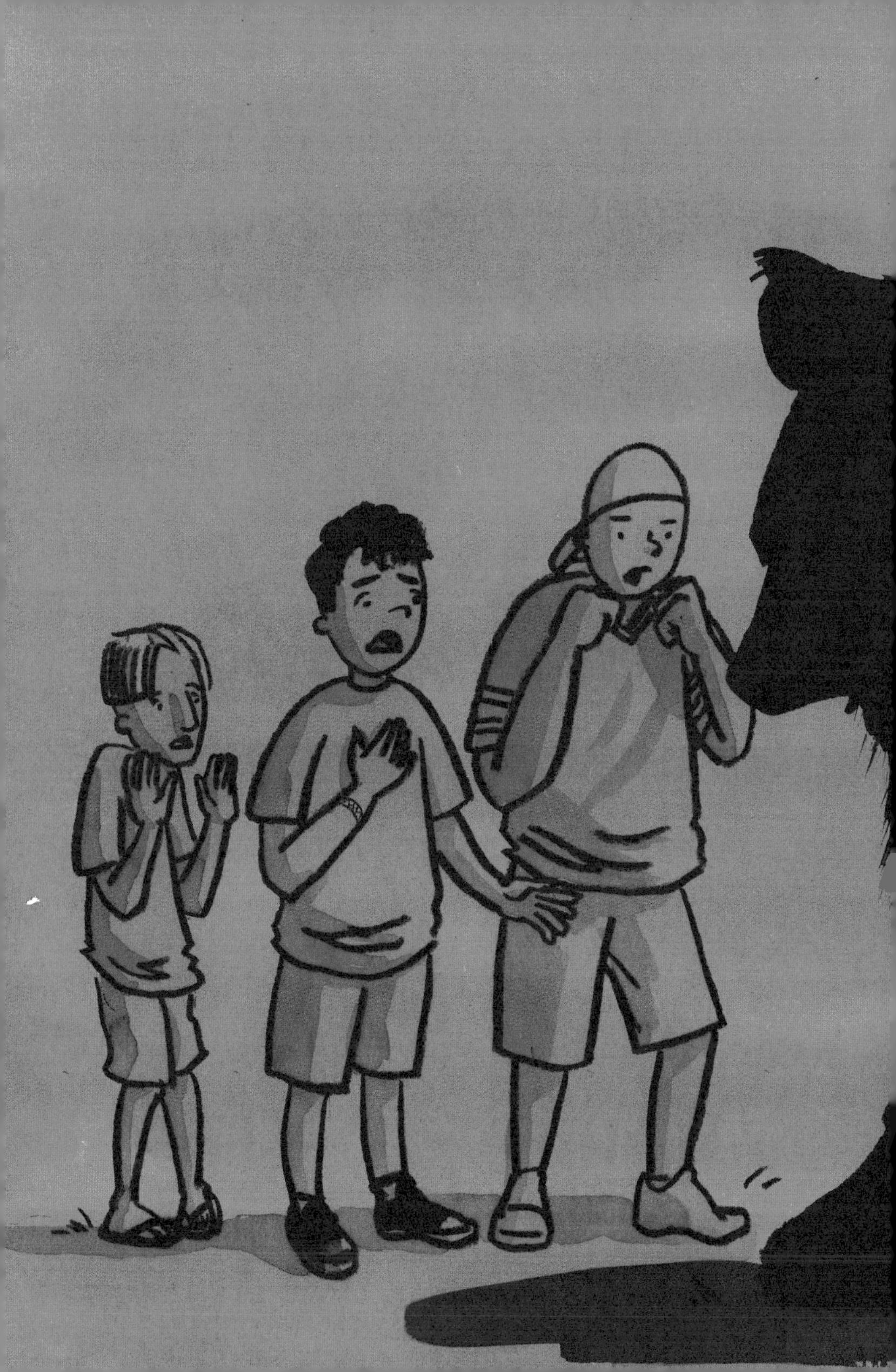

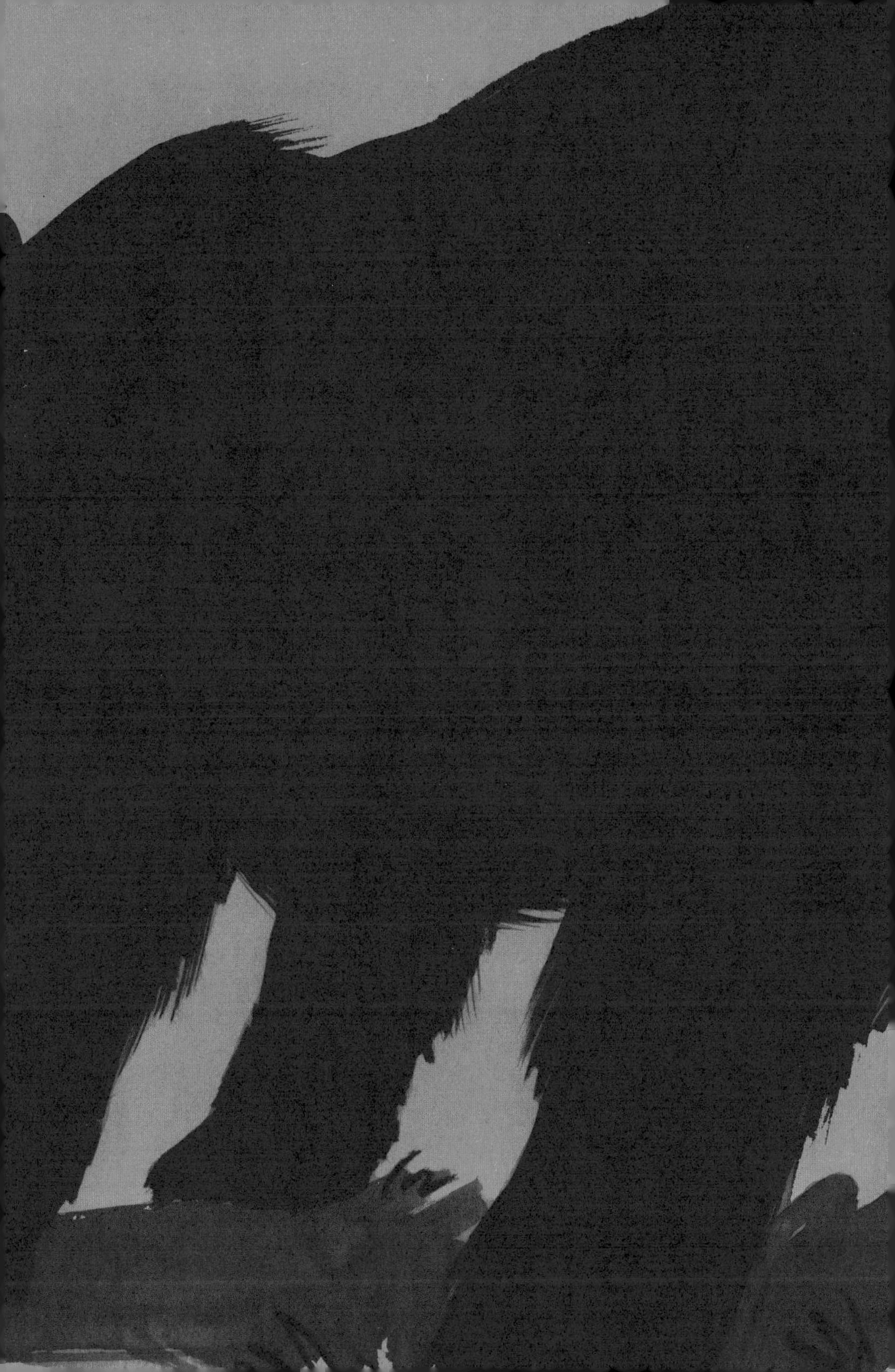

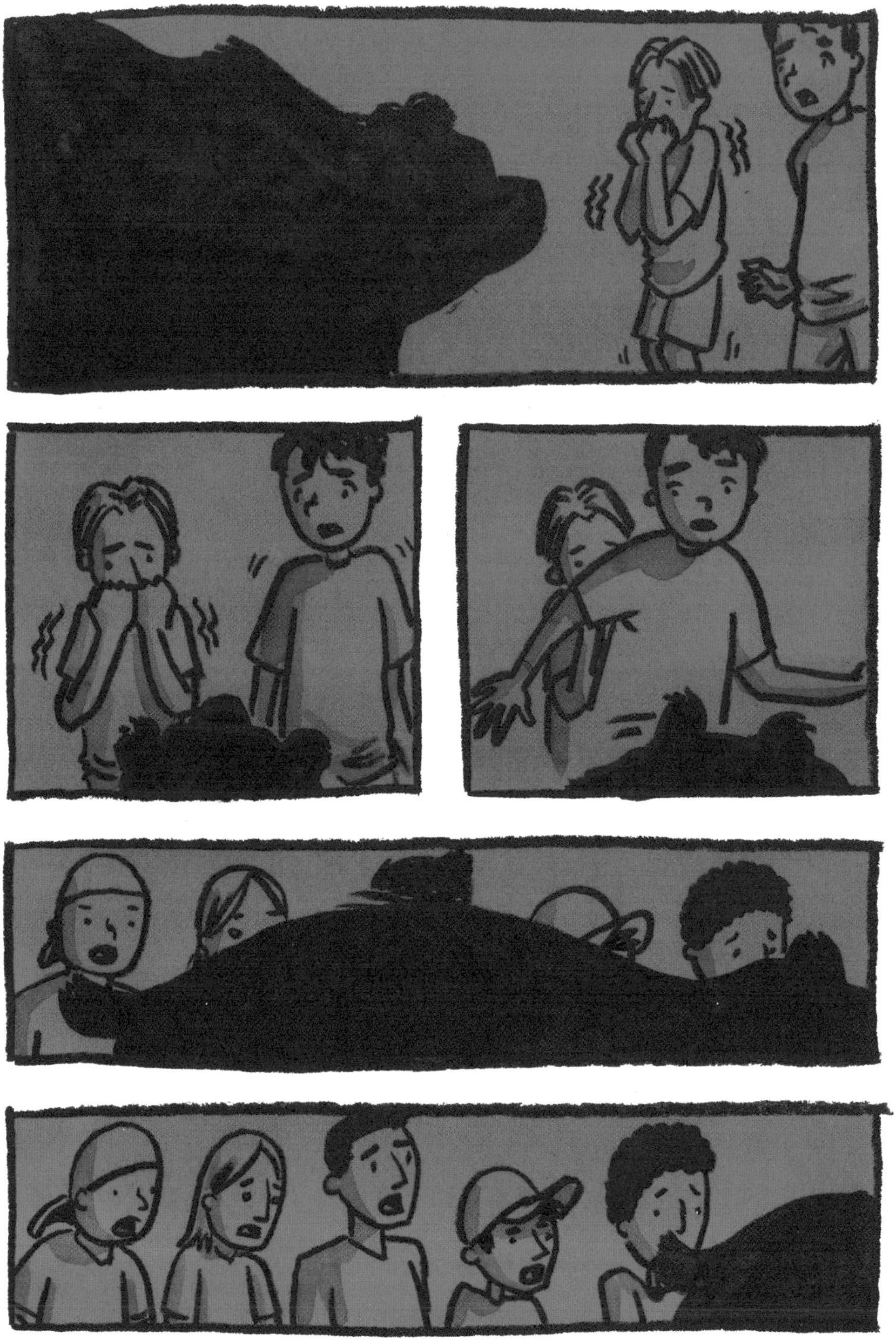

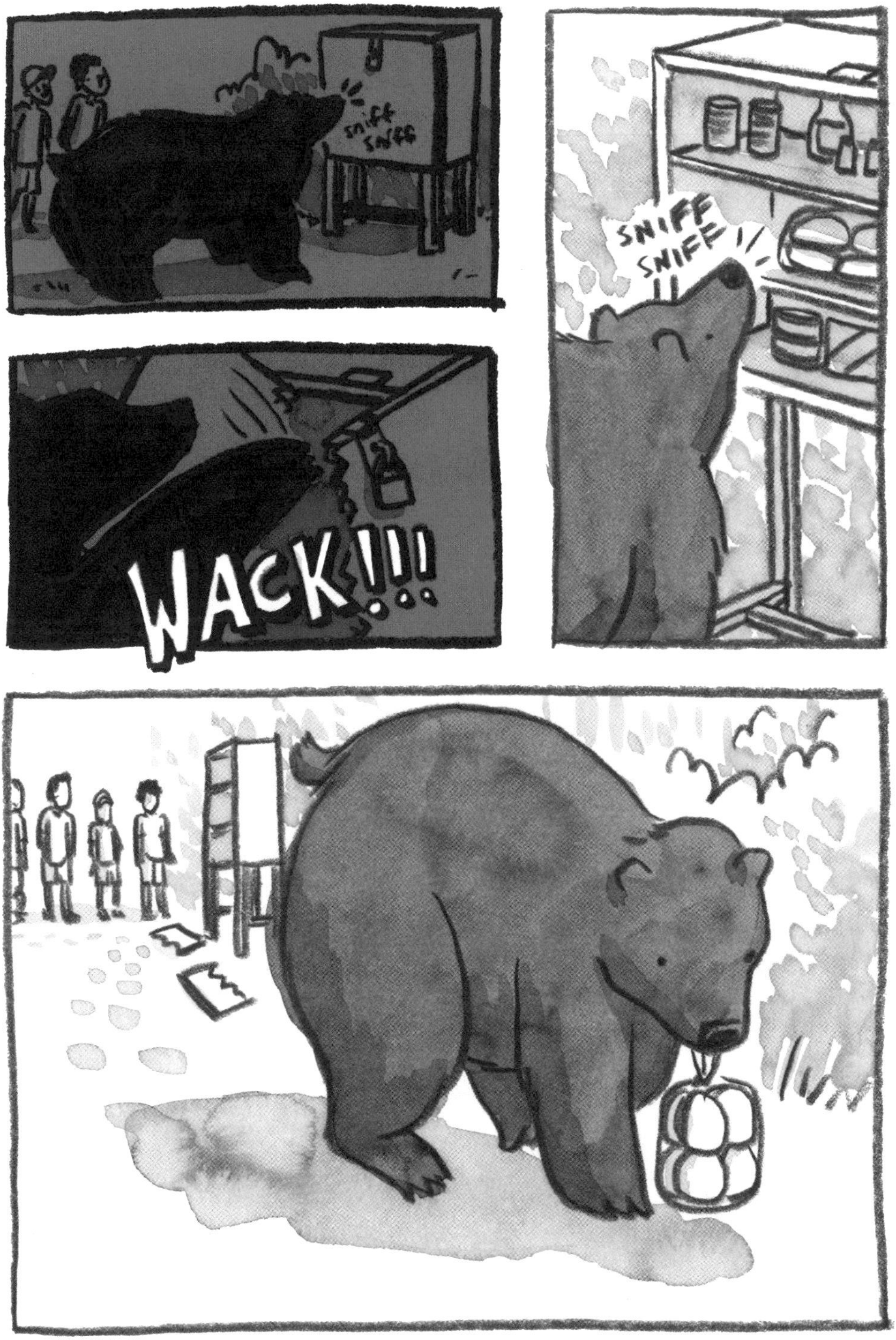
sniff sniff
SNIFF SNIFF
WACK!!!

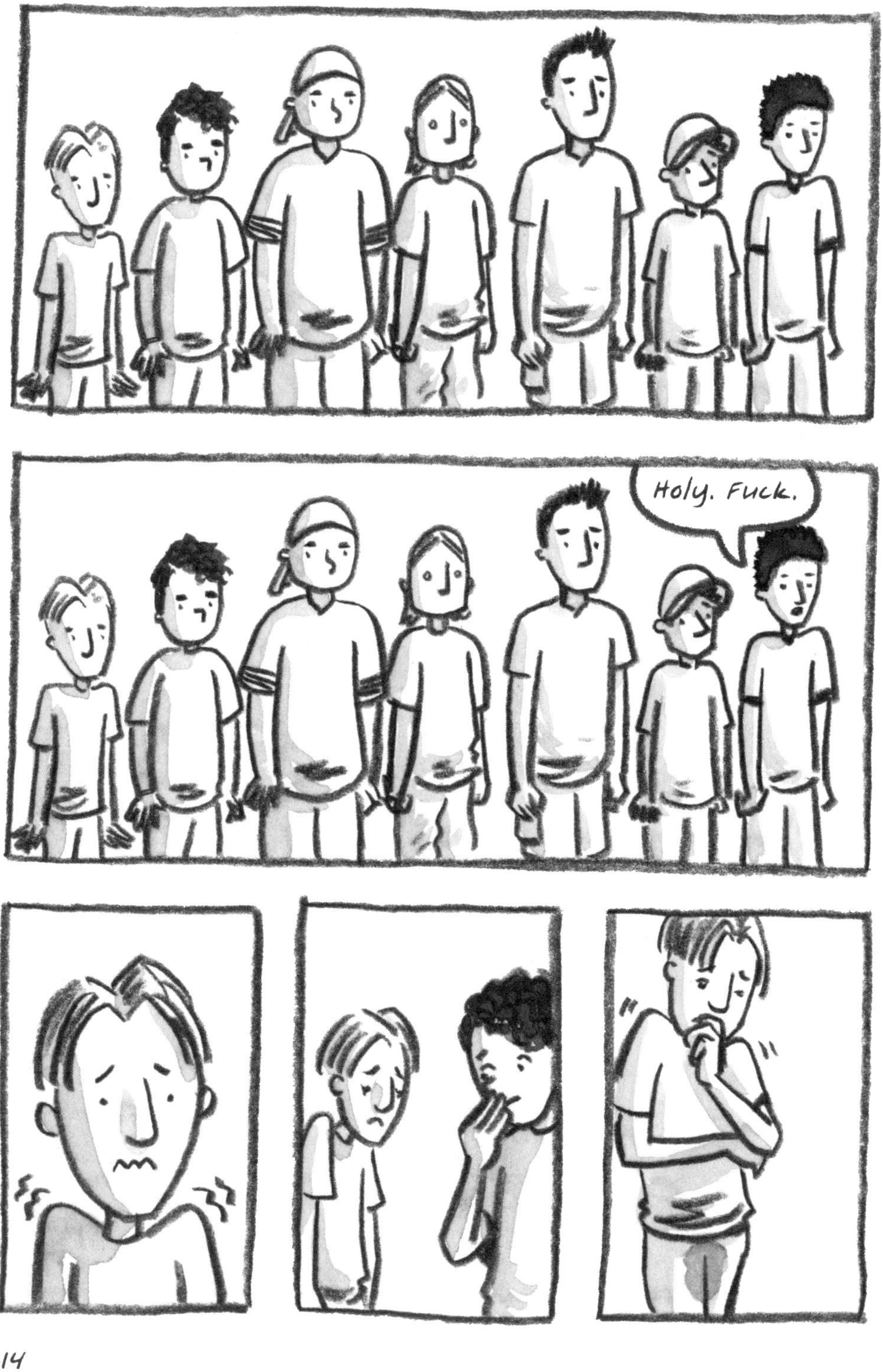
Holy. Fuck.

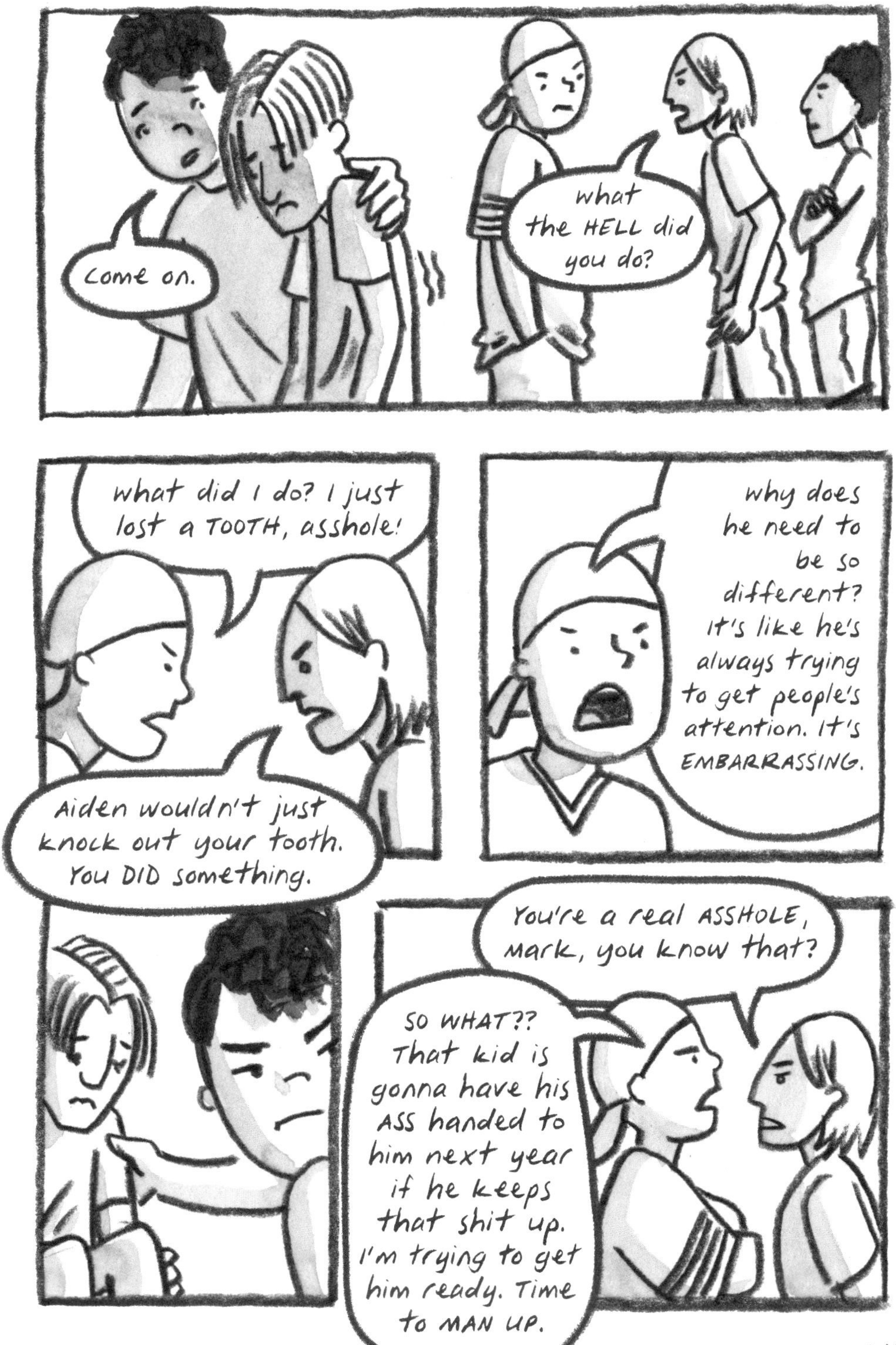
Come on.
what the HELL did you do?
what did I do? I just lost a TOOTH, asshole!
Aiden wouldn't just knock out your tooth. You DID something.
why does he need to be so different? It's like he's always trying to get people's attention. It's EMBARRASSING.
You're a real ASSHOLE, Mark, you know that?
SO WHAT?? That kid is gonna have his ASS handed to him next year if he keeps that shit up. I'm trying to get him ready. Time to MAN UP.

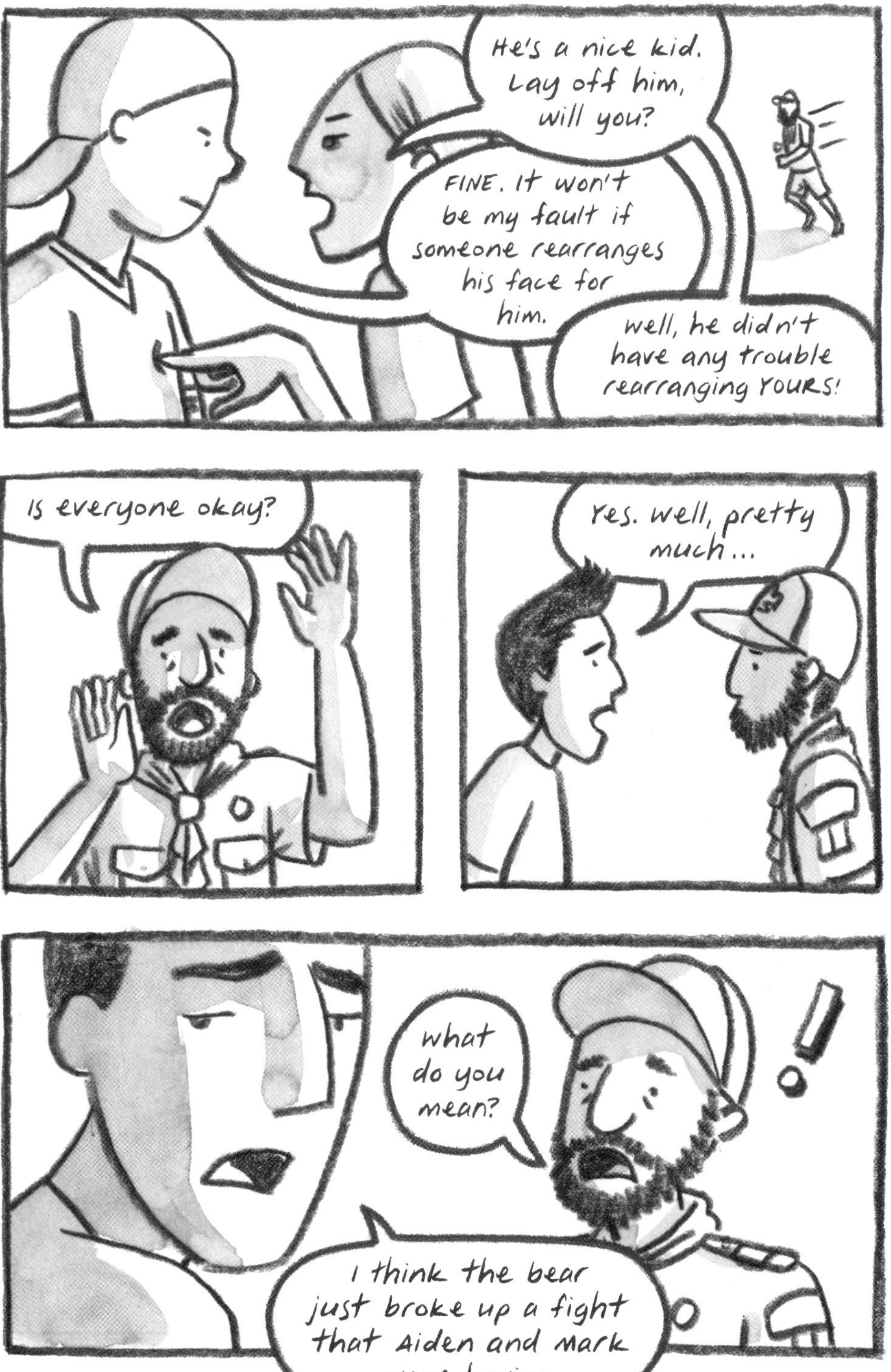
He's a nice kid. Lay off him, will you?
FINE. It won't be my fault if someone rearranges his face for him.
Well, he didn't have any trouble rearranging YOURS!
Is everyone okay?
Yes. Well, pretty much...
What do you mean?
I think the bear just broke up a fight that Aiden and Mark were having.

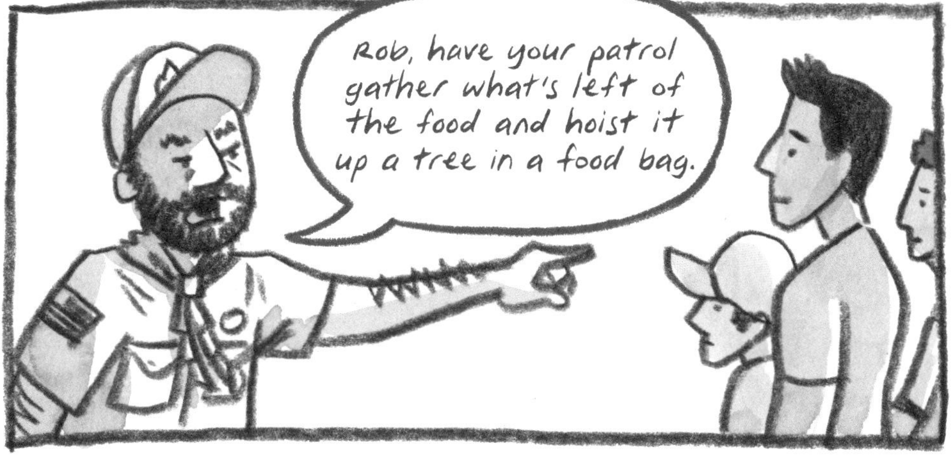
Rob, have your patrol gather what's left of the food and hoist it up a tree in a food bag.

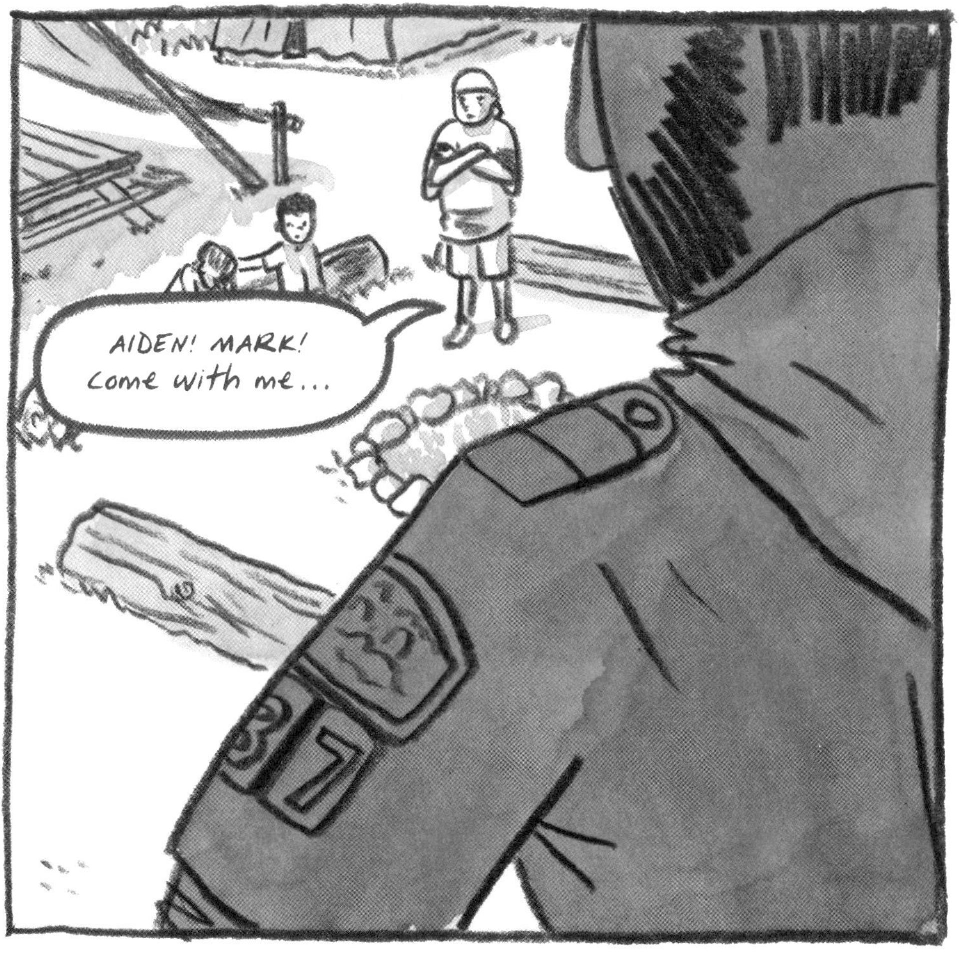
AIDEN! MARK! Come with me...
37

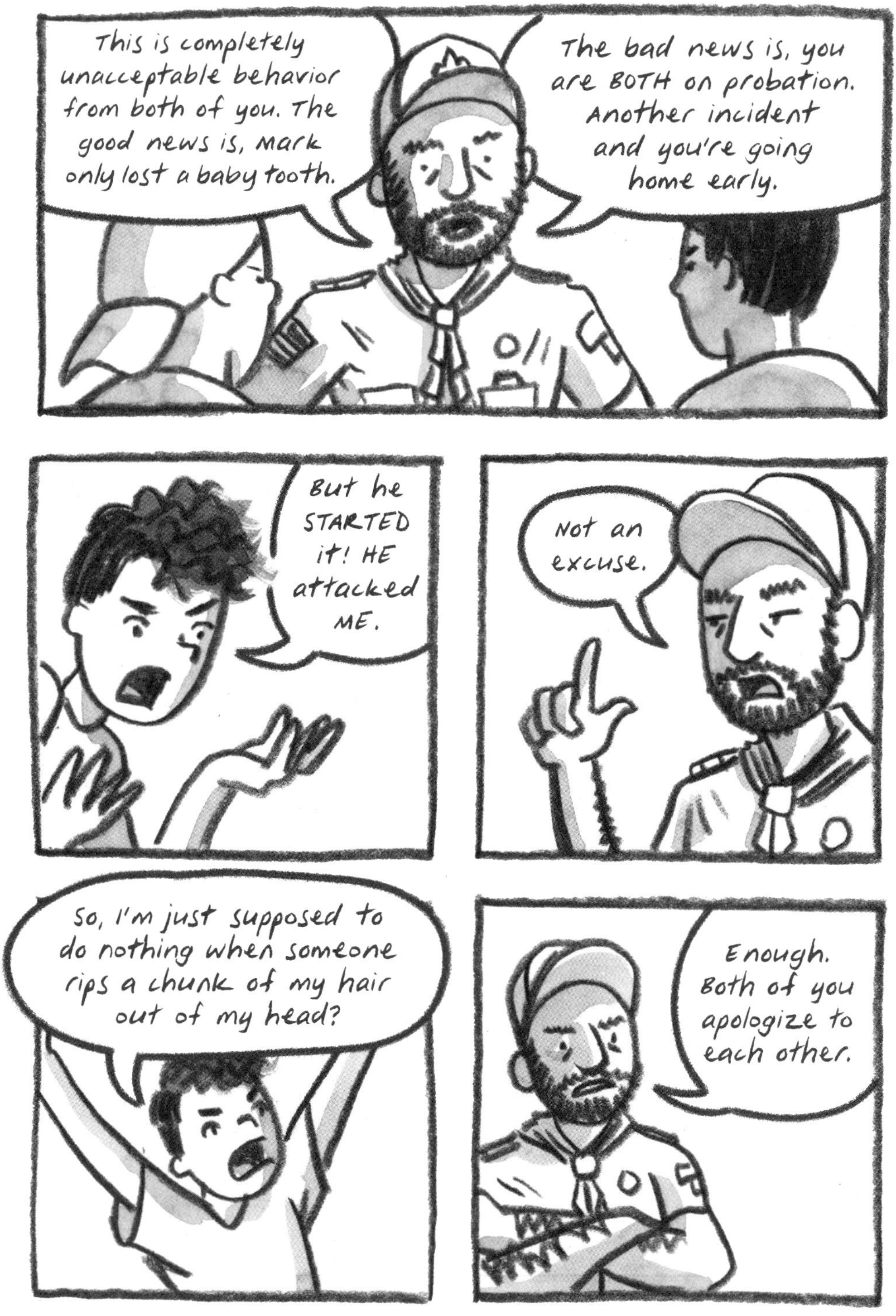
This is completely unacceptable behavior from both of you. The good news is, Mark only lost a baby tooth.
The bad news is, you are BOTH on probation. Another incident and you're going home early.
But he STARTED it! HE attacked ME.
Not an excuse.
So, I'm just supposed to do nothing when someone rips a chunk of my hair out of my head?
Enough. Both of you apologize to each other.

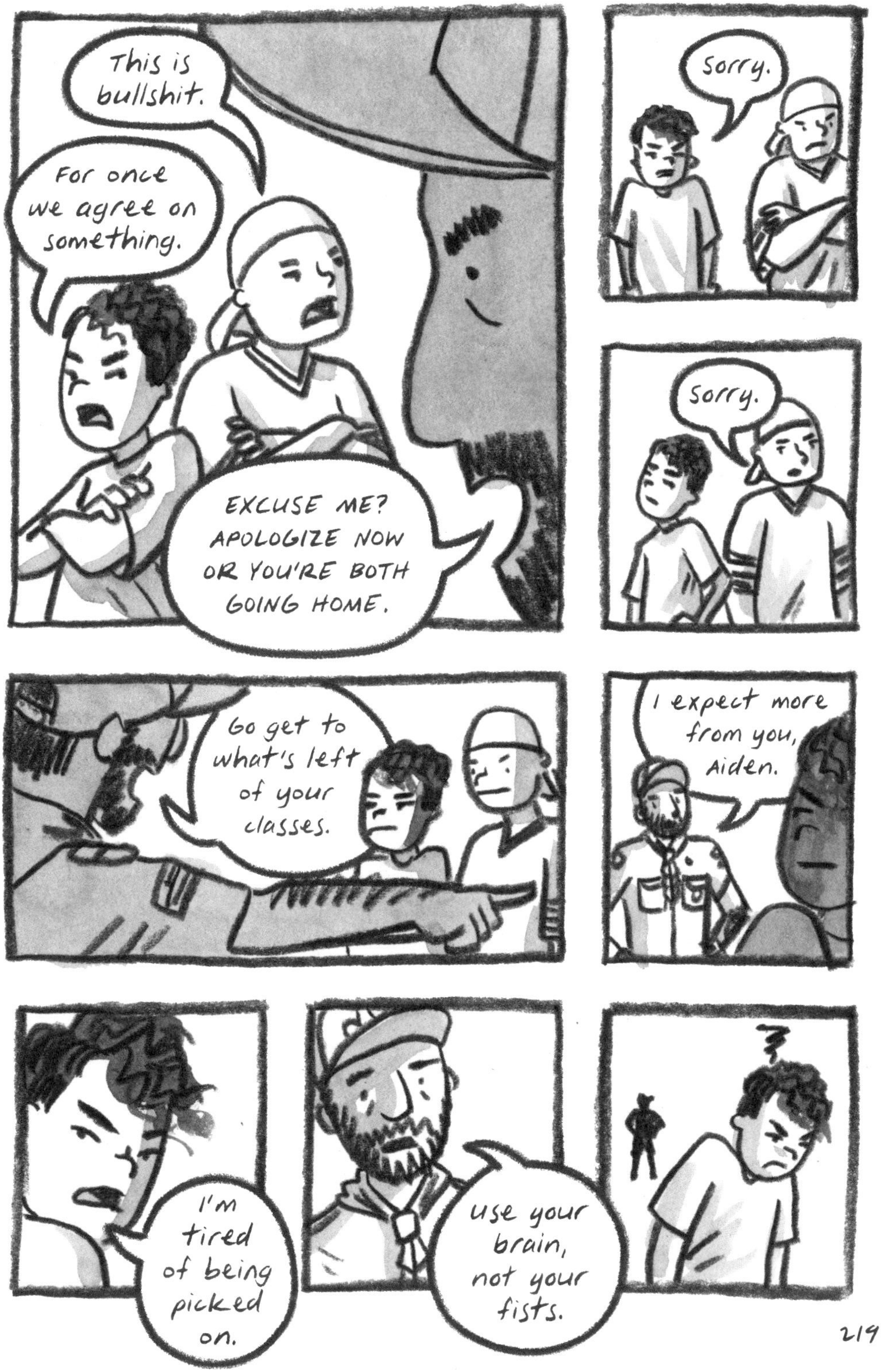
This is bullshit.
For once we agree on something.
EXCUSE ME? APOLOGIZE NOW OR YOU'RE BOTH GOING HOME.
Sorry.
Sorry.
Go get to what's left of your classes.
I expect more from you, Aiden.
I'm tired of being picked on.
Use your brain, not your fists.

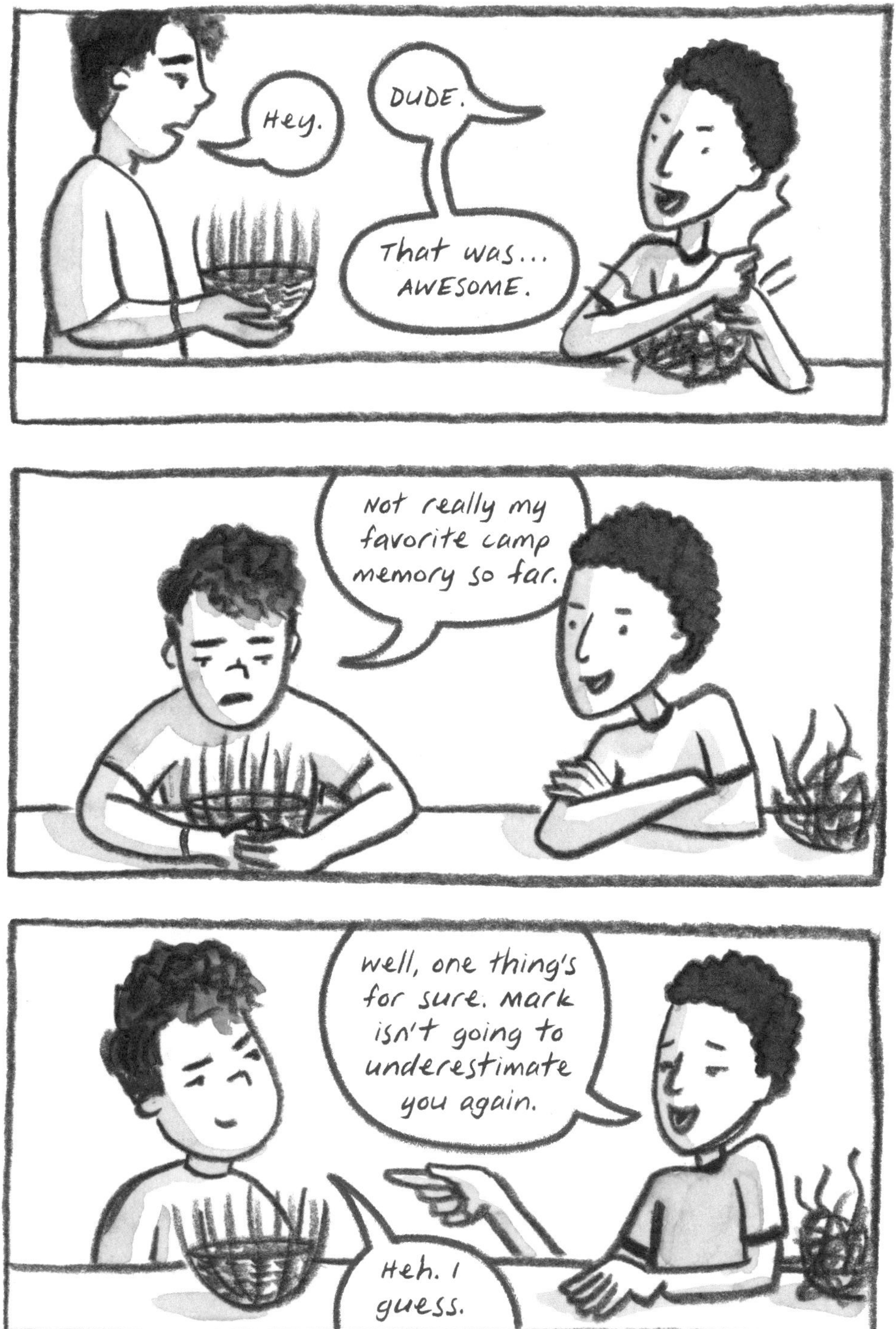
Hey.
DUDE.
That was... AWESOME.
Not really my favorite camp memory so far.
well, one thing's for sure. Mark isn't going to underestimate you again.
Heh. I guess.

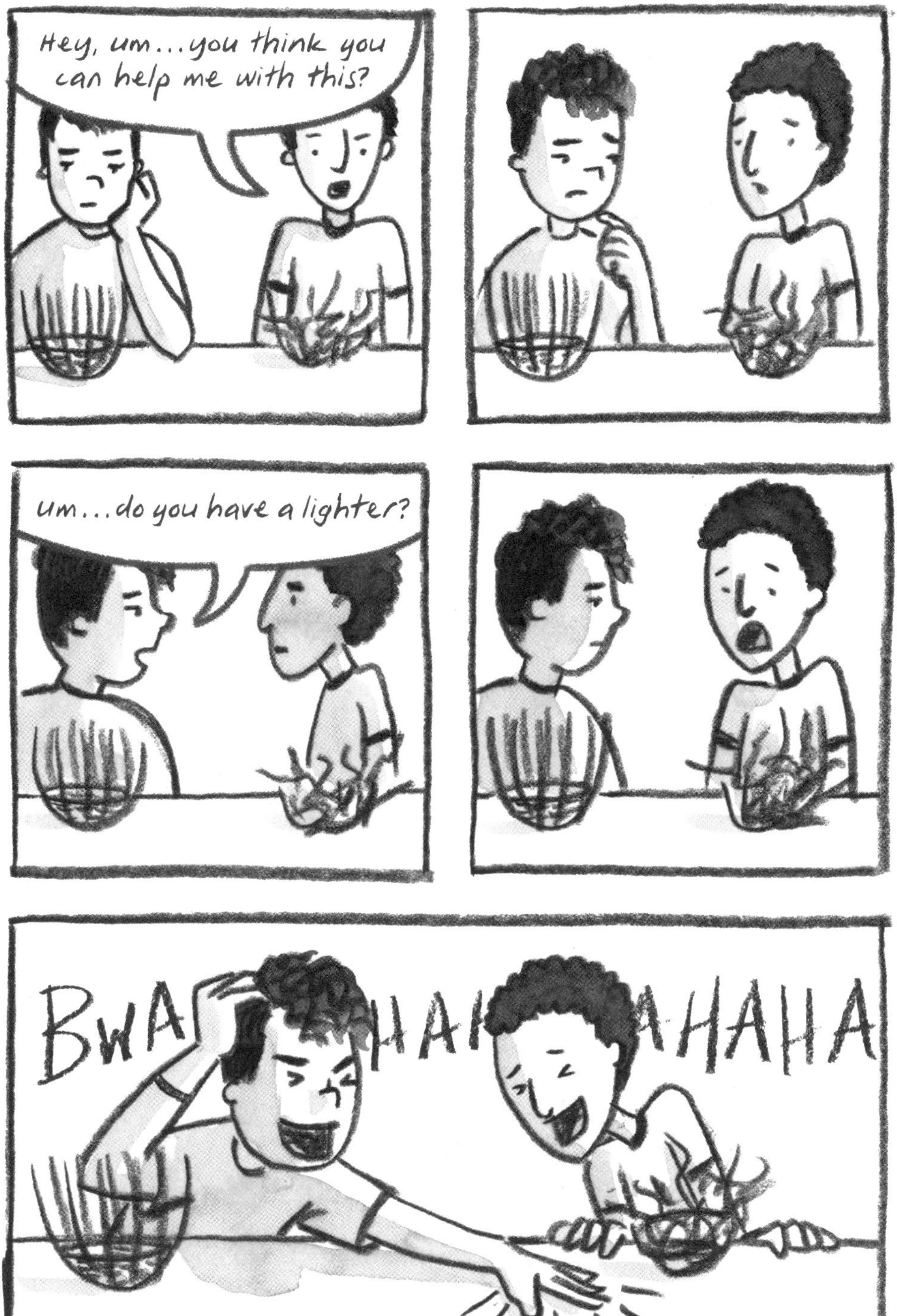
Hey, um...you think you can help me with this?
um...do you have a lighter?
BWAHAHAHAHAHA

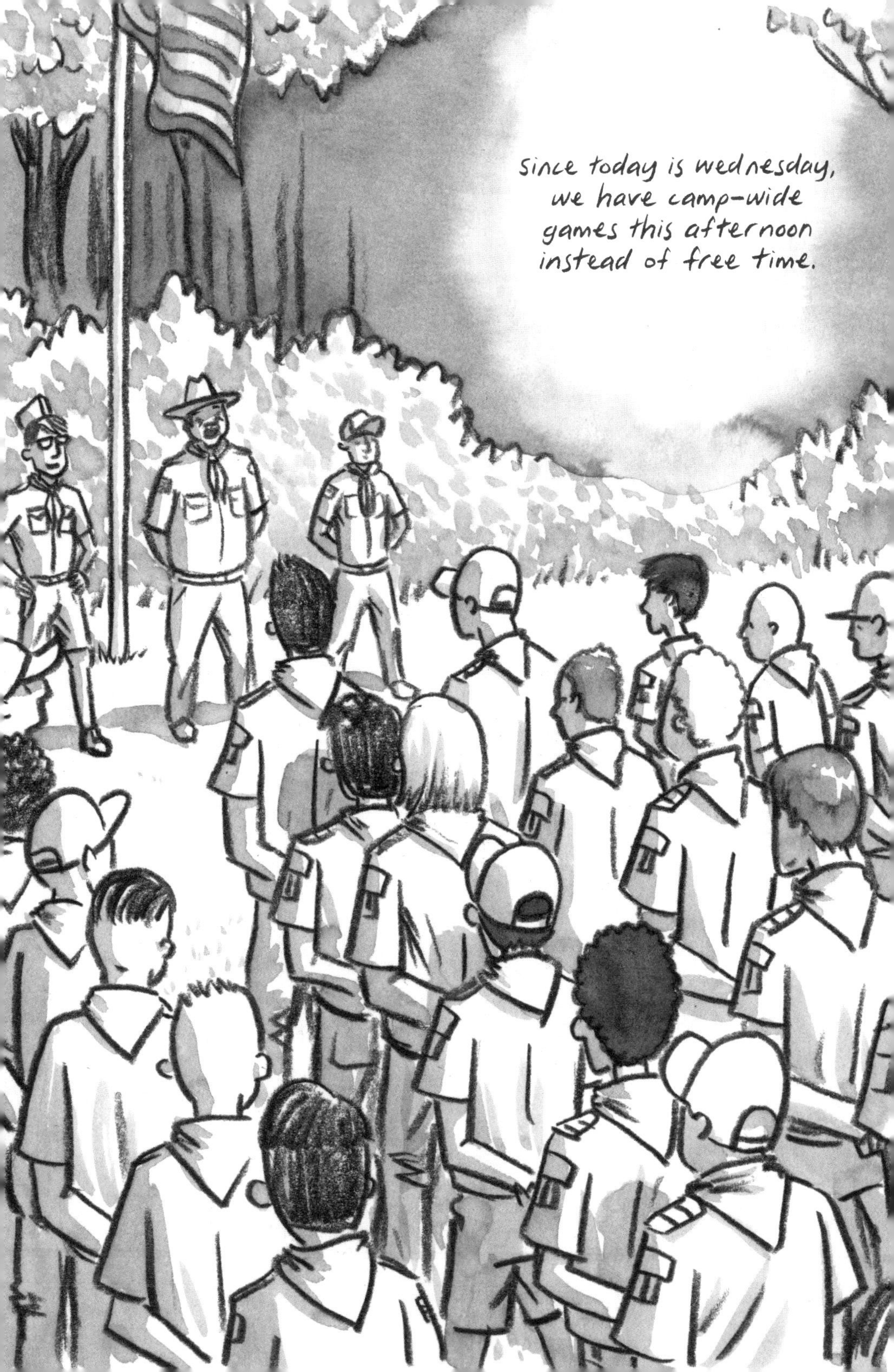
since today is wednesday, we have camp-wide games this afternoon instead of free time.

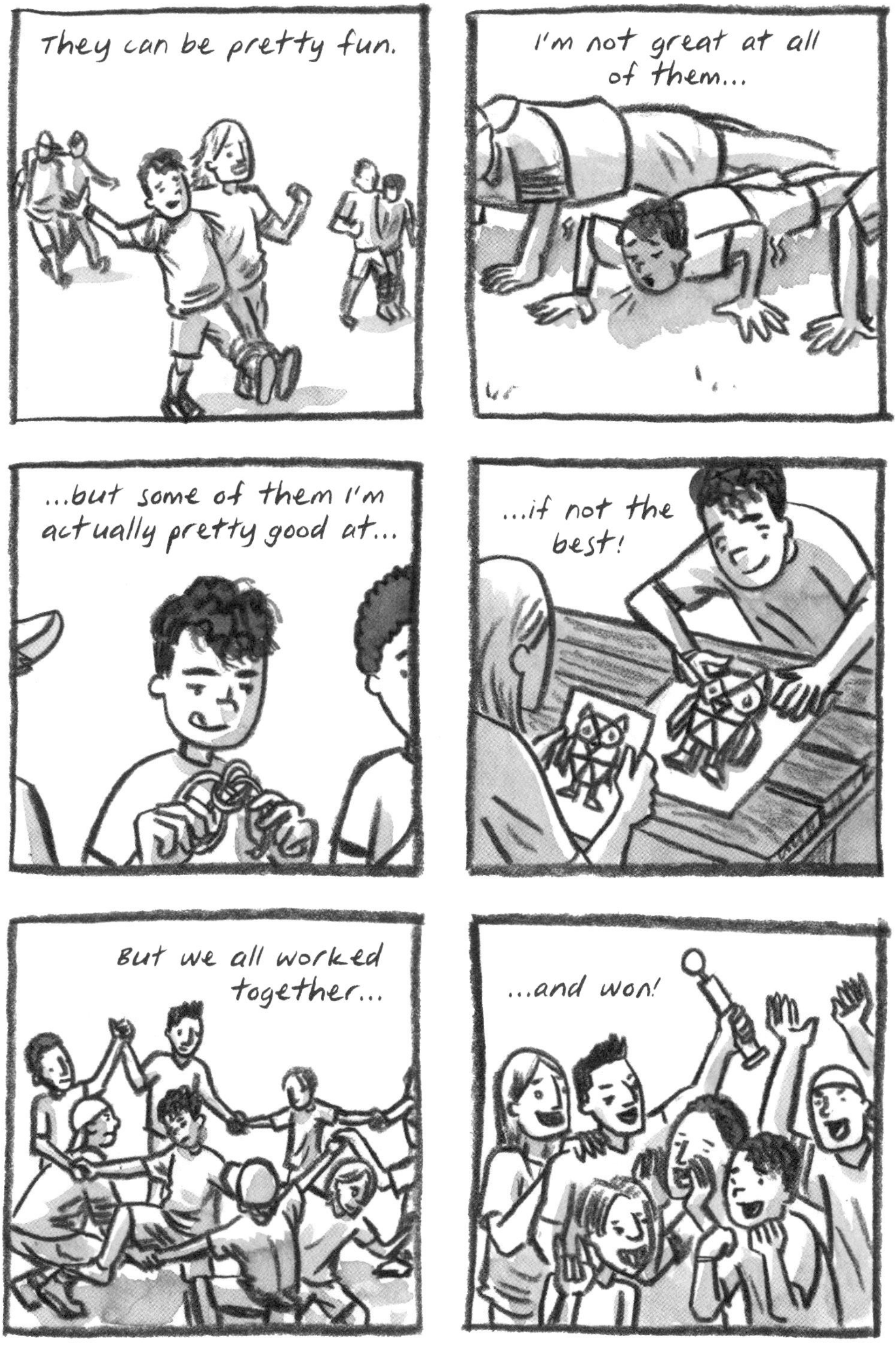
They can be pretty fun.
I'm not great at all of them...
...but some of them I'm actually pretty good at...
...if not the best!
But we all worked together...
...and won!

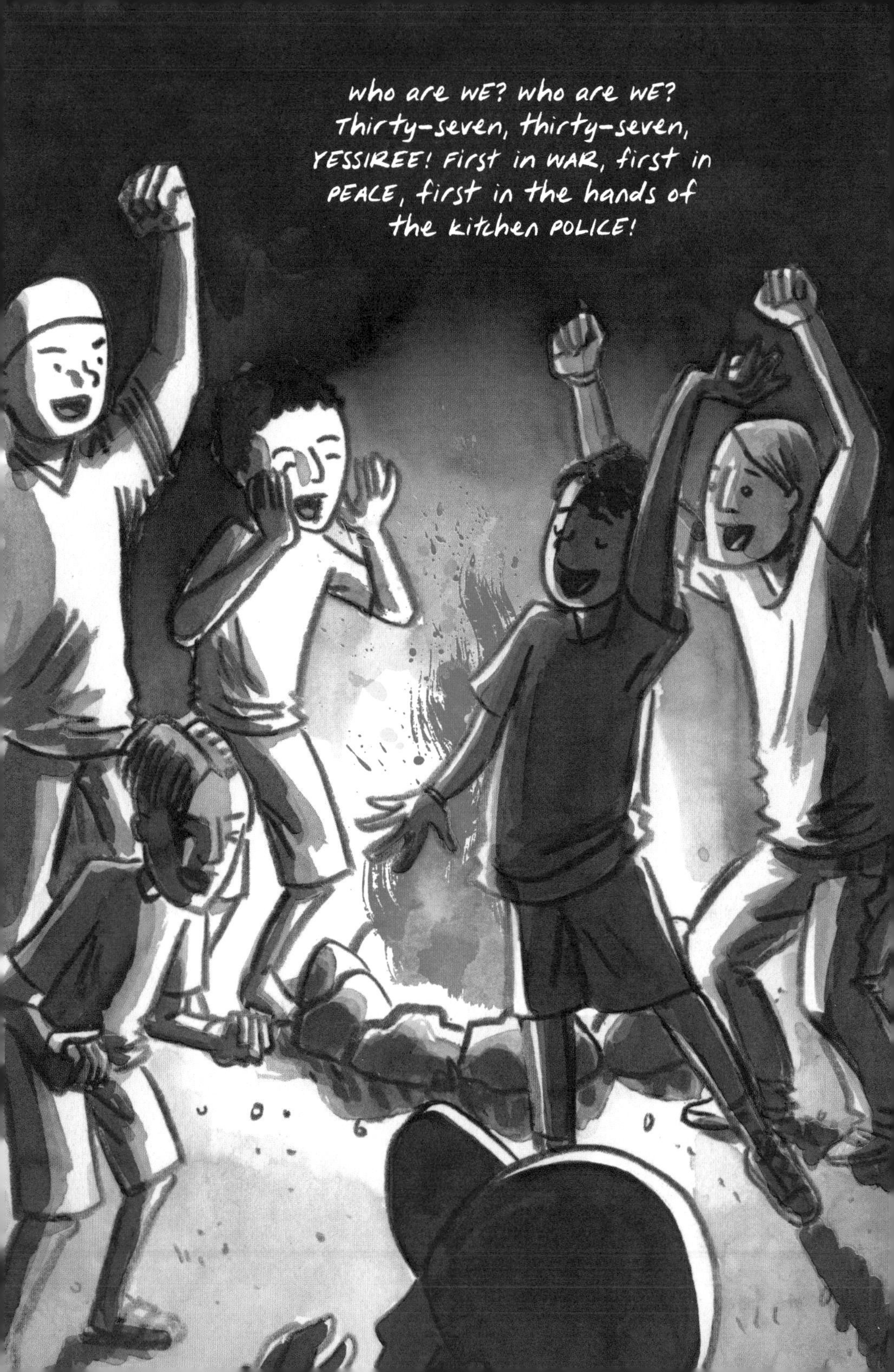
who are WE? who are WE? Thirty-seven, thirty-seven, YESSIREE! First in WAR, first in PEACE, first in the hands of the kitchen POLICE!

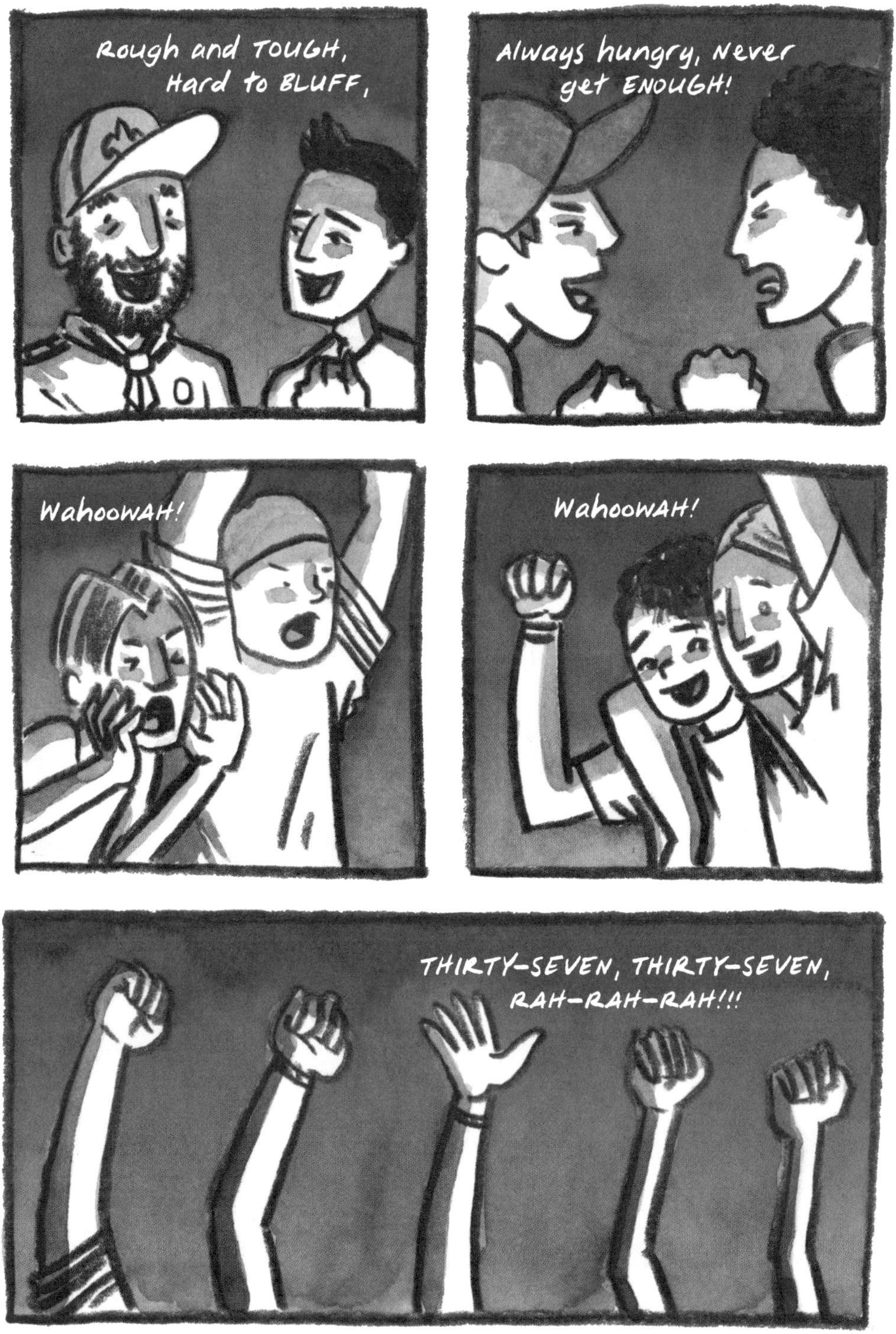
Rough and TOUGH, Hard to BLUFF,
Always hungry, Never get ENOUGH!
WahooWAH!
WahooWAH!
THIRTY-SEVEN, THIRTY-SEVEN, RAH-RAH-RAH!!!

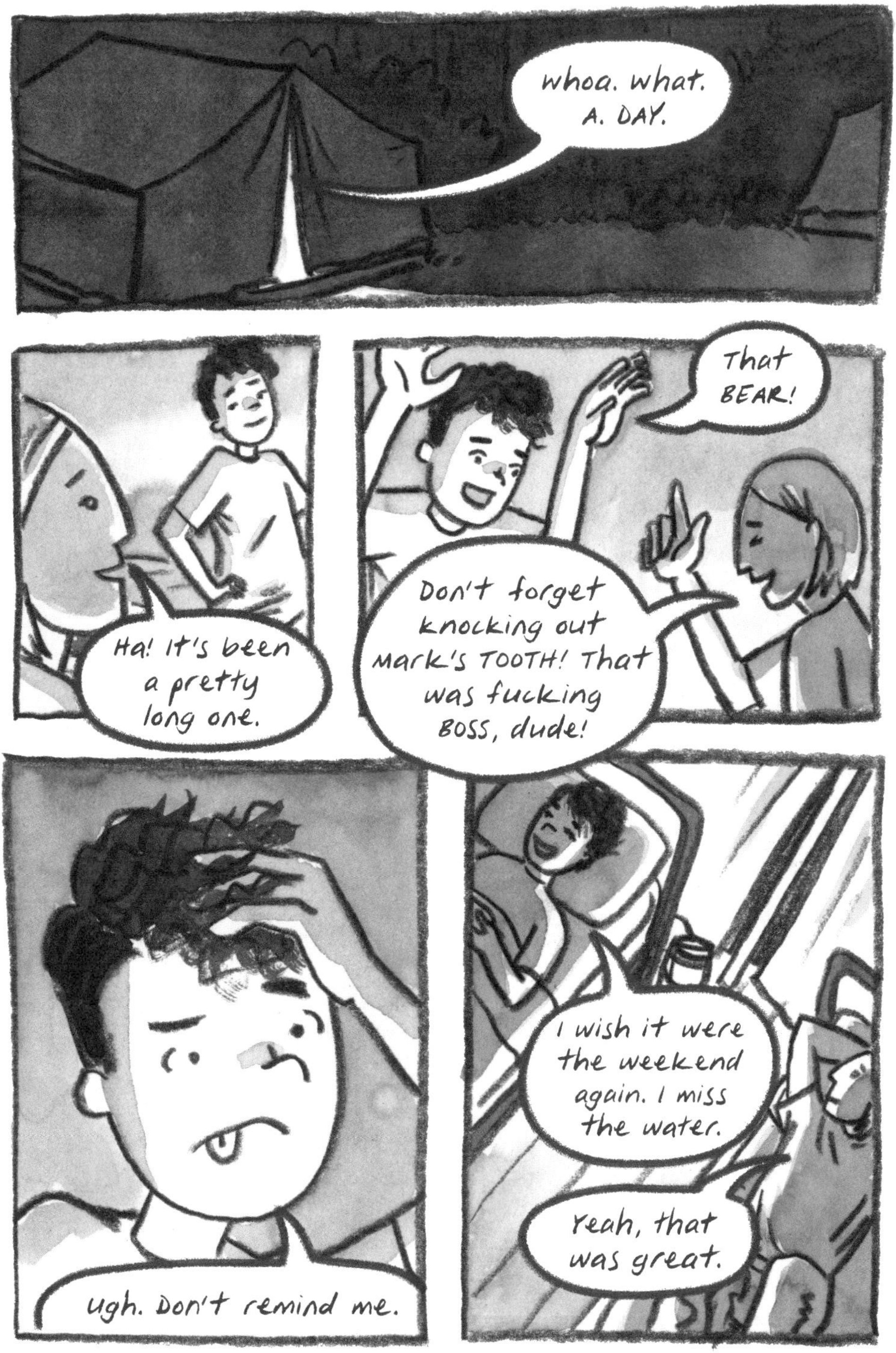
whoa. what. A. DAY.
Ha! It's been a pretty long one.
That BEAR!
Don't forget knocking out Mark's TOOTH! That was fucking BOSS, dude!
ugh. Don't remind me.
I wish it were the weekend again. I miss the water.
Yeah, that was great.

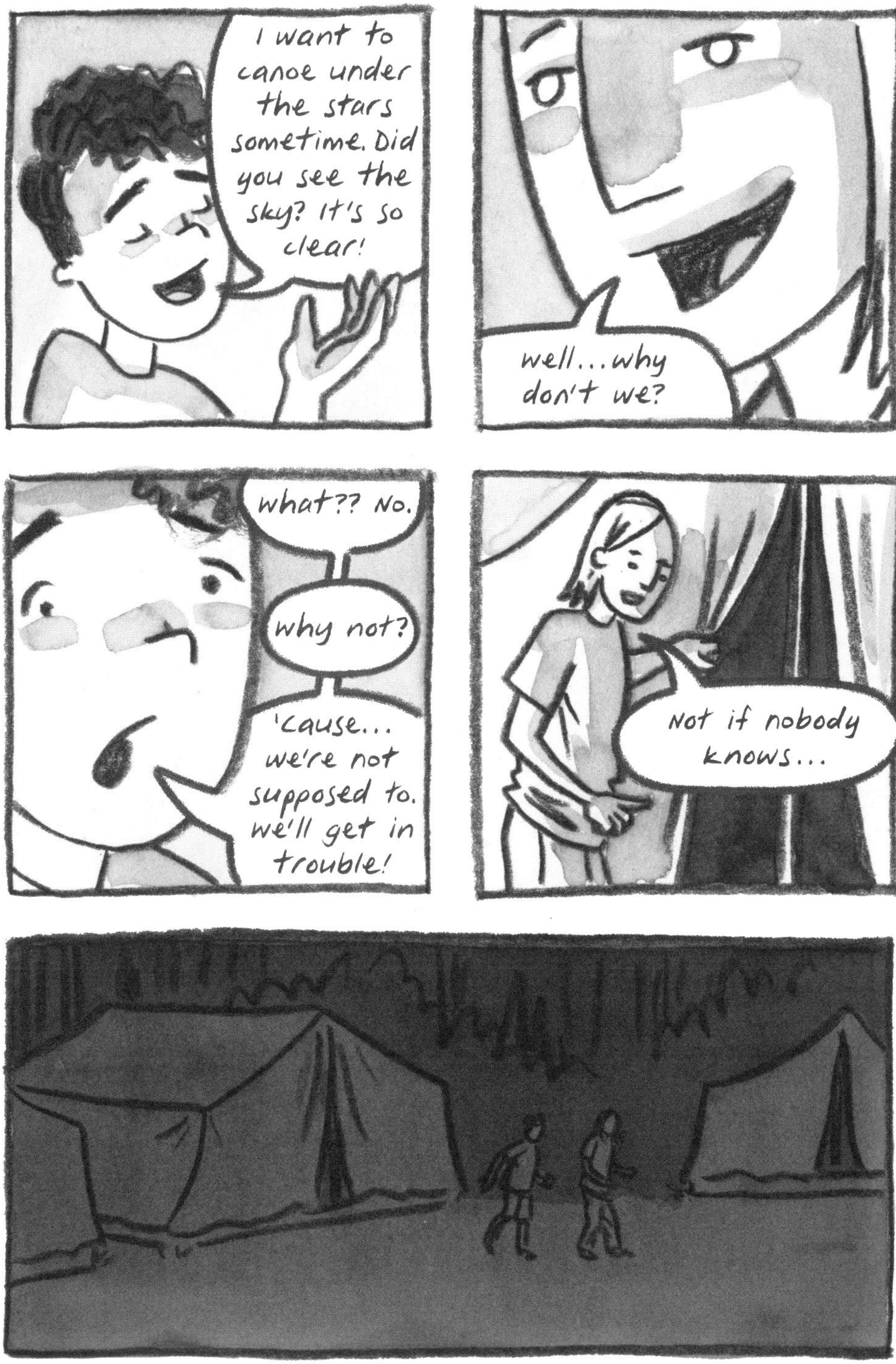
I want to canoe under the stars sometime. Did you see the sky? It's so clear!
well...why don't we?
what?? No.
why not?
'cause... we're not supposed to. we'll get in trouble!
Not if nobody knows...

SCLICKS

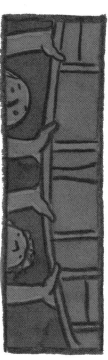

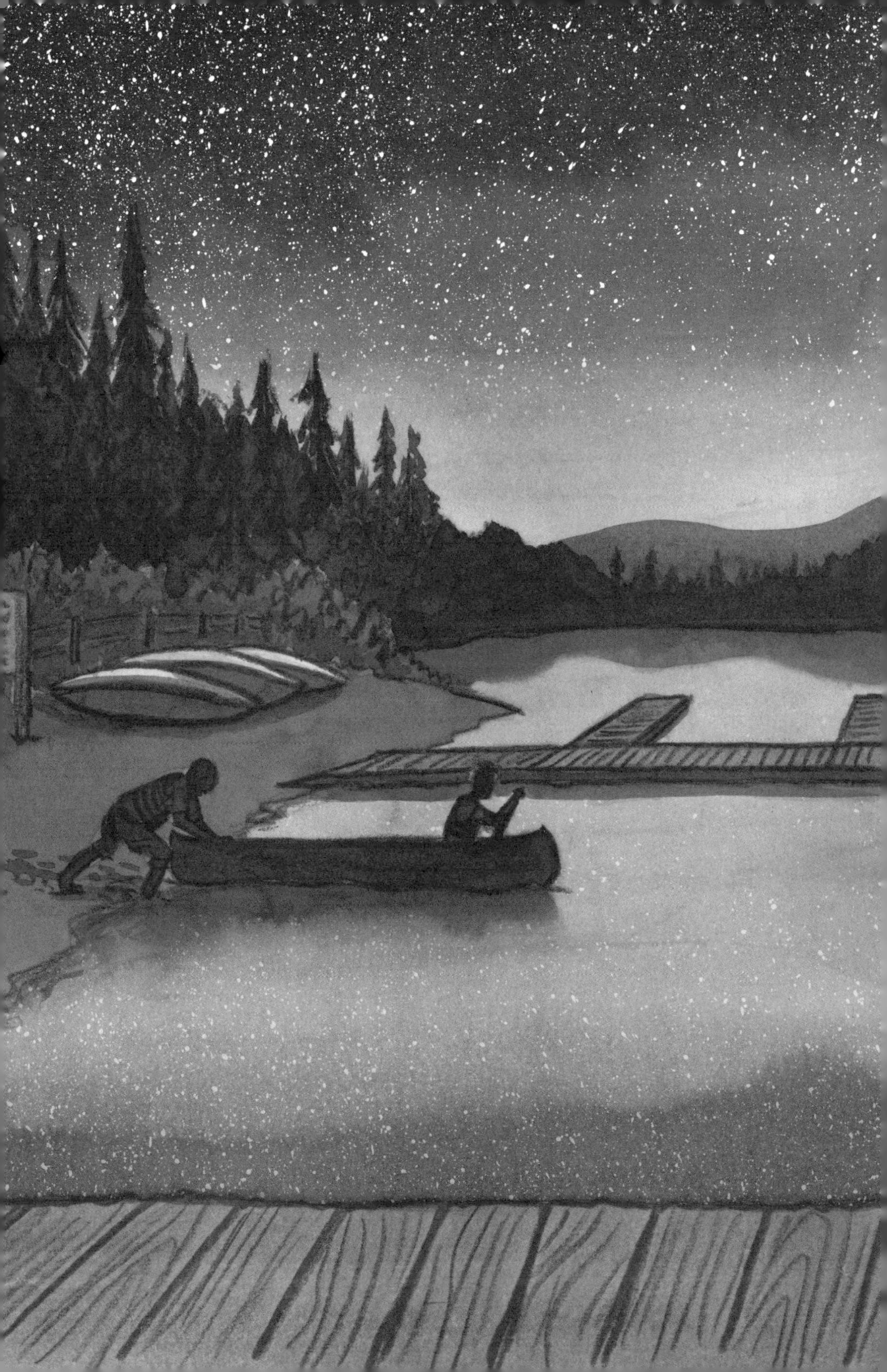

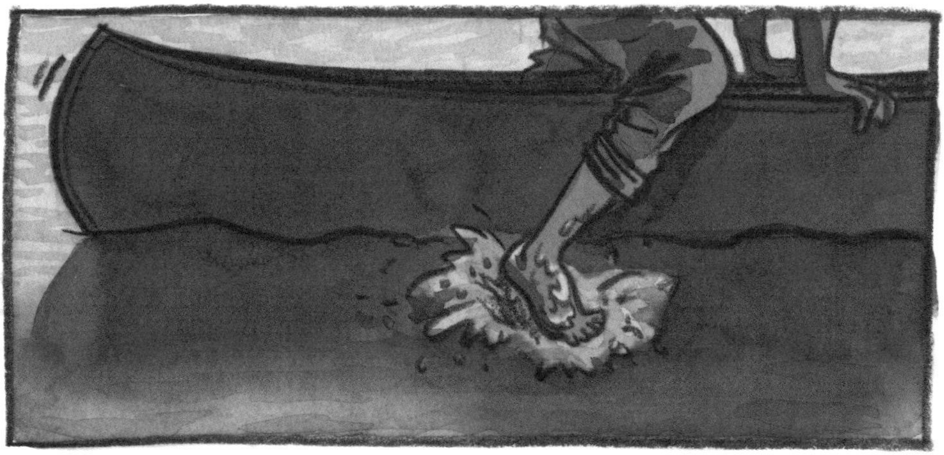

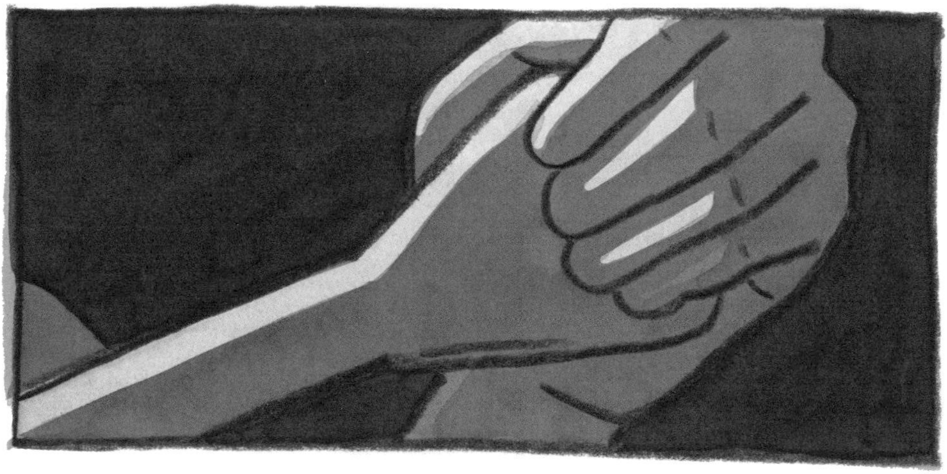

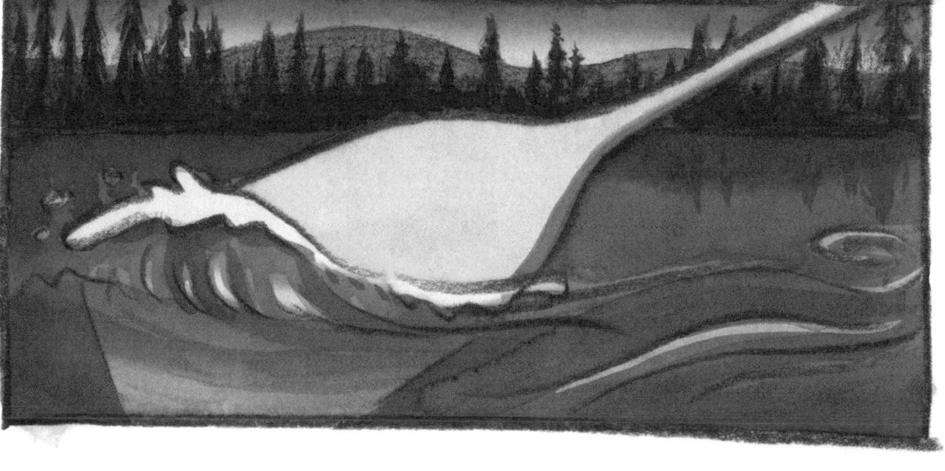

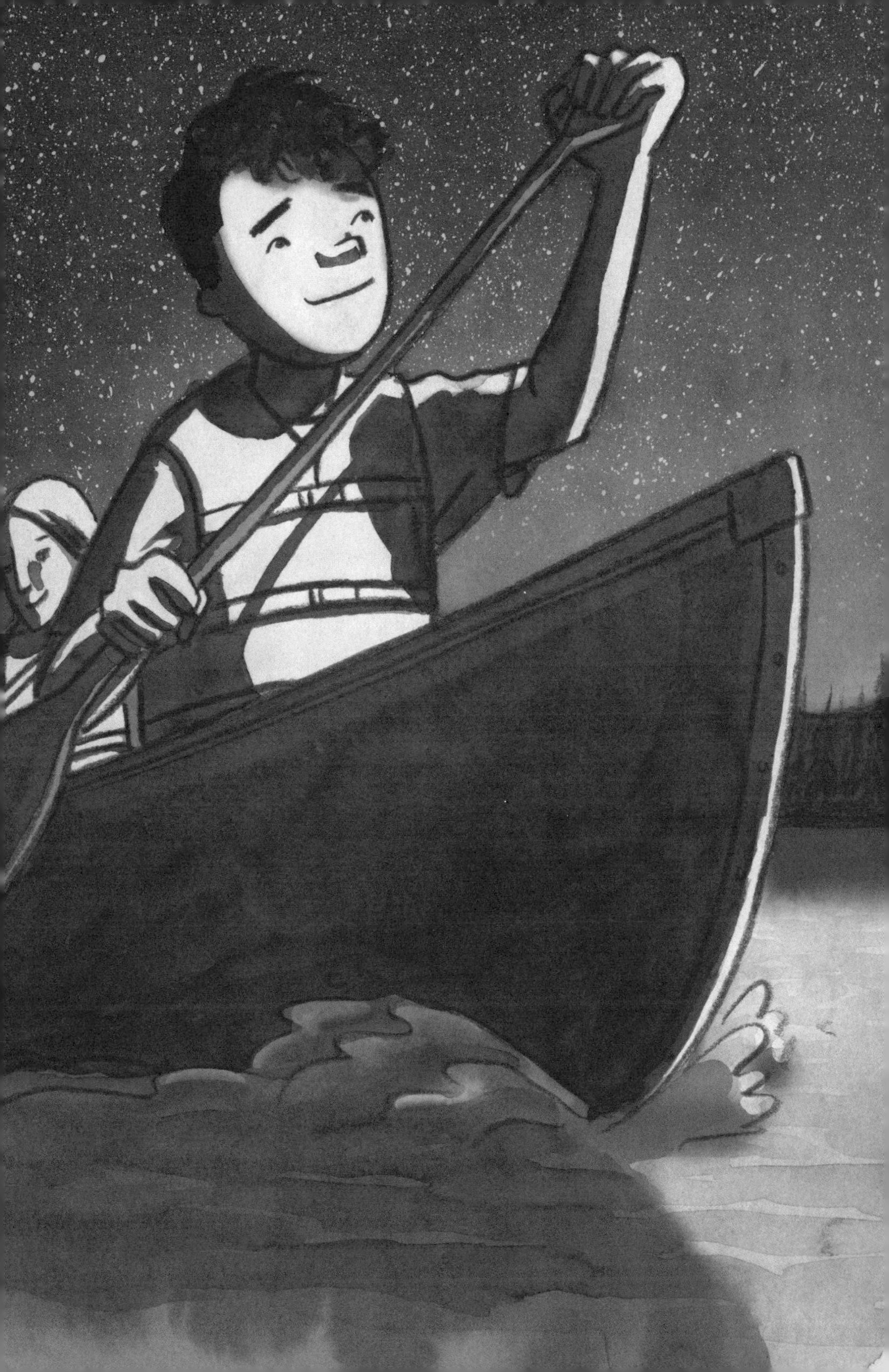

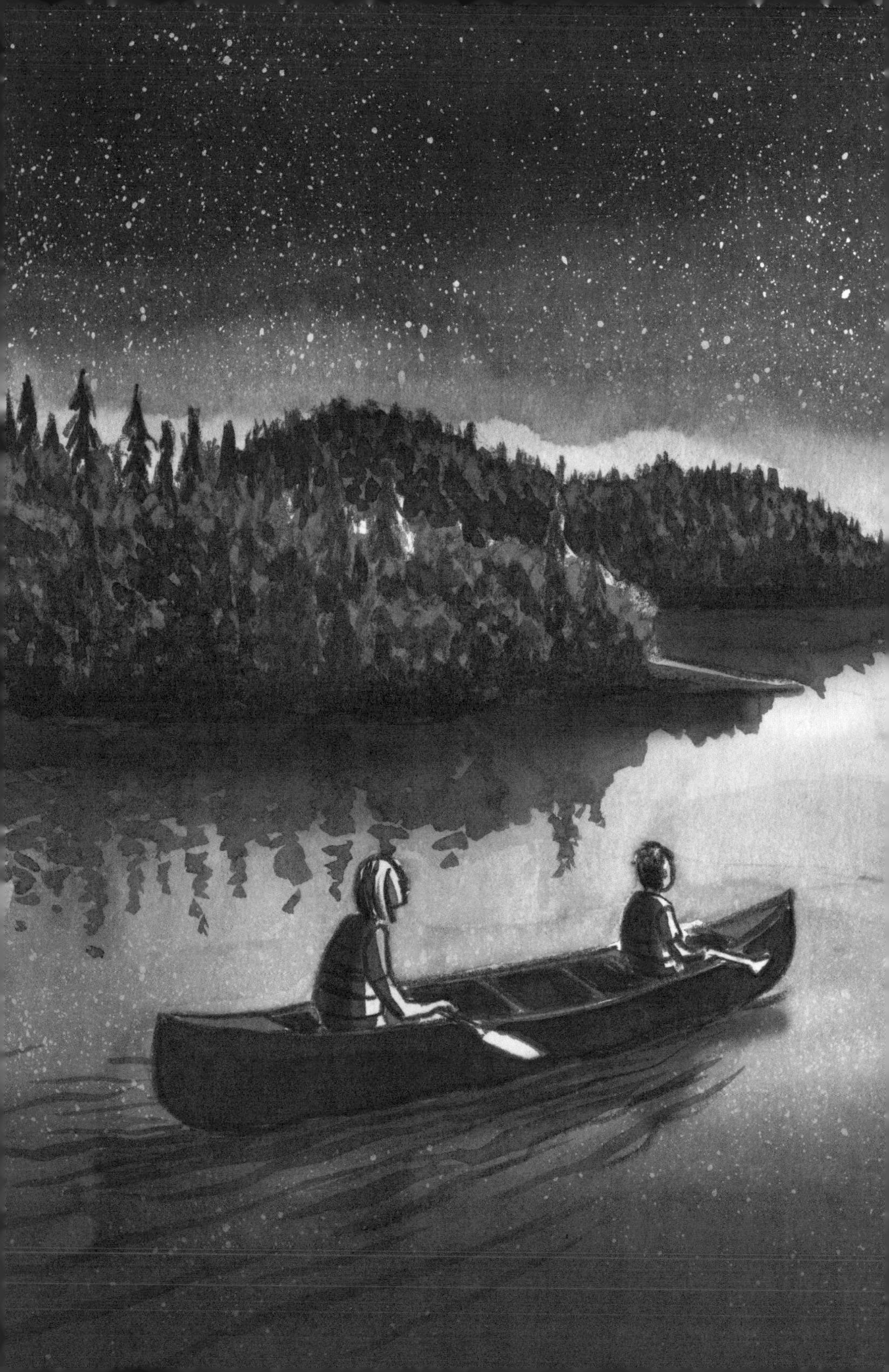

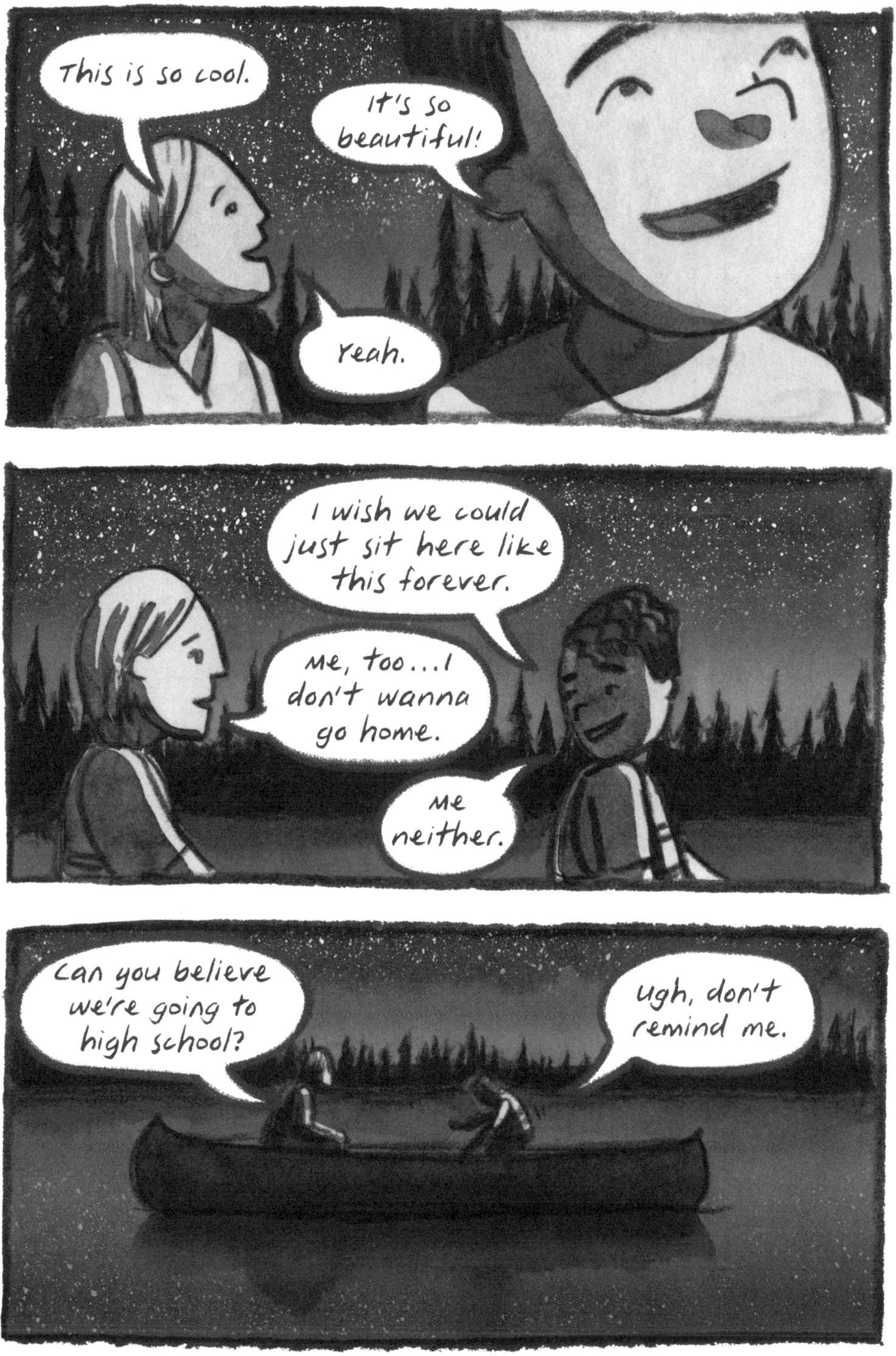
This is so cool.
It's so beautiful!
Yeah.
I wish we could just sit here like this forever.
Me, too... I don't wanna go home.
Me neither.
Can you believe we're going to high school?
Ugh, don't remind me.

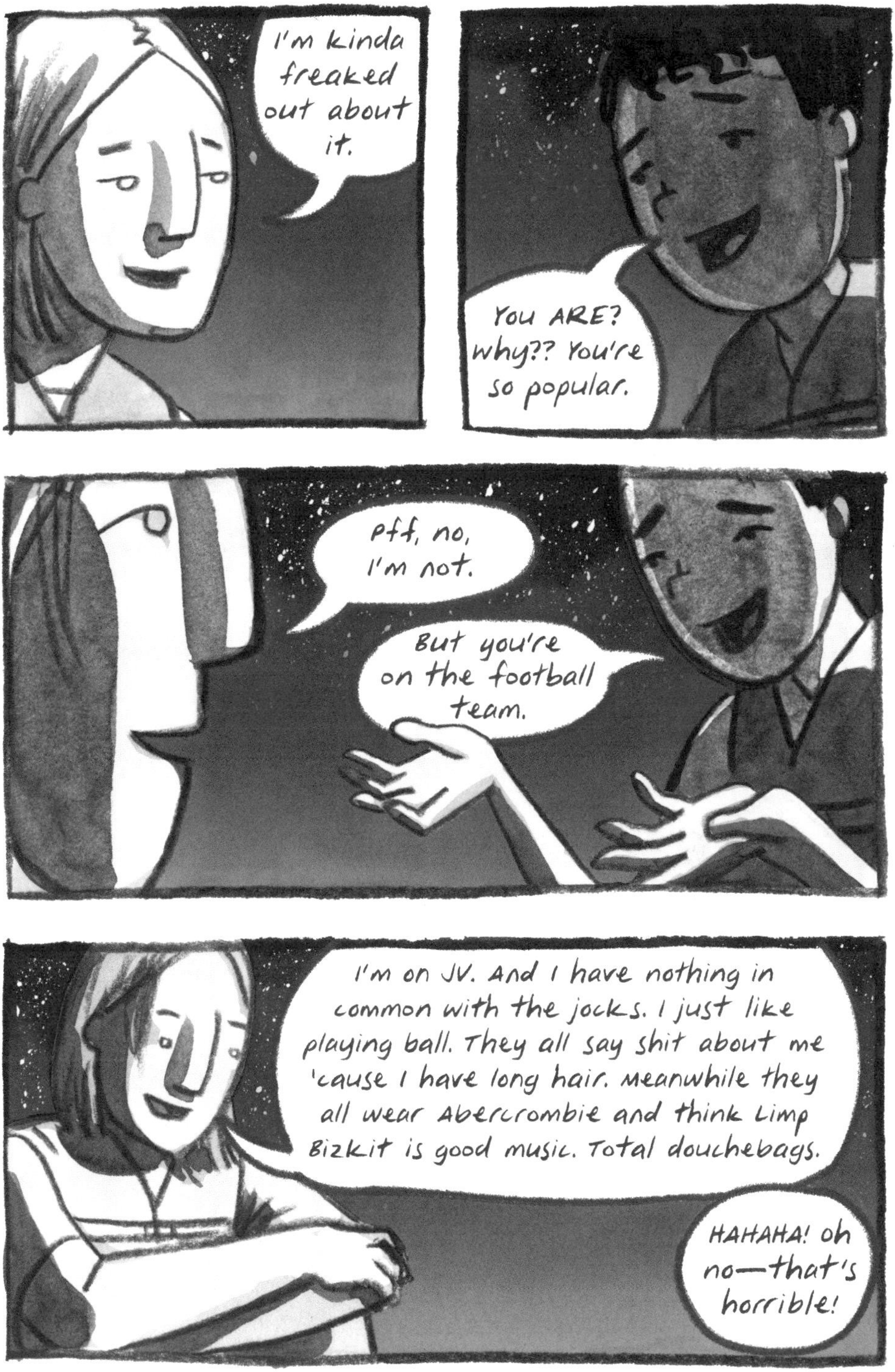
I'm kinda freaked out about it.
You ARE? Why?? You're so popular.
Pff, no, I'm not.
But you're on the football team.
I'm on JV. And I have nothing in common with the jocks. I just like playing ball. They all say shit about me 'cause I have long hair. Meanwhile they all wear Abercrombie and think Limp Bizkit is good music. Total douchebags.
HAHAHA! Oh no—that's horrible!

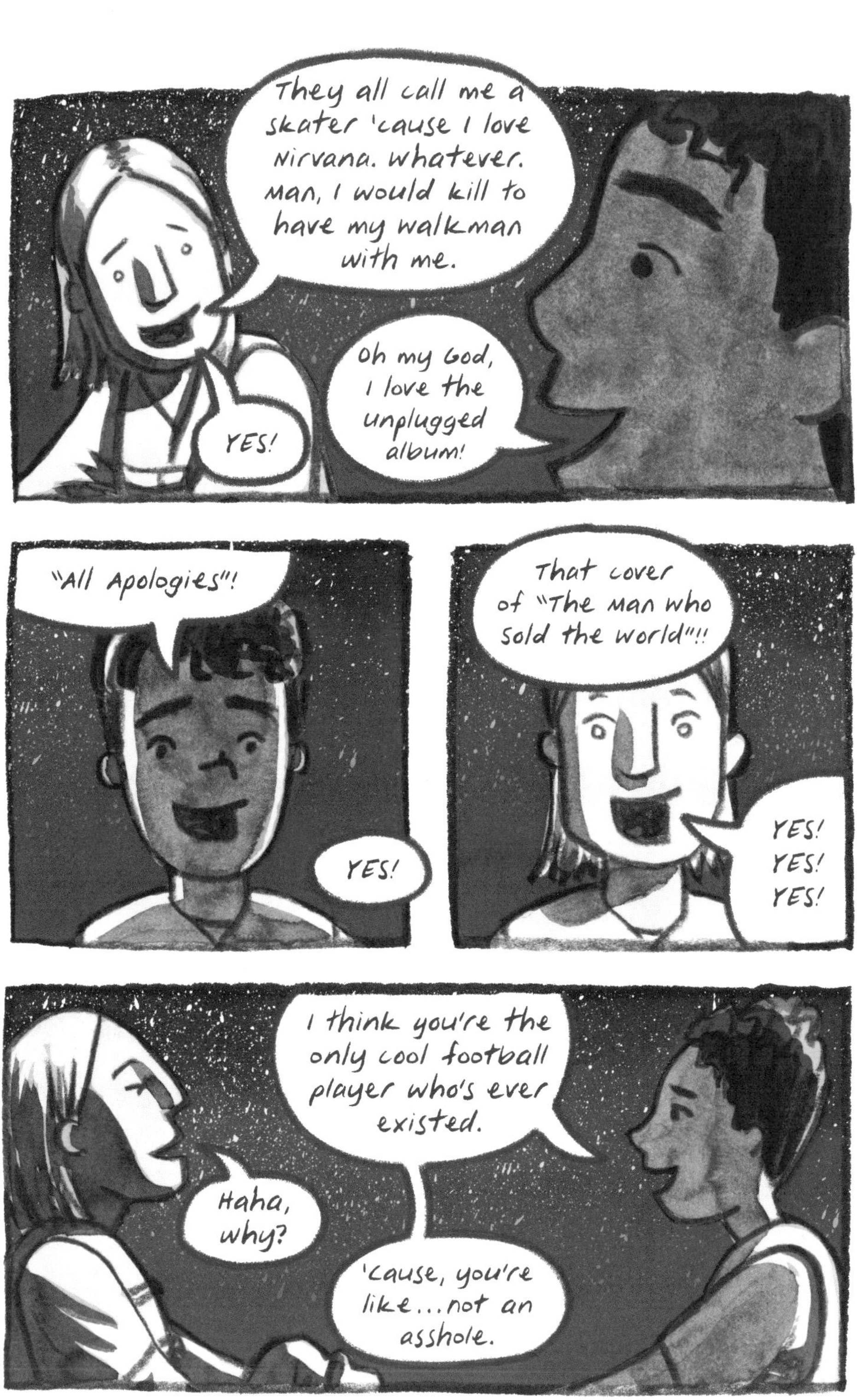
They all call me a skater 'cause I love Nirvana. whatever. Man, I would kill to have my walkman with me.
YES!
Oh my God, I love the unplugged album!
"All Apologies"!
YES!
That cover of "The Man who Sold the world"!!
YES! YES! YES!
I think you're the only cool football player who's ever existed.
Haha, why?
'cause, you're like...not an asshole.

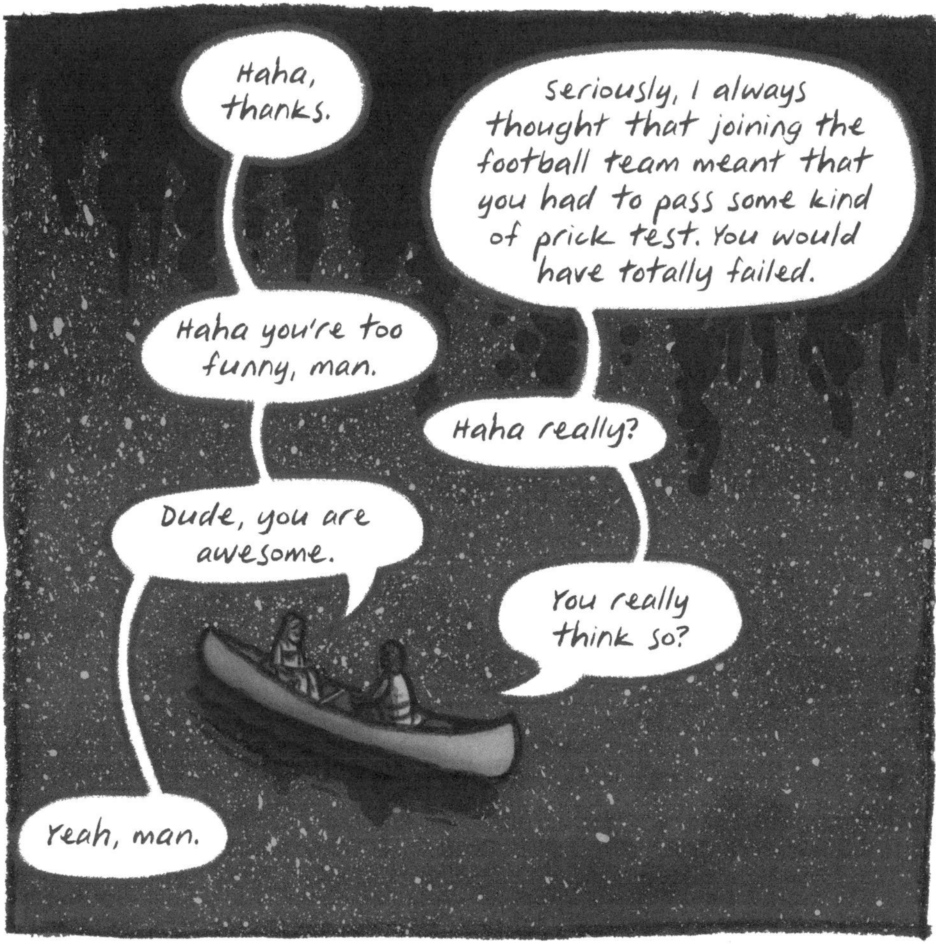
Haha, thanks.
Seriously, I always thought that joining the football team meant that you had to pass some kind of prick test. You would have totally failed.
Haha you're too funny, man.
Haha really?
Dude, you are awesome.
You really think so?
Yeah, man.

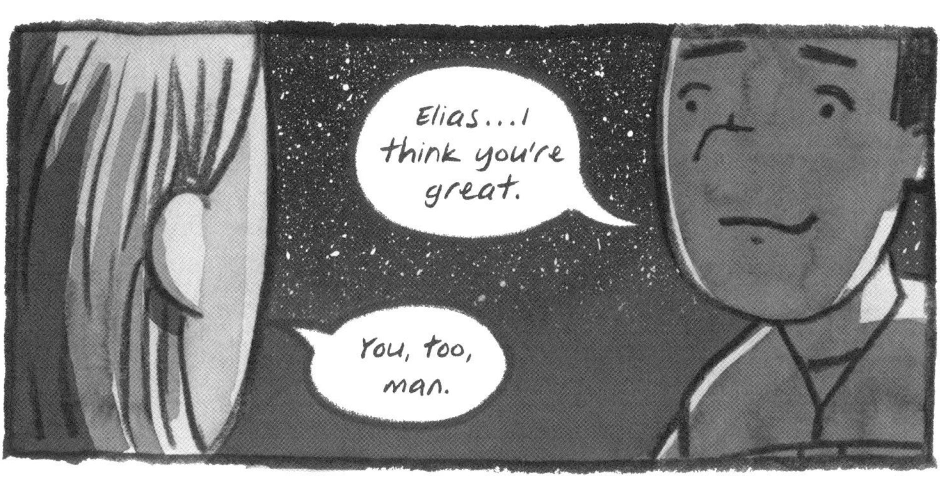
Elias...I think you're great.
You, too, man.

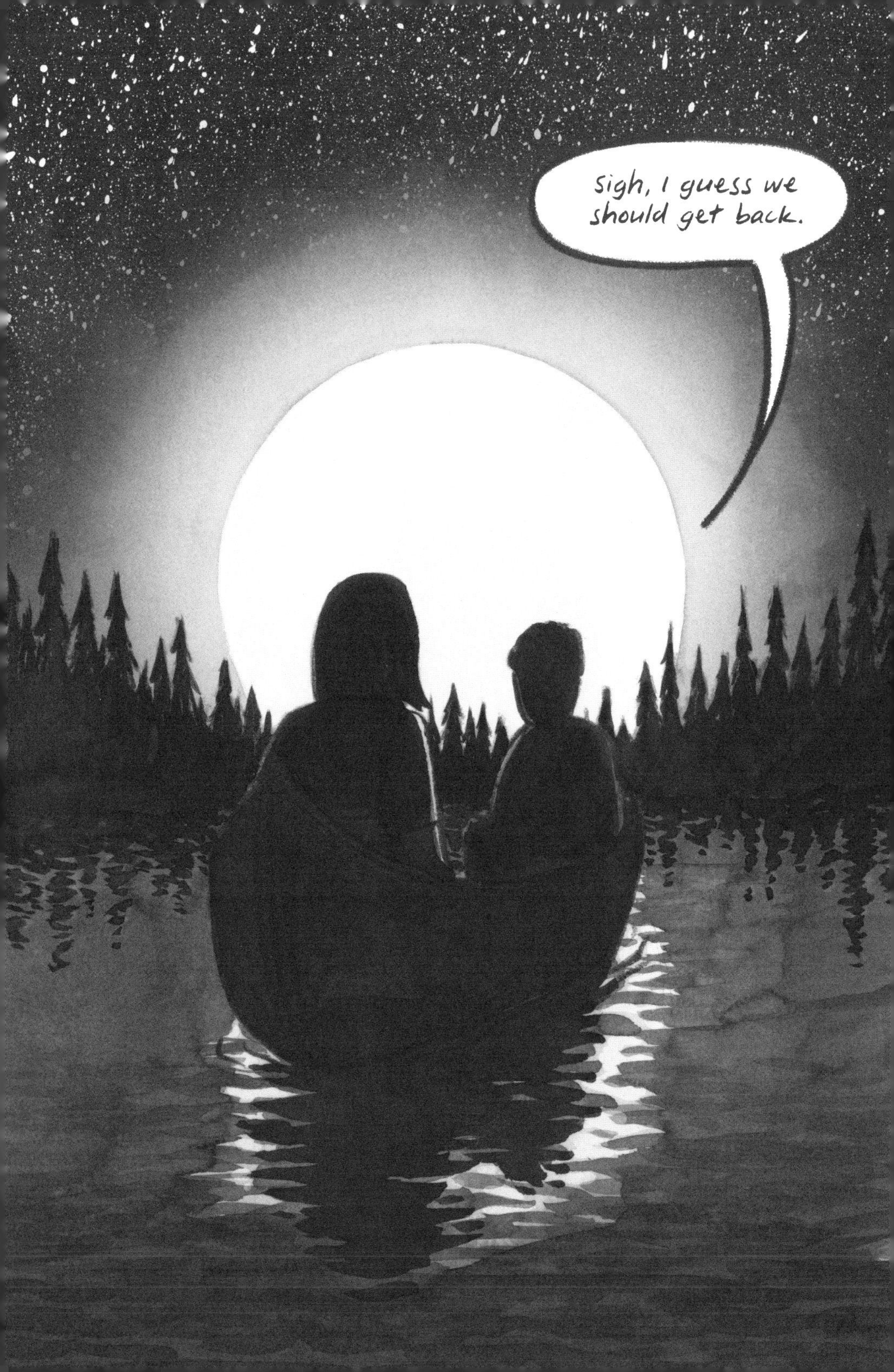
Sigh, I guess we should get back.

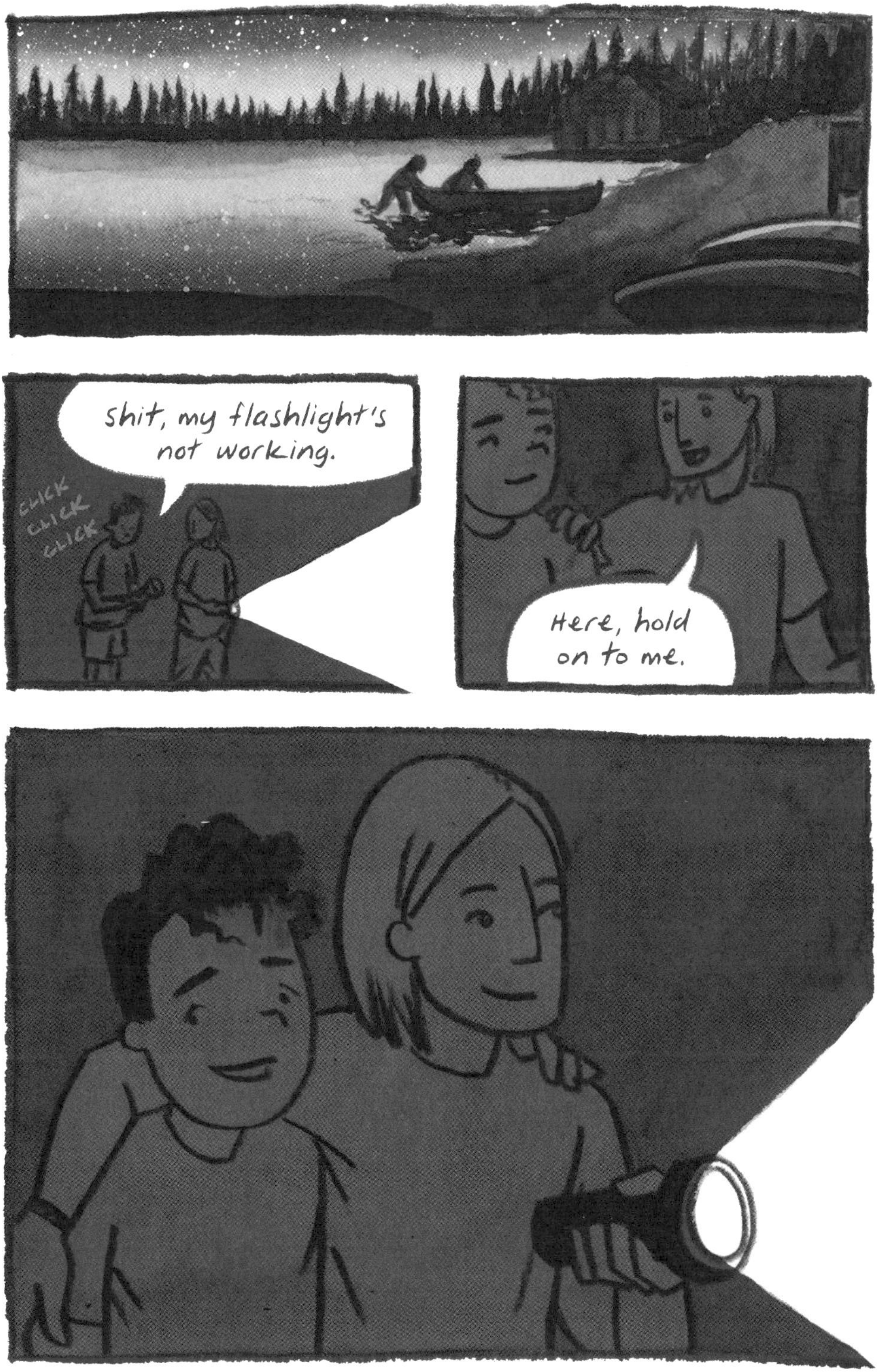
shit, my flashlight's not working.
CLICK CLICK CLICK
Here, hold on to me.

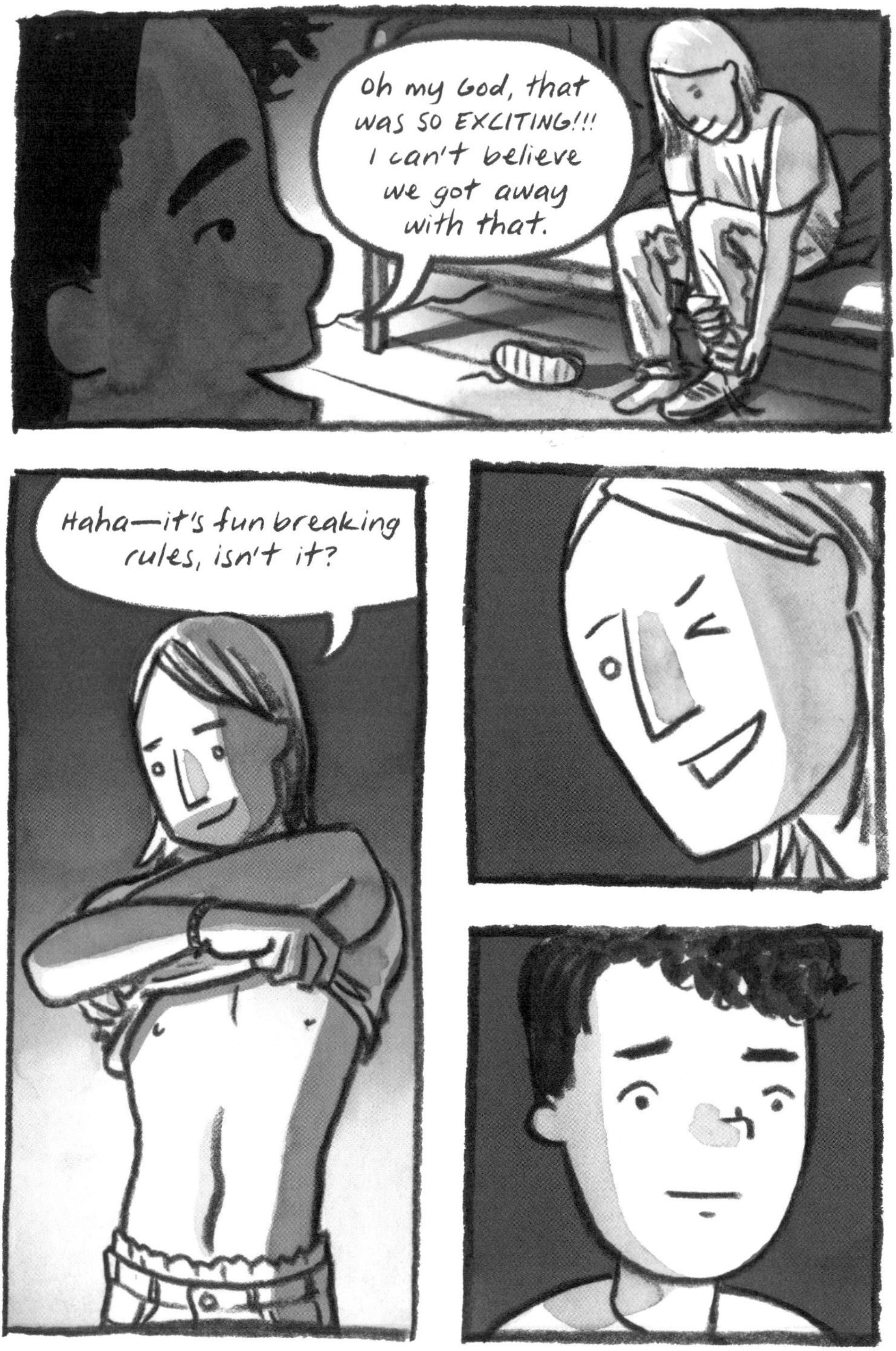
Oh my God, that was SO EXCITING!!! I can't believe we got away with that.
Haha—it's fun breaking rules, isn't it?

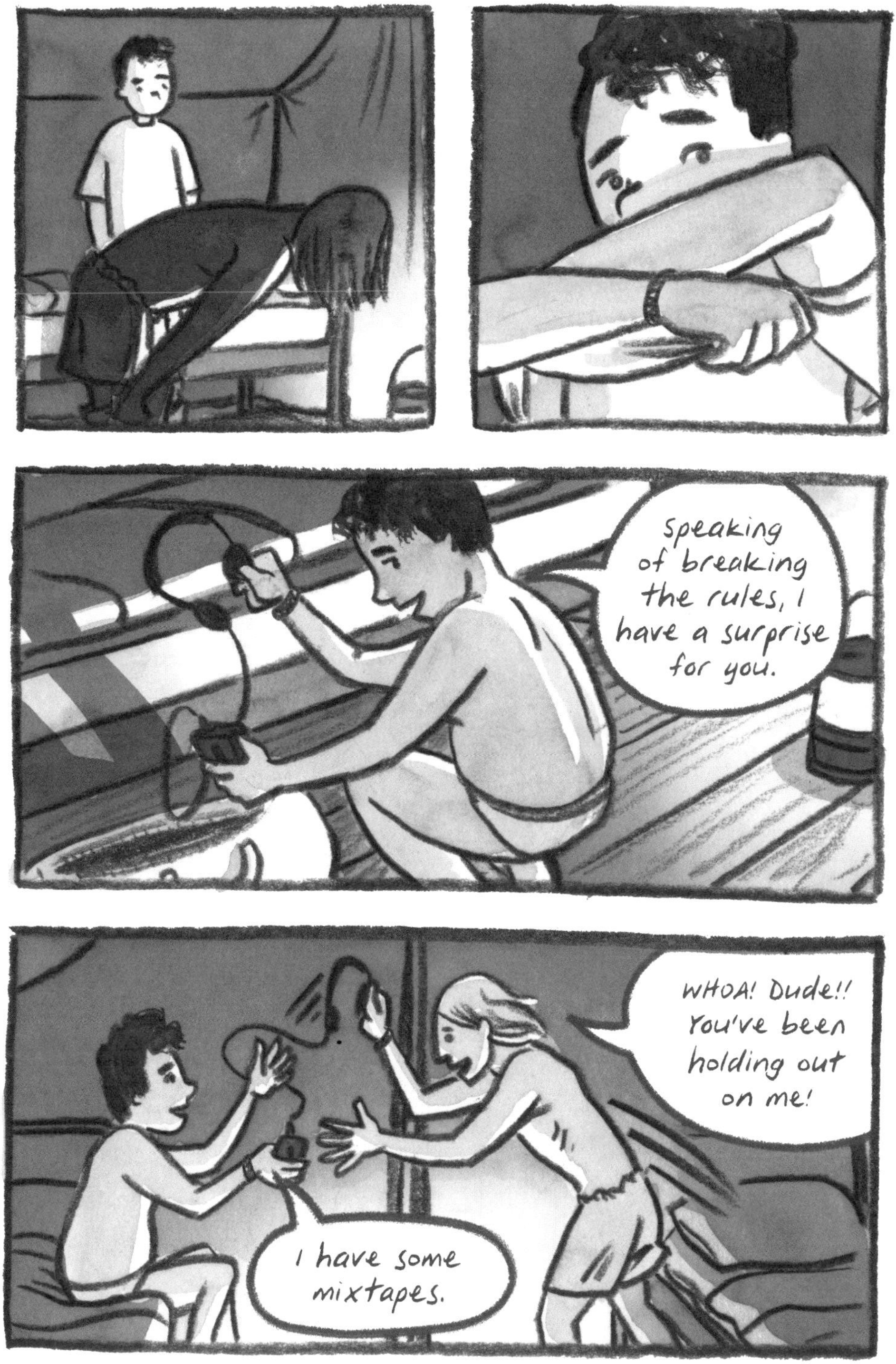

Speaking of breaking the rules, I have a surprise for you.
WHOA! Dude!! You've been holding out on me!
I have some mixtapes.

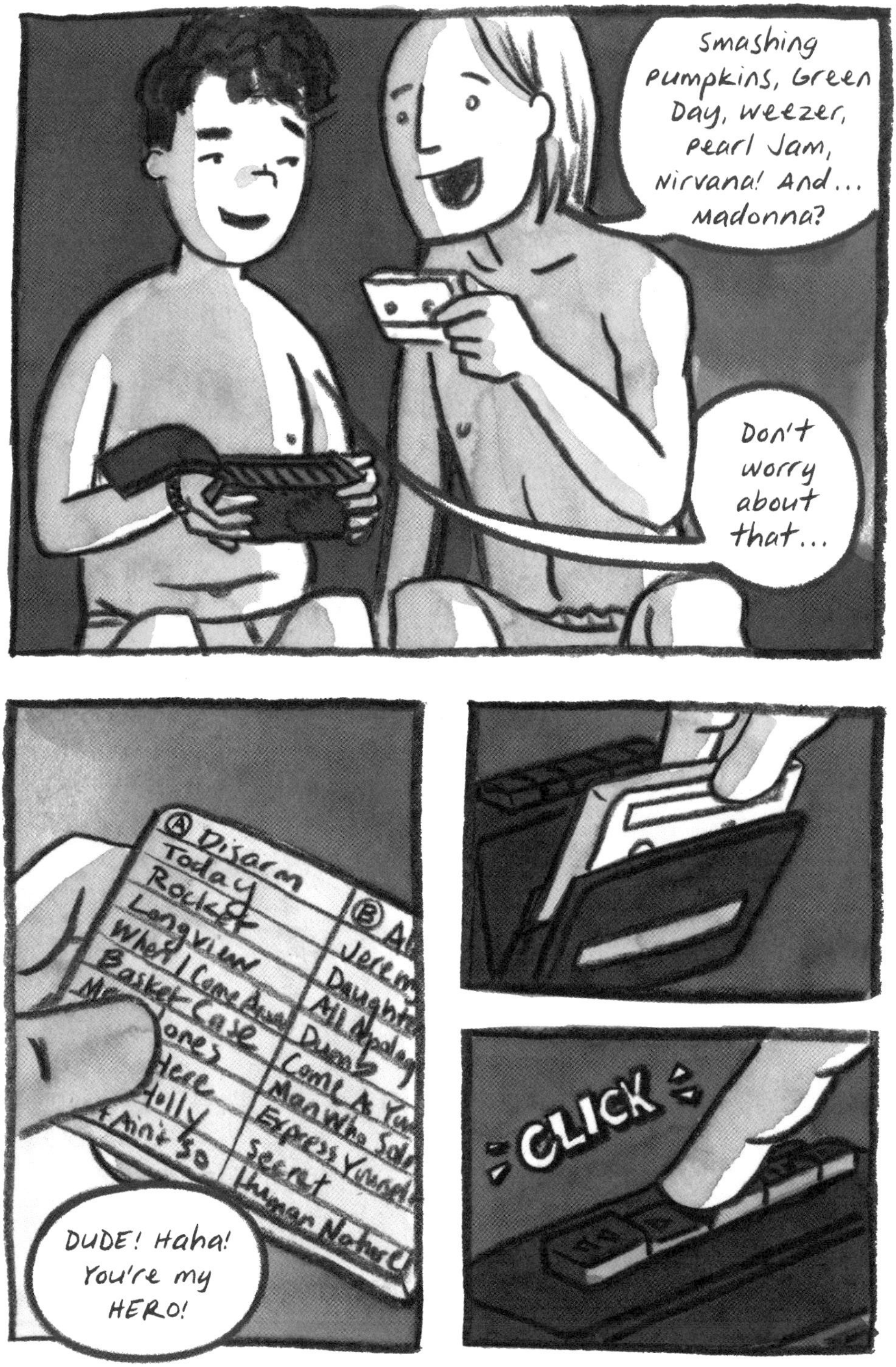
Smashing Pumpkins, Green Day, Weezer, Pearl Jam, Nirvana! And... Madonna?
Don't worry about that...
Disarm
Today
Rocket
Longview
Basket Case
Secret
DUDE! Haha! You're my HERO!
CLICK

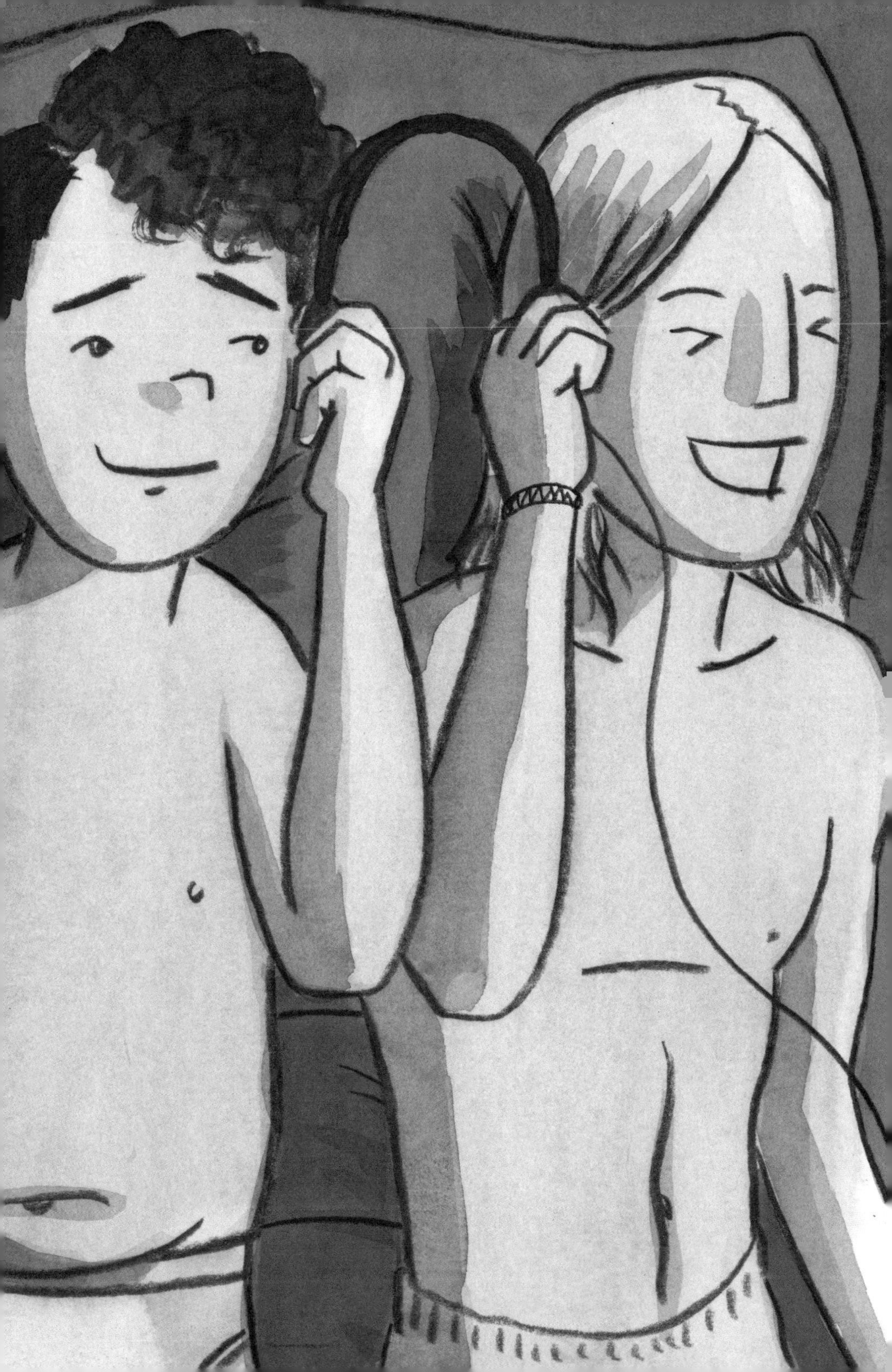

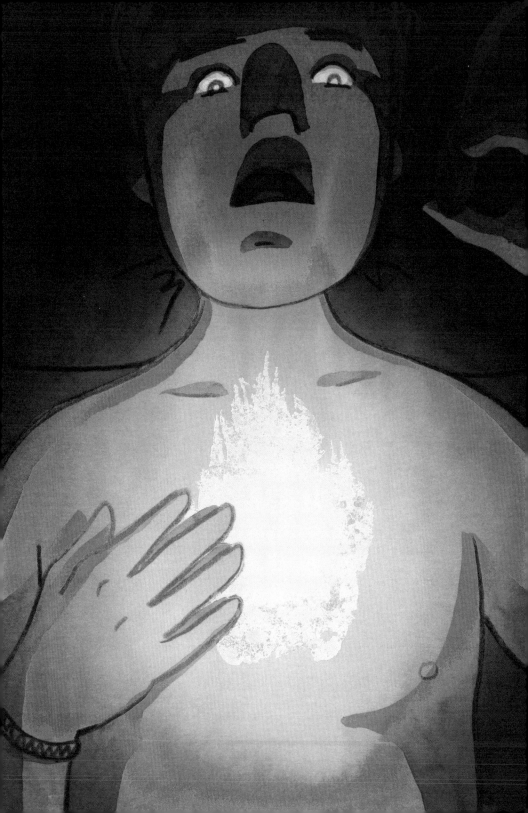

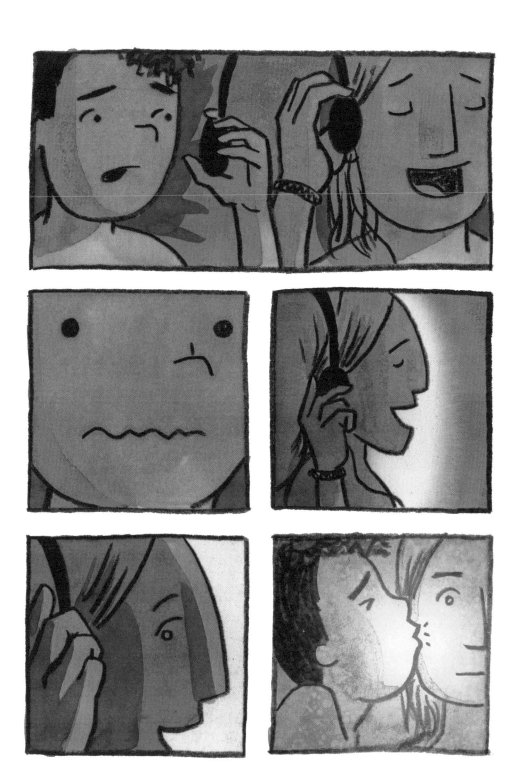

245

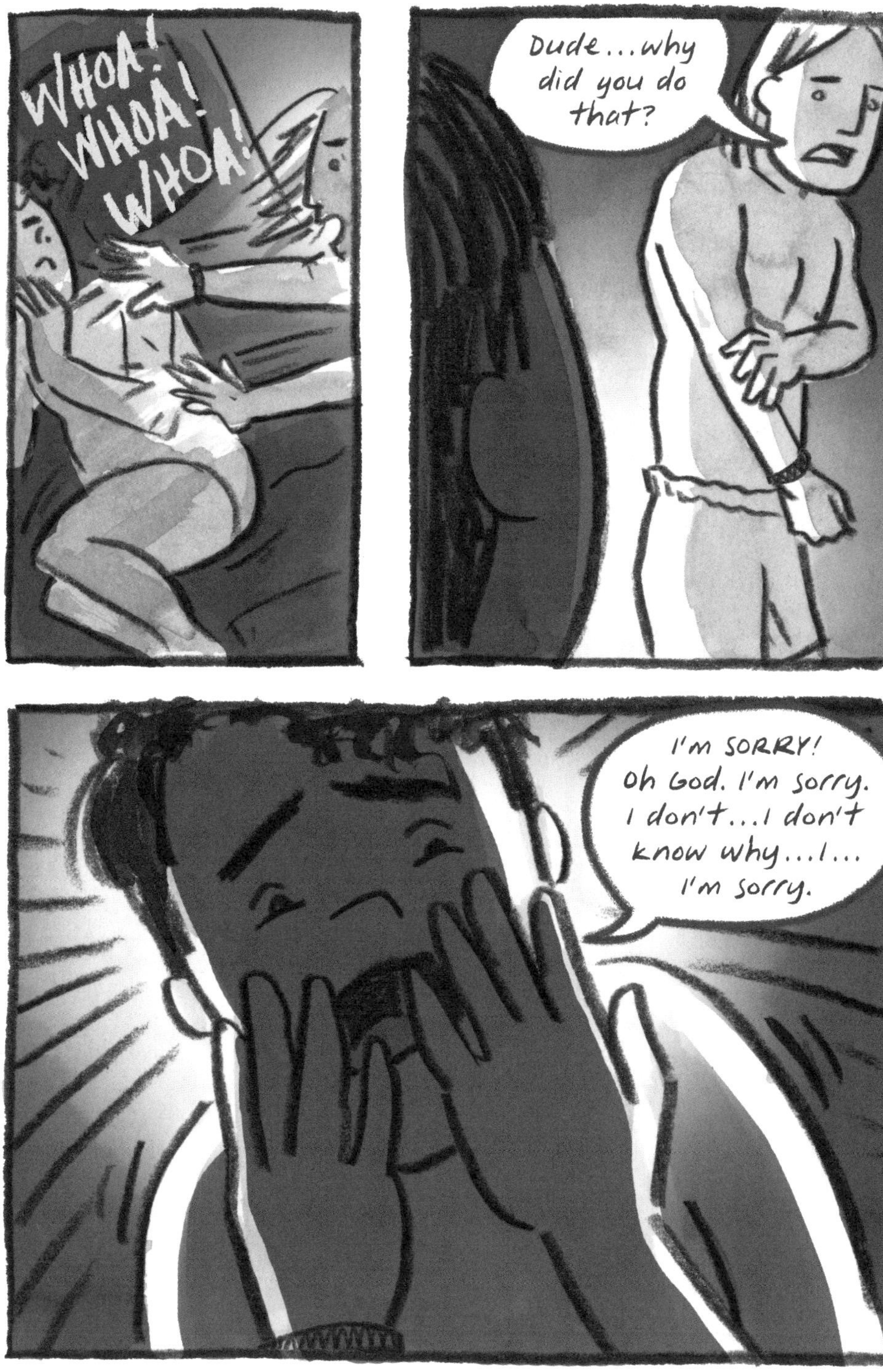
WHOA! WHOA! WHOA!
Dude...why did you do that?
I'm SORRY! Oh God. I'm sorry. I don't...I don't know why...I... I'm sorry.

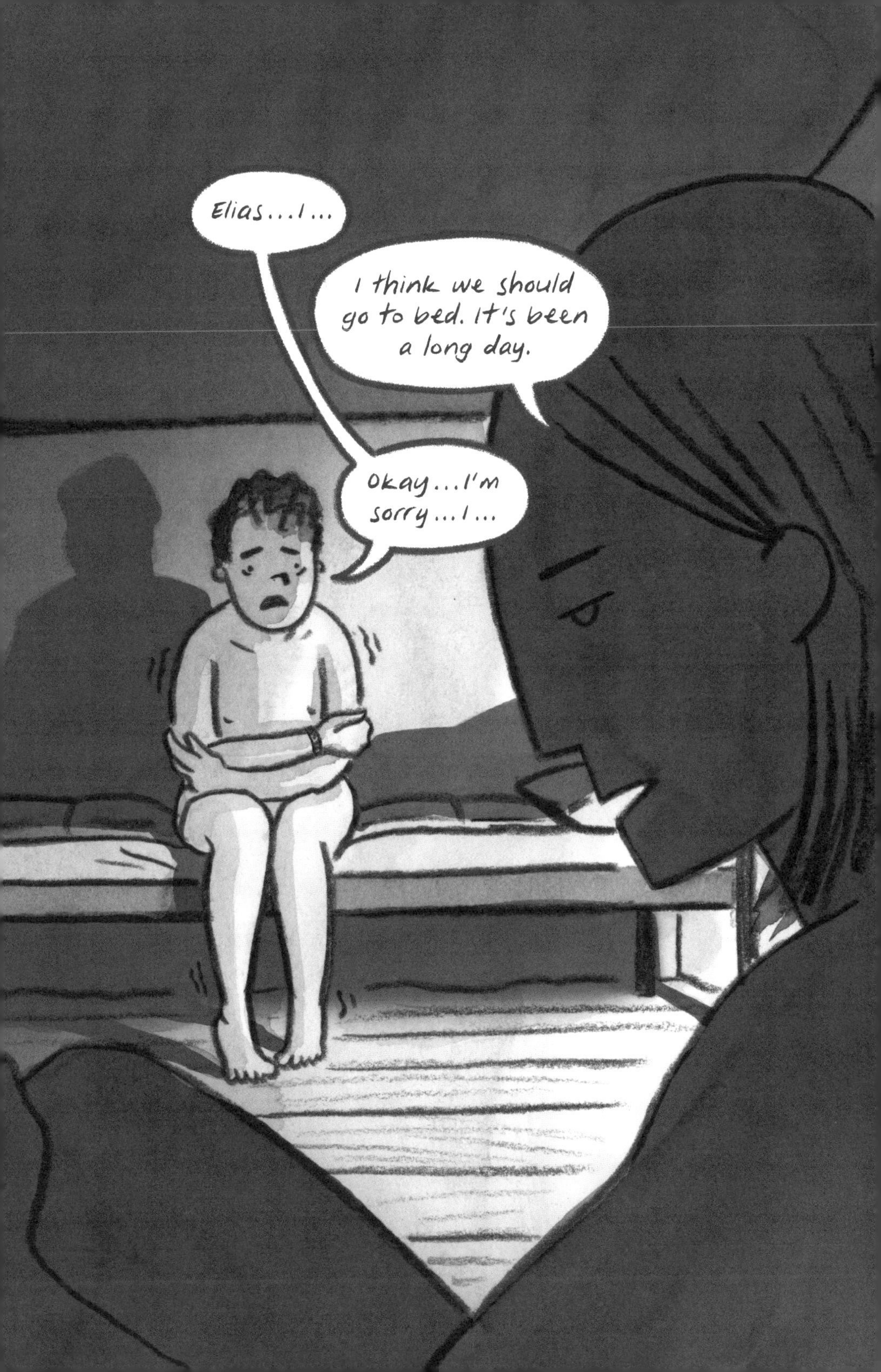
Elias...I...
I think we should go to bed. It's been a long day.
Okay...I'm sorry...I...

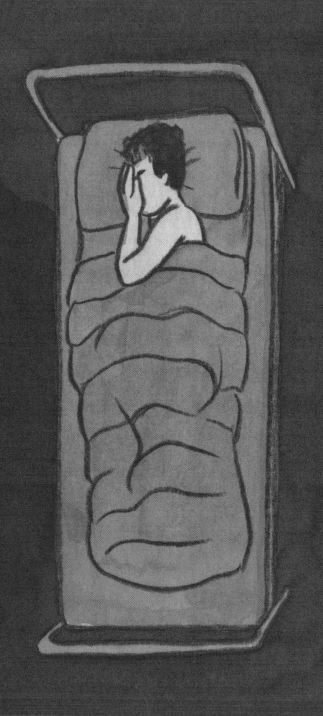

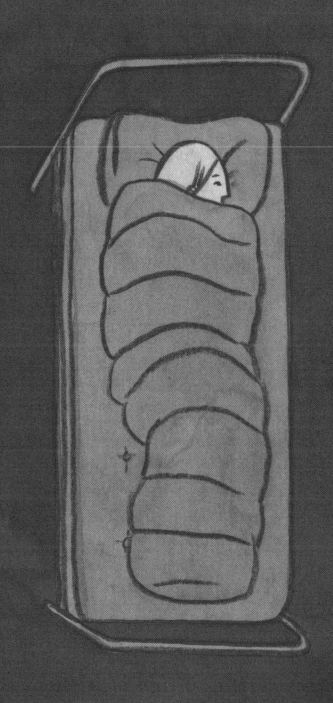

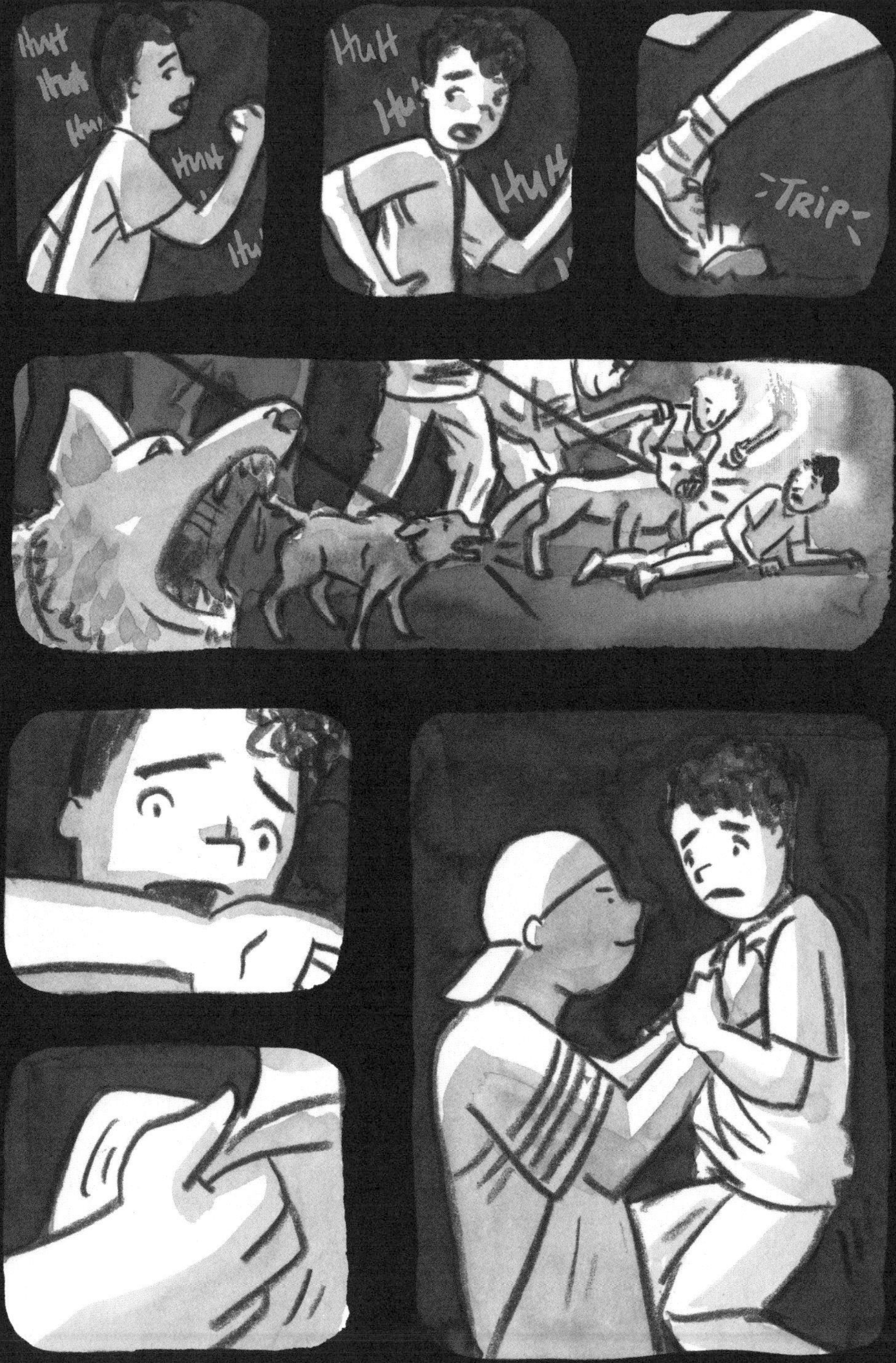
HUH
HUH
HUH
HUH
HUH
HUH
HUH
HUH
TRIP

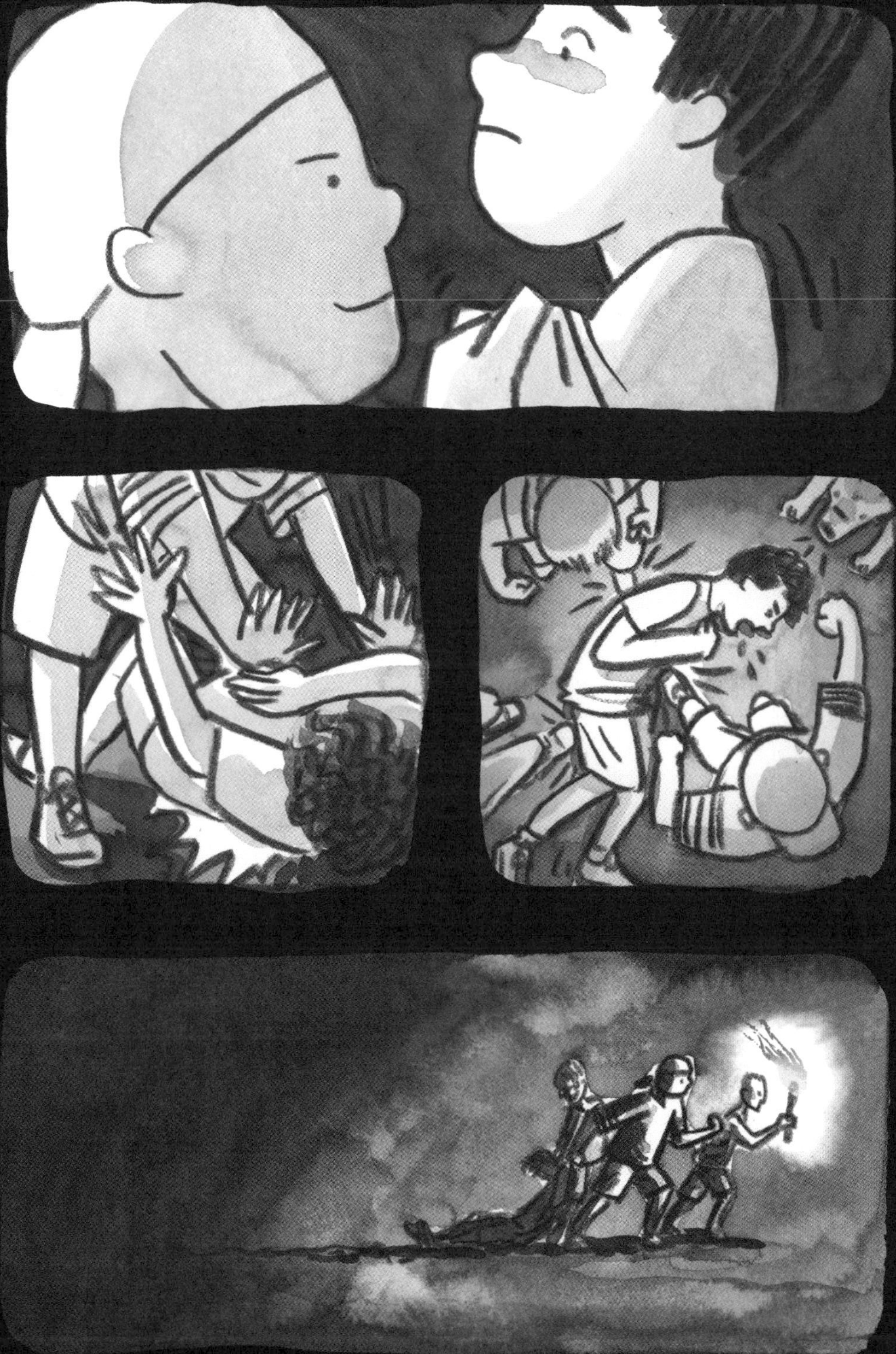

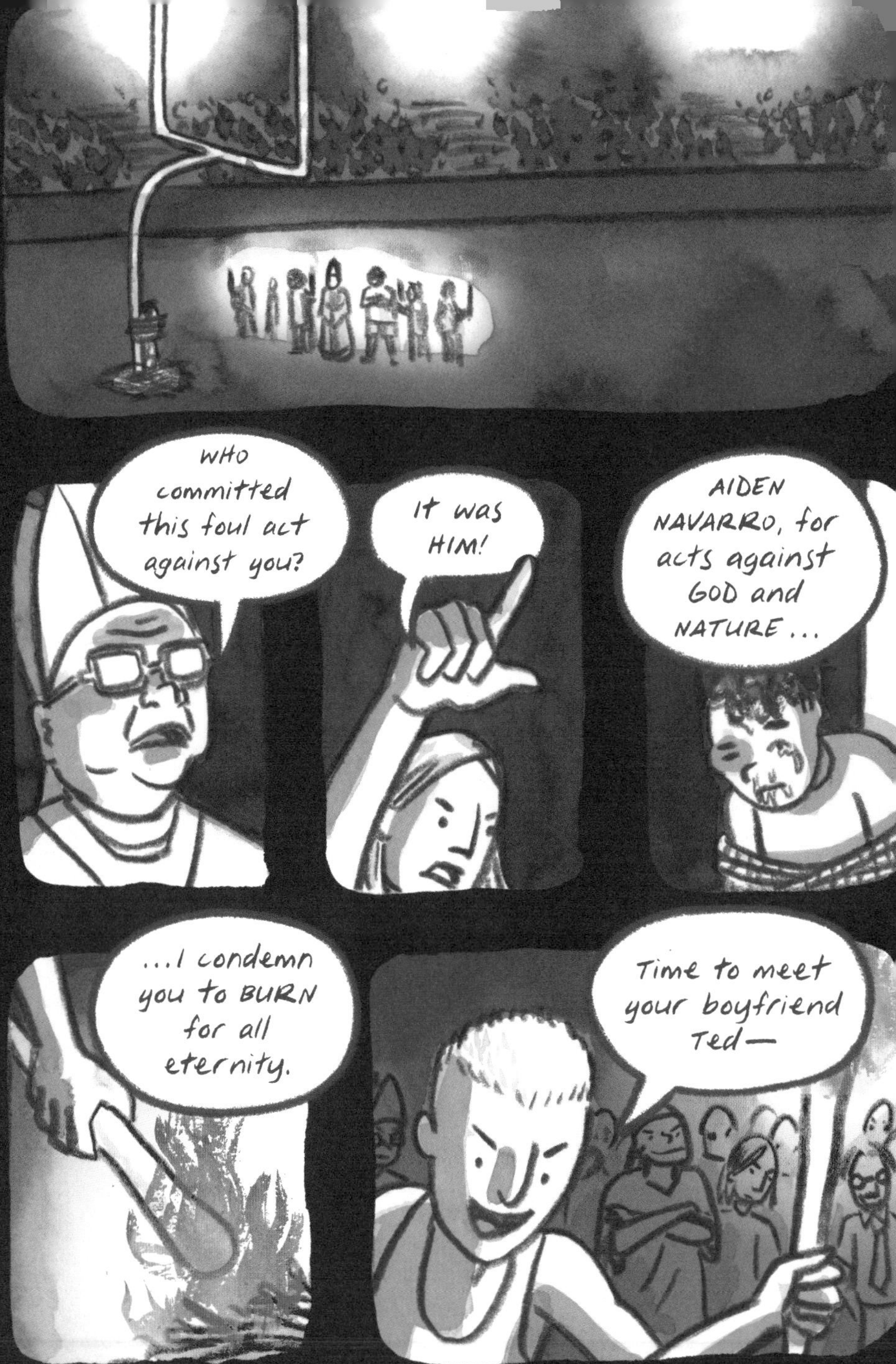
WHO committed this foul act against you?
It was HIM!
AIDEN NAVARRO, for acts against GOD and NATURE...
...I condemn you to BURN for all eternity.
Time to meet your boyfriend Ted—

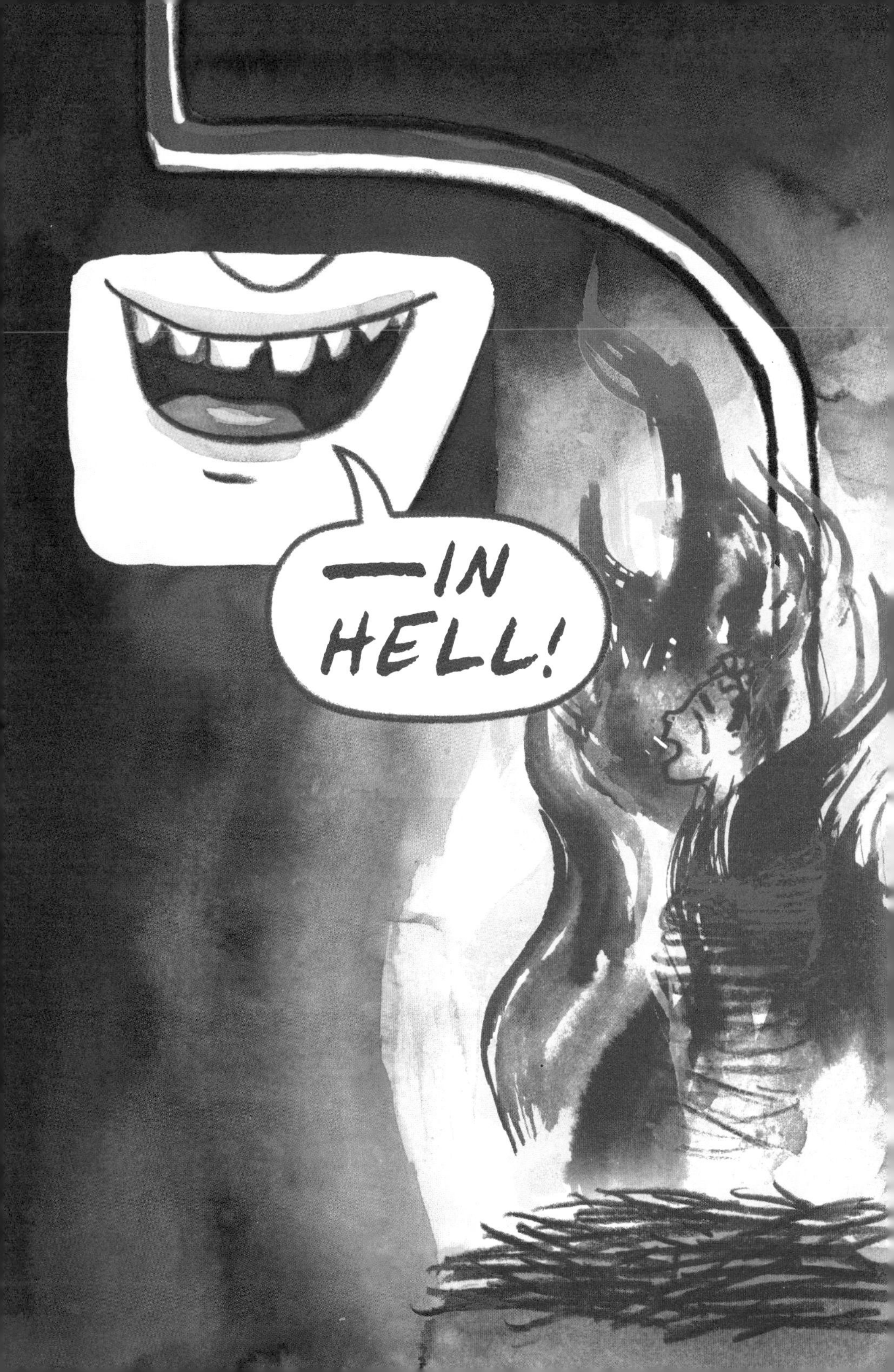
—IN HELL!

THURSDAY

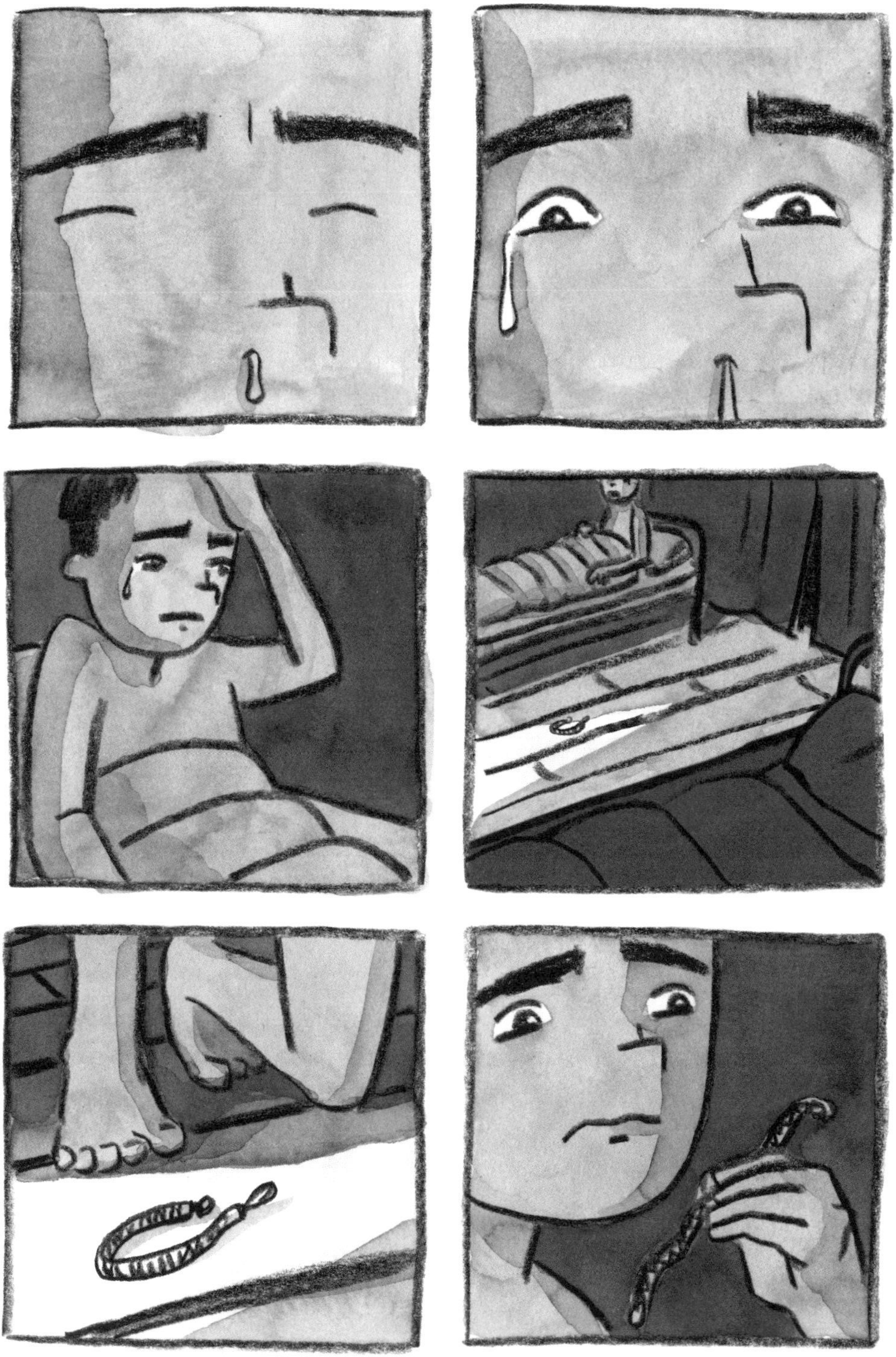

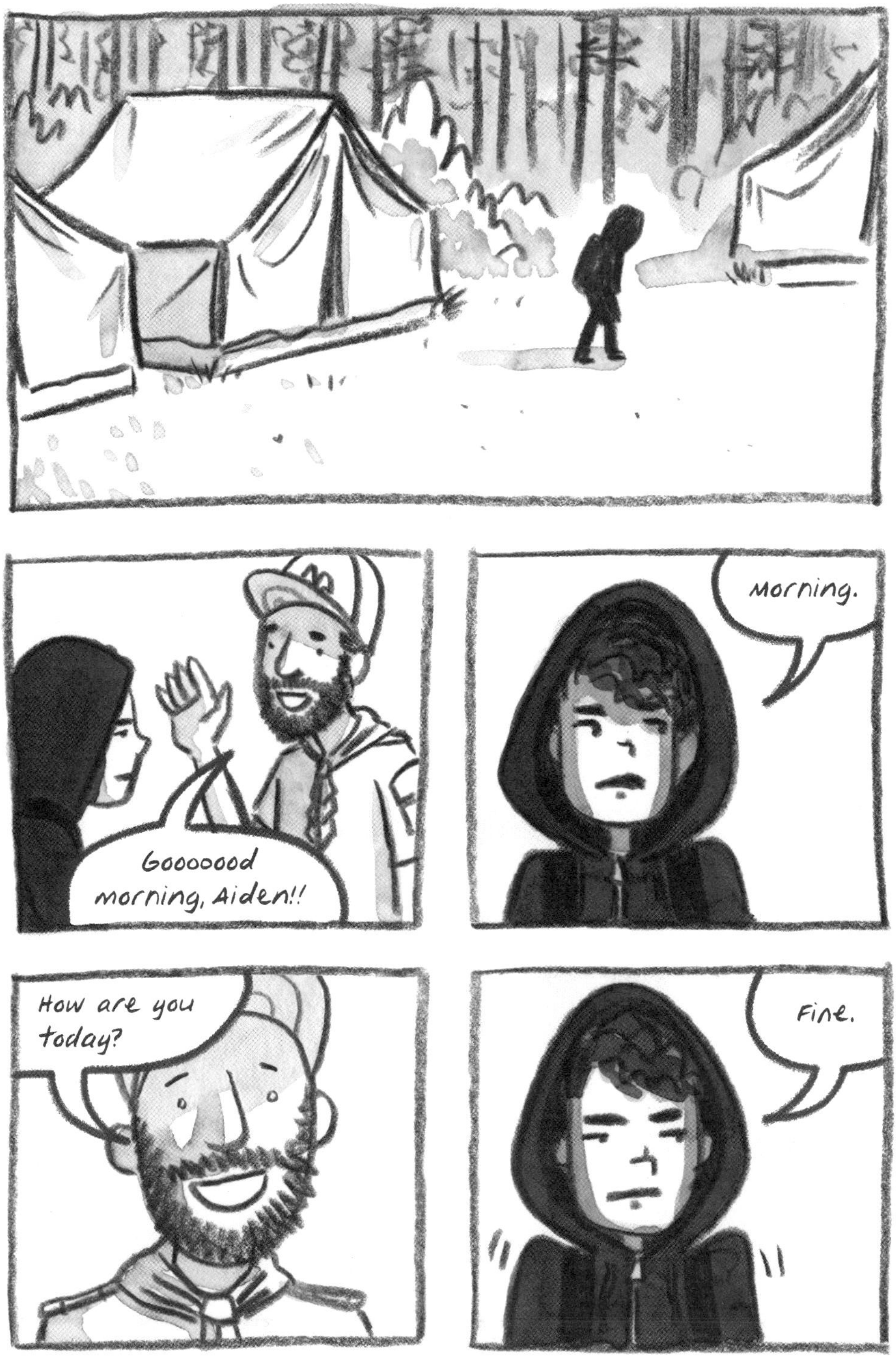
Gooooood morning, Aiden!!
Morning.
How are you today?
Fine.

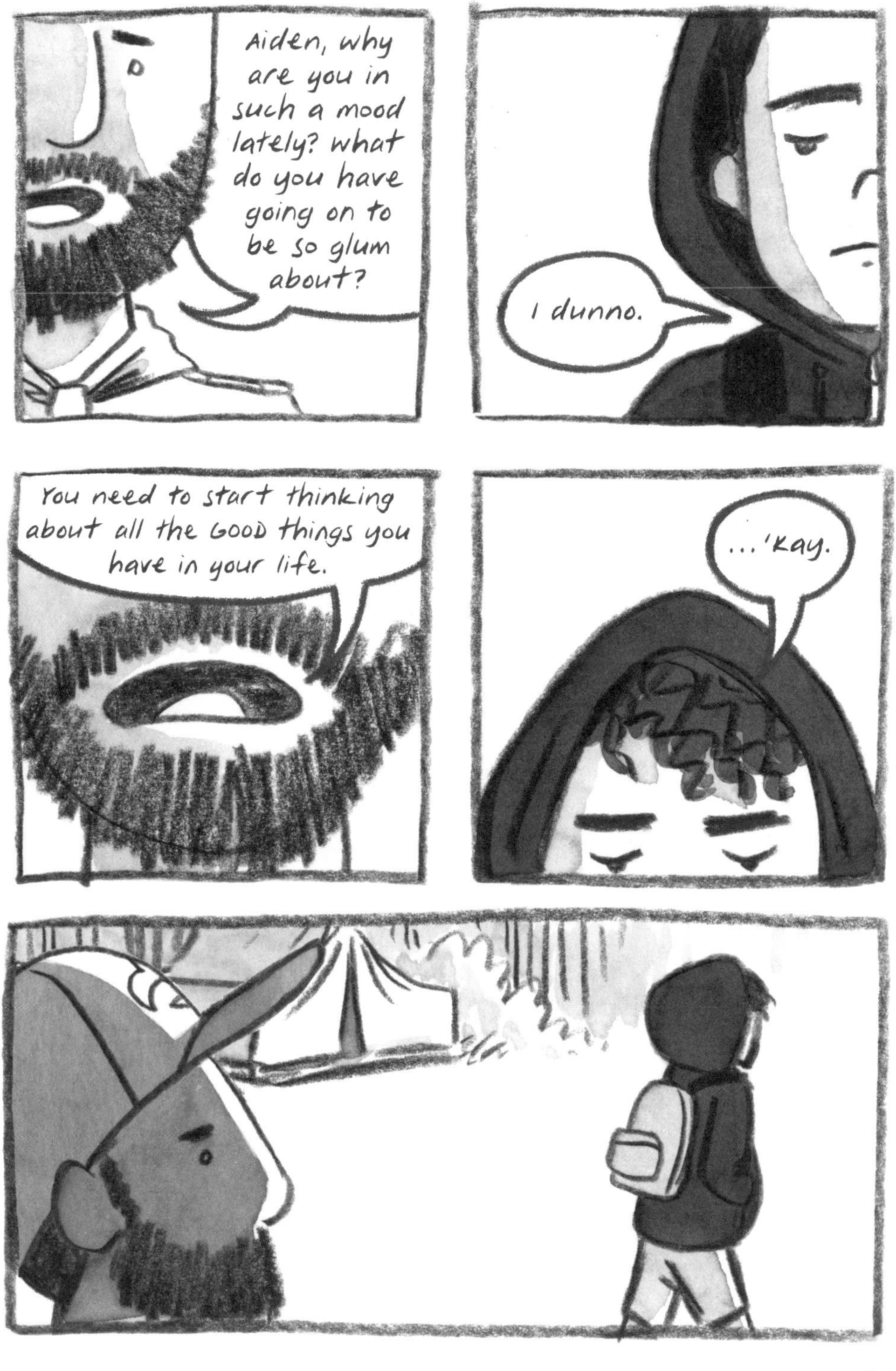
Aiden, why are you in such a mood lately? what do you have going on to be so glum about?
I dunno.
You need to start thinking about all the GOOD things you have in your life.
...'Kay.

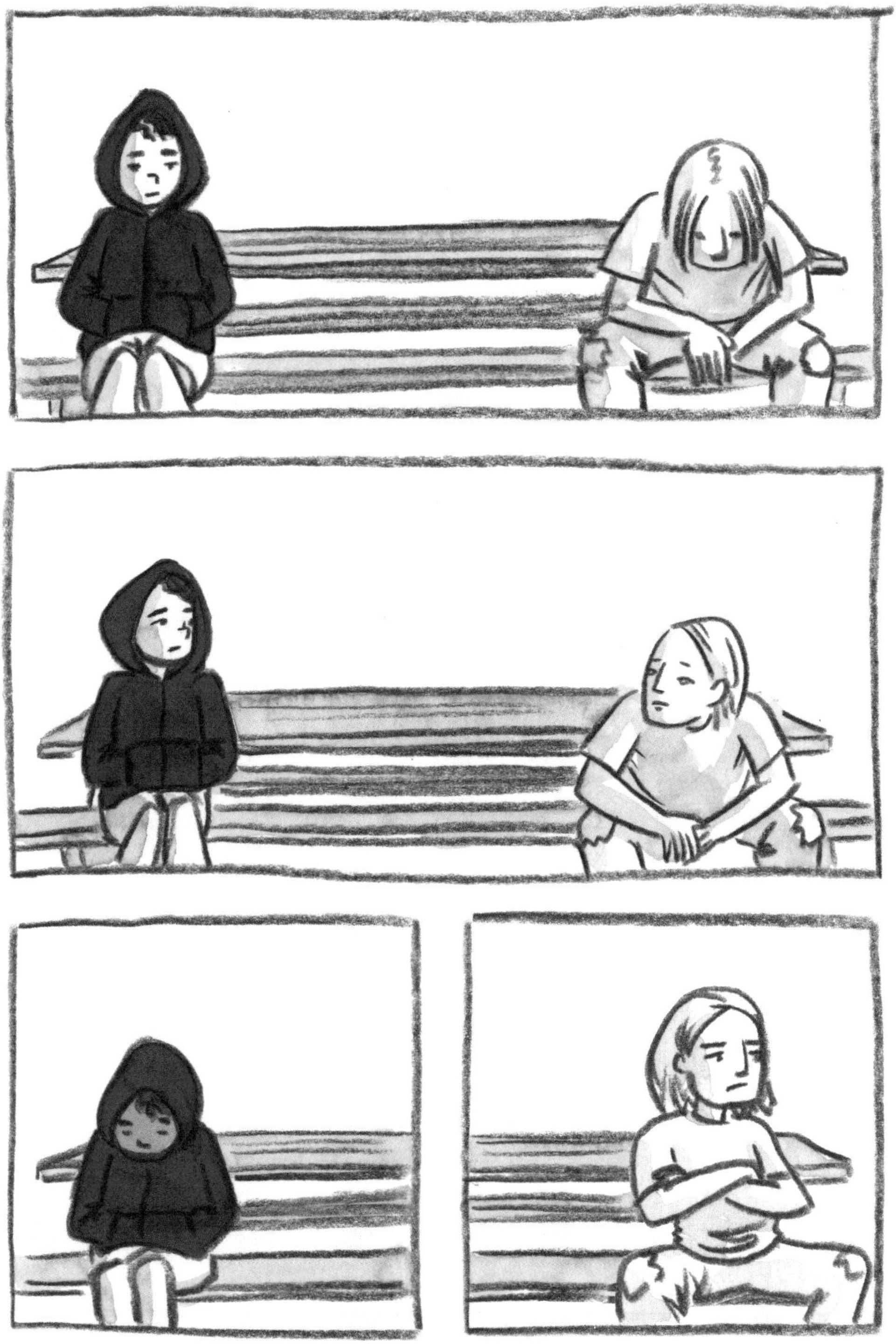

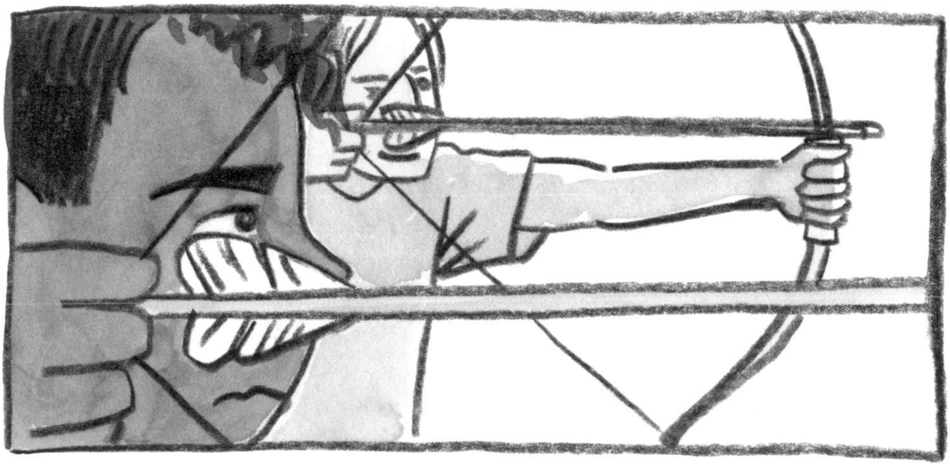

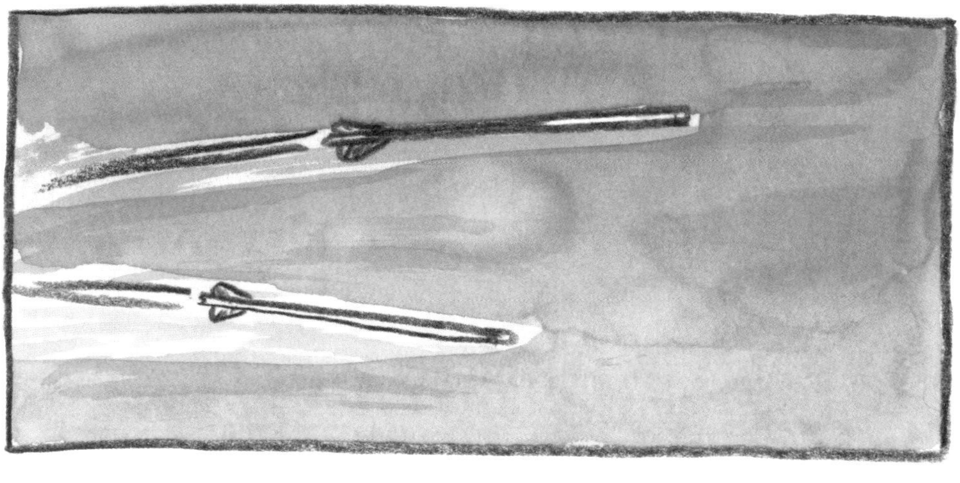

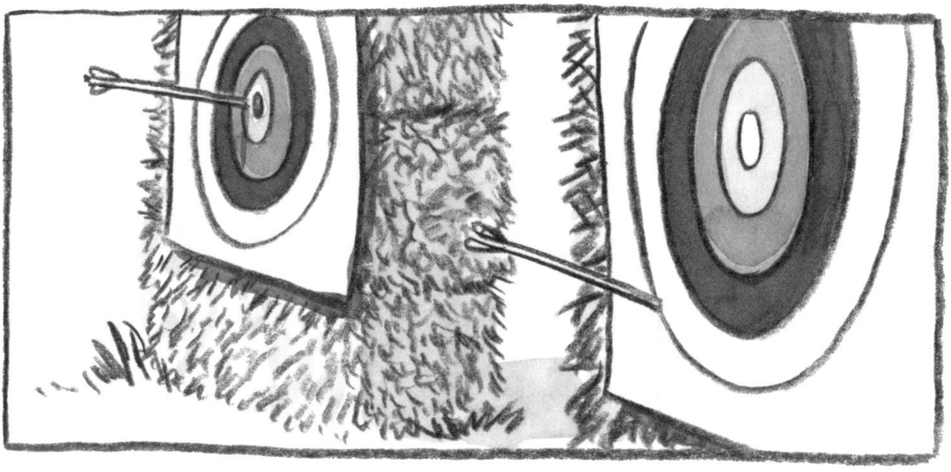

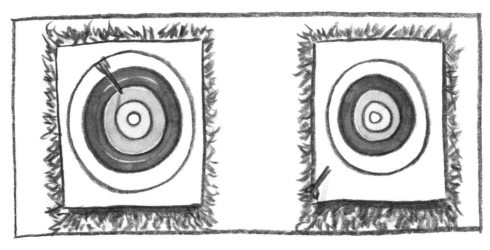

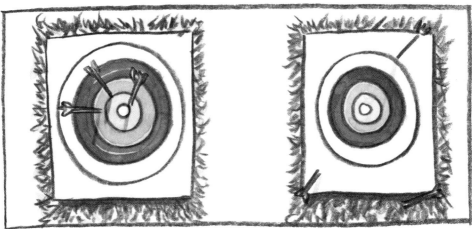

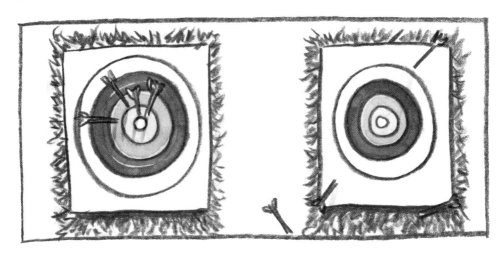

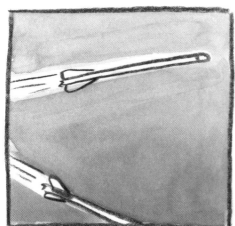

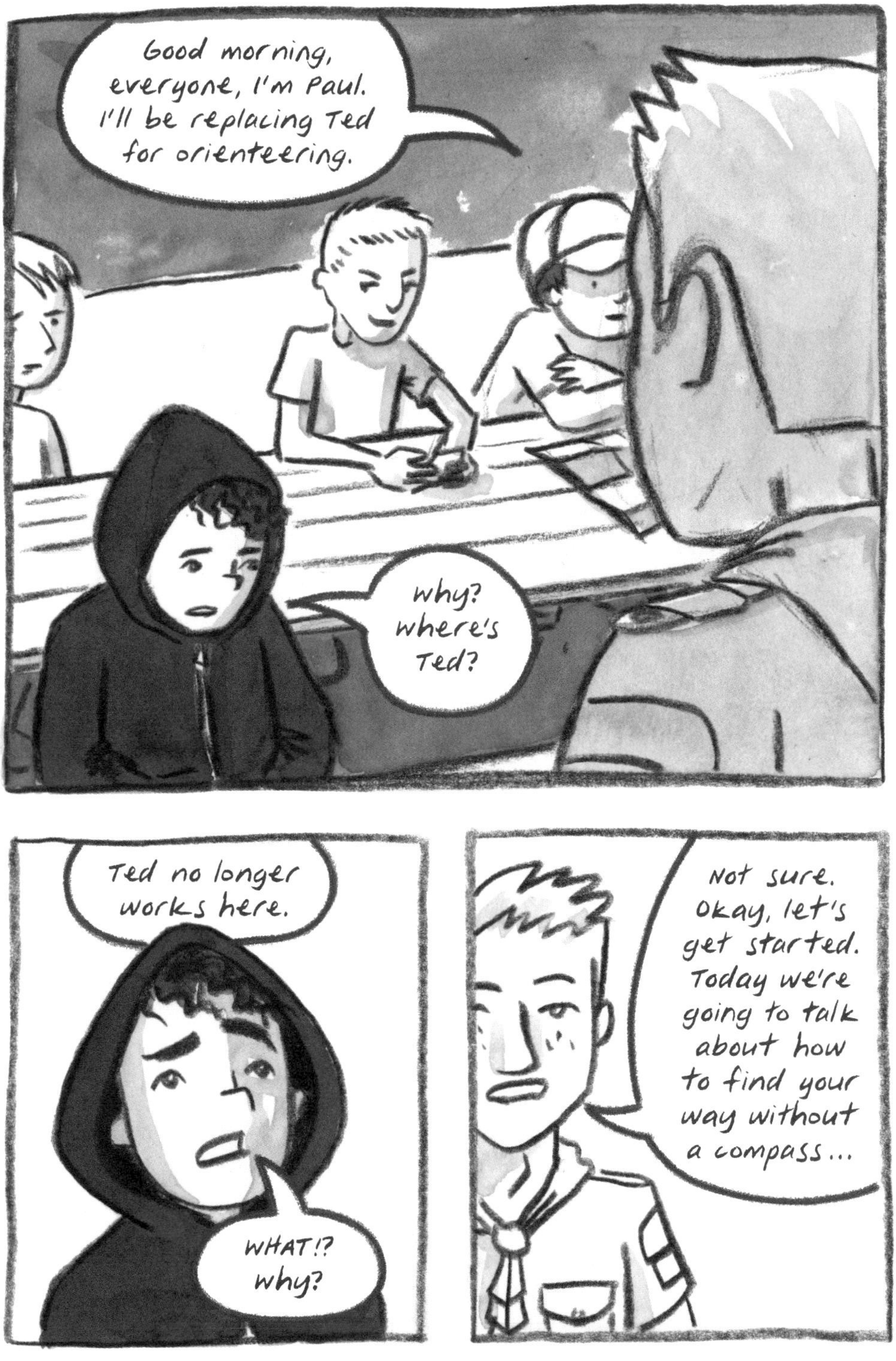
Good morning, everyone, I'm Paul. I'll be replacing Ted for orienteering.
Why? Where's Ted?
Ted no longer works here.
WHAT!? Why?
Not sure. Okay, let's get started. Today we're going to talk about how to find your way without a compass...

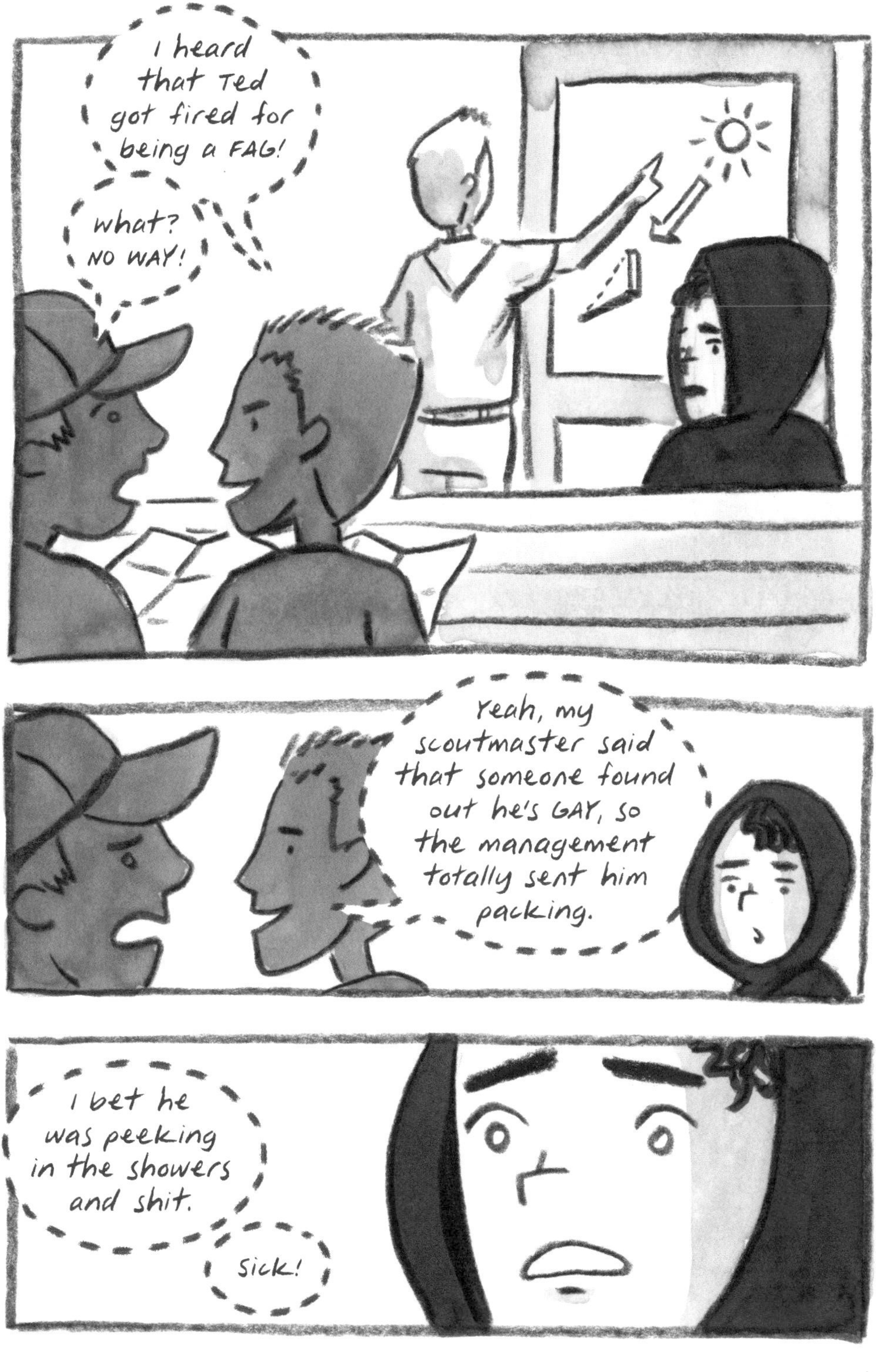
I heard that Ted got fired for being a FAG!
What? NO WAY!
Yeah, my scoutmaster said that someone found out he's GAY, so the management totally sent him packing.
I bet he was peeking in the showers and shit.
Sick!

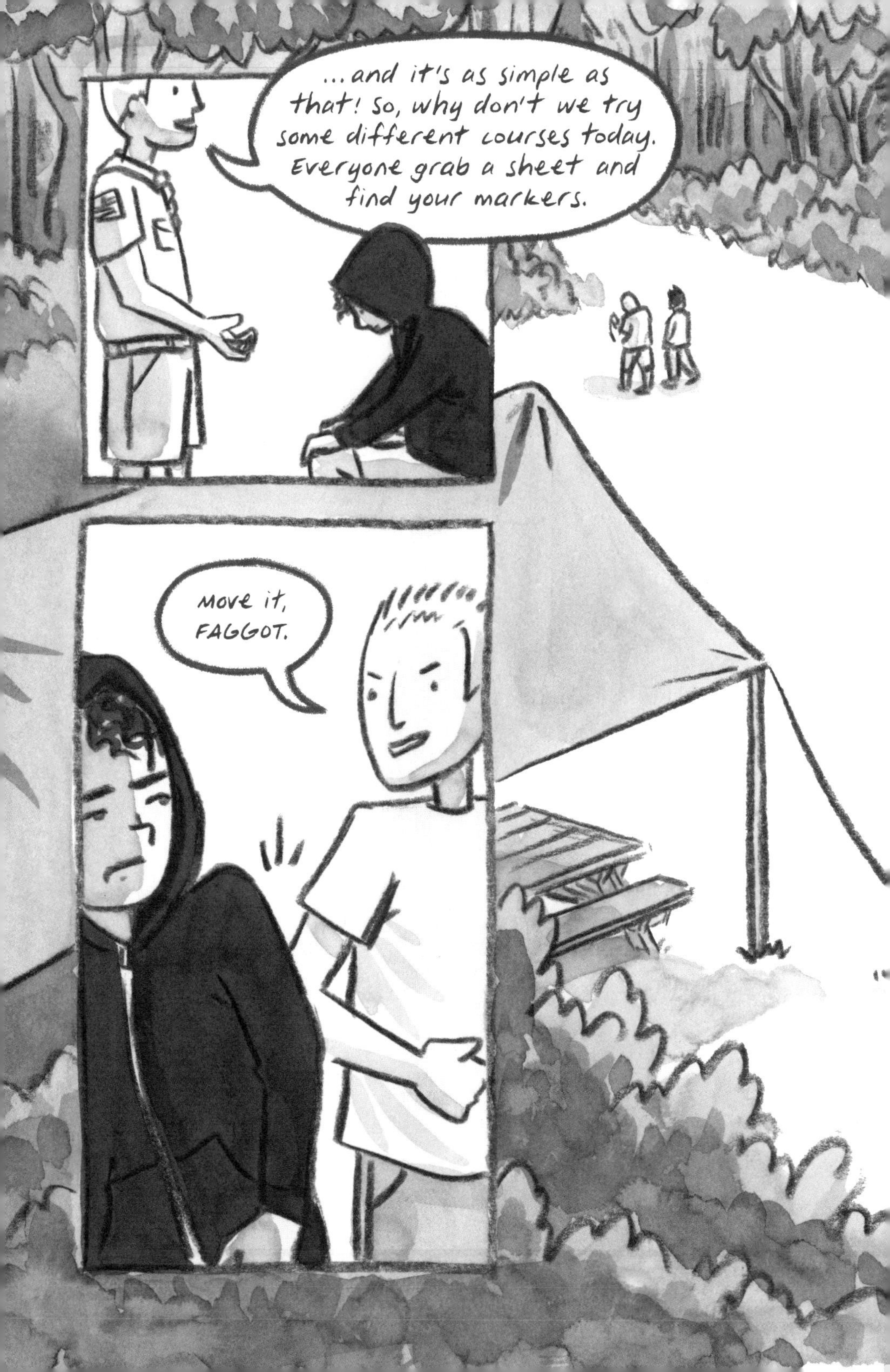
...and it's as simple as that! So, why don't we try some different courses today. Everyone grab a sheet and find your markers.
Move it, FAGGOT.

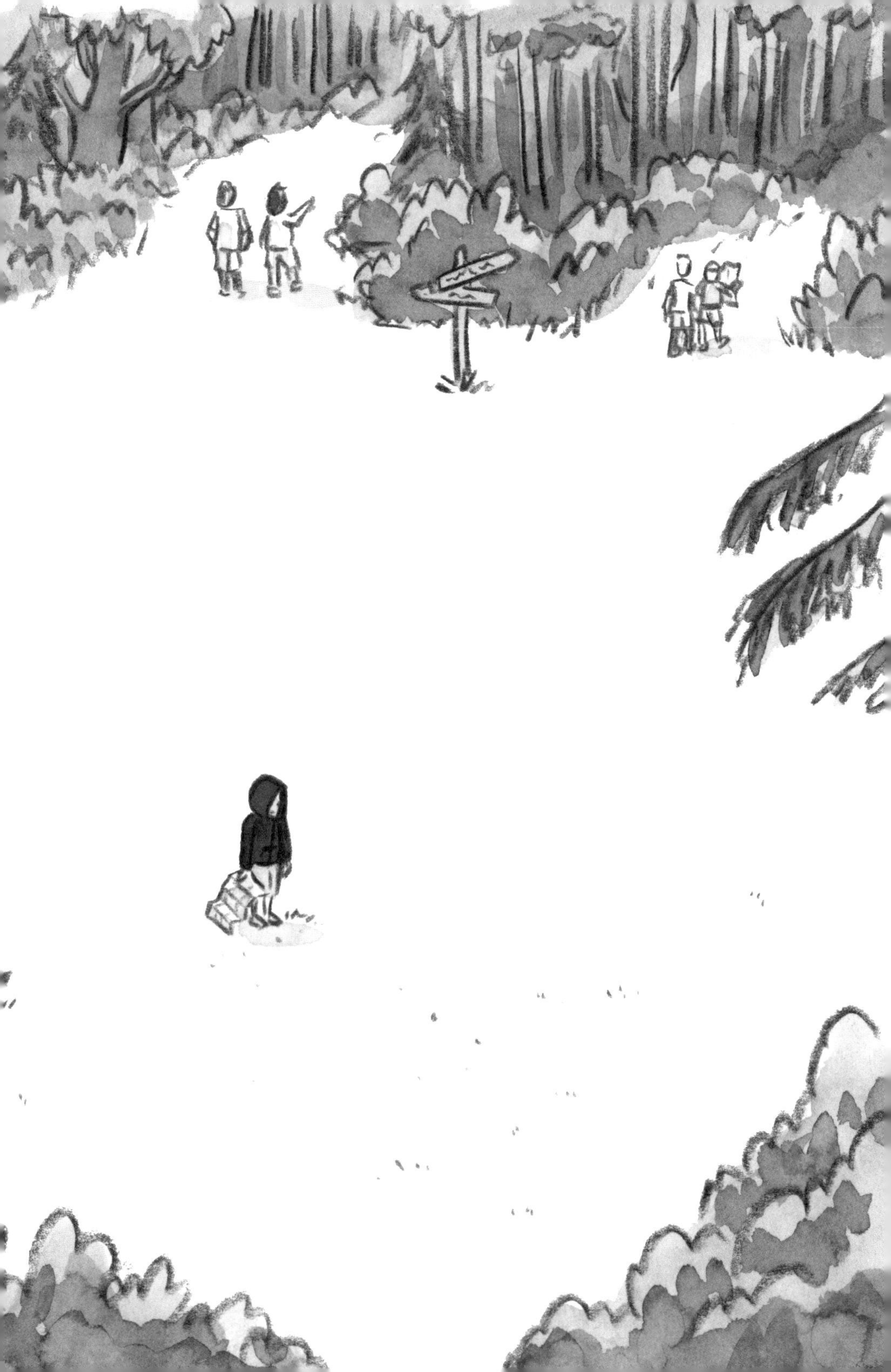

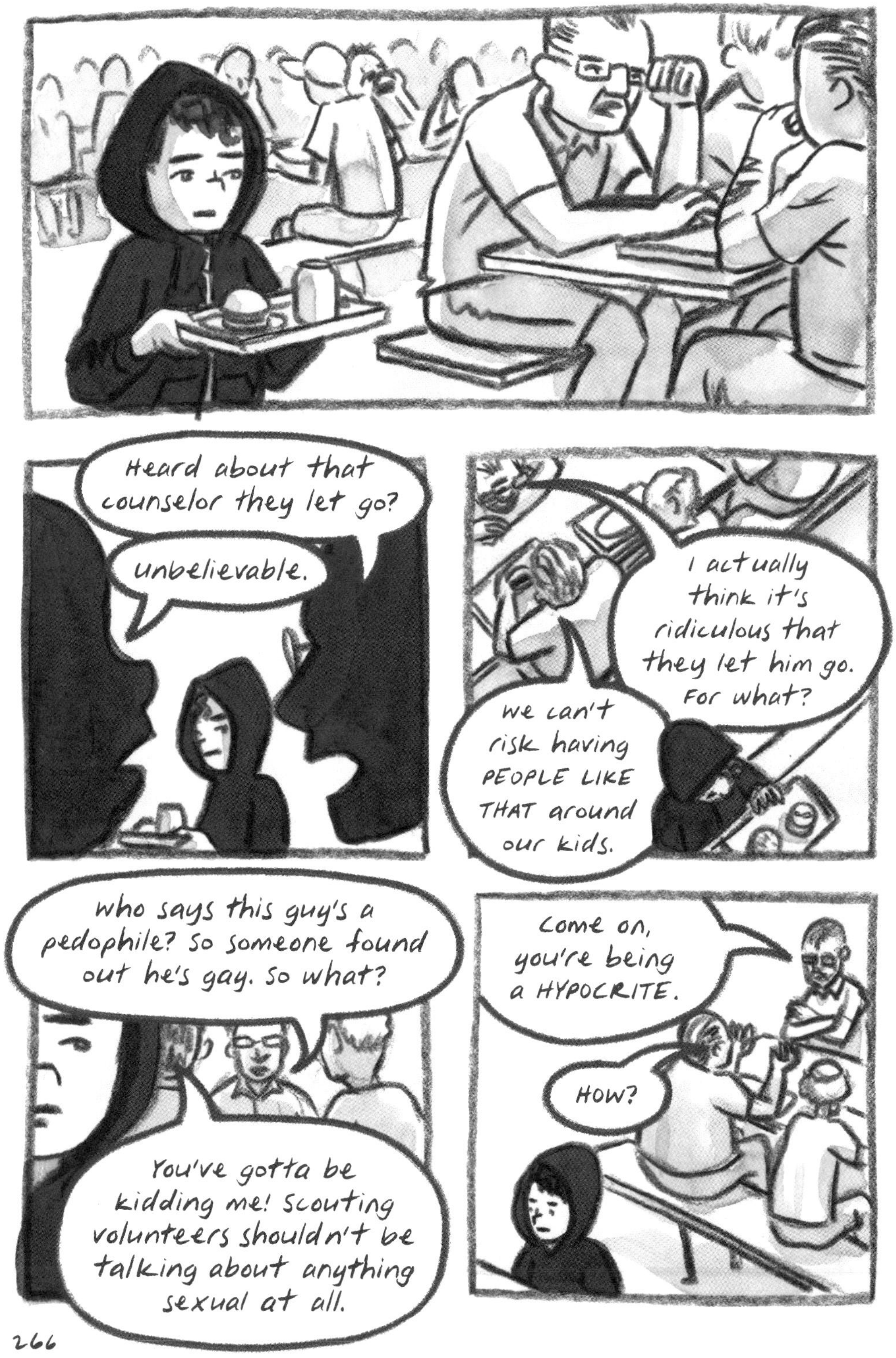
Heard about that counselor they let go?
unbelievable.
I actually think it's ridiculous that they let him go. For what?
we can't risk having PEOPLE LIKE THAT around our kids.
who says this guy's a pedophile? So someone found out he's gay. So what?
You've gotta be kidding me! Scouting volunteers shouldn't be talking about anything sexual at all.
Come on, you're being a HYPOCRITE.
HOW?

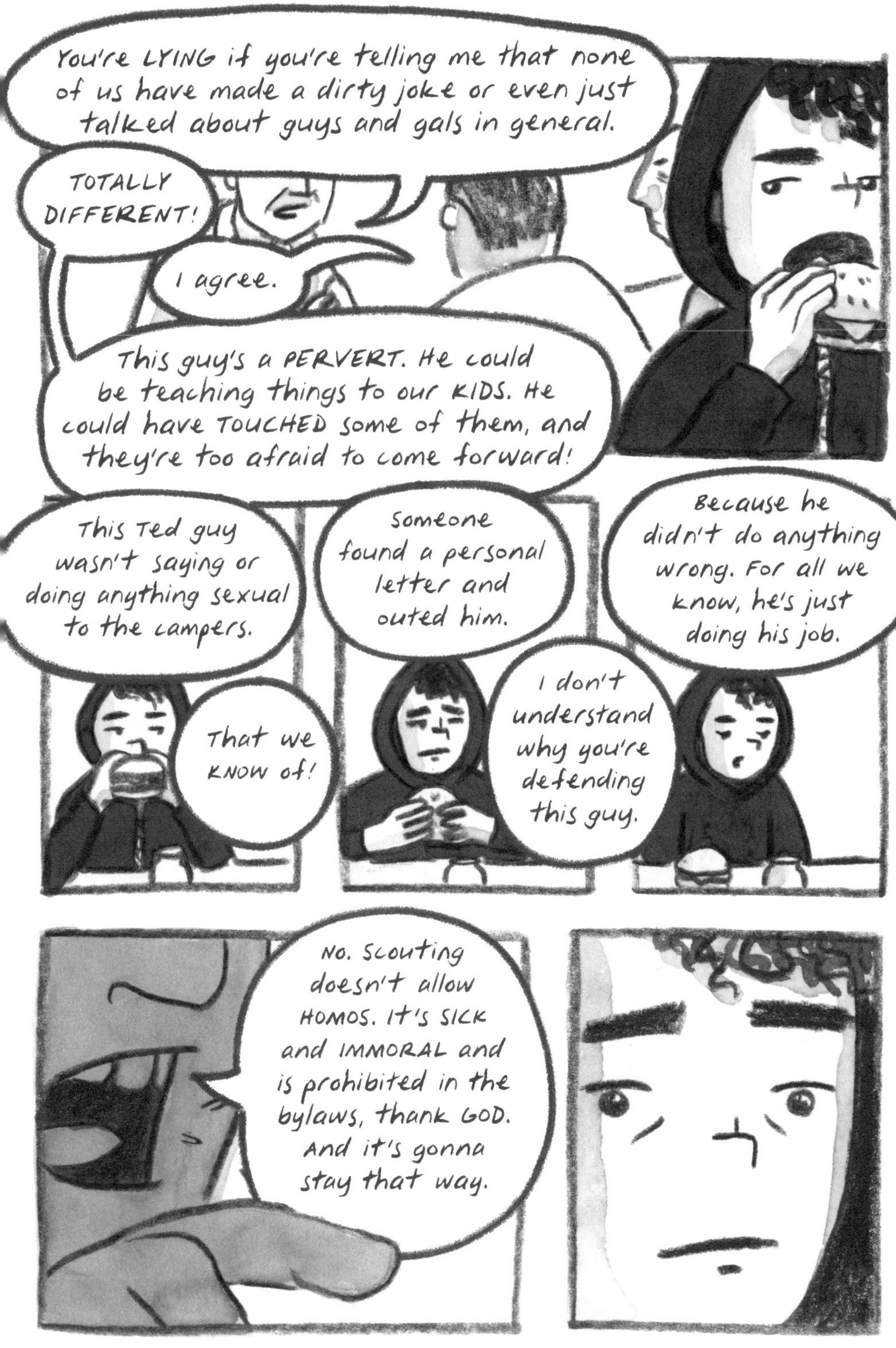
You're LYING if you're telling me that none of us have made a dirty joke or even just talked about guys and gals in general.
TOTALLY DIFFERENT!
I agree.
This guy's a PERVERT. He could be teaching things to our KIDS. He could have TOUCHED some of them, and they're too afraid to come forward!
This Ted guy wasn't saying or doing anything sexual to the campers.
That we KNOW of!
Someone found a personal letter and outed him.
I don't understand why you're defending this guy.
Because he didn't do anything wrong. For all we know, he's just doing his job.
No. Scouting doesn't allow HOMOS. It's SICK and IMMORAL and is prohibited in the bylaws, thank GOD. And it's gonna stay that way.

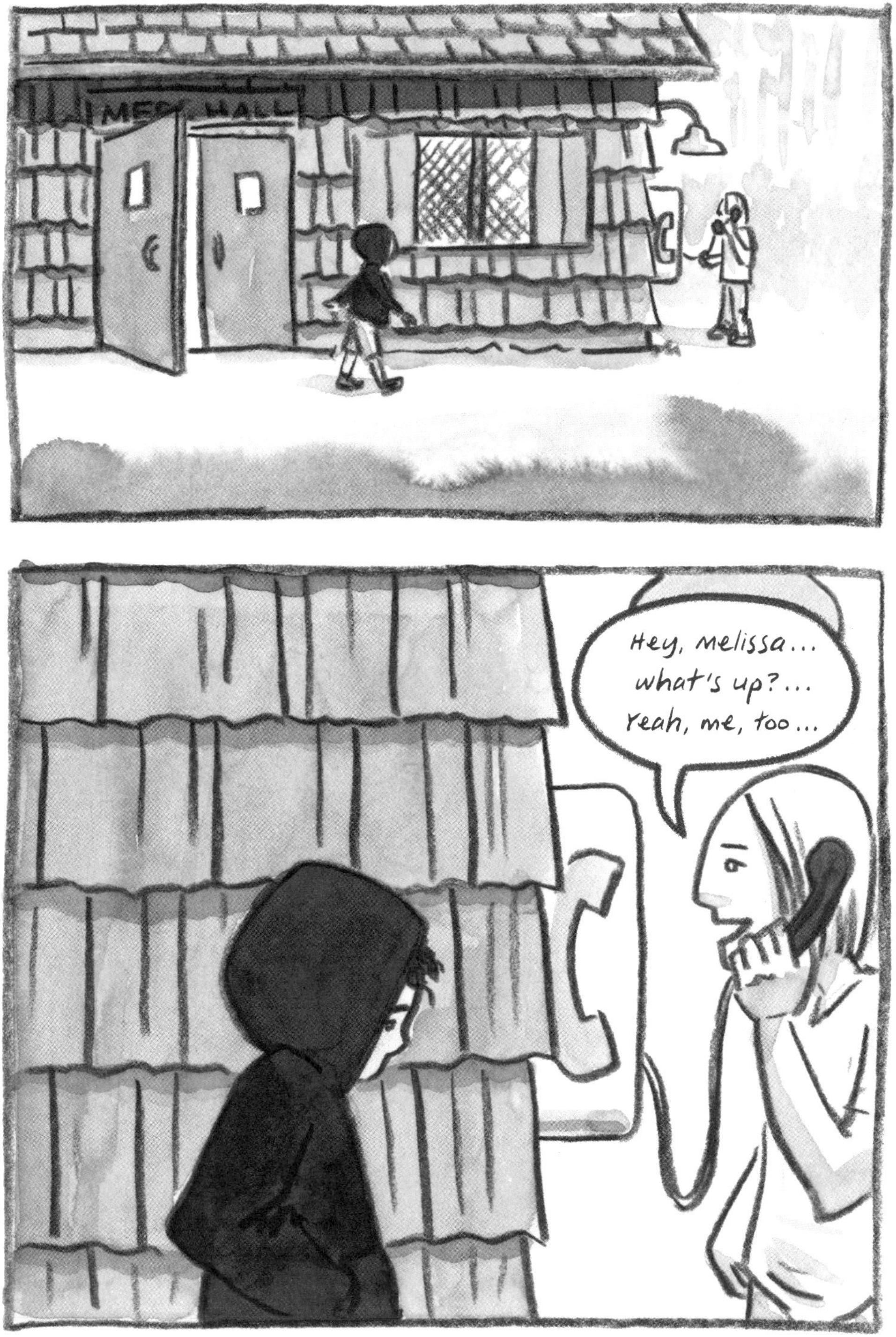
Hey, Melissa... what's up?... Yeah, me, too...

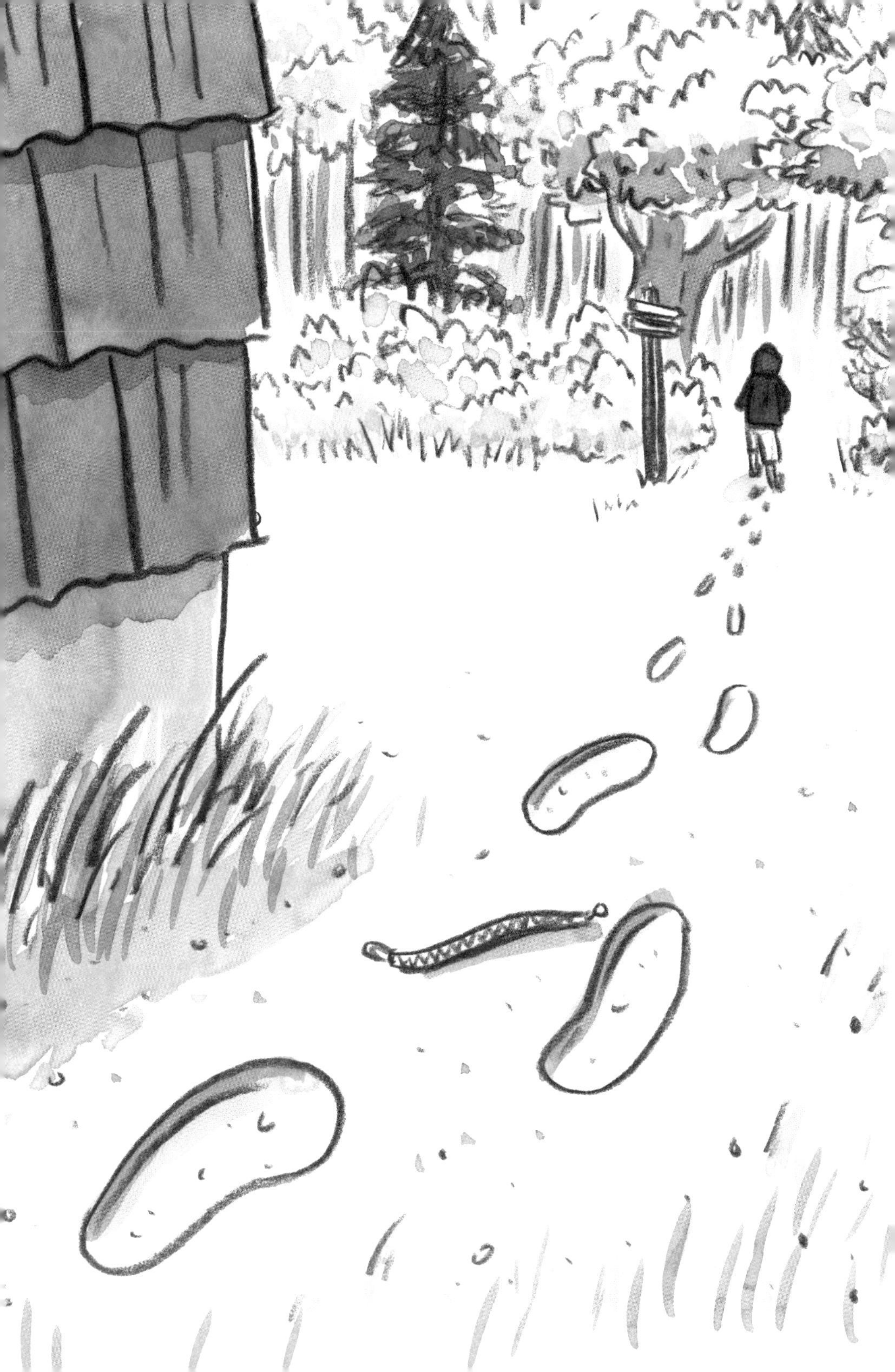

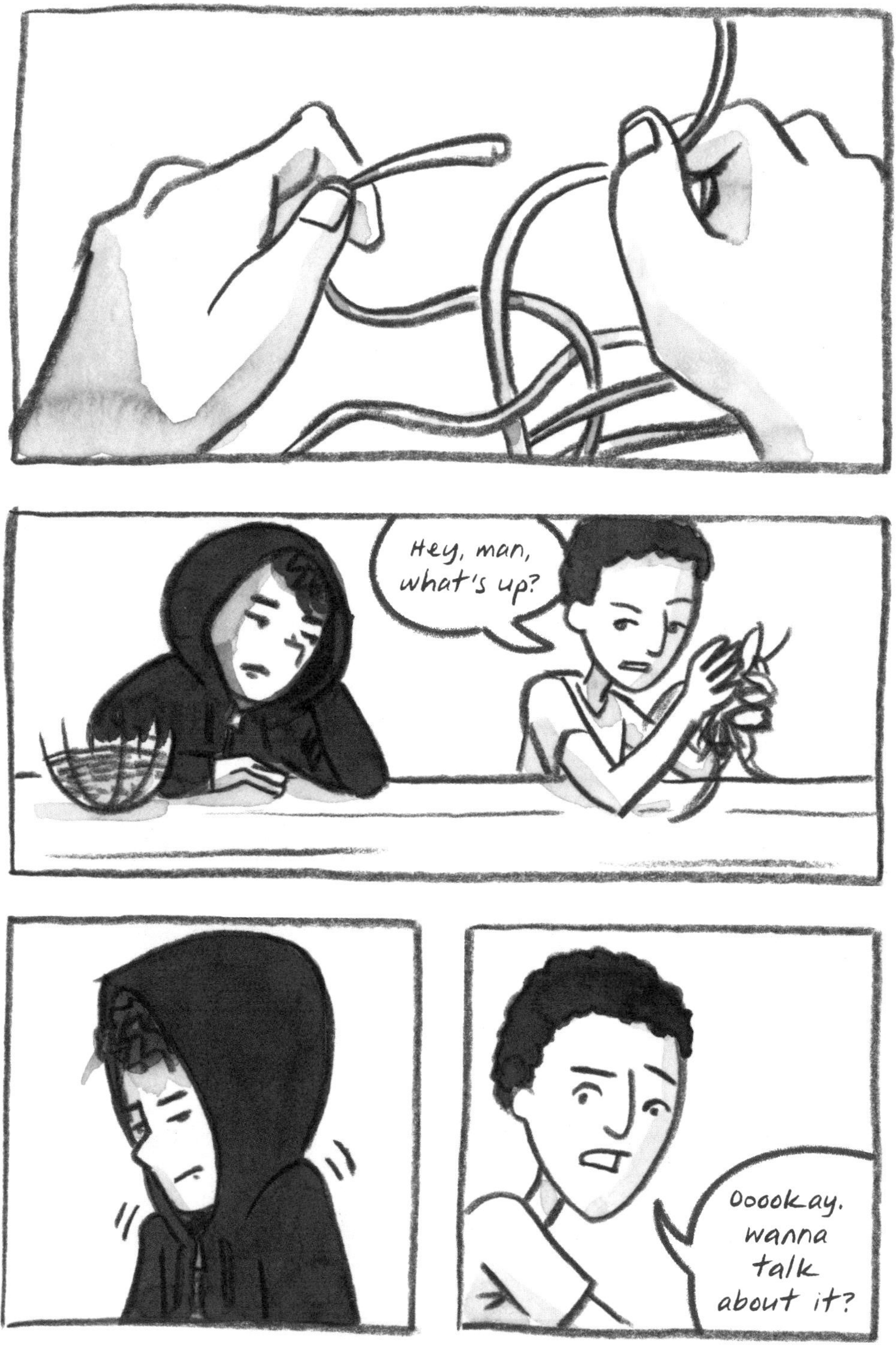
Hey, man,
what's up?
Ooook ay.
wanna
talk
about it?

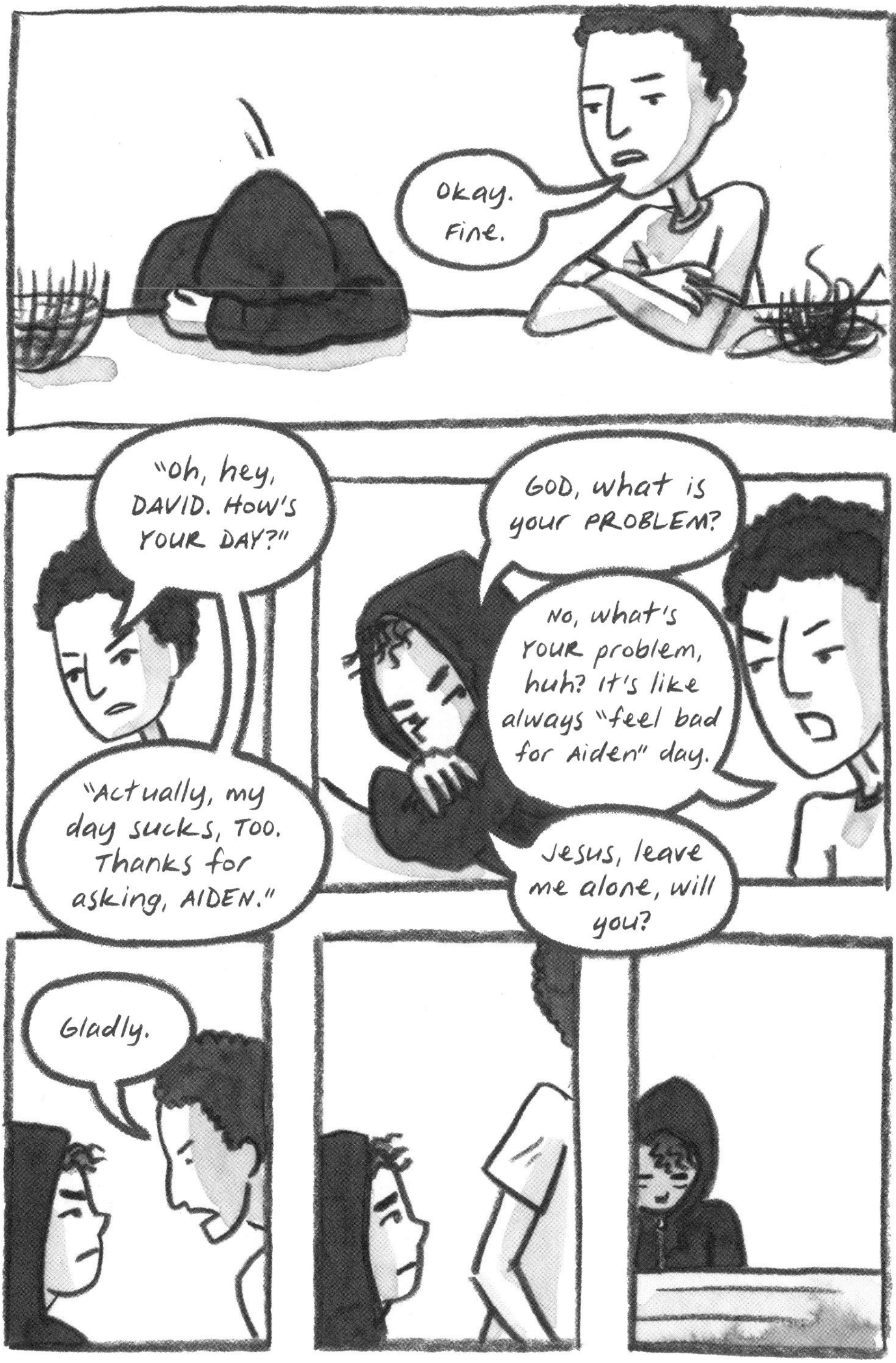
Okay. Fine.
"Oh, hey, DAVID. How's YOUR DAY?"
"Actually, my day sucks, TOO. Thanks for asking, AIDEN."
GOD, what is your PROBLEM?
No, what's YOUR problem, huh? It's like always "feel bad for Aiden" day.
Jesus, leave me alone, will you?
Gladly.

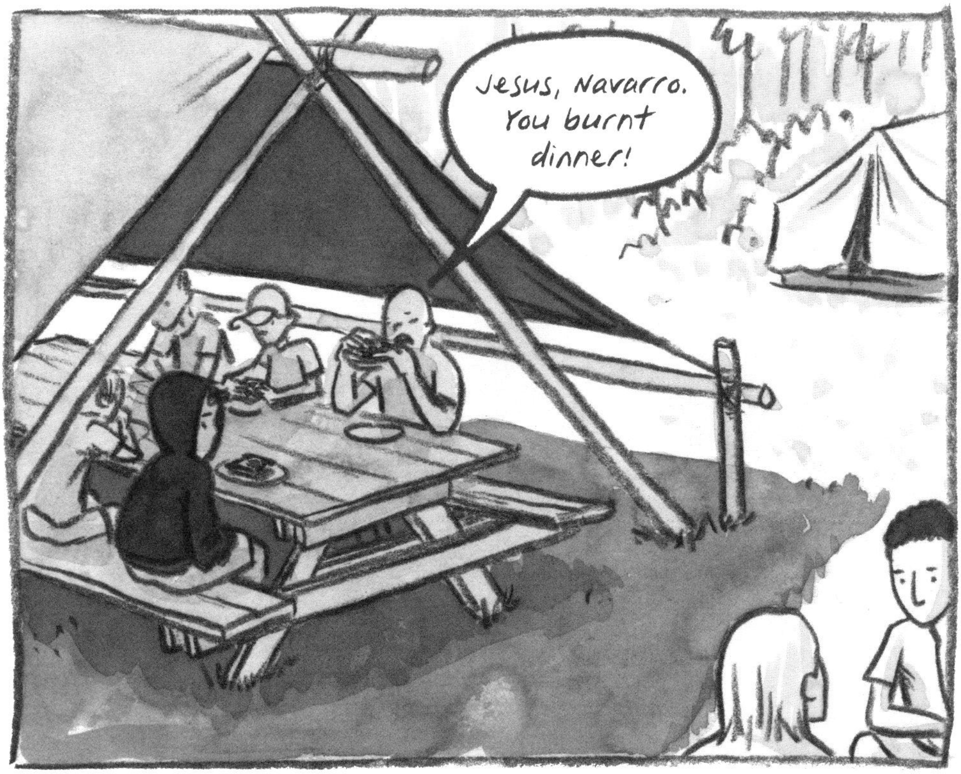
Jesus, Navarro. You burnt dinner!

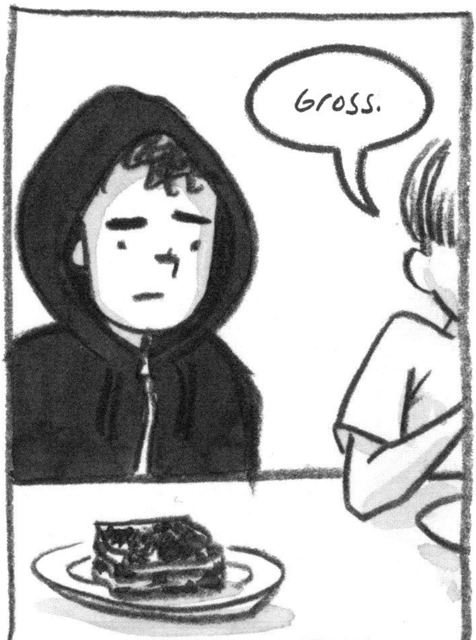
Gross.

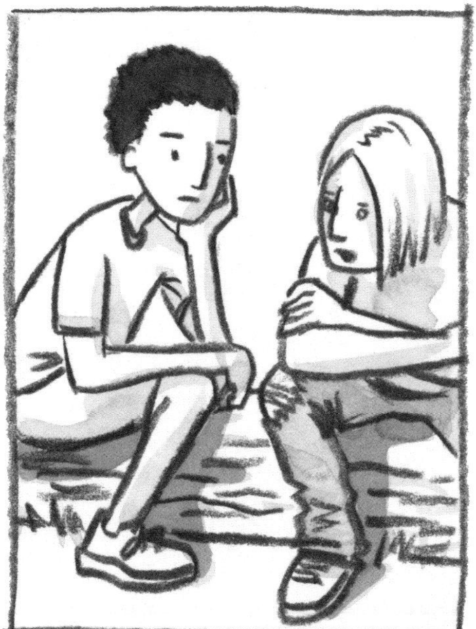

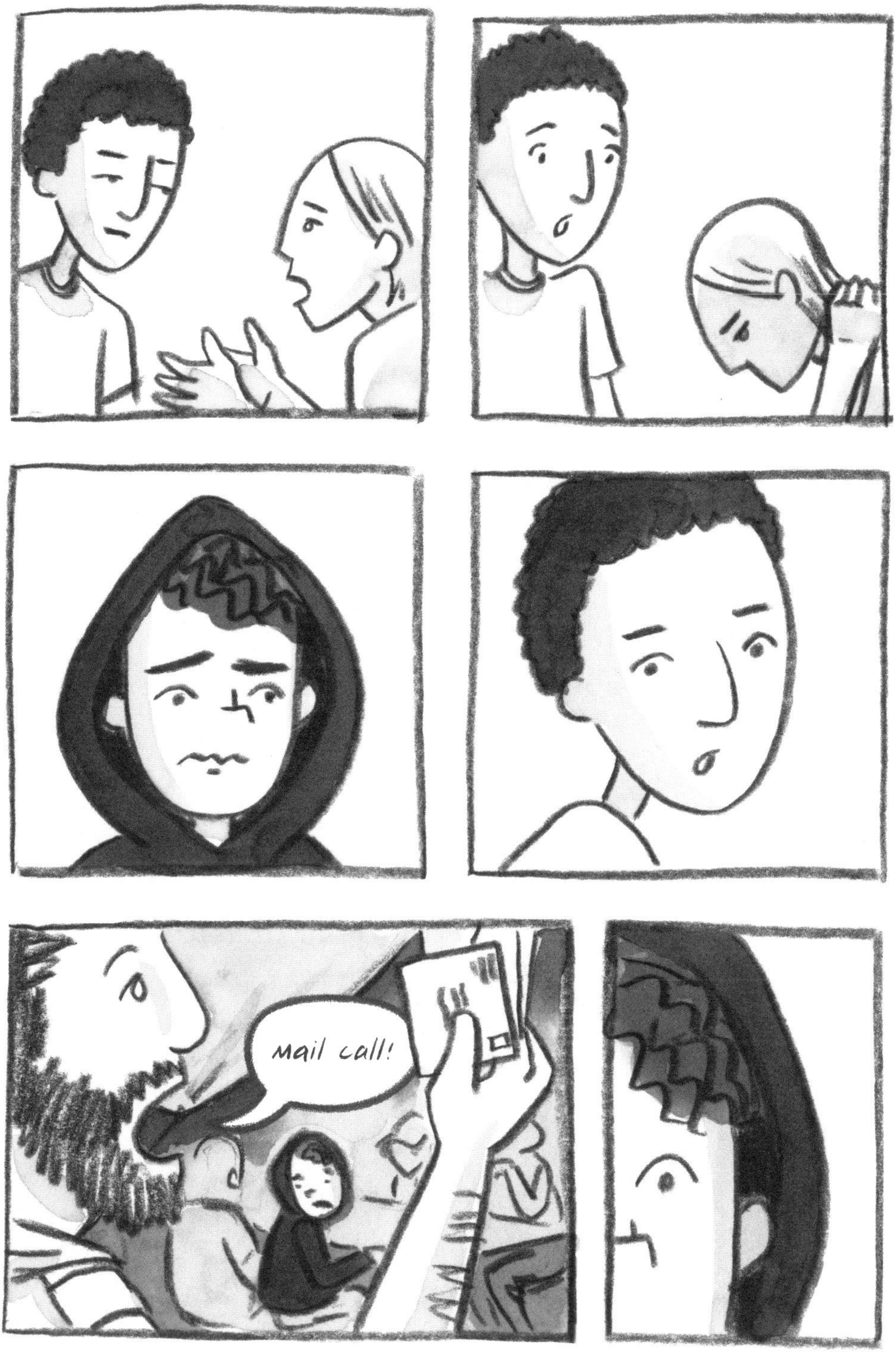
Mail call!

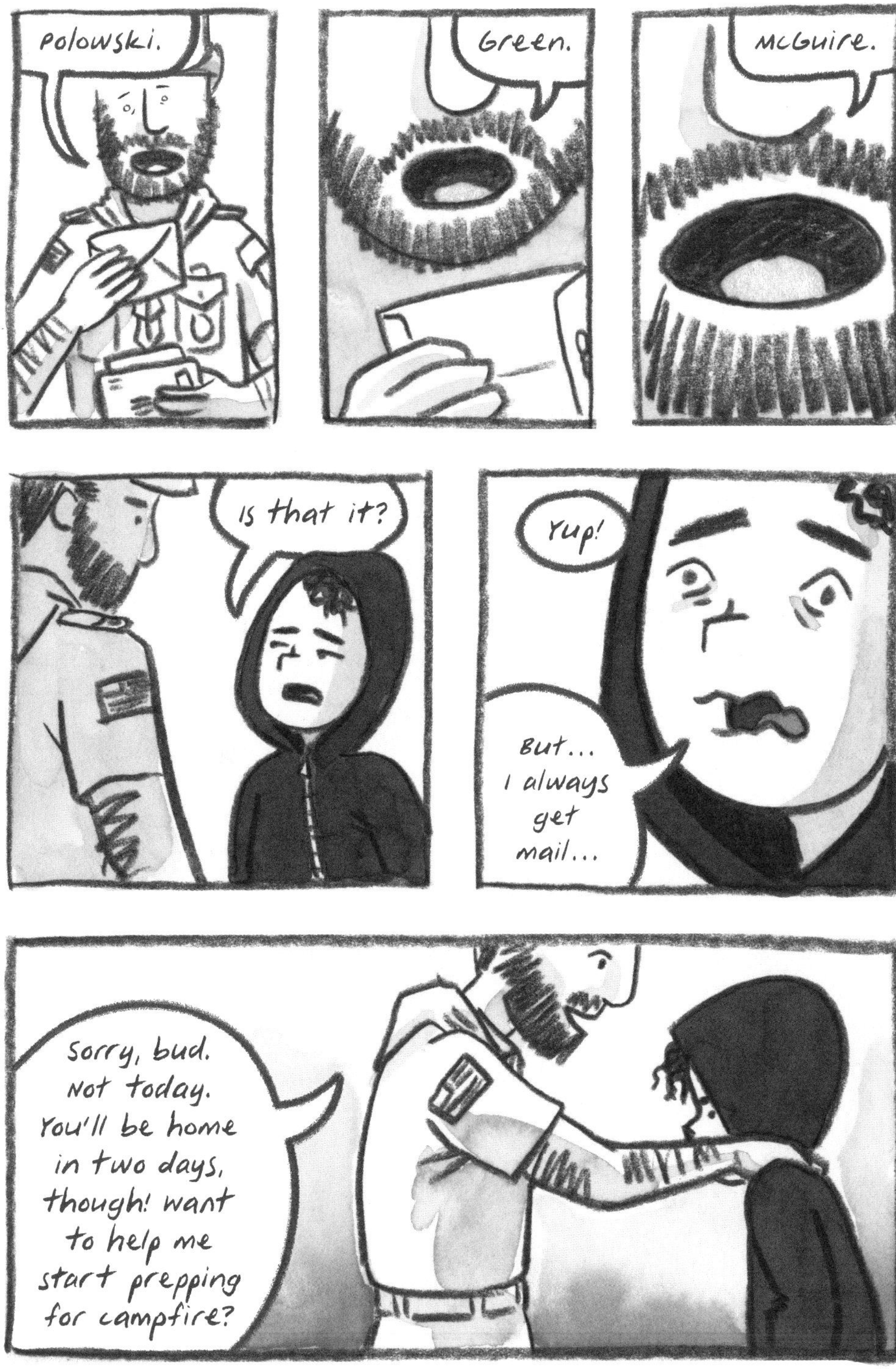
Polowski.
Green.
McGuire.
Is that it?
Yup!
But... I always get mail...
Sorry, bud. Not today. You'll be home in two days, though! Want to help me start prepping for campfire?

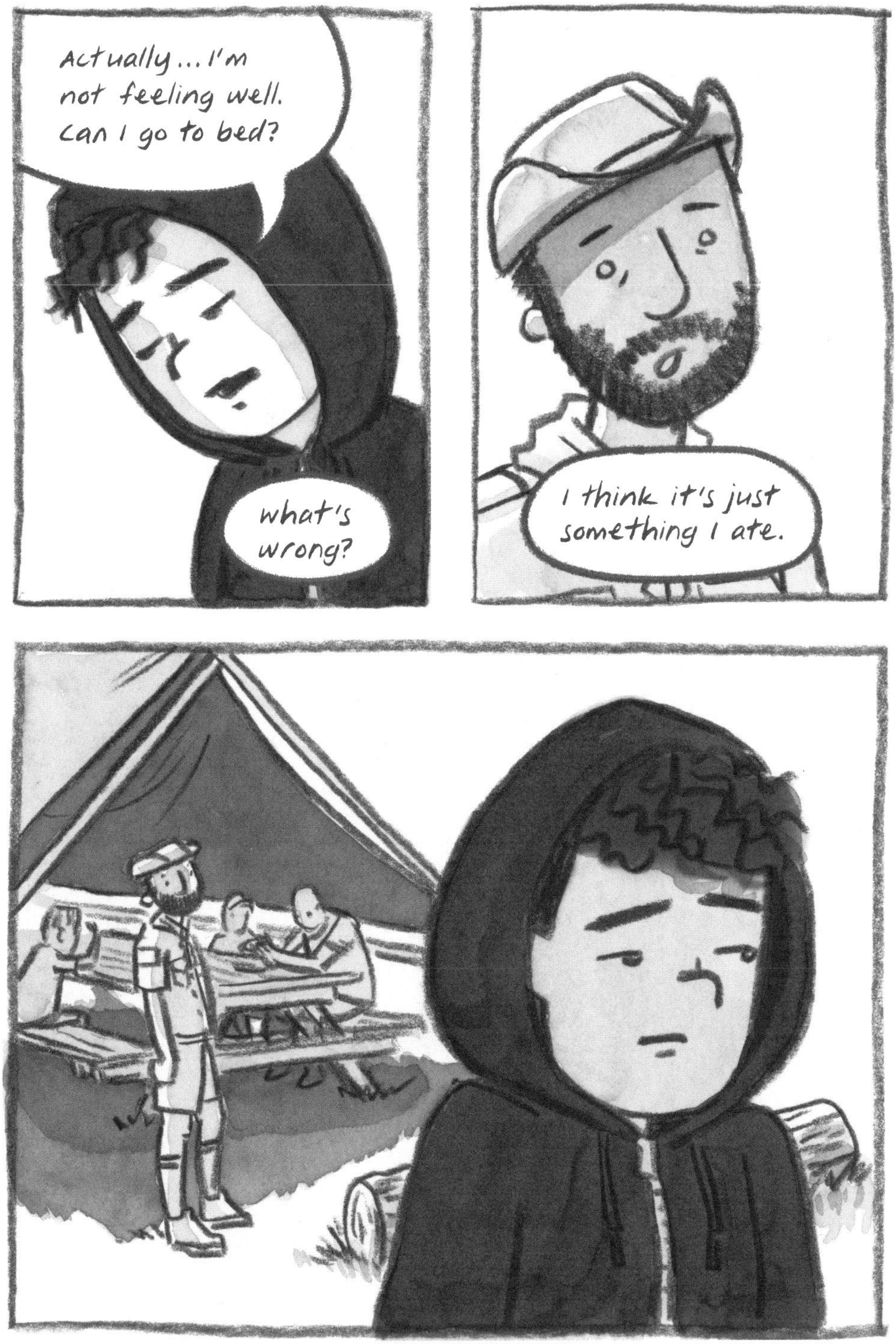
Actually... I'm not feeling well. Can I go to bed?
What's wrong?
I think it's just something I ate.

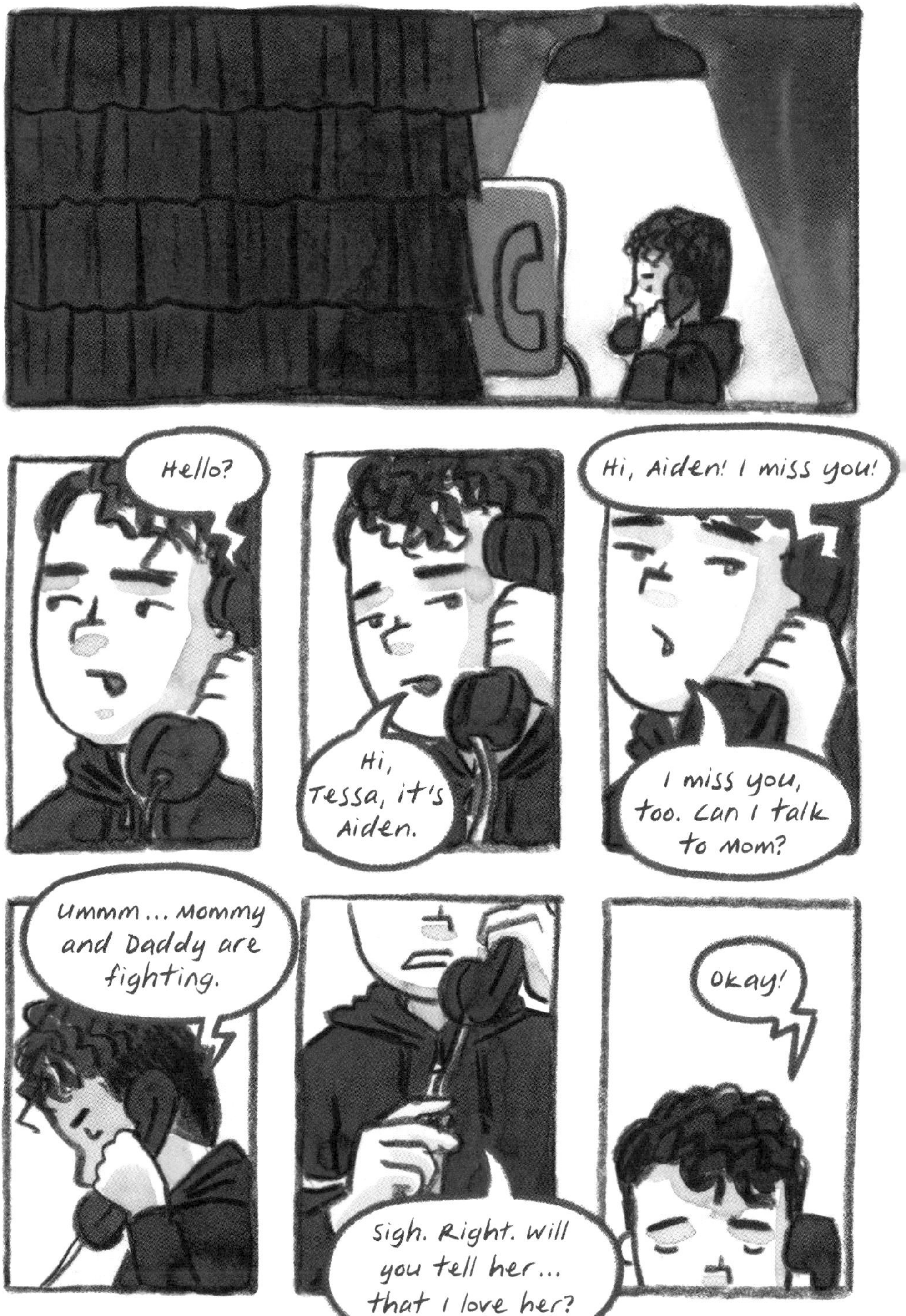
Hello?
Hi, Tessa, it's Aiden.
Hi, Aiden! I miss you!
I miss you, too. Can I talk to Mom?
Ummm... Mommy and Daddy are fighting.
Sigh. Right. Will you tell her... that I love her?
Okay!

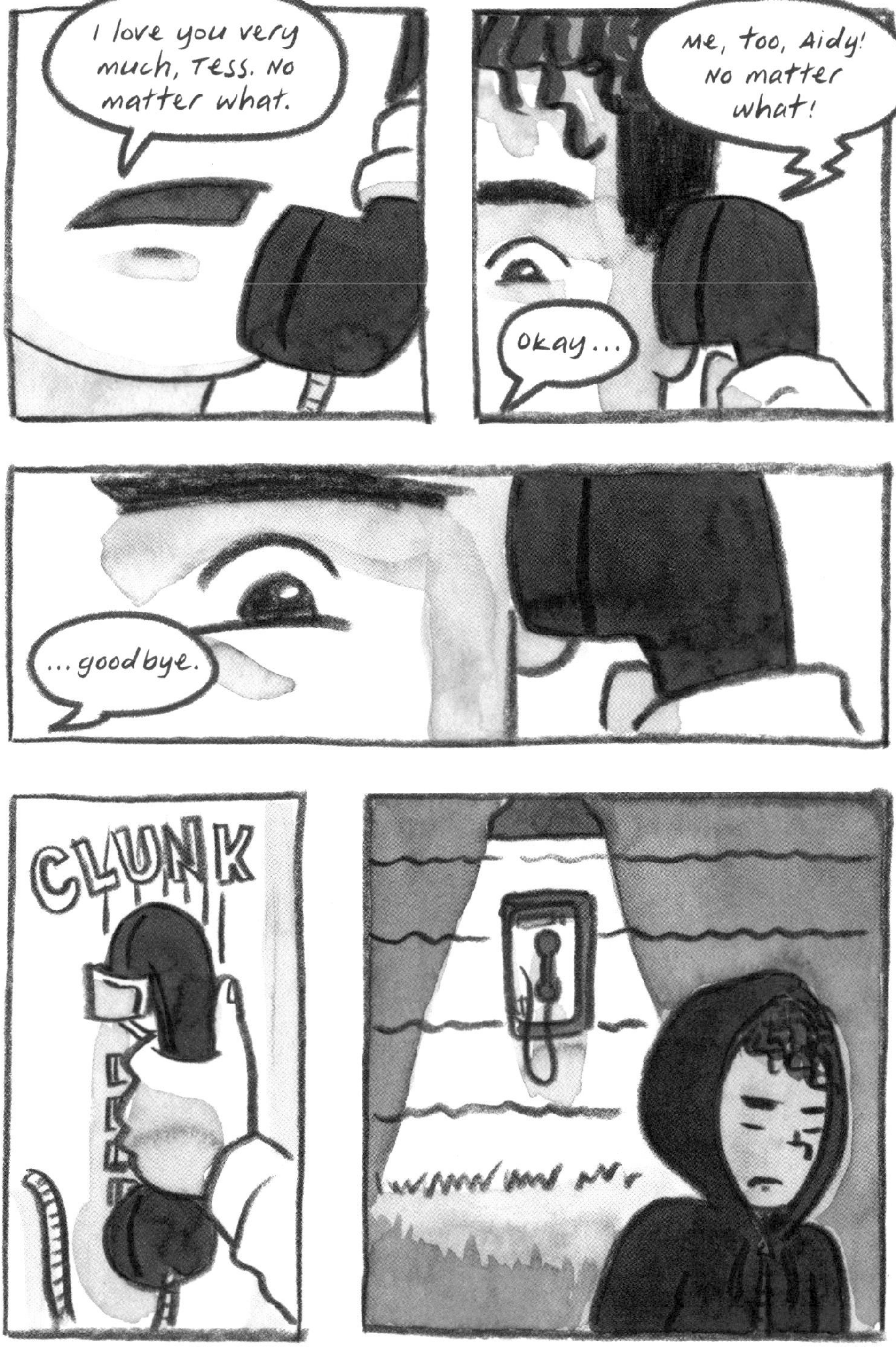
I love you very much, Tess. No matter what.
Me, too, Aidy! No matter what!
Okay...
...goodbye.
CLUNK

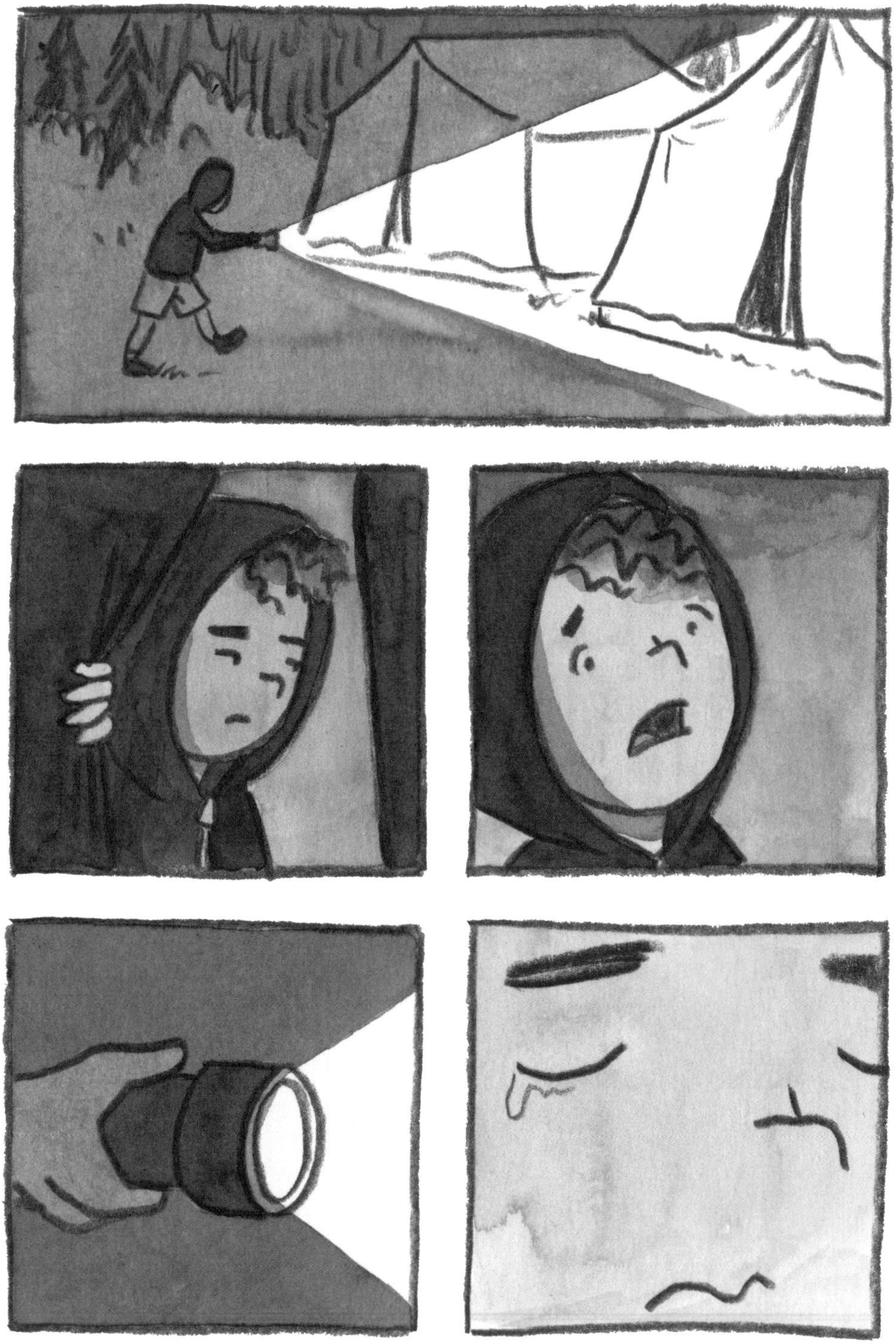

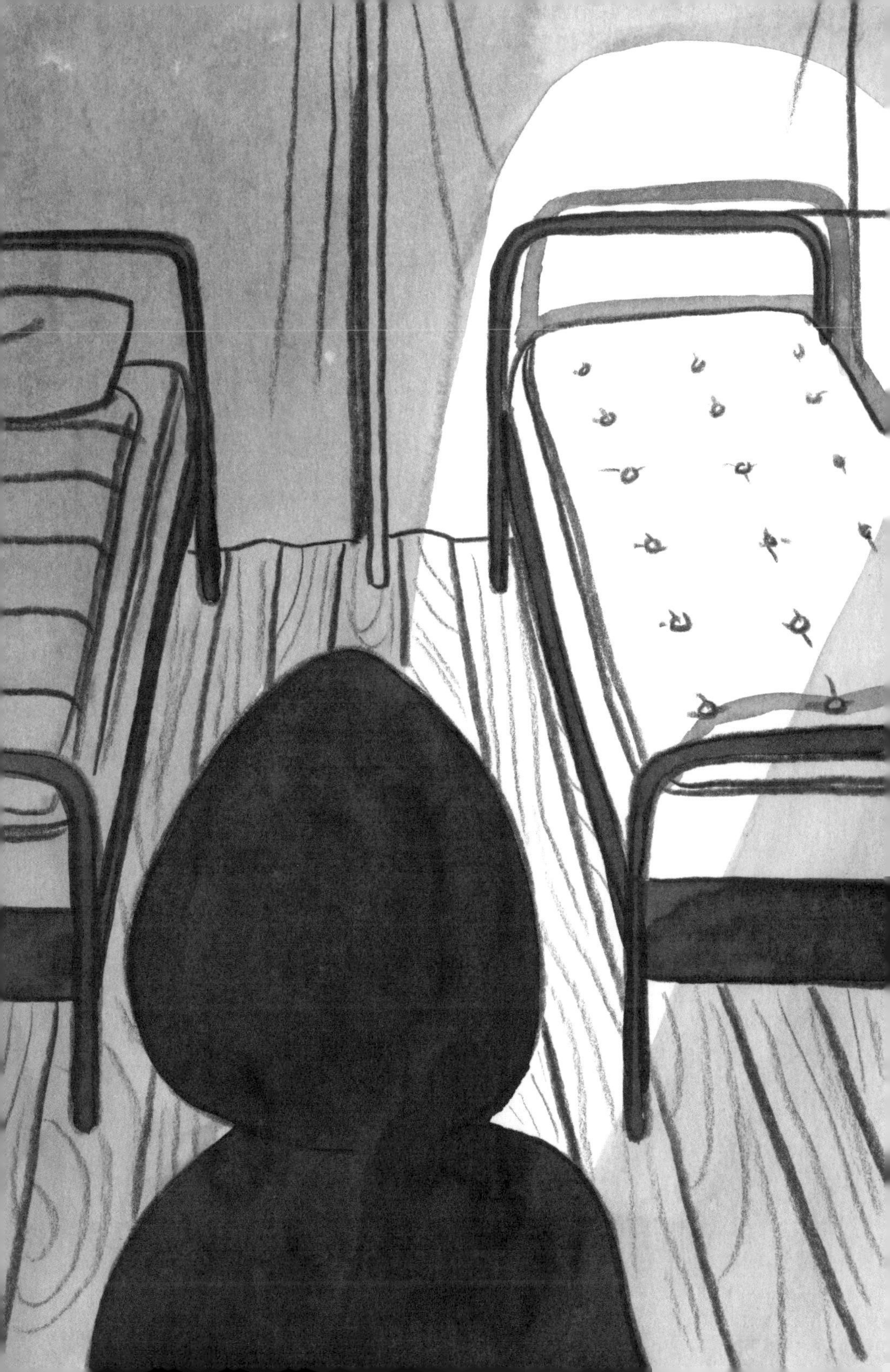

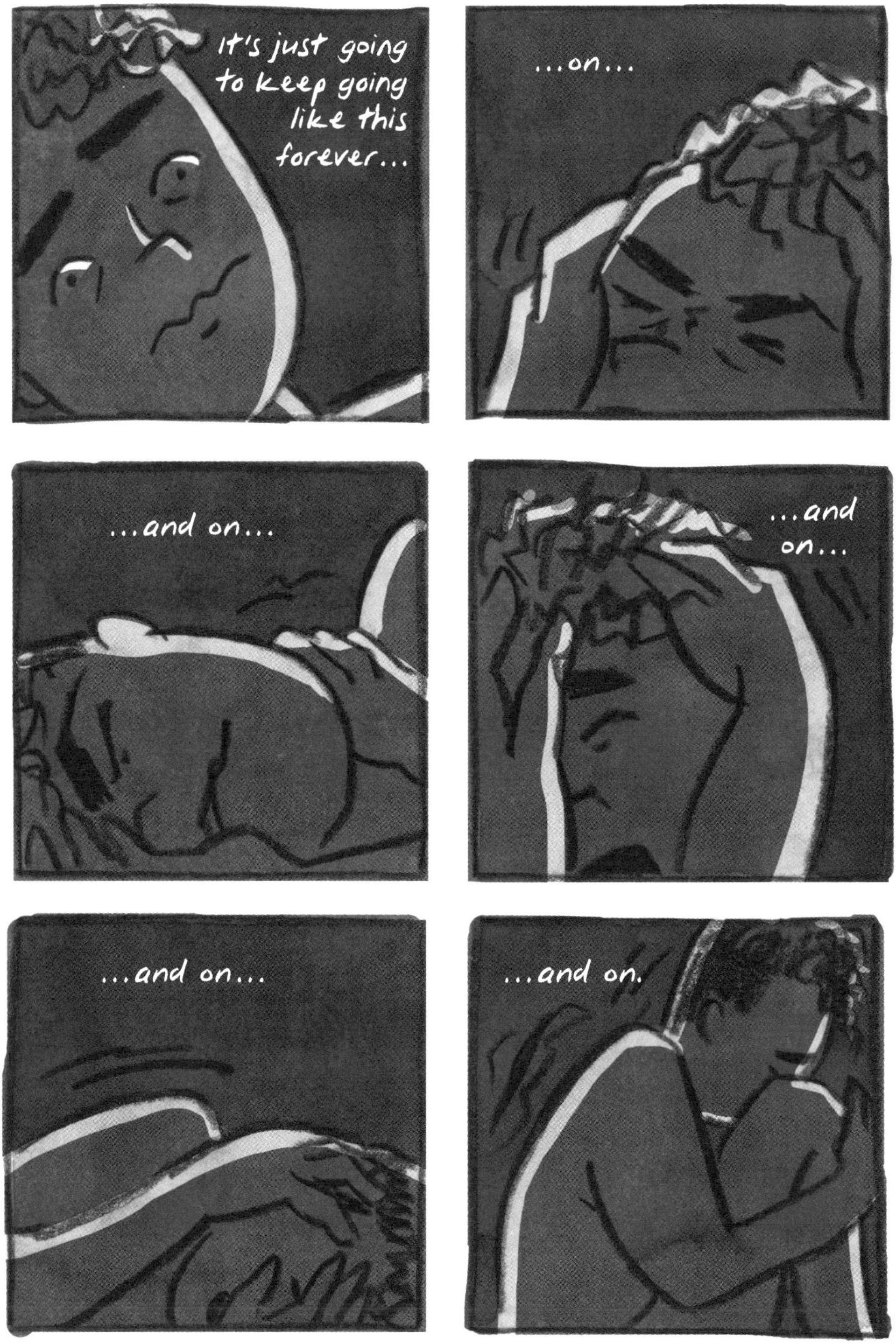
It's just going to keep going like this forever...
...on...
...and on...
...and on...
...and on...
...and on.

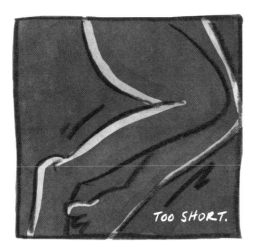

TOO SHORT.

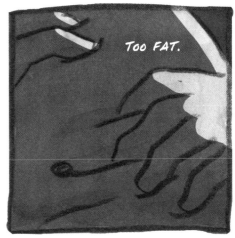

TOO FAT.

Not MAN enough.

Not WHITE enough.

Not STRAIGHT enough.

I'll never be safe ANYWHERE.

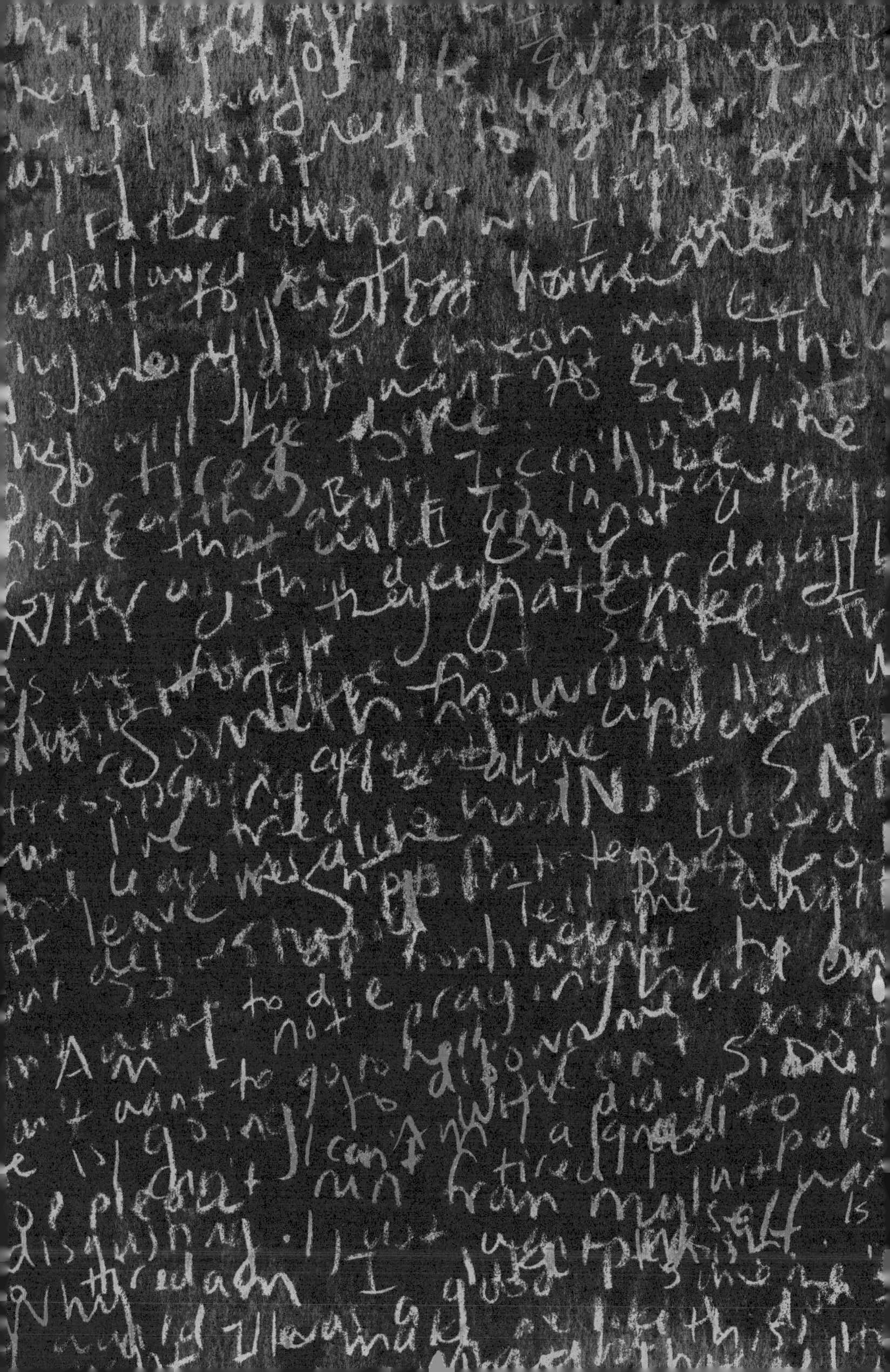

to die
Am I
not
Tell the
from myself

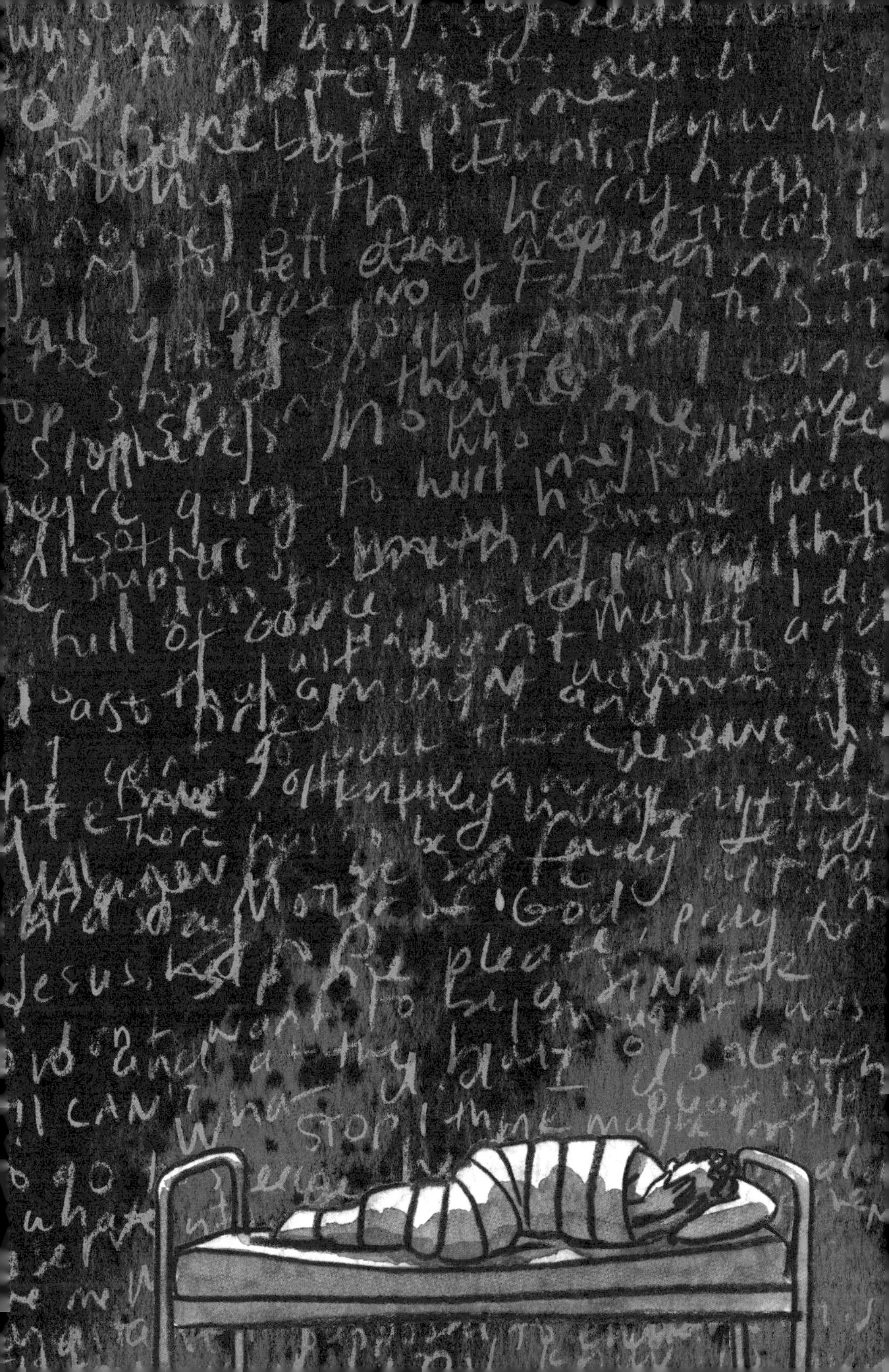

...I hate myself... I know... I don't know how... going to tell them... please no... that... stop staring... they're going to hurt me... who... stupid... full of... Jesus, keep me please... to be a SINNER... STOP I think maybe... I CAN'T... what if... pray to God...

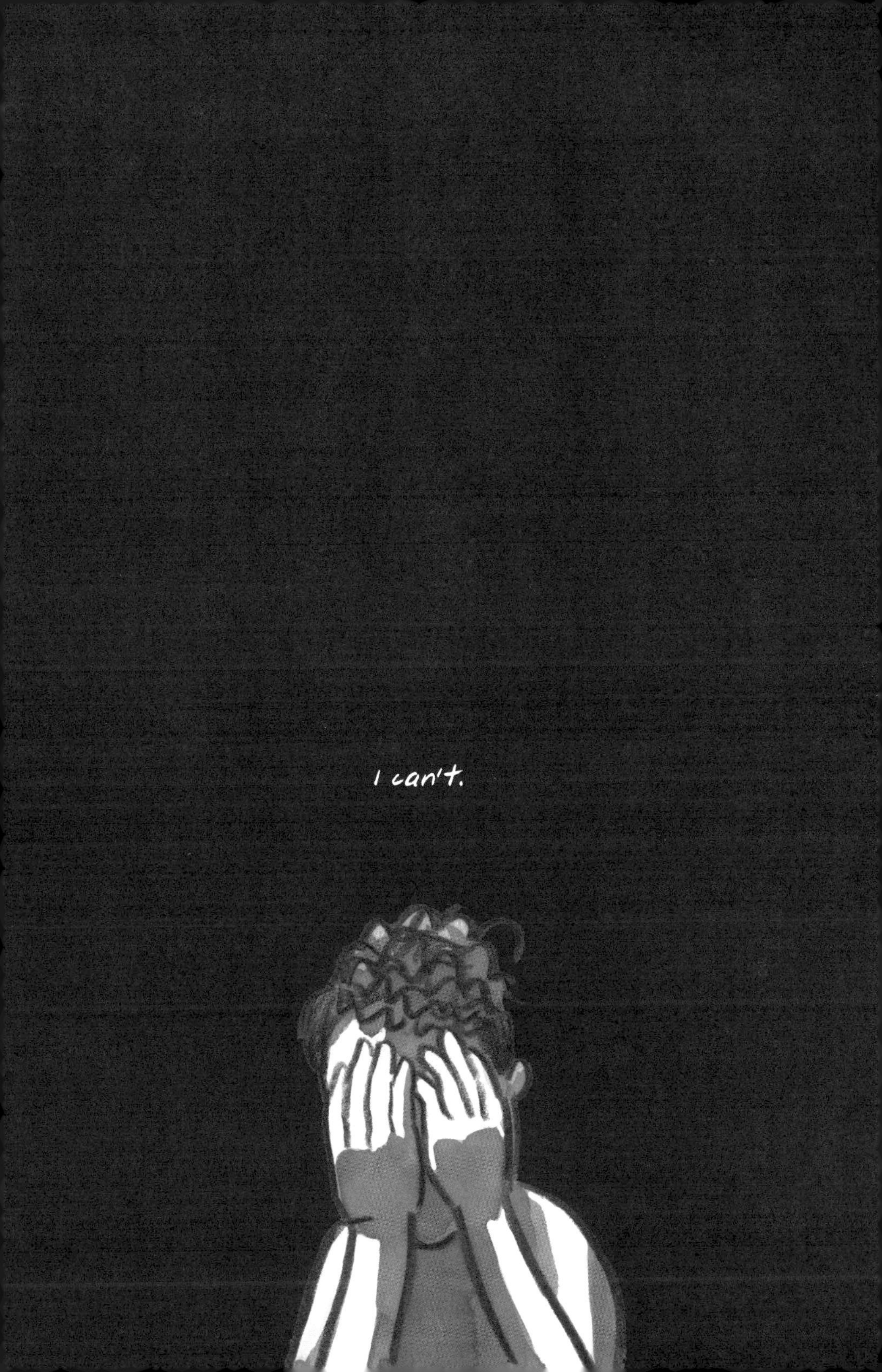
I can't.

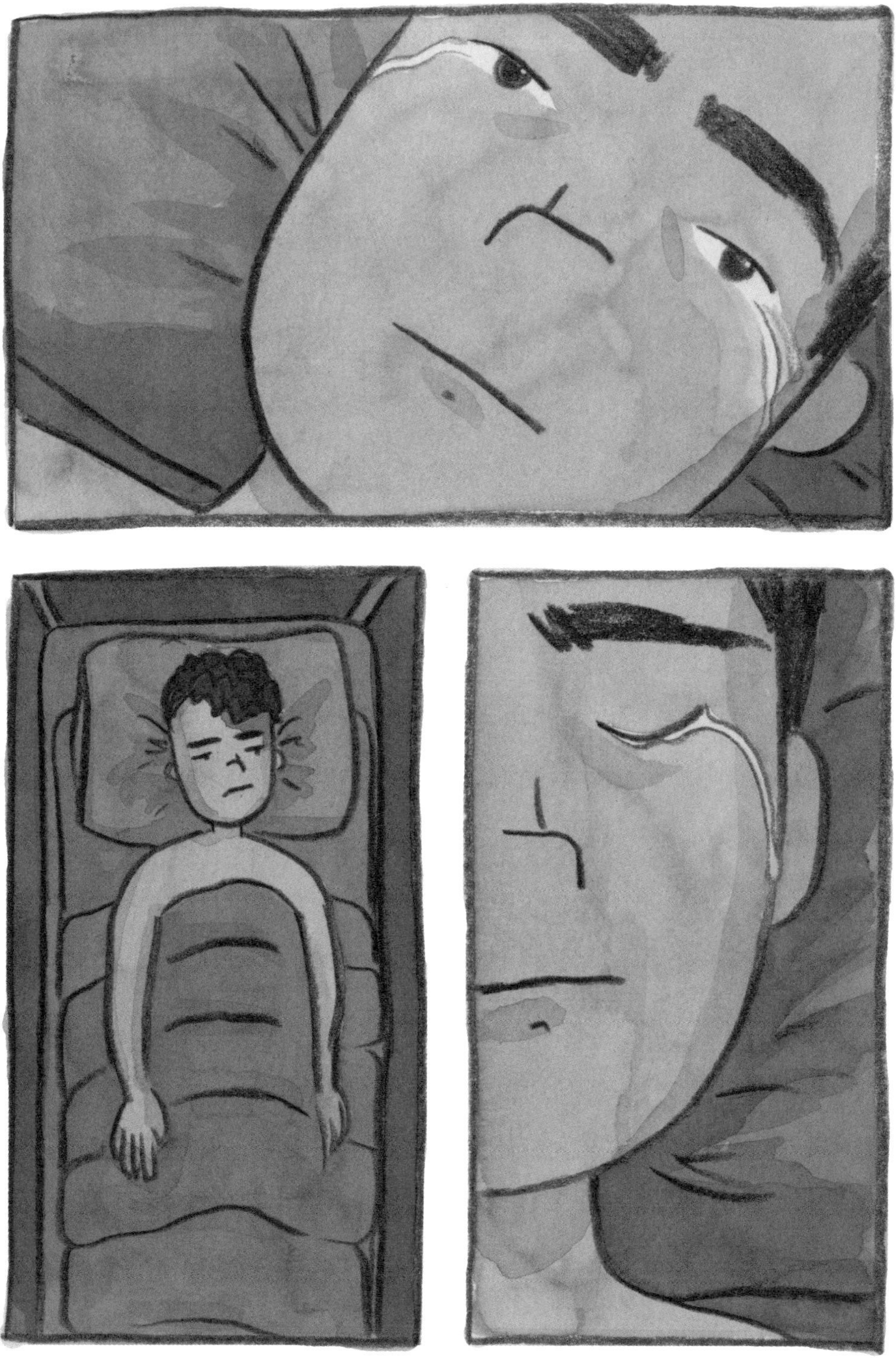

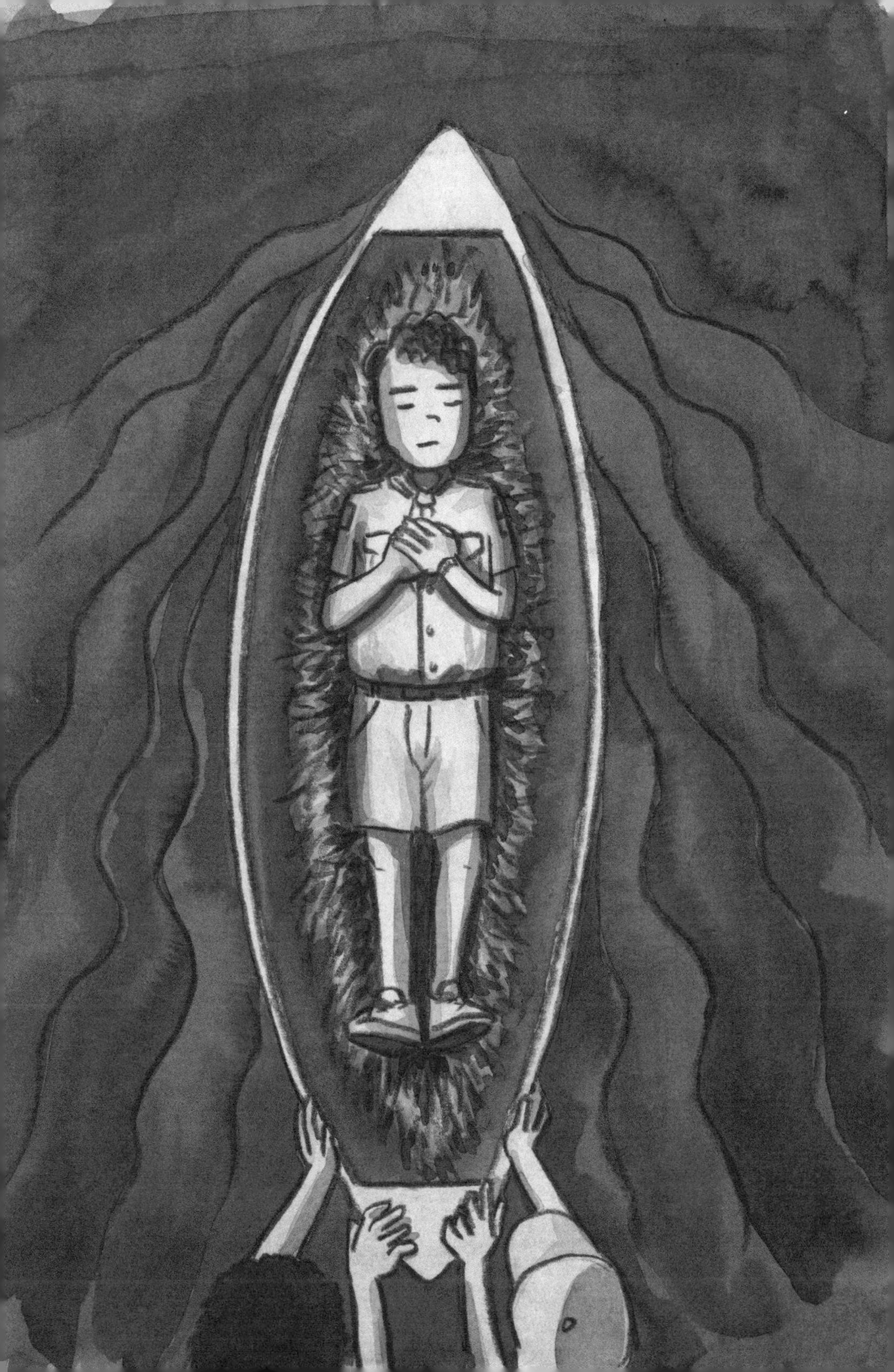

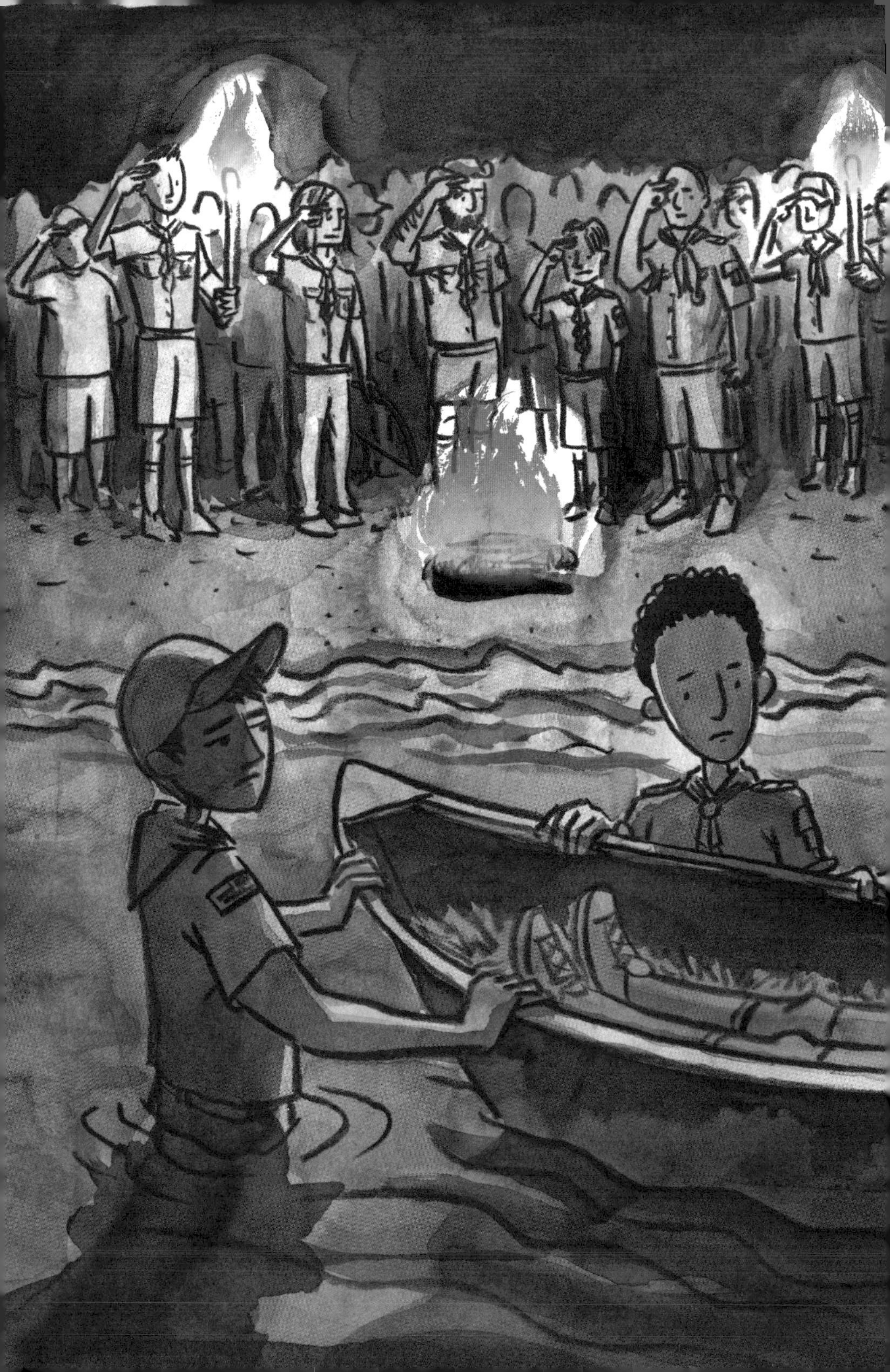

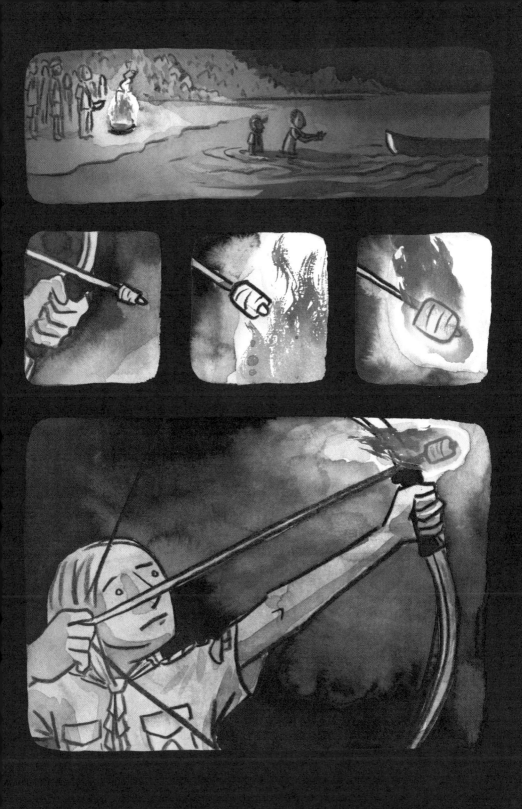

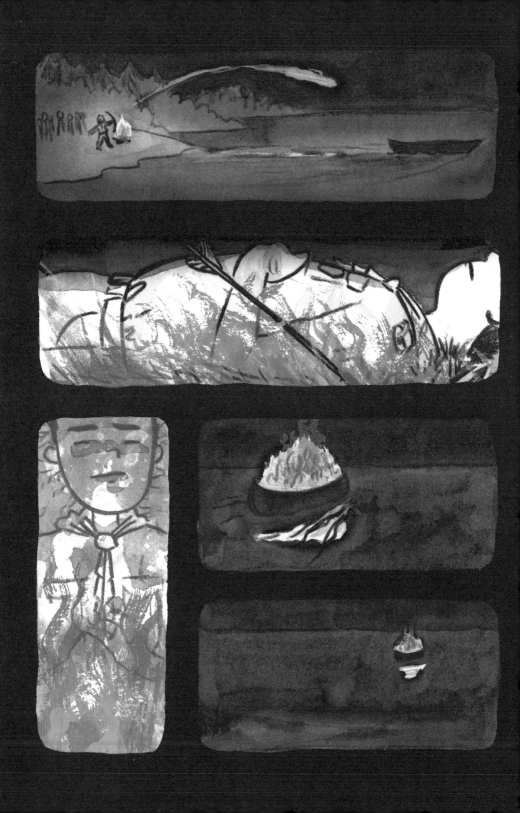

FRIDAY

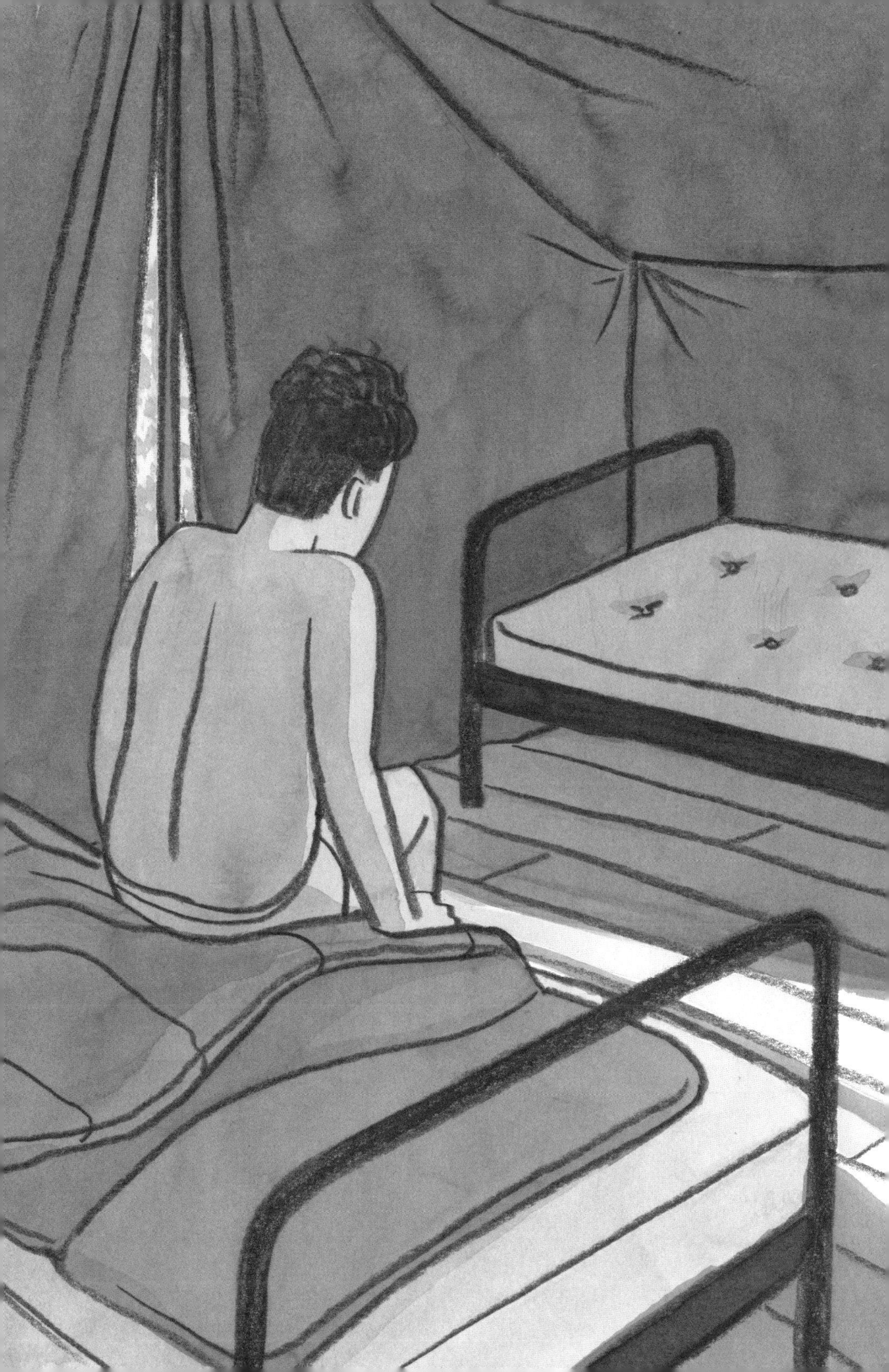

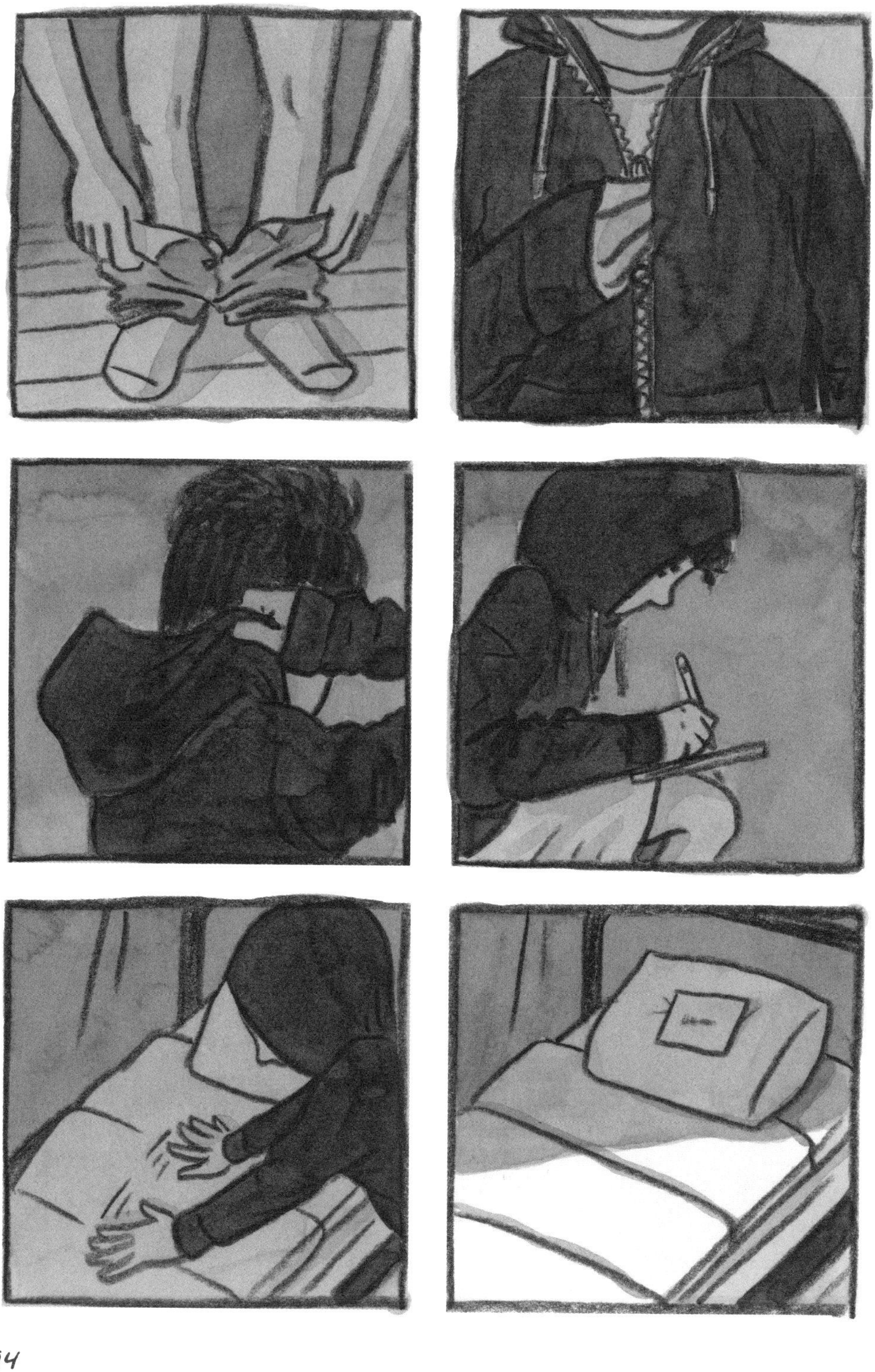

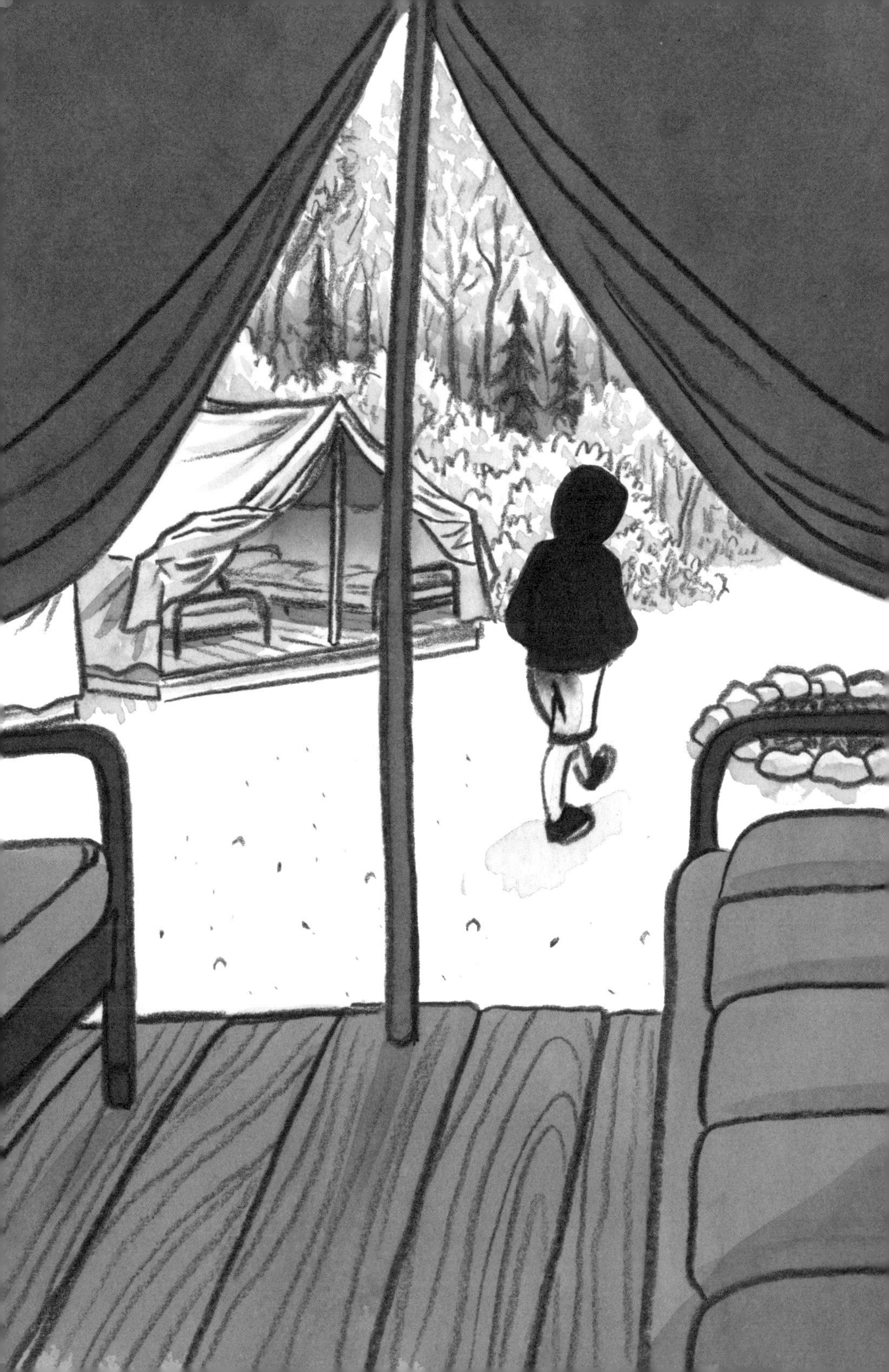

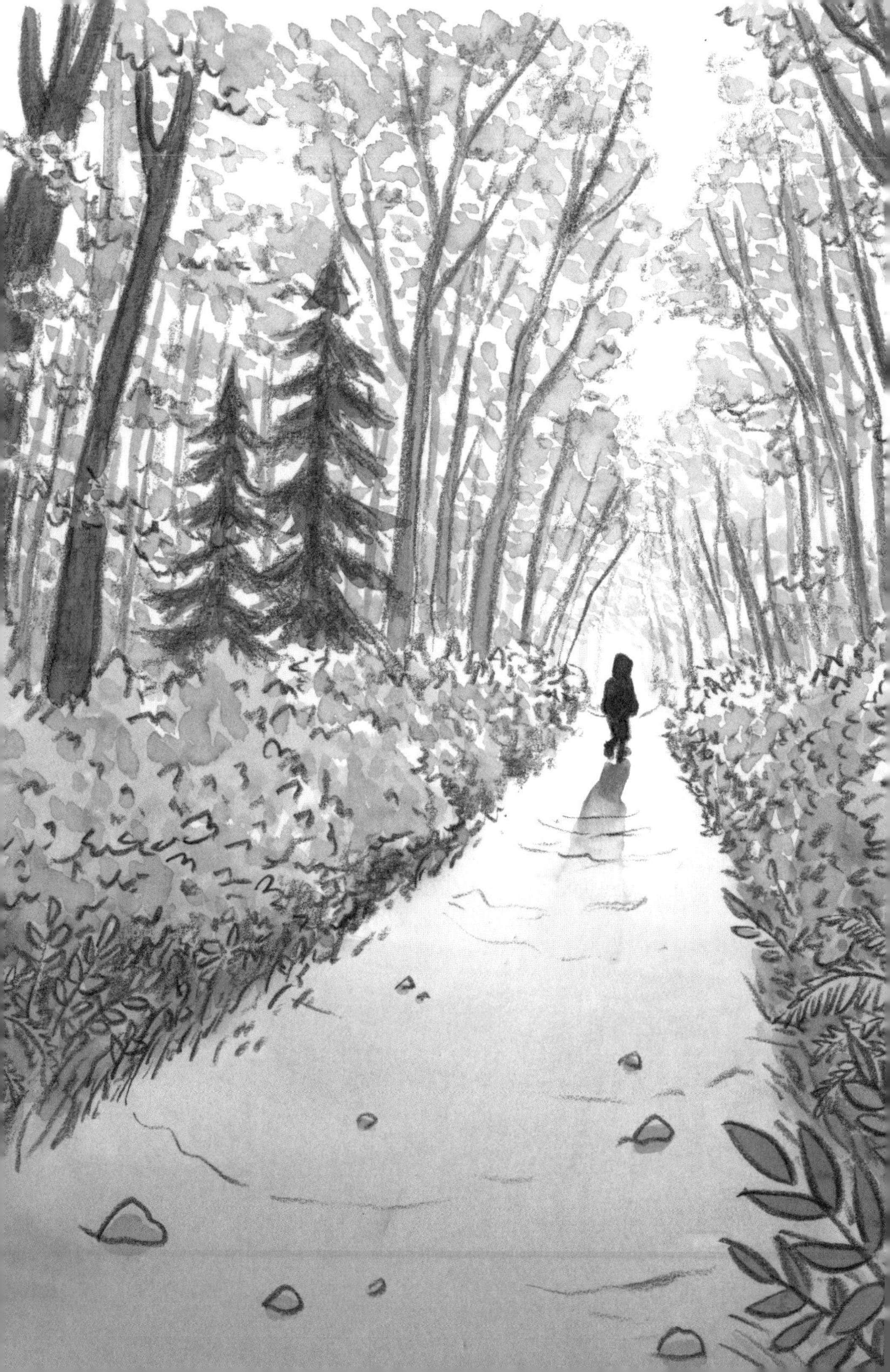

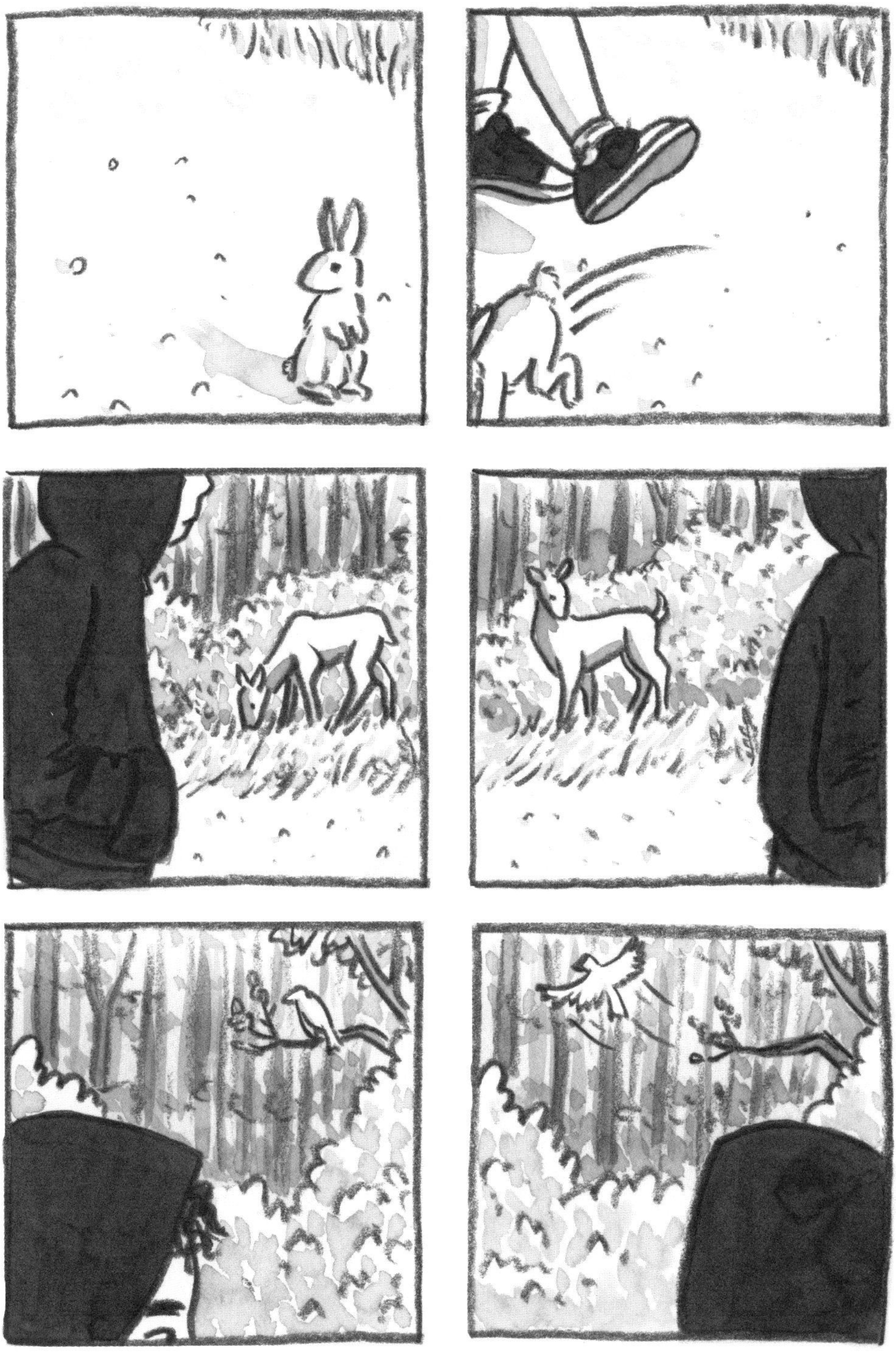

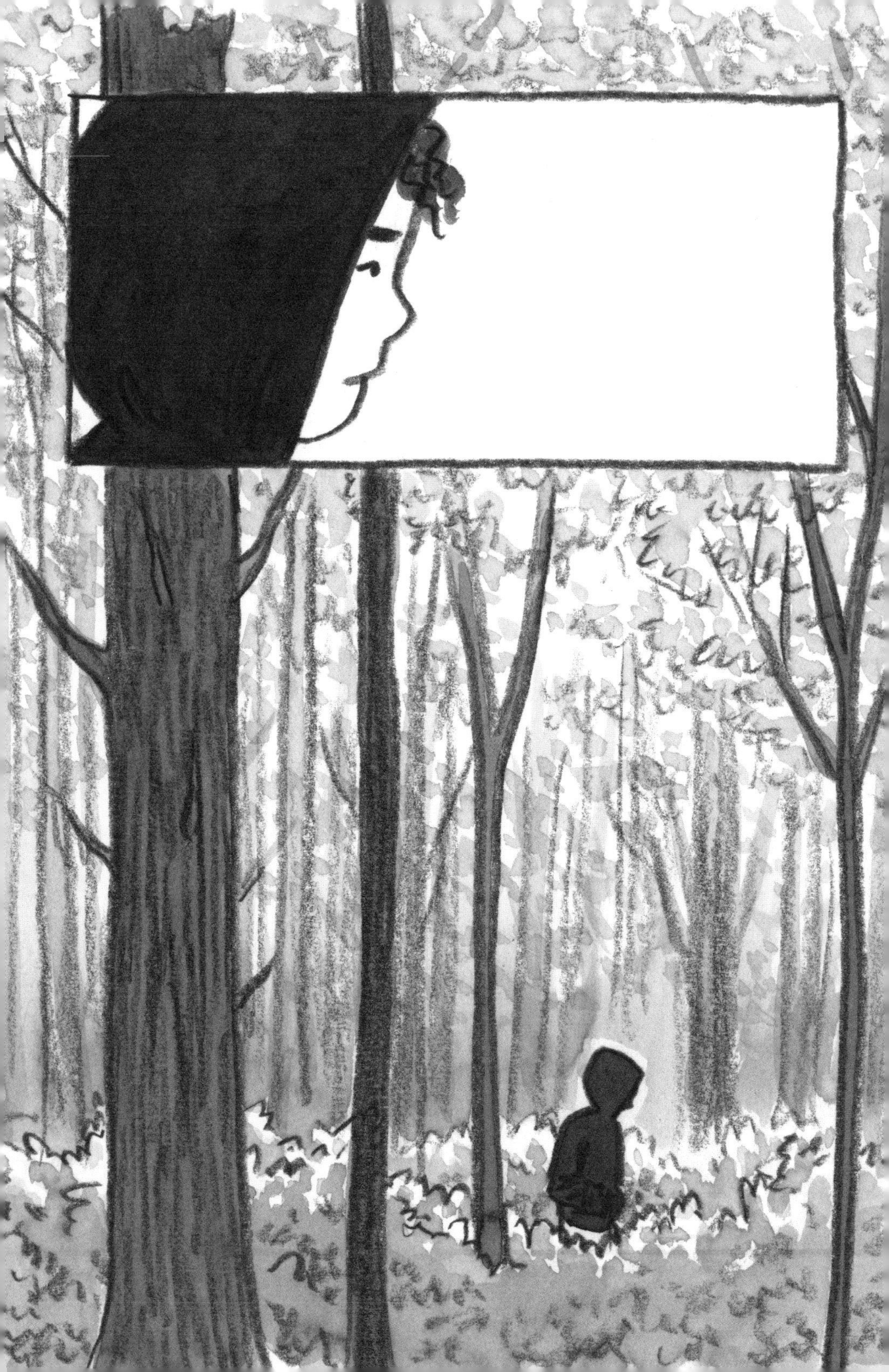

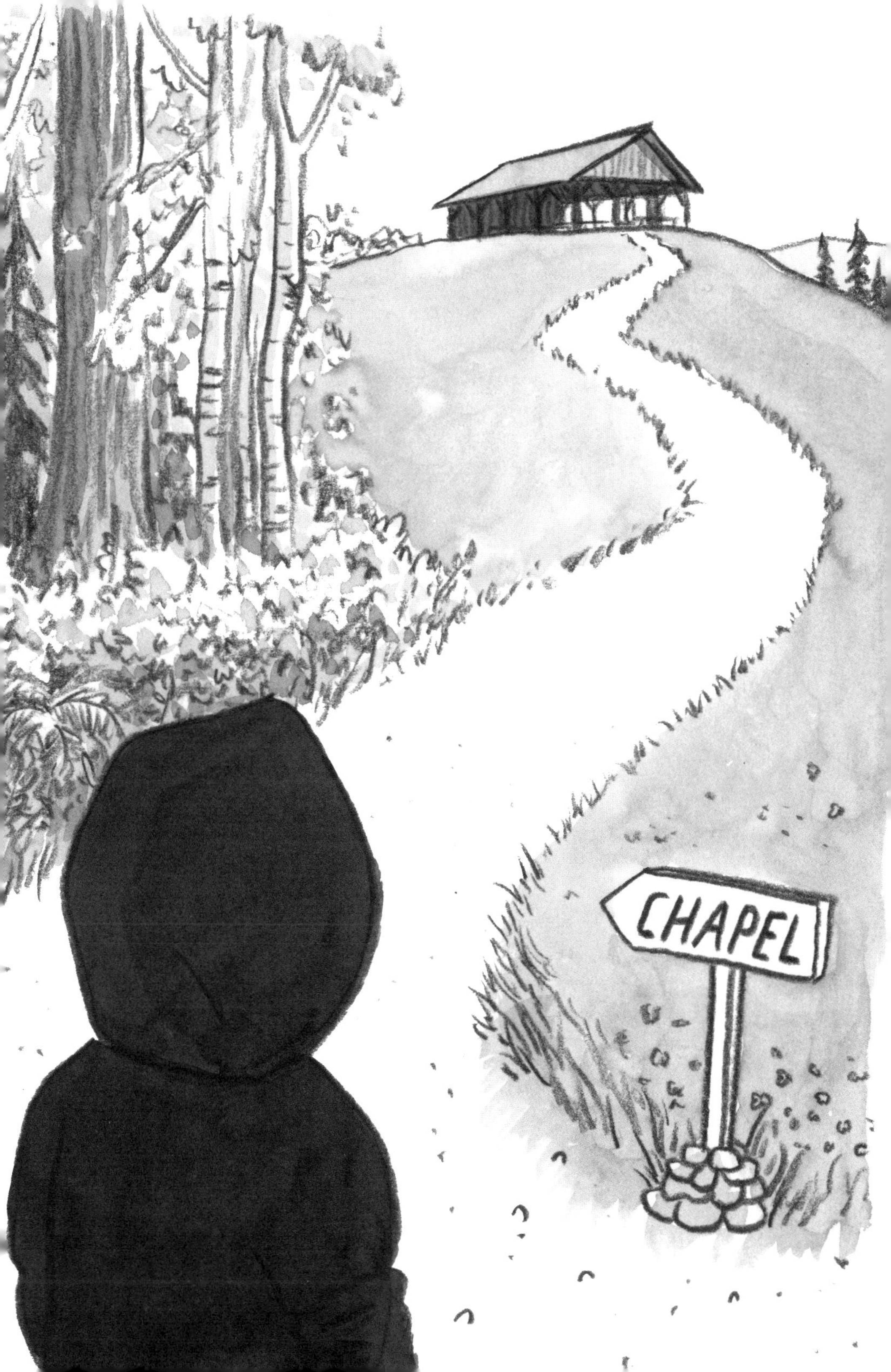
CHAPEL

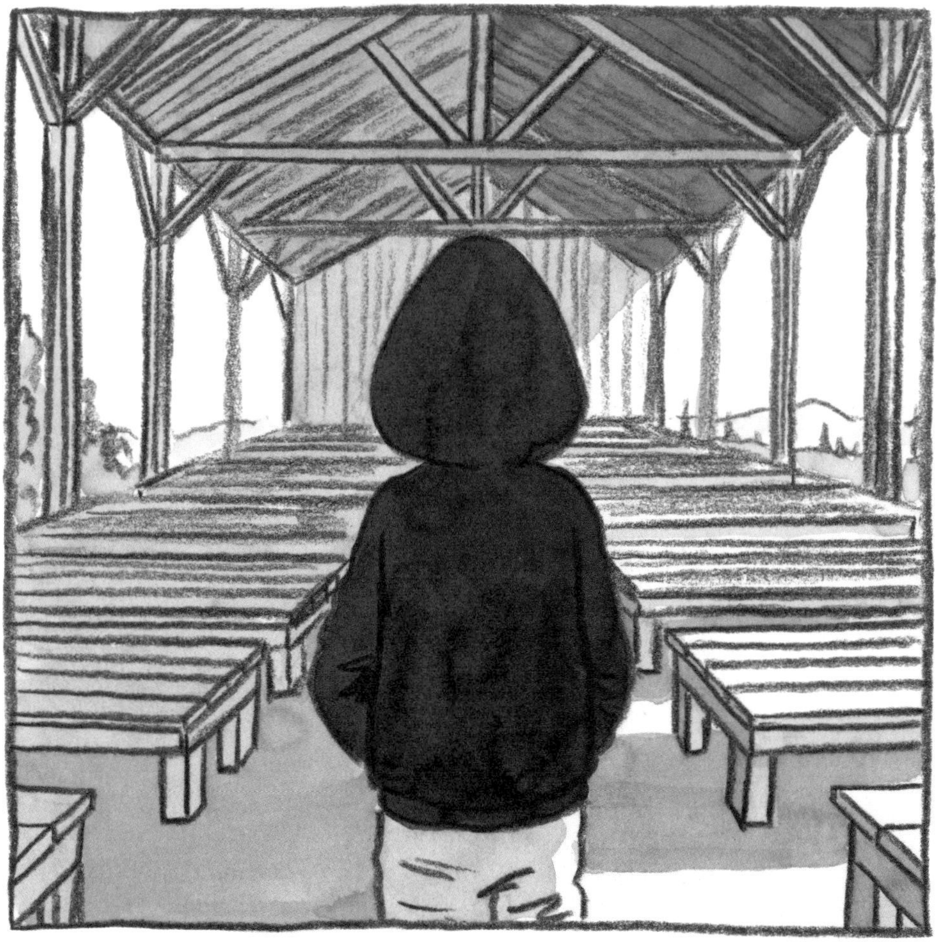

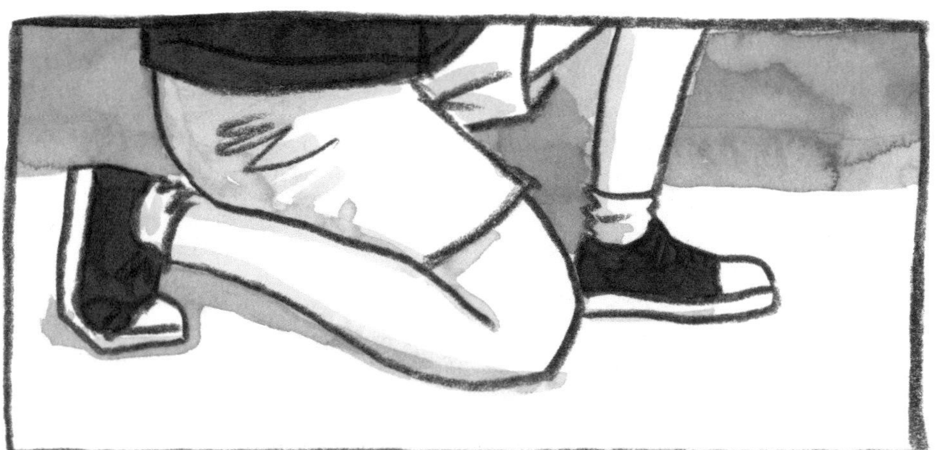

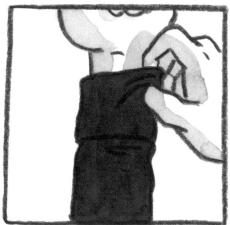

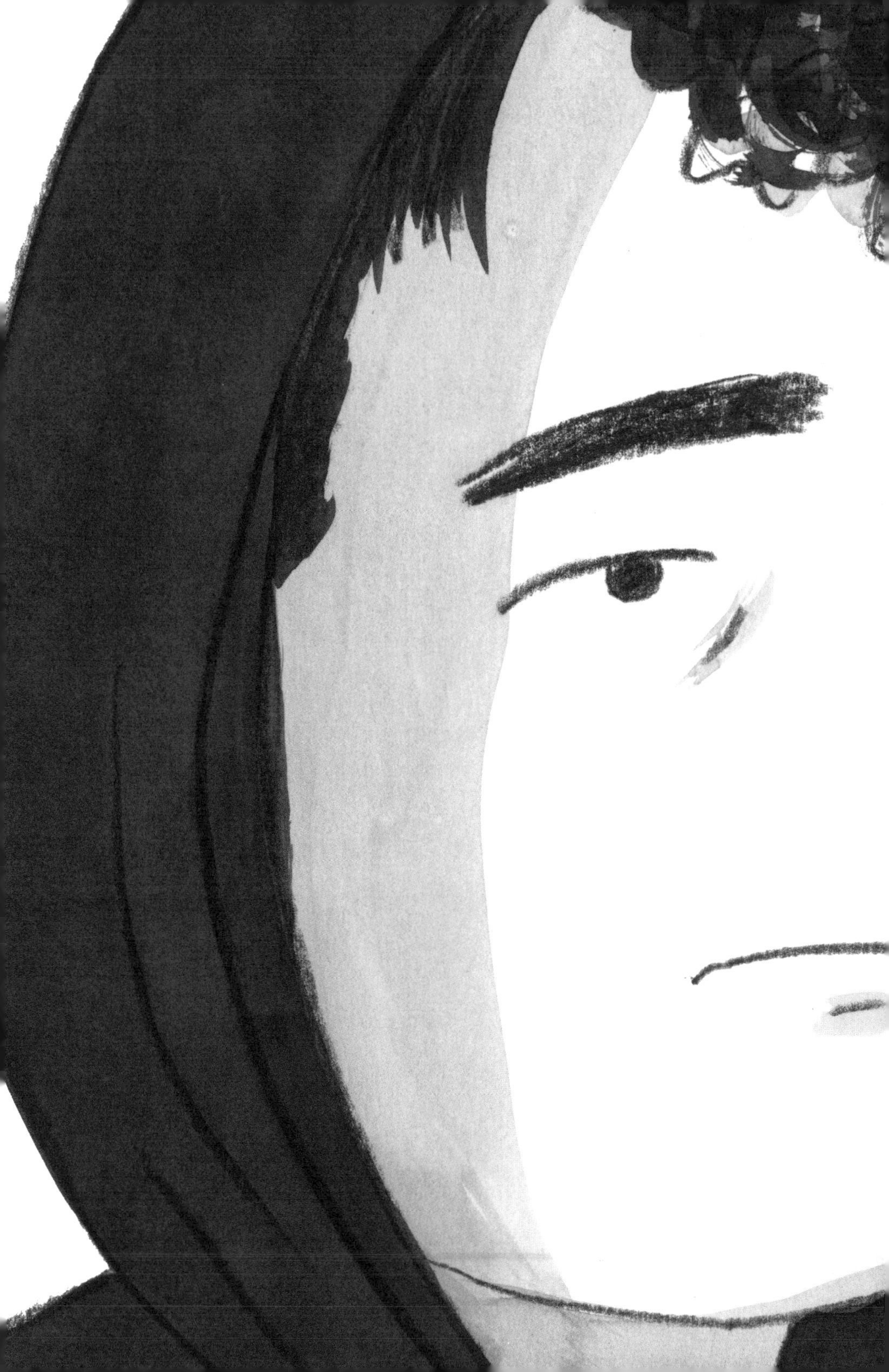

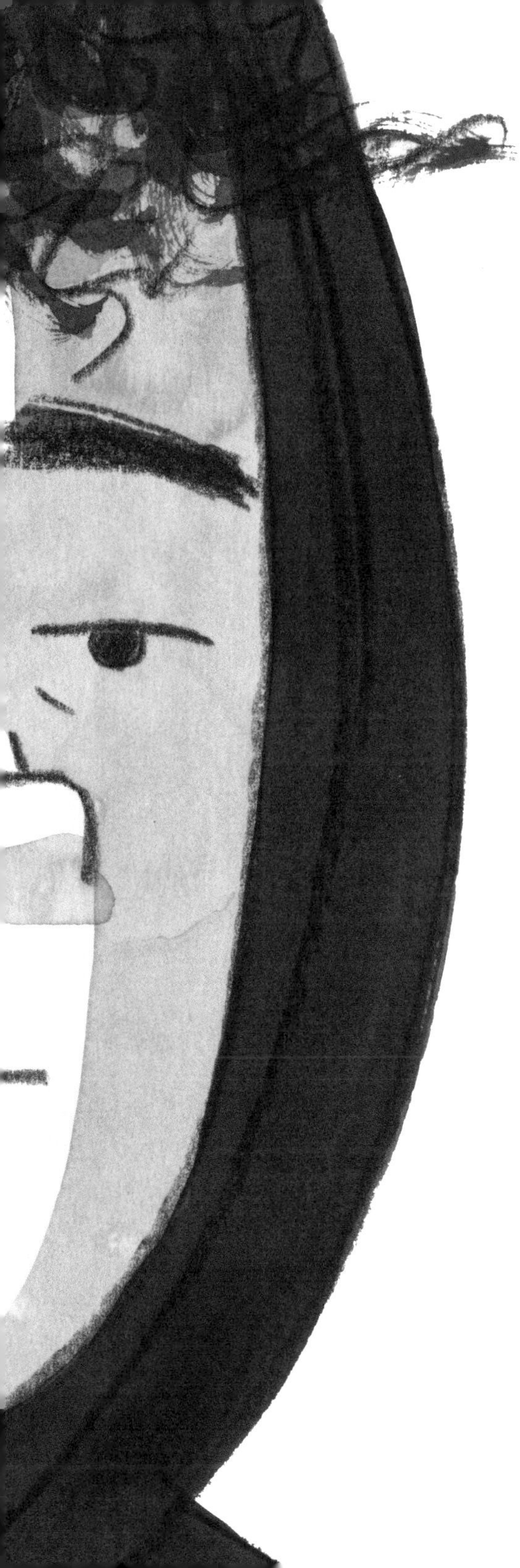

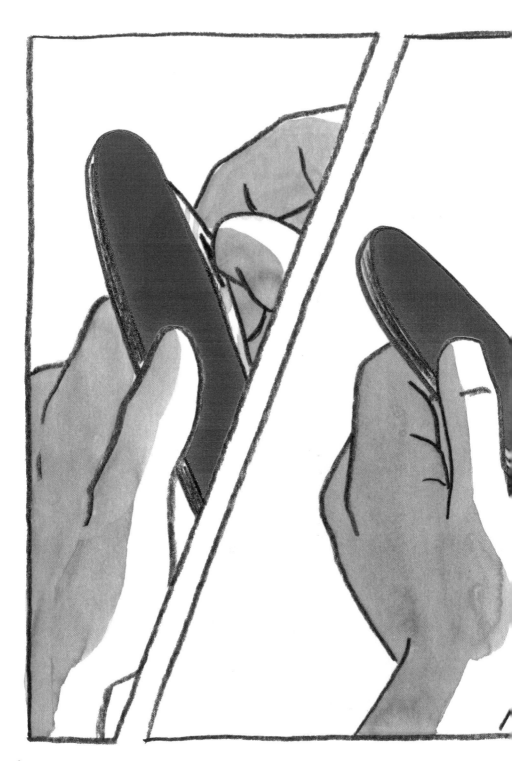

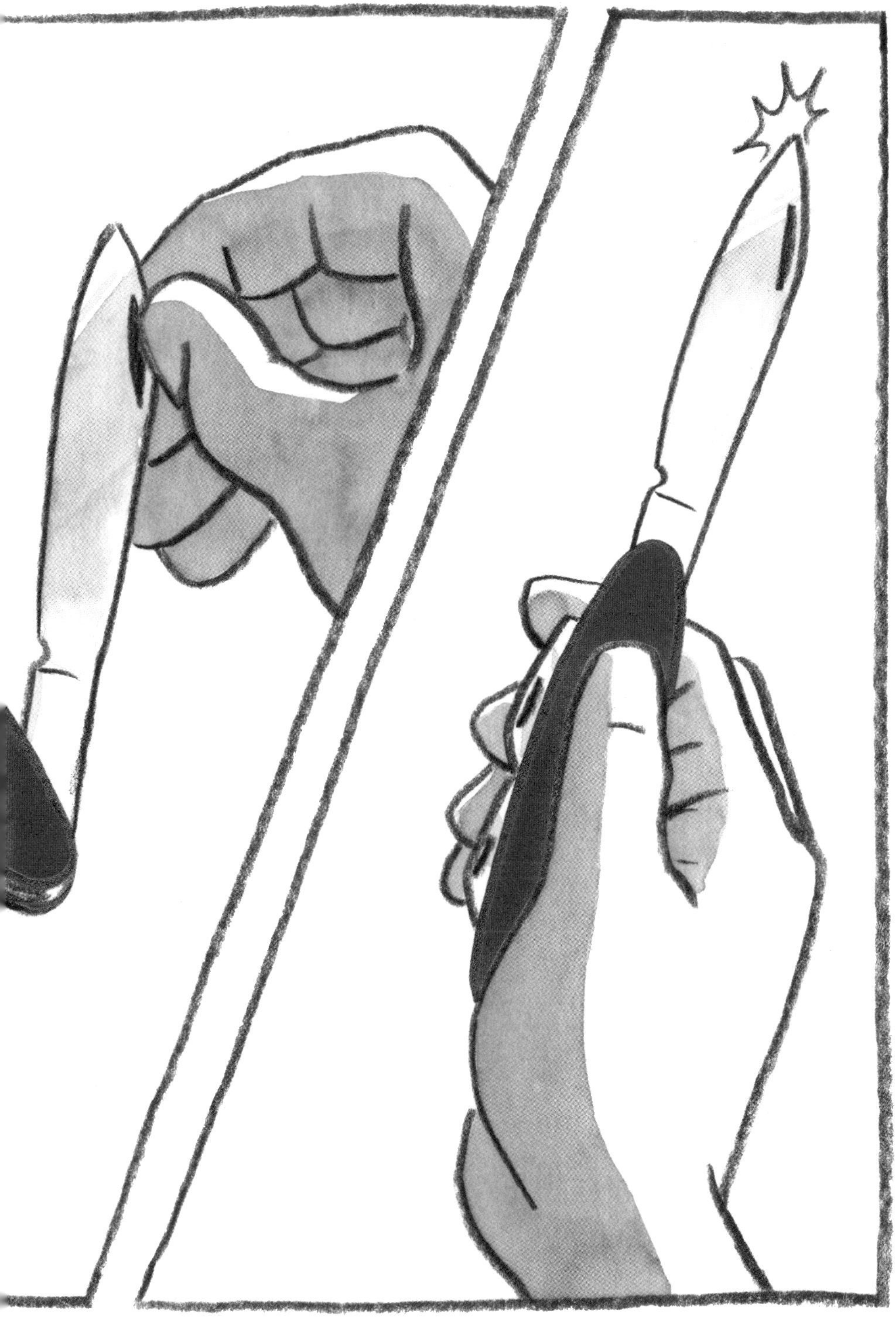

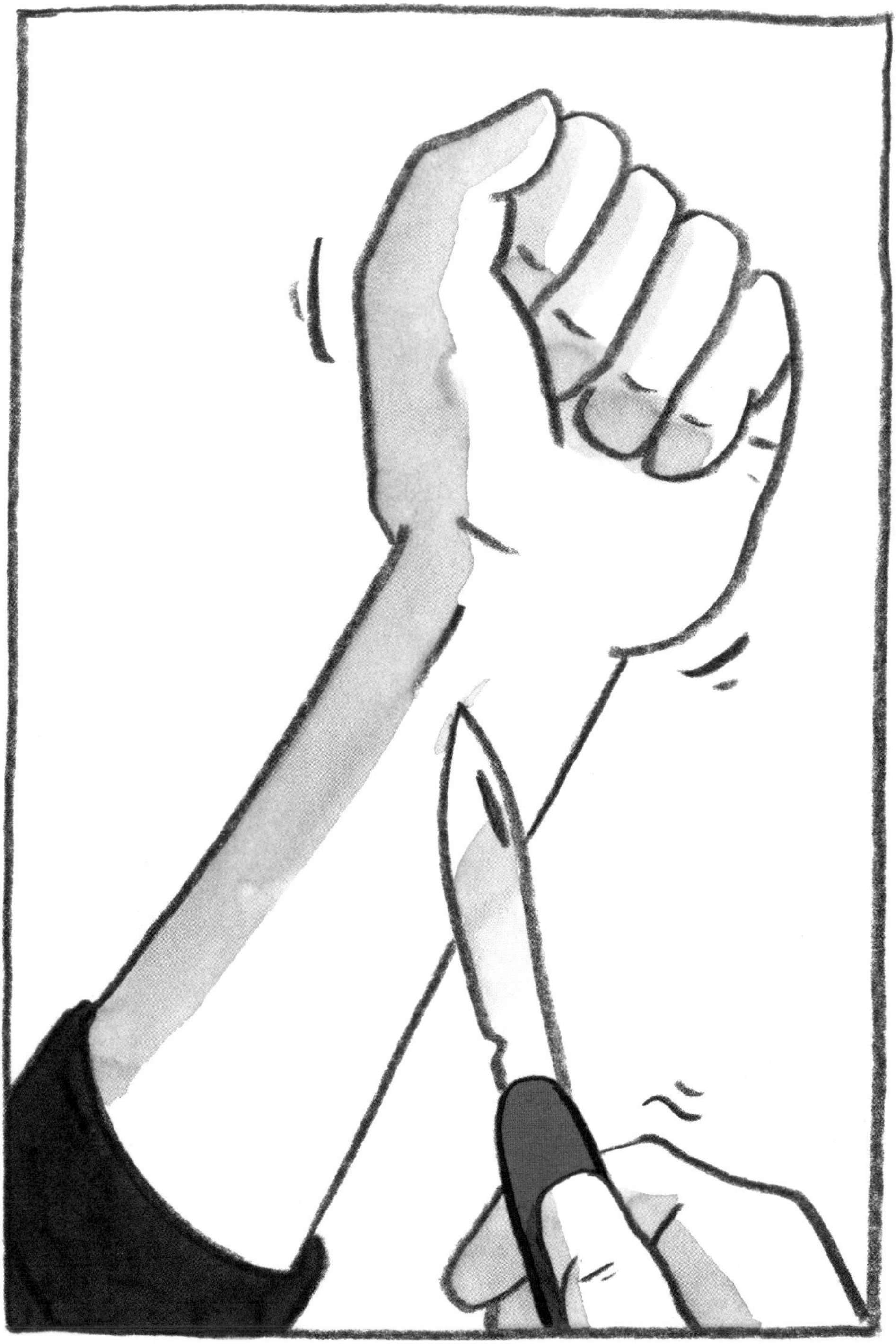

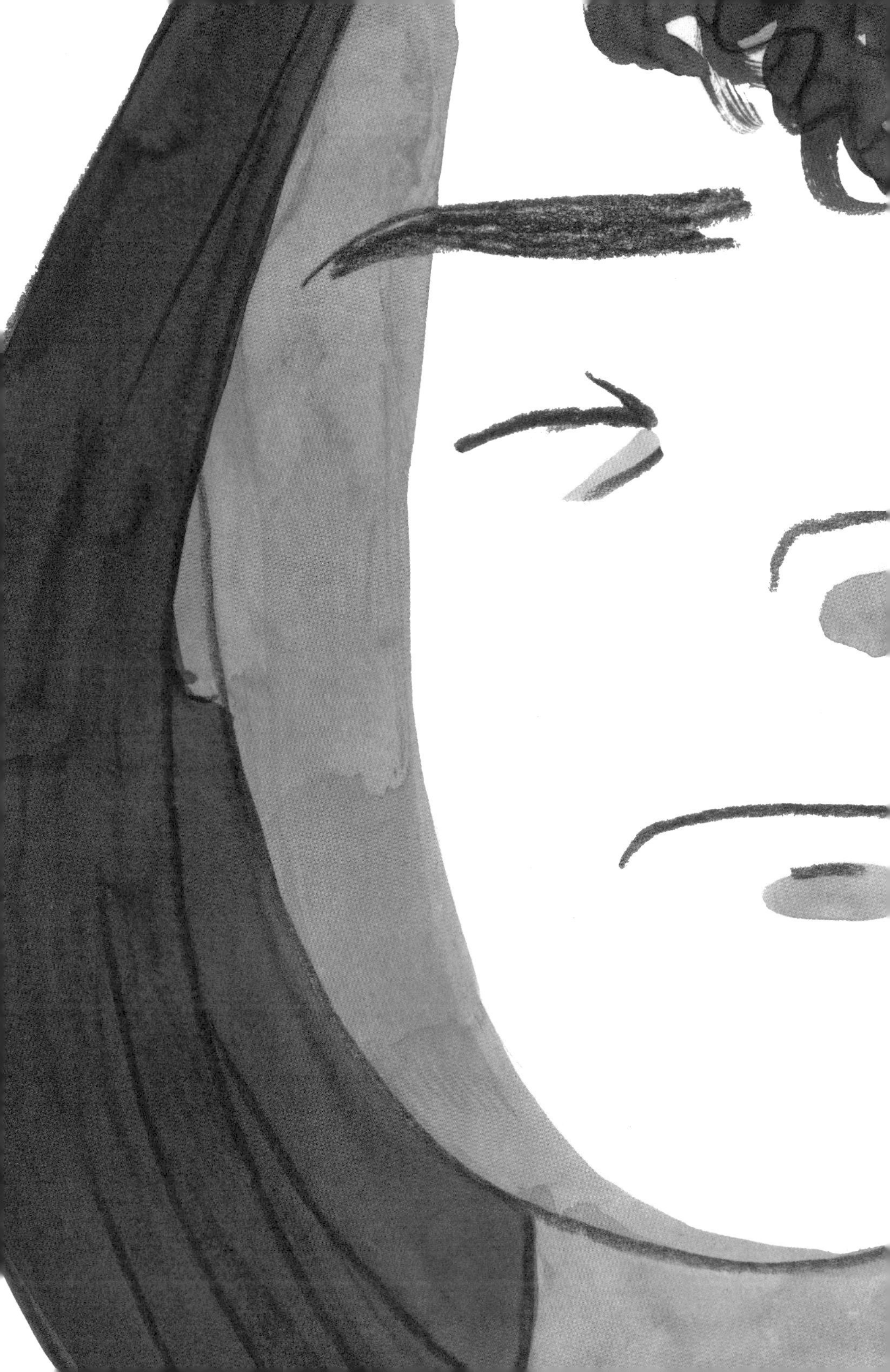

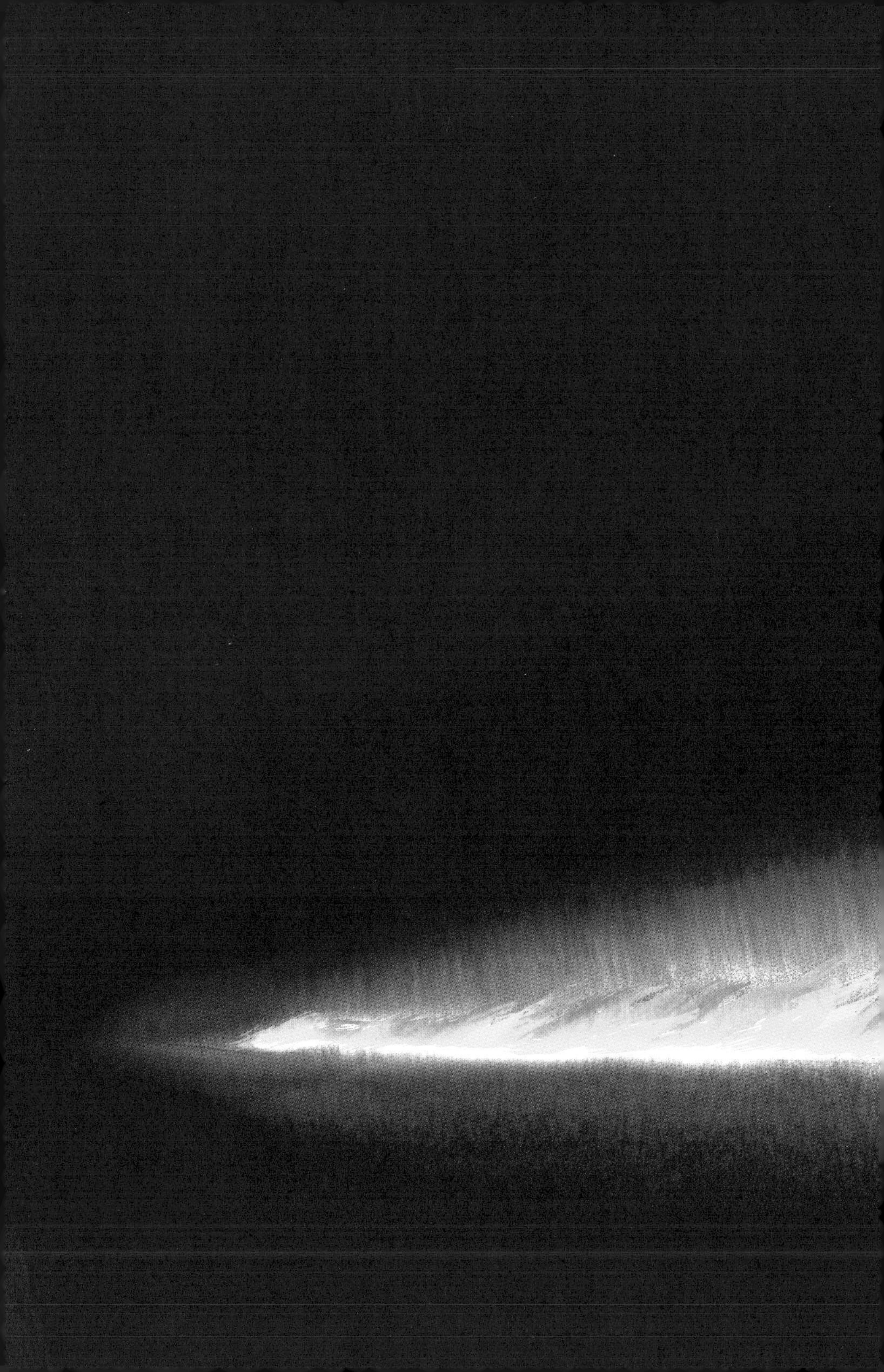

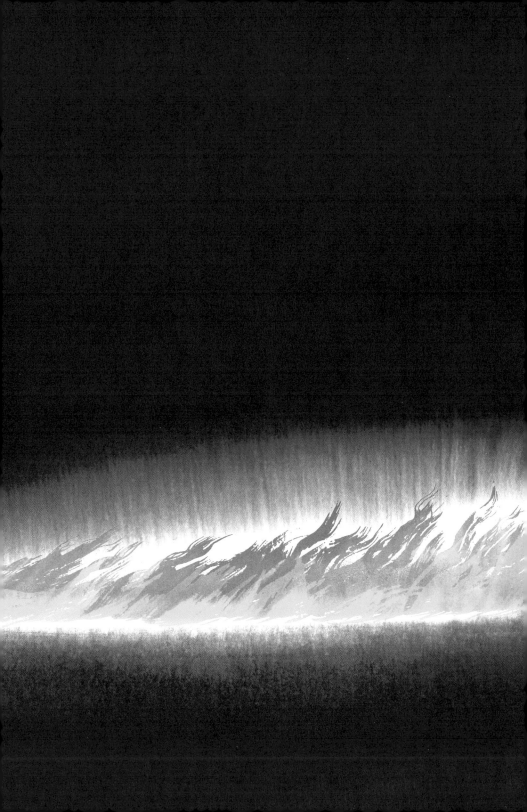

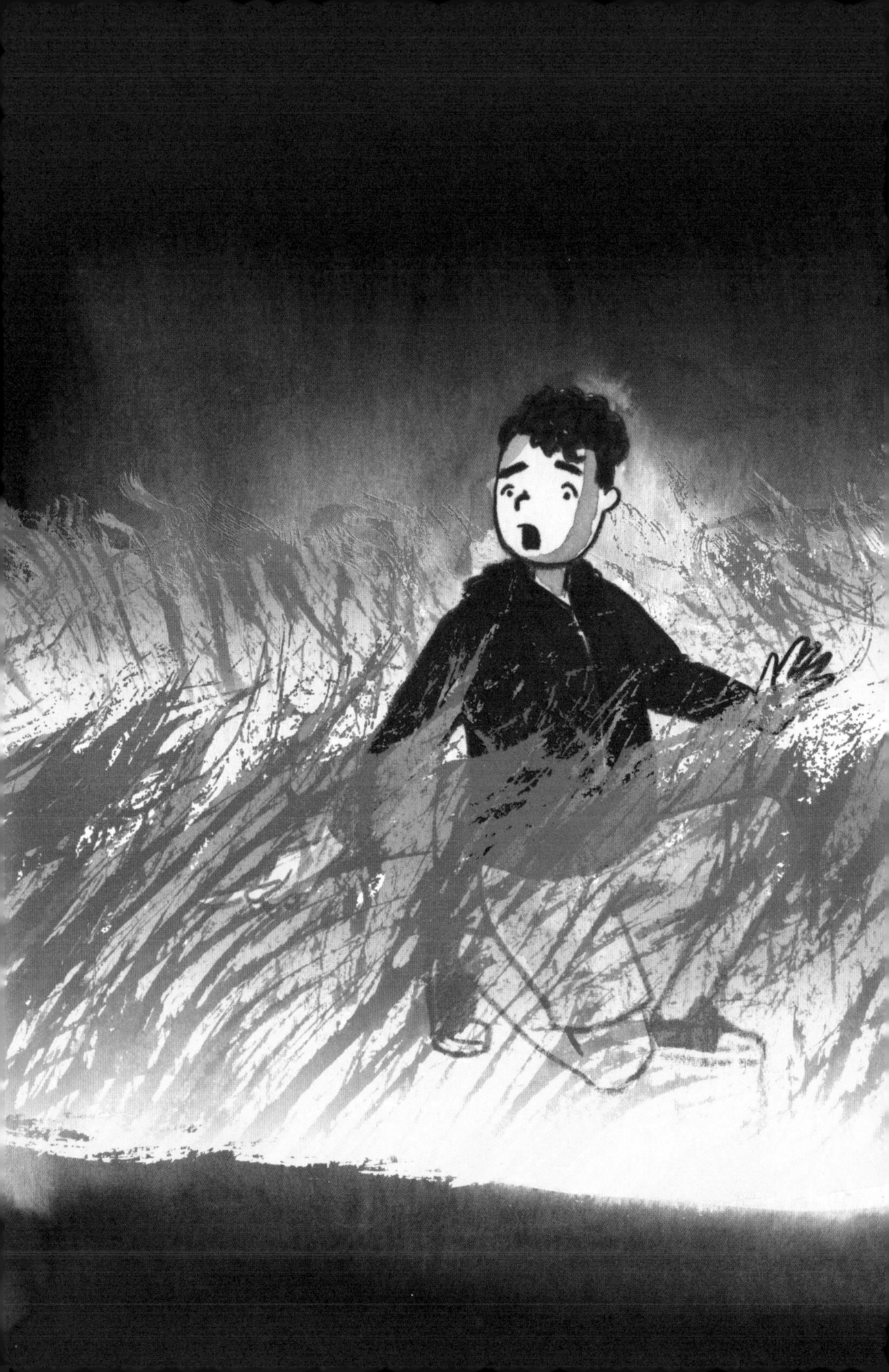

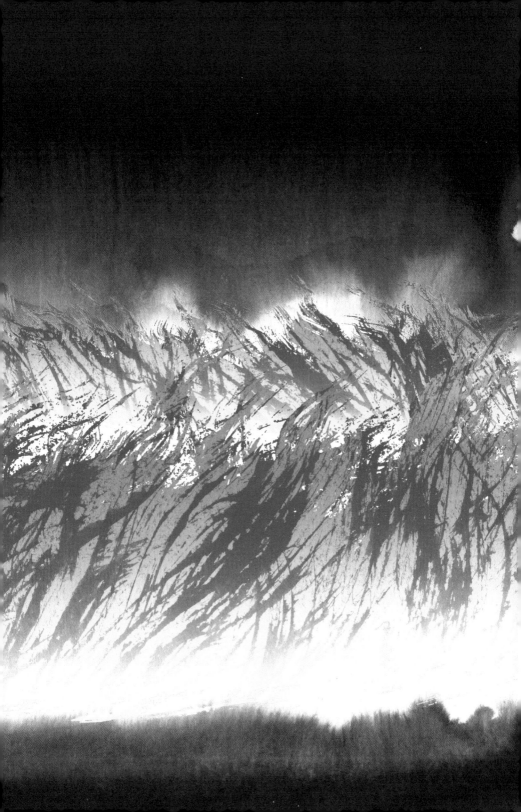

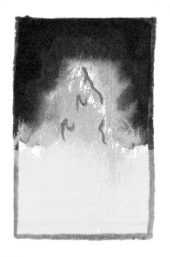

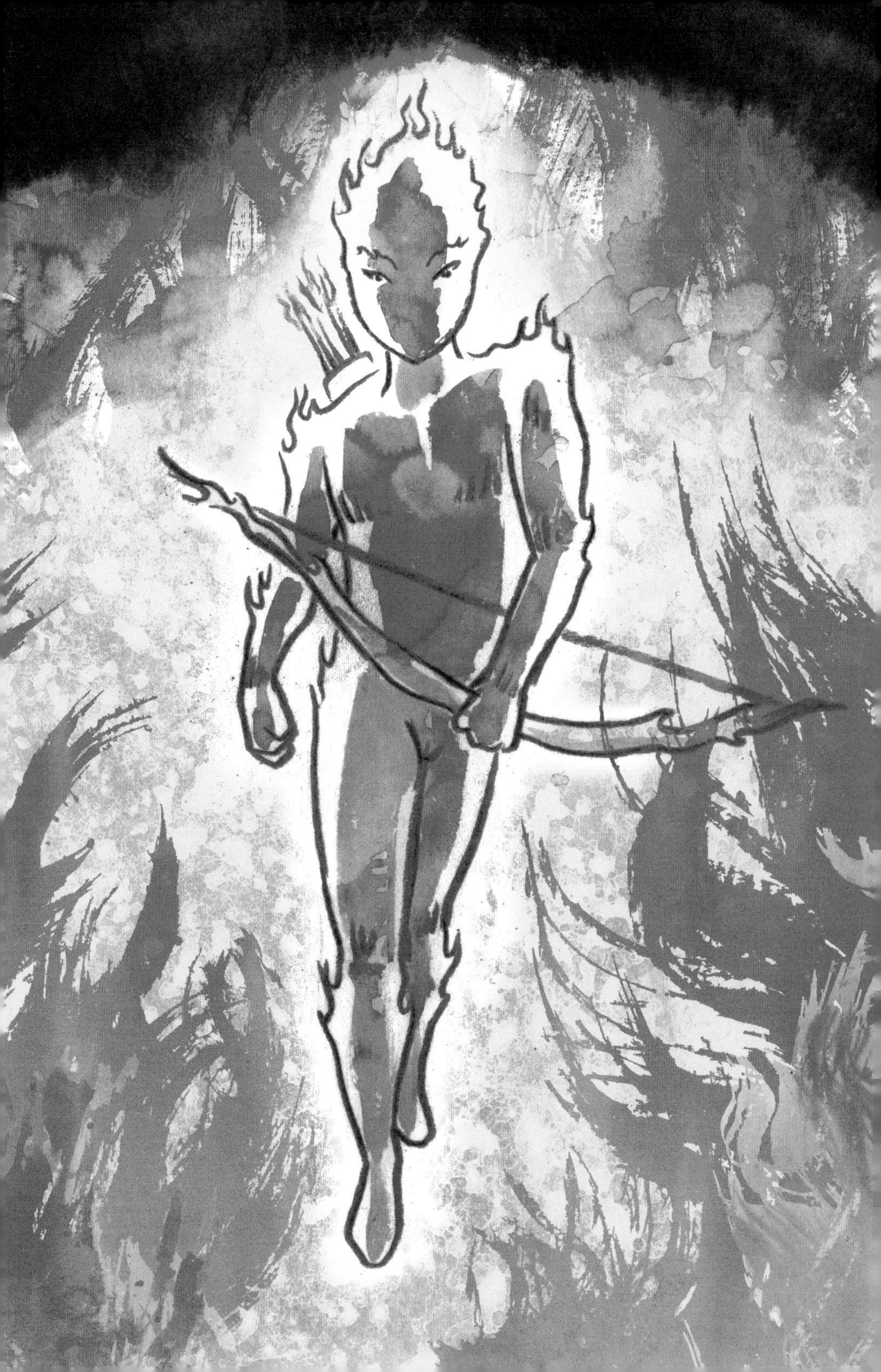

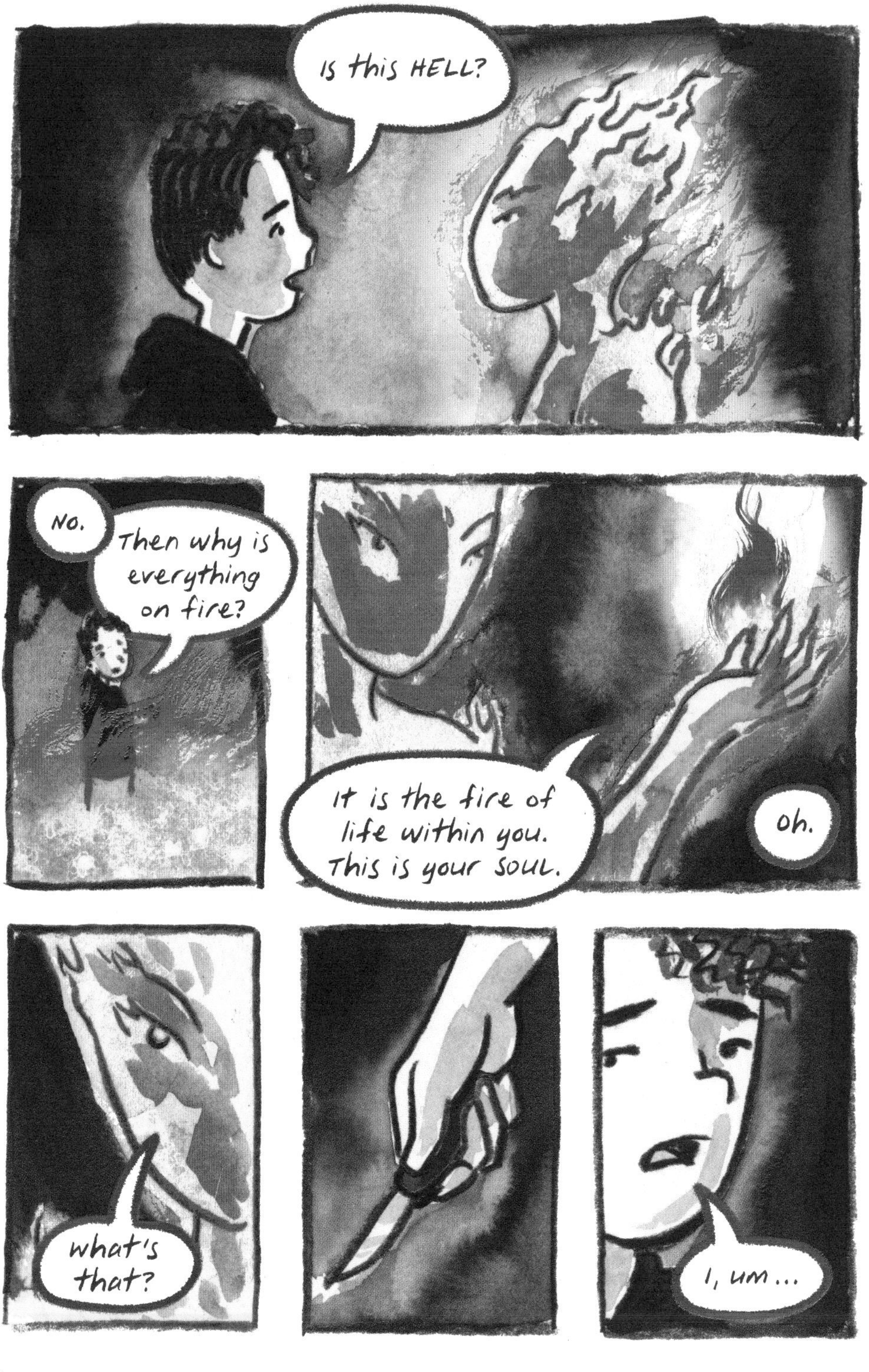
Is this HELL?
No.
Then why is everything on fire?
It is the fire of life within you. This is your soul.
Oh.
What's that?
I, um...

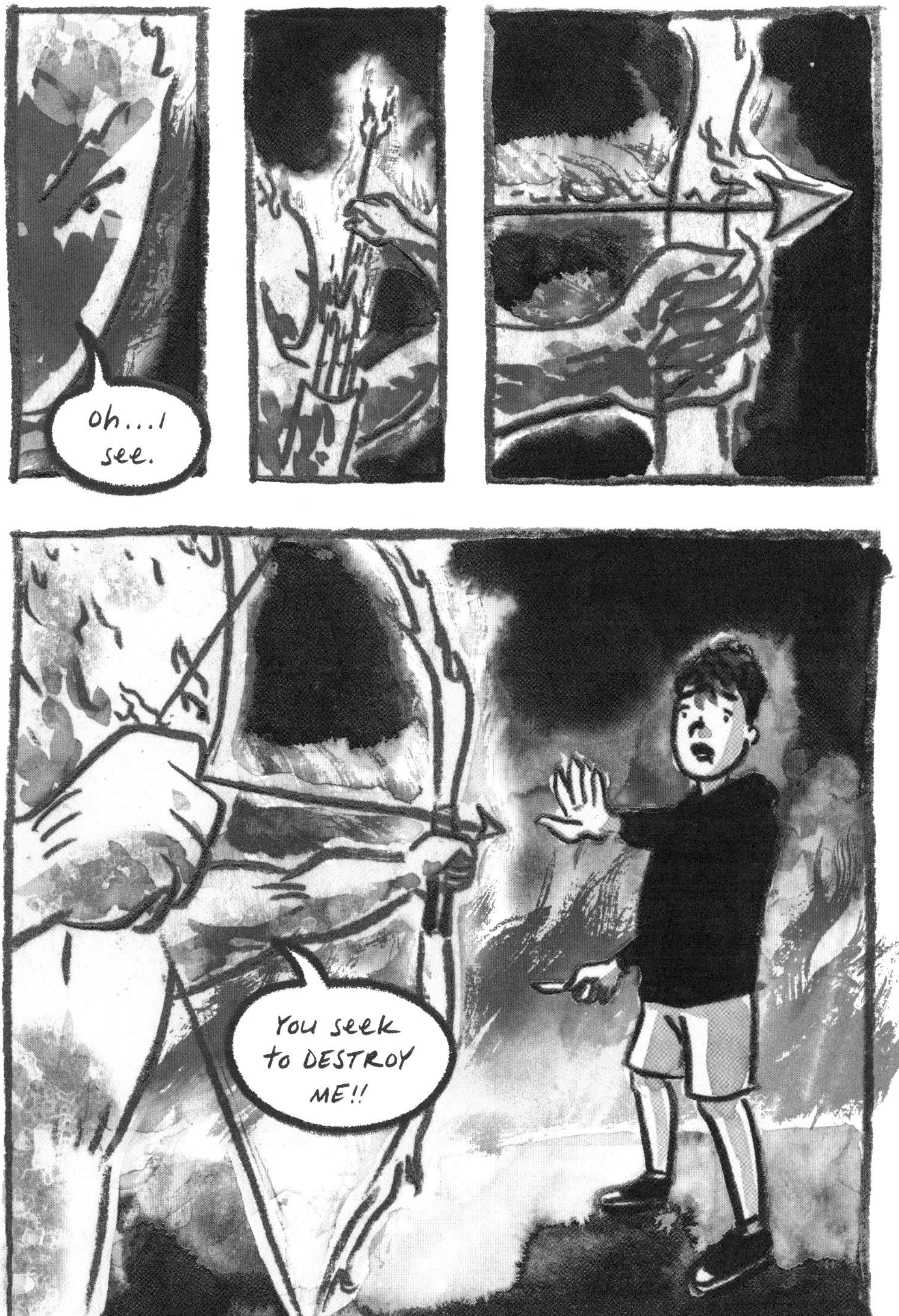
oh...I see.
You seek to DESTROY ME!!

I...I'm just so TIRED. I can't do this anymore! I'm WEAK.

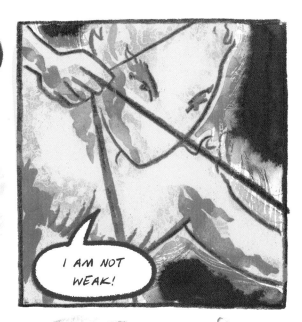

I AM NOT WEAK!

WHOOSH

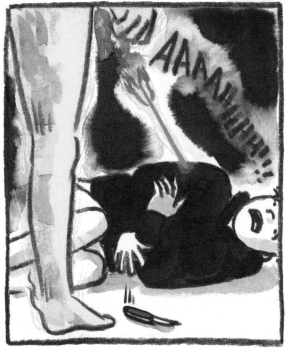

AAAHHHHH!!

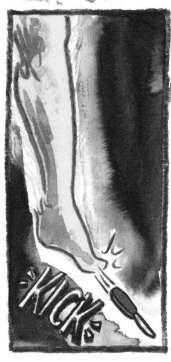

KICK

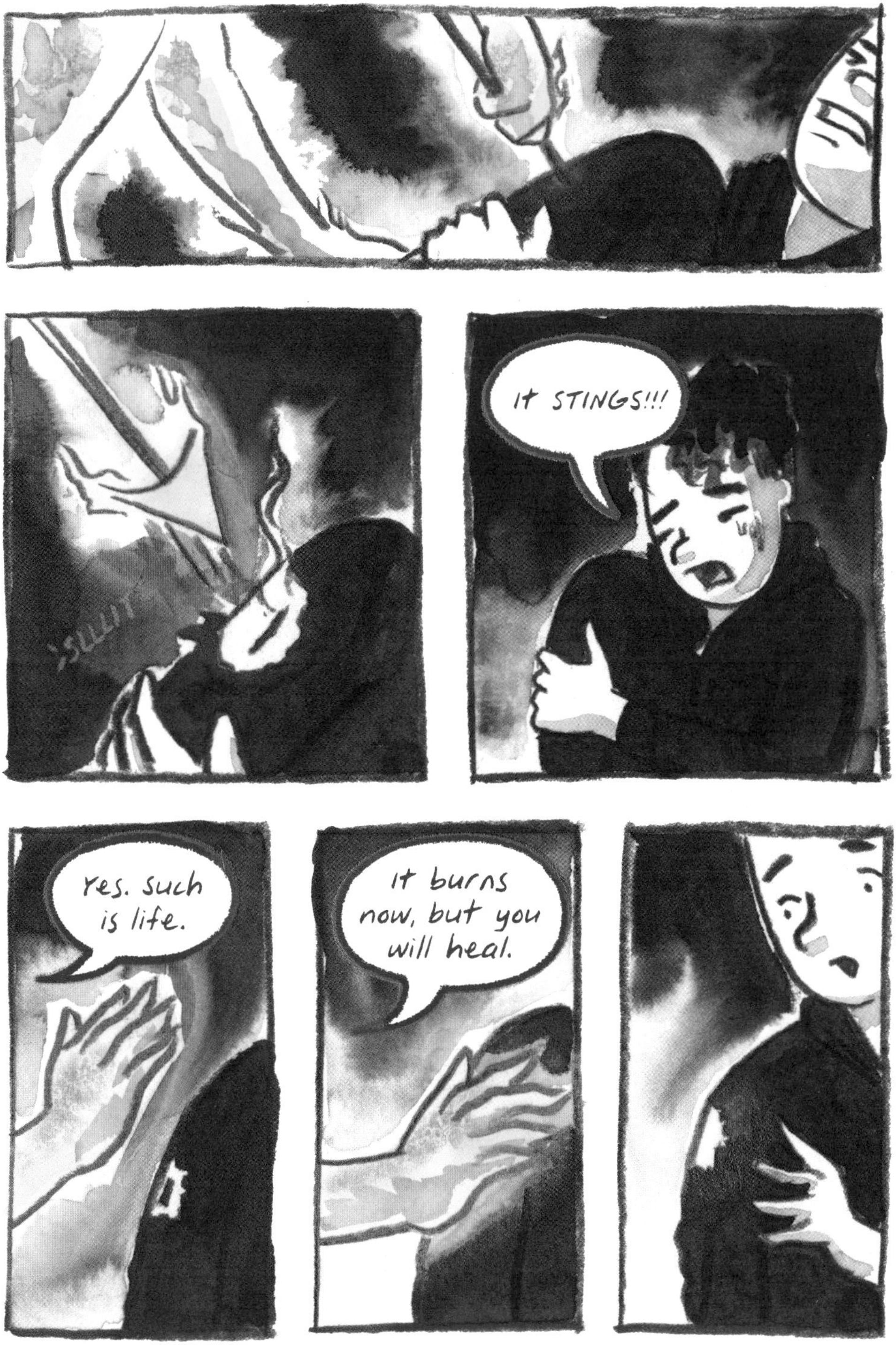
SLLLIT
IT STINGS!!!
Yes. Such is life.
It burns now, but you will heal.

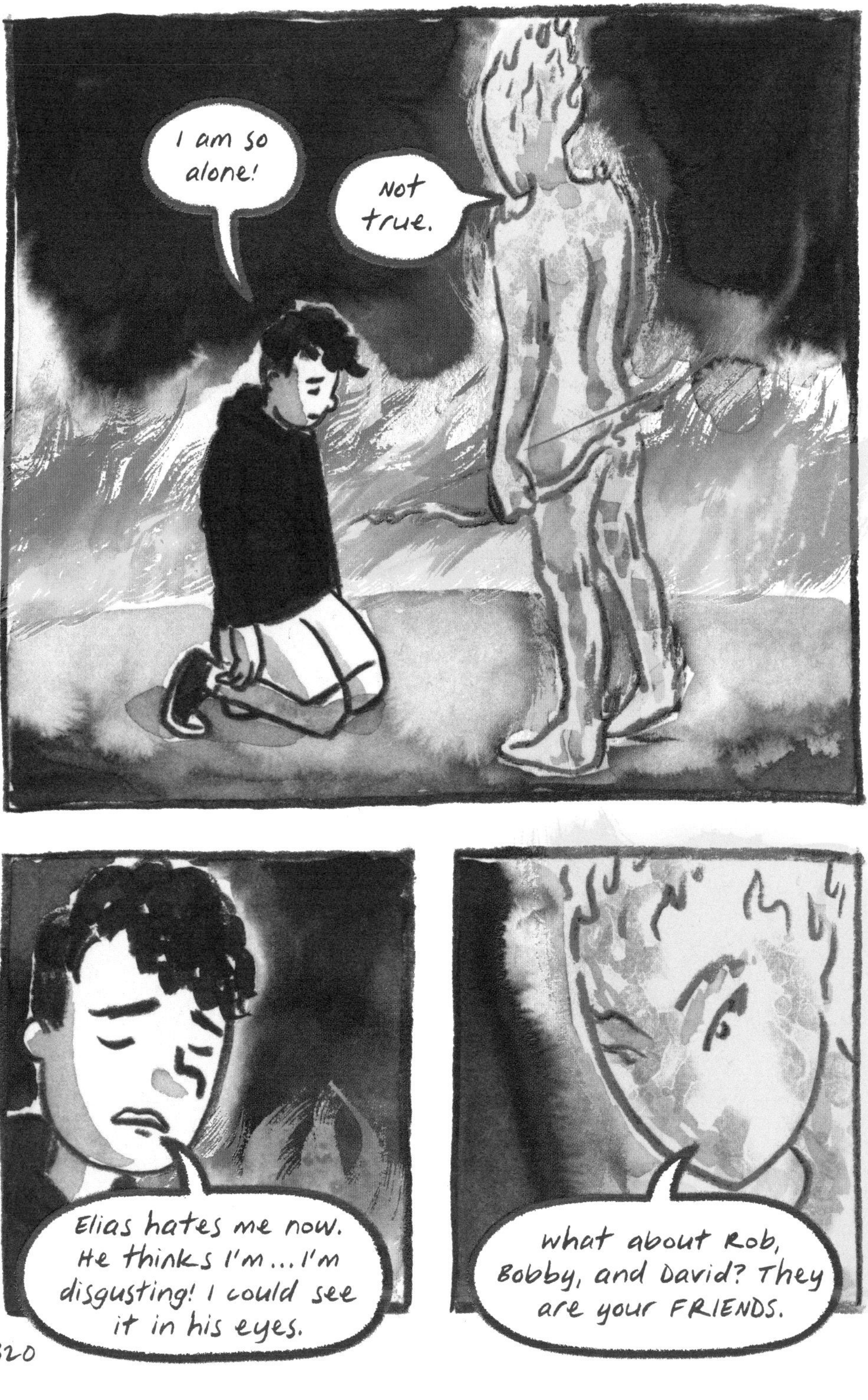
I am so alone!
Not true.
Elias hates me now. He thinks I'm... I'm disgusting! I could see it in his eyes.
What about Rob, Bobby, and David? They are your FRIENDS.

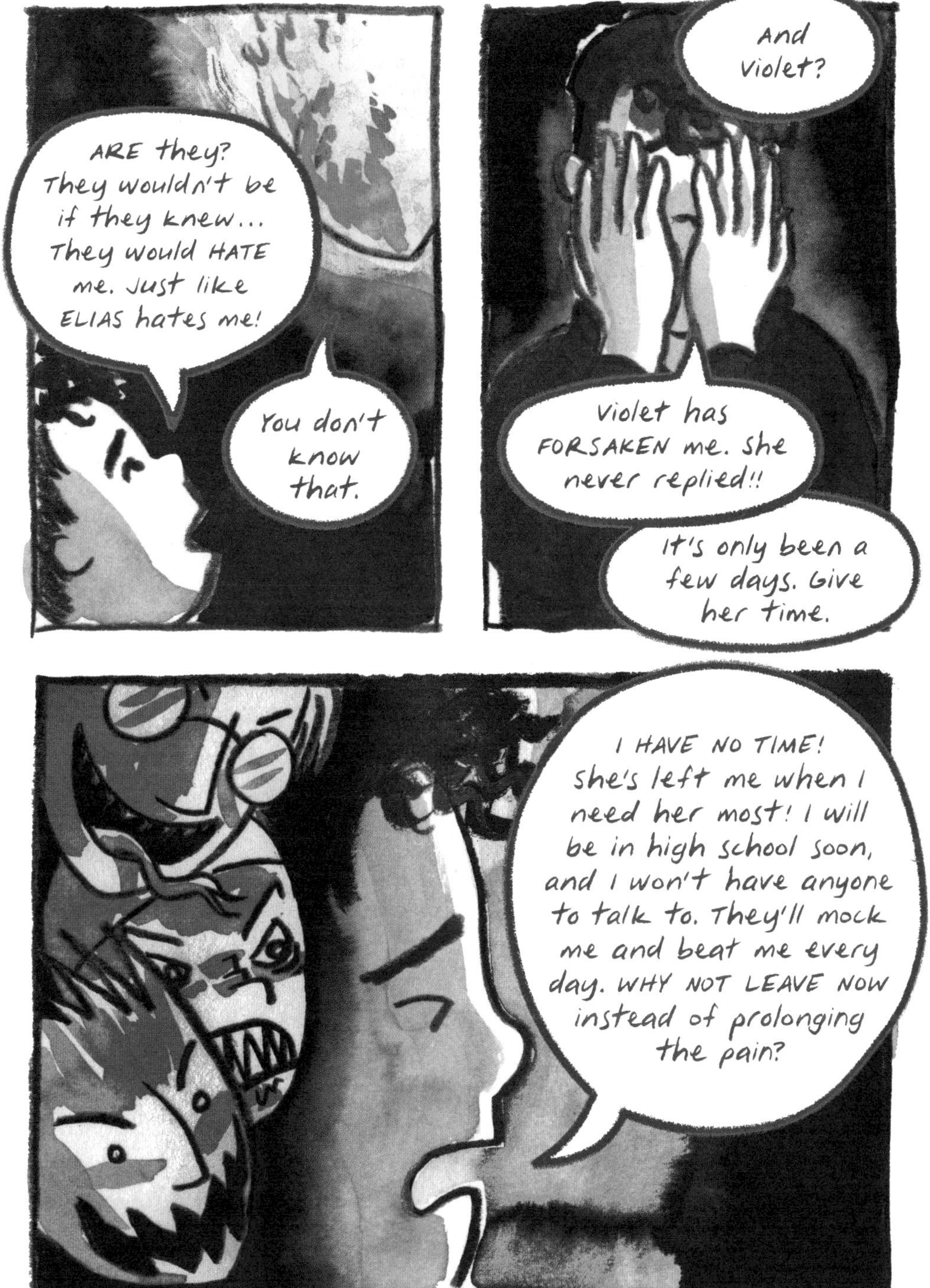

ARE they? They wouldn't be if they knew... They would HATE me. Just like ELIAS hates me!
You don't know that.
And Violet?
Violet has FORSAKEN me. She never replied!!
It's only been a few days. Give her time.
I HAVE NO TIME! She's left me when I need her most! I will be in high school soon, and I won't have anyone to talk to. They'll mock me and beat me every day. WHY NOT LEAVE NOW instead of prolonging the pain?

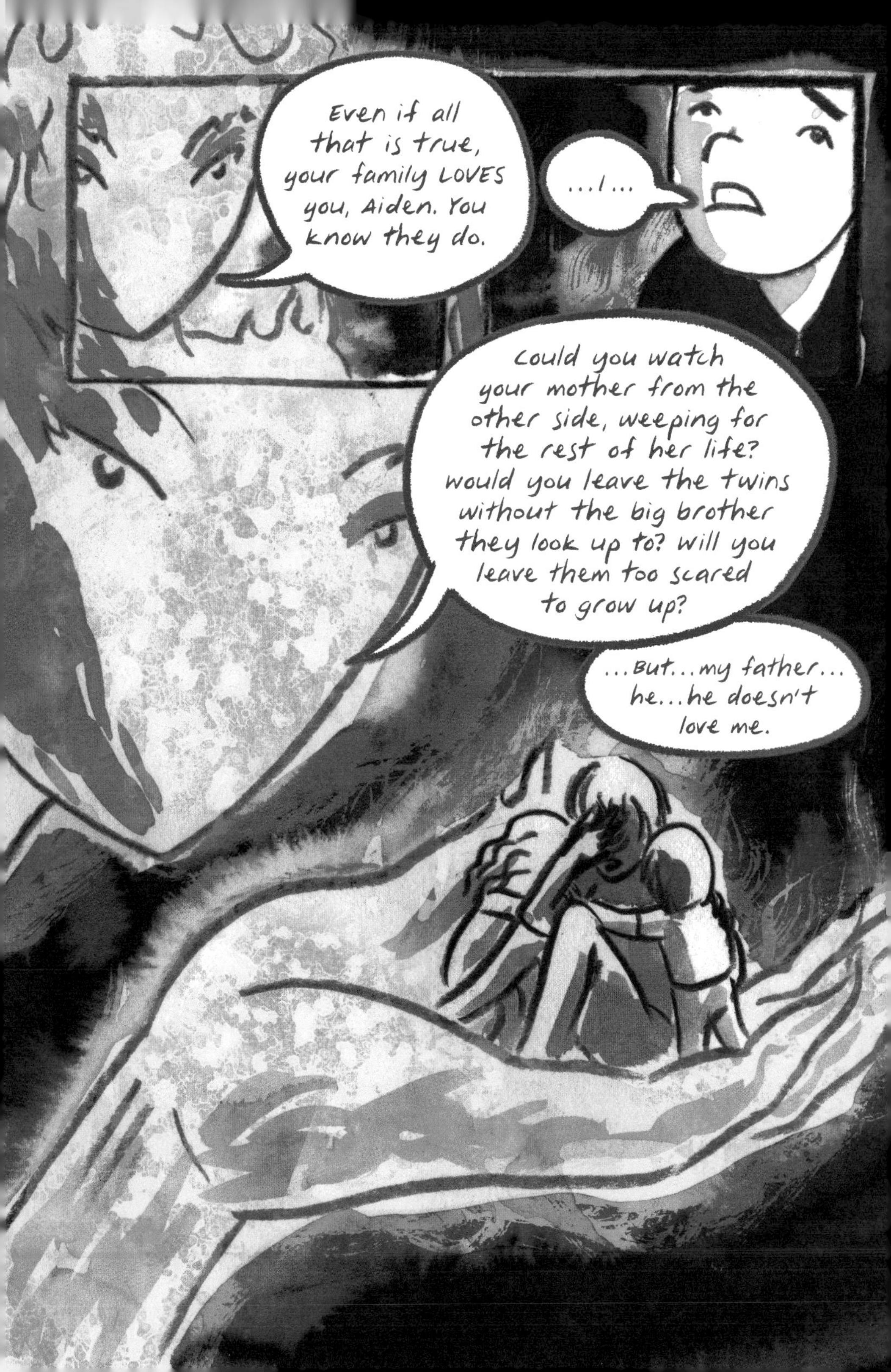
Even if all that is true, your family LOVES you, Aiden. You know they do.
...I...
Could you watch your mother from the other side, weeping for the rest of her life? Would you leave the twins without the big brother they look up to? Will you leave them too scared to grow up?
...But...my father... he...he doesn't love me.

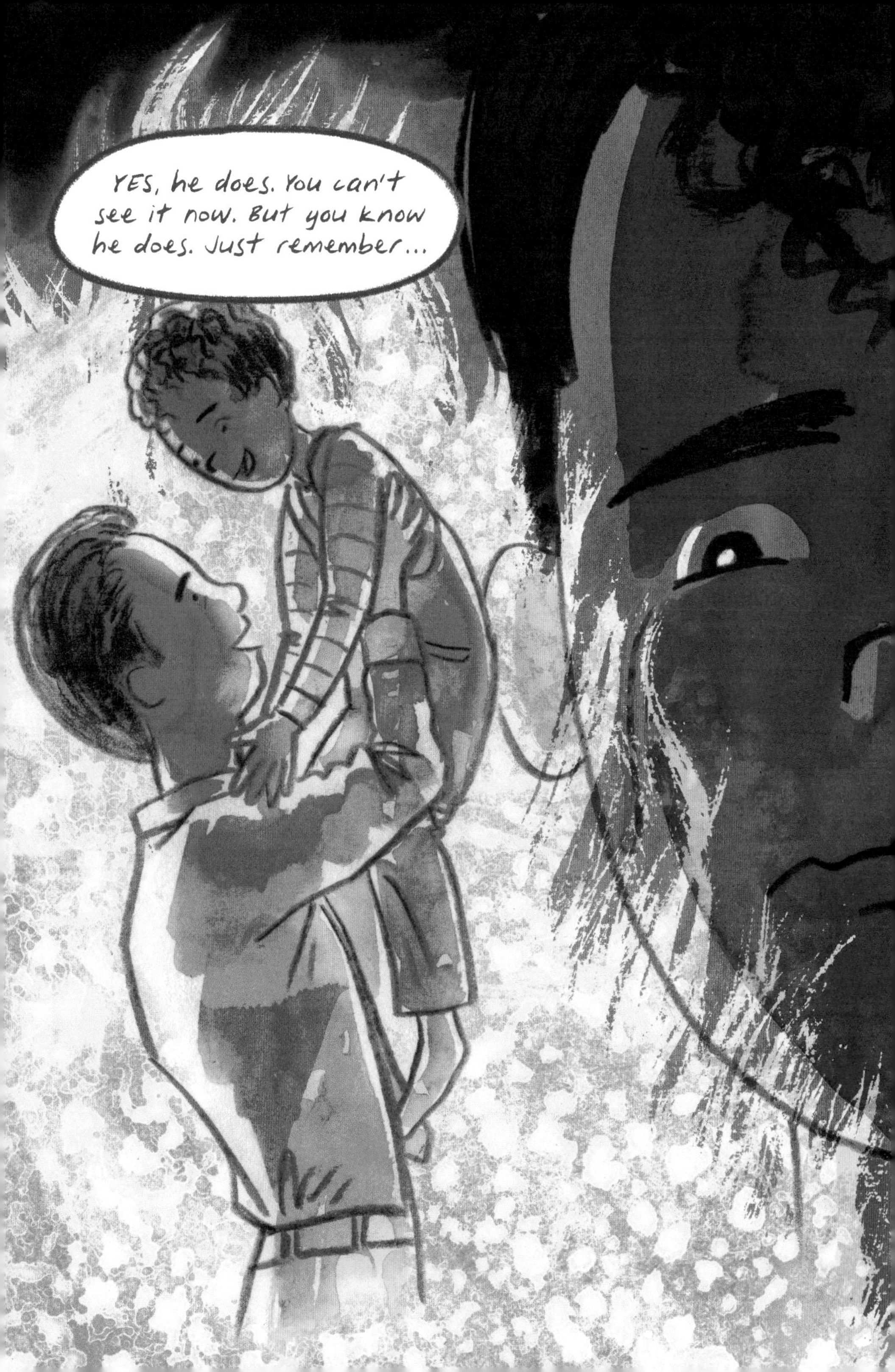
YES, he does. You can't see it now. But you know he does. Just remember...

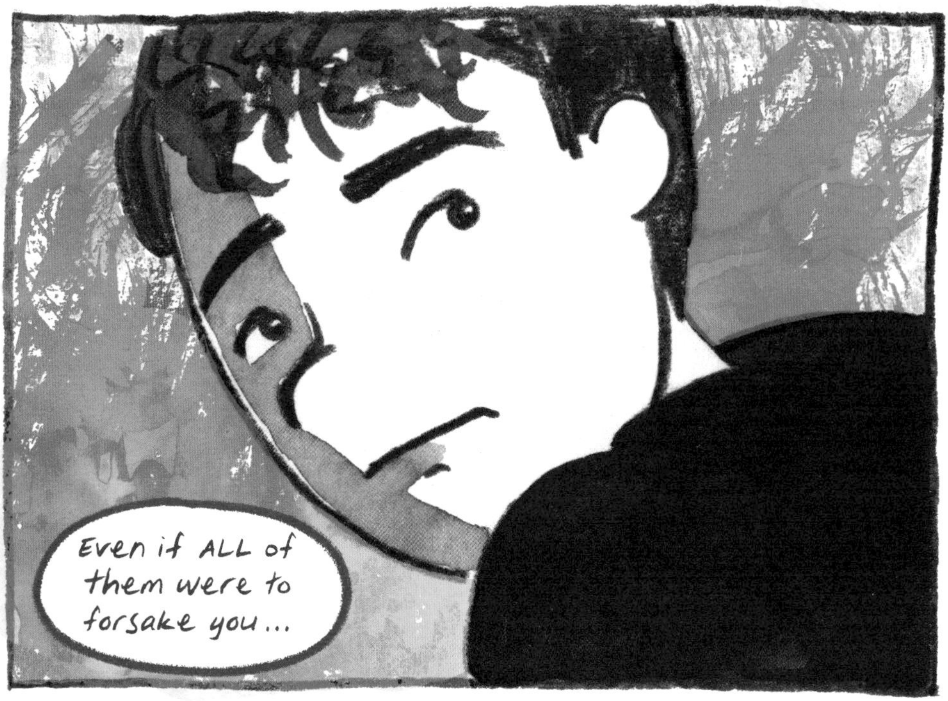
Even if ALL of them were to forsake you...

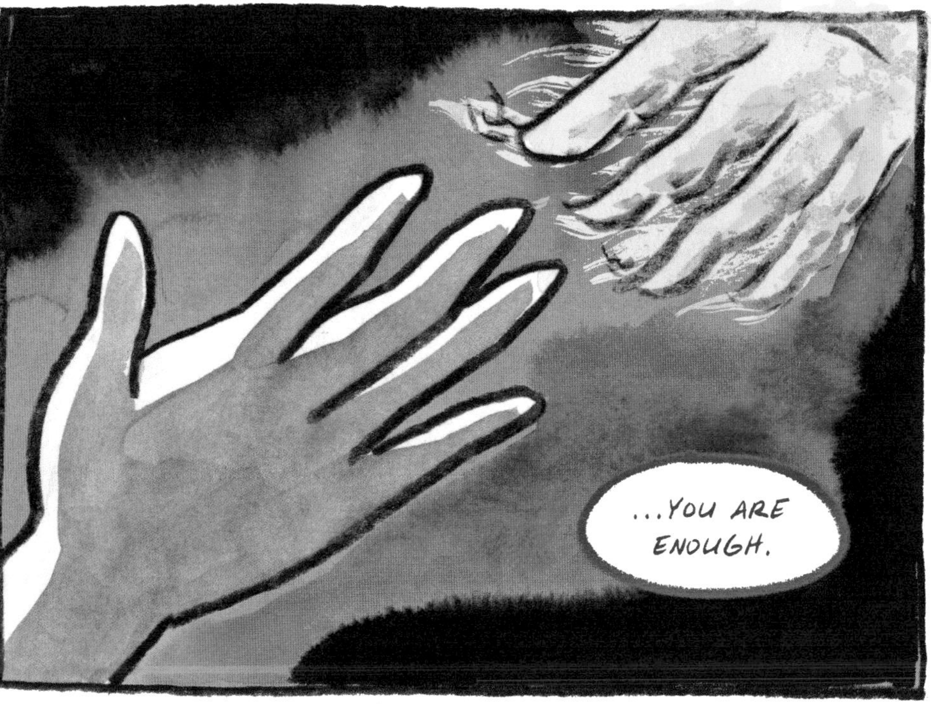
...YOU ARE ENOUGH.

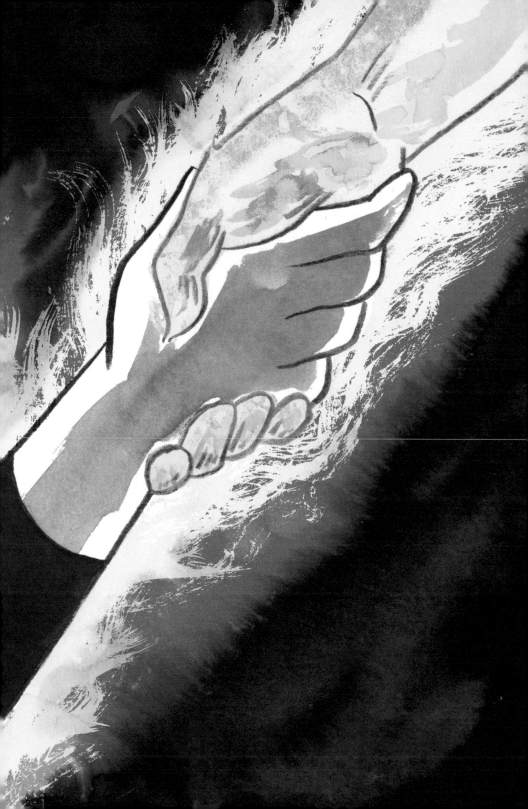

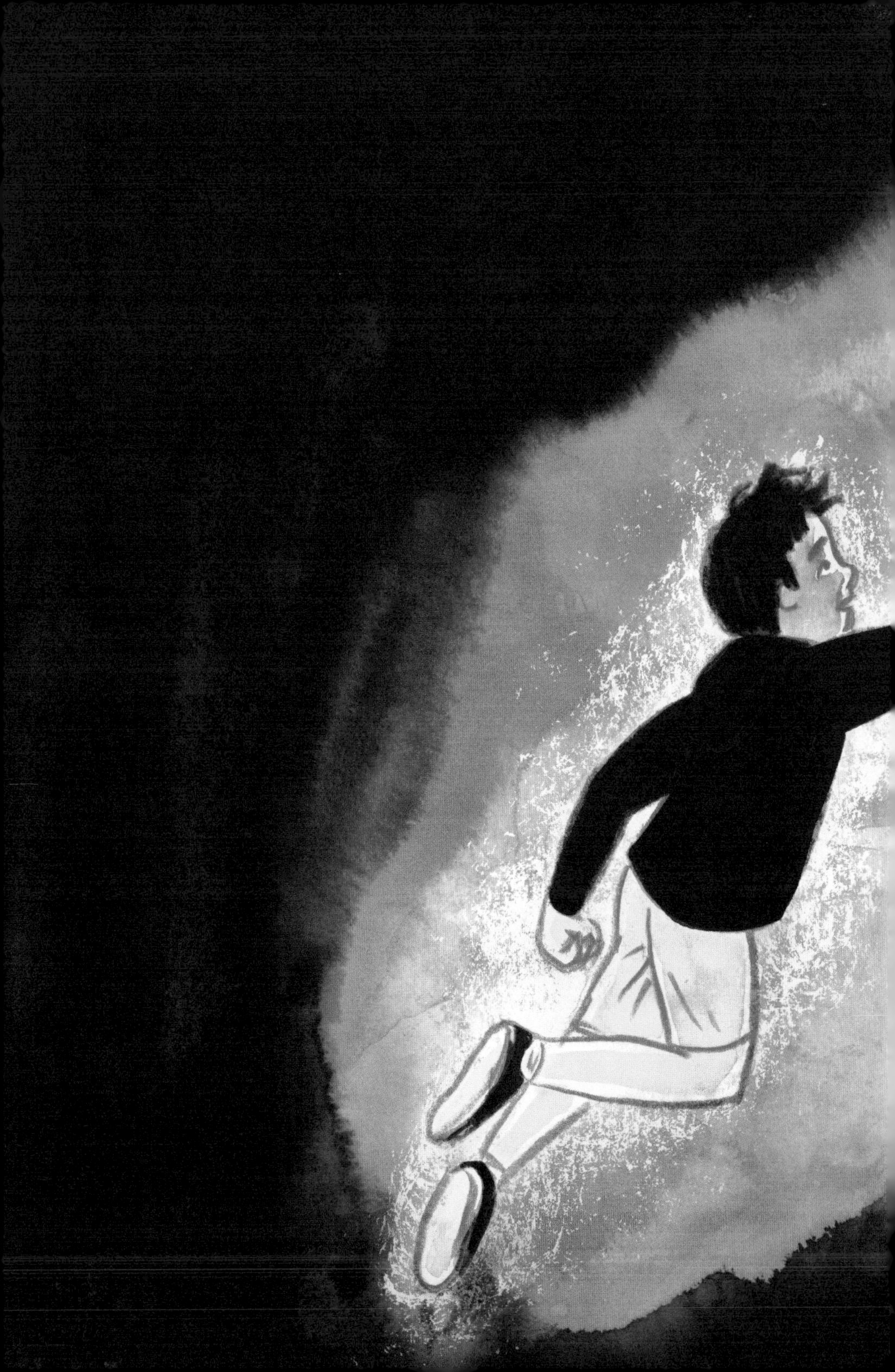

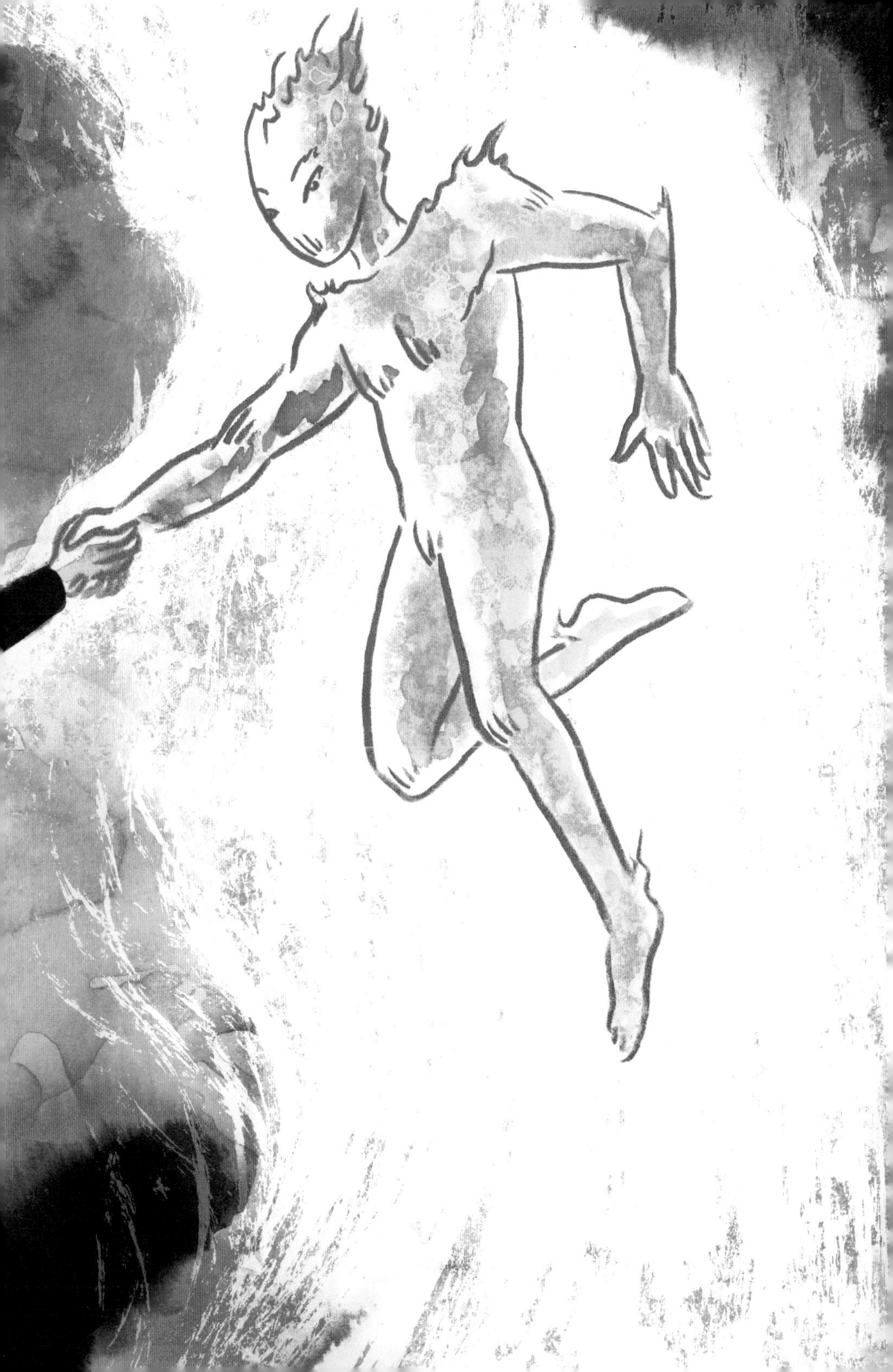

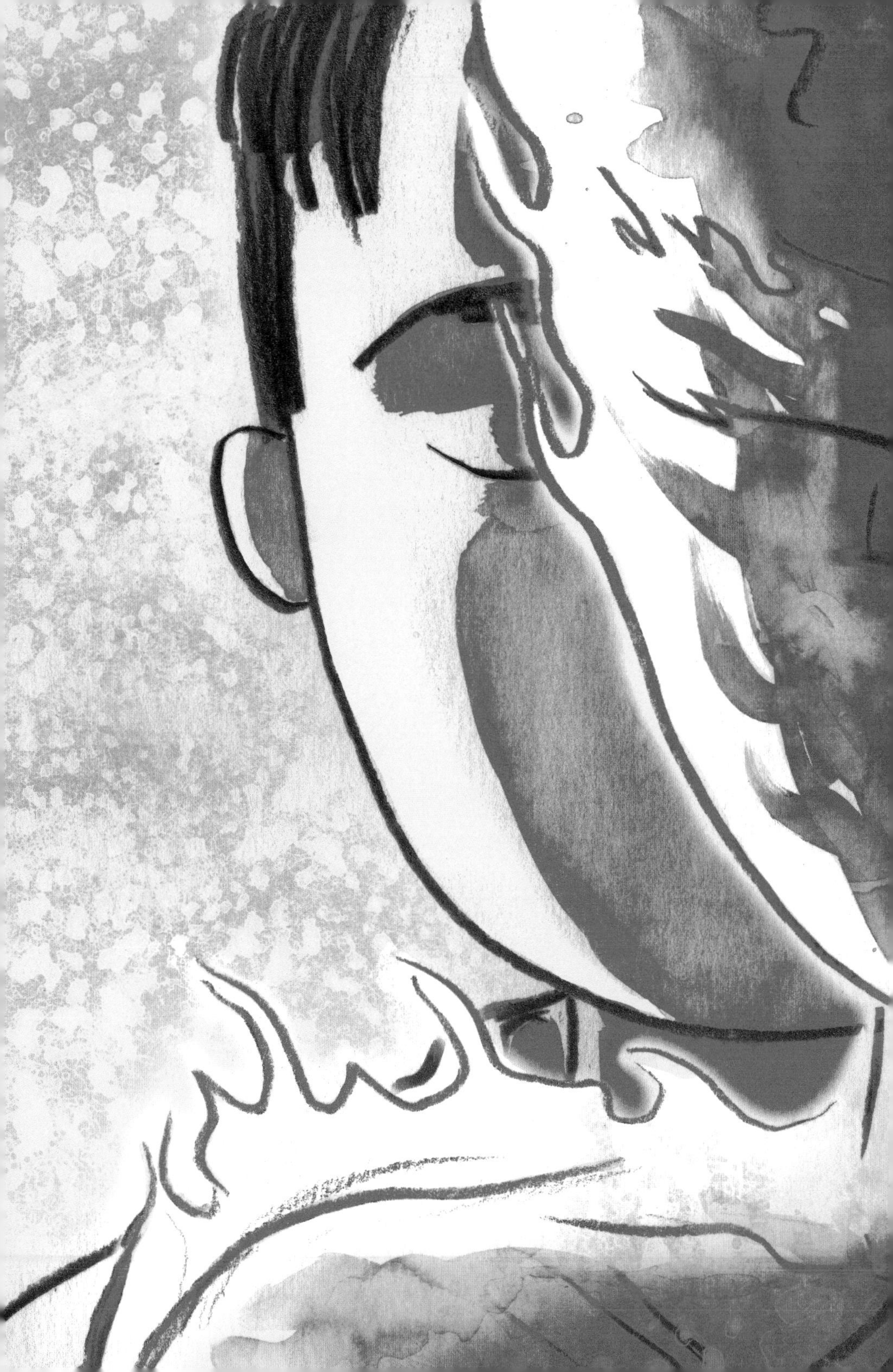

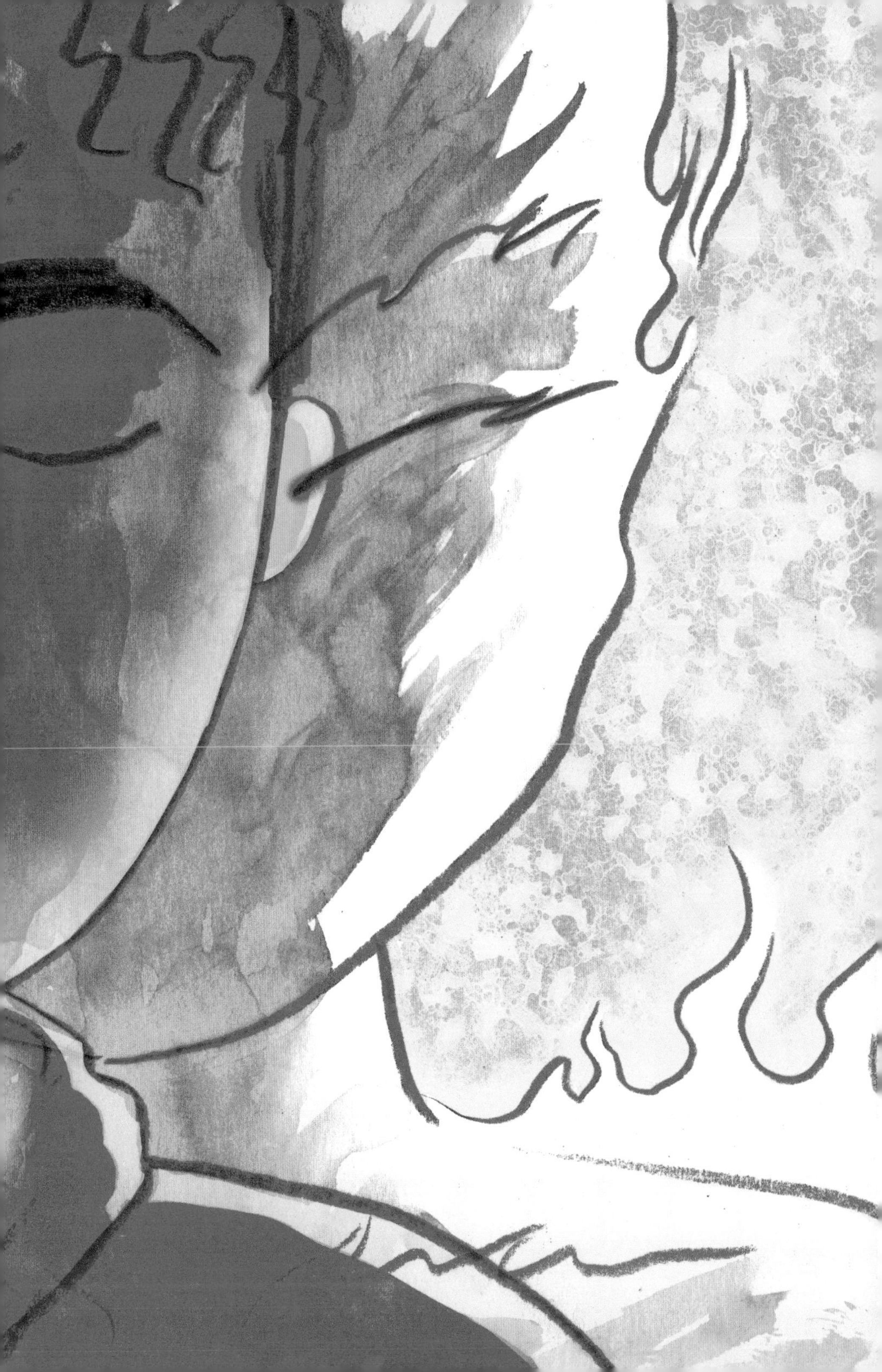

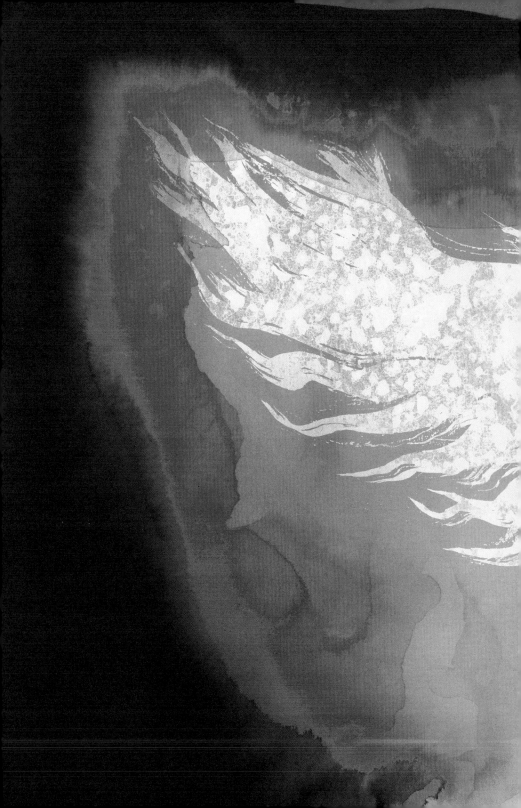

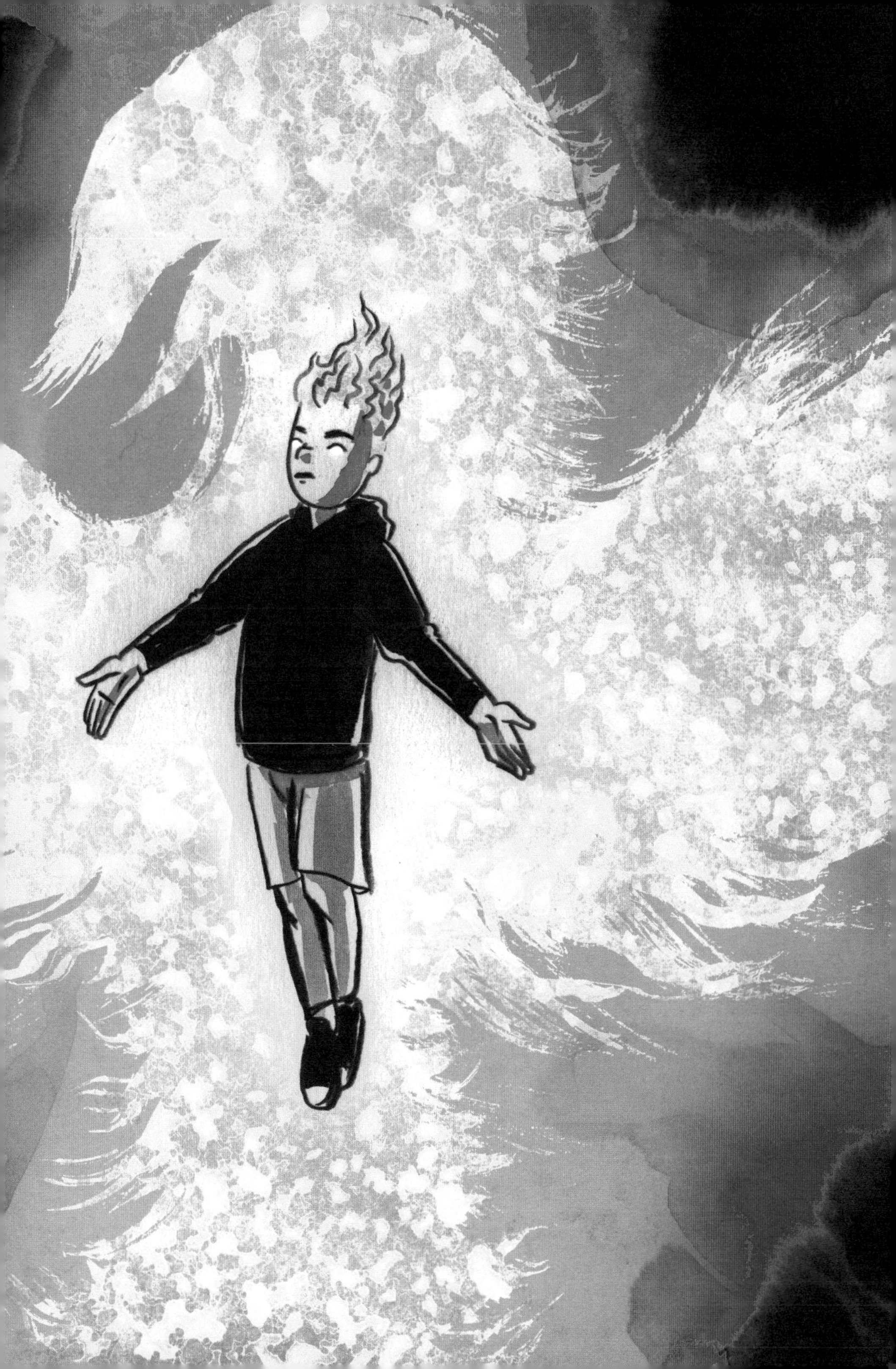

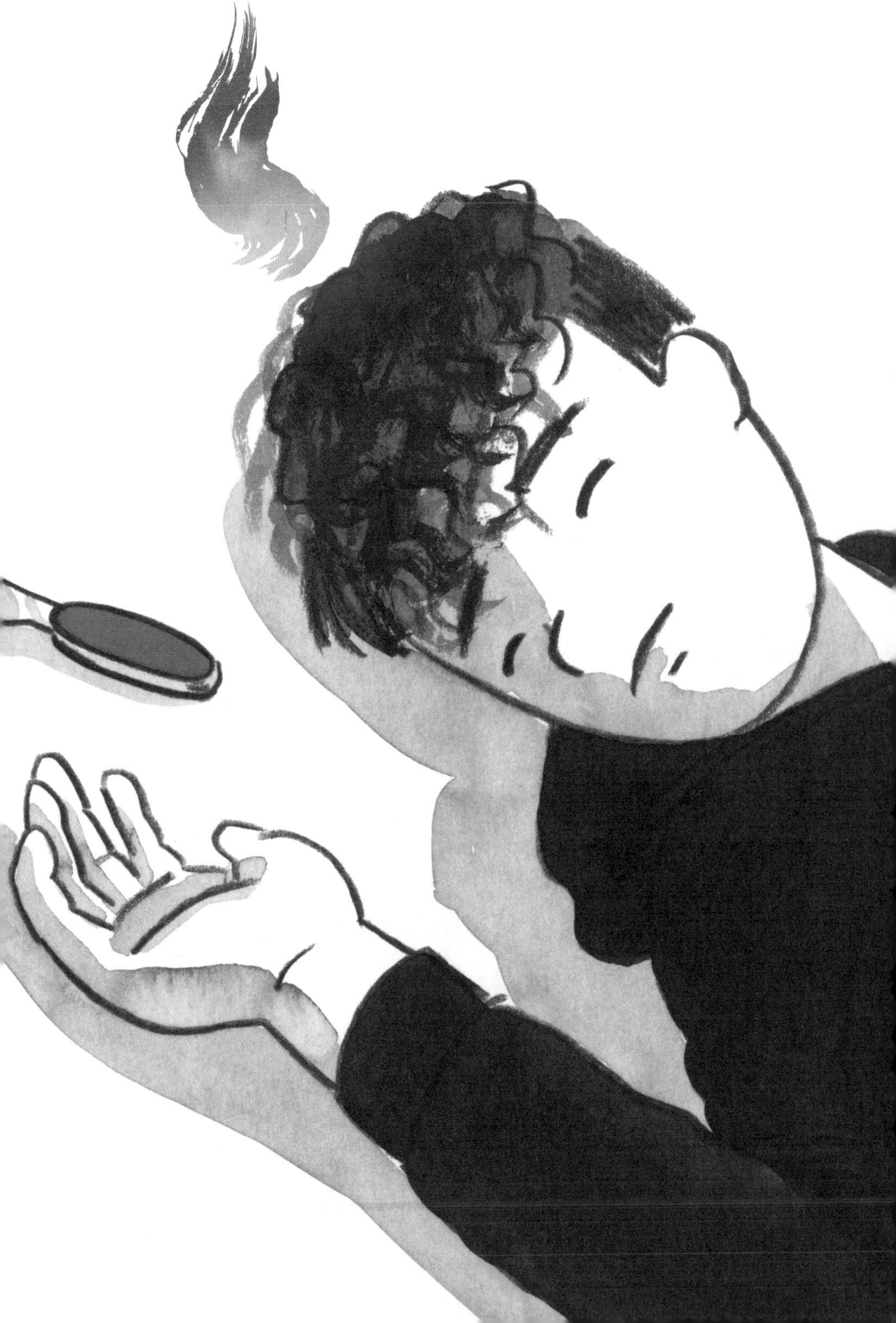

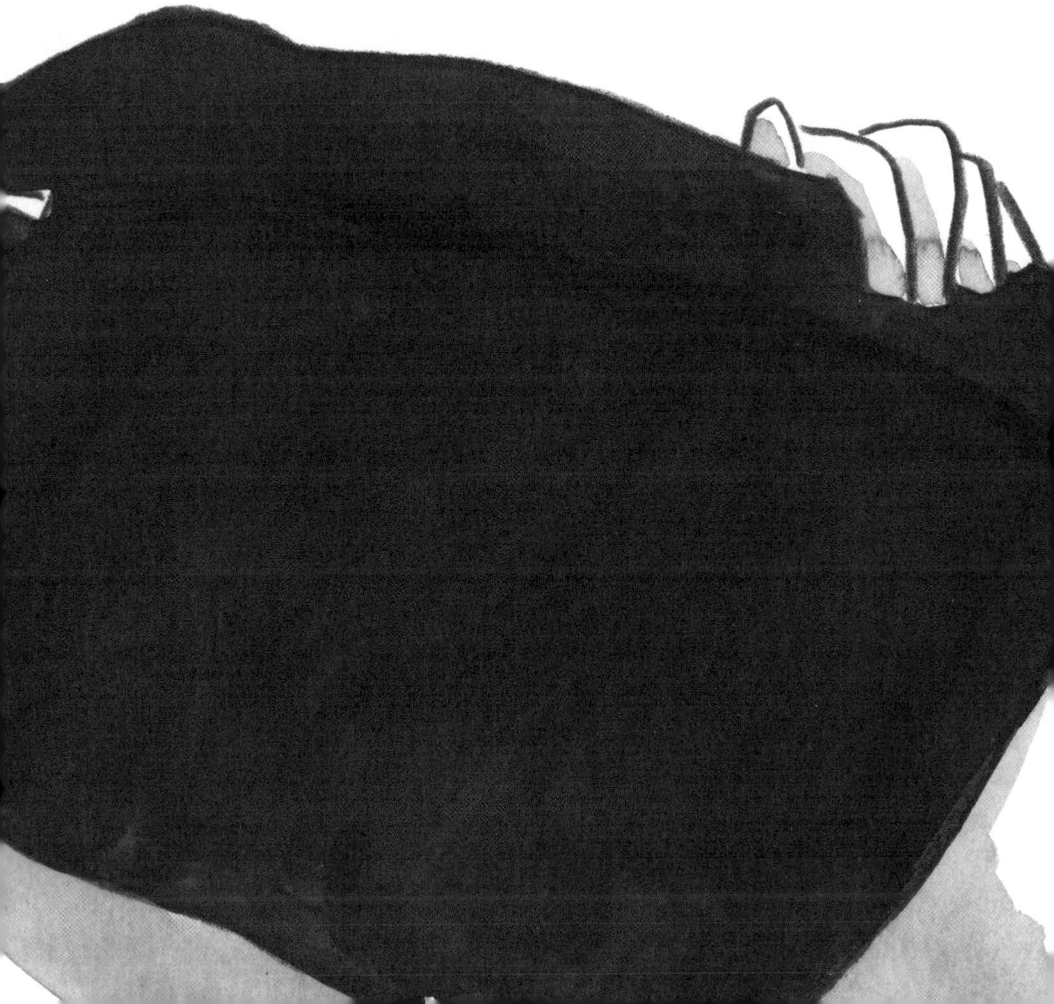

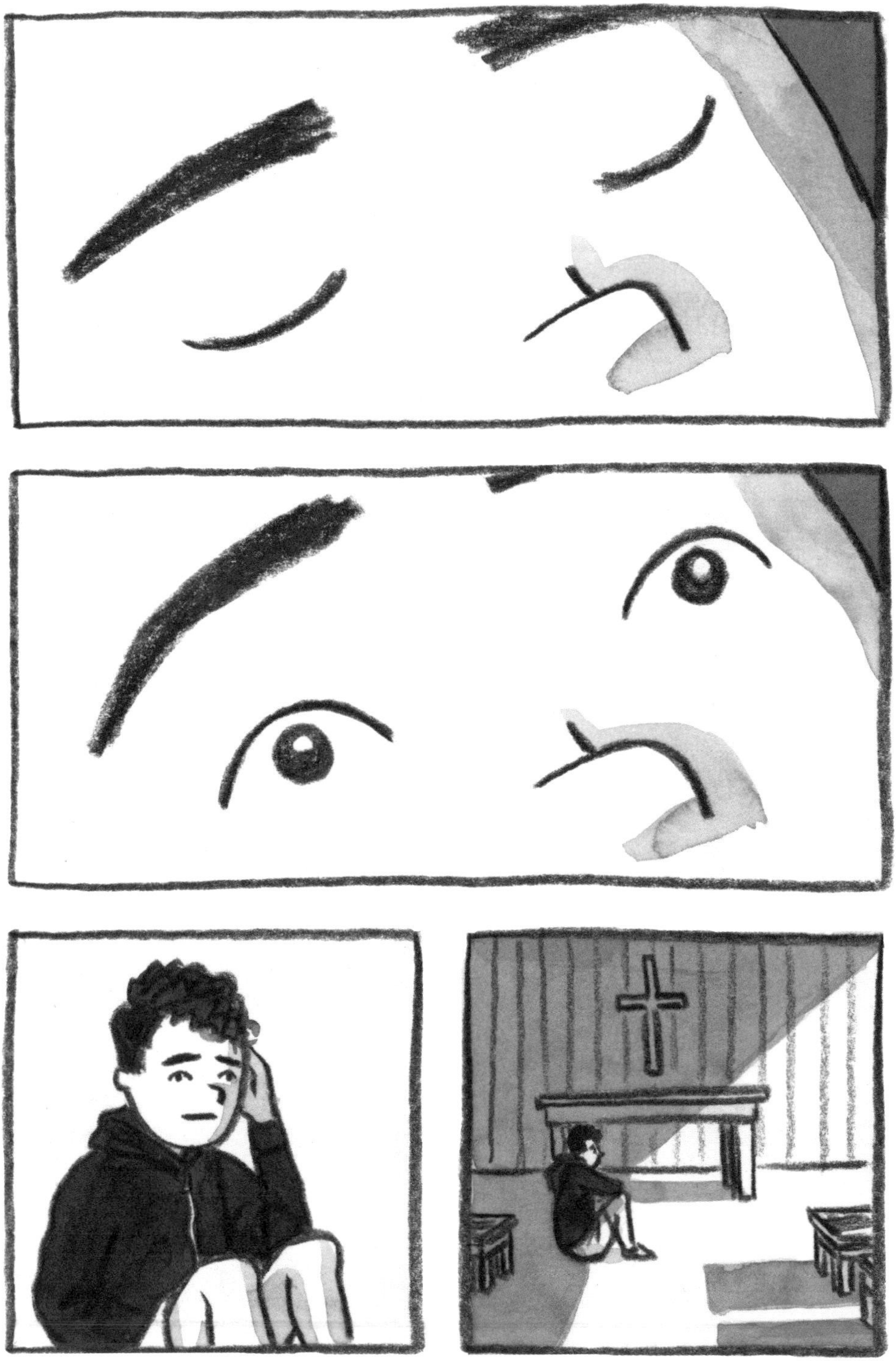

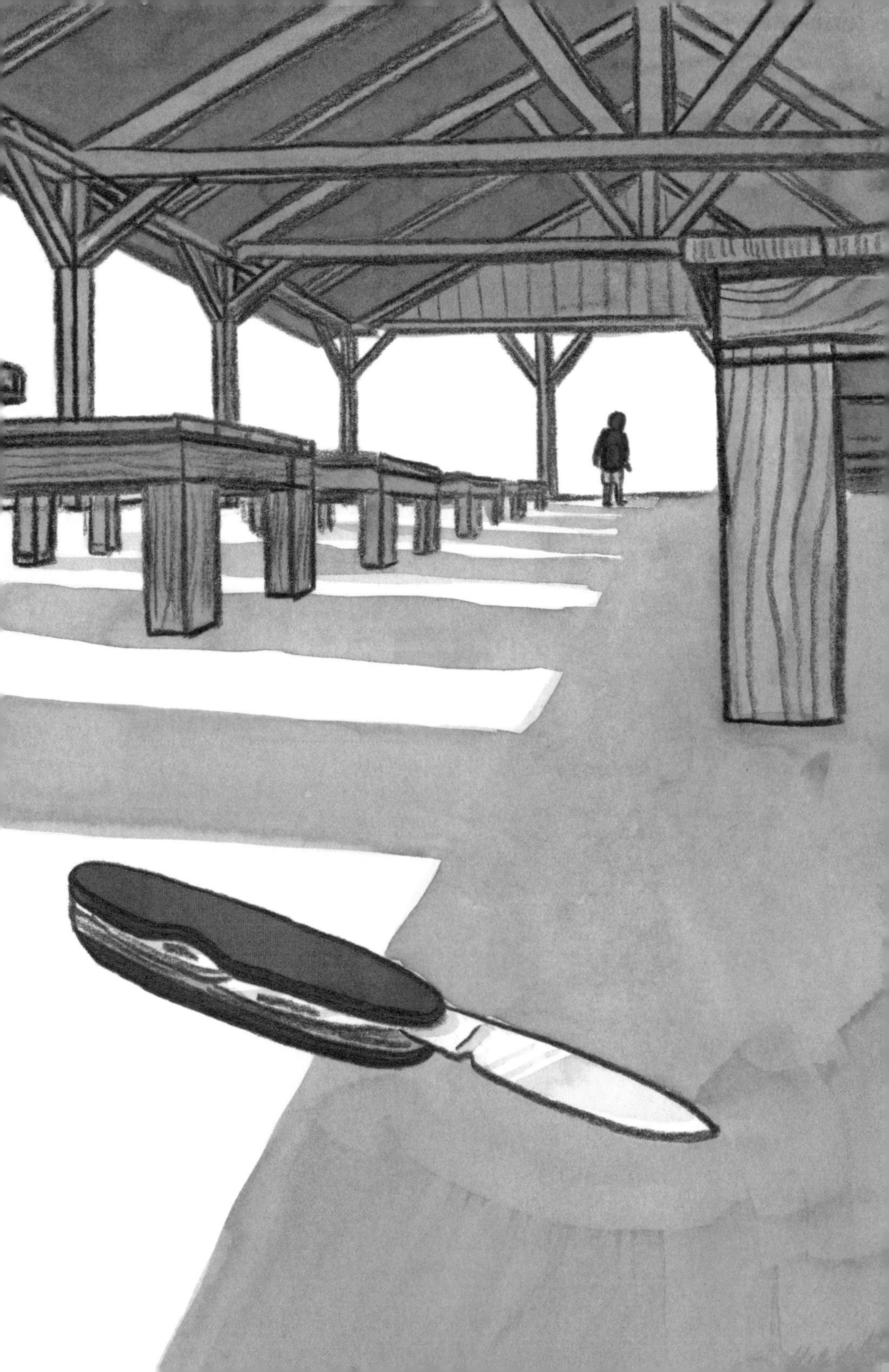

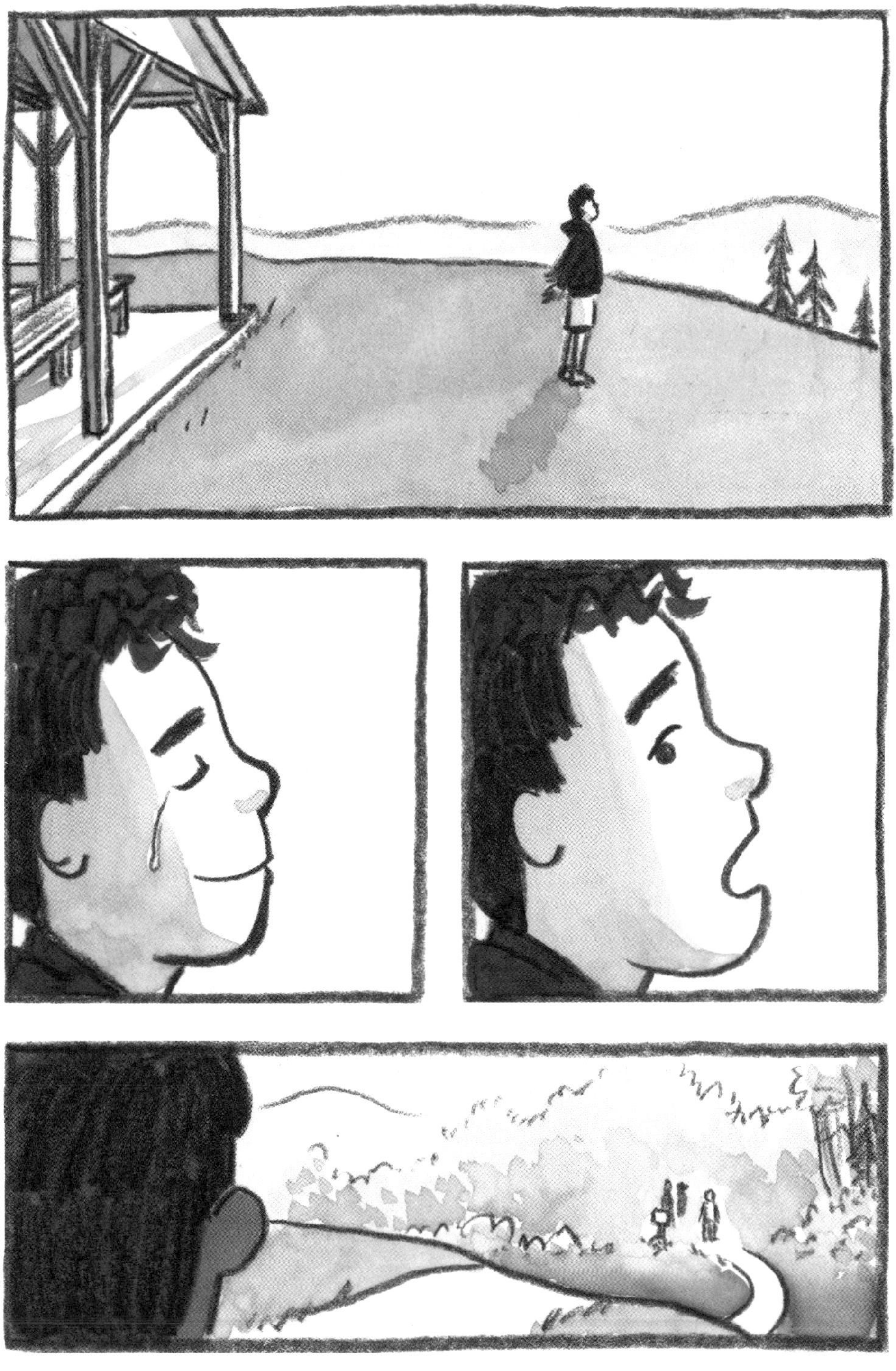

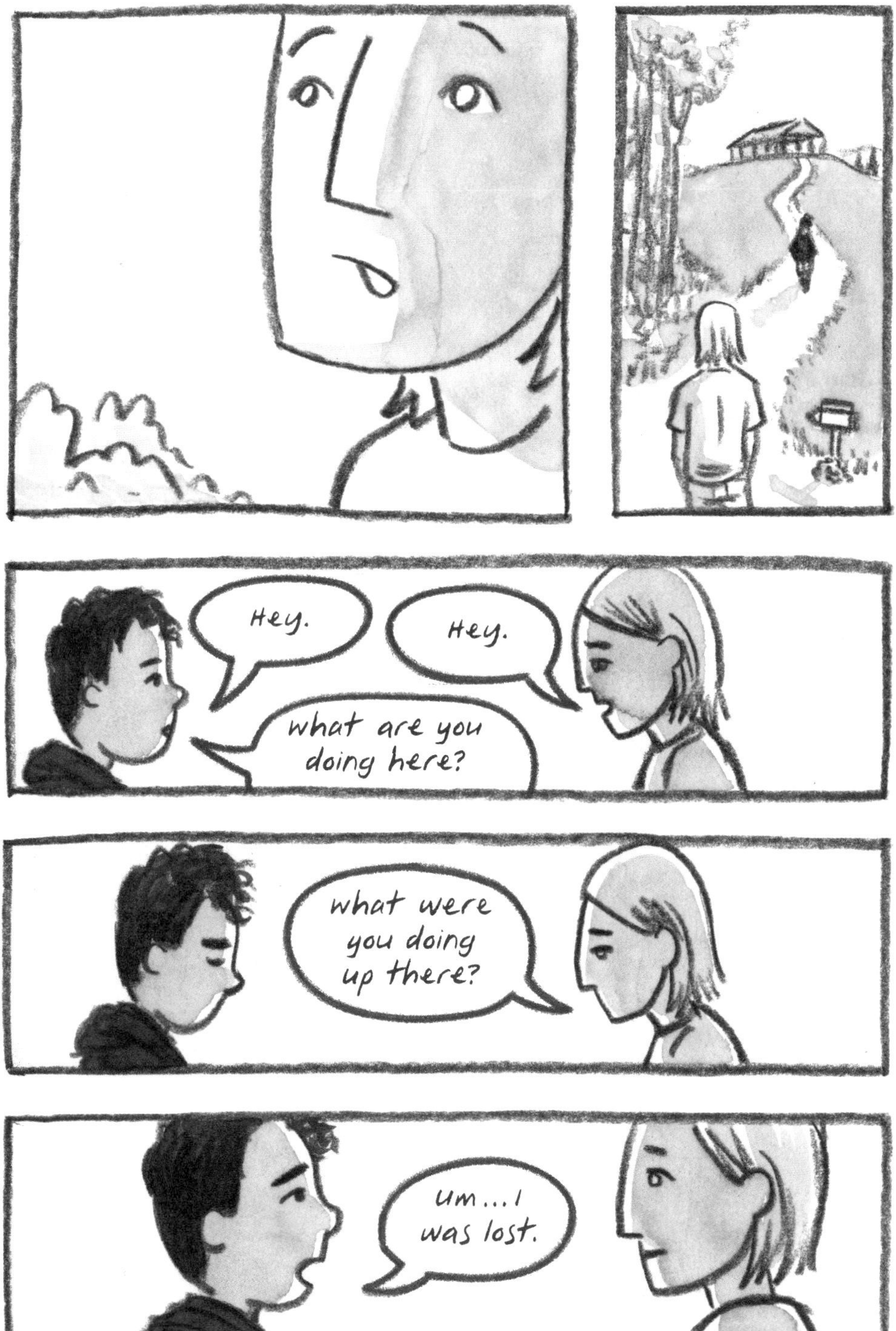
Hey.
Hey.
what are you doing here?
what were you doing up there?
um...I was lost.

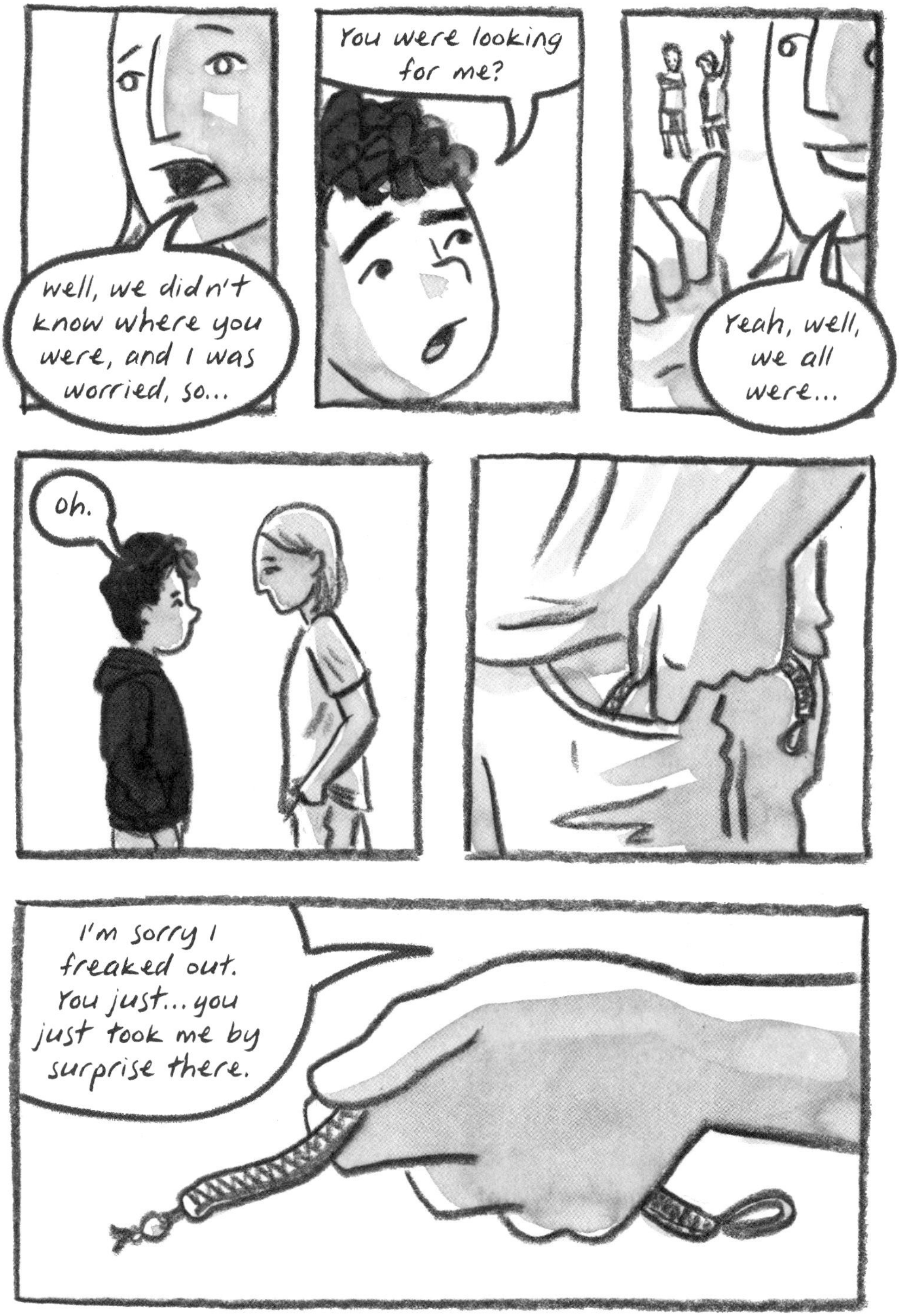
Well, we didn't know where you were, and I was worried, so...
You were looking for me?
Yeah, well, we all were...
Oh.
I'm sorry I freaked out. You just... you just took me by surprise there.

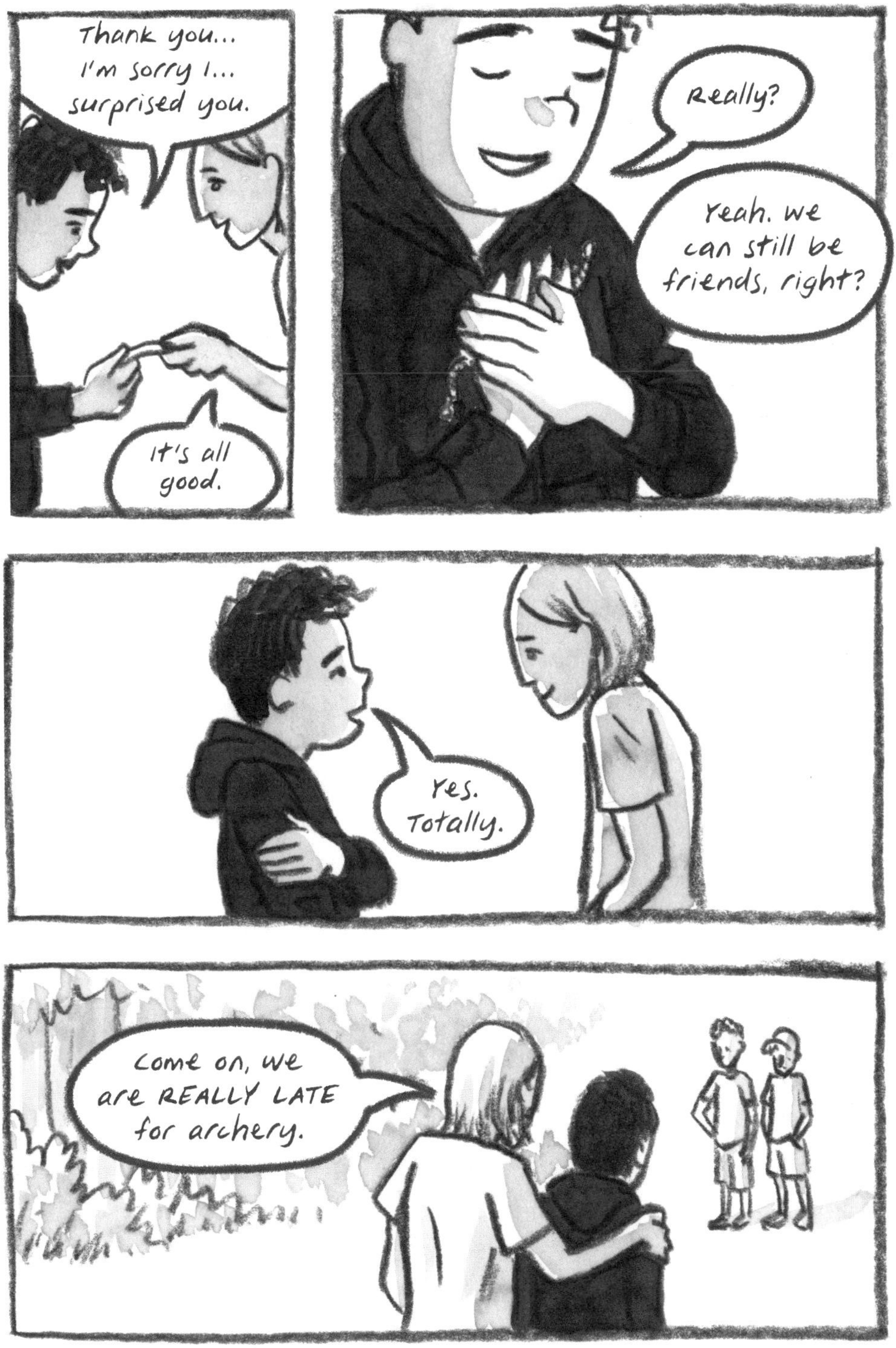
Thank you... I'm sorry I... surprised you.
It's all good.
Really?
Yeah. We can still be friends, right?
Yes. Totally.
Come on, we are REALLY LATE for archery.

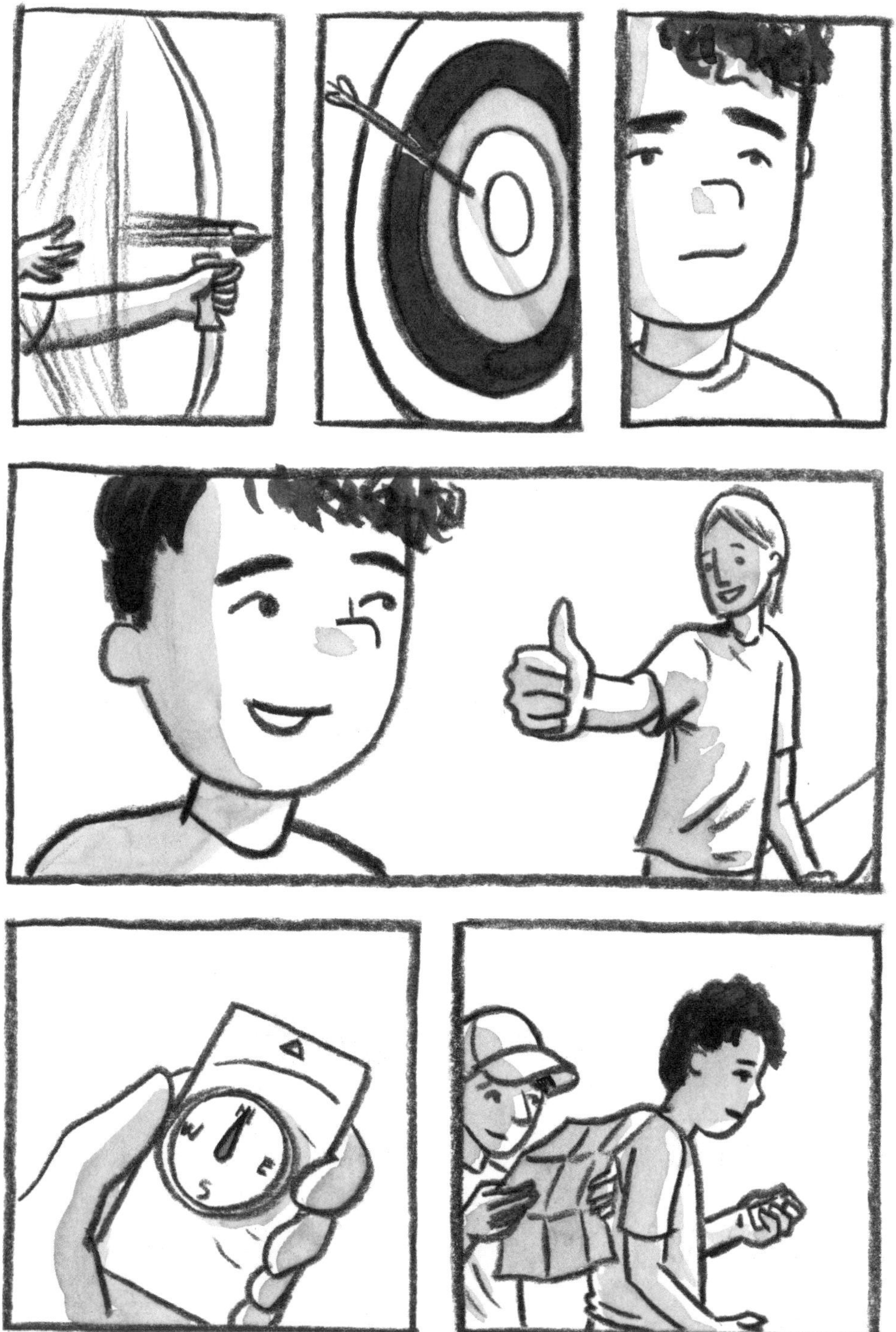

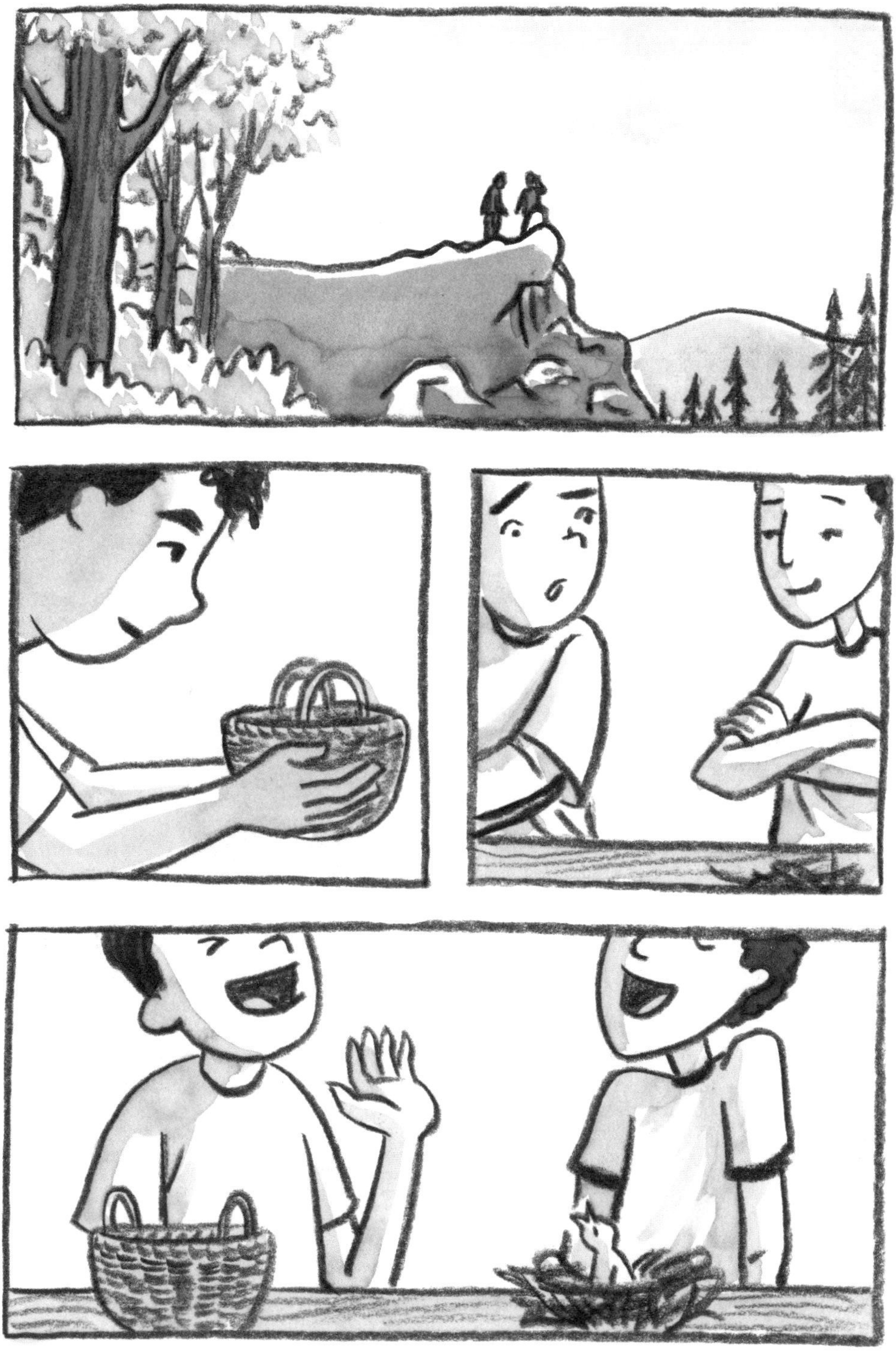

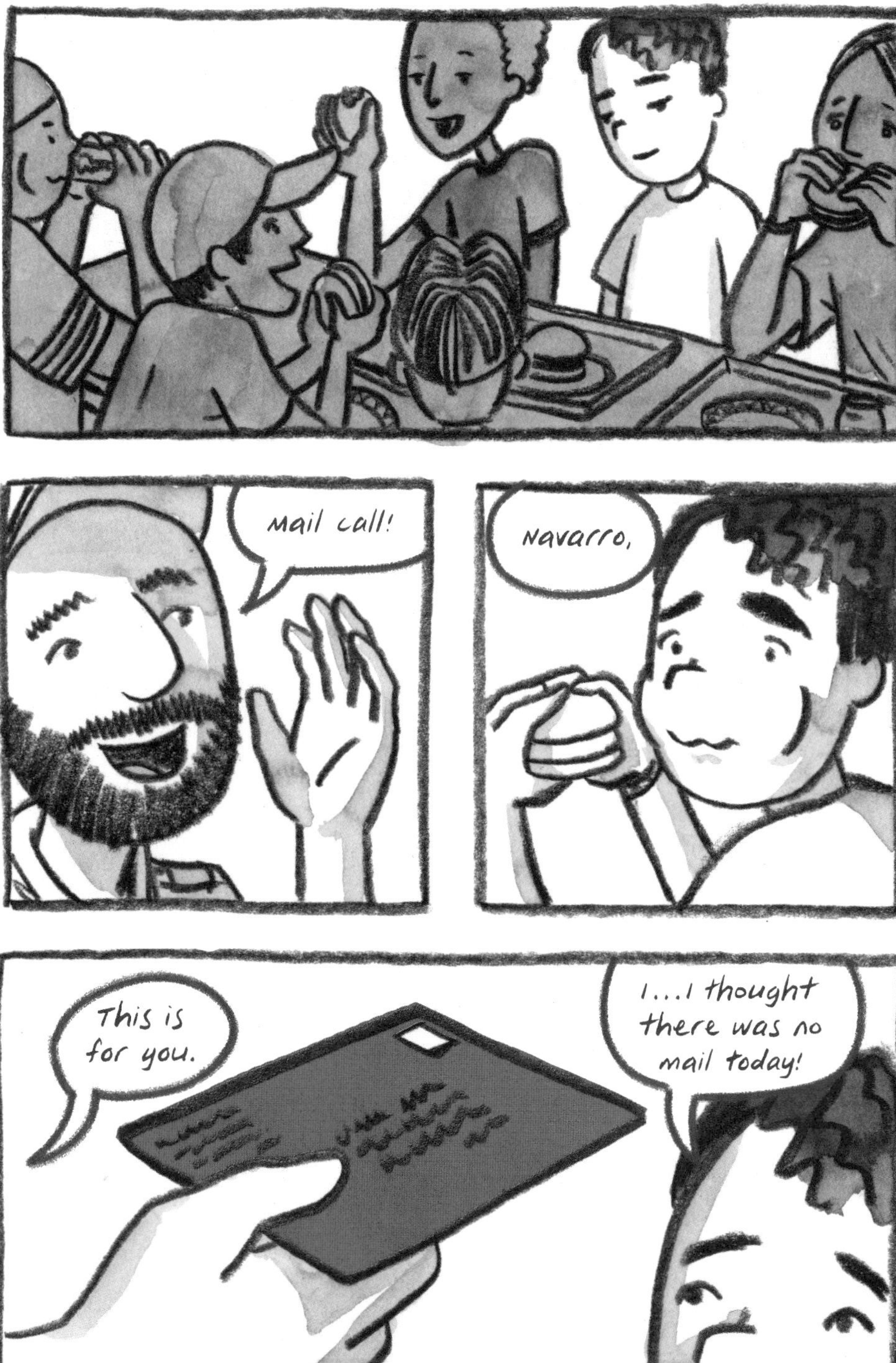
Mail call!
Navarro,
This is for you.
I...I thought there was no mail today!

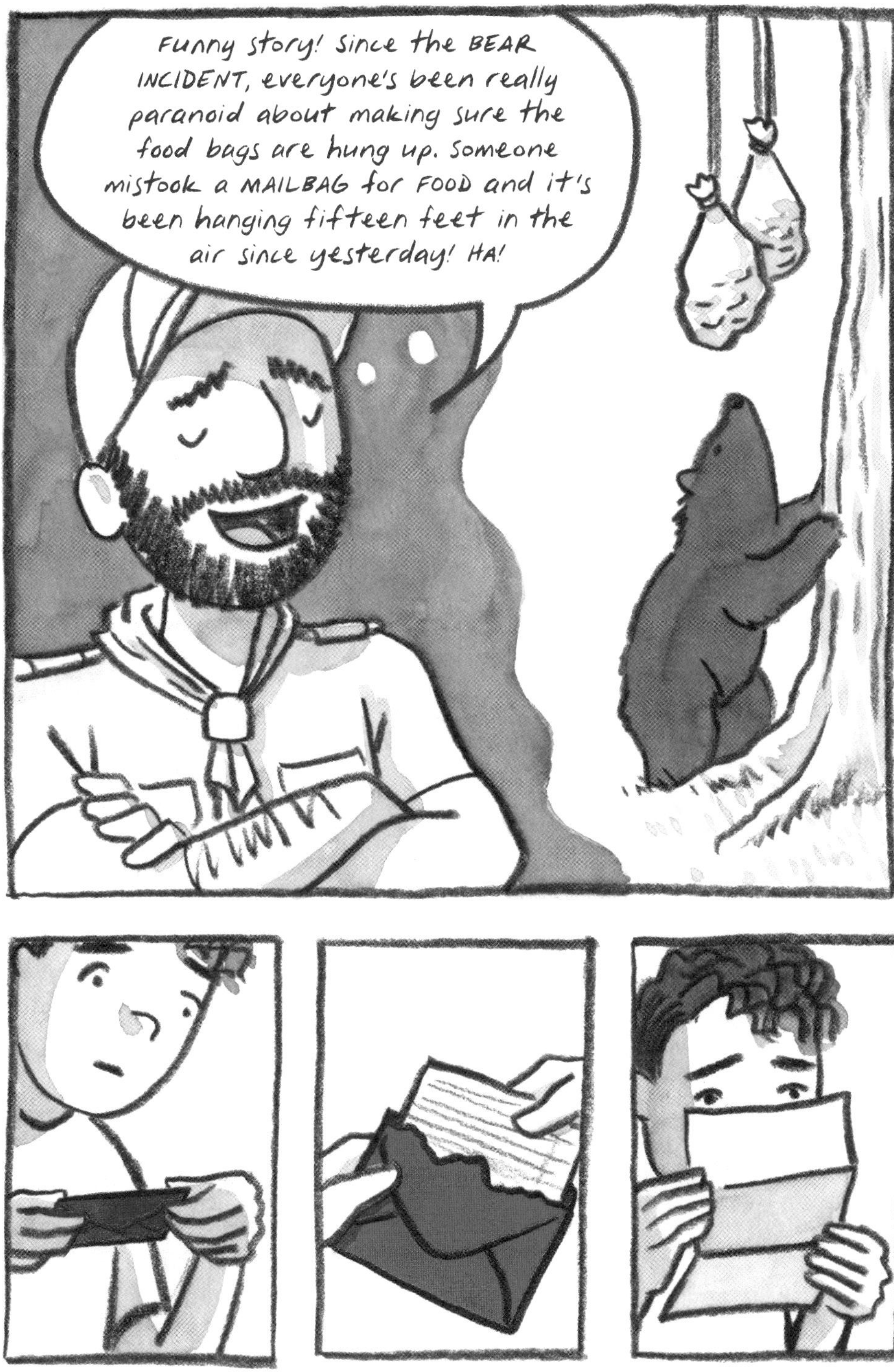
Funny story! Since the BEAR INCIDENT, everyone's been really paranoid about making sure the food bags are hung up. Someone mistook a MAILBAG for FOOD and it's been hanging fifteen feet in the air since yesterday! HA!

Dear Aiden,
There is nothing
wrong with you. You
are my best friend
in the whole world.
I would never ever
abandon you.
I am here, and
always will be.
Lylah,
Violet

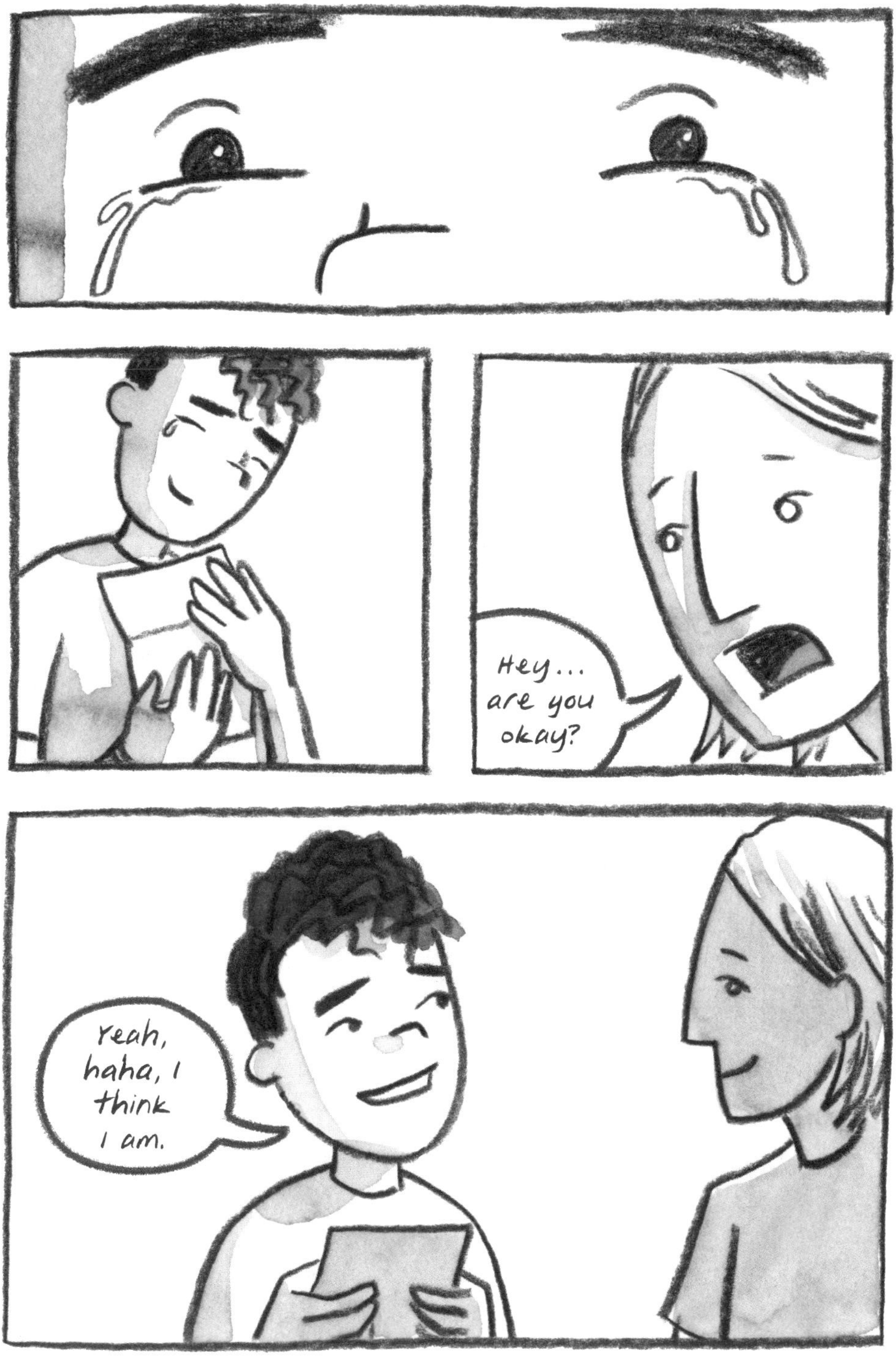
Hey... are you okay?
Yeah, haha, I think I am.

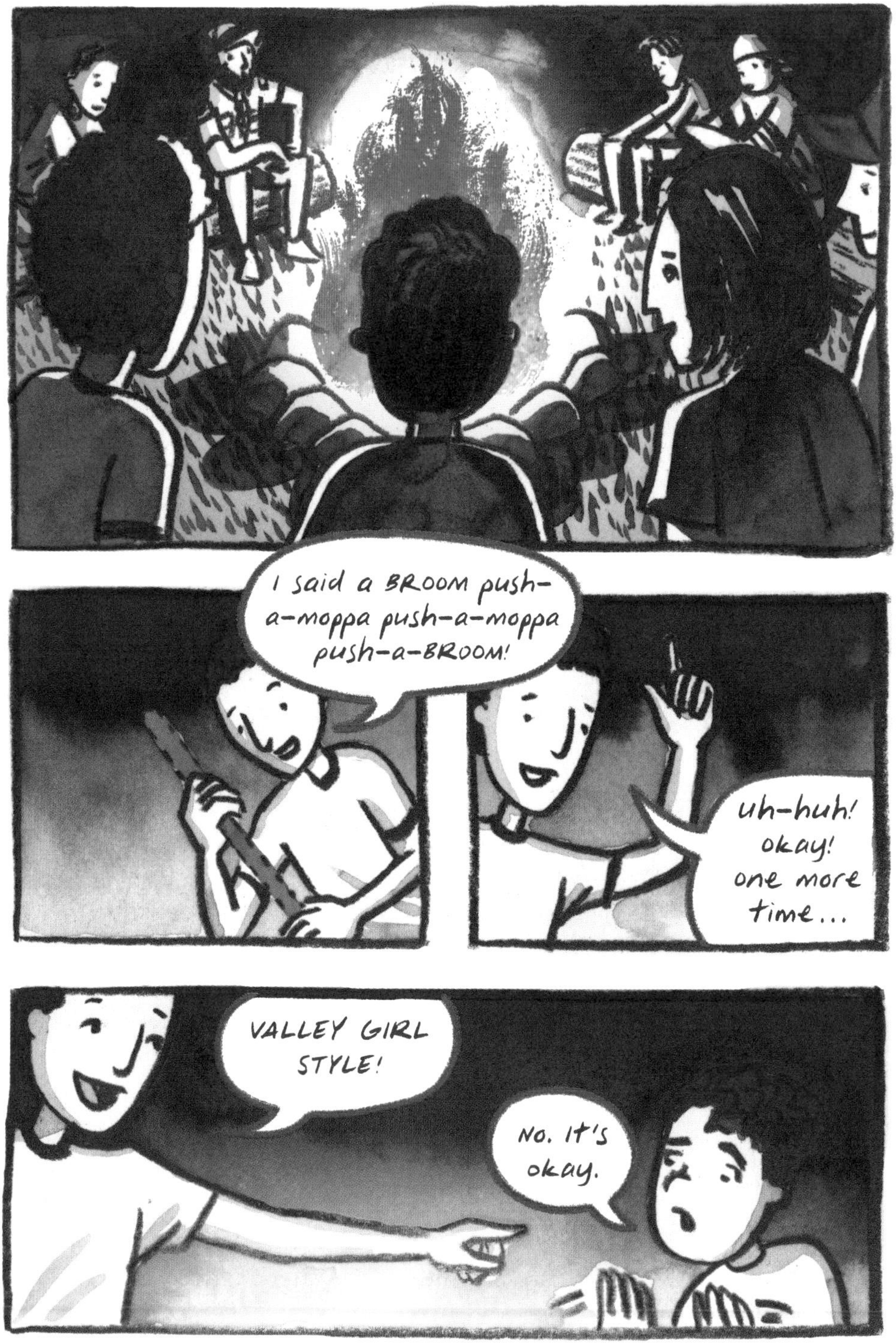
I said a BROOM push-a-moppa push-a-moppa push-a-BROOM!
uh-huh! okay! one more time...
VALLEY GIRL STYLE!
No. It's okay.

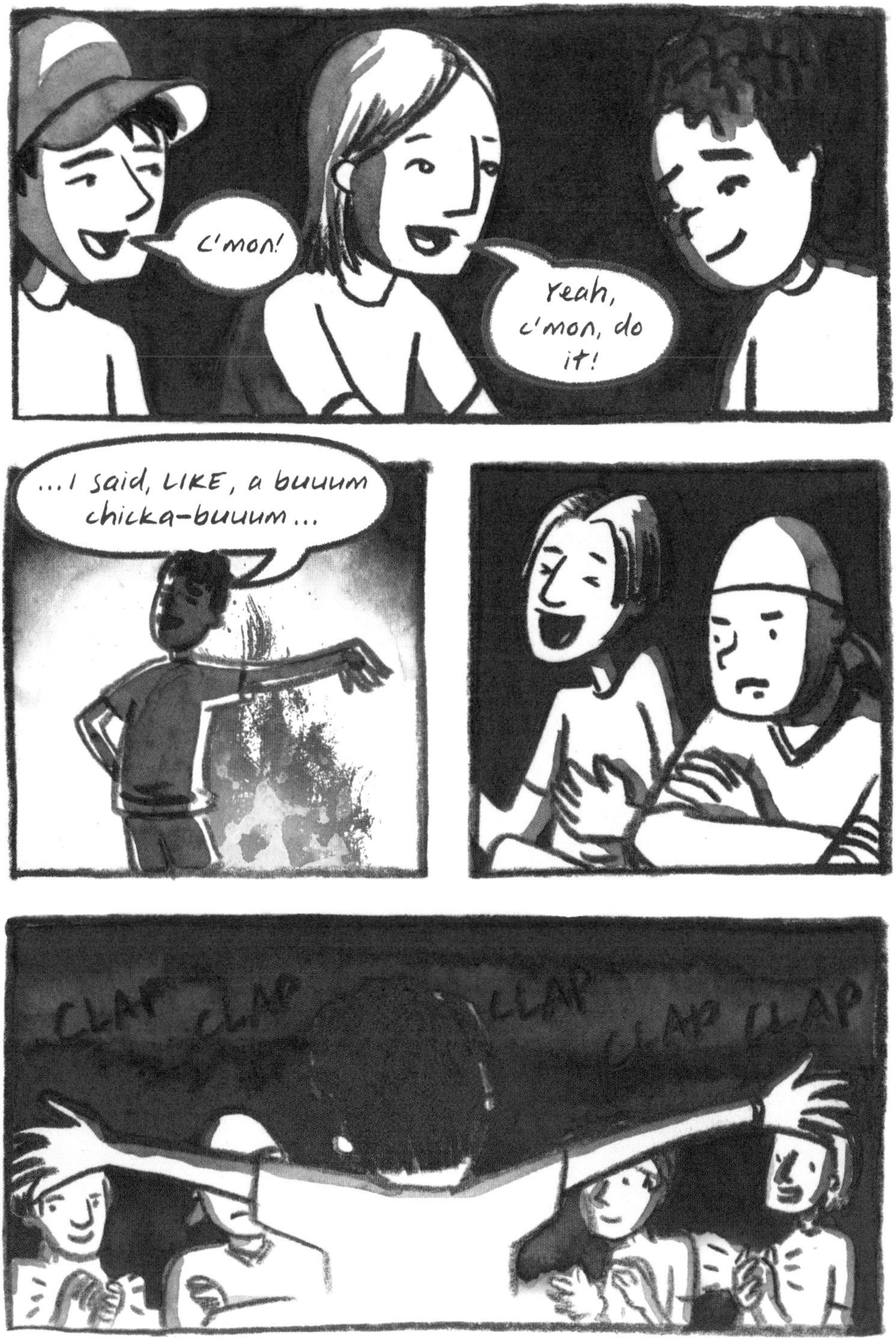
C'mon!
Yeah, c'mon, do it!
...I said, LIKE, a buuum chicka-buuum...
CLAP CLAP CLAP CLAP CLAP

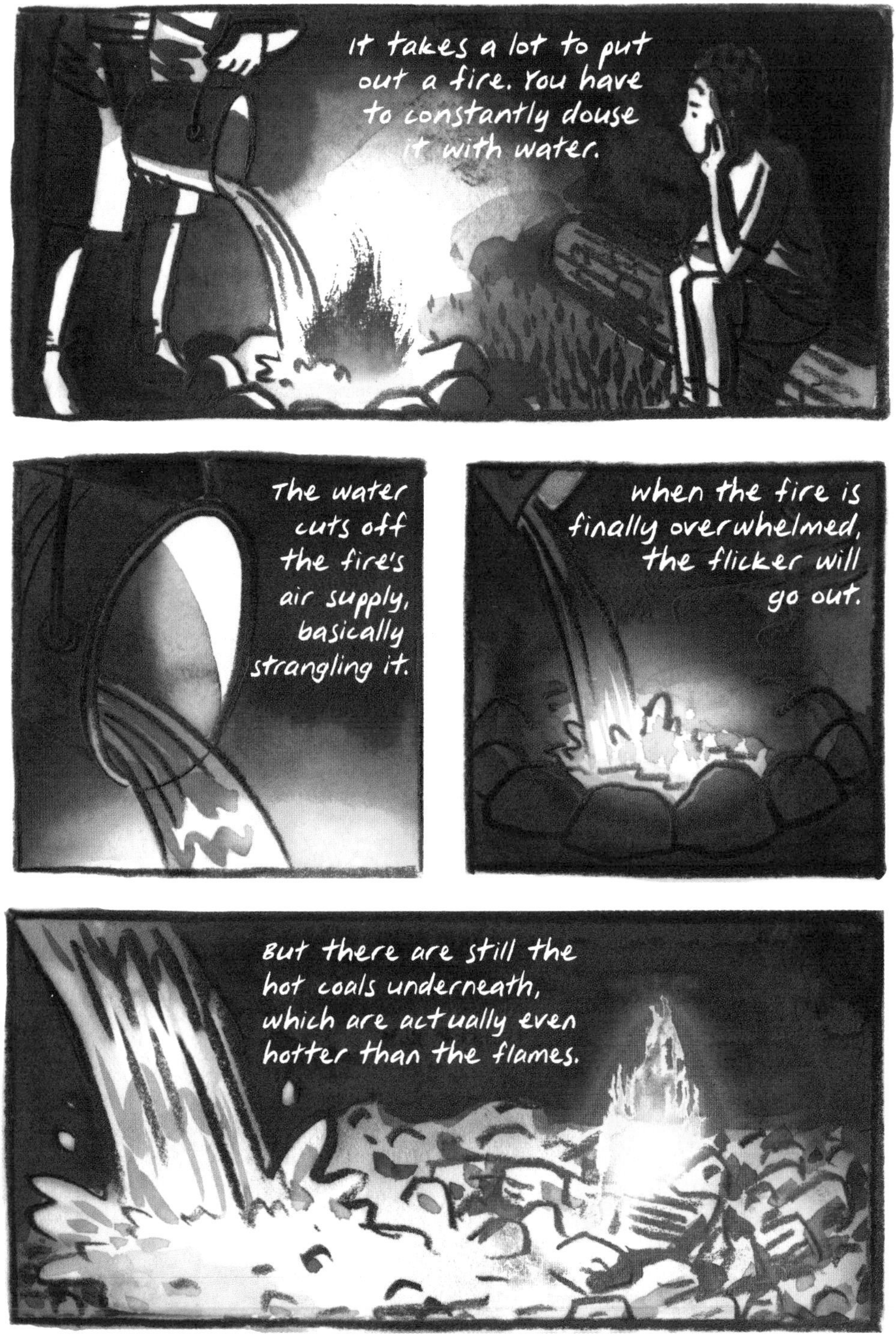
It takes a lot to put out a fire. You have to constantly douse it with water.
The water cuts off the fire's air supply, basically strangling it.
When the fire is finally overwhelmed, the flicker will go out.
But there are still the hot coals underneath, which are actually even hotter than the flames.

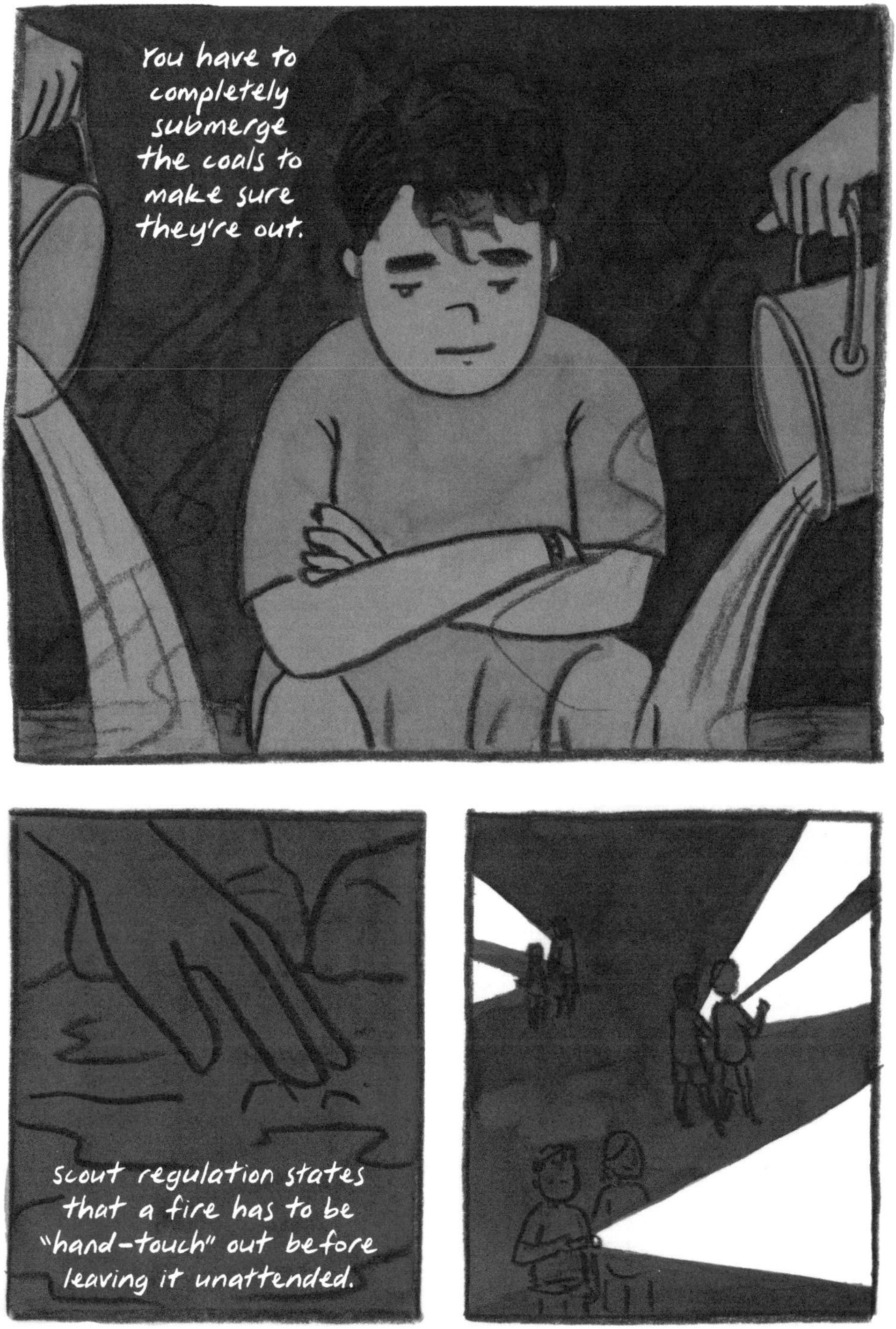
You have to completely submerge the coals to make sure they're out.
Scout regulation states that a fire has to be "hand-touch" out before leaving it unattended.

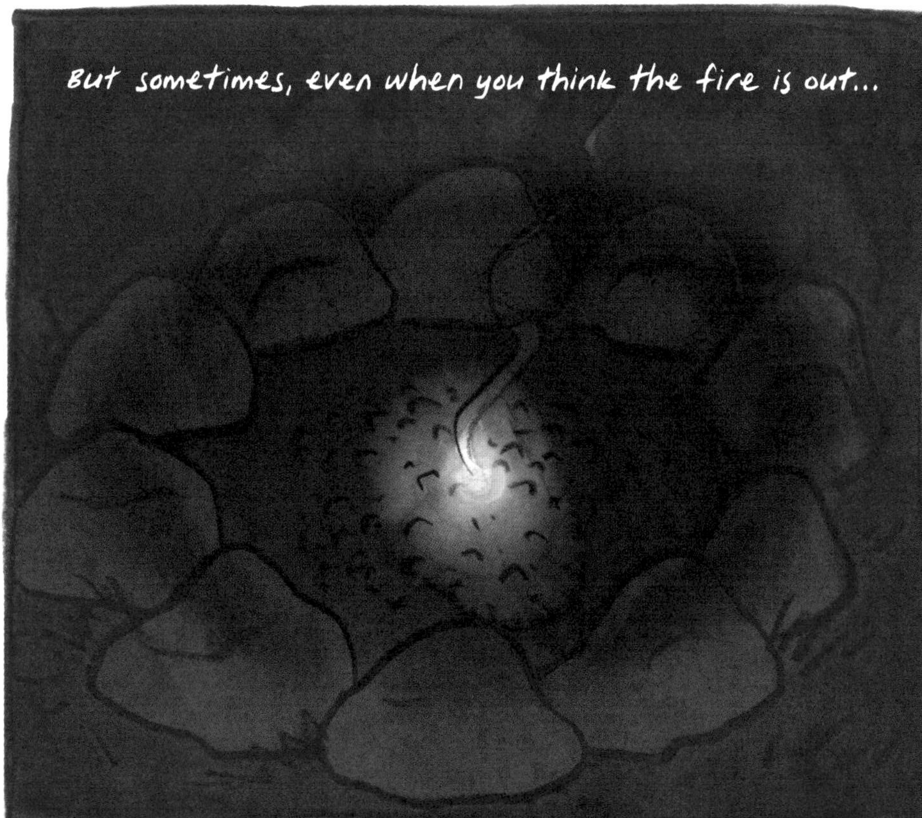
But sometimes, even when you think the fire is out...

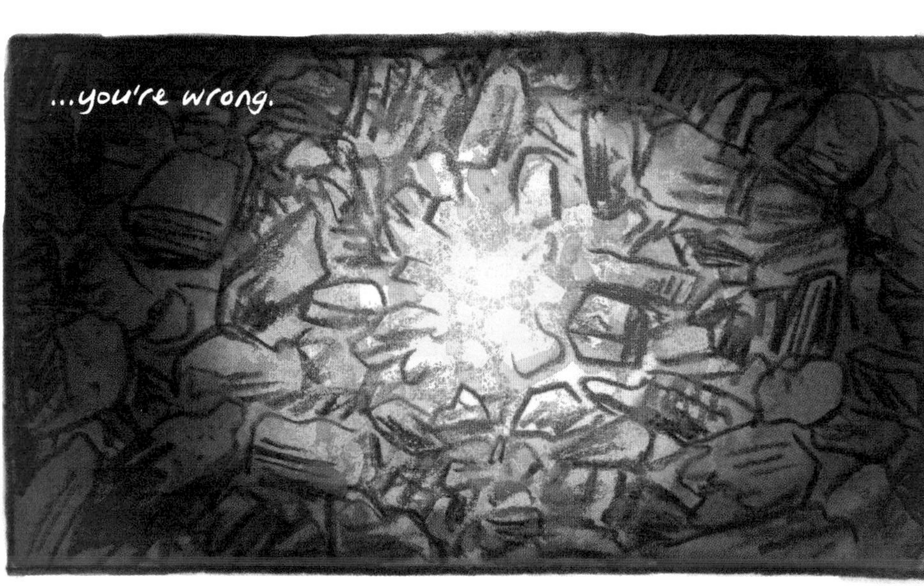
...you're wrong.

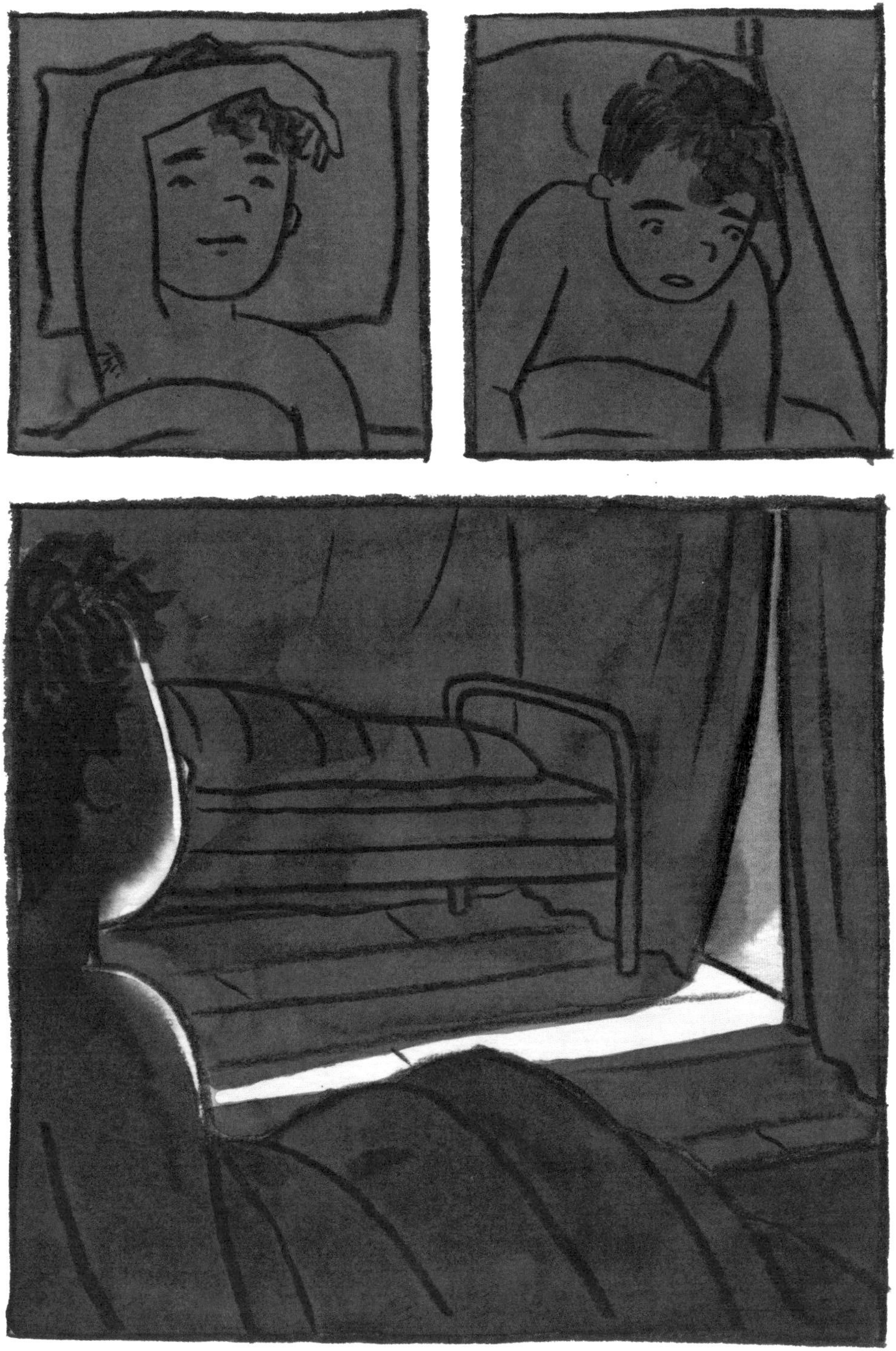

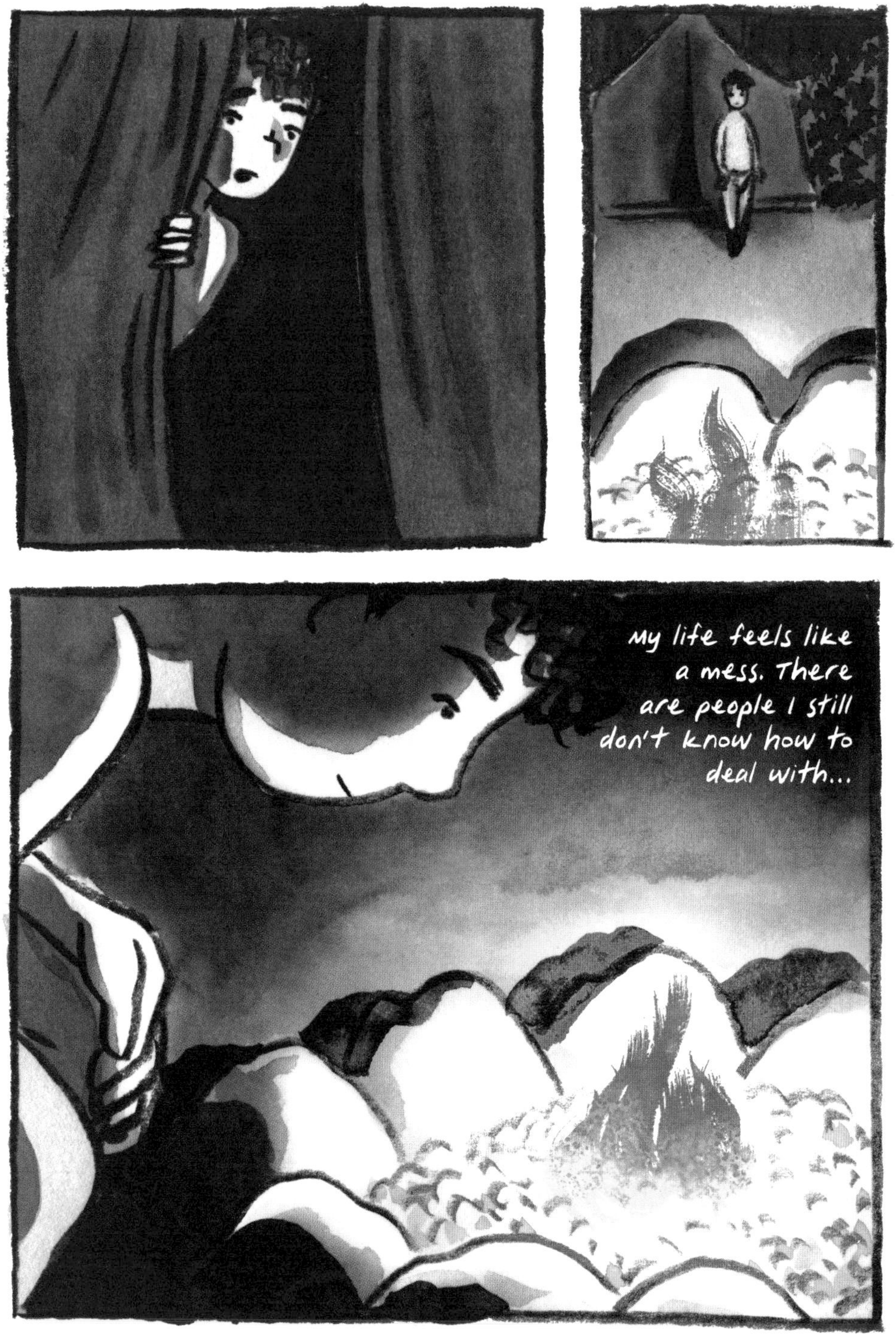
My life feels like a mess. There are people I still don't know how to deal with...

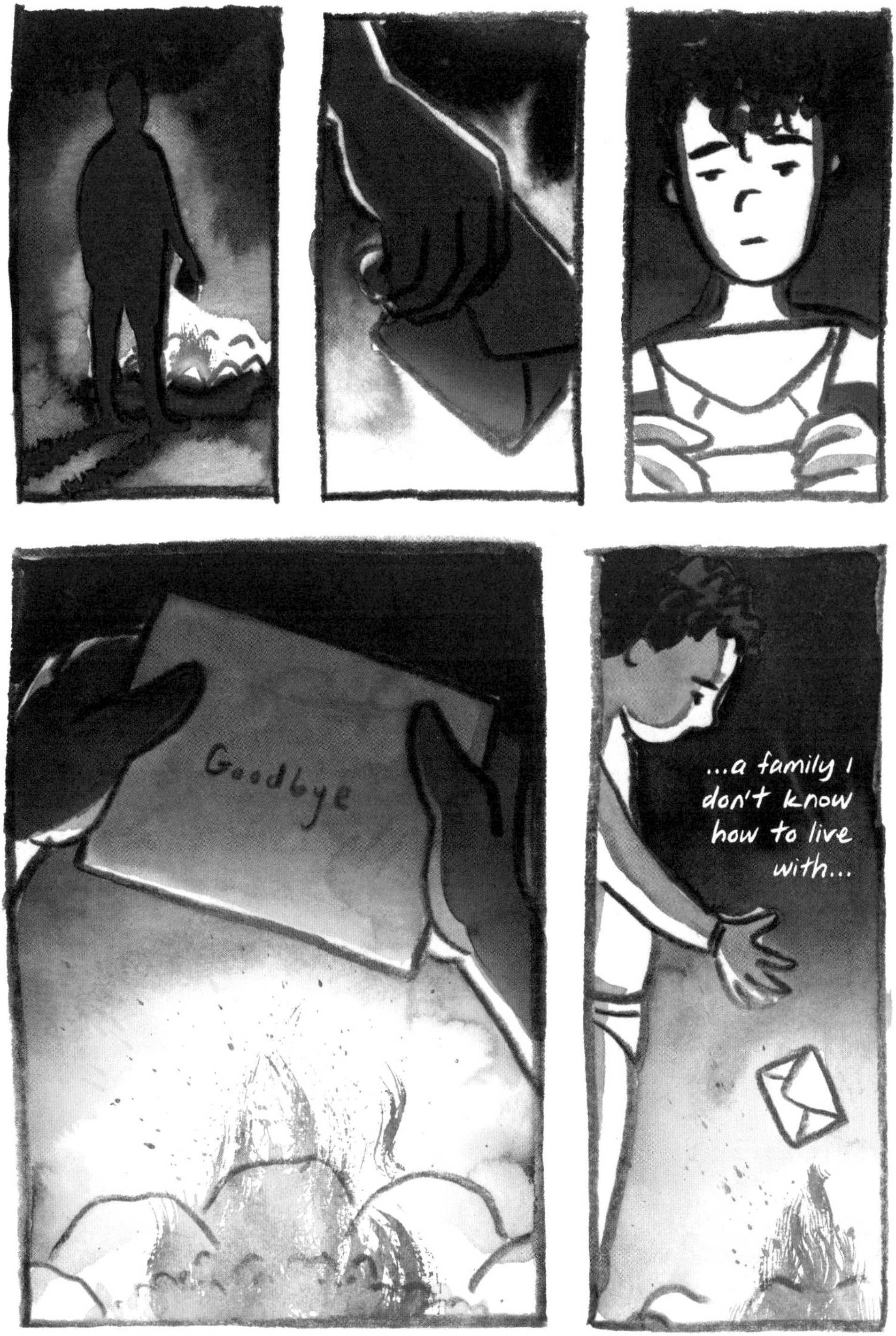
Goodbye
...a family I
don't know
how to live
with...

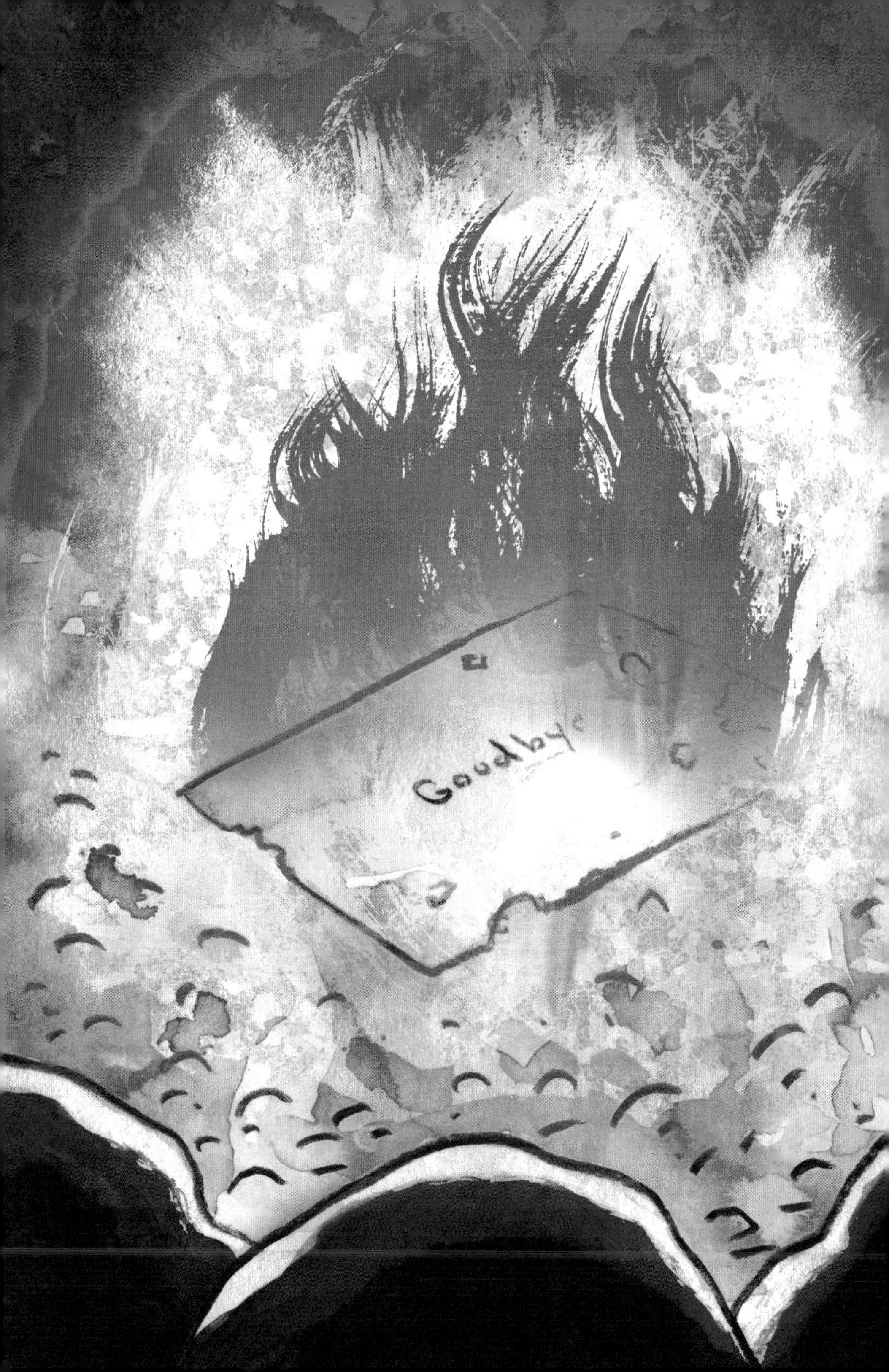
Goodbye

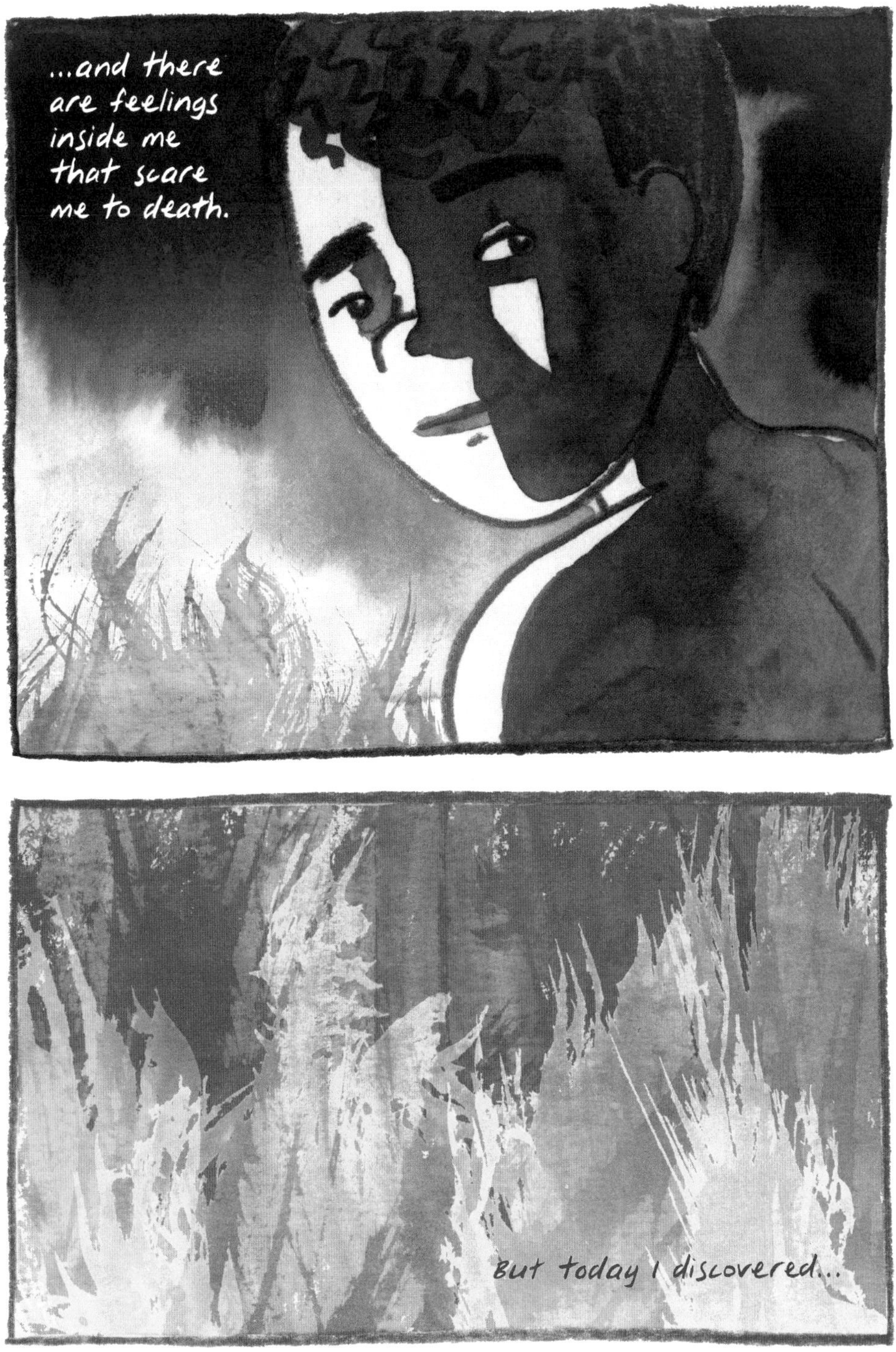
...and there are feelings inside me that scare me to death.
But today I discovered...

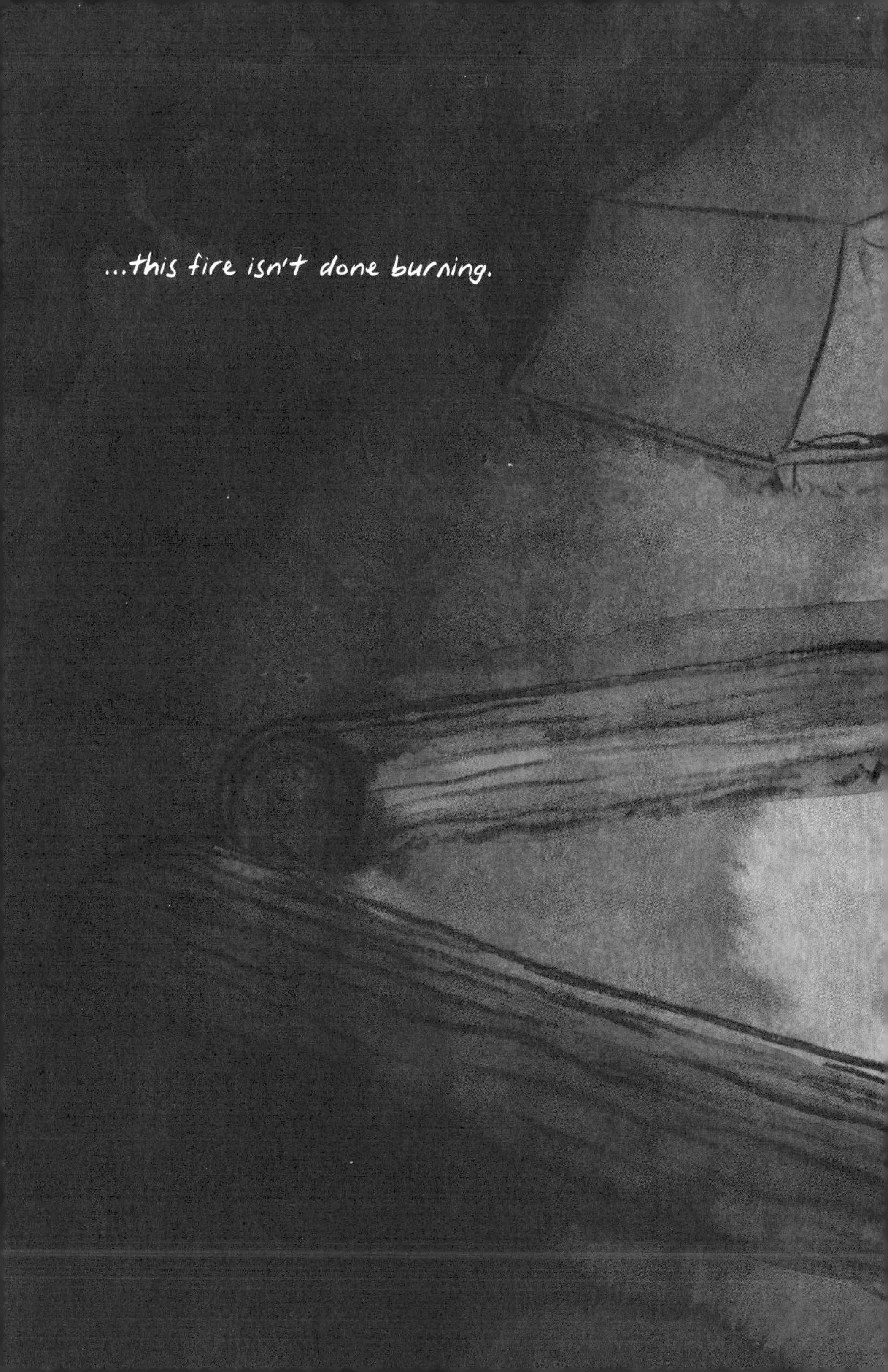
...this fire isn't done burning.

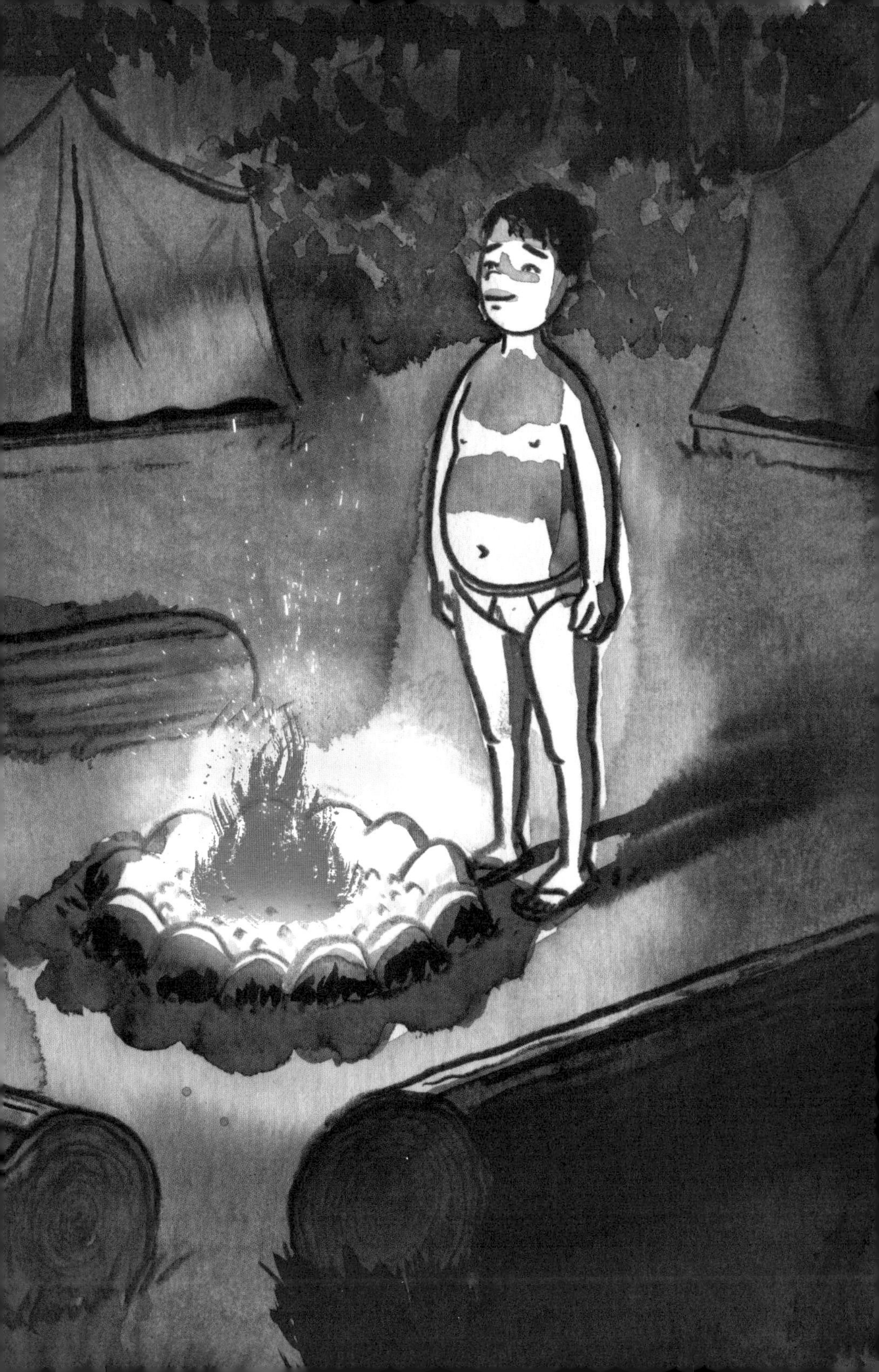

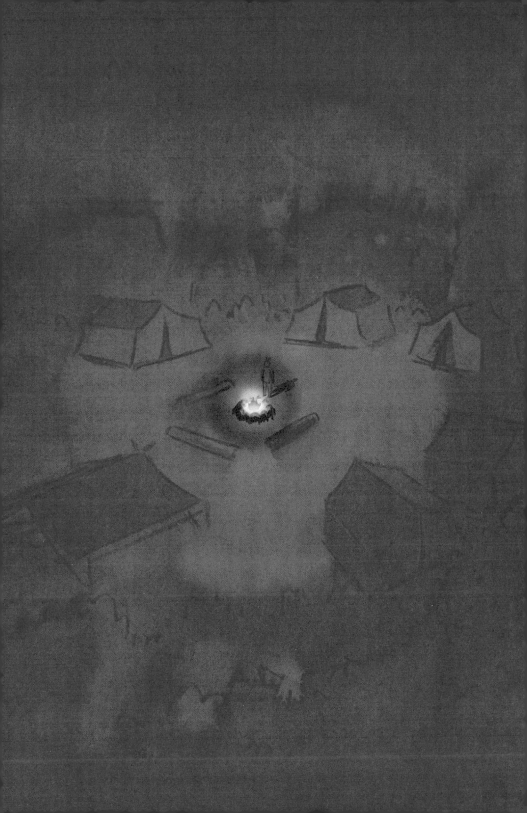

AFTERWORD

This book is a work of fiction, and yet much of it is based on my personal experiences. I grew up in scouting from a Tiger Cub all the way up to an Eagle Scout and Assistant Scoutmaster. There are many things I am grateful for. Scouting got me outside. It taught me how to work with others. It gave me self-confidence. It was a way to meet people who did not go to my school. I made friends. And though I don't see those people for years at a time, when I do, that bond is still there.

However, there were experiences I had during my time in the Boy Scouts that were very hard as a closeted kid. Over the years, the Boy Scouts have become more inclusive of sexual orientation and gender thanks to people in and out of scouting who made their voices heard. But when I was a kid, it was not okay to be gay. In 1995, the year in which this book is set, gay and queer people were routinely villified, ridiculed, and hated. Fear of AIDS only fueled the bigotry. Back then, gay adult scout leaders who came out were immediately removed from their post. Though scout bylaws have become more inclusive, homophobia still exists in many troops today, because homophobia is nationally and internationally a systemic issue.

Like my character Aiden, I felt overwhelmed by this culture of hatred. Also like Aiden, I once kneeled in a camp chapel with a knife against my wrist. I wanted my anguish to stop. I wanted to silence my fears. I was so scared of high school that I thought I would not survive it. Worst of all, I hated myself. But like Aiden, I found the strength to live. And although living is scary when we continue to suffer, I would do it all over again to be able to write this book for you. To hope. To dream. To want love. These are dangerous acts. Fear and hope are bound up together inside of us, alongside our flaws and our divinity. In this darkness, we can find an inner light to guide us. And there is light in you, even if you can't see it.

Mike Curato

RESOURCES

While my journey has led me far away from that chapel on a hill, I have known some dear people who did not survive. Their loss is a void that can never be filled. And they give me strength to say these things to you.

If you or someone you know is contemplating suicide, ask for help. Call the National Suicide Prevention Lifeline at 1-800-273-8255.

There is also TrevorLifeline, 1-866-488-7386, for specifically LGBTQ support.

Coming out is hard. For resources to support you in your self-discovery, go to thetrevorproject.org and glsen.org.

ACKNOWLEDGMENTS

I want to thank . . .

my editor, Laura Godwin, who has always believed in me and who cheered me on when I wanted to try something I've never done before.

my agent, Brenda Bowen, whose love and support have seen me through the best and worst of times, in writing and in life.

my assistant, Sabrina Montenigro, whose hard work and diligence helped make this book happen. I am forever grateful for the endless hours of scanning that I did NOT have to do.

my art director, Mallory Grigg, and designer Colleen AF Venable for helping me make this book look spectacular.

Tara Hardy, the first person to read my rough ideas. Thank you for saying "Yes, you do need to make this, and yes, you can."

Lynda Barry, whose Writing for Artists workshop gave me the confidence to take on such a huge project.

my fellow authors/illustrators for their time and incredible advice: Samantha Berger, Ruth Chan, Brian Selznick, and Sarah Jane Lapp, and all the support from Molly Burnham, Jarrett Krosoczka, Grace Lin, Lisa Yee, Dave Roman, and Craig Thompson.

my other dear friends, of whom I'm blessed to say I have too many to list here. You know who you are. I don't know where I'd be without you.

my old friends from Troop 37. I can't express how much our time meant to me. Our troop was the first group of people I felt accepted by. I can't smell a campfire without thinking of you. I miss you.

my family, for my mother's unconditional love, for my father's hard work and sacrifices, for my sister and brother's laughter.

Lara Robbins, my real-life Violet, to whom this book is dedicated. Thank you for showing me the power of friendship. You saved my life.

and Dan, for everything.